GW01275771

आ नो भद्रा: क्रतवो यन्तु विश्वत: ।
Let noble thoughts come to us from every side
—Rigveda, I-89-i

BHAVAN'S BOOK UNIVERSITY

RAMAYANA

by

KAMALA SUBRAMANIAM

BHAVAN'S BOOK UNIVERSITY

RAMAYANA

KAMALA SUBRAMANIAM

Foreword
SWAMI RANGANATHANANDA

2017
BHARATIYA VIDYA BHAVAN
Kulapati Munshi Marg
Mumbai - 400007

© *All rights reserved*
Bharatiya Vidya Bhavan
Kulapati Munshi Marg
Mumbai - 400007

First Edition : *1981*
Second Edition : *1983*
Third Edition : *1983*
Fourth Edition : *1988*
Fifth Edition : *1990*
Sixth Edition : *1995*
Seventh Edition : *1998*
Eighth Edition : *2003*
Ninth Edition : *2007*
Tenth Edition : *2009*
Eleventh Edition : *2012*
Twelveth Edition : *2014*
Thirteenth Edition : *2017*

Price ₹ 750/-

PRINTED IN INDIA

By Atul Goradia at Siddhi Printers, 13/14, Bhabha Building, 13th Khetwadi Lane, Mumbai - 400 004, and Published by P.V. Sankarankutty, Joint Director, for the Bharatiya Vidya Bhavan, Kulapati Munshi Marg, Mumbai - 400007.
E-mail : bhavan@bhavans.info
web-site : www.bhavans.info

FOREWORD

After presenting to the English-reading public two great books of the Hindu tradition earlier, namely, The Mahābhāratam and The Śrimad Bhāgavatam, Srimati Kamala Subramaniam is now offering to the readers a third great book of the Hindu tradition, namely, The Ramayanam of Vālmīki. Like the two previous books, this one also is an abridged edition of the large epic, retaining, however, all the essential parts of the book and its inspirational flow of epic narrative.

Eulogizing the two great epics of India, Swami Vivekananda says (Complete Works, Vol. IV, p. 96):

"In fact, the Rāmāyaṇa and the Mahābhārata are the two encyclopaedias of the ancient Aryan life and wisdom, portraying an ideal civilization, which humanity has yet to aspire after."

The Rāmāyaṇa has been the perennial source of spiritual, cultural, and artistic inspiration for these thousands of years, not only to the people of India but also to the peoples of South-East Asian countries. It has enriched the national literatures of these countries, and has also provided themes for every form of their art – dance, drama, music, painting and sculpture. Its heroic characters have helped to mould the Hindu character; and its three great personalities, namely, Rāma, Sītā, and Hanumān, have inspired millions of her people, high or low in the socio-economic scale, with the deepest, tenderest, and holiest love, reverence, and devotion.

All Hindu spiritual teachers, ancient and modern, have responded ecstatically to this great book and its heroes. Says Swami Vivekananda in the course of his lecture on The Sages of India (Complete Works, Vol. III, pp. 255-56):

"Rāma, the ancient idol of the heroic ages, the embodiment of truth, of morality, the ideal son, the ideal husband, the ideal father, and above all, the ideal king, this Rāma had been presented before us by the great sage Vālmīki. No language can be purer, none chaster, none more beautiful, and at the same time simpler, than the language in which the great poet has depicted the life of Rāma."

"And what to speak of Sītā? You may exhaust the literature of the world that is past, and I may assure you that you will have to exhaust the literature of the world of the future, before finding another Sītā. Sītā is unique; that character was depicted once and for all. There may have been several Rāmas perhaps, but never more than one Sītā! She is the very type of the true Indian woman, for all the Indian ideals of a perfected woman have grown out of that one life of Sītā. And here she stands, these thousands of years, commanding the worship of every man, woman, and child, throughout the length and breadth of Aryāvarta (India). There she will always be, this glorious Sītā, purer than purity itself, all patience, and all suffering."

Rt. Hon. the late V. S. Srinivasa Sastry, India's distinguished scholar and statesman, in his famous Lectures on the Rāmāyana delivered in Madras in 1944 and published by the Madras Samskrit Academy, invited the Indian youth to benefit from this great and immortal epic of their country (p. 2):

"Perhaps, The Rāmāyana is not quite as familiar to the younger generations that are coming up, as it was to us of an older day. Is it not true, alas, that great numbers of our youth at school and college are being brought up without adequate knowledge of the very springs of our civilization and culture? .... Is it an exaggeration to say that a student of the Rāmāyana, not out of touch with its sanctity and its unequalled importance to the study of our civilization, can talk to an audience largely composed of the younger generation with some hope of profiting them? I believe there is, and in the coming years there is going to be, a greater need than ever of our going back with reverent hearts to this most beautiful and moving of all stories in literature."

I cannot conclude this Foreword better than by quoting the two popular verses which salute, in highly elevating poetic imageries, the greatness of the intensely human sage-poet Vālmīki and the heroic and self-effacing devotee Hanumān :

Kūjantaṁ rāma rāmeti madhuraṁ madhurākṣaram;
Āruhya kavitā-śākhāṁ vande vālmīki-kokilam

"I salute Vālmīki, the cuckoo, who, perching on the tree of poesy, melodiously sings the sweet syllables –Rāma, Rāma!"

Sītā-rāma guna-grāma punyāranya vihārinau
Vande viśuddha-vijñānau kaviśvara-kapiś varau

"I salute the master of kavis, i.e. poets (Vālmīki) and the master of kapis, i.e. monkeys (Hanumān), who are endowed with pure Reason and who move freely and joyously in the sacred grove of the myriad virtues and graces of Rāma and Sītā."

The author and publishers have done a great service to humanity by bringing out this immortal epic in a pleasantly readable edition.

Janmashtami,
August 22, 1981
Ramakrishna Math
Hyderabad-500 029   SWAMI RANGANATHANANDA

PREFACE

It has been universally accepted that the three epics, *Mahabharata, Bhagavata* and *Ramayana,* comprise our cultural heritage. It has been my dream to render all three of them into English in a manner which will appeal to the young people and my dream seems to have come true. I have finally managed to complete the narration of the *Ramayana* in the same vein as I have the other two.

What is fascinating about these three treasure-houses is the fact that each is completely different from the other. One cannot but think of the river Ganga in this context. Ganga, hurtling through space, rushing down in a torrent towards the earth from the heavens, makes one think of the great epic *Mahabharata* which is full of action, full of passions, full of force, full of emotion. There is nothing placid about the flow of the narration.

Now think of Ganga as she enters the sea, when she becomes one with her lord. There is a feeling that the long tortuous journey is ended: that the strife is over: that at last, at long last, all passion spent, she has found Peace. This, to me, seems to compare with *Srimad Bhagavatam.*

Let us watch Ganga between these two extremities. Flowing calmly, placidly, in an unruffled manner, like the *Mandakranta* metre, chastening everyone who comes in contact with her : this Ganga makes me want to compare her to the *Ramayana.* There is, in the *Ramayana,* everything that is beautiful and the very atmosphere is purifying.

"Drama" is the first word which comes to the mind while reading the great epic, *Mahabharata.* "Bhakti," on the other hand, is the thread running through the entire narration of the *Bhagavata.* "Pain" is the predominant emotion in the *Ramayana.* Pain is the monochord which can be heard throughout : and yet, this very pain is ennobling, purifying and satisfying. *Ramayana* is a threnody filled to the brim, with noble thoughts, noble sentiments, noble characters, not one of whom is spared the experience of pain.

The *Bhagavata* has a mystic veil which shrouds it throughout. The *Ramayana,* however, has less number of "characters", but each is so clearly and sharply portrayed that we can almost see them. It is full of word-pictures which reveal the sufferings of the different characters.

The morning of the proposed coronation of Rama when the young prince is summoned to the apartments of Kaikeyi where he sees his father, the very picture of woe, while Kaikeyi is 'different', to quote Rama. This was one of the most painful days in the life of Rama and how calm and composed he is when he is told about the banishment! The death of Dasaratha, and the moment when Bharata comes to know of it : all these three scenes are so clearly described, one cannot forget them easily.

Can one forget the other scene when Rama comes back to the *ashrama* at Panchavati and finds it empty? And we see Sita in Lanka, in the Ashokavana, like a figure carved out of suffering.

Consider the later scenes when Ravana's pride is humbled day after day and the ultimate heartbreak when he hears of the death of Indrajit. Ravana rises to tragic heights during the end when he faces the consequence of his 'tragic fault' and we see the truth of the Greek proverb : "Character is Destiny."

Ramayana has been called the *Adi Kavya*. If one were to try and look at it as one would at a Sanskrit drama and search for the predominant 'Rasa', it is evident that the *Ramayana* is, in essence, full of 'Viraha', 'Vipralambha Shringara' in a very wide sense. It is not just the separation of a husband and wife but several partings of different kinds. The predominant motif of the epic is : "Separation".

The killing of the *krauncha* bird and the curse of Valmiki strike the keynote of the entire epic. Consider the number of partings. In the very beginning Rishyashringa is parted from his father who was doting on him. Later, Rama is taken away from his father by Vishvamitra though the duration of the separation is short. Then comes the time when Bharata and Shatrughna are parted from their father as they go to Kekaya. Nothing is the same when they come back to Ayodhya. Bharata's father is dead and his mother so changed that he refuses to consider her his mother any longer. And Rama was far away. There is the exile of Rama to the Dandaka forest, the great separation from his father and mother which kills the king and breaks the heart of his mother.

We come to the poignant scenes in the Aranya Kanda when Rama suffers the pangs of separation from Sita. The Kishkindha Kanda is filled to the brim with sublime poetry when Rama pines for Sita on the banks of the Pampa and later, at Prasravana when the rainy season visits the hill.

We see Sugriva parted from his wife. Then follows the death of Vali and the lament of Tara. Again, later, we are confronted with the painful scene when Mandodari grieves for Ravana.

Rama's coronation takes place and, with Sita, he spends a short happy time : and again, separation. Sita is sent away and Rama spends the rest of his life in loneliness.

The *Ramayana* is a sad story. At the same time, like a Greek tragedy, it is the very summit of poetic art.

"Unarm, Eros, the long day's task is done," says Mark Antony. Even so, I am in a mood to say: a task which I undertook thirty years ago has now been completed and I feel a strange contentment stealing over me. I have but one regret. I only wish Pujya Munshiji had been with us. He would have been happy. But for his words of encouragement I would never have been able to do what I have done.

I am extremely grateful to Swami Ranganathananda for having been gracious enough to write the Foreword to the book. I feel very happy that he has blessed this book, and highly honoured.

KAMALA SUBRAMANIAM

CONTENTS

Chapter		Page
Foreword		v
Preface		ix

BALAKANDA

1.	Valmiki And Narada	3
2.	The Coming of Brahma	10
3.	Valmiki Composes The Great Poem	13
4.	Dasaratha, and His Grief	15
5.	The Ashvamedha Yaga	19
6.	The Devas in Distress	21
7.	The Birth Of Rama	23
8.	Vishvamitra Comes to Dasaratha	27
9.	Vishvamitra and the Young Princes	33
10.	Tataka Vana	36
11.	The Killing of Tataka	39
12.	Siddhashrama	41
13.	The Yaga of Vishvamitra	45
14.	To Mithila	48
15.	Ganga	50
16.	Bhagiratha's Penance	55
17.	Towards Gautama's Ashrama	57
18.	Mithila	61
19.	Vishvamitra	64
20.	Vasishta Hosts the King	64
21.	A Frustrated King	67
22.	The power of the Brahmin	70
23.	Trishanku of the Solar Race	72
24.	A New Heaven	76
25.	Sunashepha	78
26.	Kaushika's Lapses	82
27.	Vishvamitra, the Brahmarshi	85
28.	The Bow of Mahadeva	87
29.	Dasaratha Leaves for Mithila	90
30.	In Mithila	91
31.	Sita Kalyanam	94
32.	Parasurama, the Bhargava	95

AYODHYA KANDA

1.	Rama	103
2.	The Desire in the Heart of Dasaratha	105

CONTENTS

Chapter	Page
3. "Tomorrow" — Said the King	110
4. Preparations	113
5. The Maid, Manthara	114
6. Kaikeyi's Decision	119
7. Dasaratha Comes to Kaikeyi	122
8. The Dawn of the Terrible Day	129
9. Kaikeyi Talks to Rama	133
10. Lakshmana's Anger	142
11. Rama's Firmness	147
12. A Mother's Bleesings	151
13. Rama and Sita	153
14. Laksmana's Request	161
15. In the Presence of Dasaratha	163
16. Kaikeyi Brings the Valkalas	168
17. A Painful Farewell	171
18. Dasaratha's Despair	174
19. On the Banks of the Tamasa	177
20. The Journey	179
21. Guha, A Chieftain of Hunters	181
22. The Third Night of the Exile	188
23. The Ashrama of Bharadvaja	190
24. Chitrakuta at Last	194
25. Sumantra Returns to Ayodhya	196
26. The Curse of a Rishi	199
27. The Death of Dasaratha	203
28. Bharata has Bad Dreams	205
29. Bharata in Ayodhya	208
30. The Wrath and Sorrow of Bharata	212
31. Bharata's Oath	215
32. The Last Rites for the King	217
33. Manthara Again	220
34. The Throne is Yours	222
35. Bharata on his Way	225
36. Bharata Meets Bharadvaja	230
37. Lakshmana is Worried	233
38. Bharata's Quest	236
39. Bharata Meets Rama	237
40. Bharata's Appeal	242
41. Bharata Asks for the Padukas	250
42. Bharata's Return	251

Chapter	Page
ARANYA KANDA	
1. Rama Abandons Chitrakuta	257
2. Atri and Anasuya	259
3. The Dandaka Forest	263
4. The Killing of Viradha	265
5. The Sage Sharabhanga	268
6. The Sage Sutheekshna	272
7. Sita's Admonition	273
8. The Greatness of Agastya	276
9. Agastya's Ashrama	279
10. Panchavati	284
11. Shurpanakha	287
12. Khara, Dushana and Trishiras	291
13. Ravana is Told About Janasthana	298
14. Shurpanakha and her Tale of Woe	301
15. To Maricha's Ashrama Again	305
16. The Golden Deer	313
17. The Killing of Maricha	315
18. Ravana in Ochre Robes	319
19. Jatayu's Death	325
20. Sita in Ravana's City	329
21. Rama's Lament	331
22. The Fruitless Search	336
23. Meeting With Jatayu	340
24. Ayomukhi and Kabandha	343
25. A Ray of Hope	346
26. Shabari's Ashrama	348
27. The Lake by Name Pampa	350
28. Rama's Grief	351
KISHKINDHA KANDA	
1. Sugriva Sends Hanuman to Rama	359
2. A Friendship is Forged	364
3. Vali and Sugriva	368
4. The Valour of Vali	372
5. Sugriva has Doubts	375
6. The Killing of Vali	377
7. Vali's Censure	380

Chapter	Page
8. Rama Justifies his Action	383
9. Tara's Grief	386
10. The Coronation of Sugriva and Angada	391
11. Rama and Lakshmana in Prasravana	392
12. Rama's Impatience	394
13. The Fury of Lakshmana	397
14. Lakshmana is Pacified	401
15. The Beginning of the Search	406
16. The South-Bound Vanaras	408
17. The Despair of the Vanaras	412
18. Sampati, the Old Eagle	416
19. How to Cross the Sea?	421
20. The Greatness of Hanuman	423

SUNDARA KANDA

1. The Magnificent Leap	429
2. Hanuman Enters Lanka	433
3. Lanka	436
4. Hanuman Sees Mandodari	438
5. Hanuman Sees Sita	443
6. The Coming of Ravana	446
7. A Ray of Hope	451
8. Hanuman Meets Sita	455
9. Sita Hears About Rama	459
10. Sita's Message to Rama	465
11. Destruction of the Ashokavana	469
12. The Brahmastra	473
13. Hanuman in the Court of Ravana	474
14. Conflagration in Lanka	479
15. The Return of Hanuman	485
16. Sugriva's Madhuvana	489
17. The Narration of Hanuman	492

YUDDHA KANDA

1. Preparations	499
2. The March Southwards	502
3. Ravana is Worried	505
4. Ravana Loses Vibhishana	510

Chapter	Page
5. Vibhishana and Rama	516
6. Preparations for the War	520
7. Rama's Anger	524
8. The Building of the Bridge	527
9. Speculations	530
10. Ravana Tries to Distress Sita	534
11. In the Council Hall Again	538
12. Rama with His Men	541
13. Sugriva's Impulsiveness	543
14. Angada's Mission	545
15. The Nagapasa	547
16. Sita Sees Rama on the Field	550
17. The Recovery of the Princes	553
18. Ravana Sends Prahastha	554
19. Ravana on the Field of Battle	557
20. Kumbhakarna is Woken Up	562
21. Kumbhakarna on the Field	570
22. The Death of Kumbhakarna	576
23. The Young Heroes	577
24. The Valour of the Princes	579
25. Indrajit	581
26. The Sanjivini	585
27. Kumbha and Nikumbha	587
28. Indrajit to the Rescue	589
29. Maya Sita Slain	591
30. Yaga at Nikumbhila	593
31. Lakshmana Accosts Indrajit	596
32. The Killing of Indrajit	599
33. Rama's Joy	603
34. Ravana's Grief	605
35. The Moolabala of Ravana	608
36. Ravana Sets Out to the Field of Battle	611
37. Sanjivini Again	616
38. The Final Encounter	618
39. The Killing of Ravana	624
40. When Ravana Died	627
41. The Lament of Mandodari	630
42. The Funeral Rites	632
43. Rama Sends Hanuman to Sita	634

Chapter	Page
44. Rama and Sita	636
45. The Ritual of Fire	640
46. The Gods Speak	642
47. Homeward-Bound	646
48. Hanuman in Nandigrama	651
49. The Home-Coming of Rama	653
50. The Coronation of Rama	655
Phalashruti	658
Glossary	660

BALAKANDA

1. VALMIKI AND NARADA

Tamasa was the river on the banks of which was built the ashrama of Valmiki, the great sage. He was famed the world over for his great tapas, for his Gurukula which had many disciples learning the sacred lore under him.

Once the rishi was sunk in reverie and to him came Narada, the divine rishi: Narada, the son of Brahma, the Creator. Watching Narada's fingers strumming the strings of the Veena Valmiki sat without speaking a word. Narada asked him what his thoughts were and the rishi replied: "You are the son of Brahma and you are like Vayu the god of wind. You can enter everywhere, even into the minds of men and know what thoughts there are in the innermost hearts of living beings. You must be knowing what has been teasing me for quite, some time now. I wonder if there is, in this world of men, a single individual, a man blessed with all the many good qualities which one can think of."

"Tell me what these qualities are," said Narada, "and I will try and tell you if there is one endowed with all of them and thus satisfy your curiosity."

"Integrity," said Valmiki. "Integrity, bravery, righteousness, gratitude, truthfulness, dedication to one's principles, character without blemish, concern for all living beings, learning, skill, beauty, a pleasing appearance, courage, radiance, ability to keep anger under control, perfect control, a lack of jealousy at all times, undaunted heroism which can frighten even the celestials."

Valmiki paused for a while after enumerating all these many qualities and then said with a smile: "I know I am expecting perfection in a human being. But I wonder if there *is* such a person! Is it possible for a single man to have *all* these qualities? Even gods have not been able to possess them and how can a human being aspire to perfection? Yet this mind of mine has been aching to know of such a person: hoping that there *is* a perfect man."

Narada, who knew the past, the present and the future, was very pleased with the speculation of Valmiki and he replied: "Listen to me carefully. I happen to know of such a man." He looked thoughtful as though he were trying to collect his memories and said: "As you rightly observed, it is very hard to find a single individual endowed with all these glorious qualities which you have enumerated. But I will tell you about one who can be said to have attained perfection in this world of men.

"In the line of the Ikshvakus there is a king by name Rama. He is the man you are looking for. He is unruffled by the sway of the emotions. He is powerful, and he has a very attractive personality. He has charm and, at the same time, he is firm in his mind. He is highly intelligent and just. He has no foes since he has subdued all of them. As for his looks, he is broad-shouldered, with long arms, a wide chest, a large and beautiful forehead and a very attractive gait. He is neither too tall nor too short. He has large and liquid eyes. He is well-versed in the shastras and is very jealous of his personal honour. He is a great archer and he is ever pondering on the great Truth beyond the comprehension of all human thought. He is dear to everyone. He is very noble and good; and all gentle people gravitate towards him like the rivers flow continuously towards the ocean.

"Rama knows no partiality and he is ever gentle and pleasant in his speech. All the good and great qualities which you are looking for in a man, are found in this king who is the son of Kausalya. In nobility he resembles the mighty ocean and he is firm in his convictions like the great Himavan. In prowess he is like Narayana and he is as pleasing to the sight as the moon. If his anger is aroused, he will be like the fire which burns up the Universe at the end of Time. Patient like mother earth, he is generous like Kubera. He is like Dharma, the lord of righteousness in truthfulness: and, in short, he is a paragon of all the virtues which adorn the human being."

Valmiki, who had been sitting quiet all the while, became greatly excited at the words of Narada and his eyes flashed with a great happiness. Loth to interrupt the flow of words from the lips of Narada his eyes beseeched the divine rishi to tell him more. Sensing his eagerness Narada, with a smile lighting his young face, continued his talk. "Dasaratha, the father of Rama," said Narada, "was very eager to crown his eldest son Rama as the yuvaraja of the kingdom: Rama who was noble, who was the home of all virtues, the great qualities we spoke of just now. The king began, to make all preparations for the coronation. His younger wife, Kaikeyi, however, was against the coronation. With the help of two boons which she had been granted long ago, she made the king agree to her stipulations. One of them was the crowning of her son Bharata as the king and the other was the banishment of Rama to the dreaded Dandaka forest. The unfortunate king, bound as he was by his promise, had to conform to her wishes and he banished Rama to the forest. The noble prince Rama agreed to go away to please his father and to fulfil the promise of the king. Rama's brother Lakshmana who was born of Sumitra was devoted to Rama and he decided to accompany Rama in his exile.

"Rama had a wife by name Sita. She was dear to him as his very life. She was the daughter of Janaka. Born, as she was, of a noble race, this jewel among women followed her lord Rama even as the star Rohini does the moon.

"On the banks of the river Ganga dwelt a hunter by name Guha. Rama spent the first night of his exile in Shringiberapura, the capital of the hunter king. After sending the charioteer Sumantra back to Ayodhya, the capital of the Ikshvaku kings, Rama, Lakshmana and Sita crossed the river Ganga with the help of Guha. They then arrived at the ashrama of Bharadwaja. The rishi advised them to go to the hill by name Chitrakuta and to build a hermitage there. They crossed many coppices and fords and small rivers and finally arrived at the hill by name Chitrakuta. Lakshmana built a hermitage and the three of them were dwelling happily there in the midst of so much natural beauty.

"Even as Rama was approaching Chitrakuta, Dasaratha, his father, unable to bear the separation from his beloved son Rama, abandoned his mortal frame and was gathered to his forefathers. Bharata had all the while been with his uncle Yudhajit, the brother of Kaikeyi. Vasishtha the royal preceptor sent for him and when the funeral obsequies were completed, the wise man told Bharata about the danger of a country which was without a ruler and asked Bharata to take up the reins of the kingdom and rule it as his father had done.

"Bharata refused to do so. Instead, he made up his mind to go to the forest, meet Rama and bring him back to Ayodhya. He went to Chitrakuta accompanied by his subjects and the ministers and Vasishtha. He met Rama and beseeched him to accept the kingdom. He said: 'My Lord, you are the king and you must come back and take up the responsibility of ruling the kingdom.' But Rama who was ever famed for granting anyone his wish was firm in this one instance and refused to grant Bharata his wish. He would not accept the kingdom since that would falsify his father's promise. Finally, as a compromise, Bharata asked for the sandals of Rama and told him that he would place them on the throne and rule the kingdom in the name of Rama, as his representative. Rama agreed to it. Bharata took an oath that he would enter Ayodhya only with Rama. He therefore stayed in a small village by name Nandigrama which was on the fringe of the city of Ayodhya. There he stayed dressed in tree-bark and deerskin and with his hair matted even as Rama's and Lakshmana's were. He was governing the country waiting eagerly for the coming of Rama.

"Rama, in the meantime, felt that he should abandon Chitrakuta since the people of Ayodhya knew his whereabouts. Therefore he decided to penetrate into the Dandaka. The first event in the Dandaka was his slaying of the rakshasa by name Viradha. He then proceeded to the ashramas of Sharabhanga, Sutheekshna, Agastya and the brother of Agastya. Agastya made a gift of the great bow of Indra to Rama. He also gave him a beautiful sword and two quivers which were inexhaustible.

"The rishis in the forest approached Rama with a request. They told him about their being harassed by the rakshasas who were dwelling in their midst and asked Rama to protect them. Rama listened to them and told them that he would do so. He said that he would destroy all the rakshasas. It was a solemn promise made by Rama.

"They went to a spot by name Panchavati. It was on the banks of the river Godavari and it was beautiful. There Lakshmana built an ashrama and they spent a happy time there. By now thirteen years had been spent in exile.

"When they were in Panchavati, Surpanakha, a rakshasi who was dwelling in the Janasthana came to Rama and expressed her love for him. Incensed at this, Rama caused her to be disfigured. Lakshmana took up his sword and cut off her nose and ears. She went to her brother Khara and complained to him about the insult to herself by two *mere men*. At her instigation Khara, Dushana and Trishiras, with an army made up of fourteen thousand rakshasas accosted Rama. Rama killed all of them single-handed and thus rid the Janasthana of all the rakshasas.

"Khara and the other two were cousins of Ravana, the lord of Lanka. Hearing about the incidents in Janasthana, Ravana decided to avenge the deaths of his cousins and the destruction of the army and also the insult to Surpanakha. He went to Maricha, a rakshasa, for assistance. Maricha tried in many ways to convince Ravana of the prowess of Rama and about the dangers of arousing his anger. But Ravana paid no heed to his words. Prodded as he was, by fate, Ravana took Maricha with him and arrived in the neighbourhood of the ashrama of Rama. With the help of his maya at which he was an adept, Maricha lured Rama and later Lakshmana away from the ashrama. And, when Sita was alone in the ashrama, Ravana carried her away. Jatayu, the king of eagles, was a friend of Rama and he tried in vain to prevent Ravana from abducting Sita. He was fatally wounded and Ravana went away with the princess.

"When they came back to the ashrama Rama and Lakshmana found it empty. With Sita abducted and with seeing Jatayu who was dying, Rama was beside himself with grief and anguish. He heard about Ravana from the lips of dying Jatayu and, when the eagle died, Rama performed the funeral rites for him as he would, for his own father.

"The brothers then went southwards in search of Sita. While

they were proceeding thus, they were caught in the arms of a gruesome-looking rakshasa by name Kabandha. His arms were a yojana long each and his head was in his stomach. His mouth was wide open to swallow his victims. Kabandha was, in reality, the son of Kubera who had been cursed to assume this form. When he was killed by the brothers he regained his celestial form and returned to the heaven. Before leaving him Kabandha told Rama about Shabari, a devotee of Rama who was waiting for the coming of Rama. Kabandha also said that on top of the Rishyamooka hill dwelt a vanara by name Sugriva who would help Rama to find Sita.

"Rama went to the ashrama of Shabari, was worshipped by her and he gave her leave to reach the heavens which she had earned by her tapas.

"Rama and Lakshmana proceeded on their journey and reached the lake known by the name Pampa and, after passing it, they were wandering around at the foot of the hill Rishyamooka. They were accosted by Hanuman, the minister of Sugriva. Hanuman took them to the presence of Sugriva. A great and lasting friendship was formed between these two, Rama and Sugriva, and this was forged by fire which was kindled by the wise Hanuman. Rama recounted to Sugriva about himself and about the misfortune which had befallen him: the abduction of Sita by some rakshasa. Sugriva came out with his story and the unfortunate condition he was in, banished from his city by his brother Vali. Rama promised to kill Vali to please Sugriva. The vanara was dubious about the prowess of Rama and he recounted the many acts of valour performed by his brother. To assure him of his own superior strength Rama lifted the skeleton of one Dundubhi with the tip of his toe and flung it to a distance of ten yojanas. And again, with a single arrow he pierced seven glorious sala trees. Sugriva was ashamed of himself for his lack of faith in Rama and said: 'This arrow of yours has pierced the seven salas, split the earth open and, after entering the nether regions it has returned to your quiver. Never before have I seen such valour. Forgive me for doubting you.'

"They went to Kishkindha, the capital city of Vali. Sugriva called out to the great warrior Vali and challenged him to come out and fight with him. Rama killed Vali with a single arrow and established Sugriva on the throne of the dead Vali.

"Sugriva then summoned his entire army and despatched his men to all the four quarters to search for Sita. Hanuman, accompanied by Angada, the son of Vali, went towards the south. There, directed by Sampati, the eagle king who was the brother of Jatayu, Hanuman crossed the sea which was a hundred yojanas wide. He reached the island by name Lanka. There, in the king's pleasure garden by name Ashokavana, Hanuman found Sita who was kept there as a captive. Thinking only of Rama, the princess was a picture of woe. Hanuman announced himself to her, gave her the signet ring which Rama had sent and comforted her with words of encouragement. He gave her news about Rama and Lakshmana and he told her that Rama, assisted by Sugriva and his army, would soon arrive in Lanka and rescue her from Ravana.

"Hanuman then destroyed the Ashokavana. Ravana sent his army to capture him. But five of his commanders and seven of their sons, as also the brave Akshaya, the son of Ravana, were killed by Hanuman. Indrajit, another son of Ravana, came and he despatched the Brahma astra at Hanuman. The vanara did not want to insult the great Brahma and so he allowed himself to be bound by the astra. He was then taken to the court of Ravana. Thereafter he burnt the city of Lanka and returned to the presence of Rama. He carried with him the good tidings that Sita was alive and that she was a captive of Ravana.

"Accompanied by Sugriva, Rama came to the shores of the sea. When the lord of the seas would not make way for him and his army Rama was highly incensed and threatened to burn up the entire sea. The king of the waters appeared in front of Rama and asked him to build a bridge across the sea which would take them to Lanka.

"Accordingly, Nala, the architect, built the bridge. Crossing the sea, Rama went to Lanka, killed Ravana and rescued Sita. However, he spoke harsh words to her. Unable to bear the stinging insults Sita entered fire. Agni, the god of fire brought her to Rama out of the flames and told Rama that he should accept her since she was without any taint.

"The world above and the world of men praised the prowess of Rama. They celebrated the great achievements of Rama. After crowning Vibhishana, the brother of Ravana as the king of Lanka, Rama made up his mind to turn his steps homewards. With the blessings of the devas the vanaras who had died in the war came back to life and there was great rejoicing. In the celestial chariot by name Pushpaka, Rama, along with his friends, proceeded towards Ayodhya. He went to the ashrama of Bharadwaja first to pay his respects to him and from there he sent Hanuman to Bharata to inform him of his return. Rama then went to Nandigrama with Sugriva. In Nandigrama he was reunited with his brothers Bharata and Shatrughna. After getting rid of his matted locks Rama assumed the garments of a king and was crowned king of Kosala. The people were thrilled with the return of Rama and there was great rejoicing in the city of Ayodhya.

"Rama rules the kingdom righteously and there is not a breath of adharma in the rule of Rama.

"After performing a hundred ashvamedhas Rama will reach the heavens. He will establish dharma on the earth. He will rule for eleven thousand years before he leaves the earth. One who hears this tale of Rama will be assured of a place in heaven."

Having recounted the story of Rama to Valmiki, Narada took leave of him and went away from his ashrama.

2. THE COMING OF BRAHMA

After the departure of Narada, Valmiki was sitting quiet for a while, thinking on the glorious personage, Rama, and his mind was dwelling on Rama. The rishi suddenly realised that it was time for him to perform his morning worship and so, accompanied by his disciple, he went to the banks of the river Tamasa which was very near the more famous Ganga.

He saw a spot where the water was pellucid and he stopped in his tracks. He spoke to his disciple and said: "Son, the water here is clear and pure like the mind of a good man. Look how beautiful it is! I have decided to perform my ablutions here, in this spot. Place the water-pot here, on the ground, and give me the tree-bark."

The disciple did as he was bid. With the Valkala in his hand the rishi looked all around him, his eyes pleased with the beauty of the surroundings. He took a few steps here and there and smiled to himself as he saw how lavish mother nature had been in her bounty in this particular place. Looking up at a tree the rishi saw a couple of Krauncha birds. They were singing happily in their sweet and melodious voices and they were very much in love with each other. They were making love and Valmiki's eyes rested on them with tolerant amusement.

Even as he was looking, he saw the male Krauncha fall down, hit by an arrow. Valmiki saw a hunter, sinful and cruel, who had just shot an arrow at the bird. The bird was lying dead on the ground drenched in blood and the female Krauncha was wailing piteously, and her joyous song of a moment ago had turned into a mournful dirge. The small bird with its red head was full of sorrow. Valmiki saw the cruel act of the hunter and its sad consequence and his heart was filled with compassion.

He knew what an adharmi the hunter had been and he spoke in an impassioned voice: "You have been merciless in your action. You killed one of these two birds when they were making love. Your act is unforgivable. You will therefore be denied the long span of life granted to man."

Valmiki then turned away from him and left the spot in a hurry. His heart was still full of sadness and he thought over the incident long after he had gone away from there. He kept remembering the words he had spoken to the hunter and he repeated them in his mind. He told his disciple: "I was very sad because of what had happened to the Krauncha birds. And I spoke some words. Born as they were out of my sorrow, these words are so arranged that they follow a metre. They seem to form a sloka which can even be sung to the accompaniment of the drone of the Veena. I am amazed at the sloka which I seem to have composed." The disciple learnt the sloka and when he repeated it there was wonder at the formation of it.

Valmiki then entered the river and performed the ablutions, the worship of the sun and all the daily rituals. But his mind was all the while dwelling on the sloka. They returned to the ashrama, the rishi in the lead and the disciple carrying the water-pot filled now with the pure water from the Tamasa. Valmiki entered the ashrama and, with his other disciples, pursued with them the study of the sacred lore.

While he was thus engaged he found the hermitage filled suddenly with a heavenly glow. He looked up and saw Lord Brahma himself standing there. He got up with a feeling of awe and stood with folded palms. He could not speak a word, so overcome was he with the suddenness of it all. He then worshipped the Creator in the proper manner, fell at his feet and offered Arghya Padya and a befitting seat.

Brahma honoured him by accepting his homage and the seat offered by him. After seating himself at the command of Brahma, Valmiki sat silent and his mind was pondering on the event of the river bank. He could not still grasp the cruelty of a hunter who could deliberately kill the happy bird without any cause whatever. Again the sloka came to his mind and he repeated it to himself silently.

Brahma smiled at him and divining his thoughts said: "Do not wonder any more about the words you spoke. *IT IS A SLOKA* and there is no doubt about it. I willed you to speak thus. I want you to compose a great poem in the same metre. Relate the story of Rama. Narada told you the story of Rama who is famed the world over for his righteousness, for his nobility, his intelligence, his courage. I will grant this boon to you: you will be able to know what passed in the minds of everyone of them: Rama, Lakshmana, Sita and the many participants in the strange tale. In short, there will be nothing which is a secret withheld from you. You will know everything which happened and every thought in the mind of each of them.

"In this kavya which you are going to compose there will not be a single word of untruth spoken. I command you to relate to the world of men the sacred story of Rama set in the same metre in which you composed the sloka you are thinking about: the Anushtup metre. The world will be the richer for the composition of yours. So long as the story of Rama is remembered in the world, you will also be remembered. Your name will be immortal because of what you are going to do." Brahma vanished from the presence of Valmiki after he had spoken these words. Valmiki was still in a daze and so were his disciples. They repeated the sloka again and again and with each repetition the wonderment grew.

3. VALMIKI COMPOSES THE GREAT POEM

Valmiki touched water to purify himself. He then spread darbha grass on the floor and sat on it facing the east. He closed his eyes and went into a deep trance. He thought of the task assigned to him and he told himself: "As the Lord has commanded, I will compose the poem in the metre which came to my mind and in the sloka form. It will be the story of Rama and his achievements and I will name it the *Ramayana*."

The more he thought about it, the clearer became his vision and his intellect, and he could see with his mind's eye all the many events which had taken place. He could visualise the old king Dasaratha with his wives around him, looking at his four sons with eyes filled with joy and pride. And he saw Rama and Lakshmana with Sita in the Dandaka forest. It was as clear to him as the palm of his hand. The great rishi related to the world the glorious story of Rama and the poem was full of noble thoughts and noble deeds like the ocean is full of rare and costly gems.

Valmiki remembered the manner in which Narada had spoken of Rama and in the same strain he composed the kavya. It was made up of beautiful sounding words, words which were pleasing to the mind as well as to the ears, words which were faultless in their formation, and their meaning was as clear as the waters of a placid lake in the Himalaya. In a short while he was able to compose the poem. He had completed the epic *Ramayana* which spoke of the story of Rama, of the killing of Ravana. There were twenty-four thousand verses, slokas, in the kavya and the rishi was pleased with what he had done. He divided the kavya into six sections: five hundred chapters were needed to relate the story in its completeness.

After the completion of the kavya Valmiki was wondering about the proper person who would be able to recite the poem and thus propagate it. Even as he was thinking on it two youngsters, Kusa and Lava, came to his presence, prostrated before him and took the dust of his feet. The youngsters who were princes had been with the rishi to learn the sacred lore. They had very attractive voices and since they were twins their voices blended together very well. To them Valmiki taught the kavya by name *Ramayana*. They learnt it and they sang it to the accompaniment of the Veena. They sang like gandharvas.

These two handsome, sweet-spoken boys with their large eyes were the sons of Rama. After they had learnt the entire kavya the youngsters began to travel from ashrama to ashrama singing all the while the story of Rama.

Once, Rama was performing the great yaga by name Ashvamedha, the horse sacrifice. The young princes, dressed in tree-bark and deer-skin, went to the spot and there, in the midst of the many rishis assembled there, they sang the *Ramayana*. The rishis listened, with tears in their eyes, to this glorious tale filled with all the nine emotions which a kavya should have. And they praised the youngsters. The fame of these two young boys was the only topic of conversation among the rishis and others who had heard them and the news reached the ears of Rama, the king. He saw them too with their Veenas and he heard their voices from a distance. His curiosity was soon kindled and he sent for them. They came to his palace and he welcomed them. In the council hall was seated Rama surrounded by his ministers and his dear brothers. He had assumed the garb proper for one performing the yaga and he was charmed by the looks of the youngsters. He spoke to his brothers and said: "They glow with a radiance which is unearthly and their voice is heavenly too. Let us listen to them singing."

The song, which was accompanied by the hypnotic drone of the Veenas filled the hall. As the tale progressed, Rama, who was seated on the throne descended unobtrusively from there step by step and sat on the floor with the others listening to the glorious kavya. He sat spellbound and he listened as though it were the story of someone else and not himself. Tears were flowing from his eyes when he sat down to listen to the *Ramayana*.

"This story concerns the great line of kings whose founder was Manu and which has been immortalised by the name of Ikshvaku, the son of Manu, and, later, by Sagara and others." Thus began the kavya and Rama sat and listened as though he were a figure carved out of a block of marble.

4. DASARATHA, AND HIS GRIEF

There was a country by name Kosala and on the outskirts of the country flowed the river Sarayu. The land belonged to the Ikshvakus, the descendants of Manu, one of the Prajapatis. Kosala was beautiful and it was famed for its beauty, the richness of its soil, its luscious greenery, the abundance of its crops, its wealth and its prosperity. The kings of the solar race who had always ruled it were famed the world over for their valour and for their righteousness. The capital of the land of Kosala was Ayodhya.

Tradition had it that Manu, the great law-giver, had created the city. It was a wondrous city with flowering trees and with wide beautiful roads where the king rode everyday. The roads were well laid out and the royal pathway was ever beautiful with flowers and scented water sprinkled on it all the time. Ayodhya was like Amaravati, the city of Indra.

Ayodhya was ruled by Dasaratha even as Amaravati was by Indra. Dasaratha had earned for himself the name Rajarshi since he had always been a god-fearing man. He was a wise king. He had charmed his subjects by his good nature. As befitted a scion of the race of Ikshvaku, he had earned the praise of all the many rishis and good people for his prowess coupled with gentleness. He had performed all the yajnas which a king had to perform and he was a king beloved by all. The people were happy and contented. None of them was jealous and not one was avaricious. They were all rich and they spoke nothing but the truth. Everyone was wealthy and everyone was noble. There was no meanness, no lust, and even ugliness was absent. The people were all well-read and no one was an atheist. There was no unhappiness in the mind of even one of them: such a good king was Dasaratha, the descendant of Ikshvaku.

Dasaratha had eight ministers who were well-versed in the art of advising the king in matters of importance. They were highly intelligent, great diplomats, and they were all the time interested in the well-being of their king and his subjects. The ministers were: Dhriti, Jayanta, Vijaya, Siddhartha, Arthasadaka, Asoka, Mantrapala and Sumantra. The king also had great priests to advise him on matters pertaining to religion and religious rites and rituals. The chief of them were Vasishtha and Vamadeva. They were great scholars and they were famed for their learning, for their pride and self-respect, for their self-control, their penance. They were glorious men who had thoughts only for the good of others, the king and his subjects.

The king's ministers were so efficient that there was nothing which escaped their notice. They knew about the happenings in all the neighbouring countries. The treasury of the king was ever full and so was the granary.

Such a great king, who had everything he could wish for, was not perfectly happy. He had no son to make him happy. The line of the Ikshvakus threatened to terminate with him since he had no one to succeed him. King Dasaratha was unhappy because of this and this sorrow ate into his vitals day and night. And, as he grew older, his sorrow increased too.

One day, while thinking on this, the king thought: "Why should I not perform the yaga by name Ashvamedha? I have been told that it is a rewarding yaga. Perhaps my prayers may be answered if I perform the horse sacrifice." He called for a meeting of his counsellors. When they had all come the king asked them to be seated and sent Sumantra to fetch the rishis who surrounded him during the performance of religious rites. He said: "Sumantra, bring to me the revered gurus, Vasishtha, Vamadeva, Suyagnya, Jabali, Kashyapa and their disciples too." Within a short while Sumantra brought all of them to the great council hall. The king received them with all due honour and after seating them properly, paying attention to their status, the king spoke to them.

"Surrounded as I am by the wealth of this land and by many beautiful objects of pleasure, still, my mind is sorely troubled by sorrow. I have no son and that makes me unhappy. I feel that the performing of the Ashvamedha may be an answer to my prayers. This is just a thought that has occurred to me. It is up to all of you to weigh it carefully and tell me if I have thought right."

They approved of his suggestion and said: "O king! this desire of yours to perform the Ashvamedha for the purpose of continuing the glorious line of the Ikshvakus, is, indeed, commendable. That you should have thought of it is, in itself, a sign that your wishes will be granted. It is but right that we should hasten and make preparations for the yaga to be performed. Let us, from now, collect the materials for it. The horse should be found. Let the yajnasala be built on the northern side of the river Sarayu."

The king was very pleased with the spontaneous approval of those assembled in the hall. With his eyes wide open with joy he spoke to his ministers: "Take the advice of my acharyas and make all the arrangements. Construct the yajnasala on the northern banks of Sarayu as has been suggested. All the rituals must be performed properly. Any lapse will cause severe repercussions on all of us. Be very careful to listen to the biddings of the mentors, Vasishtha and the others." "We will obey you and the great ones," said the ministers and the great hall emptied itself slowly. There was a strange glow of happiness on the face of the king. Something inside him seemed to assure him that he would be blessed with a son and, with that thought uppermost in his mind, he entered the inner apartments and told his wives about his decision.

When he was alone in his chambers, came to the king, his charioteer Sumantra. He said: "My lord, I remembered suddenly something which I had heard long ago. I thought it but right that I should come to you immediately with the information I have. The news is very ancient and so it had slipped from my memory till now. But when you spoke of the yaga, I remembered it.

"Many years ago, the famous rishi by name Sanatkumara had spoken about the birth of your son in the presence of several rishis. He said: 'Kashyapa, the revered sage, has a son by name Vibhandaka. He will be the father of Rishyashringa. This son of Vibhandaka will live in the forest with his father. He will not know any other human being and he will look to his father for the smallest action which he has to perform. He will be innocent in the ways of the world. In course of time a king will be ruling the country by name Anga. His name will be Romapada. Because of a slight misdeed of the king his country will suffer. A terrible famine will visit the country of Anga and the king will ask the advice of holy men as to how he can pacify the gods and bring rain to the country. And the holy men will say: "O king! if the son of the sage Vibhandaka is brought to the country rain will follow in his wake. The young man is called Rishyashringa and if you bring him to your country and give your daughter Shanta to him in marriage there will be an end to the dread famine." The king will wonder as to how this can be achieved. He will request his wise ministers and preceptors in his court to go to the forest to bring the young sage. But the anger of Vibhandaka is too well known and no one will have the courage to go. They will advise the king to send the courtesans of the palace to the forest and they will succeed where others are afraid to venture. Rishyashringa will, later preside over a yajna which will be performed by Dasaratha and, because of this, the king will be the father of sons.' Sumantra continued: "My lord, if you should, with the permission of guru Vasishtha, approach the rishi Rishyashringa and beseech him to perform a yajna for you, the prophecy of Sanatkumara is certain to come true. Let me assure you that Sanatkumara has said that you will be the father of four sons who will be valiant and who will be famed the world over. Please go to the kingdom of Anga and do not hesitate or delay."

5. THE ASHVAMEDHA YAGA

King Dasaratha spoke to Vasishtha and Vamadeva about the words of Sanatkumara which had been repeated to him by Sumantra. The gurus were only too happy to have Rishyashringa among them during the performance of the yaga. The king, therefore, accompanied by a large army and by his chief ministers and preceptors began the journey to Anga and, after travelling through forests and several countries arrived at the city where Romapada lived. Hearing about the coming of the great emperor of Kosala, Romapada hurried out of his city and went to the city gates to welcome Dasaratha with great enthusiasm. The two kings greeted each other with great affection and, together, they went to the presence of Rishyashringa. The rishi was glowing like a flame. The king of the Kosala fell at his feet and honoured him. Romapada told him about the great friendship which had existed between himself and King Dasaratha.

They spent seven days together happily and on the eighth day Dasaratha told his friend: "I have a boon to ask of you, my friend. I want you to allow your daughter and her husband, the great rishi, to come to my kingdom for a while. This is to help me achieve something for which I have been praying for the last so many years." He then told Romapada about the yaga which he was planning to perform. Dasaratha now approached Rishyashringa and requested him to preside over the function. "So be it," said the rishi and went with Dasaratha to Ayodhya. The friends parted after affectionate farewells.

Dasaratha sent a host of messengers in advance asking them to prepare the city for the arrival of the illustrious guest. When the royal entourage arrived in the city the streets had been decorated with banners and flags and flower garlands and the entire city had a festive look. The king took the rishi and his wife to his antahpura and made them stay in the apartments set apart for them. When he had brought them to his city the king felt that he had already achieved the goal for which he was striving.

The season Vasanta had now made its appearance. The rivers were filled with pure and sweet waters and the trees were covered with fresh green leaves. Dasaratha approached the honoured guest Rishyashringa and requested him to undertake the performance of the yaga. The rishi said: "Now that the season Vasanta is here I feel the time is perfect for the beginning of the yaga. You should instruct the ministers and your servants to collect the materials for the yaga and you can now send the sacrificial horse for its sojourn round the entire Bharatavarsha."

The king listened to him with respectful attention and he instructed Sumantra to take care of all the details. He sent him first to fetch his guru Vasishtha accompanied by Vamadeva, Suyagnya and the others. They came, the masters of all the Vedas and all the sacred lore. Honouring them and placing them on their seats the king spoke in his characteristic humble manner: "You know only too well how much I have been pained at the thought that I have no son to continue the mighty line of the Ikshvakus. I have told you about the prophecy that my sorrow will be at an end if I perform the yajna with the great Rishyashringa to preside over it. I now stand humbly in front of all of you asking you to grant me permission to commence the yaga and to bless me." Vasishtha and the others were pleased with the humility of the king and knowing what a righteous man he was, they were happy that he was about to perform the yajna which would be the crowning glory of his life. Along with Rishyashringa they began to make all the preparations for the yajna. And they told the king: "We can assure you that the yajna will be performed without any hindrance and your wishes will certainly be granted."

On the northern bank of the Sarayu the yajnasala was soon constructed and the materials necessary for such an elaborate yajna were assembled methodically and very quickly. The seasons passed quickly and once again Vasanta heralded its approach by the fresh green buds on the branches of the barren trees. The very air seemed to breathe more freely and there was happiness in the city and in the heart of the king and his queens since the yajna was due to begin.

Dasaratha took the dust of the feet of Vasishtha and the others and spoke to his guru: "My lord, you have been my preceptor. You have been like a father to me since you were the one to initiate me into the great Gayatri. It is up to you to make this yajna successful and make me happy."

Attended by all the kings of Bharatavarsha the yajna was performed without a single fault and the Ashvamedha yaga was drawing to a close. The king then requested Rishyashringa to help him perform the yaga by name Putrakama which would grant him the son he desired. The rishi pondered for a moment and then said: "There is a certain rite which is described in detail in the Atharva Veda. I happen to know all about it and I will perform it for you."

The Putrakama Yajna was begun at an auspicious moment and the heavenly host assembled in the skies to receive their share of the *havis*.

6. THE DEVAS IN DISTRESS

While the Ashvamedha was in progress the devas led by Indra went to Brahma, the Creator. They said: "My Lord, we are sorely distressed and only you can help us."

Brahma wanted to know what was troubling them and they said: "We are unable to bear the valour of Ravana. He has been harassing us no end and we have reached a point when we can bear it no longer. Your gracious self has granted him boons which have made him powerful: so powerful that we have to behave like his menial slaves. Because he has been favoured by you we have to suffer the many indignities he has been heaping on us. We have to bear the many atrocities he has been committing. But then, my lord, we have reached the limit of endurance. You must devise for us some means of escape from Ravana and his persistent ill-treatment of us. He frightens all the three worlds and he has been wanting to insult me in my Amaravati. Yakshas, gandharvas and rishis are all scared of him and his cruelty. The sun is afraid to glow too brightly lest Ravana should punish him. Vayu does not blow too hard since he is in great fear of the asura king. When his eyes rest on it, even the sea with its ever-rolling waves comes to a standstill. You have granted him such a powerful boon that he cannot be killed by any of us. It is up to you to think of some method by which his destruction can be brought about."

Brahma listened to them and said: "You are right. I have granted him immunity from the hands of devas, danavas, rakshasas, gandharvas, yakshas and so you are all helpless. In his arrogance, however, Ravana did not deem it worthy of himself to ask immunity from the hands of a mere man. And, that is how he will be killed: by a man."

When they were talking thus, there came to their presence Narayana, the Lord of lords, Narayana with the Shanka and Chakra. He was borne by Garuda and seated on Garuda with his golden silk glowing softly. Narayana looked like the sun surmounting a cloud.

Brahma and the devas were overwhelmed by the coming of Lord Narayana and they worshipped him with folded palms. They said: "Please protect us from suffering. Protect the world from evil. We look to you for succour. We do not have to tell you what is worrying us since you have come to us with the sole purpose of helping us and the entire Universe. You will be born as a man, we gather, to destroy Ravana." Narayana stood smiling and looked at them as though he were asking them to continue. Brahma said: "My lord, the good king Dasaratha of the Surya Vamsa is performing the yaga by name Putrakama and it is being presided over by the sage Rishyashringa. Dasaratha has three wives. If I may make a humble suggestion, please make us happy by being born as the son of Dasaratha. It has been prophesied that he will be the father of four sons and all the four sons will be the amshas of you. Your Avatara is essential for the good of mankind and for the good of the heavens. You, and only you, my lord, will be able to vanquish Ravana. He is too powerful for anyone else."

Narayana listened to the words of Brahma and said: "Have no fear. I have made up my mind to be born in the world of men. I will destroy this tyrant Ravana with his entire clan and I have but this one purpose to fulfil when I descend into the world. After killing him I will rule the world for eleven thousand years before coming back to my abode."

Narayana had thought over this problem of the Avatara he had to undertake to save the world from Ravana. He had been wondering as to who was worthy enough to be his father and he knew that Dasaratha, the ever-righteous, who was performing the Putrakama yaga would be his father. He told the devas and Brahma about his decision and they were overjoyed. A few more years and their sorrow would be at an end. They prostrated before him and praised him and his glory in words full of adoration.

Narayana said: "To assist me in my mission you should all be born in the world of men too. Ravana has forgotten to ask for immunity from monkeys and bears also. I would, therefore, like you all to be born as monkeys and help me when the time comes."

7. THE BIRTH OF RAMA

The Putrakama yaga was almost drawing to a close. Everyone was watching and, all on a sudden, the fire seemed to burn with an unearthly glow. Out of the fire rose a divine form. He was dark and he was clad in crimson silk. His hair was tawny, golden, like the mane of the lion. He was wearing ornaments made of gold and set with precious stones. He was like the sun in radiance and his arms were decked with bracelets of gold. A chandrahara adorned has immense chest and his smile was as soft and charming as the radiance of the moon. The entire yajnasala was illuminated by his presence. The king looked at him and stood with his palms folded. He saw that the divine being held in his hands a golden bowl with a silver covering. The celestial form spoke to the king in the midst of everyone. He said: "I am a messenger from the Creator, Brahma. I have been commanded by the gods to hand you this vessel filled with payasa. Give it to your queens and they will bear you the sons for whom you have been aching since so many years."

The king prostrated before the divine being and accepted the bowl of payasa with great reverence. When he had taken it in his hands the divine being blessed him and vanished from his presence.

The yaga had come to a glorious conclusion and the rishis blessed the king and asked him to go into the inner chambers and distribute the payasa to the queens.

The king went to Kausalya, the eldest of the queens and told her: "Look, my queen, the gods have answered our prayers and a son is to be born to you." And so saying, he gave half the payasa to her and asked her to partake of it. He then gave half of what was left to Sumitra and half of what was left, to Kaikeyi, the youngest queen. Seeing that there was still some left, he gave this again to Sumitra and there was great joy in the hearts of the queens and that of the king.

The devas, after receiving their shares of the *havis*, went back to their abodes. The yaga had been completed and the citizens followed the king and the rishis into the city of Ayodhya. The kings who had attended the yaga went back to their kingdoms after having been honoured by the king. Rishis from different parts of the world returned to their ashramas after taking part in the two yagas.

THE BIRTH OF RAMA

Sage Rishyashringa accompanied by his wife Shanta went back to the kingdom of Anga.

The king Dasaratha was happy in the anticipation of the births of the children. He felt that he was a god and not a human being: so great was his happiness.

The month of Chaitra was once again heralding its approach. Vasanta made its appearance felt by the pleasant breeze which was wafted across the ponds filled with lotuses and by the trees which were clad in soft fresh green.

The month was Chaitra. It was the fortnight when the moon was waxing—Shuklapaksha—and it was the ninth day after the new moon. Five planets were in very auspicious positions. The lagna was Karkataka and the planet Guru was rising with the moon. The star was Punarvasu. The Lord of lords had assumed the form of a human being for the good of mankind and was born as the son of Kausalya. Kausalya glowed with radiance like Aditi did, when Indra was born to her.

When the next star Pushya appeared, under the Meena lagna was born a son to Kaikeyi.

The gentle Sumitra gave birth to twins when the next star appeared, the star Ashlesha.

The four sons of king Dasaratha were all the amshas of Narayana and Kausalya's son was Narayana himself.

There was joy and nothing but joy in the hearts of all the people in Ayodhya. The great king Dasaratha who had been childless was now the father of four sons and great were the rejoicings in the country of Kosala.

When the children were born divine instruments made music in the heavens and the gandharvas sang and danced out of happiness. They danced and they sang because soon, very soon, their woes would be at an end since Ravana would be killed. Flowers rained on the divine children.

The city of Ayodhya was dressed in her best. All the people were thronging to the palace gates. Music and dancing and various expressions of joy were to be found wherever people gathered. It was like Indra's festival for them and the streets were filled with men and women and children dressed in their finery.

The king gave away gold and gifts of cows to brahmins and others. Eleven days passed after the sons were born to the king. It was the day when the children should be named. The preceptor Vasishtha named Kausalya's son as Rama. The son of Kaikeyi was named Bharata and Sumitra's two sons were named Lakshmana and Shatrughna. After the ceremony had been completed the king performed the Jatakarma and other rites associated with a new-born child.

The children grew up like the moon during Shukla paksha.

Ever since they were born, ever since they were children, Lakshmana, who was very beautiful and gentle, became greatly attached to Rama. Rama too, was extremely fond of Lakshmana. It seemed as though Lakshmana was Rama himself: as though his very life had taken up a form and was moving about with the name Lakshmana. Rama would not go to sleep unless Lakshmana was placed by his side and fed with the same milk and rice. And, later, when they grew up, whenever Rama went out to hunt Lakshmana had to be by his side with his bow and arrows.

Even as Lakshmana was dear to Rama, Shatrughna, his twin became the alter ego of Bharata. King Dasaratha was in the seventh heaven of happiness surrounded as he was, by his four sons who were all handsome, strong, powerful, righteous, respectful to their father and mothers and their Guru, their Kulaguru who taught them the sacred lore, sage Vasishtha.

They were heroes, all four of them and their learning was great, taught as they were by the great Vasishtha himself. They were well versed in the art of fighting like all kshatriya princes and they were very humble and very soft-spoken. They were proficient in riding on the elephant, on the horse, and in driving a chariot. They were all four of them good archers and they were very fond of their father.

Of the four, Rama was the favourite of his father. He was as sweet, beautiful and gentle as the full moon and his father was inordinately fond of Rama. And Rama was ever engaged in pleasing his father in every way.

The princes were like lions among men and the king was extremely proud of his sons. They were now nearing the age of sixteen and Dasaratha was the happiest man on the earth, surrounded as he was, by these four sons.

8. VISHVAMITRA COMES TO DASARATHA

The sons of the king were now grown up. They were nearing sixteen and entering manhood. As was the custom, sixteen was the age when a young man was to be married and, accordingly, the king thought of it. The king Dasaratha was wondering as to who the bride of Rama should be. Since Rama was the favourite son the king could think only of Rama and his mind was ever thinking of the many ways and means of pleasing Rama. Rama, on his part, thought of nothing else but making his father happy in every way. The kinship between them was so great that everyone in the palace or even Ayodhya knew about it.

One day in the council hall the king spoke to his ministers about the subject uppermost in his mind: the marriage of Rama and his brothers. Even as he was thinking thus, there arrived at the doorsteps of the king the sage Vishvamitra. He accosted the doorkeepers and said: "Go and announce to the king about my arrival. I am Kaushika, the son of Gadhi. People call me Vishvamitra." The name was so well known that even the doorkeepers knew about him. They were greatly excited and, with hurried steps, went to the presence of the king. Entering the council hall they rushed to the king and told him about the arrival of Vishvamitra. The king was greatly pleased that such an illustrious rishi should have come to see him. He got up from the throne and, accompanied by his preceptors, he went to receive the rishi.

Padya in hand Dasaratha stood before the guest and washed his feet. He then offered Arghya and other prescribed objects used for worshipping such guests. Accepting the welcome of the king with grace and with a smile Vishvamitra entered the palace of the king. He made the conventional enquiries about the kingdom, about the subjects, about the welfare of the people and, in return, Dasaratha spoke about the ashrama of the rishi, his tapas and the welfare of the inmates of the ashrama. When the formalities were over Vishvamitra paid his respects to Vasishtha and the others. He accepted the seat offered to him. The king then spoke to Vishvamitra. He said:

"Your coming is like a godsend to me: like the divine nectar to a human being: like rain water to one who is thirsty: like the birth of a son to a man and his good wife: like the finding of a treasure to one who has lost his entire wealth. I am indeed thrilled at the coming of a great personage like your gracious self. Can it be possible that I will be granted the privilege of doing something for you? Something to please you? That a Brahmarshi like you should have come to me on your own, means some great good fortune to me. With the grace of the Lord above and with the blessings of men like you, I am in a position to offer the entire earth to you if you are so inclined. Please let me know if I can do anything for you." The rishi was pleased with the devotion, affection and humility of Dasaratha. He said: "I am not surprised at your words. Born as you are in the line of the Ikshvakus and, having the great Vasishtha as your Guru, it is but natural for you to speak such words. Only men like you will carry out what they have promised. I have, indeed, come to ask a favour of you. I will give you the background.

"I have taken the Diksha for a yaga. It has to be completed. But I am not able to do so. Two rakshasas who are able to assume what shape they will, are proving to be a hindrance to my yaga. They are extremely skilful in fighting the 'Maya' type of warfare, fighting without being seen. And they rain blood and flesh and such unclean objects into the yajnasala and on the platform itself where I perform the yaga. All my endeavours to perform the yaga have gone waste and I have come away from the spot without finishing the yaga. The yaga itself is of such a nature that there is no place for anger in my mind during the performing of it. I am not able to curse them and I have to hold back my anger. I have come to you for help so that I can complete the yaga."

"Tell me, my lord," said Dasaratha. He was greatly excited. He had fought on the side of Indra when there was war in the high heavens between the devas and the asuras and the king from the earth had been able to assist Indra during the war. That was when he was granted the boon that he would be able to drive his chariot in all the ten directions. The king was eager to hear more. "Tell me how I can help you," asked the king.

"I want you to give me Rama, your eldest son: Rama, that charming youngster who is a great warrior," said Vishvamitra. Before the king could put in a word he said: "I will protect him, you need have no fear of that. This young man is sure to destroy those rakshasas. I am certain of that. Have no doubt that this will mean nothing but great good fortune for your son. He will be famed in the three worlds for this act of valour and I predict nothing but good for your son to follow in the wake of this act. The two rakshasas will not be able to withstand Rama's powerful arrows. And again, Rama, and only Rama, is capable of destroying them. They are eaten up with pride and they have come to the end of their lives. Dasaratha, do not let your fatherly affection make you hesitate in granting me my boon. The yaga is for ten days and only ten days. The evil ones are destined to be killed by Rama and you can rest assured that they are dead already. I know Rama: I know his true nature. I know him and his unswerving devotion to truth. These great rishis led by Vasishtha also know the truth about him. If you desire fame in this world and a great future in the next, you must give Rama to me for these ten days. If you do but look at your ministers you can see that they are wanting you to grant me my wish."

Dasaratha thought of the youth of his beloved son Rama and to his mind came the dreadful forms of the rakshasas who could assume what form they chose and who were Mayavis. He fell down senseless and, for a while, for the duration of a muhurta, he was like that. He regained consciousness and then said: "My lord, please be merciful. My Rama, my child with the eyes like the lotus is hardly sixteen years old. I am not able to imagine him fighting with rakshasas you speak of. I am an old veteran in the art of fighting. My entire army is at your service, my lord. I will accompany you and with my army to assist me I will fight with the rakshasas. I have fought before in the war with the danavas when the devas were harassed by them and I am sure I can vanquish these two trouble-makers. They are able to use astras and I will be able to give them good fight. I will protect your yaga and help you bring it to a successful conclusion. Please do not ask Rama to face the rakshasas. His education is hardly over and he is not strong enough to know how fierce the proposed fight will be. As for me, even if an hour passes without seeing my beloved child, my eyes become blurred with tears and I feel as though my very life is ebbing away from me. Please do not ask me to send my Rama with you. If you insist on Rama coming with you then let me also come along with my army. Rama is my very life. After so many years of childlessness he has been granted to me and he is very dear to me. I have four sons but Rama is most dear to me as is well known the world over. Tell me about the rakshasas. Who are they? How did they acquire so much power? Who protect them? Where do they come from?"

Vishvamitra said: "In the line of the famed Pulastya is born a rakshasa by name Ravana. He is a very powerful warrior and a brave fighter. He has pleased Brahma with his penance and has obtained boons from the Creator. He is now bent on persecuting rishis and all good people. He has defeated Kubera, his half-brother in battle and has snatched from him the Pushpaka, a chariot which can fly in the air. Ravana is the son of Vishravas and he is famed in all the three worlds. These two rakshasas, Maricha and Subahu, are his henchmen. They are bent on doing harm to people like me who are bent on tapas and actions which spell good for the world. Rama has to rid the world of them."

The king's expression was piteous when he heard about the rakshasas. He said, "Unfortunate man that I am, I am in danger of losing my beloved son. My lord, how can I assume that this youngster will be able to stand in front of such powerful rakshasas and fight with them? I have been told that the devas and the gandharvas and all the denizens of the heavens are not able to stand up to Ravana. How then can this child of mine, my Rama who is not yet sixteen, how can he fight with the henchmen of Ravana? I have heard it said that the valour of those who fight with him is absorbed into him and his opponents lose all their prowess. Rama is the scion of my race. I dare not give him to you. I will not give him to you. Subahu and Maricha are not the proper adversaries he should encounter in his first taste of fighting. I will fight, my lord. But please do not ask me to give my child."

Vishvamitra's patience was at an end. Like a sacrificial fire which burns brighter when ghee is poured into it, the words of the king made him more and more angry and finally his anger knew no bounds. He looked at the king with his eyes glowing and said: "You made elaborate promises and now you are trying to go back on your word. This does not bring credit to the illustrious Raghuvamsha of which you are a descendant. If you think you are doing the right thing, I will go back to where I came from. Having broken your promise to your guest, you can live happily with your kinsmen surrounding you."

When he spoke thus the earth trembled in fear since his anger was known to all. Still the king sat silent. Blinded as he was by his love for his son he did not realise what he was doing. Vasishtha, his mentor, now spoke to him. He said: "Dasaratha, you are born of the line of the Ikshvakus. You are expected to be a personification of Dharma himself. You are a righteous man and are well versed in the rules of conduct. You should not behave thus and stay away from the path of dharma. The world calls you 'Dharmatma' and you should not besmirch the name of your ancestors and yours too by this action of yours. Once you say that you will do a thing and then hesitate to do so, it is an act unworthy of good men and it will rob you of all the punya you have accumulated so far. Send Rama with the rishi and save your name and that of your family. This illustrious son of Kushika will guard Rama like the Wheel of Fire does the pot filled with Amrita. No rakshasa can approach this son of yours however mighty he may be. I am sure of that. Vishvamitra is the very image of dharma and he is a great man.

He is a man of great intellect and his tapas is his wealth. He is proficient in all the shastras and the sacred lore. No one in all the three worlds can gauge the greatness of Vishvamitra. He knows the past, the present and the future. Please send your son with him without any qualms. Do you think it is hard for this great man to kill those two rakshasas who are wisps of straw in his presence? He can do it. But he wants your son to achieve greatness and that is the reason why he is honouring you by asking you for Rama. Please realise the honour which has been granted to you and wake up from this delusion called "Putrasneha."

When Vasishtha spoke thus Dasaratha was convinced and woke up from his mental stupor. He fell at Vishvamitra's feet and craved his pardon. He then said: "In my blind love for my child I spoke hastily. Please forgive me and accept my son. I am sending him with you and I am happy to do so. Rama is never alone and Lakshmana will always be with him. Please take both of them."

The words of Vasishtha had convinced the king that the prince was taken by Vishvamitra for the good of the youngster and his words of apology to the rishi were sincere. He sent for Rama and Lakshmana. Kausalya had heard about the decision of the king to send the children with the rishi and even as the word reached her that the king wanted them she had prepared them for the journey. Taking leave of their mothers, the handsome young men came and stood before their father. They saluted all the rishis in the great hall and then they prostrated before their father. They were so handsome that Vishwamitra could not take his eyes off their faces. Rama was dark like a blue lotus and Lakshmana was fair. Both had long liquid eyes and their smiles were bewitching. They stood with folded palms in front of their father.

Dasaratha said: "My dear Rama, Lakshmana, the great sage Vishvamitra has come to me with the sole purpose of taking you with him. Go with him and obey his commands in every way as you would mine." The children spoke not a word but went and stood by the side of the rishi after saluting their father and the others in the hall.

The wind blew softly and gently and all the omens were good when they left the palace. All those in the hall went up to the doorway to bid adieu to them and they were amazed to see the rain of flowers from the heavens and the distant music of heavenly drums. Vasishtha looked at the king as if to say: "I told you that it is for the good of your sons that the great Vishvamitra came to you asking you to lend them to him."

9. VISHVAMITRA AND THE YOUNG PRINCES

Vishvamitra walked in front and he was followed by Rama with a bow in his hand, with a sword at his waist and quivers fastened to his shoulders. Attired similarly, Lakshmana walked just behind Rama and the citizens saw with their eyes wide with wonder at the beautiful spectacle: the rishi like a sacrificial fire and the two young men like smokeless flames leaping out of it. They looked like five-headed serpents, accoutred as they were for fighting. Several thought of the Ashvini twins following Brahma when they saw the two princes walking behind the sage. Their fingers were protected by guards made of skin and their scabbards which had been set with precious stones gleamed in the sunlight.

Soon they reached the banks of the river Sarayu, the southern side of it. There, in a very sweet voice Vishvamitra called out: "Rama". There was a wealth of affection behind it. He said: "Child, fill your palms with water. I will teach you the mantras, Bala and Atibala. Once you know them neither hunger nor fatigue nor thirst will trouble you while walking with me and there will be no trace of tiredness bothering you when you walk this long distance to the ashrama. You will not be at a disadvantage if the rakshasas should accost you when you are tired.

"Rama, I know there is no one on the face of this earth to equal you in prowess, in bravery, in all the many qualities that make up an ideal kshatriya. Why, even in the three worlds I am yet to see the like of you. There is no one to equal you in handsomeness, in skill, in wisdom, in the art of conversing with people. Fortunate indeed is Dasaratha to have you as his son and I am fortunate too that you will be with me constantly for a while.

"As for these mantras, Bala and Atibala, they will make you respected by everyone in all the three worlds. They are the daughters of Brahma. I know that only you are worthy of learning them. Listen to me carefully and learn the mantras."

Rama touched water and meditated on the Lord with great humility. He then learnt the mantras from the rishi. Rama looked more powerful than ever after his initiation into the mantras. The young men then paid their respects to the great man as was the custom and they proceeded to make the preparations to spend the night on the banks of Sarayu. They spread dried grass and leaves on the ground and, after seeing to the comforts of Vishvamitra, the royal sons spent the night comfortably on the beds to which they were not accustomed.

When the night waned into daylight Vishvamitra approached Rama who was still asleep and paused for a while to drink with his eyes the beauty of Rama. He then said: "Rama, Kausalya's beloved child, the first Sandhya is approaching. Rouse thyself from sleep and perform the morning ablutions." The princes got up at once, bathed in the waters of the river and offered Arghya to the sun standing in the waters. They then approached the rishi and prostrated before him. They began to walk again in pursuit of the journey. They reached the spot where the Sarayu joined the divine river Ganga. They looked at the glorious sight with wonderment in their eyes. They saw there several ashramas and the rishis were bent on tapas. The princes approached Vishvamitra and asked him: "Whose ashrama is this holy place? Who dwells here? Please tell us."

A gentle smile lit up the face of Vishvamitra when he saw the eagerness of the young men. And he said: "I will tell you how this ashrama came into existence. Aeons of time have passed since then. But then, there was a time when Kama, the god of love, had a form and features. Once lord Mahadeva was performing tapas here. He had lost his wife Sati and with his mind filled with anger and sorrow he came here, all alone, and was absorbed in meditation. Parvati, the daughter of Himavan was serving him. The devas were desirous that he should wed her since Parvati was Sati born again as the daughter of Himavan. The gods had been told that the son born of them would be the commander of the army of the devas.

"Indra asked Kama to go to the neighbourhood of the spot where Mahadeva was, and he was asked to aim his arrows at the Lord. When Parvati was standing before Mahadeva he had just opened his eyes and Kama thought it was an apportune moment to shoot his arrows made of flowers. The Lord was hit and he turned to see who had the audacity to do this and his eyes lighted on Kama. Mahadeva was furious and he opened his third eye, the eye of Agni and burnt Kama. Kama was, from then, without a form and is now famed as Ananga, the formless one. The spot where his ashes were wafted to, is known as the country Anga. As for this ashrama, you must have guessed that this is the spot where Kama was burnt to ashes and these rishis are all disciples of Mahadeva. It is rightly named 'Kamashrama'. Let me take you to the rishis there. They will be pleased to see you both and they will bless you. In the place where the two holy rivers become one, let us spend the night and we will cross the Ganga tomorrow. After purifying ourselves we will enter the ashrama."

The rishis who knew all that had happened in the past and who could look into the future beyond the Veil of Time knew who had come to their ashramas and were immensely pleased. They welcomed Vishvamitra with great affection and they were thrilled to see the young men who were so humble and so gentle in their speech and in their conduct.

The guests spent a happy time in the Kamashrama with the rishis and Vishvamitra entertained them with stories about the many spots which they were to visit.

10. TATAKA VANA

Day dawning, the warriors led by Vishvamitra reached the banks of the river Ganga. The rishis who were there secured for them a boat and told Vishvamitra: "Please use this boat to cross the river with the princes. Do not tarry." "So be it," said Vishvamitra and the three travellers sat in the boat and crossed the river Ganga which was flowing towards the sea.

When they were crossing, in the midst of the river they heard a great noise. Rama and Lakshmana were impressed by the thunderous noise which was continuous and Rama said: "Lord, where is this roar from? It is wondrous and, at the same time, fearful." "I will tell you," said the sage. Brahma once created out of his mind a lake which is rightly named Manasa Sarovara. This river Sarayu which flows all along the edge of your city Ayodhya, was born out of this saras. At this spot actually, she is blending with the golden waters of the Ganga. Salute the two rivers." They did as they were bid and soon they reached the southern banks of the river. They resumed their walk.

After a while they reached a dark forest. It was dense and damp. No light from the sun could filter into the forest, so thickly were the tree branches intertwined. But what surprised Rama was the beauty of the forest and a strange lack of habitation there. This spot, which seemed ideally suited for any number of ashramas, was empty and there was an eerie and frightening silence pervading the entire place. Only animals seemed to make their presence felt. Rama said: "My lord, what strange noises! Beetles are making shrill music and the wild animals are roaring and making characteristic noises. Even the birds seem to cry harshly and there is no music emanating from their throats. The trees are all dense and they have darkened the place. I am not able to see anything. I cannot see the sun at all. Tell us what forest this is, and why it is deserted by human beings."

Vishvamitra was pleased with the natural curiosity of the youngsters and he said: "I will tell you. This forest was not really a forest before. Two countries by name Malada and Karusha were existing here. They were fertile and they were well populated. Indra, when he slew Vritra, was guilty of Brahmahatya. He was purified by the heavenly host of rishis with waters from all the sacred rivers. And he was rid of the sin. This was the ground on which the waters flowed from the body of Indra and the lord of the heavens, pleased with the earth for having received the polluted water said: 'I bless this ground. The countries will be called Malada and Karusha and they will be extremely fertile.' The fame of these two was a byword in the three worlds since they had been blessed by Indra.

Now, several years later, a terrible rakshasi by name Tataka took possession of this place. She is ugly, horrible to look at, cruel by nature. She can assume any form she likes and she has the strength of a thousand elephants. She is the wife of a good yaksha by name Sunanda and her son is Maricha who will bring you fame in later years. This rakshasi has occupied the entrance to the two countries and no human being dares to enter here since she is extremely fond of human flesh. A yojana and a half from where we are standing now, is her dwelling place. I am asking you to kill her. Kill this Tataka and make this land habitable once more. You and only you will be the man who has courage enough to enter the land occupied by the dreadful woman and, as for the number of human beings she has consumed, there is no count. This Tatakavana does not boast of a single inhabitant. Still she will not abandon this place and go elsewhere."

Rama was listening to the words of Vishvamitra very carefully. He then asked in a soft and gentle voice! "My lord, you tell me that she is the wife of a yaksha. I have been told that yakshas are not so powerful as the other heavenly beings like the devas, for instance. How then can a mere woman be so strong? You say that she has the strength of a thousand elephants. How can that be possible?

"It is a pertinent question," said Vishvamitra. "It is because of a boon which she was granted. Once there was a powerful yaksha by name Suketu. He had no sons and so he performed a very intense tapas. Pleased with him Brahma granted him a daughter by name Tataka. She was granted the strength of a thousand elephants. But the yaksha did not get what he had prayed for—a son. But it was the will of the gods and so, satisfied with the gift which had been granted him, the yaksha brought up his daughter as he would, a son. She grew up to be a beautiful maiden and when she was of marriageable age he gave her to Sunanda, the son of Jarjara. In course of time she gave birth to a son by name Maricha.

"Sunanda died and, after his death, Tataka's nature underwent a change. She went with her son to the ashrama of Agastya and began to harass that great man with her advances. She desired him and with this desire evident by her progress Tataka went towards Agastya. Looking at her and her behaviour which was entirely against all modesty expected of a woman, Agastya, who was radiant as lord Agni himself, became very angry and he cursed her to become a rakshasi. 'You will lose these attractive feminine looks and you will be ugly and formidable. You will eat human flesh and be despised by all,' said the rishi.

"Furious with Agastya for this curse Tataka has occupied this country and she has been killing anyone and everyone who has been foolish enough to enter this forest without knowing about her. Rama, for the sake of protecting the human beings in the neighbourhood, the hermits, the cows and other gentle animals, you are to kill this rakshasi. No one but you will be able to kill her. I know that you are not very keen. You are not happy about it since she is a woman. But then the duty of a kshatriya, as I know only too well, is to protect the oppressed and the good. It has been the glory of the House in which you are born that no one has shirked in his duty, which is doing good to others. Several people have killed women for the common good. Why, Indra himself killed Mandara, the daughter of Virochana who had been wanting to destroy this entire world. Bhrigu's wife, the mother of Sukra, once desired that there should be no Indra and Lord Narayana himself killed her. Several other women who have been sinful have been killed in the past. Do not hesitate to kill Tataka."

The prince stood humbly in front of the rishi and said: "My father, when he sent us with you, said: 'Go with him and obey him in all things as you would my commands.' He spoke to me in the presence of the elders of his court and I will never disobey my father. I will certainly do as you ask me to. I will kill Tataka since you have asked me to. It is a command and it should be obeyed. For the sake of protecting the hermits and the cows and for the good of the country, I am prepared to do your bidding."

11. THE KILLING OF TATAKA

Even as he was saying so, there arose the glorious noise of the bow string which he had been drawing. Rama held the bow in his left hand and his head was flung back. The entire forest reverberated with the sound. Hearing it Tataka was surprised. It was a long time since anyone had dared to enter her forest. She thought for a moment and, incensed beyond measure, rushed in the direction from which the noise came. From atop the hillock there appeared the frightening female who was ugliness personified. Looking at her looming up like another hillock, whose face was old and fearful to look at, Rama turned to Lakshmana and said: "Lakshmana, look at this dreadful woman. The very sight of her will make weak hearts stand still with fear. It will not be easy to subdue her. I am going to cut off her nose and ears at the tips and see the fun."

As he was talking to Lakshmana, Tataka rushed towards them with both her arms uplifted. Vishvamitra made her halt in her tracks by scolding her and he said: "May the two sons of the Raghuvamsa succeed in their attempt."

Tataka was spraying stones and mud on the young men and the sky was filled with the dust. It was dark for a long while and they could see nothing. She then sent a real rain of stones which made the gentle prince extremely angry. With his arrows Rama destroyed the stones and cut off her arms. Lakshmana, in the meantime, heard her roar with anger and pain and he cut off the tips of her nose and ears. Tataka suddenly vanished from their sight and, from out of nowhere, there rained on them a number of stones hurled by her. Both the brothers pulled the strings of their bows and the noise was so frightening that she forgot all about her maya warfare and fell on the ground senseless. Vishvamitra said: "Rama there is no need for you to have any compunction about slaying this dreadful sinner. Evening is fast approaching and it is only too well known that the strength of rakshasas increase with the setting of the sun."

Rama felt that the time had come when he should kill her. Not heeding the stones which were being hurled at him, Rama took an arrow, pulled it as near his ear as possible and released it. The arrow hit Tataka's chest, entered it and she fell dead on the hill.

The heavenly host rejoiced when Rama accomplished this task which had seemed impossible. Indra with his attendants came to Vishvamitra and said: "All our gratitude for bringing the son of the great Dasaratha to rid the world of this sinful woman. You know there are many such tasks which have to be accomplished by him. May your blessings be showered on him fully." The denizens from heaven went back. Evening drew near and Vishvamitra raised Rama who had prostrated before him and said: "Rama, we will spend the night here and in the morning we will be on the last lap of our journey. We will soon reach my ashrama."

As soon as the rakshasi Tataka was killed the forest changed its complexion completely. It was a startling sight. When they woke up in the morning Vishvamitra and the young princes saw the forest freed from the taint of Tataka. Flowers were blooming everywhere: Champaka, Ashoka, Punnaga, and Mallika. Mango trees and Panasa trees and many palm trees could be seen bearing fruits. Ponds could now be seen everywhere with clear water and it seemed to be as beautiful as Chaitra, the garden of Kubera. Vishvamitra's eyes rested lovingly on Rama. They strayed away from there to the beautiful surroundings and came back to Rama. He said: "I am extremely pleased with you. May you be famed the world over for your prowess. Accept my blessings. I am so pleased with you that I am going to make a rare gift to you."

Rama and Lakshmana were intrigued by the words of Vishvamitra. They said: "You have blessed us and you have told us that you are pleased with us. Is there any other gift greater than this, my lord?"

Vishvamitra smiled and said: "You may know about it or you may not. But I am telling you now that I am in possession of all the divine astras you can think of. I will give them to you. With the help of these astras you will be able to vanquish all the enemies you will come across later. I will now grant all of them to you. Learn the incantations carefully from me and you will be able to master them very soon."

Rama sat facing the east after purifying himself and the rishi taught him the astras which he had obtained from Mahadeva after performing intense tapas. Those were the days when he thought he needed them. He had passed those days and he needed them no more. Smiling to himself at his earlier struggles, the sage Vishvamitra taught them all to Rama one by one: the method by which he should invoke the astra, the manner in which it should be despatched and the manner of withdrawing it. And all the presiding deities came and stood before Rama. Folding their palms they said: "Noble Rama, we are now your slaves and will do your bidding." Rama told them: "Reside in my mind all the time and come to me when I want you."

Vishvamitra asked Rama to teach the astras to Lakshmana now and he did so. The three of them hastened towards the ashrama of Vishvamitra with a chastened look. The young men were still under the euphoria of the sight of the presiding deities of the astras and the rishi, realising this, gave them time to get used to the possession of the astras.

12. SIDDHASHRAMA

As they were walking along, Rama again asked Vishvamitra: "There is a beautiful mountain there and, nestling at its foot, is a grove which is pleasing to the eye. Even at this distance I can see deer dark as rain clouds. Birds with sweet voices are singing in the grove. This green grove of trees captures my mind. Tell us what the place is. We just came out of a forest which was fearful and uninhabited and this is all the more exciting since it seems to be a happy place. How far away from here is the ashrama of your gracious self? I have become very impatient since I am eager to see those sinners who are causing so much discomfort to you. When will I see those wicked rakshasas who kill hermits without compunction? When will I be able to kill them?" Vishvamitra was only too eager to answer the questions of Rama. He said: "This grove has a long history behind it. I will relate it to you.

"Ages back, the great Lord Narayana, the all-pervading, who is the cause of the creation, the preservation and the destruction of this entire Universe, performed tapas here. And again, this is the place where Vamana had his dwelling place and hence it is called 'Siddhashrama'.

"Bali, the son of Virochana, was the emperor. He had defeated all the rival danavas as also the Maruts and Indra too. He was famed all the world over for his prowess and for his generous nature. He once performed a yajna. The yajna was to confirm his position as the lord of the three worlds. It was in this ashrama that the devas led by Agni approached Narayana and said: 'Lord, Bali the son of Virochana is performing a yajna. You must somehow stop it for the good of those who dwell in the celestial regions. Bali is well known for his generosity. He has never said 'No' to anyone who has asked him for anything. You must make use of this characteristic in him and help us to regain the world which we have lost to him.'

"In the meantime Kashyapa, the great Prajapati who was like the god of fire, so radiant was he because of his tapas, desired a son. His wife Aditi was like his other self in glory and this great man once performed tapas with the image of Narayana deeply engraved in his mind. To him came the Lord in person and asked him what he desired. Kashyapa the son of Marichi said: 'Please do not think it audacious on my part when I ask you to be born as my son. You must be born as the son of Aditi and you must wipe her tears which are flowing because of the unhappiness of her children, the devas. Our purpose should thus be served and this ashrama where you will be born will be famed the world over as the *Siddhashrama* since we would have attained our desires."

"So be it," said Narayana with a smile. Aditi became the mother of the Lord in human form. He was so small and so much like a miniature of a man that he was called 'Vamana' along with his other name 'Upendra'. When the yajna of Bali was in progress Vamana went to the yajnasala.

"Bali stood up and greeted this young brahmin who was like a heap of gold. He said: 'What will you have, my young brahmin? You look so beautiful and so radiant, I have a feeling you do not belong to this earth but to the heavens. No human being can look so glorious. Ask anything of me and I will give it to you. I am eager to please you.' "

"Vamana was gratified by the generous nature of the king and said: 'O king! it is but proper for the son of Virochana to talk thus. The world talks of nothing but the great yajna you are performing and so I came to you hoping that you will give me something. I want very little but I will ask only if you assure me that I will be granted my wish.' "

"The king smiled at the young child—for so he thought!—and said: 'It is my great good fortune that you should come to me asking me to give you something. My tapas has been sanctified only now. My very life seems purposeful only now and I feel that I have been born for this only task, granting you what you ask for. My kingship, and all the many good acts which I may have performed seem to bear fruit at this moment when you have come to me. My treasury, my granary, my army, my entire kingdom, all these are at your disposal. Ask of me anything you please and it is yours.' "

"A beautiful smile lit up the face of the young brahmin and he said: 'Of what use is all this to me, O king? I am but a poor dweller in an ashrama and my needs are few. All I want is a bit of land: a piece from your kingdom which can be covered by three paces of mine.' "

"The king was amused at the request of Vamana. He smiled tolerantly at Vamana and said: 'But certainly. I will grant you three paces of land as you wish.' "

"Sukra Acharya, the Bhargava, was the preceptor of Bali and he stopped the king from taking water in his hand preparatory to the gift and said: 'Bali, this is no ordinary brahmin. He is that TRUTH which cannot be known even by Brahma or the devas or by yogis who spend years and years in tapas. He is Narayana. You should not grant him his wish. If you do, you will be destroyed. Narayana, as is well known, is ever partial to the devas and their good will be the consequence of your gift.' Bali would not listen to him."

" 'If the Lord of lords has assumed this form to bless me with the request, my yajna has been fulfilled to a glorious degree. What greater good fortune can befall one like me?', said the king and, with his wife pouring the water into his hands he gave away 'three paces of land' to the youngster who was standing with his little right hand held out to receive the gift. When the water touched his hand and when the gift had been granted, Vamana grew. Narayana assumed his Visvarupa. With one blessed foot he covered the entire earth and with the other, the heavens. Bali worshipped him with great gladness in his heart and he spoke to himself: 'Narayana Himself came to me with a request and I was able to grant it. Can anyone be more fortunate than me?' He stood with folded palms, with tears streaming from his eyes."

"Narayana thus regained for Indra his kingdom and restored to him his throne. That grove which seems to thrill you so much was where Vamana was born. Since it is a Siddhashrama where everyone will get what he wants I have chosen it as my ashrama for performing this yaga for the good of mankind. The dreadful rakshasas come only to this ashrama and it is here, my child, that they must be killed. Children, we are nearing the Siddhashrama. This spot is mine which means that it is yours too."

Even as they were talking and walking they reached the ashrama. With the two young princes on either side of him

Vishvamitra entered the ashrama and he looked like the moon with the star Punarvasu on a cloudless clear sky.

The rishis worshipped him and welcomed the princes. After they had rested for a while since this last lap of the journey was long, the brothers went to the presence of Vishvamitra and stood before him. They said: "My lord, you can resume your Diksha. Your yaga will proceed uninterrupted. We can assure you of that. As you have said so aptly the ashrama cannot lose its name and we cannot let it go waste."

Vishvamitra assumed Diksha that night and the princes slept throughout the night without any worry. When the night had passed they rose up early and purifying themselves they went to the presence of Vishvamitra who was seated on holy darbha grass after performing Agnihotra, the worship of the fire.

13. THE YAGA OF VISHVAMITRA

The young princes went to the presence of the rishi and asked him: "We would like to be told when the rakshasas will make their appearance. We want to be prepared for their coming." Looking at them eager to fight with the rakshasas and to kill them, the rishis in the ashrama of Vishvamitra, were pleased beyond measure. They spoke gently and softly: "From today, the yaga will last for six days. Since he has taken up the Diksha the great saint Vishvamitra is silent. He has to observe the vow of silence. For six days and six nights you will both have to be alert and guard the yajnasala." "We will do so," said Rama. The brothers took up their bows, strung them and stood grasping them firmly with their left hands and with the arrows poised in their right hands they stood, alert, ready and eager.

Day and night they went round the yajnasala guarding it like the eyelids guard the eyes from danger. Five days and five nights passed without any mishap. Rama said: "Lakshmana, be very careful. Today is the last day and we have to be prepared for the coming of the two evil-doers." The fire in the yajnakunda was burning with a greater brilliance as Rama spoke. It was a great and glorious sight: the fire, presided over by the noble Vishvamitra and surrounded by all the rishis. The music of the recital of the Vedas, sonorous, slow and dignified, filled the four quarters with a feeling of awe and, at the same time, peace. It purified the very air which carried it everywhere.

There was a sudden noise like the clap of thunder at the coming of monsoon. Like a rain-cloud darkens the sky during the rainy season the sky was suddenly dark. Rama and Lakshmana knew that the rakshasas had appeared. They had their myrmidons with them and there rained a ghastly rain made up of blood and flesh. The rakshasas did not expect any opposition and they had not assumed the maya tactics and Rama could see them clearly. Angered beyond measure at the manner in which they were trying to pollute the holy yajnasala Rama told Lakshmana: "Look, Lakshmana. Look at these flesh-eating rakshasas who are trying to molest these good men. Watch me scatter them and their associates like the rain-clouds will be, by a fast wind."

Angry with the act of the intruders Rama took up the astra called Manavastra and aimed it at the chest of Maricha. Taken unawares, unused to opposition from anyone at any time, Maricha felt as though lightning had struck him. Before he could even think, the astra carried him to a distance of a hundred yojanas and threw him into the sea. But it did not kill him. Rama said: "Look at this Manavastra and its power, Lakshmana. It has carried this sinner to a distance of a hundred yojanas and has thrown him into the sea. But it has not killed him. This is a compassionate astra. It punishes but does not kill. The noble Vishvamitra had told us much and it is true. But, I am not giving so much of latitude to the others. I will kill all of them."

Rama took up the Agneyastra, the astra presided over by fire and aimed it at the chest of Subahu, the other miscreant. Subahu fell to the ground dead. With the help of Vayavastra, the astra presided over by the god of wind, Rama killed the rest of the rakshasa host.

The yajna was protected only too well by Rama and Lakshmana and there was great joy in the hearts of all the rishis in the Siddhashrama. That night was the last night of the yaga.

The next morning, after the conclusion of the yaga with the proper rituals, Vishvamitra called the young men to his side and said: "Rama, you are indeed a great warrior and your fame will now spread in all the four quarters. With your help I have been able to complete the yaga which I had begun some time back. Siddhashrama is Siddhashrama today."

Rama and Lakshmana were happy that they had accomplished the task which they had undertaken and they spent the night in a happy frame of mind. When the night had passed and when the sun's rim brightened the eastern sky they rose up from their sleep. They went to their Guru Vishvamitra who was surrounded by a crowd of rishis. Everyone was looking radiant since the yaga, which at a time seemed an almost impossible task to have been taken up, had been completed with the help of the young princes from Ayodhya. As soon as they saw the young men they all blessed them in unison with the words: "Jaya Vijayi Bhava!" "May you be ever victorious!" Vishvamitra sat with a gentle smile on his lips.

Rama spoke to him in a respectful and soft voice. He said: "We are here waiting for further commands from you. Please, my lord, tell us what we should do now."

Vishvamitra said: "In Mithila, King Janaka is performing a yaga. He is a very righteous king, a Rajarshi. We are all going to Mithila and I would like you to come with us. There is something in Mithila which will interest princes like you. The famed bow of Mahadeva is there with Janaka and, I am sure, you will like to have a look at it. That bow is very powerful and it is said to glow like the sun. It was given to the ancestors of Janaka during the performance of a yaga. It is also well known that no deva, nor an asura, nor a gandharva or a man has been able to lift and string the divine bow. Many were the kings and princes who tried to, but they failed miserably. You must see this bow, Rama. It is a wonderful bow. It is placed in the palace of the king and is worshipped with flowers and incense everyday. We will soon begin our journey to Mithila."

14. TO MITHILA

Vishvamitra addressed the demigods who guarded the ashrama and the forest. "I have completed what I had undertaken. The Siddhashrama has retained her name. After visiting Mithila I will proceed towards Himavan, the mountain where the sacred Ganga has her source. I wish you well and this place will always be a blessed spot."

Accompanied by the rishis and by Rama and Lakshmana, the sage Vishvamitra made a pradakshina to the ashrama and began his journey towards the north. Several people followed them: even the birds and the deer which were living in the ashrama. With gentle persuasive words Vishvamitra coaxed them back and proceeded with the journey. After covering a considerable distance, when the sun was sloping westwards, they reached the banks of the river Sona and remained there. They sat around Vishvamitra when they found a charming spot to relax. Rama, with his brother, sat very near the rishi. He asked Vishvamitra: "This country is beautiful. I see nothing but green everywhere and evidently it is a very fertile and fruitful land. Tell me whom does it belong to?"

Vishvamitra was only too eager to answer his question. He began: "Lord Brahma had a son by name Kusa. He was a great tapasvin and he married the daughter of the king of Videha and four sons were born to him: Kushamba, Kushanabha, Adhurtarajas and Vasu. All of them were valiant like their father and equally righteous. The king asked his sons to follow the dharma of kshatriyas and to rule the world. They founded four cities and each ruled one. Kushamba's city went by the name Kaushambi. Kushanabha's city was Mahodaya. Adhurtarajas named his city Dharmaranya and Vasu was the ruler of the city by name Girivraja.

"This country which you admire so much is called Vasumati and it belongs to Vasu. There are five mountains here and the river which has its source in the Magadha kingdom, flows in between the mountains like a garland of flowers flung on the earth. Kushanabha had a hundred daughters who were given to Brahmadatta, a noble rishi. The king was desirous of a son and he asked Brahmadatta to perform a yaga for him. During the performance of the yaga Kusa, the father of Kushanabha said: 'Do not worry. You will be the father of a son by name Gadhi. Because of him your name will be famed throughout the world.' After some time, a son was born to Kushanabha and his name was Gadhi. Rama, Gadhi was my father.

"My elder sister was Satyavati and she was given in marriage to a saintly man by name Richaka. She was so pure and so good that she reached the heavens with the human body. She became a sacred river by name Kaushiki. This pure woman, my sister, was born into this world only to do good to others. This is the reason why I spend all my time on the banks of Kaushiki in the Himavan mountains. When I am there unbelievable peace enfolds me and I am extremely happy. Because I had a duty to perform I left the banks of that pure river and came down south. I came to Siddhashrama and, with your assistance, I was able to achieve what I had set out to do. Now you know whose country this is.

"Look! half the night has passed by! I have been talking unaware of the passing of time! The trees have gone to sleep, perhaps! Even a leaf does not move, so still is the night. Animals and birds have covered themselves with this dark night and have gone to sleep. The first half of the night is gradually disappearing and the sky, studded with the myriad stars, seems to have a thousand eyes with which to look at us. The moon is just now brightening the east and his soft rays will soon embrace the world and banish the enveloping darkness. Only the night-birds, the pishachas, rakshasas and bhutas are making use of the darkness. You must sleep now, children. We must continue the journey tomorrow. We will set about it early in the morning."

15. GANGA

The music of the birds and the rustling of the waters of the river Sona were waking them up and soon they were awake. Even before they could get up Vishvamitra was by their side and he said: "Children, the dark night has passed and the dawn is fast approaching. Let us hurry and make preparations for the journey."

Rama with his brother soon went to Vishvamitra, ready to leave with them. He asked Vishvamitra: "My lord, this river does not seem to be fed enough with water. I can see sandy islands here and there breaking the even flow of the river. Where are we planning to cross the river?"

"We will follow the path of the rishis who have gone this way before," said Vishvamitra and the troupe walked fast towards the north. After a long trudge, when the sun had reached the zenith, they saw in front of them, the broad expanse of the sacred river Ganga. They were thrilled at the sight of the river with swans and lotuses floating on its surface. They stood for a while looking at the beauty of the waters and they made up their minds to spend some time on her banks.

As usual in the evening they sat round Vishvamitra. Rama asked the rishi: "I want to hear the story of this sacred river Ganga. She is called *Tripathaga*—the river with the three paths. How did she purify the three worlds and finally reach the sea, the lord of all rivers? I am very eager to listen to the thrilling story."

"There is a mountain by name Himavan," began Vishvamitra. "Himavan is the lord of all mountains and he had two daughters who were unrivalled in beauty. Their mother was Mena, also known as Manorama. Ganga was the elder of the two daughters and the younger is known by the name Parvati and also by the name Uma. The devas wanted Ganga for themselves. They went to Himavan and asked him to make a gift of his daughter to them. Himavan agreed and Ganga who converted herself into a river flowed in the heavens and her waters purified whatever it touched. She was famed as Mandakini in the heavens and is also known as Akasha Ganga.

"The other daughter Uma performed severe tapas and her devotion was rewarded. Her father gave her to Lord Mahadeva. These two daughters of Himavan are worthy of the worship of the three worlds.

"Rama, one of your ancestors was a king by name Sagara. He was, for a long time, childless. He had two wives. One was Kesini, the daughter of the king of Vidarbha. The second wife was Sumati, the daughter of Kashyapa. She was famed for her beauty. With a desire for a child, the king went to the slopes of the Himavan with his wives. There he performed tapas. After a hundred years had passed the rishi Bhrigu came to him and said: 'You will certainly become a father and because of them your name will be ever remembered by the world of men. One of your wives will be the mother of a son, only one son, who will continue the line of the Ikshvakus. The other will be the mother of sixty thousand sons, all valiant, powerful and brave." The princesses were very happy and they stood before him humbly and said: 'Which of us will be the mother of the sixty thousand sons? and which of us will bear the son who will continue the line? We are eager to know.'"

"Bhrigu said: 'The choice is yours. One of you will have to choose, the single progeny while the other will have the sixty thousand sons.' Kesini, the elder queen, chose to be the mother of the only son while Sumati, the younger, was happy in the anticipation of her many sons who were to be born to her. King Sagara took leave of the rishi and went back to his kingdom.

"In course of time a son was born to Kesini. He was named as Asamanja. To his dismay the king realised that this son was wicked in the real sense of the word. He enjoyed doing evil acts. When he was a young boy he would catch hold of young children and throw them into the river Sarayu. He would stand watching them struggling in the water before they were drowned. He would clap his hands in glee. Sagara thought that he would improve as he grew older. But no. He became more and more unpopular. The townfolk finally came to the king and told him about the atrocities performed by the prince. Righteous man that he was, Sagara did not hesitate even for a moment; he meted out punishment for such a miscreant: banishment from the kingdom.

"The one consolation the king had was that Asamanja's son, by name Amshuman, did not inherit his father's nature but was a good, sweet, gentle child, ever devoted to his grandfather.

"The other wife of the king, Sumati, became the mother of the sixty thousand sons as had been prophesied, lusty young men who were very powerful, handsome and extremely arrogant. They were the pride of the mother.

"Once Sagara wanted to perform the Ashvamedha. The location of the yajnasala was beautiful. The north is proud of the powerful Himavan and, facing it, in the middle of Bharatavarsha, is the mountain Vindhya which is a large range. These two mountains stand as though challenging each other in greatness. The land between these two was chosen as the site for the yajnasala.

"The youngster Amshuman was asked to accompany the sacrificial horse in its triumphant march through all the kingdoms. Indra, who is ever jealous of the kings of the earth who perform the Ashvamedha, was very prompt in stealing the horse and he disappeared with it.

"The pundits who were performing the yajna could not proceed with the rituals until the horse was found and they told the king about the urgency of the matter. They said: 'Unless the horse is found and the yaga is completed grave disaster will follow!' Sagara called his powerful sons and said: 'You have heard the words of the rishis. Please make haste and go in search of the horse. This sacrifice can be performed without any fault by only very few people and, once begun, it has to be concluded. Please go at once and search in all the four quarters and in the nether world also.' "

"The lusty kshatriya princes, the Sagaraputras, were very happy to do as they were told. They set out in quest of the horse. With their powerful arms they dug up the earth. Each prince allotted to himself one yojana of ground and dug into it. The entire surface of the earth had been dug up and they could not find the horse. The earth groaned under the fierce onslaught of the princes. Serpents, animals and even the rakshasas suffered and the air was filled with their cries of pain which were piteous to hear.

"When they did not find the horse on the surface of the earth Sagara's sons entered the nether regions. They saw the diggajas, the elephants bearing the earth on their mighty heads: Virupaksha, Mahapadma, Saumanta and Bhadra. But they were not able to see the horse. Finally they went deep into the nether lands and they came to the vicinity of a cave. When they were wondering as to who was inside they heard the neighing of a horse. The princes were surprised at this. Promptly they went inside the cave. It was an ashrama which was more like a cave than usual hermitage.

"When they went inside, the valiant brothers saw Kapila Vasudeva, the great rishi, who was lost in meditation. Beyond him, beyond where he was sitting, they saw, tied to a tree, their father's sacrificial horse. They were happy that their search was at an end.

"The sons of Sagara shouted: 'This is the thief. He has stolen our horse and, having reached this underground retreat, he has assumed the garb of a sanyasi and pretends to be in deep meditation. Let us punish him.' With their minds completely bemused because of their anger against the rishi the sons of Sagara rushed at Kapila with their hands holding different weapons. They shouted at the great man calling him 'thief' and Kapila, opening his eyes because of the noise they made, saw what was happening. He looked at them with angry eyes and that was enough to reduce all of them to ashes. The sixty thousand sons of Sagara were now just a heap of ashes. The rishi went back into trance as though nothing had happened.

"Sagara, in the meantime, waited in vain for the return of his sons with the horse. Finally, he asked his grandson Amshuman to go and find out what has happened. The young prince went along the path which his uncles had taken and soon reached the cave where Kapila was. Amshuman entered the cave and there he saw the horse. Amshuman stood humbly and waited for the great man to come out of his samadhi. When Kapila opened his eyes he saw a young man standing before him with folded palms. Amshuman prostrated before the rishi and taking the dust of his feet he spoke to him and told him about his errand. Kapila said: 'Here is your horse, child. Indra, as usual, has stolen it and brought it here. As for your uncles, there they are,' he said and pointed to the heap of ashes. They behaved in an unforgivable manner and with my looks I burnt them to ashes.' ."

"Amshuman looked around for water so that he could offer the funeral oblations, the tarpana to his elders. But he could find no water there. But he found Garuda, the brother of Sumati, coming towards him. And he said: 'Child, do not be too unhappy. This is but the law of nature. Your uncles, my nephews, were too arrogant to be popular. As for the Anjali you want to offer them, ordinary water will not wipe out their sin. Ganga, the elder daughter of Himavan, is the only one who will be able to purify them. Ask her to come down to the earth. The holy waters of Ganga must wet these ashes. Then, and only then, will they attain salvation.' "

"Amshuman was speechless with sorrow and with the stupendous task which he had been asked to undertake. Garuda then said: "That will be later. Now hurry with the horse to the presence of your grandfather and let him complete the Ashvamedha.' "

"Amshuman returned to the kingdom with the horse and the sacrifice was concluded. But the king was greatly unhappy at the turn of events. He did not know how to make the divine river Ganga flow on the earth. After some time he left the kingdom in the hands of his grandson Amshuman and King Sagara accompanied by his wives went to the forest to perform tapas and then to reach the heavens.

"Amshuman ruled the kingdom well and he had no time to try and woo Ganga to come down to the earth. He had a son by name Dilipa. Amshuman left the kingdom in his hands and went to the slopes of the Himavan to perform penance in order to get Ganga. But it was in vain. He died without accomplishing his object. Dilipa also suffered the same way. He could not, during his reign, achieve the desire in the hearts of all of them: the coming of Ganga to the earth and the salvation of the sons of Sagara."

16. BHAGIRATHA'S PENANCE

"Dilipa had a son by name Bhagiratha. Dilipa ruled the kingdom until illness overtook him and, crowning Bhagiratha as the king, Dilipa died.

"The one purpose in the life of Bhagiratha was to make his ancestors reach the heavens. He left the kingdom in the hands of efficient ministers and went to perform tapas. Brahma was pleased with the intense tapas which the king was bent on, and he appeared before Bhagiratha and said: 'The devas and I are pleased with your penance. Ask what thou wilt of me. I will certainly grant it.' "

"Bhagiratha, with his eyes filled with tears of gratefulness, spoke in a voice choked with tears. 'My lord, if you want to grant me a boon, grant me this: grant that my forefathers reach the heavens. I have to perform the Nirvapanjali for them with the waters of the Ganga. And, my lord, the line of the Ikshvakus should not terminate with me. These are the boons I ask of you,' said Bhagiratha."

"Brahma said: 'Have no fear. Your line will not stop with you. You will be the father of a son. As for Ganga, you know that she is the daughter of Himavan. When she descends from the heavens no one will be able to bear the force of her descent except Lord Mahadeva. You must pray to him.' "

"Bhagiratha now addressed himself to Mahadeva and spent a whole year fasting, with just air for food. Mahadeva was pleased with the devotion of the king and appeared before him and said: 'My mind is pleased with you and your desire to win for your forefathers a place in the heavens. I will take Ganga on my head and break the force of her descent.' "

"Ganga, the daughter of Himavan, had, at the command of Brahma, agreed to come down to the earth. According to the promise he had given Bhagiratha, Lord Mahadeva stood on a raised plateau of the mountain by name Himavan. All the heavenly beings had assembled in the skies to see the great and glorious sight. Bhagiratha was standing with his eyes lifted to the skies from where Ganga was to descend.

"They were waiting and suddenly they heard a mighty roar. Ganga was in the sky and an immense sheet of water began to rush towards the earth. It seemed as though the sea had reached the heavens and was rushing back to the earth in a hurry. Ganga had become very proud of the fact that she was indispensable. She told herself: 'I will rush down with such fury that I will sweep Mahadeva into the Patala and the earth too.' Gauging her mind Mahadeva knew that her pride had to be humbled. He stood with his trident held behind his back with both his hands, with his head slightly raised and a beatific smile shadowing his lips. So he stood when Ganga came down to the earth.

"The sacred Ganga fell straight onto the hallowed head of Mahadeva. Everyone was watching her descent. Then they saw a strange sight. Ganga's waters were coming down from the sky but when they reached the matted locks of my lord Mahadeva, they were absorbed by them. Ganga was lost there and no one could see her. Try as she might, she could find no way out of the tangled mass of the Lord's locks.

"Bhagiratha was desperate and he praised the Lord and prayed that he should have compassion on him. Mahadeva felt that he had punished her enough and he allowed Ganga to emerge from his Jata along a single strand of hair. Drop by drop she came and a pool was formed which was named Bindusaras. Ganga was thus called Alakananda. When the pool became a lake and when it was full, the river flowed in seven streams. Three of these flowed eastwards and three, towards the west. The seventh followed Bhagiratha as his chariot rushed towards the south, towards the cave where the Sagaraputras were waiting for their deliverance.

"The earth looked like the sky with swans flying around: so white was the foam of the river as she followed the king's chariot. She was so wilful. Here she would flow straight as an arrow and there she would wind like a serpent. She would rush fast at some spots and, at others, she would just meander like a woman walking in her pleasure garden. She would flow smoothly on the ground for a while and, suddenly, she would tumble like a child at play. So she went to purify the earth. She had washed the feet of Narayana and she had passed the region of the moon. She had been borne on the head of Mahadeva and thus, thrice purified, she had come down to the sinful earth to grant salvation for a fistful of ashes. Such is the greatness of the heavenly-borns.

"Ganga reached Patala and finally Bhagiratha's dream came true. He saw the ashes of his ancestor drenched in the waters of the divine Ganga.

"Brahma came to Bhagiratha and said: 'Child, you have achieved something which was by no means easy. So long as the waters remain in the ocean your forefathers who gave the ocean its name Sagara will remain in the heavens. Ganga will be your eldest daughter in the eyes of the gods and she will be called *Bhagirathi.*' "

Vishvamitra's narration was complete and he said: "Rama, my child, as usual, I have been talking for so long. I have told you the story of how Ganga came down to the earth. Ganga who is *Tripathaga* since she was in the heavens, on the earth and in Patala too. Evening is fast approaching. Let us prepare to rest for the night."

"What a thrilling tale!," exclaimed Rama. Neither he nor his brother could get over the thrill of it. They spent the whole night thinking of the strange things which had happened long ago, and so passed the night.

17. TOWARDS GAUTAMA'S ASHRAMA

Early in the morning the party of rishis headed by Vishvamitra, who had the princes by his side, went towards Vishala, a beautiful city. They had crossed the Ganga with the help of a boat and had reached the other bank. Rama was still thinking of the glorious narration of the descent of Ganga. On the northern banks of Ganga they saw the city by name Vishala. As was natural to him Rama wanted to know whose city it was and who was ruling it now. Vishvamitra said:

"The history of this city goes as far back in time as the churning of the ocean of milk when Amrita was found. The devas and the asuras vied with each other to be the sole possessors of the bowl containing nectar. Narayana, with his guile, managed to let the devas have it. There ensued a war and several of the famed asuras were killed in this war. And so, Diti, the mother of the daityas, was very unhappy. She asked her husband to help her to be the mother of a son who would be able to kill Indra. Kashyapa taught her the incantations and there was one condition which she had to obey with great care: she had to be very pure and clean and should never make a single mistake regarding this rule. A lapse would mean that her desire would not be granted. Diti listened to it all carefully.

"She observed all the rules well and Indra was by her side all the time. He was attending to her wants and, by and large, making himself useful to her. He was her sister's son and, on that pretext, he was with her. She was extremely careful. But one day she was careless and Indra, who was waiting for this chance, took advantage of it and managed to cut the little child inside her into pieces. Try as he might he could not destroy the pieces and they began to cry. He had cut the child into seven pieces and all seven of them were crying. Diti was asleep and he did not want her to wake up and so he told the crying children: 'Do not cry! 'Maa Ruda.' Meanwhile Diti was awake and found that calamity had overtaken her. Indra said: 'Mother, you wanted me to be destroyed and, as a matter of self-preservation, I had to resort to this. But your children are not dead. See, I could not kill them; so powerful is the effect of your Vrata. My Vajra was ineffective. There are now seven children instead of one. Forgive me and take your sons. I could not kill them.' "

"Diti knew that they were not going to kill Indra since her Vrata had been tainted by her lapse. She said: 'No one can conquer

Fate and it is destined that no evil should befall you. Since you were responsible for these children, partly, you can take them with you. Though born of me they will be your brothers. Since you went on saying 'Maa Ruda' to them they will be famed as the seven 'Maruts' and let them be the associates of Vayu and be with him for ever.' " "Rama," said Vishvamitra: "This is the spot where Diti performed her tapas and this is where the seven Maruts were born. Later the city Vishala was built here by Alambusa, one of the sons of Ikshvaku. His descendants have ruled this country since then. At the present moment Vishala is being ruled by the king by name Sumati.

"We will spend the night here in this pleasant city and proceed to Mithila tomorrow."

Hearing about the arrival of Vishvamitra and his disciples, Sumati, the king, came to where he was and paid his respects to him. He looked at the young princes and asked Vishvamitra who they were and how it was possible for these young men, evidently princes, to be accompanying the rishis. Vishvamitra told him about the yaga and how the young sons of Dasaratha had protected the yaga from getting polluted by the rakshasas and about how Rama had killed the entire host. Sumati was amazed at the thrilling narration and after talking to them for some time, went back to his palace. The rishis spent the night there and, early in the morning, they resumed their walk towards the city Mithila.

They reached the outskirts of Mithila and they felt that they were already in Mithila. It was a beautiful city and they all exclaimed: 'How beautiful! What a lovely city!" On the way Rama discerned a very pleasant-looking ashrama. It was isolated, situated in a garden which was almost touching the edge of the city. Rama looked with admiring eyes at the ashrama. He saw that there was no smoke pluming towards the sky and he realised that there was no one in the ashrama. This was very strange and, with wondering eyes, he turned to Vishvamitra and asked him: "Yonder, there seems to be an ashrama. I think it is very beautiful. But it seems to me as though it is empty. This beautiful ashrama seems to be uninhabited. How is it possible, my lord? Why is it, there is no one in this ashrama situated as it is in such sylvan surroundings?"

"It is empty because of a great man's anger," said Vishvamitra. He continued: "I will tell you how it came to pass. This same spot was once like the very heaven itself. It was the ashrama of the great rishi Gautama. He performed tapas here for many years.

"Brahma had created a beautiful woman and he called her Ahalya. To Gautama was this Ahalya given in marriage. And they lived here for a long time.

"Once Indra, who is famed for his weakness for beautiful women, came to the neighbourhood of this ashrama. After making sure that Gautama was away from the hermitage, Indra, assuming the guise of the rishi, entered the apartment where Ahalya was and said: 'You are a very beautiful woman and my mind is lost in you. I desire you.' Ahalya could see that it was not the rishi though the guise was there. She knew too that it was Indra. She was flattered and pleased that the lord of the heavens desired her and she decided to conform to his desire. She agreed to his love-making.

"When it was time for Gautama to return from the river then Ahalya realised the extent of her sin and also the danger which beset her and Indra. She told him: 'Go away from here as quickly as you can. I am afraid of the anger of my husband. Please protect yourself from his wrath.' Indra laughed and said: 'Have no fear. I will take good care of myself and of you too.' "

"Indra hurried out of the ashrama bent on escaping the eyes of Gautama. He was just late. He saw the rishi entering the ashrama even as he was trying to depart. Gautama had just bathed in the river. He was wearing wet clothes and with his body covered with ashes he looked like Lord Mahadeva. Gautama was able to know the truth about everything which was happening around him and with the samit and darbha in his hands he stood still looking at the apparition before him: Indra assuming the garb of Gautama. It did not take very long for Gautama to guess what had happened. He bent his angry eyes on Indra and said: 'Your vanity about your being irresistible to women has made you commit this crime. I now curse you. You will lose your manhood.' "

"Gautama then entered the ashrama and looked at his wife who was shivering with terror. He said: 'You will remain here, unseen by anyone and you will lie on the ashes and the air will be your food. Years later, when Rama, the powerful son of Dasaratha, enters the ashrama, it will become sanctified and you will regain your form and you will also be cleansed of this sin which you have committed.' "

"Gautama left the ashrama and went off to perform tapas while Ahalya is waiting for the touch of your blessed feet to purify her and to sanctify this ashrama. Come, let us enter the hermitage and end the torture of this beautiful woman who is now penitent."

Rama, Lakshmana and Vishvamitra entered the ashrama of Gautama and saw the beauty that was Ahalya. Rid as she was of her sin, Ahalya radiated beauty and charm like the moon which has emerged from a screen of clouds. She looked like a sudden flame which leaped out of a cloud of smoke. She was like the sun reflected in a sheet of water.

Rama and Lakshmana saluted her and flowers rained from the heavens on them. Gautama came there and blessed the princes. The rishis spent some time together and then they parted. The princes took leave of Gautama and his spouse and with glad hearts the entire group of rishis walked towards Mithila.

18. MITHILA

They walked northwards and soon reached the yajnasala of Janaka. Rama was staring with wondering eyes at the elaborate arrangements which had been made for the yajna. He said: "Look, my lord: Thousands of well-read brahmins have now assembled here and they are all scholars in the Vedas. The ashramas for the rishis have been constructed and they are so many in number. All the provisions and other materials for the yajna are there and they look like miniature hills. Tell me, where are we supposed to stay? I am so excited at the sight of all this."

Vishvamitra chose a spot which was near the water and which was not too crowded. They were settling down there. Janaka, in the meantime, heard about the arrival of the sage Vishvamitra and he was greatly excited. Accompanied by his preceptor Sadananda he walked fast to where the great man was. He received the sage with great humility. Vishvamitra accepted his homage with graciousness and asked Janaka about the yajna he was performing. After the exchange of formalities they spent some time together. Janaka was immensely pleased that his yajna was to be blessed by the presence of Vishvamitra. He stood humbly before the rishi and said: "All the preparations are being made for the yajna. But before it is performed I feel that I have found the fruits of the yajna since it is blessed by your gracious presence. I am greatly honoured. All my desires will be granted, I know, since you have been pleased to come here in person to bless me. The pundits say that twelve days more are left for the conclusion of the yajna. I am hopeful that you will be with us all the while and be present when the devas come to receive their shares of the *havis*." Janaka prostrated before the sage and accepted the seat indicated by him.

Janaka then said: "My curiosity has been kindled by the sight of these two young men. They seem to be as valiant as the gods. They walk like young elephants: their gait is as noble as the gait of lions and as graceful as that of lithe tigers or wild bulls. Their eyes, my lord, are wide and beautiful like the petals of the lotus. They are carrying bows and arrows along with swords. They are like the Ashvini twins, glowing with a handsomeness which is not of this earth. It seems to me as though these two are some gods who have come to the earth by chance. What beautiful eyes! How long! How liquid! Their fingers are protected by guards made of leather and they look as though they are sons of Agni. They are young men who have just entered manhood. Their beauty is such that even men wish they had been born as women. Such is the charm of these two. It seems to me they have come here to make me happy and my family too. How is it these, who seem to be princes used to luxury: how is it they have walked all this distance? Why have they undertaken this journey and who are these blessed youths? Who is the fortunate king who has them for sons? They are making this entire yajnasala beautiful with their handsomeness, like the sun and moon beautify the sky. They seem to be kshatriyas and since they resemble each other so much they must be brothers. Tell me who they are."

Vishvamitra said: "They are the sons of Dasaratha, the king of Kosala." He then recounted to the king about the yaga at Siddhashrama and the later journey to Mithila. He spoke about the visit to the ashrama of Gautama and he concluded: "They heard me talk about the Shivadhanus you have with you. I brought them with me so that they can feast their eyes on the great bow of Mahadeva which you have been worshipping for generations. They are archers as you can see, and they are naturally eager to see this bow which is famed the world over."

When he heard the words of Vishvamitra, Sadananda, the preceptor of Janaka, was greatly excited. He was a rishi rich in tapas which he had performed and he was the son of Gautama. He could not take his eyes off Rama who had granted purity to his mother and he addressed Vishvamitra: "My friend, my mother who had been suffering for all these many years has been seen by the princes. She has worshipped them and my noble father has come back to his ashrama. They have been reunited after a very long time. Great indeed is my happiness at the events which have taken place." He then turned to Rama and said: "Welcome to you. You are a scion of the Raghuvamsa and you have come here accompanied by the renowned rishi, Vishvamitra. This man has achieved what cannot even be imagined by ordinary mortals. By the power of his tapas he has become a Brahmarshi. This great man has assumed the role of guardian to you. You are extremely fortunate in your godfather. He will not talk about himself. So I will tell you about his magnificent efforts and his achievements."

19. VISHVAMITRA

"Pururavas, the ancestor of the Lunar race, had six sons, the eldest of whom was Ayu. His descendants were Nahusha, his son Yayati and, after Yayati, Puru and the later kings who were more famed as Pauravas.

"Vijaya was the name of the youngest son of Pururavas. Vijaya was the father of a son by name Bheema. Bheema's son was Kanchana and his son was Jahnu, who later swallowed the river Ganga when she rushed in tumult following the king Bhagiratha. Jahnu's son was Pooru and his son was Balaaka. His son was Ajaka. Ajaka had a son by name Kusha who had four sons, the youngest of whom was Kushanabha. Gadhi was the son of Kushanabha. This Vishvamitra is the son of Gadhi. He was known in those days as Kaushika and he was a famous king. He ruled his subjects well, and he was reputed to be a very good king.

20. VASISHTHA HOSTS THE KING

"Once, the king had gone to the forest with a large army. He was visiting several places. He visited cities which were ruled by him and in the course of his journey he saw many beautiful rivers, hills and ashramas nestling at their sides. One such ashrama was that of Vasishtha, the son of Brahma. From a distance Kaushika could see the flowering trees and shrubs and he could see the orchards and there was a small stream flowing slowly past the ashrama. Several deer and other tame animals could be seen and he was very surprised to see siddhas and charanas as well as gandharvas and kinnaras. The place was resounding with the music made by the birds which had nests on the trees and there was peace reigning in the ashrama and in the forest which surrounded the ashrama.

"On going nearer, the king saw several rishis performing tapas and there were many who were bent on meditation and who

VASISHTHA HOSTS THE KING

seemed to be lost to the world. It seemed to him that Brahmaloka of which he had heard was not in the heavens, but here, on the earth where Vasishtha was.

"It is a rule among kshatriyas that they should not pass the ashrama of a rishi without paying respect to him and, in return, the rishi has to welcome him and honour him since a king is said to be Narayana Himself.

"Kaushika entered the ashrama of Vasishtha and prostrated before the great man. The rishi was very pleased with him and welcomed him with great excitement. He sent for a seat noble enough to befit a king and he made the king sit on it. He offered fruits and water. Kaushika received all these with a humility becoming a great king and they spoke to each other about general things. Vasishtha asked the conventional questions which should be asked. He said: 'I hope your subjects are happy under your rule which is sure to be righteous. I hope your servants are well-behaved and obedient, all your enemies are subdued. Is your army large and powerful? Is your treasury full? Are your children well and happy and obedient?' "

"Kaushika answered them all in the affirmative. Each had great respect for the other and they spent a long time talking about many things. After a long time had passed Vasishtha said: 'I want you to accept my hospitality. It is a rare and great honour that you have visited our ashrama with your army. I want to entertain you. You are a righteous king and a good man. I am pleased with you. You are to be honoured and give me the pleasure of doing so.' "

"Kaushika was touched by the words of the rishi and spoke very humbly and said: 'Your words full of affection have done more than a feast can do. You have already given us fruits and milk. The sight of you has made us pure for birth after birth. What need is there for a feast? You are the person who should be honoured as a god and it is not right that you should say I deserve to be honoured. I will soon be taking leave of you to continue my journey.' "

"Kaushika felt that it would only embarrass the rishi to feed so many of them and to save him this he rose up very tactfully as if to go. Vasishtha would have none of it. Again and again he insisted that the king with his retinue should stay and accept his hospitality. Finally Kaushika had to accede to his request and said: 'So be it, my lord. You are so eager to play host to us and I have not a chance to escape from your goodness.' Laughing together they walked out of the ashrama.

"Vasishtha called out: 'Surabhi! Child! Shabale! come here.' Kaushika was wondering whom he was calling and even as he was thinking about it a beautiful cow came and stood before Vasishtha and said: 'You called me, father.' Kaushika saw that the cow was unbelievably beautiful. She was of a lovely shape and her hide was mottled black and white. Her eyes were soft and gentle and Vasishtha said: 'Shabale, this is the king of the country and his name is Kaushika. He has come with his army and I wish to entertain him and his retinue. Prepare for them a feast with all the things necessary. Let there be nothing wanting and I want them all to go back satisfied. Hurry and create everything.'"

"Shabala was Kamadhenu, the divine cow which rose up out of the milk-ocean when the devas and asuras churned it for Amrita. She had been given to Vasishtha.

"She created a feast for the royal guest and his attendants. There were all kinds of food and drinks of every type imaginable. The food was such that it suited every palate. There were heaps and heaps of all the edibles they could think of and the guests were served with affection and care so that everyone had his fill of food and was satisfied. Kaushika was extremely happy and he saluted the rishi with his men.

"He then said: 'My lord, never in my life have I been so entertained and never have I tasted food like what I ate today. I want to ask a favour of you. I was greatly impressed by the power of Shabala, your cow. A cow such as she should be in the possession of the king of the country. Bounty like hers should benefit everyone. Please give her to me and, in return, I will give you a hundred thousand cows. This cow is a jewel and any precious jewel rightfully belongs to the king. Please give her to me.' "

"Vasishtha was taken aback at the words of Kaushika. But he composed himself and softly said: 'I hate to refuse anyone anything. But Shabala is someone different. Not even in exchange for a hundred thousand cows will I give my Surabhi. You may say that you will give me heaps and heaps of silver and gold. But it will be of no use. I will not part with Shabala and that is certain.'"

"Kaushika stood as though stunned. Vasishtha's eyes were now wet and he said: 'O king: Shabala is part of me and I cannot be separated from her. It is like trying to part the fame from a man who is famous. All my religious rites are performed because of the gifts of Shabala. I cannot give her to you.' "

"Kaushika would not give up. He said: 'I will give you a thousand elephants fully caparisoned, in gold and silks. I will give you eight hundred horses and chariots. I will give you more if you so desire. I will give you a crore of Kapila cows. Please give this one cow Shabala to me. If you are so desirous, I will give you gold and precious stones without number.' "

"Vasishtha shook his head sadly but firmly and said: 'No. She is my jewel and she is my wealth. She is my everything and she is my very life. My tapas is all comprised in her. What is the use of dilating on the subject? I will never part with her and it is futile on your part to offer me wealth. I have no use for any of the things you mention. I have Shabala and she will be with me for ever.' "

21. A FRUSTRATED KING

"Kaushika was a kshatriya and anger was second nature to him. He had never before been baulked in his desire and he had set his heart on this wonderful cow. He became very angry and he walked out of the ashrama. He commanded his servants to take the cow by force and they led her out of the shed where she was stationed. She thought to herself: 'Why has the noble Vasishtha abandoned me? What have I done that he should punish me thus? The servants of the king are dragging me away from here and my father has not done anything about it.' She was crying and her tears were falling fast. Her sighs were audible and she told herself: 'I will go now to him and ask him why he has allowed this insult to me by the servants of the king."

"She suddenly broke away from the hands of her captors and ran with the speed of wind and reached the presence of Vasishtha. She fell at his feet and asked: 'Why have you forsaken me, father? Even as you are looking on, these men are carrying me away. Why are you allowing this?'"

"Vasishtha said: 'Child, you have not been in the wrong and I am not punishing you. I will never forsake you. This king is powerful and he is dragging you away forcibly from my ashrama. This army of his, one akshowhini in number is his and he thinks he is invincible and hence his action.'"

"Shabala said: 'My lord, what is the power of a mere king in the presence of a brahmin? Brahmabala is far superior to that of a kshatriya. Your greatness is unequalled in all the several worlds. Kaushika is powerful, no doubt, and a great kshatriya. Give me permission, father, to show him that even a weakling like me, when blessed by you, can be more powerful than he is. I will punish his arrogance and humble his pride.'"

"Vasishtha looked at the cow whose breath was coming in gasps: so angry was she. Her eyes had become red and her tail was lifted up in anger. The rishi smiled at her and said: 'Alright, I grant you permission. Create in a moment, an army which can tackle the king's army.'"

"Surabhi just shook her body once and there appeared a huge army: hundreds of warriors and they went to fight with the army of Kaushika. Finding that his army was being defeated by this one created by the cow, Kaushika, with his eyes red with anger, entered the fight and fought with the army of Surabhi. Seeing her army suffering at the hands of the king, Surabhi created more warriors to join the fight. Even as the army got thinned out Surabhi kept on creating more and more. Kaushika was now joined by his sons and all together they attacked Vasishtha himself. The rishi, with a 'hunkara' burnt all of them and only a heap of ashes was left of the sons of the king. Kaushika was heart-broken. His army was gone and his children were dead. He was completely broken. He was like the ocean without its power: like a serpent with its fangs pulled out: like a bird whose wings had been severed. His pride was humbled and his face was like the setting sun: all its fierceness was gone.

"Without a word, with his head hanging down, with his eyes bent on the ground Kaushika left the ashrama of Vasishtha and went back to his kingdom."

"Kaushika's anger was unappeased and his thoughts were always hovering around the humiliating defeat at the hands of the cow's army in the ashrama of Vasishtha. Kaushika was disgusted with everything and he made a son of his stay and mind the kingdom. He then went to the forest. He went to the slopes of the Himavan where the kinnaras were, and he began to perform a great tapas with a desire to please lord Mahadeva. After a time the Lord was satisfied with the penance of Kaushika and he appeared before him and asked him: 'Why are you performing this tapas? What is it you desire? I will grant you anything you ask for.' "

"Kaushika prostrated before Him and, singing his praises, he said: 'My lord, if you are pleased with me then grant me this boon: I should be proficient in archery. Grant me that I am master of all the divine astras. Please be gracious enough to accede to my request.' Mahadeva said: 'I have given them all to you. Go in peace.' "

"Kaushika went back to his kingdom. His self-respect was restored and with it, his pride came back to him. It grew tenfold now. He told himself: 'Vasishtha, the great rishi, is as good as dead. How can he withstand the astras which are presided over by the gods?' "

22. THE POWER OF THE BRAHMIN

"Kaushika went to the ashrama of Vasishtha and, without any warning, he began to despatch the astras one after another. The birds and animals which were in the ashrama rushed out in panic. The disciples who were living with the rishi were also startled by the sudden harassment and they fled from there in fear. The ashrama and its surroundings were now as bare as soil which is salty and fit for nothing. There was silence reigning and it was frightening. Vasishtha was extremely angry with this cruelty on the part of Kaushika. He told himself: 'For no reason at all, this king is bent on troubling me again and again. I will destroy him like the sun burns up snow.' "

"Vasishtha came and stood before Kaushika and said: 'This peaceful hermitage, the haven of mental peace, has been destroyed by you and I am very angry with you. You do not know anything about proprieties and you are a fool. I am going to kill you.' "

"Vasishtha lifted up his staff which began to glow like the staff of Yama, the lord of death: like the fire which burns without smoke at the end of the yuga.

"Kaushika was not frightened by his words since he had the divine astras with him. He invoked the astra presided over by Agni the god of fire. Vasishtha hurled his danda at Kaushika and said: 'So you have come to challenge me with your 'divine' astras! Let me see your prowess. I am here standing in front of you and let me see what you can do. Show me. Let us see if your Kshatriyabala is great or if my Brahmabala is. You fool! you are a disgrace to the kshatriya clan to which you belong. You will now see the superiority of the divine powers of a brahmin.' "

"The astra sent by Kaushika was rushing towards Vasishtha spitting fire in all directions. When it touched the Brahma Danda which Vasishtha had planted in from of him, the fire was extinguished like when it is touched by water. Kaushika then sent the astras, Vaaruna, Raudra, Aindra, Paasupata, Aishika, and his brows were knit with anger and frustration when he found each one of them swallowed up by the Brahma Danda. Manavastra was sent in vain: and Gaandharva, the great Jrumbhana, and Swaapana. Even Vajra, the astra presided over by Indra, was futile. Kaushika sent the Paashas: Kaala Pasha, Varuna Paasha, and Brahma. The chakras followed and many other astras which were reputed to be invincible. Not one of them was capable of superseding the Brahma Danda of Vasishtha.

"By now the devas had assembled in the skies to witness this glorious scene where the power of the brahmin was proving itself to be greater than all the other powers in the three worlds. In despair the king sent the great Brahmastra and everyone was watching its progress with bated breath. Even the Brahmastra was swallowed and followed the same path as the others. Vasishtha was now glowing like the god of fire and every pore in his skin was spitting fire. The Brahma Danda was resplendent: it was like a pillar of fire. The rishis from the skies and from all over the heavens proclaimed: 'Vasishtha, your power is the greatest power we have ever known. You are capable of bearing any of these fires and making them pale into insignificance because of your glory. The good king Kaushika has been vanquished by you. Please abandon your wrath and let not the world suffer because of your anger.' "

Vasishtha accordingly calmed himself and his Brahma Danda also. As for Kaushika he threw down his bow and arrows and, with a long sigh, exclaimed: 'Fie on the bala of a kshatriya! The only bala worthwhile is the bala of a brahmin. With his mere staff this man has been able to hold at bay all the astras which had been given to me by Mahadeva. I have decided to perform tapas so that I will become like him. I will be equal to him in bala and that will be Brahmabala and not Kshatriyabala. I will realise Brahmatva with my tapas.'

"Kaushika's heart was full of diverse feelings. His heart was sore with the defeat he had met with at the hands of Vasishtha. His sighs were like the hisses of a serpent which had been angered by the beatings by a stick. His hatred for the rishi was also immense.

"With so many emotions raging in his heart Kaushika proceeded towards the south and began to perform intense tapas with the desire to become a Brahmarshi. Years passed. When a thousand years had passed Brahma the Creator came to him and said: 'Kaushika, your tapas has been so intense that the heavens are very pleased with your concentration. You have achieved what seemed to be impossible. You will, from now on, be known as *Rajarshi Kaushika*.' Having granted the boon Brahma went back to Satyaloka.

"Kaushika, however, was not as pleased as he ought to have been. On the contrary, he was very unhappy. His grief was intense and so was his frustration. He wanted the world and he was granted a handful of sand! He told himself: 'After all these years of tapas I have been called a *Rajarshi*. I feel that I have not done enough. I will try again."

23. TRISHANKU OF THE SOLAR RACE

"In the solar race was a king by name Trishanku. He was a good king famed for his righteousness as all the kings of the race were. All on a sudden he was filled with a strange desire. He wanted to reach the heavens with the human body. He approached his Guru Vasishtha with this desire in view and asked him to perform a yaga which would help him realise his dream. Vasishtha refused saying: 'This is an unnatural and impious desire on your part. I cannot help you to reach the heavens with this body.' "

"Trishanku was sorely disappointed. He renounced his throne and travelled to the south. There he met sons of Vasishtha and asked them to help him achieve the impossible. They were hundred in number and they had performed tapas for several years and they were rich in the wealth of tapas. Trishanku approached them and saluting them with reverence he stood with folded palms and said: 'I have surrendered myself to you. I am the king whose Guru is your dear father. I request you to perform for me a yaga which will make me reach the heavens with this human body. Guru Vasishtha, the famous rishi, refused to help me and asked me to look for someone else to do it for me. I have no one else but the sons of my Guru and so I have come to you for help. Rich as you are with tapas I beseech you to help me. It is well known that your ancestors have been the gurus for the line of Ikshvaku all these years. You are like gods to us and you should grant me my prayer.' "

"The sons of Vasishtha were very angry with the king. They said: 'You are very stupid and also sinful. When our father has refused to perform a sacrifice saying that it is against all dharma, how dare you approach us with the same request? Vasishtha has been the kulaguru for the line of kings ever since Ikshvaku, as you rightly observed and this Vasishtha has not approved of your ambition. He has told you that it is not possible to do such a thing. How did you expect us to agree to do something which our father has not sanctioned? You are indeed childish in your desire. Go back to the city and resume your kingly duties. We are not prepared to insult our father by taking up your cause.' "

"The king was very unhappy at their reply. He said: 'If my Guru refuses to help me and his sons too, what am I going to do? I have only one course open to me. I will go in search of another Guru who will grant me what I want.' "

"The sons of Vasishtha were furious with him. They could not brook the insult to their father and to themselves. Therefore they cursed him and said: 'You will, from this moment, become a chandala.' Having cursed him they returned to their ashramas."

"The unhappy king returned to his city with his heart filled with pain and disappointment. When the night had passed the king found that he had become a chandala. His clothes had turned black and his skin was black. His neck was adorned with flowers which were wild and the ornaments of gold which he had been wearing had turned to crude ones of iron. When he entered the city the people jeered at him and they could not recognise him. Even his ministers were unable to believe him when he told them who he was. He was chased out of the city by the citizens who made fun of his appearance."

"Trishanku thought for a while and decided that there was one rishi who would surely help him. He had heard so much about the intense tapas which Kaushika had performed and about his becoming a *Rajarshi* because of his tapas."

"Trishanku hurried towards the spot where Kaushika was and saw him absorbed in his tapas. The king stood by and Kaushika felt someone standing near him and opened his eyes. He looked at the dark and ugly chandala standing at some distance. His eyes and his face were the very picture of woe and Kaushika whose heart was always ready with sympathy felt that this man was suffering intensely. He called him near and asked him: 'I can see that you are Trishanku, the king of Ayodhya. You are a great warrior and a good king. What can I do for you? I know that this chandala form of yours is the result of a curse. Tell me what I can do to help you.' "

"Hearing the words of affection which were spoken by Kaushika the king was overcome with gratitude and his eyes filled with tears. He said: 'My Guru Vasishtha and his sons have refused to grant me my desire. I asked them to make me reach the heavens with this human body and they would not grant me my wish. I have performed a hundred yajnas. But, evidently, that is not enough. I have never once, in my life, spoken an untruth and I will not do so hereafter. I swear that I have ruled my subjects with great care and I have never once transgressed the rules which a kshatriya should follow. I have always tried to please the elders and have always set my mind on dharma. Seeing that all this seems to be futile when it cannot grant me a small desire, I realise that man's attempts are always useless and Fate is the only powerful factor. Everything is controlled by Fate and Fate is the ultimate refuge of all. I have now come to you to ask you if you will help me realise the dream in my heart: to reach the heavens with this mortal body. I have no one else to whom I can go with this request and it is up to you to help me and prove that even Fate can be subdued by the attempts of man.' "

"Kaushika was filled with pity and compassion for this king who had been so unfortunate. He spoke in a soft and gentle voice and he said: 'O king! you are welcome to be with me in my home. The world knows what a righteous monarch you are. I have decided to help you. Do not be afraid. I will summon all the rishis and ask them to help me perform a yajna. With this form, with this chandala form, which your Guru's curse has given you, with this form, I say, I will make you ascend the heavens. Kaushika has been approached as a refuge by you and you cannot be sent back empty handed. I will do what you want me to.' "

"Kaushika then instigated his sons to collect all that was necessary for the performance of a yajna. He summoned his disciples and said: 'Go and ask all the rishis to come here at my request. Let them bring their entire ashramas with them.' The disciples went to all the quarters to bring the many rishis. They came, all of them, except the sons of Vasishtha and the father too. Vasishtha's sons' words were: 'Very comical indeed! A strange sight this yajna will be with a kshatriya to perform the yajna and with a chandala as the object of the yajna. We wonder how the participants will react: the divine beings who have to receive their shares of the *havis* at the hands of one who is not a brahmin. They will have to eat the food touched by a chandala and served by a kshatriya since Kaushika is not a brahmin.' "

"When he heard these words Kaushika was highly incensed and with his eyes red with anger he cursed them to be nishadhas."

"Kaushika then addressed the rishis who had come there at his request and said: 'This is the king Trishanku, a descendant of Ikshvaku. He is a righteous king famed in all the three worlds. He has come to me with a request. He wants to reach the heavens with this body. I have promised to help him and I appeal to all of you to assist me in this my attempt to help a good king.' "

"Hearing his words the rishis said to themselves: 'Kaushika is a man with a very short temper. His anger is dangerous. If we do not assist him as he asks us to, he is sure to get angry and we can never guess what he will do if his anger turns against us. It is better to help him perform the yajna.' "

"Kaushika was the yajaka and the rishis were all willing to do the needful. The yajna proceeded in the proper manner. At the final stage when the *havis* was to be offered Kaushika summoned the devas one by one to accept their shares. But not one of them came. Their disapproval of the yajna was obvious. Kaushika was furious at this insult. But he composed himself and, with his eyes blazing with anger and with his frame trembling with fury, he raised the *sruva* (the spoon with which ghee is poured into the sacrificial fire) aloft and said: 'Look on the power of my tapas. I will raise this king to the heavens with this human body. I command you, Trishanku, rise in the air and reach the heavens with this body of yours. If at all I have performed any tapas I give the result of all that with this end in view: to raise you to the heavens.' "

'Rise, O king! and reach the heavens!'

24. A NEW HEAVEN

"Everyone was watching with bated breath. Suddenly Trishanku began to rise above the ground. He folded his palms and he saluted the rishi. He rose in the air and even as they were all looking, he vanished into the clouds."

"Indra was not pleased with this intruder. He said: 'Trishanku, go back to the earth. You are not fit to dwell in the heavens, cursed as you are, by your Guru. We are not prepared to consider you as one of us.' "

'Trishanku was pushed rudely and he found himself falling downwards. He called out to the great Kaushika and said: 'My lord, they have thrown me out and I am falling down. Save me, save me.' Kaushika was very angry and very sad too. He could not brook the cruelty of the devas and their selfishness. He said: 'Stay where you are.' "

"The fall of Trishanku was arrested half way. Then, in the presence of all, Kaushika, like another Brahma, began to create a new heaven for Trishanku. In the southern direction he created the seven rishis and other stars. He created the clusters of stars. He then said: 'I am going to create another Indra who will eclipse the present Indra.' "He began to do so and to create other devas too. There was great commotion in the heavens and the devas and rishis from the heavens approached Kaushika with humility and said: 'Please listen to our words, Kaushika. It has been said that one who has been cursed by his Guru cannot reach the heavens and so we did what we did. It was in no way meant to cast aspersions on you or your greatness.' Hearing their words Kaushika said: 'You are jealous of him and so you treated him thus. I will not let him come back to the earth. He is a righteous king and he does not deserve punishment.'"

"The devas said: 'We will agree to anything you say.'" "I will not go back on my promise to Trishanku,' said Kaushika. 'The heaven I have created for him will be permanent. The stars and the seven rishis and the entire galaxy which have been created by me will be permanent. Indras may come and go but the heavens I have built for Trishanku and the world of Trishanku will last for ever.' "

" 'So be it,' said Indra and the devas with great humility. "This world of stars and gods which you have created out of your tapas will remain for ever proclaiming your greatness. Trishanku will rule the heaven built for him like another Indra. All the stars will move in their orbits for him and his fame and name will last for ever.' "

"Kaushika was satisfied by their promise and Trishanku was happy. The devas went back to their abode, and the rishis to theirs."

"Only Kaushika was left all alone and his treasury of tapas was empty. He had given it all for the sake of a king whose suffering could not be borne by Kaushika."

25. SUNASHEPHA

"Trishanku had reached the heavens which had been created by Kaushika. He told himself: 'This tapas which I performed in the south has had interruptions and I have used it all up. I will go towards the west and begin all over again. I will choose a spot where I will be concealed from every one. I will be hidden from the sight of people and on the shores of some lake I will have my ashrama and perform tapas there, undisturbed,' "

"On the shores of a lake Kaushika began his tapas again in the holy spot by name Pushkarakshetra."

"Trishanku had a son by name Harishchandra. He had no sons and he prayed to Varuna, the lord of the oceans. He said: 'All I want is to have a son. When a son is born to me I will perform a yajna with my son as offering and give him to you.'"

"In course of time a son was born to the king: and he called him Rohita. Varuna came to him and asked him to keep his word. He said: 'You must keep your promise. You agreed to perform a sacrifice with this child as the offering.'"

"The king said: 'A new-born child is not clean. It is only after ten days that it becomes clean. I will give him to you after that.' "

"Ten days later Varuna came to claim the child and the king said: 'A yajna pashu has to have teeth. So wait till the child cuts his teeth.'"

"When Varuna came again the king postponed the gift by saying that the milk teeth should fall: and then, that they should grow again. And so it went on. In his attachment to his son the king kept on thinking up excuses. 'Let my son wear armour. A kshatriya is pure only when he wears an armour.' "

"Rohita, in the meantime, came to know about all that had happened. He wanted to escape his doom by running away to the forest with a bow in his hand."

"The king was afflicted with the dread disease called Mahodara which Varuna caused as a punishment. Hearing about it the prince Rohita started to go back home, to save his father. Indra stopped him. He told the young prince that he should go and visit all the holy rivers. One year passed and again it happened and again. Five years passed and finally he made up his mind to go back to his kingdom and see his father."

"On the way Rohita met a brahmin whose name was Ajigartha. He was travelling with his wife and three sons. The prince thought that his father's disease would be cured and that he himself could escape death by sacrificing someone else. He saluted the brahmin who stood silent to find out what the prince wanted. Rohita said: 'My lord, I will give you a hundred thousand cows. Are you willing to trade one of your sons for it?' The brahmin wanted more details and the prince told him about the predicament of his father and himself. Ajigartha said: 'My eldest son will not part from me. He is too dear to me and I will not be able to live without him.' The wife of the brahmin said: 'My husband, the Bhargava, has said that our eldest son is dear to him and therefore cannot be given. I want you to know that the youngest child is dear to me and I cannot bear to give him up. It is always the way of the world that the eldest is the father's favourite and the youngest, that of the mother.'"

"The second son was called Sunashepha. He spoke in a soft and sad voice: 'Listen to me, O prince. My father favours my elder brother and my mother, my younger brother. It is as good as understood that I have been sold to you by my parents for a hundred thousand cows. Take me with you.' The prince gave the number of cows to the brahmin and was happy since he had the young boy with him who would be sacrificed instead of himself."

"It was noon when Rohita and Sunashepha reached the holy spot named Pushkara. There the young boy saw Kaushika who was absorbed in his tapas. The child was hungry, thirsty and very depressed because he realised that he was unwanted by his parents, or else would they have sold him for a hundred thousand cows? And they knew that he was going to be killed and yet they gave him away! He knew that this rishi Kaushika was distantly related to the Bhargava clan and he felt that he had a claim on him. Impulsively he rushed to the presence of Kaushika and fell on his lap sobbing. Rudely awakened from his trance Kaushika looked at the intruder. He saw a young boy with a woe-begone face and he was sobbing his heart out."

"The child said: 'I have no father and no mother. As for kinsfolk I have none. You are my only refuge. You must save my life. I have been told that you are very noble, powerful and compassionate, that you can never bear to see anyone who is unhappy. I saw you and I have come to you for help.' Kaushika wanted to know what was worrying the young boy and he told him the entire story. Kaushika's heart was full of love for this foundling. Sunashepha said: 'My lord, since my father has sold me for the purpose of a yajna I do not want that yajna to be spoilt nor do I want to lose my life. Only you can work things in such a way that both these can be accomplished. I want to live long, perform tapas and then reach the heavens. You are the succour for unfortunate beings like me and you are a father to me since I am now an orphan.' "

"Kaushika pacified the weeping boy with gentle words and promises and he summoned his sons and said: 'Parents create their children so that they will guide them to heaven: to assure them of a place in the other world. I want you to justify your births. Here is this child who has come to me to save him. You are all well-read and you have acquired wealth in the form of tapas. Do what is expected of you by me. One of you should become the yajnapashu, for the sacrifice of King Harishchandra. Thus I will save this child and the yajna will also come to a successful conclusion. Will you do it?' "

"The sons led by Madhuchandas considered it a big joke and laughing at their father said: 'Father, how can you find it in your heart to abandon your sons for the sake of a foundling who weeps his heart out? It is as improbable that we should accept your suggestion as it is to eat the flesh of a dog.' Kaushika's anger rose to the surface and he said: 'Your behaviour and your words are unworthy of your birth and you are not fit to be my sons. Those who disobey their father are not fit to be honoured. Like the sons of Vasishtha you will also be chandalas and eat the flesh of dogs for a thousand years.' "

"Kaushika assured Sunashepha that he would save his life somehow. He pondered for a long while and then said: 'You must go with Rohita and allow yourself to be tied to the sacrificial pole, yupasthambha. They will place garlands of red flowers round your neck and smear red sandal paste on your body. They will tie you up with ropes which have been purified with incantations. I will teach you these two verses and in your mind repeat them till you have memorised them. Then, during the yajna sing these hymns. The yajna will be as good as successful in its completion.' "

"Sunashepha learnt the hymns with great care. He then went to Rohita who had been resting all the while and said: 'Let us hurry to the spot where the yajna is to be performed. I am well prepared for it.' The prince was happy to see him a willing victim. And they hurried to the presence of the sick king. Harishchandra was immensely pleased with the turn of events. He went to the yajnasala and began to perform the yajna though he was sorely afflicted with the disease Mahodara."

"The young boy was tied to the yupasthambha and when they were getting ready to sacrifice him the young boy began to sing in his childish treble, the hymns taught to him by Kaushika. The yajnasala was silent with surprise and later, with admiration for the noble hymns which were in praise of the devas, Indra, Varuna and the others who were entitled to a share of the *havis*."

"Indra was pleased and so was Varuna. They appeared in person and granted long life to Sunashepha. The king was forgiven for his lapse and he was cured of his disease. The experiences he had gone through because of his excessive attachment to his son had taught him a lesson and Harishchandra wanted to learn the Brahmavidya from Kaushika. The rishi was only too happy to tell him, and after that, Harishchandra was a changed man."

"Kaushika had a hundred sons. One of them was called by the name Madhuchandas and so all the hundred were called as the 'Madhuchandas brothers.' After the yajna performed by

Harishchandra, Kaushika adopted Sunashepha as his own and told his sons: 'He is your brother. I want you to treat him as your elder brother. He was born a Bhrigu but he is now one of you."

"The older sons of Kaushika were not happy at the suggestion of their father and they would not accept Sunashepha as their elder brother. Kaushika was of course furious and he cursed them too, to be low-born. There were fifty of them. The other fifty led by Madhuchandas fell at his feet and said: 'We are willing to obey you in everything. We are very happy to accept Sunashepha as our eldest brother.' The father was naturally pleased with them and said: 'You are good sons and I am pleased with you. Led by this new son of mine you will be known as the *Kaushikas* and our House will be famed as the Kaushika Gotra.' "

"Kaushika pursued his tapas for a thousand years. At the end of it Brahma appeared before him and said: 'Because of your tapas you have become a rishi, not just a Rajarshi.' "

"Kaushika was not pleased with becoming a rishi. He was determined to achieve the status of Brahmarshi and he began to perform tapas intensely. He went to the north and there he pursued his tapas."

26. KAUSHIKA'S LAPSES

"The devas were worried about Kaushika's tapas and the foremost of them was Indra who was afraid that his status as Indra might be in danger. He decided to disturb the tapas and he summoned to his presence Menaka, the apsara of his court. He said: 'You are the best among the apsaras. I want your help. I will tell you what I want you to do. Kaushika is performing tapas and he is glowing like the noonday sun: so fierce is the tapas he has accumulated. If he succeeds there is every danger of my being pushed out of my throne. I want you to go to his presence. He has all his senses under control and with single-mindedness he is absorbed in meditation. With your beauty, your youth and your winning ways, you should tempt him and make him succumb to the weakness which is innate in the heart of every man. Make him abandon his tapas and I will be pleased with you.' "

"Menaka was afraid to go. She said: 'My lord, I have been told that he is very powerful and that he is very easily angered. Think of the combination, power, tapas and anger! How can I survive these? You are afraid of him and yet you want a weak woman like me to go to him! How can I face him? He has cursed the sons of Vasishtha. He was a kshatriya and by his own efforts he has become a rishi now. He has been like Brahma in creating a new heaven for the sake of a king. Such a powerful tapasvin will surely have gone beyond the sway of the senses and how can I dare to go near him? What if he curses me? If you assure me that he will not curse me I will do what you ask me to do. Send Manmatha and Vasanta with me. Make the wind Mandanila to come with us. Under such pleasing conditions which are always conducive to the act of love, I will try to tempt Kaushika and let us hope I succeed in my attempts.' "

"Menaka went down to the earth and in the neighbourhood of the spot where Kaushika was, she spent her time waiting for the proper time when she could make her appearance. One day Kaushika got up from the meditation and was moving about. Menaka thought that the chance had come her way now, the chance she was waiting for. And she was not wrong. Looking at her beautiful figure and her winning ways Kaushika was bewitched and he succumbed to her charms."

"Five years passed and another five years. He woke up suddenly one day out of this bewitchment. He realised that ten years, ten precious years had been wasted. His tapas had been disturbed and he had lost much of what he had accumulated. He was full of anger and sorrow. He then realised that it was the work of the devas who were set on disturbing tapas performed by any one."

"When she saw him like this Menaka was overcome with fear lest he should vent his anger on her. She stood with folded palms and her tears were trembling on her lashes. But Kaushika was not angry with her. He told her that he was going north to continue where he had left off."

He went to the banks of the river Kaushiki and his tapas was terrible. After a long time the devas, pleased with him came there with Brahma and they said: 'Kaushika, you are now a *Maharshi*. You have performed severe penance. We say that you are the greatest of the rishis.' "

"Kaushika was neither pleased nor sad at the words of Brahma. He said: 'With my tapas I have earned the title 'Maharshi'. But tell me, have I become one who has conquered the senses?' Brahma said: 'No, you are not a Jitendriya, not completely.' Kaushika's face fell and Brahma said: 'You must try to achieve that also: perfect control of the senses.' "

"The most difficult part of his tapas was performed by him for the next few years. He held his arms aloft and he was bent on starving himself, in the midst of five fires during the summer days and in the midst of water during winter. Only air was his food. His tapas became intense and, as was his custom, Indra summoned Rambha and told her: 'Go and try to tempt Kaushika as Menaka did before.' Rambha was very much afraid of Kaushika and said: 'I dare not. His anger will be unbearable.' But Indra assured her that he would himself be with her. The nightingale would sing from the branches of the mango tree near where Kaushika was and on that tree would be stationed Manmatha and Indra."

"While he was absorbed in his meditation Kaushika was disturbed by the music of the nightingale. He smelt the scent of the flowers which bloom only during the season Vasanta. He opened his eyes and they lighted on the very beautiful woman standing before him. He knew that it was the work of Indra or else how could Vasanta come long before it was due? And again, how could a woman find her way into the heart of the terrible forest unless she had been brought there? His anger came up once more and he cursed Rambha: 'You have agreed to try and tempt me by your wiles and by your wanton ways and rob me of my tapas. You will be turned to stone and stay on the earth for a thousand years."

"The moment he said it he repented his action and said: 'Yes, Brahma is right. I am not a Jitendriya. I am not able to subdue my anger. So long as the senses are unconquered, the atman will not attain tranquillity. Hereafter I will never be angry and I will not speak a word. I will drain myself of all feelings and perform tapas once again. Then and only then, will I attain the fruits of my tapas.'"

27. VISHVAMITRA, THE BRAHMARSHI

"Kaushika abandoned the north and walked towards the east. And there again he performed his tapas. For a thousand years he was silent and the world and the heavens were all being burnt up by the fire of his penance. He had become as thin as a twig and he had surmounted several obstacles placed in the way of his achievement. He banished anger from his mind completely."

"One day he broke his fast and cooked some rice for himself. Just as he was about to eat it Indra, taking the form of a brahmin, came to him and begged him for food. Kaushika spoke not a word but gave the entire food to the brahmin and went back to his meditation without eating."

"His tapas became more and more fierce. Even the air which he was breathing he controlled so that he could stay without breathing for a long while. Smoke began to emanate from his head and the worlds were suffering because of his penance and the devas and others went to Brahma and told him: 'Kaushika now glows with the greatness of his tapas. If you do not grant him what he has been wanting all these years, his tapas is sure to destroy all the three worlds. His glory is so great that even the sun and fire have lost their lustre. The seas are lashing their waves in torment and the mountains are spitting fire. The earth is trembling and there is storm everywhere. Kaushika is like the great fire at the end of the yuga and it is up to you to save the universe from him.' Brahma hurried to the presence of Kaushika and said: 'We welcome you *Brahmarshi*! We have been pleased with the tapas you have performed. With your efforts you have achieved the status of Brahmarshi. You will live very long. May you prosper.' A thin flash of pleasure lit up the face of Kaushika. He prostrated before Brahma and said: "If what you have granted me is really true, if I am a Brahmarshi, if I am long-lived by your grace, let the Vedas accept me as Brahmarshi. I have but one desire. Vasishtha, your son, should recognise me as such.' They brought Vasishtha to the presence of the great Kaushika and he smiled with affection at Kaushika and said: 'You are a great man, Brahmarshi. There is no doubt about it."

"Kaushika honoured Vasishtha and he was free to go as he pleased. The thought that he had achieved the seemingly impossible made him happy but he was not proud nor conceited. He was ever bent on doing good to others and he was called *Vishvamitra*, the friend of the universe."

Sadanand said: "This great Vishvamitra is the very personification of tapas."

Janaka stood in front of Vishvamitra and said: "It has been an act of infinite kindness on your part to have come here to my yajna with the sons of the monarch. Today I have heard in detail the sacred story of how you became Vishvamitra, the friend of the universe. How well the name fits you, my lord. You are bent on doing nothing but good to mankind and something tells me that you have come here to do me a great favour."

The sun had nearly set and they broke up their session. The king went back to his palace and the rishis, to their hermitages. Rama was silent and so was Lakshmana.

The story of Vishvamitra and his struggle was too sublime to be talked about.

28. THE BOW OF MAHADEVA

Early in the morning King Janaka went to the presence of Vishvamitra. He spoke to him and to the princes words of welcome and added: "Lord, you have come to me with the intention of blessing me. I know that. Tell me if there is anything particular which I should do. Please command me as to what should be done to make you happy." The rishi was impressed by the humility of Janaka and he spoke in a soft persuasive voice: "As I told you yesterday, these two young men are kshatriyas, the sons of the monarch Dasaratha, and they are called Rama and Lakshmana. Their fame as archers has spread the world over. It is but natural for them to be impatient to see the Bow of Mahadeva which you have been worshipping for years. I can assure you that great good fortune is awaiting you and the bow will be the cause of it. Ask the bow to be brought here. Let them see it."

King Janaka said: "I will relate to the young men the story of the bow: about how it came about that the House of the Videhas has been honoured by its possession. Nimi was a famed monarch in our family and the sixth king after him was Devaratha. This bow was given to him. He had been asked to keep it with him and to guard it very carefully. As for this bow, in ancient times, when Daksha performed a yaga, he insulted Mahadeva by refusing to give him his share of the *havis*. The devas, who were afraid of Daksha, countenanced this insult to the Lord. Mahadeva went to the yajnasala with this bow in his hand and looking at the devas sneeringly he said: 'Since you allowed this injustice I am going to separate your jewelled heads from your bodies.' The devas rushed to him at once and they fell at his feet and craved pardon. Mahadeva is a god who is easily incensed and easily pacified. His anger vanished and the devas were saved. This bow was then given to my ancestor and he was asked to guard it as a treasure as indeed it is.

"Once, when I was planning to perform another yajna, I was ploughing the ground and when the ground was split by the plough I saw that in the furrow made by the plough was a beautiful child.

It was a delicate looking girl and since I was then childless I took her to my queen and the child grew up to be my eldest daughter. Discovered as she was by the tip of the plough, I have called her Sita. She seems to me to be the incarnation of Devi Lakshmi herself. She is no ordinary mortal."

"I decided to give her in marriage to a hero. This was after several princes came to me and asked me for her hand. I was not willing to give her away and so I told them that she can be given only to the one who can fulfil my stipulation. They asked me what it was and I said: 'She will be given to the one who will lift this bow and string it.'"

"My lord, not one of them was able even to lift it. Offended by me, as they thought, they joined together and surrounded Mithila on all sides seeking to destroy me and my kingdom. I was not able to withstand the onslaught of so many kings who had combined their forces and, for a year, I suffered. I performed tapas and the devas sent their divine army to help me. The enemies were vanquished and Mithila was saved from destruction. This is the bow which has such a long story which goes with it. I will certainly have it brought here for Rama and Lakshmana to see."

Janaka commanded his ministers to have the bow brought to the presence of Vishvamitra. They went to the palace of the king. The bow was placed so that everyone could see it. The great bow was worshipped with flowers and incense everyday. It took five thousand stalwarts to drag the cart holding the bow; the cart had eight large wheels and, with great difficulty, the cart was dragged to where the king was seated with his guests.

When the iron casket containing the bow came into view they all stood up as one man and honoured the Bow of Mahadeva. Janaka stood humbly before Vishvamitra and said: "This is that famed bow which has broken the pride of so many kings. This is the Bow of Mahadeva. No deva, nor asura nor yaksha has been able to lift it even: not to mention stringing it or using it. No gandharva nor kinnara nor a rakshasa has been able to lift it. What then can be said about a mere man? Please show the bow to the princes."

THE BOW OF MAHADEVA

Vishvamitra was listening to the words of Janaka with a great deal of attention. A moment passed, and then, with a sweet and gentle smile touching his lips, Vishvamitra said: "Child, Rama, go and look at the bow."

Rama walked towards the casket. He opened the lid and stood staring at the magnificent bow. He stood gazing at it for a long moment. He then turned to the rishi Vishvamitra and asked: "Great one, I will now touch this great bow with my hand. I will lift it and try to string it. May I do so?"

"You may," said both the rishi and the king.

Everyone was tense with excitement since Rama spoke with so much confidence. Even as thousands of eyes were watching, Rama lifted the bow as though it were just a sport. There was an audible sigh from everyone when they saw him lift it easily with his left hand. Rama stood the bow straight and, holding it with his left hand, he bent it with his right to string it.

There was a noise like a clap of thunder and those who were watching saw the great Bow of Mahadeva break into two. The earth trembled at the noise and most of the people around fell down senseless. Vishvamitra, Janaka and the princes were the only four unaffected by the noise.

When they had all recovered and when there was a semblance of normalcy restored, Janaka spoke words of great sweetness and words suited to the occasion. He said: "I still cannot believe that this has happened. I have never seen the like of it before. This Rama is the greatest among men. My dear daughter Sita is fortunate to become the bride of the House of the Ikshvakus. I had announced that I would give her to the hero who will string the bow and Rama has done it.

"Permit me, my lord, to send messengers to Ayodhya. Let them relate to the monarch about the incidents here and let the king know how his son won the hand of my daughter. Let him be told that the princes are still under your care and let him be entreated to come to Mithila as early as he possibly can."

Vishvamitra was only too happy to say: "Do so by all means."

Messengers were sent to Ayodhya on fleet horses and they hurried to the great city with the glad tidings that Rama had broken the great Bow of Mahadeva and that Sita, the daughter of Janaka, was to be his bride.

29. DASARATHA LEAVES FOR MITHILA

Three days and three nights had to pass before the messengers could reach Ayodhya. They reached the palace of the king and told the doorkeepers: "We have come from Mithila and we have a message for the king. Please take us to his presence." They went to the king and, after saluting him in a manner befitting a monarch, they spoke to him and said: "Great one! Janaka, the King of Mithila, sends his regards to your gracious self and wants to know if all is well with you and your kingdom. He asks again and again after your welfare and that of your subjects.

"He now wants you to listen to a request of his, which has been approved and sanctioned by the great rishi, Vishvamitra. These are his words: 'I have a daughter by name Sita. I had announced to the world that she is a Viryasulka. None of the kings who came were able to satisfy the stipulations which I had laid down. That daughter of mine has been won now by your blessed son who was brought to me by Vishvamitra. It is my good fortune that Rama, your eldest son, should be my son-in-law. In the presence of several rishis, kings and citizens, the great divine Bow of Mahadeva was broken by your noble son. According to my promise, Sita, my daughter, will be given to him as a prize for his prowess. Please accept my gift and honour me. Please come to Mithila as early as possible accompanied by your preceptors. Your sons are eager to be re-united with you. You must be gracious enough to let me keep my promise and let me give my child to your son.' The messengers continued: "Advised by the sage Vishvamitra and by his own Guru Sadananda, our king has asked us to convey to you this message. Please let us also add our entreaties and request you to come to our city." They waited eagerly for the king's reply.

Dasaratha, happy beyond words, looked at Vasishtha and Vamadeva and the other ministers in the court and said: "So the children have gone to Videha with Vishvamitra. As you have all heard, Rama's prowess has won the admiration of everyone. Janaka is eager to perform the wedding as early as possible. If you are all agreeable to it we will, at once, leave for Mithila. Let us not lose time."

There was nothing but happiness in the hearts of everyone in Ayodhya. It was decided to leave for Mithila early in the morning. The tired messengers from Mithila were duly honoured and they spent the night peacefully.

30. IN MITHILA

When the east was tinted red heralding the approach of dawn the royal entourage left for Mithila. The king had asked his treasurer to take as many jewels and gold with him as was necessary for the occasion. These were the gifts which a king naturally carried with him when he went to meet another king. In this instance there was also the proposed marriage of his eldest son. Chariots and palanquins to carry the members of the royal family were ready. The many preceptors led by Vasishtha were already on their way. The king ascended the chariot and the journey was on.

It took them four days to reach Mithila. Even as they were nearing the gates of the city, King Janaka hurried forward to greet the old and venerable king, surrounded as he was by his kinsmen and the rishis who were his preceptors. He spoke to the king of Kosala and said: "It is gracious on your part to have acceded to my request and to have come to my city. You must honour me by accepting my hospitality. I have been honoured by the coming of Vasishtha and he is accompanied by great rishis like Vamadeva and Markandeya.

"Your son, O king, has made my dream come true. He has saved me from breaking my oath about the proper man who should wed my child. The yajna is nearly at an end. At the conclusion of the yajna you should permit that the wedding of your son with my child takes place."

Dasaratha, with his face lit up with a smile of contentment, said: "Receiving of a gift depends entirely on the giver, Janaka. There is no need for me to tell you when the marriage should take place. You and your preceptors will know." Janaka led them to the palace set apart for them. The rishis had all assembled there for the sake of the yajna and the great Vasishtha with Vamadeva and the renowned Markandeya were honoured by all of them.

Tender was the reunion of Rama and Lakshmana with their father. For the sake of propriety the king had refrained from rushing to Rama when he saw him. Now they were alone, the king shed tears of joy and embraced them again and again. The night was spent happily with the princes recounting to their father about the many happenings during their stay with Vishvamitra. Janaka, as was the custom, spent the night in the yajnasala.

Early in the morning the king of Mithila became engrossed in the yajna which had almost neared completion. The ritviks surrounded the Vedika and the rites were performed without any disturbance or interruption or lapse to mar its perfection.

Janaka then spoke to his own preceptor Sadananda, the son of Gautama, and said: "As, you know, I have a brother by name Kushadhvaja who is ruling over the city by name Sankashya. The city has the sweet river Ikshumati flowing near her. I wish to send for him and let him share the joy of this happy occasion with me." Sadananda at once sent messengers to bring Kushadhvaja to Mithila. Soon he came and when they had all assembled in the great hall, Janaka asked his chief minister Sudhama to go to the presence of King Dasaratha and bring him to the court along with his sons.

When the old king arrived there with Rama and Lakshmana, Janaka with his brother went towards them and with folded palms, greeted them and led them to the jewelled seats set apart for them.

Dasaratha then said: "Janaka, my friend, my preceptor Vasishtha will perform everything in the proper manner. It is the custom to relate the ancestry of the young man who is to be married and I now request Guru Vasishtha to do the needful."

Kulaguru Vasishtha traced the line of Manu elaborating on the greatness of kings like Ikshvaku who was the first to rule in the city of Ayodhya. He then spoke of Trishanku, the famed Yuvanashva, his son Mandhata who was called the 'Jewel of Kritayuga', King Sagara, Bhagiratha, Kakustha, Raghu and down to Aja whose son was the present King Dasaratha. He said: "You have heard about the glorious story of this dynasty. Please be gracious enough to give your daughter in marriage to Rama, the son of Dasaratha."

Janaka said: "I would also like to tell you something about the glorious men who were my ancestors: who have shed glory on our heritage." He spoke of their first king Nimi and his son Mithi after whom the city was called Mithila. The recital went on. King after king was mentioned and his glorious achievements. The king by name Svarnaroma was the father of Janaka who had three brothers. Janaka concluded: "I now ask you to accept my daughter Sita as the bride of your eldest son Rama, and my other child, Urmila, as the bride for Lakshmana." He added: "Please make all the many preparations which are religious for these two young men, and three days from today, when the star is in Uttara Phalguni, let the marriages be performed."

Vishvamitra spoke to Janaka and said: "Janaka, the alliances which you have proposed are indeed very good and we are all immensely pleased with it. I have a suggestion to make. I have been told that this brother of yours Kushadhvaja has two beautiful daughters. I ask you on behalf of the king of Ayodhya to give them in marriage to Bharata and Shatrughna, the other sons of the king. May the two great houses be inextricably bound by these alliances."

The entire hall was filled with words of praise for the suggestion of Vishvamitra and the old king Dasaratha returned to his palace with a glad heart.

31. SITA KALYANAM

On the morning of the day fixed for the wedding, King Dasaratha surrounded by his entire host arrived in the hall which had been set apart for the wedding. The princes stood with their father and Vasishtha was the officiating priest. He smiled at Janaka and said: "King Dasaratha, accompanied by his sons, is here and they have been prepared for the solemn ceremony. They are wearing the scared kankanas on their wrists and, please hasten to perform the kanyadana which is said to benefit the giver and the one who receives."

Janaka with the rishis Vishvamitra and Sadananda to guide him, purified and decorated the platform set for the marriage by offering flowers and incense and other symbols of prosperity. These were the rites prescribed in the Vedas. He then kindled the sacred fire with incantations.

Janaka brought Sita. Words were inadequate to describe the beauty of Sita. She looked like the goddess Lakshmi who had walked out of the lotus on which she resides: as though she had left the presence of Narayana and come down to the earth. She was as bright and beautiful as a flash of lightning. Large eyes like lotus petals were cast down and her hair which was long and dark was decked with flowers and with gems. She was wearing jewels and her dress was of the colour of gold with an edging of gold which was woven as though swans were strung together. She walked slowly with her father.

Janaka brought her to the presence of Rama and said: "This Sita, my daughter, will be, from now, yours. She will walk in the path of Dharma with you. Accept her. Take her hand in yours and may you both be blessed. She is a Pativrata, a great personage and she will be like a shadow unto you."

Janaka then poured water into the hands of Rama and thus made the gift complete: the gift of his beloved daughter to the greatest among men.

When the waters touched the hands of Rama, divine music could be heard from the heavens and the devas showered flowers on the newly-weds.

Janaka then went to Lakshmana and gave his other daughter Urmila to him and said: "Lakshmana, accept my daughter as your spouse. Take her hand in yours and make her yours." Bharata and Shatrughna took the hands of the princesses Mandavi and Srutakirti and the sight was glorious: the four young men with their brides making pradakshina to the fire and taking the seven steps which is an essential rite. The excitement of the wedding was over and the night was spent in happiness. Early in the morning Vishvamitra went to the palace where the young princes were. He took affectionate farewell of them and proceeded to the north, to the Himavan and the banks of Kaushiki where he always stayed.

32. PARASURAMA, THE BHARGAVA

After the departure of Vishvamitra, Dasaratha went to the King of Mithila and, taking leave of him, began his journey back to Ayodhya with his sons and their brides. Janaka went with them for some distance and returned to his city while Dasaratha continued his journey.

As they proceeded towards Ayodhya, the king observed ill-omens on the way. Birds were making strange noises and it was fearsome. They were flying hither and thither as though in panic. The animals were also signifying that something terrible was about to happen.

Dasaratha was naturally upset by these and asked Vasishtha what these omens foreboded. The rishi thought for a while and said: "Dasaratha, something fearful is approaching us. There is no doubt about it. Since the birds are afraid it is evident. But the animals which are running in the right direction, that is, making pradakshina means that the fear will be removed and no great harm will befall you. Be rid of this fear. It will pass, whatever is to come."

Even as they were talking, a sudden gale blew across the sky and it seemed to make the earth tremble. It was like a whirlwind. The sun was covered with darkness and the quarters seemed to be covered by dust. Nothing could be visible. There was an unknown fear in the heart of every one of the men in the army of the king and Dasaratha was extremely worried as to why this was happening.

Out of the darkness and the cloak of dust there came towards them a glorious figure. He was wearing the garb of an ascetic and his hair was matted like the locks of Lord Mahadeva himself. This was Parasurama, the Bhargava: Parasurama who would strike nothing but terror in the hearts of the kshatriyas since he was known to be a hater of kshatriyas. He was as fearful as the great fire which licks up the earth at the end of time and he was an awe-inspiring personage like the peak of Mount Kailasa. He was so radiant that they were all dazzled by him. On his shoulder rested the famed axe which got him the name Parasurama. His hands held a glorious bow and he was like Lord Mahadeva who was setting out to kill the Tripuras.

When they saw him, the rishis led by Vasishtha placed their palms together and greeted him with reverence. Their minds were filled with misgivings since this hater of kshatriyas was in the midst of the scions of a famed line of kshatriyas. They thought to themselves: "Bhargava has already completed his tarpana to his father with the blood of the kshatriyas and we have been told that he has abandoned his anger and his hatred of the kshatriyas. And so there may not be any danger to the king or to his sons. But then, why this anger which sits like a thunder-cloud on his noble brow?"

They offered Arghya to the guest and he accepted it. He went to Rama and said: "Rama, I have been hearing about your prowess with the bow and arrow. People have been talking of nothing else. I was also told about your visit to Mithila and about your breaking the sacred bow of Lord Mahadeva. I am curious to know how great is this power and prowess of yours which people are talking about. I have, therefore, brought another bow to test you."

Parasurama held out the bow which he had been holding in his hands and said: "This bow belonged to my father, the noble Jamadagni. Everyone is afraid even to touch this bow. Let me see you lift it, string it and shoot an arrow with it. Then and only then, will I believe the stories I have been hearing about you. If you are able to do so, to do what I have stipulated, I will then consider you to be a worthy opponent and we can fight a duel.

"If, however, you are afraid, then accept that you have been defeated by me. You should either accept my superiority or fight with me."

Bhargava stood with his eyes blazing and to the old king he looked like an avenging fury all set to kill his beloved Rama. With his face pale with fear the king said: "I have been told that your anger against kshatriyas has been appeased and that your hatred is now like a fire which has been extinguished. Why then, this anger? My son should be left unharmed, for my sake. I beg you to spare my child to me. You have promised to Indra that you would lay down your arms. You did so and went to live in the mountain by name Mahendra. Why then have you assumed this angry look? If Rama, my child, is killed, that will be the end of all of us. You have, evidently, come to destroy the entire family of Dasaratha."

Parasurama paid no heed to the piteous pleadings of Dasaratha. He was looking only at Rama and he said: "These two bows, were made at the same time by Vishvakarma. They are great bows, famed throughout the three worlds. They are firm, strong, and it is not possible for ordinary mortals to handle them. One of these was given to Mahadeva, the three-eyed god, and the other was offered to Narayana. What I am holding in my hands is the bow of Narayana. It has never known defeat. It is as famed as the bow of Mahadeva. Once the devas wanted to know who was more powerful, Mahadeva or Narayana. They went to Brahma, the Creator and he sowed the seed of dissension between the two gods. A thrilling fight ensued between Narayana and Mahadeva. Narayana sent the astra by name Jrumbhana at Mahadeva and with his bow slightly broken, the lord Mahadeva was non-plussed for a moment. But he resumed the fight. The devas regretted their curiosity and appeased the angry gods and made them stop their fight.

"Mahadeva left his bow with the ancestors of Janaka and that was the bow which was broken by you. The other bow was given to the rishi Richaka who gave it to his son Jamadagni who was my father. I inherited it from my father who was killed by Kartaviryarjuna, the kshatriya, who was swollen with pride. It was with this bow that I killed innumerable kings, kshatriyas, and avenged the death of my father. I was the possessor of the entire earth at one time. I performed the tarpana for my father and then a yaga to rid me of the sin of killing so many anointed kings. At the end of the yaga I gave away the entire earth to Kashyapa and ever since then I have been spending my time on the Mahendra mountain with my mind bent on tapas.

"I heard the celestials praise you and your prowess and that prompted me to come down to the plains to accost you. If you are a real kshatriya, accept my challenge and string this bow as I suggest. If you do that, you can then be fit enough to fight with me: I concede that."

Rama was standing silent during the entire harangue of the angry Parasurama. He looked reassuringly at his father and then addressed Parasurama: "Bhargava, I heard you and I heard your challenge also. I will only be too happy to accept your challenge. You seem to be under the impression that I am a weak man who has not courage enough to fight with you. You have insulted me. I will show you how powerful my arms are, and how much of a kshatriya I am."

Rama held out his hand and, casually he took the bow from the hands of Parasurama. He strung the bow and fixed an arrow to it. He then said: "Bhargava, Vishvamitra is my beloved guru and I respect him immensely. He was very fond of his sister Satyavati and your father happens to be her son. And because of your kinship with him and because you are a brahmin, respect is due to you from me. That is the sole reason why I am not trying to aim this arrow at your life. No arrow of mine has ever come back to me without getting some victim. Tell me, what will you give me to satisfy this arrow from this bow? This bow, as you have told me, is powerful since it is sacred to Narayana and it is not right that I should let the arrow go unappeased. Tell me what you will give this arrow? Will it be the wealth of all the tapas you have performed or the world to come which you have earned? Tell me and I will aim my arrow to get me that."

As was their custom, the divine host headed by Brahma himself had assembled in the skies to watch the encounter between the two Ramas. Parasurama felt strength ebbing away from his limbs and he spoke in halting words. He said: "I have realised that you are superior to me, Rama. I will, this very moment, return to Mahendra where I will dwell for ever. I will grant you the wealth of my tapas which I have accumulated. When you took up the bow in your blessed hands I realised that you are Narayana Himself. I have been vanquished and, strangely enough, it is not galling to my pride to accept defeat at your hands."

When Parasurama spoke these words Rama released the arrow from the bow. Parasurama went back to the mountain by name Mahendra after having abandoned his tapas and his strength to Rama. The heavens rejoiced when Parasurama made a pradakshina to Rama and walked away from there toward the north where Mahendra was.

It took a while for Rama to control his anger. When his wrath was appeased, Rama gave the bow to Varuna, the lord of oceans.

Rama then spoke to his father: "Come, father, Parasurama has been sent back by me and we can continue our journey towards Ayodhya." Dasaratha who had been in a daze all the while roused himself and with great joy embraced his beloved child, Rama.

They came to Ayodhya and the citizens welcomed them with great excitement and happiness. Music sounded everywhere and the king and his sons with their brides entered the palace of the king.

Rama was the ideal son to his father. He would ever be attentive to the slightest wish of the king and would obey him even before the king mentioned it. He was the beloved of everyone in Ayodhya.

Sita and Rama were an extremely devoted couple. Sita was the ideal wife for Rama. She was his equal in beauty, in her modesty and in her love for the elders. She was very dear to Rama. Each dwelt in the heart of the other and her beauty and his were like those of Lakshmi and Narayana and they lived happily in the city of Ayodhya.

AYODHYA KANDA

1. RAMA

Kaikeyi was the younger queen of Dasaratha and the mother of Bharata. Her father Ashvapati was now old and Dasaratha thought that it would please him if he sent his son Bharata to Kekaya. He called Bharata and told him that he should go and spend some time in Kekaya with his grandfather and his uncle Yudhajit. When Bharata left for Kekaya, with him went his brother Shatrughna who was so fond of him that he would never be separated from him. Shatrughna was a noble prince who was able to keep the six enemies at bay: the enemies by name Kama, Krodha, Lobha, Moha, Mada and Matsarya. He was indeed Shatrughna as his name implied and he was Bharata's alter ego even as Lakshmana was, Rama's.

Ashvapati, the old king, was very happy that the young men had come to him to spend some time with him. Though they were treated well, entertained very well by their uncle and their grandfather, Bharata and Shatrughna thought of their old father very often. The king also remembered them and their gentle ways.

All his sons were dear to the old King Dasaratha. To him they were like four arms and he was happy, the more so since they were born to him when he was no longer young. Still, though he was fond of all of them, Rama was dearer to his father than his other sons. It was perhaps his beauty and his charm, or perhaps the many good qualities, noble qualities in him which made the king love him as he did. Only the devas knew that he was Narayana Himself who had deigned to be born on the earth for the sole purpose of destroying Ravana. Kausalya was contented and proud of her son Rama and she looked like Aditi, the mother of Indra.

As for Rama, he was unparalleled in the qualities which make a man great. He was handsome, very pleasing and charming to look at. He was a very brave young man and yet his bravery was combined with mercy. He was ever tranquil, unruffled by the sway of emotions. He would be friendly with everyone. He would talk first and talk softly, with affection. Even if, by some chance, someone spoke harshly to him, he would never reply in the same tone. If anyone did him any favor, even if it were a small task, he would always remember it with gratitude while his own good acts would be forgotten by him even if they were hundreds in number.

Engaged in the Ayudhasala practising his archery and other arts befitting a kshatriya, Rama would still find time to spend with elders, those who were elder to him because of age, because of their greater wisdom, because they were old enough to teach him the ways of the world. He was highly intelligent and he had learnt the art of conversing with people. His voice was pleasing to hear and, though he was a warrior, he never once prided himself on his prowess. Rama would never tell a lie. It was, with him, almost a religious compulsion, that he should not utter an untruth even in the most trying situation. He was ever bent on honouring elders and scholars. He would spend a long time with them humbly learning all that they had to teach. Rama was greatly attached to his father's subjects and the people of Ayodhya loved him. Each man loved him as his own son: so dear was the prince to everyone. Rama was compassionate and he would always sympathise with anyone who was in trouble. He was the first to shed tears if anyone was in pain or suffering. He was ever righteous and he had conquered the greatest of enemies, anger. He would never willingly hurt anyone with his words and he could never countenance words which were against the code of living. He knew how to listen patiently to others and to make the proper reply when questioned: in this art he was like the heavenly preceptor Brihaspati himself. He was loved by everyone, this young son of the king. Words could not describe the wealth of goodness that was Rama. He was the very life of the men in Ayodhya. He was well versed in the arts which a kshatriya had to master and he was also very proficient in the knowledge of the Vedas and all its Angas. He was greater than even his father in the art of warfare.

Born of a line of kings all of whom were paragons of virtue, Rama was the jewel of them all. Righteous and ever truthful, he was firm in his convictions. He was trained by great teachers and he would never forget what he had been taught. He would always think of new ways of doing things and his name was used as an example for everything: for every good quality that should adorn a human being.

Rama firmly believed that the path of Dharma was the only pathway to Artha, Kama and Moksha. Humble when he had to be humble, Rama knew how to keep his thoughts to himself and until it was completed, he would not talk about any task which he had undertaken. He was a sincere friend and he was wise as to the proper use of wealth : when it should be acquired, and when it should be spent.

He was a great devotee of the Lord and his wisdom was unrivalled. He had never been known to speak a word which was unfitting to any occasion. Never fond of laziness, he was ever alert. Rama could never be deceived by any one. He was fully conscious of his own shortcomings as well as those of others. He was well versed in the shastras and he had studied the nature of man well: man and his behaviour and the variations of his nature in its various aspects. He knew how to choose his friends and once they were chosen, his friends were never abandoned. Protecting the good and punishing evil-doers was the ultimate aim of Rama and it was his nature to do every act at the proper time and never once had he done a wrong act or spoken a wrong word.

Well-read as he was in the sacred lore, Rama was equally proficient in the fine arts. He could play on the Veena and the flute and he was an expert in judging the merits of sculptures and other forms of art. He could control horses and elephants just as well as he could, his own feelings. A great warrior, he knew all the many methods of arranging the vyuhas, riding in the chariot, fighting from a horseback or on foot. He was greater than all the devas and asuras in the intricacies of warfare.

He was never jealous and anger had no place in his heart. He had never once insulted his dependents. He knew when to be angry and with whom. Never selfish, Rama knew how to act according to the situations in which he found himself. In short, Rama was the home of all the many qualities that can be enumerated and he was the beloved prince of the citizens of Ayodhya. He was ever dear to his father and to the people of the country. The earth herself was so much enamoured of him that she desired to be ruled by him.

2. THE DESIRE IN THE HEART OF DASARATHA

King Dasaratha would often think of the greatness that was Rama and his heart would be filled with happiness. There was, in his heart, a great desire to make Rama the Yuvaraja. He felt that it would be ideal since Rama was dear to all. He told himself: "If I crown Rama as Yuvaraja now, I will have the happiness of seeing him drenched in the waters of the abhisheka and there will be no one to equal me in my joy. I know that he will rule the kingdom even better than I have been doing all these years. He will do good to the people even as the rainbearing clouds water the earth with a desire to make it more fertile. In prowess Rama is like Yama and Indra and in wisdom he is like the divine Guru Brihaspati. My son is far superior to me in every way. I must leave the earth to be ruled by my child and I can depart to the other world in peace."

The king knew that the good qualities found in Rama were not to be found in anyone else. He was the best among men, a rare soul and he was best suited to rule the kingdom. Dasaratha decided to consult his ministers and ask them for their opinion and then proceed further in the matter.

The king had been worried of late. He knew that he was getting old and added to this was the worry caused by evil omens in the heavens, in the sky and on the land also. He knew that some dire calamity was in store for him and he thought that it was his own death which was imminent. To set his mind at rest and for the sake of his beloved subjects, this righteous monarch decided to make haste and make Rama the crown prince during his own lifetime.

To think was to act, and Dasaratha gave instructions for the subjects who lived nearby and for all the chiefs and kings to be brought to Ayodhya. The two rulers of Kekaya and Mithila, however, were not sent for. The king told himself: "I am in a hurry. They will hear about this later and rejoice. It is of no great importance if I do not send for them now."

The guests began to arrive soon and the king welcomed them as was befitting their status and his. There was a gathering of all of them in the immense council hall and the people of Ayodhya had thronged there too. There was a roar as of the sea during full tide. The king came with his ministers and took his seat on the throne. Surrounded as he was by the lesser luminaries, Dasaratha looked like Indra surrounded by the devas in his court.

Dasaratha, the king, who was more like a father than a king to his subjects, now spoke in a deep and powerful voice. He said: "It is well known to all of you that this kingdom of Kosala has been ruled by my ancestors ever since the time of Ikshvaku. To the best of my ability, I have tried to follow in the footsteps of my ancients and to rule the country. I have never consciously swerved from the path of dharma and I have been a father to you all. But this body of mine, sheltered as it has been for the last so many years by the white umbrella, has become old and tired. I feel weak. I have spent innumerable number of years in this task of ruling the land and I want to be relieved of this responsibility. I have devoted my mind and all my thoughts to this sole task and it is now time for me to place the burden on younger shoulders and to take leave of you. With the approval of the kings and the wise ones here and all of you, I wish to appoint my son Rama as my next of heir and be without worries.

"Rama is my eldest son. He is like Indra in valour and he cannot be conquered by anyone. He is superior to me in all the qualities needed for ruling a country. I wish to make him the Yuvaraja. He is capable of accomplishing easily any task assigned to him and he is the ideal man to be the ruler of the land. I am eager to make him take over from me the great task of kingship. I have spent a lot of time before coming to this decision.

"If it is approved by all of you, I will pursue the matter further. If you do not, I ask of you to suggest an alternative. I desire to make only Rama the Yuvaraja but it has to be decided by all of you as to whether my decision has your approval and approbation."

There was a roar when the king stopped talking and the noise made by the happy crowd made the entire palace resound with echoes. They did not have to consider the matter at all, they said: "O king! you are right in the thought that you have ruled the kingdom long enough and that you are tired of it since you are getting old. We fully approve of the suggestion that Rama be crowned as the heir. We are eager to see Rama, drenched with the waters of the abhisheka, with his face sheltered by the white umbrella, riding on the elephant."

The king, pleased with the general enthusiasm of the crowd, spoke as though he did not know the reason for their ready assent and said: "I have been ruling this land for many years and I have been righteous all the time. Never once have I transgressed the rules of conduct. Have you not been happy all these years? Your eagerness to have Rama as your king makes me pause and ask you why. Have I not done my duty? What makes you so excited at the thought of Rama's coronation as the Yuvaraja?"

"The reason is your son," said the people. "His good and noble qualities have endeared him to us. We will tell you why he is dear to us. He is truthful. His religion is Truth and that is his strength. He is the best of the descendants of Ikshvaku. He is a personification of all that is good and great. He will never swerve from the path of truth and of dharma. He is like the moon in charming everyone: like the earth in patience, in his forgiveness of others' faults. He is like Brihaspati in intellect and like Indra in valour. He is righteous and has never been known to break his word. His conduct is faultless and he is happy to see and recognise greatness in others. Forgiving the faults of others is second nature to him and he will never anger anyone by his thoughts, or his words or by his action. He knows no guile and he is ever grateful to those who do him a favour. Those who come to him for protection can be sure that he will never abandon them. Pleasure and pain are treated alike by him and he is unaffected by the sway of these.

"Rama speaks lovingly to everyone at all times and his words have never been untrue. He respects elders and wise men. He is proficient in the use of all the astras and his fame is not only of this world. He is famed in all the three worlds for his greatness. He is well-read and he is a master of the Vedas and the Vedangas. He is well acquainted with music and all the fine arts.

"He is blessed with an ancestry which is faultless and he is the jewel among kings of his race. He has courage and his mind is so firm that nothing will make him weaken because of the sway of the emotions. Never once has he been defeated in any war which he has fought.

"He is genuinely interested in the welfare of others. When he is riding on a horse or in the chariot he stops and talks to the man in the street and enquires about his welfare and those of his kinsmen even as a father does to his son. Rama thinks of the well-being of every one of us. He shares our joys and our sorrows. Ever devoted to speaking the truth, Rama, your son, is respectful towards elders and he has his senses under perfect control. There is smile on his face when he talks to people and as for his looks, there is no one to equal him. He charms everyone with his beauty. His eyebrows are long and his eyes under his arched eyebrows, with the slight red tint in them, are large and liquid. He seems to us to be Lord Narayana Himself who has assumed the form of a human being. He is unequalled in the art of ruling and he can rule not only this land but the three worlds. His anger will not be wasted nor will his grace be spent on undeserving people. The earth is eager to have Rama as her lord, endowed as he is with all the qualities needed for a ruler.

"Everyone of us thinks of Rama everyday. Every morning when we get up, whether it is a man, woman, young or old, or even a young child, the first thought is Rama and the prayer which we send up to the heavens is:

'May Rama live long. May no evil befall him.' We want to see Rama, dark blue as a lotus, crowned as the Yuvaraja. Please perform the coronation as early as you can and make the three worlds happy."

Dasaratha was thrilled with the words of his subjects. Tears of joy rose to his eyes and he said: "I am gratified to know that my wish is the same as yours and I will try to perform the crowning ceremony as early as I can." He then turned to Vasishtha and Vamadeva and said: "This month Chaitra is a beautiful month. The blessed forests will be wearing garments of flowers. Please be good enough to make all the arrangements for the coronation."

The words of the king brought shouts of joy from the crowd which had assembled. After it had subsided, the king spoke again to Vasishtha and said: "Please, my lord, take care of the religious aspect of the coronation."

Vasishtha called for the attendants of the king at once and asked them to collect the various accessories for the function. He also ordered that the decoration of the city should begin as early as possible. He said: "Let the doorways of the palace be decorated with flowers and let there be incense kindled everywhere. Let the royal pathway be sprinkled with perfumed water and with flowers. Let the musicians and dancers assemble in the hall of the palace itself. Flowers and fruits should be available in abundance."

The king called Sumantra and said: "Go and bring Rama to me immediately." Sumantra went in the chariot of the king. Dasaratha went up to the terrace of his palace and waited for the coming of Rama. The king had his eyes glued to the distance to perceive the Kovidara banner of the chariot which was to bring Rama to him.

It came into view and Dasaratha could see Rama. It was his Rama who was coming to him. Rama was like a gandharva in beauty, whose fame was known to all the worlds, who was so strong with long and beautiful arms, who walked like a young elephant, so noble was his gait. His face had the charm of the moon and he was extremely handsome. He pleased the eyes of the people like the first sight of the rain-cloud which promised rain to the earth. Dasaratha was so pleased with the sight of his son, he kept on looking at him as though his eyes could never be satisfied. Rama was his very life to Dasaratha.

Sumantra helped Rama to descend from the chariot. With his palms folded, Rama went to the presence of his father and Sumantra followed him. Rama climbed the terrace which was as beautiful as the peak by name Kailasa, came to the presence of the king and prostrated before him. The king looked at his son who was standing before him with his face full of respect and embraced him warmly. He made him sit on a jewelled seat and said: "Rama, my son, you are my eldest son, born of my queen Kausalya and you are very dear to me. These subjects of mine desire that you should be their ruler. I want you to be crowned as the Yuvaraja on the day when the moon and the star Pushya are close. You are good-natured and you are well-read. And I do not have to teach you how to rule a kingdom. You have been groomed for that role and I ask you to take it up."

People who were around went to the apartments of Kausalya and told her about the decision of the king. Pleased with the news, she gave away gold and ornaments and costly silks to her attendants as a sign of her happiness.

When he heard the commands of his father, Rama spoke not a word but stood still. He prostrated once again before his father and ascended the chariot which had brought him to the court.

The crowd also dispersed slowly, each man thinking only of the glad event which was to happen soon.

3. "TOMORROW"– SAID THE KING

When the crowd had all dispersed and when he was alone in his chambers the king thought to himself and said: "Tomorrow happens to be

Pushya and why should I not arrange the coronation to take place tomorrow?"

Dasaratha entered his palace and went to his innermost apartments. He summoned Sumantra and asked him to bring Rama once again to him. Sumantra went to the palace of Rama and he asked the doorkeeper to announce his arrival to Rama. The prince was puzzled when he heard about the desire of the king to see him again. He took Sumantra inside the palace and asked him: "You seem to be in a hurry. I have just returned from the presence of the king and you say that he wants me there again. Can you tell me why?"

Sumantra said: "I do not know. The king went to his inner chambers, summoned me and asked me to bring you to him immediately. That is all I know. He did not tell me why." Rama hurried into the chariot and went to the presence of the king and stood as before, waiting for him to speak. Holding him close to his chest, the king embraced Rama again and again. He said: "Rama, I wanted to talk to you for a while. That is why I sent for you. Child, I am getting old. I have tasted all the joys which life has to offer. I have performed yagas and I have been a good king. Because of my good fortune and as a reward of my good actions you have been born as my eldest son. I have done my duty well and your coronation is the only task which I have not attended to, yet. I want to do it as early as possible. I have been having bad dreams, my child, and they have begun to worry me. I dreamed that a big burning torch fell on the ground with a noise like a thunder clap. This means that a calamity is in store for me. And again, the astrologers who have studied my horoscope tell me that my star is now being attacked by planets Surya, Angaraka and Rahu. These evil omens spell either the death of the king or some misfortune to the king. He may even lose the power of sane thinking. I would like you to take up the reins of the realm before life leaves this frail old body of mine.

"Man's mind is full of uncertainties. Today the moon is in conjunction with Punarvasu and tomorrow he will be with Pushya. My mind can think of nothing else unless and until you are crowned. You must be crowned on the day when Pushya is with the moon and that is tomorrow. From today you must observe all the necessary rituals, guided by Vasishtha. You must fast tonight with your wife and sleep on the floor where darbha grass has been spread. Great events like this are apt to be beset with hindrances. I therefore ask you to surround yourself with well-wishers.

"Bharata has been sent away from here and I am of opinion that this is the proper time for your coronation. I know Bharata and his nature. I know that he is devoted to you, his eldest brother. He is righteous and he is a compassionate man, one who can enter into the hearts of others. He is able to keep his senses under control. But then, having lived in this world for years, I have come to know one truth: even the minds of those who follow no other path but that of dharma who have been taught all the rules of conduct: even they, I say, are very rarely happy at the sight of the good fortune which has befallen others. The mind of man is very unsteady and so I have decided to hold the coronation tomorrow."

Still Rama spoke not a word but went back after taking the dust of the feet of his father.

After leaving the apartments of his father, Rama went to his mother Kausalya. He found her in the place set apart for the worship of the household gods. She was dressed in pure white silk and she was reciting slokas in praise of Lakshmi, the spouse of Narayana. Her eyes were closed and he stood by, waiting. Sumitra and Lakshmana too, having heard the great news, had come there to be with the queen and they were also standing by, waiting for her to conclude her prayers. Sita had come there long ago.

When she opened her eyes, Kausalya saw them all standing by her. Rama approached her and he prostrated before her. He then said: "Mother, father has commanded me to be the ruler of his subjects. He now told me that I am to be crowned tomorrow. He asked me to fast tonight along with Sita. I have come to you to ask you to bless me and Sita." Kausalya whose heart had been waiting for this moment for the past so many years, spoke to Rama in a soft voice: "Rama, my child, may you live long. May your enemies perish, enemies who wish to stand in the way of your coronation. May you please me and Sumitra. You were born under an auspicious star and your father is pleased with you and your excellent qualities. I am indeed very fortunate. My prayers to Narayana have not been in vain."

Rama smiled gently at the words of his mother and he then looked at Lakshmana and said: "Lakshmana, this kingdom, this honour bestowed on me by my father is only for you: since you are my very life to me. Rule this world along with me. I am happy to be the king for your sake. I want you to enjoy the pleasures of kingship." He then prostrated before his mother and went back to his palace accompanied by Sita.

4. PREPARATIONS

After Rama had gone away, Dasaratha sent for Vasishtha and spoke to him about the coronation which had to take place in the morning. He said: "Please take care that Rama adopts Diksha and fasts tonight with his wife. This will, I know, assure him of wealth, kingdom and fame." Vasishtha who knew the past, the present and the future spoke not a word and took his seat in the chariot which was waiting for him and he went to the palace of Rama.

Rama stood up from the seat where he was reclining and he welcomed his teacher. He gave him his right hand and helped him descend from the chariot. Vasishtha was very fond of his pupil who was so full of respect for the elders and who did not know what it was to be arrogant. Ever humble and gentle, Rama had won the heart of the old man long ago.

They sat down on seats covered with costly silk. Vasishtha said: "Rama, like Nahusha crowned Yayati your father has decided to make you crown prince. You have to observe all the religious rites which are preliminaries to the great event which is to take place tomorrow." He initiated Rama and Sita into the Diksha. Rama honoured him and the kulaguru left Rama after blessing him. Rama had many people to talk to, people who had come to see him after hearing about the coronation of the morrow. After spending some time with them Rama entered his inner apartments.

Vasishtha, when he left the palace of Rama, came out into the streets. Wherever his eyes rested he saw nothing but men and women, some dancing, some singing and everyone expressing joy in some way or other. The city was already decorated and flowers were sprinkled on the roads and garlands of flowers festooned the pillars and terraces of the houses. Banners were fluttering everywhere and the entire city was waiting for the coming of the morning when their beloved Rama would be the Yuvaraja. Rama, in the meantime, purified himself by the rituals dictated by Vasishtha and, accompanied by his wife Sita, performed the puja for Narayana. Later they spent the night on the floor where darbha grass had been spread.

Early in the morning he was roused from his sleep by the Vandya Magadha and Sutas. He woke up and performed the morning ablutions and recited the sacred Gayatri. He was wearing white silk and he worshipped the brahmins who were in the palace.

Even as the east began to lighten as a forerunner of the dawn, the city began to assume a festive look. Music could be heard everywhere and there was dancing and singing in the streets. The people were delirious with happiness and there was joy and nothing but joy in the heart of everyone in Ayodhya.

5. THE MAID, MANTHARA

On the day the king announced his intention to crown Rama, the city began to don the garb of gaiety and happiness. That evening, a servant maid of Kaikeyi, Manthara by name, happened to go up to the terrace of the palace. It was sheer chance which prompted this woman to do so since usually, she was not in the habit of doing so, deformed as she was, because of a hunch in her back. The terrace which was as white and beautiful as a stream of moonlight attracted her, perhaps, or perhaps it was Fate which made her ascend the steps of the terrace of the queen's palace.

She stood near the parapet of the terrace and looked down at the city of Ayodhya. Something out of the way struck her. The streets were covered with flowers and the scent of the water which had been sprinkled on them reached her. There were banners fluttering everywhere. The people were all looking greatly excited and there seemed to be excessive joy writ on their faces. She could hear music and she was intrigued as to what the great event was, which the people seemed to be celebrating.

Even as she was wondering, she saw a maid passing by. This maid was wearing white silk garments and her eyes were dancing with joy. Manthara accosted her and asked her: "Tell me, what is all this excitement about? What is to happen? Rama's mother seems to be giving away gifts to everyone around. I have never seen it happen before. The citizens seem to be very happy too. What is the provocation?"

The maid who was standing by, smiled happily and said: "How is it you do not know about it? Tomorrow, early in the morning, the emperor is desirous of crowning noble-minded Rama as the Yuvaraja. There is nothing but joy in the heart of everyone and that is why the city is looking so happy." Manthara could hardly stand there listening to her words. Uncontrollable anger filled her heart and with the maid watching her with wondering eyes, she hobbled down the steps of the terrace without speaking even a word in reply.

Manthara went straight as an arrow into the chambers of Kaikeyi, the young queen. She was the beautiful mother of Bharata lying down on a couch half asleep. Manthara rushed up to her and said: "Get up, you stupid woman. This is not the time to lie down. Great danger is approaching you. You will soon be drowned in a sea of sorrow and, without being aware of it, you recline on the couch as though nothing has happened. You are blinded by the assurance that the king is lost in you: that he loves you more than he loves anyone else. Can you not see that the love of the king is like a summer stream short-lived?"

Kaikeyi paid no attention to the words of Manthara. Evidently she knew the old woman who had come to Ayodhya with her when she was married. She had been with her ever since she was a child and she was granted certain privileges because she had brought up Kaikeyi. After a while the queen looked at her and said: "Manthara, I hope you are well. Your face looks as though you are sick. You seem to be unhappy about something. What is bothering you?"

Manthara stood fuming with anger. After a while, composing herself she said: "Madam, the king is contemplating your destruction even at this very moment. He is planning to crown Rama as Yuvaraja tomorrow. As for me, concerned as I am about you and your welfare, I feel I am being burnt up by grief and anger. You will be destroyed, my queen, and I have come to you hoping to find a way to save you. Kaikeyi, you know how much I love you. Your happiness is my happiness and when, danger threatens you it threatens me too. You were born as the daughter of a king and you have been the dear queen of an emperor. How is it then, you do not know about the intrigues in the royal court? Your lord, the king, talks glibly about dharma but he is deceiving you. He speaks words steeped in honey but at heart he is cruel. You are very simple, trusting and very innocent. You are not able to perceive the truth about the nature of the king. All these years he has been talking to you words of such sweetness that you have not been able to see through his deception. Look, he is now granting all good fortune to Kausalya and not to you.

"With evil designs forming in his mind he has sent away your son to the kingdom of Kekaya and when there is no obstruction in his path he is going to establish Rama on the throne. You do not know it but the king is really your enemy. He is like a serpent. Since he is your husband you have never questioned his actions and, like a mother does her child, you have taken this serpent in your hands and placed it on your lap. And, an enemy or a serpent, when unnoticed, is sure to hurt and that is what the king is doing now. You are a mother and your motherhood is being ignored. It is time for you to wake up from this dream of security. Seek the good of your son and thus save yourself from calamity and me too, along with you."

Kaikeyi had not even bothered to get up from her couch. The words of Manthara, "the king is crowning Rama as the Yuvaraja tomorrow," were all she heard. She would not listen to anything else. She was full of happiness and her face became as charming as the moon during the season by name Sharat. Pleasure and surprise were writ on her face.

Impulsively she removed a costly necklace from her neck and gave it to Manthara saying : "O Manthara! what a glorious thing to happen! and *you* have brought me the good news! Take this as my gift for making me happy. If you want anything more, ask of me. I am so happy. My Rama is to be the Yuvaraja tomorrow." She paused for a moment and continued: "I am very pleased by the decision of the king. I have never made any difference between Rama and Bharata as far as my love is concerned. They are both my sons. I am well pleased with this event. You could not have given me any news more welcome than this."

Manthara, filled as she was with hatred, anger and grief, flung the jewel on the floor. Kaikeyi could not understand why she was behaving like this. She stared with her eyes wide open in wonderment. Manthara said: "How careless about yourself and your future can you be, that you can rejoice at this! You still do not seem to realise that it means nothing but sorrow for you. You are, indeed, very childish. Only a woman like you will rejoice at the good fortune that has befallen another queen of the king. Tomorrow, during the time when the star Pushya is in the ascent, the wise men of the court will perform the abhisheka of Kausalya's son. Is it not evident that the king really favours Kausalya and not you? With the obstacle in her path wiped away, Kausalya will be the favourite of all. Everyone will attend on her hereafter since she will be the queen-mother and as for you, you will also stand by as one of her handmaidens. Your son Bharata will have to be a serf to Rama."

Manthara paused for breath. She was still fuming with rage and frustration since Kaikeyi would not listen to her. The queen intervened and said: "Manthara, Rama is righteous and he has been trained in the path of dharma by the best of men. He is a noble and gentle soul. He is not enamoured of wealth or kingdom. He is the eldest son of the king and it is but right that he should be crowned as the Yuvaraja. Throughout his lifetime he will protect his brothers and all his kinsfolk like a father will, his children. Why do you feel so strongly about this? After a hundred years of Rama's rule, Bharata will become the king. The present event, Rama's coronation, is welcomed by all as a happy event. Why should you and only you, be unhappy? Bharata is no doubt dear to me. But Rama is greater than even Bharata. He loves me more than he does his mother Kausalya. He loves his brothers so much that it is immaterial whether Rama is the king or Bharata. The kingdom will belong to both of them and to their brothers too."

Manthara sighed as though her heart had already been broken and with her voice choked with tears she said: "What am I to do with you and your foolishness? You are surrounded on all sides by the terrible danger which will lead you to eternal sorrow. This sea is threatening to engulf you and you refuse to realise it. Listen to me very carefully, Kaikeyi. Rama will become the monarch. It will be *his* son who will rule after him and not *your* son. Bharata will be just an object of ridicule.

"Remember, all the sons of the king are not entitled to be the heirs. If it were so, there will be many difficulties which have to be faced and that is why the rule has been laid down that the king should be allowed to use his discretion to choose one of his sons as his successor. Your son is destined to be ignored by all and be treated as an underling. I came to you because I wish you well: and you do not seem to understand me.

"Your rival Kausalya seems to have come into her own and you rejoice so much over it that you reward me with a jewel for bringing you the dire news. I assure you of one fact: once he is firmly established on the throne, Rama will either banish Bharata from the country or even seek his death. Bharata is a pure-minded youngster and he is away in his uncle's house in Kekaya. Do you not know the simple truth that love thrives only when the persons are with you all the while? Shatrughna is devoted to Bharata even as Lakshmana is to Rama, and Shatrughna has gone with Bharata. The world knows well the affection which exists between Rama and Lakshmana. Rama will never injure Lakshmana, but the same cannot be said about his treatment of Bharata.

"I assure you, Rama will try to harm Bharata. I suggest that you send word to your son to go away to the forest from the palace of the Kekaya king. However, if it is possible for Bharata to be made the heir to this ancient kingdom of Kosala, then it will be a matter of pride to you and to those who are devoted to you.

"It stands to reason that Rama will not treat your son as a brother since Bharata will be a rival to him. Accustomed as he is to luxury and comforts, how can Bharata expect the same life after the coronation of Rama? He will be like an elephant in the forest oppressed by a lion. You are the only one capable of saving him.

"Again, think of yourself. What have you been doing all these years? The king has chosen you as his favoured queen and pride had gone to your head so much that you have constantly insulted Kausalya. Now that she has a chance to retaliate, do you think the queen-mother as she soon will be, will hesitate to assert herself and punish you for your arrogance? The moment Rama is crowned, all your privileges as the dear queen of Dasaratha will be at an end and insults will be heaped on you and your son. Bharata will be destroyed. I hope you have realised the truth of my words at least now. Make haste and think of a method by which Bharata will be crowned and Rama banished from Kosala."

6. KAIKEYI'S DECISION

The poison began to work. Manthara's words had the desired effect and Kaikeyi who was all love for Rama, changed suddenly. Her face was now flushed with anger and sighs escaped her. She said: "You are right, Manthara, you are right. Rama has to be banished. I will today, at this very moment, send Rama away to the forest. I will summon Bharata from Kekaya and crown him as the Yuvaraja. Manthara, tell me how I am to accomplish this. Rama should go and Bharata should be king. How am I going to do it? Think deeply and advise me as to how I can do it."

The sinful hunchback spoke slowly and deliberately. "May the gods be praised that you have come to your senses finally. I will tell you how to achieve the crowning of Bharata and the exile of Rama.

"Kaikeyi, have you forgotten something which happened long ago? You confided it to me then and evidently you have forgotten it or perhaps you do not remember having told me about it. If you wish that I should repeat what you once told me, I shall do so to please you."

Kaikeyi rose up a little from the couch where she was leaning and said: "I am not playing a game with you nor do I remember anything which I told you. I am impatient. Tell me how I can make Bharata king instead of Rama."

Manthara spoke with a wicked smile lighting her ugly face. "I want you to go back several years. Do you remember the war in the high heavens when the devas fought with the asuras? King Dasaratha had been asked by Indra to help and he went: and with him, you. Sambara was the asura who was the chief enemy of Indra. During the night the asuras entered the encampment and they began to kill the men there. Your husband fought with all of them and finally he fell down senseless. Dasaratha was hurt. You carried him away from the site of danger. Hurt as he was by the arrows and rendered senseless by his wounds, Dasaratha was nursed by you and his life was saved by you.

"Pleased with you and your devotion he granted you two boons then. You said: 'I do not need them. If at any time I need them very badly, I will ask you for them.' 'So be it,' said the king and there the matter ended. You once told me about this and I have not forgotten it.

"Kaikeyi, the time has come when you must ask the king to grant you these two boons. One of the boons will be the crowning of Bharata as the Yuvaraja and with the other you can have Rama banished to the Dandaka forest for a duration of fourteen years. This is the way to force the hand of the king and to assure yourself that Bharata will be king."

Kaikeyi was listening silently to the words of Manthara. The wicked mentor continued: "Kaikeyi, you must enter the chamber called Krodhagriha—the chamber where you stay when you are angry about anything. Remove these beautiful silks you are wearing and dress yourself in soiled clothes. Lie on the bare ground as though you have been weeping for a long time and that you are unhappy.

"The king will surely come to see you tonight. Behave as though you are very angry. Do not talk to him. Do not receive him when he comes to you nor should you reply when he talks to you. You are very dear to the king and he will even fall into the blazing fire if you so desire. I have no doubt about his love for you. He cannot bear to see you angry or unhappy. He will try to pacify you in every way. He will say that he will even give up his very life if it will please you. Remember that the king loves you to distraction. He cannot refuse you anything.

"When he sees you on the ground he will try to placate you with gifts of gems and pearls and lovely ornaments. Be very careful and do not be distracted by these.

"Remind him of the boons he granted you in the days of yore and make him promise you that he will grant you anything you like and then make him grant you these boons. Everything depends on you and on your firmness. He must promise to give you anything you ask for and then, and only then should you mention the boons and ask for them. When the boons are granted you should tell him what they are: you should say: 'Send Rama to the forest for the duration of fourteen years and make my son Bharata the Yuvaraja.'

"If Rama is away in the forest for this long time your son will be able to establish himself firmly on the throne and nothing can dislodge him. Remember, you must make sure that Rama is banished. That is the one and only way to make your son's future secure. Rama, who will be away from the kingdom for fourteen years, will soon be forgotten by the people and that boon should be granted by the king at any cost. You must make sure of that. Do not let your mind weaken when the king appeals to you to change your mind."

Kaikeyi listened to the words of Manthara carefully and she decided to do as she was told. Alas, this princess had, till then, been famed for her sweet nature. The entire city of Ayodhya knew about the affection she had for Rama and about the respect with which Rama treated her. He spent more time with her than with Kausalya and Kaikeyi was pleased with it. Even Bharata did not enjoy the privileges which Rama did at the hands of Kaikeyi. But, because of the evil genius in the shape of the sinful Manthara she agreed to do something which she would never have done on her own. Evil was so disguised that it appeared to be good and Manthara, who was clever enough to know the workings of the mind of Kaikeyi, took advantage of her weakness and killed the goodness in her. With a glad heart Kaikeyi spoke to her. She said: "You are my well-wisher and no one has thought of my future as you have. You are a very wise woman and I did not know it till now. But for you, I would never have known the real nature of the king. Manthara, my beautiful Manthara, when my Bharata becomes king I will decorate this hump of yours with golden ornaments. I am very grateful to you."

With a smile Manthara brushed aside all her words and said: "Kaikeyi, that is all in the distant future. At the moment you must hurry and set about the task ahead of you. Evening is fast approaching and this is the time when the king comes to you. Prepare yourself before he arrives."

Kaikeyi, the proud and beautiful queen of Dasaratha, went to the sulking room and Manthara went with her. She took off her precious jewels, necklaces of pearls, golden bracelets, earrings, and all the many auspicious jewels which a woman wears. She removed her costly silks too and dressed herself in an old soiled silk.

She then spoke to Manthara and said: "Manthara, my mind is made up. When Rama goes to the forest, Bharata will rule the kingdom. If I am not able to achieve this, consider me to be dead. You can rest assured that the king will not be able to make me change my mind with offerings of gold and gems. Until Rama leaves for the forest I will not wear flowers, I will not use perfumes and I will not darken my eyes with collyrium. I promise you, I will succeed in my attempt."

Kaikeyi removed all the auspicious jewels and, with the flowers and gems and jewels lying about her, this beautiful queen of Dasaratha lay on the ground and looked like a Kinnara woman who had lost all her punya and had been flung down to the earth.

7. DASARATHA COMES TO KAIKEYI

The king, in the meantime, had made haste to make the final arrangements for the coronation. When he felt that he had attended to everything, Dasaratha, assured that Rama's coronation was certain to take place in the morning, hurried to the apartments of Kaikeyi to tell her himself about the morrow knowing full well that she would be happy.

He entered the chambers and looked around and did not see her. Lost as he was in his love for her, the king felt very disappointed that he could not see her at once. Even a single moment seemed to him like a year. He looked around again and still he could not find her. This had never happened before. Never once had she failed him. Kaikeyi would always be found at the doorway waiting for her lord and this was the first time this had happened.

The watchman there came to presence of the king, stood humbly before him and said: "My lord, the queen is very angry about something and she has entered the Krodhagriha."

Dasaratha was taken aback at the words of the attendant. His mind was in a turmoil and he hurried to where Kaikeyi was. To his dismay he saw the queen lying on the ground. Around her lay her jewels and flowers gleaming in the dark like stars in a sky bereft of the moon. The old king looked at his young wife who was dearer to him than his very life. She looked like a creeper which had been uprooted and had lost its hold on a tree: like a goddess who had been hurled down from heaven: like a deer caught in a hunter's net, like an elephant hurt by a poison arrow.

Dasaratha went near her and stroked her with his hands. He spoke to her with a voice full of affection and concern. He said "I cannot guess what has happened to you. What has upset you? Have you been insulted by anyone? Did anyone hurt you with cruel words? My dearest queen, it pains my eyes to see you lying in the dust on the ground. Maybe, you are unwell. Shall I send for the physicians? Has anyone wronged you? Should I punish anyone? Please do not weep. These tears do not become you. Do you desire to send to his death anyone who is innocent? Or do you want me to leave unpunished one who deserves to be punished? If you want me to live, please make haste and tell me what you desire. I cannot live without you and your smiles. You know the wealth of love I have for you. I swear by all the punya I have accumulated, to do as you please. Evidently you want something and you feel shy to ask me. Do not hesitate. First get up from this floor and then tell me what is worrying you."

Reassured that the king would grant her what she desired, Kaikeyi began to talk. "I am not unwell," she said, "nor have I been insulted by anyone. I am eager to get something done and only you will be able to satisfy my wishes. You told me just now that you would do so. If you swear that you will do what I ask you to do, then, and only then will I tell you what I want."

The poor king, smitten with love for this beautiful woman, smiled a little at her elaborate preface and caressing her head with his hands, he said: "Kaikeyi, you know how much I love you. You mean everything to me. If at all there is anyone dearer to me than you, it is Rama, my child. I now swear in the name of Rama that I will grant you anything you ask for. Rama is my very life to me and I repeat, I do swear by him that you can ask what you want and get it from me. Ask and put an end to my suffering." He paused for a moment and said: "Kaikeyi, if I do not see him for more than a few moments, my life threatens to leave my body: so dear is Rama to me. Can you still doubt my words when I have sworn by him that I will grant you your wish? Do not have any doubts about my words. It is a solemn promise."

Like a king cobra uncoiling itself, Kaikeyi raised herself from the floor and looked at the king. There was triumph in her glowing eyes since she knew that her desire would be fulfilled. The king had sworn in the name of Rama.

She said: "You have promised to grant me my wish. Let Indra and the devas bear witness to your words. Let the sun, the moon, the sky and the planets be my witnesses. Let the heavens and the earth listen to me. This great king who has never once swerved from the path of dharma, who has never spoken an untruth, has agreed to give me what I desire."

Dasaratha was listening to her with a smile on his lips and wonderment because of the words she was using to make sure of his promise. Kaikeyi said: "Listen, my lord. If you will take your mind back several years, you will remember the war between the devas and the asuras when you were asked to fight with Sambara. During that war there was a time when I saved your life and in appreciation you granted me two boons. I had told you that I would ask you for them when I needed something badly. The time has come when I want them. Please be good enough to give me those two boons. If you refuse to grant them after promising to, I will give up my life. I will now tell you what I desire. Please listen to me very carefully.

"You have made all preparations for Rama to be crowned as the Yuvaraja. Let the preparations remain as they are. Only, I want Bharata to be crowned instead of Rama. As for the other boon, wearing deerskin and tree-bark, Rama should spend fourteen years in the Dandaka forest. I want my son Bharata to be crowned and it is up to you to keep your word and do the needful. I want Rama to be banished today, this very moment.

"You have been famed the world over for your truthfulness and for your walking in the path of dharma always. You belong to a line of kings well known for their righteousness. Do not disgrace the name of your House by refusing to grant me my boons after promising to give me anything I ask for."

Dasaratha was too surprised by her words to react at once. He was stunned. Suddenly he realised what she had said and he fell down in a faint.

He recovered after a while and then said: "Am I dreaming? Is this a nightmare? Or am I losing my reason? Is it an incident which happened in my previous birth which I am remembering now? Am I sick and is this a distortion of my mind which makes me think I heard these words from Kaikeyi?"

He looked at Kaikeyi and she stood silent as though waiting for an answer from him. He trembled like a deer which is threatened by a tigress. He realised that it was no nightmare but reality which faced him. He was sorely distressed and he could not speak a word. He was like a serpent which had been bound by the chanting of spells and had been rendered immobile. He sighed as though his very life were ebbing away from him and then sat on the ground. He tried to talk but fainted again, unable to bear the sorrow which had visited him. So he lay for a long time, and came to his senses again.

Anger now took the place of sorrow and he spoke to Kaikeyi: "What a cruel woman you are! I had not realised what a wicked woman you are, until now. You seem to be set on the destruction of my entire house. What have I done that you should punish me thus? What have you against Rama that you wish him to be banished? He did you no wrong. He is ever devoted to you and he considers you to be as dear to him as Kausalya. How then can you think ill of him? I brought you to my home as my bride and made you my favourite queen. I did not realise that I had brought a poisonous serpent and foolishly clasped it to my bosom. The entire world is all praise for the goodness that is Rama. What fault have you found in him that you should hate him so? How will I justify my act when I am questioned about Rama's exile? I can live without Kausalya or Sumitra. I am prepared to give up even my kingdom. But I can never give up Rama. When my eyes light on Rama's face, my heart becomes full of joy, and when he is not with me I am the most unhappy of all beings. The world may live without the sun. Plants may be able to live without water but I will not be able to live once I am parted from Rama. Abandon this sinful thought from your mind. If you so desire, I will fall at your feet and ask you to have pity on me.

"Kaikeyi, tell me, how did this sinful thought come to your mind? Are you trying to test the extent of my love for Bharata by asking me to grant this boon to you? You love Rama as much as I do! Often you have told me: 'Rama, your eldest son, is dear to me and he is my eldest son too. He is righteous, truthful and very dear to me.' You have ever been pleased with Rama. Someone has been poisoning your mind against him and you have been led astray by others. That is why you are torturing me like this. A great blot will taint the name of the Ikshvakus if I agree to your wish. I still cannot believe that you can speak such harsh words. You have ever been so thoughtful about my happiness and this is unlike you. You do not realise the extent of your foolishness in behaving thus. Bharata and Rama are both dear to you. How then can you think of Rama spending fourteen years in the forest?

"There are so many women in my harem and among all the inmates of this palace, not one has found fault with Rama about anything. He is loved by everyone. He is devoted to truth and that is why he is dear to the elders. He is a great warrior and the enemies are afraid of him because of that. He has conquered the minds of the people by his affection and by his generosity.

"Kaikeyi, think for a moment of Rama and his noble traits, selflessness, ability to control his senses at all times, humility, intelligence as well as wisdom and, above all, pleasing everyone by his behaviour. You have known all these and often have you spoken about them. How then can you find fault with him suddenly and find him to be such a sinner as to deserve exile from the country? I have never once spoken harshly to my Rama and now, to make you happy, you want me to do him this injustice. How is it possible? What is left for me in this world if Rama goes away from me? Kaikeyi, I have reached the end of my life on this earth. I am old and my mind is sorely distressed by your words: Please have pity on me and change your mind. I will give you everything I can lay hands on. But grant me this: Rama should never leave me and go away."

The king was drowning in the sea of sorrow and his appeal was piteous. Again and again he appealed to her, beseeched her, but it was all of no avail. She stood firm and he heard her harsh words: "You gave me two boons and now you are full of regret for having done so. How can you consider yourself to be righteous? When good people hear about this what will they say? You will have to tell them: 'This Kaikeyi once saved my life and, pleased with her devotion, I granted her two boons. But I refuse to keep my word because it does not please me to do so.' You are an untruthful man. You are born in a line of kings famed for their truthfulness. The great Sibi and the incident of the hawk and the dove are too well-known for me to talk about them. Alarka, to keep his word, gave away both his eyes to a brahmin since he had promised to do so. I have been told that the ocean does not break its boundary because of the dharma of the kings who ruled before you. Born in such an illustrious line of kings, you wish to transgress dharma. You wish to abandon truth and righteousness and after crowning Rama as the Yuvaraja you wish to be happy with Kausalya. You are a wicked-minded king and your mind follows only the path of adharma. I am not concerned about your opinion of me. You may consider my request to be unjust. But the fact remains that you should keep your word and give me what you promised. If, however, in spite of all this, you decide to crown Rama, I will kill myself by drinking poison. I prefer death to the indignity of seeing another woman becoming the queen-mother. I swear to you in the name of Bharata, I will be satisfied only by one gift: the exile of Rama. Nothing short of it will please me."

Kaikeyi paid no heed to the king who was crying piteously. He lost consciousness for a long time and she was quite unconcerned. When he woke up he set his eyes on her but he spoke nothing. He had been bound by his oath and he could not find any way of extricating himself from it. He was mumbling to himself as though he were demented and again and again he spoke Rama's name.

Once again he spoke to her and said: "Kaikeyi, someone has been trying to influence you and someone has made you behave like this. By nature you have never been cruel. Some demon seems to have entered into your mind and you seem to be under its sway. All these years you have been like an innocent child and this is something uncalled for, in you. Why this sudden decision to see Bharata as king and to see Rama banished from my presence? If you wish to save the lives of your husband and the citizens of Ayodhya, please think again and withdraw your request. Save me, my queen."

He realised that she would not relent. His sorrow turned to anger and he said: "You are a cruel woman and your mind thinks up only sinful thoughts. You have been born just for the purpose of destruction. You have been nursing this hatred for Rama and me since ever so long and I did not know about it. You are only dreaming about the crowning of your son Bharata. He is righteous and he will never accept the kingdom when Rama has been banished. I know him, but you do not. As for Rama, I know how much he loves me. When I tell him: 'Rama, go to the forest,' he will not speak a word in protest. How can I bear to see his face after I tell him this? Today I called him to my presence and in the midst of everyone I told him that he should be the Yuvaraja. And now you ask me to speak these harsh words to him, taking back what I had promised to give him. What will the many kings of the world say when they come to know of this? They will talk disparagingly of me. If they question me about the reason for the banishment of Rama, what shall I tell them? If I say that I have done so since my wife Kaikeyi wished it, I will then be breaking my promise to the people of the city. How will I pacify Kausalya, Rama's mother? Because of my love for you I have been neglecting her for the last so many years. She has been a perfect wife in spite of my indifference to her. Now, when I make her lose her son she will not be able to bear it. Sumitra will not respect me any more. As for Sita, the young wife of Rama, how will she react to this act of mine? You will see the death of several of us. You can be sure that I will die the moment Rama goes away. You can rule the kingdom with your son. Kosala will be ruled by a widow.

"I must have sinned in my previous birth and that is the reason why I have to listen to you and your sinful wishes. I know what the world will think of me. 'This king, in his infatuation for a woman, lost all count of dharma and banished his son to the forest for no fault of his. What a foolish man!'

"I wish Rama had not been such a good son. If only he would refuse to obey me, it will be a source of great happiness to me. But Rama is noble. The moment he hears my words he will say: 'It is my duty to obey you in all things. I will do your bidding immediately.' I am dreading the future of my country. I will be gone and Rama will also be sent away. What you are planning to do with the subjects of this land makes me feel for them. I wish to stress one wish of mine. If, after my death and the exile of Rama, your son Bharata accepts the throne, he should not perform my obsequies since I will disown him. My Rama who has never once walked in the streets of the city will now walk in the dreadful forests. I have never seen him without his golden bracelets and earrings. And he should wear tree-bark and deerskin. He has to live on the fruits and roots gathered by his own dear hands in the forest. My mind reels at the thought of my child's plight. It seems to me women, as a whole, are wicked, ungrateful, selfish, bent only on achieving their objectives and unconcerned about the feelings of others.

"But I am wrong. All women should not be condemned thus. I can only say this about Bharata's mother. Can you not realise that I cannot live without Rama? The sun may cease to shine and Indra may forget to moisten the earth with rain and the world may still go on. But I cannot exist even for a moment without Rama. It is true of the people of Ayodhya also. No one can bear the thought of the exile of Rama. Once again, Kaikeyi, I fall at your feet. Kaikeyi, will you not relent?" Dasaratha held out his hands to her and walked towards her. Without touching her feet the king fell down senseless on the ground.

Kaikeyi was adamant and realising that it was so, Dasaratha lamented his fate. He spoke of the beauty of Rama and his many qualities and he shuddered to think of the morning when he would have to face separation from him. The sun had set long ago and the night had advanced. To the king the night seemed interminably long and he watched the sky and began to talk disjointedly: "May this star-studded sky never get brightened by the red light of dawn. I do not want the night to come to an end. Once the sun rises, my son will leave me. Or else, let the night pass soon. I am not able to bear the company of this sinful woman. Let me go away from here as early as possible."

He tried again and again to talk her out of the promise and he could not. Finally, with a sign of sheer pain and hopelessness the king lay down senseless. So passed the terrible night.

8. THE DAWN OF THE TERRIBLE DAY

Early in the morning the Sutas and others began to sing at the doorway of the chamber of Kaikeyi to wake up the king as was the custom in any royal household. The king was roused and he signalled to them to stop the music. Kaikeyi, who was impatient to precipitate the final act, made the king sit up and said: "You promised me something and I told you about my dearest wish. After agreeing to do what I asked you to, you are now being untruthful: you are not helping matters by lying on the ground making much of a minor matter.

"Truth is as sacred as the mystic letter 'AUM'. Truth is the pathway for the achievement of all the four purusharthas: Dharma, Artha, Kama and Moksha. Truth is the essence of the Vedas. It is shameful on your part to abandon this truth and behave like this."

The king looked all around like a stricken deer. He was helpless, bound as he was by his oath. He said: "The night has passed and the world is bright once again with the rays of the sun. The elders in the court will now approach me with the desire to take me to the hall where the coronation is to be performed. With the waters collected for the abhisheka let Rama perform the funeral rites for me who will die very soon. I have no desire to face my people whose wishes I have thwarted." Kaikeyi's eyes flashed with anger. She said: "Enough of this mourning, O king. Please send for my son and crown him. Banish Rama and your task is complete. I see no reason for your dalliance."

Like a high-born horse which is hurt by the unexpected whip wielded by the rider, Dasaratha winced at the words of Kaikeyi and said: "I wish to see my son Rama."

In the meantime, when the sun's rim appeared in the east, Vasishtha, surrounded by his pupils and disciples entered the palace. People had already begun to assemble in the hall and in the courtyards as also in the streets waiting for the great event. Vasishtha met Sumantra, the favourite charioteer of the king. He said: "Sumantra, the king has not arrived yet. Go at once and tell him that everything is ready and that we are waiting for his coming. Tell him I have already kindled the fire and that the auspicious moment has arrived." Sumantra hurried to the chambers of Kaikeyi and entered the apartments singing the praises of the king as a Suta should. He then said: "Please wake up, my lord. Prepare yourself for the great event. The sun has risen, the entire city has gathered to witness Rama's coronation. Everything has been done as per your wishes and we are waiting for your coming. Vasishtha is here with the other priests. The hall, filled as it is with people, still looks empty without your presence, your majesty. It is like a herd of cattle without the cowherd: like an army without a commander: like the night without the moon: like a kingdom without a ruler." His words hurt the unfortunate king. It was like the twisting of a wound. The king looked at the Suta, Sumantra. His eyes were red with weeping and with the sleepless night he had spent. He was a picture of woe.

Dasaratha looked at Sumantra who stood before him and said: "My tears, Sumantra, flow all the more when I hear your words." The charioteer could not understand what was happening. He was able to make out that something was amiss, but beyond that he could not guess. He moved a few steps away from the king who was unable to talk even a word after that. Kaikeyi, who saw what was happening, came near Sumantra and spoke in her arrogant and imperious voice: "Sumantra, all through the night the king spent sleeplessly since he was worried, worried because of his extreme love for Rama. Just some time back sleep overcame him and he is dozing. Go at once and bring Rama to the presence of the king. There is nothing here to be concerned about."

Sumantra's worried look of a moment ago was wiped out by the words of the queen and, pleased with the thought that he would be meeting Rama soon and that the king would perform the abhisheka at once, Sumantra hurried away from the presence of the king. He told himself: "Evidently the king wants to discuss some matters of importance with Rama before the coronation and that is why he has asked Rama to be brought to the chambers of the younger queen."

Karkataka Lagna under which Rama was born was fast approaching and the star Pushya was already said to have reached the neighbourhood of the moon. The time was approaching for the coronation and there was an incessant noise as of the roar of the ocean when Sumantra left for the palace of Rama. Several people asked him on the way: "Where is the king? Why has he not come to the council hall yet? The sun is rising higher and higher in the heavens and still the king has not come out of his sleeping chambers."

Sumantra said: "The king has asked me to fetch Rama from his palace and that is where I am going. I will certainly inform the king about the fact that you have all assembled here and that time is fast approaching when the coronation should take place." Sumantra came back to the doorway of the apartments of Kaikeyi and tried to wake up the king once again. Dasaratha looked at him with his sad eyes and said in a feeble voice: "Sumantra, you were asked to bring Rama. Have you not gone yet? I have to see my child at once. Bring him to me."

Puzzled by the general atmosphere, Sumantra did not pause to think. He went fast towards the palace of Rama. It took him some time to cross the dense crowd. Soon he reached the mansion where Rama lived.

Rama's palace was like the peak of Kailasa and like the dwelling of Indra himself. It was decorated with flowers, festoons, perfumes, and all the beautiful things that could be found on the face of the earth. The carved doorways, the sculptured figures which were placed here and there, the jewelled entrances to the several chambers, the birds which were making music in the gardens, the beauty of the peacocks which were strutting in the gardens, all lent charm to the glorious palace of Rama.

The citizens of Ayodhya saw Sumantra in the chariot proceeding towards the mansion of Rama and there was great excitement since they knew he had come to fetch the prince. Sumantra reached the palace and entered it. Shatrunjaya, the famed elephant which was the favourite of Rama, was there and Sumantra imagined Rama seated on it and a smile lighted up his face. He went inside the palace and finally reached the innermost chambers where the prince stayed. He sent word through the doorkeeper: "Please announce to Rama that Sumantra is at the doorstep and wants to pay his respects to the prince."

The message was carried to Rama and he asked for the Suta to be brought with the respect due to an old and trusted attendant of his father. Sumantra went inside. He saw Rama seated on a couch which was inlaid with gold. Rama stood up as Sumantra entered the place and his charm and beauty made Sumantra close his eyes for a moment and then open them: so overpowering was the effect of Rama's presence.

Rama had dressed himself in silk and by his side stood Sita with a chamara in her hand. Rama and Sita looked like the moon and the star Chitra. Sumantra fell at the feet of the young prince and stood humbly before him. He said: "Rama, the king, your father, is desirous of seeing you. He is with his queen Kaikeyi and I have been asked to take you there at once." Rama received the summons with a pleasant smile and turned to Sita saying: "Sita, the king and my mother want to consult me about something related to the event which has to take place now. This mother of mine, Kaikeyi, is ever thoughtful about my welfare and she has evidently thought of something new and the king wants to tell me about it. She is a princess from Kekaya and she is ever devoted to my father. Never once has she displeased him. As for me, I have always seen her with a smile and Sumantra has come to take me there for some good fortune which awaits me there. It has to be good since the two people who has been discussing my future are my well-wishers and this Sumantra who has been sent to fetch me is another of my father's friends. I will at once go and pay my respects to my father. Wait for me here. I will come to you very soon."

Sita did not speak a word. She walked with Rama to the doorway and stood watching him enter the chariot. She sent up prayers to all the gods silently, saying: "The king has decided to crown my lord today. Protect him, all of you. I ask Indra, Yama, Varuna and Kubera to be his protectors. He will take up the Diksha and you must all be by his side and guard him."

Rama came out of the mansion like a lion does out of its cave and Lakshmana, who was always with him stood at the doorway waiting to accompany him.

The glorious chariot was on its way. Making a noise like distant thunder, with horses of great beauty and speed yoked to it, the jewelled chariot was making but slow progress through the crowd which had collected in front of the palace and in the streets leading to the great hall in the king's palace.

It was a glorious procession and women from the many terraces and windows of the houses sprinkled the chariot with flowers and Rama, with a smiling face, acknowledged the affectionate shouts of the people. Each one spoke something in praise of the prince and the progress of the chariot was slow. They were talking amongst themselves: "Fortunate indeed are we since this prince, this young man who is the home of all virtues, will be our king from today. It is a day to be remembered by all of us."

The chariot reached the palace of the king. Rama descended from the chariot and, led by Sumantra and followed by his beloved brother Lakshmana, he entered the palace.

9. KAIKEYI TALKS TO RAMA

Rama went fast towards the apartments of Kaikeyi. He was eager to see his father. Lakshmana stood near the doorway and Rama entered the chambers. Rama looked at his father. Dasaratha was seated on a jewelled couch and Bharata's mother, Kaikeyi, was standing at a little distance from him. An unnatural silence pervaded the place. Rama was puzzled and he looked again at his father. The king's face was like that of a rishi who had uttered an untruth. Rama could perceive that the king was suffering from some great mental torture. His face had no evidence of happiness on it as it would always have, when Rama came to his presence. The king's eyes were closed and he was looking as though sorrow had taken shape and become a human being. Such a picture of woe was the king.

Rama went to the presence of the king, announced himself and falling at his feet, clasped his feet in his blessed hands. He prostrated before Kaikeyi and did the same thing. The king could not open his eyes. Tears flowed from them and he said "Rama". He could proceed no further. His eyes remained closed and words would not leave his lips. Rama was taken aback at this strange sight. It was frightening and Rama was like one who had stepped unwittingly on a snake. The king was sighing like one in great pain. His senses did not seem to be functioning at all. He looked like the sun eclipsed by Rahu, the dread planet. Rama could not guess the reason for the king's unhappiness and he stood with his mind in a great turmoil. He thought to himself: "This is the first time that such a thing has happened. My father has never once failed to greet me with a smile, an embrace and a loving word. I have ever tried to obey him in all things. Why does he not look at me? Why does he refuse to talk to me? Have I offended him in any way? Even if he is angry with someone, he would smile when I went to him. But today he is different."

Rama stood for a long moment looking at his father. He went near Kaikeyi and said: "Mother, father seems to be angry with me." As he said it Rama's voice was full of sadness and his pain could be seen on his face. He was sorely grieved to see his father thus. He asked her: "Tell me how I have offended my father, the king. I have never once done anything to displease him. Please, if I have unwittingly done so, please, on my behalf, plead with the king and pacify him. He has ever been sweet to me and today he seems to be very unhappy, displeased and unwilling to speak to me. I am not able to bear it. Is he unwell? Or is he mentally upset? He is not like ordinary human beings to be affected by the usual sorrows which bother others. He is far above all that. I am afraid, mother. I hope no bad news has reached you from Kekaya about my beloved brother Bharata or Shatrughna. Unless and until I do what my father wants me to do, I cannot rest in peace. I am unable to live with this fear in my mind: that I have displeased my father. A father is divinity incarnate to a man and my father is the god whom I worship daily. How can I bear to see him so unhappy? I know I should not ask this of you, but have you, by any chance hurt him with harsh words spoken thoughtlessly? Mother, please tell me what makes him look like the moon under an eclipse?"

When she heard Rama, Kaikeyi spoke words which were harsh and heartless. She had no hesitation to speak the words which were like a thunder-clap when they were first heard by the king. She said: "Rama, the king is not angry with you nor is he unwell. Bharata and Shatrughna are well too. A matter of grave importance, of great moment, is now lodged in his mind. He is not able to talk to you since he is afraid you may not be pleased with his words. He is extremely fond of you, Rama, and these words refuse to leave his lips." Kaikeyi paused for a while. Her face was calm and unruffled. She had no thought of the censure of the world which would condemn her for ever nor did she feel that she was doing something unforgivable, an act which was unparalleled in the history of the Raghuvamsa. She continued: "What has been promised to me by him should be fulfilled by you."

Kaikeyi looked at Rama and his beautiful face which was full of concern for his father and impatience to know what she was trying to say. He listened with eager eyes. Kaikeyi said: "Once this king had granted me two boons and that was when he was extremely pleased with me. Now, when he is asked to live up to it, he is repenting his gift like an ordinary illiterate man. After committing himself he is trying to go back on his word like a foolish man who is trying to build a bridge after the floods have damaged everything. His love for you is making him untrue. Rama, I do not have to tell you that the true sign of good men is to walk in the path of dharma, to speak the truth, never to swerve from it. This, I am told, is the only pathway to heaven. Since that is so, the king should not transgress the rules of dharma even for the sake of the love he has for his son. If you agree to fulfil the conditions of my boons, whether they are pleasing to you or displeasing, I will tell you all about it. I will relate to you the desire in the heart of the king and it is up to you to save the honour of your father. He will never speak to you about it. But knowing you as I do, I have no doubt that you will do what is desirable, and I will talk to you." Rama was listening. He was as still as an image carved out of stone. He saw his father suffering and he was himself quite upset by the words of Kaikeyi. He had never heard this harsh, hard tone in her voice before. Her face had lost the charm and softness which he was wont to see always. "Mother," said Rama, "Mother, you should not say this to me. You should not say: 'If you will do it.' You know my devotion to my father. If the king wishes me to do something, nothing will stop me from obeying him. I will fall into the blazing fire, drink poison without hesitation or drown myself in the sea if my father so wishes. I am hurt that you should have doubted it even for a moment. It is my misfortune that you should have thought so. I am but the slave of my father who is my elder, who is my guru, who is everything good and great to me. Tell me, mother, tell me what the king desires me to do. I promise to do so immediately and you must know that Rama speaks but once and no one need ask him to repeat what he said, for assurance. Please tell me about my father's commands."

Kaikeyi spoke to the great prince who was devoted to one thing and only one thing and that was the path of dharma: whose religion was Truth. Kaikeyi who had now passed beyond caring for the opinion of the world, spoke in a calm and emotionless voice: "Long ago, Rama, there was war in the heavens between the devas and the asuras. Your father had gone to help Indra and I had gone with him. I happened to save the life of the king and he, pleased with me, granted me two boons. I had told him that I would ask for them when I needed them. I asked him now, for the two boons. It is not as though he cannot grant them.

"All I wanted was that Bharata, instead of you, should be crowned the Yuvaraja: and, that you should spend nine years and five more in the Dandaka forest. Rama, if the king should prove truthful it is up to you to help him do so. If you accept these conditions and fulfil his promise to me, he will be saved from being called an adharmi. You must go away to the forest and spend these years away from Ayodhya. Bharata must be crowned. Wearing deerskin and tree-bark, you must spend seven years and another seven in the Dandaka forest. Bharata will rule the land of the Ikshvakus. Love for you is blinding this king and he is in danger of following the path of adharma by breaking his promise. He is not able to look you in the face since he is bound by his word. You should do what I have told you just now. You are a jewel among the sons of this House and you must undertake the task of saving your father's name."

Unperturbed as he always was by pleasure or pain, happiness or sorrow, by the sway of the opposites, Rama stood calm. There was not even a trace of disappointment or anger in his face. Her harsh words had no disturbing effect on the face of the great prince Rama. It was the king who looked more unhappy than before and he was moaning in pain.

Rama looked at Kaikeyi and said : "But certainly, my mother, I will go at once to the forest dressed, as you say, in tree-bark and deerskin. I will not let my father break his word. I am unhappy only about one fact: why does the king refuse to look at me with love as he always does? Mother, please have no doubt about me. I swear to you that I will definitely do what you have asked me to. I will go away from here, to the forest. Your wishes are granted by me on behalf of my father. This, my guru, has stipulated that I should go, and do you think I will even dream of disobeying this god among men? What hurts me most is this: why could the king not tell me the good news himself—that Bharata, my beloved brother Bharata, is to be crowned? As for my love for Bharata, for the sake of Bharata I am prepared to give up my kingdom, my kinsmen, Sita and even my very life without being asked to do so. I will gladly do so. When such is the case, did you think I would hesitate when the king himself desires it? Let the king look happy at least from now. Why does he bend his eyes on the ground and shed tears? Why, mother? Please despatch messengers to Kekaya immediately and ask them to fetch Bharata as early as possible. As for me, I will at once leave for the forest as per my father's commands."

Rama stood with folded palms and Kaikeyi, with a triumphant toss of her head, looked at the king and then at Rama. "Rama," she said, "I will arrange about fetching Bharata from Kekaya. Messengers will certainly be sent soon. I do not see any need for you to tarry till the arrival of Bharata. It is imperative that you leave at once for Dandaka. The king does not speak to you because of his love for you which is making him feel slightly shame-faced. That is the only reason why he is not talking to you. Unless and until you leave this city, your father, the king, will neither bathe nor eat."

Rama closed his ears with his hands and said: *"Shantham Papam"* to himself and the king spoke in a feeble voice: "What a shameful thing this is : I am helpless and I am not able to talk to my child." With a sigh which seemed to shatter his entire frame, the king fell back on his couch in a faint. Rama hurried to his side and raised him up with great concern.

Like a high-born horse wincing under the stroke of a whip, Rama, spurred by Kaikeyi, spoke to her with a smile and with sadness in his voice: "Mother, still you have not understood me. I have never been fond of riches, nor do I want to live in luxury like ordinary men. I wish you to know that I am like the rishis, bent on following the path of dharma and nothing else is desirable to me. If it is humanly possible to please this godly man who is my father, I will do so. I will give up my very life and save my father's name from ignominy. As I see it, the utmost dharma of a man is to serve his father and to worship him as his god and to obey him in everything. Though I have not been spoken to by the king directly, I have been commanded by you to spend the next fourteen years in the fearful forest by name Dandaka. I will certainly do so, have no fear.

"Devi, Kaikeyi, you did not credit me with one thing. I would have obeyed you if *you* had asked me to do this. Because of your lack of faith in me and in my love for you, you have approached the king. I am only sorry you have underrated me. Are you not as dear to me as my father? I would have obeyed you implicitly. But it is no matter.

"I will at once go to my mother and take her blessing. I will have to comfort her and convince her that this is not a calamity which has befallen me. I will then speak to Sita about this. After that I have nothing left but to leave for Dandaka, situated between the rivers Narmada and Godavari. After all, the forest once belonged to Dandaka, the son of Ikshvaku. Bharata can take over the service which is due to my father. Service to one's parents is the first, and, in fact, the only path which leads to the other purusharthas. Mother, you must take good care of my father and make certain that Bharata does not fail in his duties as a son and as a ruler."

The king was now sobbing loudly and his grief was uncontrollable. Rama had to steel his heart against staying there and comforting his father. Without a word he fell at his father's feet, clasped them in his hands and placing them on his head, he stood up. He went to Kaikeyi and, taking the dust of her feet, walked out of the chamber without another word. He could hear his father's sighs and his lamentations but he walked away with firm steps.

Lakshmana had been standing near the doorway and he had heard everything. Rama looked at the angry face of his brother. Lakshmana's lips were throbbing with anger and his eyes were filled with tears. Rama walked fast towards the antahpura of his mother Kausalya controlling the unhappiness in his own heart and his senses too, and Lakshmana followed him silently. They had to pass the great hall where preparations were made for the coronation. Rama went round the vessels full of the waters from the many sacred rivers of Bharatavarsha, waters which had been gathered in a hurry for the coronation.

There was not even a shadow of disappointment on the face of Rama as he did this. His face was like the full moon, charming and pleasing. The loss of the kingdom and the banishment which was imminent had no effect on this great soul who was the beloved of everyone, and his face was just as it was the previous day when the king had summoned him to his presence and told him that he should be the Yuvaraja. Rama looked like a great sanyasi who had renounced the world. He had made up his mind to abandon willingly all the glory which should have been his, and he had decided to proceed to the forest.

Rama did not even look at the white umbrella, the chamaras, nor the chariot which stood at the doorway of the palace. Rama managed to avoid the people and friends who were awaiting him but walked towards his mother's chamber. His mind was engaged only in one thought : how to break the news to his dear mother whose grief would be unbearable. His face did not reveal any of the feelings inside his mind. He walked with the same firm step which was usual with him and his face was looking as though nothing untoward had happened.

Some people spoke to him on the way and Rama spoke sweetly and calmly with them and went towards Kausalya's chambers. Lakshmana, whom Rama would call "my life which has taken a form and is with me always," walked with him. He managed to keep under control the great sorrow and the greater anger which were seething inside his heart, and walked with Rama. Ever since he was born, Lakshmana had shared everything with Rama, and the two brothers walked towards Kausalya's chambers, each busy with his own thoughts.

News was already spreading about the impending disaster. Cries of dismay and distress could be heard vaguely from inside the apartments of several of the women in the palace. "Rama, the prince who is dear to us, who has been a son to all of us, who has treated us with the same love and respect he has for Kausalya devi, Rama who is the refuge of all those who are in trouble, Rama our child, is today leaving us and will depart for the forest. He has never angered any of us with his words or acts and even those who were angry would be pacified by him. The king has taken leave of his senses or else how can he contemplate such an act? How will he live without Rama after he is gone?" These and similar words were filtering through the walls of the many chambers. Some were sobbing, some were wailing and some were talking angrily about the injustice of the king. Rama paid no heed to all these disturbances. Like an Ashvattha tree which stands firm and unconcerned about the twittering of the birds seated on its branches, he reached the palace of his mother followed by Lakshmana.

The old doorkeeper was squatting at the doorway and some others were standing by. Seeing Rama, they rushed towards him with excitement and said: "Jaya Vijayee Bhava". Rama accepted their greeting with his beautiful smile and walked on. The women in the inner chambers went towards, where Kausalya was, to announce the arrival of Rama.

The queen-mother Kausalya had spent the entire night praying to Lord Narayana. Her one thought was the welfare of Rama. Early in the morning she sat before the image of the Lord and was even then performing pooja to Him. Dressed as was her custom in white silk, she was worshipping fire with oblations poured into it.

Rama walked into his mother's pooja room. He saw his mother seated before the fire with her mind set on offering up prayers. All the accessories for the pooja were placed by her side: curds, rice, ghee, sweet preparations, havis, fried rice white like moonlight, butter, Payasam (rice cooked in milk with sugar to sweeten it), flowers and garlands of flowers, and samit along with pots and pots of gold filled with sanctified water. When Rama entered, Kausalya was offering Arghya to the Lord. Rama stood still and he looked at her. Constant Vratas and fasting had made her very thin. There was a sadness on her face which had been there ever since Rama could remember and he knew of the sufferings she had undergone. He knew only too well that he was the only bright star in her firmament. His face was very grave when he thought of her reaction to the news which he had brought her.

Kausalya turned and she saw Rama. Like a mare rushing to her young colt Kausalya went to Rama with a smile of infinite sweetness lighting her face. Rama, who was ever bent on attending to her slightest wish, was now standing before her with his palms folded when she came to him. Rama fell on the ground, clasped her feet in his hands and she lifted him and embraced him. She looked at him with swimming eyes and spoke to him: "Child, born as you are in the illustrious race of the Ikshvakus, you are a worthy scion of that race. May you follow in their footsteps and be as famed as they were and may you live long. The noble king will crown you as the Yuvaraja today. You must ever pay respect to your father who is righteous and good."

Kausalya led him to a jewelled seat and placed before him eatables which had been prepared for the morning. Rama was sorely distressed. Because he could not refuse her anything he made a pretence of accepting the seat by placing his hand on it and leaning against it. Rama had made up his mind to leave for Dandaka that very day and he thought the moment had come when she should be told.

With a slight hesitation, with a faltering in his stoic calm, with his head bent down, with his eyes seeking the ground Rama stood and, after a moment, spoke in a firm voice. "Mother, a great misfortune has befallen you, my Sita, and my beloved brother Lakshmana. It happened just now and you do not know about it yet. Mother, this jewelled seat does not befit me now. What I need is an asana made of darbha grass. The time has come when I should abandon all this and go to the Dandaka forest and remain there. I am leaving for the forest very soon. I must withdraw my mind from all thoughts of kingly comforts and live in the forest for fourteen years with my mind set on the other world. I must live on fruits and roots gathered by myself in the forest and how can I accept the food you have placed before me? The king will crown Bharata as the Yuvaraja and he has asked me to dwell in the forest like a tapasvin. Mother, six years and eight more will I spend in the forest."

Kausalya was listening: for a moment she could not grasp what he was saying. And, like a god who had been pushed to the earth, like a branch of a sala tree felled by an axe, she fell senseless on the ground. Rama went to her, lifted her up tenderly and placed her on a seat. He sat stroking her with loving hands. She regained consciousness and she looked at Rama. She said: "Rama, if only you had not been born to me, I would not have had to suffer this grief. The only pain I was then suffering was the thought that I was a barren woman. I now feel that would have been infinitely better than the state I am now reduced to.

"You know only too well that I have never been dear to the king. I was confident that you would make up for the loss by your love for me. I am the eldest queen, no doubt. But I have been insulted by the younger queens of the king and now, after you have gone, indignities will be heaped on me. How can I express the depth of the pain and unhappiness in my mind? Tears will now flow constantly from these eyes which will be longing to see you. Death will certainly be welcome. All these years I have been slighted by Kaikeyi and her maids since the king has never treated me well. Even the few loyal friends and companions I have, will now avoid me since Kaikeyi's son will be the king hereafter.

"Rama, it is seventeen years since you were born and I have been able to bear a great deal of unhappiness as you are here by my side. How can I live without looking at your beautiful face? How can I live in midst of all these painful surroundings? I performed so many Vratas and I have worshipped the Lord daily without fail. All my prayers have been for your welfare and they have proved to be fruitless like seeds sown in salty soil. I am the most unfortunate of all beings and that is why, perhaps, my prayers have been unanswered. My heart is indeed made of stone or else it should have broken down like the banks of a river which is suddenly filled with water during the rainy season. Maybe, it is made of iron. It does not break nor do my limbs give way under the great grief which has suddenly beset me. It is because life will not leave the body until the appointed time for death. If it were possible for one to abandon one's life when beset with unbearable grief, then like a cow parted from its calf I would give up this fruitless life of mine at once. Child, Rama, what is the use of living without you by my side? I will come with you to the forest. I cannot be here without you."

Again and again she repeated herself and cried without restraint and Rama stood by her side trying to pacify her and wipe her tears.

10. LAKSHMANA'S ANGER

Lakshmana could bear it no longer. He had been standing near Rama listening to the words of the heart-broken queen. He now intervened and said: "Mother, I do not like this at all. I do not see why Rama should give up all this glory because a woman's whim has dictated the terms. Our revered father is now old, and senility has set in, no doubt. His mind is not his own and, blinded by his love for a woman, the king has forgotten what dharma is as far as the ruling of the kingdom is concerned. He has lost the power to discriminate between the good of the country and the course which will be harmful. A king should remember what is good for his country and what is not, and he should have the acumen to consider these impartially and come to a quick decision. Our king has lost that power. So much so, he has granted this woman everything she has asked for. I do not see any reason for the banishment of Rama from the country and for the command that he should live in the Dandaka. Rama, the sinless one, cannot be condemned to such a punishment without reason. The king is so shameless that he has become an adharmi, because of this woman. I am going to kill my father. Even an enemy of Rama, an enemy who has been hurt by Rama's arrow and is dying, even he will not impute any sin to Rama. My brother has never once swerved even by a hair's breadth from the path of dharma. He is firm in his convictions and nothing can move him to do anything wrong. He is like a god and such a son is being banished for no reason at all. The king, who has lost sight of the difference between dharma and adharma, who is but a slave to his senses, has to be judged rightly. No one is prepared to accept his commands as righteous. Rama, there are three arthas, as you know. Treading the right path is named Shuklartha: the path which has a slight admixture of adharma but is, by and large, right, is named Chapalartha and the path which is entirely unrighteous is Krishnartha.

"Our king belongs to the second category. Before adharma runs rampant in the country because of this king, please take up the reins of the kingdom in your hands. Just command me. The kingdom is your birthright and I will stand by your side bow in hand. Tell me if there is anyone who has the courage to oppose me. If it is necessary, I will kill every one of the citizens of Ayodhya if they dare to side with the king. If there is even one single individual who sides with Bharata, and is his well-wisher, I will destroy him and his clan. Rama, my brother, you are gentle and soft by nature and you are being deceived because of it. If our father, influenced as he is by Kaikeyi, persists in this shameful behaviour, he will have to be imprisoned. If he actively supports your enemy he should then be killed without compunction.

"If a man is so bereft of his senses that he is unable to know the difference between dharma and adharma, if he chooses to be an adharmi and harms others, it is imperative that he should be punished. With what assurance has the king now dared to make a gift of this beautiful land to Kaikeyi? What prompted him to do so? He will not be able to resist the combined power of you and me. No one can have the courage to prefer Bharata to you and try to crown him: least of all, the king.

"There are several powers a king has. The first is Prabhu Shakti. This is the power wielded by a man purely because he is a king and a good and righteous king. There is the second type which is known as Prabhava Shakti. This is the power of the king who is righteous by nature and who is assisted in ruling the kingdom by good and capable ministers. The third is Utsaha Shakti. This is trying to achieve something which is wrong in every way with the assurance born of arrogance. Tell me Rama, which Shakti, which power has prompted the king to act thus?

"Mother, I swear by my sacred bow, by the truth which I have tried to follow, by what little punya I have earned by the deeds I have performed, that the only aim in my life is to please my beloved brother. I am his slave and there is no place for anyone else but him in my heart. I am his devotee and I will not allow any injustice to be done to my god. If Rama were to enter raging fire, you can be sure that I will also be there and that, even before my brother enters it. I am only waiting for my brother to think it over and command me. I will then wipe away your tears like the rising sun does the darkness of the night. You will see the deadliness of my arrows then. I will kill the king along with Kaikeyi. He is old, has lost his reasoning power and the only aim in his life seems to be to please Kaikeyi. He has now become the object of scorn as far as the entire world is concerned."

Kausalya, who had been drenched in tears and whose heart was heavy with sorrow, listened to the words spoken by Lakshmana and she said: "Rama, you have also heard all that child Lakshmana has been saying. If it is pleasing to you, you might proceed in the manner as per his wish. You shall not go to the forest leaving me to the mercies of the younger women in the palace. You know what is right and what is not. Remain here and serve me. Am I not as dear to you as your father? Even as you obey your father you should obey me, and I say that you *shall not go* to Dandaka leaving me alone, here, in Ayodhya.

"My happiness, nay, my very life is bound up in you and without you, life will have no meaning. I would prefer to eat grass and remain with you rather than live in this palace full of luxury. If, in spite of my entreaties you decide to go away from me I will, this very moment, remain seated on darbha grass and starve until death overtakes me. You will then be tainted by the sin of Matruhatya, killing your mother, which sin the lord of the rivers, the sea, had to suffer."

Rama was silent all the while. He allowed Lakshmana to give vent to his anger and he let his mother shed all the tears she had. She could weep no more, so exhausted was she. Rama was greatly distressed to go through all this pain. He could not, bear to see any one suffer without his sharing their pain and now, it was his mother and his brother who were unhappy. He was trying to think up words which would pacify her and, at the same time, let her be convinced that he was doing the right thing.

He spoke in a soft, gentle and persuasive voice: "Mother, it is not possible for me to disobey the words which my father has spoken. I have neither the power nor the desire to do so. I prostrate before you, mother, and assure you that I have made up my mind to go to the forest. You must bless me and send me. I need your blessings. Implicit obedience to one's father has been the law set down by the rishis, and all our ancestors have followed this rule. Think of Parasurama, mother. His father, the saintly Jamadagni, asked him to kill his mother Renuka and the son obeyed his father because that is the only dharma to be followed. Please do not think that I am the first person to follow this path of obedience to the father. Many of my predecessors have done the same thing and I am only following in their footsteps. I have been taught early in my life that the son who obeys his father is sure of a place in heaven. The rules of dharma taught by the great ones cannot be false. I believe in the shastras and I will obey my father in everything."

Rama then turned to Lakshmana and spoke to him. Rama, who was a great archer was well-versed in the art of talking too, and he had to convince Lakshmana that he was uttering words which were wrong. "Lakshmana," he said, "I know the love you have for me. It is a devotion which is unparalleled in the three worlds. I know your prowess too, very well. I am aware of your firmness, your determination to do what you have decided to do and your valour which is unbearable to the enemy. My mother's grief is intense and it cannot be cured soon. It will last for a very long time. She speaks wild and incoherent words since she is unacquainted with the nuances of dharma. A man who has his senses under control will take everything as it comes, whether it is good fortune or ill-luck, with an equanimity which is the heritage of rishis. Such a man will say, 'It is the Will of heaven that this should happen', and accept anything which befalls him in a calm manner. But mother has not learnt that secret and so she is suffering thus.

"But you, my Lakshmana, you are different! Along with me, you have sat at the feet of the Guru and you too have learnt the rules of conduct.

In this world, Lakshmana, dharma is the ultimate goal. It is the observance of dharma which will grant the other three purusharthas: Artha, Kama and Moksha. Dharma has been established in truth and truth is the ultimate religion. A well-read man should not break his word after he has promised to do something. When he is commanded by his father or mother or by his Guru, he should keep to his word and not break it. I do not, therefore, wish to disobey what my father and Kaikeyi have asked me to do. Abandon these wrong thoughts, Lakshmana. It is not right. It is not the dharma you should follow. It will seem as though you are trying to prove to the world that you are a great warrior. Do not give in to these feelings of wrath. It is wrong to be violent. Violence, I repeat, is wrong. You must listen to me and let me go to the forest. I have made up my mind to do so."

He turned again to his mother and prostrated before her. Standing up, he said: "Mother, permit me to go to the forest. Please recite the mantras which will bring me good fortune and which will keep evil spirits away from me. I will come back soon, mother, after I have satisfied the conditions of my exile. I assure you that soon, very soon, you and I with Lakshmana and Sita will be reunited and we will live happily with father as we have done all these years. Abandon this grief and prepare yourself to send me to the forest with your blessings. I am doing only what is right and you must help me do so."

Kausalya saw that her son was firm in his resolve. His mind seemed to be calm and unruffled and his face indicated it. It took her a while to speak. She said: "Rama, you speak of dharma and that very dharma says that a mother is a sacred to a man as his father. Both are your gurus. And *I command you not to go*. I say that you shall stay by my side and serve me. Without you, Rama, life will lose all meaning. With you by my side even if it be just an hour, I will be happy. I cannot live without you, Rama."

Not all her tears would move Rama to swerve from his firm resolve. Nor could Lakshmana's anger influence him. Again he spoke to Lakshmana and said: "I am aware of your valour, my Lakshmana, and I know only too well how much you love me. You have known me all these years and still, instead of trying to understand me, you are adding to my unhappiness, sorely tried as I am by my mother's tears."

11. RAMA'S FIRMNESS

The piteous words of Kausalya would have made anyone else relent. But not Rama. Like an elephant which walks with unconcern even when torches are lit by men to impede his progress, Rama, with his mind set firmly on the path of dharma, refused to be moved by the tears of his mother. He was the one person who was capable of talking to his mother who was almost demented because of excessive grief and to Lakshmana whose throat was dry with anger.

Rama spoke again: "Lakshmana, you know me so well and I know you too, since we are but two aspects of the same truth. How is it you do not understand my devotion to dharma? Simple rules of conduct have been set down for man by the elders of yore. Believe in their teachings implicitly. Man should devote himself to dharma and only to dharma. One who sets his mind, instead, on acquiring, Artha, wealth, becomes an object of the censure of the wise. The third man who is lost in Kama, the other path, is not worthy of praise. If, however, a man follows the path of dharma set down in the shastras, Artha, Kama and Moksha will follow as a natural sequel to one's actions.

"Our father has, all these years, been famed for his great good qualities, for his righteousness, and for his knowledge of all the Vedas and the shastras. Such a man commands me to do what is not pleasing to you. I will not seek the reason which prompted him to command me thus. Maybe he is angry with me, maybe he is unhappy about something, or pleased about something else. It is no matter. I am the last person to question his actions and the motives behind them. I have no right to, nor have you. I only have to obey his commands. He has promised this to Kaikeyi and it is up to me to help him keep his word. He is the very image of dharma and you and I and my mother too, must listen to his words and act accordingly.

"Mother, when such a man is alive, how can you say that you will come with me to the forest? Mother, grant me leave to go so that I will be able to fulfill my father's promise. Give me your blessings and I will come back after the term of my exile is completed. This kingdom and ruling it are not so important that I should sacrifice my good name for it. When compared with each other the rewards of the one are so inferior and so paltry while the other leads me straight to the heavens and grants me immortal fame.

Mother, you must let me go."

Rama tried to convince the two about the rightness of his decision to go to the Dandaka forest. He made a pradakshina to his mother. Lakshmana, however, refused to be convinced or comforted. Rama looked at his brother who was still fuming with anger, whose eyes were red with anger, whose sighs were like the hissing of a king cobra. Lakshmana was so fond of his brother that he could not brook this injustice done to him and all the words of Rama would not convince him. Rama touched his head with love and said: "Lakshmana, forget this wrath. Do not give in to this confusion in you mind. Rise above the level of ordinary men and be tranquil under the circumstances. Try to gain mental equilibrium. Do not think of the coronation and the attendant disappointment to you. Try and be selfless for my sake and follow my words. The same enthusiasm which was in your mind when you knew that I was to be crowned, should be in your heart since I am doing only what is right and what is rewarding to me. See to it that she is pleased, my young mother, who wishes to avert the coronation. She should have no doubts as to my decision to obey her commands. She must be assured that her wishes will come true. I have never displeased any of my mothers or my father and I do not propose to do so now.

"My father, the king, has never spoken an untruth and this incident should not prevent him from gaining a place in heaven. If his word is not kept that will hurt me more than anything else. I will not be able to bear it. I have made up my mind to go to the forest in a happy frame of mind after abandoning all thoughts of the coronation. Kekaya's daughter can now crown her son Bharata without any obstacle in her path. She will be happy only when she sees me leave for the forest dressed in tree-bark and deerskin. I am in a hurry to leave and make my father sinless."

Rama was lost in thought for a while. He then shrugged his shoulders and said: "Lakshmana, when I think of the decision of the king yesterday to crown me and the happenings of today, I cannot help thinking that Fate is responsible for our fortunes. It is Fate which makes us reap the fruits of our actions in our previous births. It must be because of something which I did in my previous birth which caused this reverse in my fortunes. Or else how could Kaikeyi have thought of giving me pain? Nothing else but Fate can explain this behaviour of the queen. Lakshmana, you know how all my mothers are dear to me and how much I love all of them. As for Kaikeyi, she has never once made any difference between me and Bharata. Today her words were so cruel and wounding, I could not believe that it was she who spoke those words. This sudden change in my fortunes is the act of Fate: I am convinced of it. Kaikeyi who has always been so well-behaved, who has always behaved like a princess, who has always been well known for her gentleness and her sweet nature, that Kaikeyi was so different, Lakshmana. She behaved like an ordinary illiterate woman who has never known what decorum is. In the presence of her lord she spoke thus.

"This is what is known as 'The Will of Providence'. Some happenings in the life of man cannot be explained away, and the course of some things can never be altered by anyone, however much he may try. This act of Providence has been proved fully in the case of Kaikeyi and me. Man is not able to defy Fate whose acts are such that man cannot satisfy himself about the happenings having any justification. He is robbed of his peace of mind and he is helpless against Fate. It is not possible to gauge the reason for one's being granted happiness, sorrow, disease, gain or loss, birth or death. Everything follows a pattern, no doubt, but we cannot understand it. This is Fate. Even the rishis who have their senses under control are not exempt from the sway of Fate. They are made to forget their daily rituals, they become slaves to the passions like Kama and Krodha and they lose all that they have gained so far. Anything which has been begun in good faith does, at times, get obstructed in its course, and takes an unexpected turn and that is the work of Fate.

"This is what has happened to us now since yesterday. But then, I am not affected by this change in my fortunes. And so, you must also adopt the same way of thinking. With these very waters which have been placed for my coronation I will have the sacred bath preparing me for the holy task of dwelling in the forest. On second thoughts, why should I have anything to do with any of these royal insignia? How can the waters meant for the purpose of coronation serve my purpose which is so different? Let me use some other water which is meant for my banishment. As for you, do not let the fickleness of the goddess Lakshmi affect you, my dear brother. Actually I prefer to roam in the forests without a care in the world. Ruling a kingdom is beset by hundreds of worries."

Lakshmana was listening with his head bent down and his eyes fixed on the ground. He was still angry. His brows were knit and he sighed like a serpent and his face was fierce to look at. He said: "I do not agree with you. How can you ascribe to Fate an action prompted by the avarice of a woman? Her desire is so great that she has made even the king agree to it. And do you not see any injustice in this? You just say it is Providence? There are people who pretend to be righteous but are, at heart, wicked. By their cleverness and by their deceitful tactics they have conspired to make you suffer this banishment and you refuse to see it. I am sure of it. Or else, why had the granting of these two famed boons been delayed all these years? It should have been done years ago. This is just a pretext. Here is an obvious intrigue to get rid of you and you insist on conforming to it by your decision to obey the king, your father. I am still of opinion that you should occupy the throne against the wishes of Kaikeyi. The king is a slave to his passions and his action is against all rules of dharma. He has no right to crown Bharata when you are here. The world will laugh at him. Only a weakling or a man lacking in valour will accept everything that comes his way with meekness and ascribe his misfortunes to Fate. A hero, on the other hand, will certainly find ways and means of overcoming the difficulties which obstruct his progress. You behave as though you are helpless against 'Fate'. Let the world see how prowess can vanquish Fate. Let the coronation take place and, with your permission, I will prove to you that the might of my arms is more powerful than Fate. No one, except our father, will object to your coronation: not even the gods who guard the eight quarters.

"The king and his young wife have conspired against you and they are the ones to be exiled to the Dandaka forest. Let me stand by your side and see that the coronation takes place. I assure you I can make it happen.

"These arms of mine, my brother, are not just for being smeared with sandal paste and for being an adornment to my body: nor is this bow an ornament I am wearing. This sword of mine is not a decoration. These arrows are not meant to support me when I am walking. They are meant for destroying enemies and I mean to use them properly: Indra himself cannot withstand my valour when I am angry. Wait and see how best I will achieve my purpose of crowning you as the Yuvaraja of the kingdom of Kosala."

Rama was standing with a sad and weary expression on his face. Distressed as he was by the many things which had happened since sunrise, he felt this to be the most trying of them all: making Lakshmana understand that he had no intention of accepting the throne even if it were offered to him now. He wiped the tears of Lakshmana and spoke words of wisdom to comfort him. He then said: "Let me tell you once and for all, Lakshmana. I have made up my mind to obey my father, since, to me, it is the ultimate dharma. I will not change my mind. I am firm in my decision and please do not give way to this anger. It is of no avail. I will not permit you to fight for the throne on my behalf nor will I allow you to talk ill of the king. Try and accept the truth. I have to go and I will go."

12. A MOTHER'S BLESSINGS

Kausalya realised that Rama had made up his mind long ago and that he would not listen to her pleadings. Sobs were stopping her from talking clearly and she said: "My child, I cannot think of the son of the emperor Dasaratha living in the forest like a mendicant. He will, from now, live on fruits and roots gathered in the forest. Will anyone believe it when they hear that Dasaratha has banished Rama to the forest, Rama, who was, till now, his very life? As you say, Fate is the most powerful of all since it has made you, the beloved of all, live in the forest. I will not be able to bear this separation from you. It will burn me like a forest fire will, a forest full of dry trees. Take me with you. I will follow you wherever you go."

Rama looked at his mother whose face was bathed in tears and said: "Mother, my father has been deceived by Kaikeyi. When I have gone to the forest he will go through a great suffering. It will take him a long time to get over this separation from me. If you too abandon him and come with me, he will not be able to live. Mother, I do not have to tell you about the dharma of a Pativrata. So long as my father is alive, it is your duty to stay by his side and serve him. That is your dharma."

With a great effort of will, Kausalya controlled herself and in a firm voice said: "Rama, you are right. I will do what you have asked me to do. I will stay by the side of the king who will be very unhappy."

Rama continued: 'Mother, these nine years and five more will pass very soon and I will come back. Actually, when I think of it, living in the forest will be, to me, like a game to play. Console yourself with the thought that I will come back to you soon, very soon." There were now tears gathering in the eyes of Rama when he said: "Mother, if you should come with me, the king will be left alone. It is not right. A woman's place is beside her lord and master. You should not abandon the king in his hour of need. Also, let me assure you of one thing. Bharata is a righteous man and a very noble youth. He will walk only in the path of dharma. He will take good care of you and please you in every way. I am certain of that. After I have gone away, my father will suffer agonies because of his separation from me. You should comfort him and make him bear the extreme grief which he is going to suffer. At this age, to suffer grief will be unbearable for my father and you should be the one to share it with him and try to lessen it. Mother, pursue your daily worship of the Lord and pray for my well-being. Wait for me to come back and take good care of my father."

Kausalya said: "Since Fate has conspired against me, I am not able to change your mind. May you be blessed all the way. You can go. I will grant you permission. May you be attended by good fortune and nothing else all the way. I will wait for you to come back. You will clear the debt you owe to your father. Having followed the dictates of dharma you will come back to me and make me happy. If it were not for Fate, you would never have disobeyed me. Go, my child, and come back well and happy. I will hear your dear voice and forget all the pain of the years I have to spend without you. Rama, do not tarry. Prepare yourself for the journey. May that dharma protect you which you have been following so assiduously with a firm mind and with a religious dedication. The gods whom you have been worshipping will protect you in the forest. May the astras given you by the noble Vishvamitra protect you. May the Samit, Kusa and the many things in the forest protect you. Vishvedevas, Maruts, Dhata and Vidhata, Pushan, Bhaga are all invoked by me to give you their grace. May the guardians of the quarters led by Indra lend their protection to you. May your path be blessed and may your valour be ever successful."

Kausalya fed the fire with havis and ghee and butter and she prayed for the welfare of her son. She said: "When the lord of the heavens, Indra, went out to fight with Vritra he was blessed by all. May such blessings attend you too. When Garuda went to the heavens to bring Amrita, his mother Vinata blessed him to be successful in his mission. May that blessing go with you. When there was war between the devas and the asuras, Aditi gave her blessings to her son Indra. May that blessing go with you, my son, when you go to the forest. I bless you as Vamana was blessed when he went to the yajna of Bali to beg for the three worlds. May the forest and all that is in the forest do nothing but good to you, my child."

Her sorrow had been controlled by her prayers and with a calm face Kausalya placed the tilaka on Rama's forehead and tied the raksha on his wrist. She embraced him warmly and said: "Go, my child, and come back to me. May you be without any illness. I will wait for the day when you will walk again in the streets of Ayodhya. After these fourteen years I will see you seated on the throne of the Ikshvakus. I am certain of that. My prayers will not remain unanswered and I will have you back with me."

With tears flowing from her eyes Kausalya completed the ritual of Svasti and embraced Rama again and again. Rama prostrated before her and held on to her feet. Again and again he took the dust of her feet and, without looking back, he left his mother's presence.

13. RAMA AND SITA

Rama entered the streets of Ayodhya after taking leave of his mother. He went straight to his own palace. He was eager to see Sita. Sita had not heard about the many things which had happened in the royal palace and her mind was dwelling on the coronation which was to take place. She performed the daily worship of the household gods and awaited the coming of her beloved Rama.

Rama entered the palace. The place was filled with people with eager expectant faces and Rama felt suddenly self-conscious and his face looked thoughtful. His usual smile was absent and, with his head slightly bent, he walked towards the inner chambers.

Sita, who had been seated, stood up abruptly and looked at Rama. His face had a worried look and there was no glow about him as was usual. He looked sad and depressed. Rama was not able to hide from her the great conflict which was raging in his mind. Sita could see that he was greatly upset about something. His face was without the smile. He actually looked angry and sweat was pouring from his frame.

With great concern Sita went to him and said: "What has happened, my lord? Why do you look so worried, angry and unhappy? Today is the day set for your coronation and you do not seem to be happy at all! Rama, I have never seen your face without the smile meant only for me. Why do you look so stern and so grim? I am afraid for you. Tell me what is worrying you."

Rama stood for a moment without speaking. And then abruptly he said: "Sita, my father, revered by all of us, has today asked me to go to the forest. Born as you are in a great line of kings famed for their righteousness, you will be able to understand my words. You have ever followed me in my path and I will tell you what happened.

"My father who is the very image of truth had, once upon a time, granted two boons to my mother Kaikeyi who had saved his life. My father had arranged this coronation for me with great enthusiasm and eagerness. While the preparations were being made, Kaikeyi asked him to grant her these two boons. The king was bound in honour to do so. The boons are simple in wording. I have, to live in the forest for the duration of fourteen years while my brother Bharata will be crowned as the Yuvaraja.. It is as simple as that. I have, therefore, come to you to bid you farewell before leaving for the forest by name Dandaka. Sita, I want to give you a piece of advice which you should remember to follow. Never, at any time, praise me in the presence of Bharata. Men in high positions cannot bear to hear the praise of other men. You should learn to behave in such a way that he is not displeased with you. The king has made him the Yuvaraja and you should be very guarded in your dealings with him. As for me, I am leaving at once for the forest at the command of the king. Be courageous and await my return with patience. When I am away, spend your time in the observance of all the Vratas and fasts and pray for my welfare. Remember to serve my father at all times and my mother Kausalya. She is aged and she is suffering because of my departure. You must make it your personal task to attend on her constantly. Do not neglect her who is full of sorrow. My other mothers should also be treated with respect because I have thought of all of them as my mothers. Bharata and Shatrughna are dearer to me than my very life and so you must treat them as though they are your brothers or your sons. You must have nothing but affection for them. Never displease Bharata by any of your actions. He will be the ruler and he will be the king who lays down the law. Sita, kings should be happy with the behaviour of their subjects and they will, in their turn, be gratified by your devotion. If, however, they are not feared and treated with respect, there is every chance of their becoming angry and that will be a sad state of affairs. If he acts against his wishes, a king will abandon even the son born of him and favour someone who is an absolute stranger to him. And so, Sita, walk very carefully in the path which will be pleasing to Bharata and, at the same time, spend all your time in observing Vratas and fasts which will be for my well-being and yours.

"I am going to the forest and you, my beloved, must stay here. You have never once displeased me or anyone so far. Remain here since I say so and you must accede to my wishes."

Sita was listening to Rama without a word. She stood silent and when he stopped talking she looked at him. They were alone and she knew that she could speak what came to her mind. Her gentle looks vanished as though by magic. Her eyes were flashing when she said: "Rama, what are you trying to tell me? Rama, my beloved husband, are you trying to make light of this which has happened to us? Very casually you are commanding me to do your bidding. Have I been in the wrong that you should talk to me thus? What have I done? How have I offended you that you should punish me thus? I have been taught the rules of dharma in a different manner. I have been given to understand that everyone, whether he is a father, a mother, a brother or a son, is meant to enjoy or suffer the results of the papa or punya which he or she has committed in the previous birth. The wife, however, is meant to share the fate of her husband. Whether it is good fortune or bad, which befalls the husband, the wife has a share in it. Accordingly when you have been banished to the forest, that means I have also been asked to go and dwell in the forest with you. Well-versed in dharma as you are, I do not have to teach the nuances of it to you. For a woman the husband is the only refuge and not her father, nor her son, or her mother, or her friends nor even her atman in this life, and in the life to come too. Why do you behave as though you know nothing of this rule?

"When you go to the fearful forest I will proceed before you and clear the path for you by removing the thorns and twigs which are likely to hurt your blessed feet. Please, Rama, please do not be angry with me for contradicting you and disobeying you in this matter. Forget it as you would water which has been left over after one has tasted it. Take me with you. I promise you I will not be any trouble. For a woman living in the glorious mansions of an emperor, or even dwelling in the heavens in the company of divine beings, or being able to achieve the eight siddhis and to be able to wander in the skies by the power of yoga, all these are as nothing compared to being with her lord. My father and my mother have constantly taught me the code of behaviour and I can boast to you that I am familiar with the rules of conduct. I will certainly go to the forest which has tigers and lions and other wild animals as its inhabitants. I will be happy only in serving you. I am not enamoured of luxury in the palace. All I want is to be with you. To me it will be like staying in my father's house. I will be happy with you, wandering in the forest perfumed with the scent of a thousand flowers. You are a lion among men and you are the protector of everyone and even a small insignificant man will be cared for by you. What then, about me? Can you not take care of me in the forest? I have made up my mind to be with you in the forest and I will not allow you to try and dissuade me from my decision. I will eat the fruits and roots with you and I assure you, I will not be a source of worry to you.

"I wish to go with you and spend all my time in the midst of the rivers, lakes, coppices; free of all care, we can wander at will in the beautiful surroundings. With you by my side, heaven will seem to have come down to the earth. With you by my side, I will enjoy seeing the lotuses blooming on the waters of the ponds and watch the swans gliding slowly on the surfaces of the lakes. To stay with you is the only path which leads me to the heavens and I am bent on following it. I will observe all the Vratas which you do and I will be by your side always. I can spend thousands of years thus, happily with you, Rama. Without you by my side, heaven will hold no charm for me. Rama, take me with you. I will not be able to live without you if I am to be separated from you. I will not find it hard to be in the forest when you are with me."

Rama did not seem to relish the words spoken by Sita. He did not want to take her with him. He tried to argue with her and tell her about the dangers which beset one who walks in the forest. He tried to comfort Sita whose tears were flowing unheeded. Wiping them with gentle fingers he said: "Sita, you are the daughter of a great man who is well-versed in dharma and you are yourself no stranger to the nuances of it. You should then know that your dharma is to obey me. Stay back here in Ayodhya and do as I tell you. Dwelling in the forest is not as easy as you seem to imagine. Abandon this desire to go to the forest with me. Uninhabited by human beings, the forest will be a fearful place to live in. I have nothing but your welfare at heart when I try to dissuade you from this impulsive decision. There is not a single ray of happiness in this forest life to which I have been condemned. Wild animals are there in plenty to frighten you and make life miserable because of the constant danger to life. You talk about sporting in the rivers but you do not seem to realise that the rivers are full of crocodiles which will grab you and will never let you go. The paths are not there at all, which you have to follow. The forest is full of thorny bushes and creepers which bar your way. At times there will not be water even for us to drink. As for sleep, you will have to make a bed of dried leaves. For a princess like you, brought up in the lap of luxury, it will not be possible to sleep in such a bed. My dearest wife, you are accustomed to wearing the softest of silks and how can you wear crude cloth made of tree-bark? Your beautiful soft hair will all be a tangled mass since you will not be able to take care of it. You may have to starve, at times, because of lack of fruits and roots in some places. And again, there will be the seasons to reckon with. The rainy season will soon be here and before that the sun will be scorching the world with his sharp rays like arrows. How can you bear the extremes of nature? How can you bear the coldness of Shisira ritu when the very trees will tremble in the cold and shed all their leaves? Think of the serpents and pythons which will catch you unawares. Infinite are the dangers that beset the path of a traveller in the forest. How can you, tender and young as you are, bear all these? In your affection for me you say that you do not mind them. But you do not know what a dreadful place the Dandaka forest is. I have considered everything well and I have come to the decision that you should not come with me but stay in Ayodhya till my return."

Sita would not be convinced. She looked at Rama with eyes which were filled with sadness as well as anger. "I am very unhappy," she said and stood silent for a while. She then spoke in a soft and persuasive voice. "Rama," she said, "all the many dangers which you have been enumerating all this while seem to me to be but the charms of the forest, since you will be with me. I have never seen all the animals and crocodiles, the trees and the lotus ponds which you described to me. I want to see them. And again, when they see you they will all resort to flight, afraid of you and your valour. My parents have told me that my place is by the side of my husband at all times and I mean to follow that rule. If, however, you insist that I have to stay behind, I will have to give up my life. When you are by my side, no one, not even Indra, the lord of the heavens, will have the courage to harm me. Oftentimes, when I have heard of dharma, when we have talked of it together, you have told me that a Pativrata, if she is separated from her husband, is not fit to be alive.

"I am also reminded of an incident when I was in my father's house. Some wise men had come there and I was told by them that I would have to live in the forest some time during my lifetime. Ever since then, there has always been this thought lying at the back of my mind, that I would see the forest some time, somehow. It is destined that I should go with you. Rama, I want to be with you. Do not try to keep me away from you. I am not a child, and I know that the forest is beset with dangers. My only thought is to serve you in the forest. I will not be a hindrance to you, Rama. You are the only god whom I worship and I will follow you wherever you go. In childhood a woman is protected by her father, in her youth by her husband and in her old age, by her son. Woman is never free. I will be your wife in the next world too.

"Rama, I have ever been devoted to you. Never once have I displeased you in any way. You are ever in my heart and in my thoughts. You know it. How then can you have the heart to ask me to be without you? How can you have the heart to be without me? Your happiness is mine and I will gladly share with you, your misfortune. I am also able to view happiness with an unruffled mind. You have taught me that. If you still persist in refusing me this desire, I will kill myself either by swallowing poison, or by falling into the blazing fire or by drowning myself."

Her tears seemed to be drenching the very earth out of which she was born and her sighs were eloquent of her grief. Rama was still trying to dissuade her. He wiped her tears and spoke words of sweetness. He spoke again of the troubles of living in the forest and asked her to stay behind. Sita spoke again. She could take liberties with Rama since she was his wife and she knew that he would not be offended. In that mood born of love, desperation and eagerness to go with him, Sita said: "My father, the king of Mithila made a mistake, perhaps. He has given his daughter to a woman dressed as a man! If the world talks of Rama thus: 'Rama does not possess the glory which is equalled only by the sun,' will it not be false, my lord? Why do you want to leave me behind, who is ever devoted to you and who has no one else to call as hers? Tell me why you think it will be difficult to take me with you. Remember, I am like Savitri who followed her lord, the son of Dyumatsena when he was taken to the very bourne of death. I am not like an ordinary woman who can amuse herself even when her husband is not with her. Rama, you are famed for the noble quality in you which says you will never abandon those who are devoted to you. You have been known to love me and only me; and, as for me, I have no thought of anything else except your love for me. And yet, you want to leave me in the hands of your enemies. Your undertaking to go to the forest at the behest of your father is indeed something which will be remembered by men everafter. Such a man should not leave his wife behind. You must take me with you, wherever you go, whether it is the forest, tapoloka, heaven, or any other place. I will be happy only with you by my side.

"Rama, the dust which will blow in the forest will seem to me to be sandal paste and the thorns will seem like the down from the breast of a swan. You have adopted the forest as a mansion to live in and so have I. We will together eat the fruits and roots from the trees and that will taste like nectar to me. I will never remember my mother or my father or this palace. I will spend all my time in the midst of the wild flowers of the forest. I will not be a burden to you nor will I displease you in anything. To me it is heaven to be with you and hell to be without you. Please understand the pain in my heart and, taking pity on me, take me with you. You know that even a moment without you is painful to me and unbearable. How then can I live for a year, three more and ten more years to follow, without you?"

Sita's grief was pathetic. She embraced Rama and wept without restraint. Out of her eyes fell tears which looked like drops of crystal falling from the petals of a lotus. Her face which was like the moon was now without its glow, like the moon drenched in frost, like a lotus which had been uprooted and thrown on the ground.

Rama embraced his weeping queen and said: "Sita, my dearest, if, by making you unhappy, I were to acquire heaven, I will not consider the thought of it even. I am not hesitant to take you with me to the forest. I am capable of protecting the entire world and that was not the reason for my refusing to take you with me. I wanted to know for certain what your desire was, and without knowing it, how could I make up your mind for you? That was the only reason why I spoke to you thus. You have been created, Sita, to spend the years in the forest with me. It is not meet that you should remain here when I go away from here. You are part of me and even as Suvarchala follows her lord Surya, even so will you be with me always. This is the dharma taught by the elders and we know it only too well.

"My father has commanded me: 'Go to the forest and dwell there for fourteen years,' and I am but obeying him implicitly. Implicit obedience to one's father and mother is the ancient rule. I will not transgress that ancient rule. Ignoring one's father, mother and guru who are gods incarnate, if a man worships some other god what is the use of such a worship? To perform yajnas and give away great wealth as gift to many will not earn for one the punya which this observance grants to man. Such a man inherits the punyalokas.

"You have made up your mind to live with me in the great and fearful forest Dandaka and I am certain that I will take you with me. When your father gave you in marriage to me he said: 'This Sita will be your Sahadharmacharee.' You shall today walk in the path of dharma which I have set my mind on, along with me. You are an ornament to your family and mine and you have proved that you are a jewel among women.

"Come, Sita, make all preparations for your journey. Give away wealth to brahmins. Feed the poor. Give away all that you have to the maids, to your servants and other attendants in the palace."

Sita's face was glowing with happiness when she heard that Rama would take her with him. She smiled happily and even as he was speaking, she decided to give away all that she possessed to the many inmates of the palace as was suggested by Rama.

14. LAKSHMANA'S REQUEST

Lakshmana who was waiting for Rama at the doorway heard the decision of Rama to take Sita with him. He was unable to bear the grief which threatened to engulf him. His eyes were red with tears and he entered the chambers of Rama. He fell at Rama's feet like a tree which had been felled by a storm. With his two hands he clasped Rama's feet. He looked up at Sita and said: "Evidently it has been decided that my lord is leaving for the forest. I am leaving for the forest too. Bow in hand I will precede you both and I will lead the way. I will be with you in the forest filled with wild animals, birds and deer too. I have known no god other than you, my beloved brother. Ever since I was a child, I have been with you and to ask me to stay behind when you are in the forest, will be cruel. Without you, I do not desire a place in the heavens nor the envied gift of deathlessness. I will refuse it even if I am asked to rule the three worlds. Take me with you, my lord."

Rama said nothing in reply and Lakshmana said: "I have been granted permission already to be with you. Why do you stand silent when I ask you now? You were asking your queen just now to be very careful in her behaviour with Bharata and you added that Bharata and Shatrughna were dear to you and that she would be treated well by them: that she should try not to displease them in any manner. When you said that you did not include my name. And that means that you have decided to take me with you. Have I, unwittingly, displeased you in any way? Have I offended you? Please let me know what my fate is. It depends on your words."

Lakshmana stood with his eyes beseeching Rama to allow him to accompany him. Rama said: "Lakshmana, you are very dear to me. You have ever been righteous like me. You are an evolved soul. You are my alter ego and there is no difference between me and you.

"Lakshmana, if you should come with me to the forest, who will take care of my mother and yours? Kausalya and Sumitra will be suffering intensely the separation when I go and if you should add to their pain, what will they do? Our father, the king, who has been like Parjanya in raining favours on all who have been depending on him, who has lived gloriously like Indra till now, has, all on a sudden, become involved in the ties of lust and Kaikeyi reigns supreme in his mind. This daughter of Ashvapati will not treat our mothers well. Bharata will have to obey his mother in every act of his, and so he will not pay attention to the comforts of your mother and mine. It is up to you, Lakshmana, to take care of my old mother with or even without the approval of the king. You must remain here and let me go in peace. You must prove your devotion to me by doing what I ask you to do. Serving one's parents is the greatest dharma and you should observe it. With both of us away, our mothers will be slighted by everyone and that is not right. You should stay behind and take care of them both."

Lakshmana heard the words of Rama and, well versed as he was in the art of saying the right thing at the right time, he said: 'I have no doubt, my lord, that Bharata who is like you in every way, will never let such a thing happen. He will cherish mother Kausalya and my mother too with the utmost love and respect. You need have no doubt about it. If it reaches my ears that swollen with pride because of his position, Bharata has lost sight of dharma and has become unrighteous, it will not take me very long to come and kill him. As for mother Kausalya, there are thousands like me, who are devoted to her and who have her welfare at heart. They will take care of her. She and my mother will be well cared for. Have no doubt about that.

"Please take me with you as your servant. There is no adharma to be seen in your doing so. I will arm myself with the bow, arrows, a spade and a basket. I will go ahead and clear the way for you. I will daily go out into the forest and collect fruits for you. You can relax on the slopes of the mountains with Sita. I will attend to your comforts day and night. Let me come with you."

Rama was thrilled with the words of Lakshmana. His eyes were moist when he said: "Lakshmana, come with me. Go at once and bid farewell to all those who are dear to you. Remember the yajna of Janaka. There, Varuna gave two immense bows which were divine, two armours which cannot be broken, and quivers which are inexhaustible. He gave us swords too, gleaming like the sun and decorated with gems. Go to the dwelling of our acharya and ask him to give these to you. Come back with them."

Lakshmana was so happy he almost ran all the way to do his brother's bidding. Very soon he came back with the famed bows of Varuna. He laid them all before Rama and said: "Here they are. Tell me what else has to be done."

Rama said: "You are ever dear to me, Lakshmana. You will now help me to perform the next act. With you by my side I wish to give away all my belongings to brahmins and to the dependents in the palace. Go at once and fetch Suyagnya, the son of our revered Vasishtha and his disciples. I want to honour all of them and leave as early as possible for the forest.

15. IN THE PRESENCE OF DASARATHA

Rama had given away all that was once his to the brahmins, to the attendants and dependents in his palace. Sita and Lakshmana had done the same thing. They now proceeded towards the palace to bid farewell to their father, the king. They were carrying the divine bows in their hands and the eyes of the people were dazzled by the brilliance of the bows. The citizens of Ayodhya had collected in the streets and on the terraces and even on the roof-tops to see the princes and Sita as they went on foot towards the palace. Rama was walking in the streets and there was no umbrella to protect him from the rays of the sun. People were sad, unhappy and angry at the course of events. Their disappointment was great. They had been waiting to see the prince borne on the elephant after the coronation and, instead, they saw him walking in the streets like anyone else. It was hard to bear.

They spoke among themselves: "Look at this prince walking in the street. An entire army made up of elephants, chariots, footmen and horses should have followed him. But alas! Only his brother Lakshmana is walking with him. Our Rama has ever been brought up in luxury and he has abandoned all the wealth and glory which ought to have been his because of his adherence to dharma. All these days Sita, the wife of Rama, has not been seen even by the celestials and such a delicate princess is now walking in the streets of the city like an ordinary person. This tender princess who is accustomed to wearing sandal paste on her arms will now walk in the forest where the sun's rays will scorch her and where the rain will drench her without mercy. The king who was once the image of dharma is now under the sway of a demon and he has lost the power of thinking. Or else how can one explain his sending his dear son to the forest? Even if he is a son without any remarkable qualities, a father will not have the heart to banish him. And our Rama is the home of all great and glorious qualities. How could the king have come to such a cruel decision? Rama has never once hurt anyone physically or with his words or behaviour: on the other hand, he has always been kind and loving towards all men. He is well read and he is righteous. He has conquered his senses and he is never fickle-minded. Because of their injustice to Rama the world is suffering like a tree which has been uprooted and left to die. Rama is the mother-root for this tree called humanity. The people form the leaves, flowers and fruits of this tree. If we should live, we should go to where Rama goes. Let us follow him to the forest. He gave up everything and let us do the same thing too. Let us desert Ayodhya. Let the city become a forest since we will not be here.

"Let Kaikeyi rule the country with no people in it. We will make the forest habitate and live with Rama. We cannot live without Rama."

Rama heard the words of the people who surrounded him but he paid no heed to their comments. His face showed no sign of any reaction to their talk. He walked without speaking a word and Sita walked beside him while Lakshmana followed the two.

Soon they reached the palace of the king. Rama walked towards the doorway and there he saw Sumantra, his father's charioteer. Sumantra's face was steeped in sorrow. Rama greeted him with his smile which came naturally to him. He knew the feeling of all the people because of his exile. He knew the sorrow in the heart of Sumantra and yet he was unmoved. He had decided to obey the commands of the king at any cost. To him, following the path of dharma was the only purpose in life and there was no disturbance in his mind since he knew that he was doing the right thing.

This scion of the race of Ikshvaku had come to bid farewell to his father and he looked at Sumantra who was at the doorstep of the palace. Rama told him: "Sumantra, be good enough to go and announce my arrival to the king." Rama, handsome and serene, stood at the doorway of the palace awaiting the permission of the king to enter, and with him stood Sita and Lakshmana. Sumantra's heart was breaking, so unhappy was he. With slow and dragging steps he went to the presence of the king and stood by his side.

The king was sighing and he looked like the sun under eclipse, like fire which was covered with ashes, like a pond without water. Sumantra could guess the pain in the heart of the king and knew that he was only adding to it. He greeted the king in the conventional manner and in a very soft voice which was full of sadness, said: "My lord, Rama, the valiant son of yours, is waiting at the doorway to see you. After giving away all his wealth to brahmins and other dependents in the palace he has come to bid farewell to you, his father and his king. He has taken leave of all those who are dear to him and now he has come to you. At your command he is going to the dreaded forest, Dandaka. Please grant him audience."

The king who was ever righteous, who was noble like the ocean, clear and true like the sky, spoke to Sumantra and said: "Ask all my wives and others who reside in the palace to be with me. I want to see Rama surrounded by all of them." Sumantra soon brought them all to the presence of the king. Kausalya came first and following her came the other wives of the king. Dasaratha said: "Sumantra, go and bring my son to me."

They were there before the king, Rama, Lakshmana and Sita, led by Sumantra. Rama entered with his palms folded and the king rose up from his seat. He walked fast towards where Rama was standing and even before he could reach him, fell down senseless on the ground. The brothers Rama and Lakshmana rushed to his side and they could see how intense was the suffering of their father. Holding him with their arms they placed him on the couch. Rama waited for him to regain consciousness. He then spoke to the king who was drowned in sorrow. "My lord, you are the lord of the world and I have come to take leave of you. I am leaving for the Dandaka forest and I beseech you, may your eyes rest lovingly on me and bless me. Lakshmana and Sita want to accompany me. I have tried in vain to prevent them but they insist on coming with me. Pray, grant them permission to do what they wish to do. Please abandon this grief and give us your love and blessings"

Dasaratha looked at Rama whose face seemed to be as calm and charming as was usual with him. He seemed to be quite unaffected by the change in his fortune. The king said: "Rama, I have been deceived by Kaikeyi. My hands are tied by my oath, because of the boons I granted her once. If you refuse to obey me, ignore me entirely and ascend the throne, which will make me happy."

Rama intervened and said: "Please do not say so. You must rule the world for many years. I will stay in the forest willingly. I will not allow you to break your word. Nine years and five more will I spend in the forest, come back to you and clasp your blessed feet in my hands."

The unfortunate king, bound by his promise and goaded by Kaikeyi into this painful situation, spoke to his beloved son. "Go, my child and come back covered with glory. May you be blessed in this world, may your fame spread to the three worlds, may you come back to Ayodhya after you fulfil the promise which your father made so rashly. My son, you are the jewel of the Raghu line and you are the very image of dharma and truth. I realise that nothing, no one can make you change your mind. I have a small desire, my child. Do not go today. Spend one day, just one single day with me and that will keep me happy for at least that time. Spend this one night with me and your mother. Stay back, and tomorrow, in the morning, you can go. Rama, you have taken on a great task. Just to save me from the sin of speaking an untruth, you are prepared to give up everything and stay in the fearful forest for a long time. I swear to you, my beloved Rama, I am not pleased at all by this happening. This wife of mine has stolen my freedom: this Kaikeyi who is like fire covered with ashes. This exile of yours and the crowning of Bharata is entirely against the code of the line of kings of which I am a descendant. Because of her deceitful nature I have become involved in this intrigue and you have agreed to guard my reputation at any cost. My child, you have done what comes naturally to you. I am not surprised at your decision."

Rama was extremely unhappy to see his father's suffering. He said: "Father, spending one night, one single night in luxury is not going to solve anything. If I enjoy them all today, who will grant them to me tomorrow when I am on my way to Dandaka? Please do not waver, but let me go. This land flowing with wealth, with grains, with prosperity, has been abandoned by me. Please give it to Bharata. I have decided to leave today, now, at this very moment, for the forest. My lord, you have granted the boons to Devi Kaikeyi. Please keep your word. I will help you to do so. According to the conditions imposed on my banishment, I will live in the forest for fourteen years. I do not desire to rule the kingdom. My only wish is to please you and to obey you. Let Bharata be lord of the world.

"Please shed this grief, my lord. It is unbecoming of you. The sea does not get ruffled by the many rivers which flow into it. Even so, you must let these pass you by and leave you untouched. As for me, I do not desire the kingdom, nor any comforts, nor even Sita! I have no desire at all for these surroundings nor even for a place in the heavens. I swear by the truth, which is sacred to me, that only one thing is dear to me and that is, to save you from the stigma of untruth. I know that it will hurt you but I will not remain here in the palace or in the city of Ayodhya even for a moment longer. Please understand me and my firm resolve. Mother Kaikeyi told me this morning: 'Rama, you must go today to the forest,' and I said I will. I cannot break that promise. I assure you, I will enjoy my wanderings in the forest. Surrounded by the deer and the birds with their sweet music I will be happy. After the lapse of fourteen years I shall come back to you. Do not give way to sorrow. Give up this distress and wait for my coming. Your grief is making everyone else unhappy too.

"I have willingly renounced the kingdom. Let Bharata rule the world and let your words come true. I am not as eager about ruling a kingdom as I am about following the rules set down by the wise. They have taught me that a father is greater than all other gods and he is to be worshipped. I am only doing what I have been taught as dharma.

"The forest will offer fruits and roots and my eyes can feast on the beautiful sight of the mountains and lakes with lotuses floating on them. I will see rare trees and sights which I have never dreamed of in the city. Please set your mind at rest. Do not think that I will suffer."

The king spoke not a word but embraced his noble son again and again and fell down senseless. Excepting Kaikeyi who stood apart with a look of utter unconcern on her face, the other wives of the king cried out loudly. Sumantra could not bear the sight and he fainted too.

The king then spoke to him and said: "Sumantra, let the army go with Rama to the forest. Load carts with costly silks and gems and ornaments for his use. Let attendants accompany him. Let those who had been his dependents go with Rama and spend their time with him, serving him. Let hunters armed with bows and arrows accompany my son." Even as he was giving these orders Kaikeyi spoke for the first time. Her face was red with anger and, standing before the king, she said: "What a king you are! How truthful! You are trying to empty the kingdom of all its riches and all its people. You want to leave nothing for my son Bharata except the empty streets. It will be like the dregs remaining at the bottom of a vessel when all the drink has been sucked. I will not allow anything to be sent with Rama when he leaves."

Dasaratha turned on her in wrath and said: "You are my enemy. Is there no end to the torture you put me through? Let me tell you something. You asked that your son should be crowned as the Yuvaraja. You did not mention these then. I can do as I please with my riches. I will, this very moment, abandon my kingdom and go with Rama to the forest. You can rule the kingdom with your son."

Rama was upset by the acute suffering to which his father was subjected. He spoke in a soft and gentle voice to the king. "I have given up all the pleasures of the palace. I have no attachment to anything here. I need no riches nor an army nor an entourage to follow me. I have promised to live in the forest like an inmate of the forest, living on fruits and roots as my mother has stipulated. Of what use will all this following be to me there? It is like a man who has given away an elephant and feels attached to the rope which is used to tie up the elephant. I do not need all these. I need but one thing and that is an apparel made of tree-bark. I also want a spade and a basket. I need nothing other than these."

A cry of distress rose like a wave and submerged the entire hall when Rama spoke thus.

16. KAIKEYI BRINGS THE VALKALAS

Before Rama had completed his request Kaikeyi went to her apartments and came out with the rough and coarse tree-bark which was to be the clothing for Rama for fourteen years. She gave it to Rama and said: "Here is what you asked for. Wear it." There was a deadly silence when Rama took it and, after getting rid of the silks he was wearing, dressed himself in the cloth given to him by his 'mother'. He looked like a tapasvin already and at the same time Lakshmana took up the other pieces of the valkala and dressed himself in them. The king was looking on and he was helpless.

Realising that another pair was brought for her sake, Sita took in her hands the valkalas held out to her by Kaikeyi. She turned them in her hands and tried in vain to wear them. With a nonplussed look on her face she spoke shyly to her husband and said: "Tell me, my lord, how do they wear it in the forest? I do not seem to be doing it properly." She was standing there, looking helplessly around with the cloth in her hand. She had wound one piece round her neck and the other was in her hand. Sita was looking embarrassed since all eyes were upon her and she could not wear it as it usually was to be worn. Rama came to her quickly and with his own blessed hands he draped it over the silk she was wearing. The sight was heart-breaking for the women of the harem and all eyes were wet as they saw Rama tying the valkala round Sita's waist. Some of them said: "Rama this young girl has not been banished to the forest. She does not have to undergo this punishment. Leave her behind with us. Take Lakshmana with you as your companion. But this young tender girl, Sita, is not meant to live in the forest and go through the many hardships of living there."

When he saw Sita dressed in tree-bark, Vasishtha was furious. He said: "Kaikeyi, you are a blot to the name of Dasaratha and to the name of Ashvapati. You have over-reached yourself in unwomanliness. You deceived the king and you are secure in the anticipation of being the queen-mother. You do not seem to set a limit to the atrocities you have been committing. Sita does not have to go to the forest. Let her be seated on the throne meant for Rama and rule the land of the Ikshvakus. It is said that a wife is one's own self taking another form. Accordingly Sita has every right to rule the kingdom. But this goddess among women is determined to live in the forest since her lord, Rama, is leaving for Dandaka. We will all follow Rama to where he goes and the forest will become a city. Ayodhya will be the forest.

"Kaikeyi, in your ambition to own the kingdom you have lost sight of one truth: you have not remembered the nature of Bharata. He will not be willing to accept the throne. I know these children of the king better than you do. Bharata and Shatrughna will wear tree-bark and deerskin too and they will live in the forest along with Rama. This city populated with trees and empty houses infested with rats and mice, can be ruled by you. Bharata will never accept the kingdom which you have won for him with so much trouble. You have done him wrong by this act of yours. There is no one in this world who is not devoted to Rama. At the moment, you must immediately give costly gems and ornaments to Sita, your son's wife and make her take off this hideous valkala. Only Rama has been asked to wear them in the forest since that was what you asked for. Sita will live in the forest since she wants to. But she need not wear anything else but the silks she is accustomed to."

The king who was now past all caring, had no desire to live nor talk to anyone. He said: "Kaikeyi, Sita should not wear the valkala which you have made my son wear. She is a young girl accustomed to nothing but luxury and, as my revered Guru said, she should not be made to dress in this coarse cloth. What has she done that she should be made to stand like a mendicant in the midst of so many people?

"This daughter of Janaka must at once take out and throw away what she has been made to wear. Sita should not be subjected to any more indignities. You have banished Rama to the forest. Is that not enough for you? Why do you want to add to my misery by these cruel acts?"

Dasaratha fell back exhausted on his couch. Rama spoke to him again and said: "My lord, my mother is old and she is devoted to you. Never once has she done anything to displease you. She will be very unhappy when she is parted from me and it is up to you to take good care of her. Unless you help her to bear it, my mother will not be able to bear this separation from me and she may lose her life."

Dasaratha could not speak. He knew the moment had come when Rama would go. He wept loudly and spoke not a word. And he mumbled: "Evidently in my previous birth I have made several lives suffer. I must have parted the young ones from their parents, perhaps. And so I am suffering thus in this birth. Life refuses to leave my body since the lord has so willed it that one should die only when the time comes. That is why I am still alive in spite of the torture Kaikeyi has meted out to me. I am looking at my sons throwing away their silks and wearing this tree-bark. They are looking like two rishis. Because of this one woman who is eager to own the land, this large expanse of mud, the entire kingdom is suffering."

17. A PAINFUL FAREWELL

The king was silent for a while. He then sighed as though his entire frame shattered. He spoke to Sumantra: "Sumantra, yoke the best horses to my chariot and bring it to the doorway. Take this noblest of men and leave in the forest which is uninhabited by men. I realise now that even when a man follows the path of dharma, the acts he had performed in his previous birth will not leave him alone. That, I think, is the reason why I am allowing this child of mine to be banished to the forest. And who is doing it–his father who has never done a wrong thing in his life, and his mother who had been loving him till today!"

Sumantra dragged his steps away from the hall and, after a while, came back to the presence of the king. He stood with his eyes downcast and with tears in his eyes. The king and all the king's wives knew that the chariot was at the door.

The king wiped the tears from his eyes and spoke in a voice which had suddenly grown firm. He said: "Go to the treasury. Calculate how much will be needed for this long stay of Sita in the forest and bring silks and jewels to last her all that while. Make sure she has enough."

Kausalya and the other women of the harem dressed Sita in silks which were brought for her. The ornaments which they made her wear made Sita glow like the goddess Lakshmi and it seemed as though she had come down to the earth to bless them all. The entire place was as radiant as the sky, lit by the rays of the sun. Kausalya embraced her and said: "My child, Sita, in this world it is common to see a woman being affectionate towards her husband and serving him well as long as he is wealthy and prosperous. But when he is in straitened circumstances this same woman does not respect him. This is the nature of ordinary women. They have not learnt the real value of things and they bring shame to the houses they are born in and the houses they are wedded to. They are foolish. However, those who know the duties of a Pativrata consider the husband as the only god whom they should worship. And it goes without saying, Sita, that you are the most blessed amongst women. You have taken on yourself the banishment of your husband and you have decided to go with him wherever he goes. He should have been the king this morning and, instead, he has become a sanyasi. And you, without any sign of sadness on your sweet face, have decided to be with him. You are an example to all women and may you live long." Sita listened to the words of Rama's mother and said: "Mother, my father and my mother have taught me how to serve my husband in such a manner that he should always be pleased with me. You have also often told me about this. I have been reminded of my duty now, by you. I will remember all that I have been told and I assure you, I will do as you have asked me to. I will not be like the women of meagre intelligence who slight their husbands when they are in trouble. Even as the moonlight will not exist without the moon, I will not swerve from dharma. The Veena will be mute without the strings. The chariot cannot move unless it has wheels. And a woman, if she is blessed with many children even, will not be happy if she is not with her husband. A father's gift will be limited: mother's will be limited too and so will be that of the son. But a husband gives his all to his wife. How can a wife do anything else but love him and honour him. Mother, I promise you I will honour and obey my husband. He is my god and he is my everything."

Even in the midst of all her sorrow, Kausalya smiled with happiness at the good fortune of her son who had been blessed with such a wife. Rama came near his mother. He made pradakshina to her and his voice faltered a bit when he said: "Mother, do not grieve too much. You must be brave and take care of my unfortunate father. He is unhappy and he needs you. Mother, time will pass fast and my exile will come to an end. Like the night passing soon when one is asleep, these nine years and five will pass and you will see me come back to you."

He then took leave of his other mothers with humility and said: "Mothers, during these many years when you have known me I might have, knowingly or unknowingly, for fun or out of ignorance or familiarity, offended you. Forgive me and be patient with me. I wish to bid farewell to all of you and I wish to carry your blessings with me." There was nothing but sobs to be heard when Rama spoke thus. The palace which would, on other days, resound with the noise of drums, bugles and other warlike instruments which would resemble the roar of thunder, was now filled with the sobs of women and the tinkling of their jewels. Women were now crying openly and their cries filled the apartment and the palace too.

Rama with Sita and Lakshmana took leave of everyone. They stood with their palms folded and finally they came to Dasaratha. They made a pradakshina to him. Rama was extremely unhappy and in that frame of mind he went to his mother again and all three of them prostrated before her. Lakshmana fell again and again at the feet of his mother Sumitra and sought her leave. Sumitra blessed him and said: "My child, you have been born to live in the forest. I know it." She tried to speak calmly but her tears choked her and she had to stop. Controlling her pain Sumitra continued: "My child, you are dear to everyone. You are devoted to Rama and it is right that you should go with him and serve him. Never displease him and remember to follow the ancient rule: serving those who are elders is the surest path to heaven. Such a man will inherit the next world. Whether your elder brother is in the midst of wealth or in the grip of poverty and sorrow it should not affect your devotion in the least. This is the path which has been pursued by your ancestors and it should be adopted by you too. Your life on this earth will be fruitful and you can rest assured that in the next world there will be a place for you. You will have nothing but good fortune in your future life. Remember, my child, you should consider Rama to be Dasaratha, your father. Sita should be to you, what I am. The forest should seem to be Ayodhya to you. May you be happy always. Go, my child"

Sumantra stood before Rama even as Matali before Indra and said: "Rama, the chariot is at the door. Tell me where you want to go and I will take you there. According to the commands of the queen Kaikeyi Devi, your exile of fourteen years begins today."

They left the Hall. Sita first ascended the chariot and the brothers Rama and Lakshmana soon followed her into the chariot which was glistening with gold and gems. The gifts which the king had ordered for Sita and the weapons which were needed by the brothers were already placed in the chariot. Sumantra took his seat and the chariot began to move.

The streets were filled with men, women and children. Nothing was heard except the wail of the people. They rushed towards the chariot which was to carry their beloved Rama away from them and they walked with it. Rama listened to their injunction to Sumantra: "Pull the reins, Sumantra. Lead the horses slowly so that the chariot does not go fast. We want to see Rama as long as we can." Their comments on the behaviour of the king and the queen were painful to hear and Rama tried in vain to shut them out. His eyes were now filled with tears. He could not fight the affection of an entire city.

Dasaratha rushed to the doorway of palace saying: "Let my eyes follow my Rama as far as my eyes can see. Let me keep on looking at him until he is lost to my sight." Rama heard the wail of the king's wives in the harem and the faint voice of his father. He could bear the torture no more. He told Sumantra: "Go fast. Make the horses go faster and let me go away from here as soon as possible." The people around were compelling Sumantra to go slow and he did not know what to do. The king who saw the receding banner of the chariot fell down in a dead faint. Rama knew what was happening. He knew that the king tried to follow the chariot on foot and that he could not do so. Again and again he asked Sumantra to hurry. Rama could no longer bear to see his mother and his father who had reached the ultimate bourne of sorrow. His mother was now trying to follow the chariot like a cow which had been parted from its calf. "Rama! Rama!", said Kausalya and Rama could hear her piteous voice. The king had now regained consciousness and he was shouting to Sumantra: "Stop the chariot! Stop!".

Rama said: "Sumantra, go as fast as you can."

He then added: "Sumantra, I know the worry which is in your mind. You are afraid to disobey the king. When you get back, if he asks you why you did not obey him, tell him that because of the noise made by the people you were not able to hear his words."

The crowd followed the chariot and surrounded it on all sides. As for the king, he stood leaning against the doorway trying to follow the chariot and Rama with his eyes. He stood staring into empty space even after the chariot was lost to view.

The king would not leave the spot where he stood with his eyes set on the path which Rama's chariot had taken. Even the dust had settled down and Rama had gone beyond the range of his vision. But still the king stood aching for a sight of his beloved son.

18. DASARATHA'S DESPAIR

It came to the mind of the king finally that Rama had really left him and gone away. He fell down and his queens rushed to hold him. Kausalya came and stood on his right and, Kaikeyi, on his left. Dasaratha looked at Kaikeyi with burning eyes and said: "Kaikeyi, you sinned against me and you have wished me ill. I do not consider you my wife any longer. Do not touch me. I cannot bear it. I do not want to set my eyes on you any longer, nor do I wish to see anyone who happens to be devoted to you. To you, this worthless wealth was greater than all the dharma which has been taught you from time immemorial. I have renounced you. Noble-minded Bharata has ever been devoted to his elders and he has never swerved from the path of righteousness. If, however, he should perchance be influenced by you, and accept the throne won for him by you, he shall not perform the funeral rites for me. I will disown him too."

Kausalya was standing by his side and she raised him up from the ground. Embracing him with her arms she stood silent by his side. They were both thinking of the same thing: the picture Rama presented dressed in tree-bark like a tapasvin. They imagined the progress of Rama on the streets of Ayodhya and at the outskirts of the city.

"Look, Kausalya," he said, "I can see clearly the track of the chariot which bore away my child from me. He is lost to my sight. He will spend tonight on a bed made up of twigs and leaves. The rishis in the forest will have the thrill of being with this child of mine who has been abandoned by his father. Janaka's daughter who is as delicate as a flower will now walk on the ground and thorns will hurt her dainty feet. That child with the eyes of a deer will be frightened by the wild animals in the forest. Even their roar will make her tremble with fear. Kaikeyi, I hope you are happy now. I will die very soon and you, the widow of the king, can rule this land flowing with milk and honey." The king entered the palace with a face like that of one returning from the burning ghat after cremating a dear one.

Dasaratha looked around him and the palace which was empty without Rama. In a weak and faltering voice the king said: "Kausalya, you are the fortunate woman who bore Rama. Take me to your house. Maybe, my bruised heart will find some comfort there with you by my side."

He was carried to her house and there he was placed on a couch covered with costly silks. To him the world seemed empty like the sky without the moon. Rama had gone, and with him, Lakshmana and Sita. He wept loudly with both arms lifted up to the skies and cried: "Rama, you have left me and you have gone far away from me. Fortunate indeed will be those who live to see you come back. I would have gone long before that. I am certain of that." They sat together all though the night. Sleep had abandoned them and they sat talking about Rama and only about Rama. Dasaratha said "Kausalya, my eyes have not come back to me from the vision of Rama seated in the chariot and going away from me. I can see nothing. Touch me gently, my queen. I will find some comfort from the touch of you who is suffering as much as I am." Kausalya was lamenting the misfortune which had visited her and the king was listening helplessly. He knew that he had wounded her by the foolish promise he had given Kaikeyi but then, he was unhappy too.

Sumitra was listening to Kausalya and she said: "My dear sister, it is not meet that you should give in to grief like this. Rama has taken upon himself this banishment to make his father's words come true and he renounced the kingdom for the sake of this one wish: to save his father's name. He is a great and noble soul and nothing untoward will happen to him. Lakshmana is with him to serve him and Sita has gone with him. Wherever he may be, Rama will spread happiness and glory. There is no need for you to feel concerned about him. The sun, knowing the greatness of Rama, will not shed hot rays on the three of them when they walk in the forest. The god of wind will blow gently where they stay and they will always be happy and comfortable. The gods in the forest, the vana devatas, will protect them. The moon will embrace them during the night even as a father will and they will spend the nights happily. Both the princes are armed with the astras which Vishvamitra gave them. You know how the yajna of the sage was guarded by our children. They are powerful, sister, and there is no danger threatening them in the forest. Soon the time will come when they will be with us, covered with glory. Rama is a god among human beings and he is more glorious than the sun or Agni. Such a man is sure to be welcomed wherever the goes and you should not be concerned about his comforts. Abandon this sorrow and accept what has happened with a fortitude becoming the mother of Rama. All you have to do is to wait patiently. Rama will come to you and place his head on these your feet and clasp them in his hands."

Sumitra spoke words which were comforting to the grieving couple and Kausalya found a semblance of peace after she listened to her.

19. ON THE BANKS OF THE TAMASA

The citizens of Ayodhya walked along with the chariot which was bearing their dear Rama away from them. They could not reconcile themselves to the truth that Rama had been banished. They were still in a daze and they followed the chariot blindly. They kept asking Rama to return to the city and he spoke to them words of gentle persuasion and he beseeched them to let him go. Rama said: "If you have genuine affection for me, you must listen to my words. I ask all of you to give this same affection to Bharata who will soon be here to take up the reins of the kingdom. He is very good, sweet-natured and generous and righteous. He will rule just as well as my father has been doing all these years. He is wise beyond his age and he is gentle. He is valiant too and you need have no fear when he is your protector. He is endowed with all the qualities needed for ruling a kingdom. As for my going away, it is the command of my father and all of us will have to obey the king in everything. You should try to please the king and the only way to do so will be to let me go and to welcome the proposed coronation of Bharata."

It was of no avail. The more he spoke, the more they bewailed his departure. The crowd was unmanageable. They began to talk to the horses asking them to stop and to Sumantra asking him to pull the reins and to let Rama remain with them. Rama stopped the chariot and descended from it. He could not bear to sit in the chariot when old and weak men walked towards him with great difficulty. He began to walk in the street and Sita was with him and Lakshmana. The brahmins and the old men said: "Rama, we are coming with you. Look, we have brought our household fire with us and we mean to spend the fourteen years of your exile with you." One old man who had been given an umbrella as a gift in some religious function rushed up to Rama and said: "Take this umbrella and hide your face from the scorching sun. Your wife looks like a wilted flower; ask her to take shelter under this. We are all devoted to you, Rama. You should come back to the city or else, you should take all of us with you. We do not want to stay in Ayodhya which is without Rama."

Rama spoke not a word in reply but he walked with speed. The men of the city walked with him too. And, all on a sudden, as though Nature herself did not want Rama to proceed any further, the river Tamasa came into view and soon they reached the banks of the river. Sumantra descended from the chariot, unyoked the horses and made them drink the waters of the river.

Rama stood staring at the river and its course with a thoughtful frown on his face. He turned to Sita and Lakshmana who were by his side and said: "The first day of the exile is almost over. Night is soon to set in and we will spend the night here, on the banks of the Tamasa. Lakshmana, you must make preparations for it. Do not let your mind dwell on anything else and do not let sadness enter your heart at any cost. Look, Lakshmana, as night draws near, the animals and the birds are coming back to their dwelling places. Listen to the noises they are making. As for Ayodhya, the city of my father will be mourning the absence of her dear sons, I am sure.

"I am grieving for my beloved father and my mother. They will be weeping incessantly. My only comfort is the righteousness of Bharata. He will certainly take care of them and serve them in every way and he will try to make them forget their grief. I know Bharata and hence my confidence in the well-being of father and mother in the days to come. I approve of your coming with me, Lakshmana, Sita and I need you. You must be with me to protect Sita. I am spending the night here with just water to quench my thirst. I do not need any fruits or roots to eat. I do not feel like eating."

Rama asked Sumantra to see that the horses were properly grazed and taken care of.

The sun was almost setting and Rama sat on the bed of leaves prepared by Lakshmana. Rama with Sita by his side slept without any worry. His face was calm and peaceful as that of a child which was sleeping.

Lakshmana could not sleep, nor could Sumantra. They sat by and spoke of the happenings of the day and about the sudden reversals of fortune they had gone through. They spoke of none else but Rama and his many qualities which had made him so precious to everyone.

Rama woke up early and he thought of the immense crowd which was still under the spell of sleep. He turned to Lakshmana and said: "Look Lakshmana, look at these men. In their love for me they have given up everything and they have come here to the edge of the river. They have decided to go with us or else, to take me back with them. They will not let me proceed. I am sure of that. Let us, therefore, go far away from them in our chariot before they wake up from their sleep." Lakshmana agreed with him and they summoned Sumantra and asked him to yoke the horses quickly to the chariot.

They ascended the chariot and crossed the river easily. Rama descended from it and he told Sumantra: "I am afraid I have to adopt a ruse to deceive the people of my city. We will stay here. You lead the chariot towards the north. After proceeding thus in that direction for a muhurta, come back to me taking care that you leave no tracks. They will think that I have gone back to Ayodhya and will follow the track of the wheels. Once they go back, they will not return. They will be sorry that they have been deceived by me but it cannot be helped. I have to resort to this for the sake of their welfare. It is not right that they should spend years on end in the forest which they will surely do, once they wake up. Hurry, Sumantra, and do the needful."

In less than an hour the chariot had come back with Sumantra. Rama and Lakshmana with Sita seated themselves in the golden chariot. Strictly in accordance with the rules to be followed when a long journey is undertaken, Rama turned his face towards the north before getting into the chariot. They began their journey to the forest.

20. THE JOURNEY

They travelled fast and every moment was taking Rama farther and farther away from his beloved Kosala. They spent the night on the way and resumed the journey the next morning even as the east was lightening with the coming of dawn. They had passed several villages and cities by now. In the morning Rama saw that they had reached the southern outskirts of the land of Kosala. Rama stood silently looking at the land spread out before him: the fields with the ploughs, still and lonely in the morning light: the flowers which had just opened their eyes to a new day: the music made by the birds in the gardens. People had begun to walk out of their huts and homes and Rama with the others hid himself behind some trees lest they should be seen by someone.

The men were talking of him and of the injustice done to him by the king and Kaikeyi. He did not want to hear any more and quickly he got into the chariot and proceeded fast towards the south. They reached the river by name Vedasruti. The river was famed for its cool sweet water. They crossed the river and went on their journey. After a long while, they reached the banks of the river Gomati. Cows were grazing on either bank of the river which was coursing fast towards the ocean. They crossed Gomati also and another river, Syandika, lay across their path. All the way, Rama was describing to Sita the different countries they were passing and also their history: about how Manu, in ancient times, had made a gift of the land to his son Ikshvaku, their famed ancestor.

Rama was overcome with sorrow when he reached the banks of Syandika. He said: "Sumantra, I wonder when I will be able to hunt once more in the forests on the banks of my beloved Sarayu! When will I be reunited with my father and mother?" He paused for a moment and continued: "Hunting in the forest has been sanctioned even by Rajarshis. It is a pastime allowed to kings. But it must not harm innocent animals. Hunting on the banks of the river Sarayu was very dear to me." Rama then spoke about many things showing them the peculiarities of some of the countries and telling them about the background of these and thus time passed for them while they pursued the long journey to the forest.

They had reached the limits of the kingdom of Kosala. Rama stood with folded palms facing Ayodhya and said: "My beloved Ayodhya, I take leave of you and of the gods who guard you night and day. When I have discharged my duty to the king, my father, when I conclude my stay in the forest, I will come back to you and live happily with my father and mother." He raised his hands towards the heavens and, with his eyes filled with tears, he addressed the citizens and said: "I know how much you all love me. Permit me to go so that I will earn wealth: the only wealth which should be gained, wealth which goes by the name Dharma. Permit me to go. I will soon come back to you."

For a while no one spoke and the only noise which could be heard was the roar of the chariot as it rushed fast across the land of Kosala. Soon they had left Kosala far behind, the land which was the heritage of the descendants of Manu.

They reached the banks of the river Ganga, the divine river, known by the name Tripathaga since she flowed in the heavens, on the earth and in the nether world also: Ganga whose water was clear and clean without any moss covering it, which granted heaven to those who bathed in her since she cleansed them of all sins, who was worshipped as a goddess by the rishis. Ashramas were found in the neighbourhood and even apsaras from the heavens would often frequent the waters of Ganga. Devas, danavas and gandharvas were to be found there frequently.

The waves made sweet music along the banks and, at places, the white foam of the waves seemed to be the smile of the river, so beautiful was the sight. There were to be found whirlpools in some places and in other spots the river flowed placidly without a noise. At times, the roar of the river was deafening. The river had a beauty which was awe-inspiring and, born as she was at the feet of Narayana and descended from the matted locks of my lord Mahadeva, this queen among rivers was sacred to everyone.

On the banks of the river was a city by name Shringiberapura. Rama saluted the river and said: "Sumantra, we will spend the night here. There, by the side of the river I can discern a big tree and that will serve as a shelter for the night when we sleep. Let us spend some time watching this glorious sight, the river which is the foremost among all rivers." Lakshmana and Sumantra agreed to his suggestion and the horses were led to the tree which Rama had indicated. They descended from the chariot. Sumantra then unyoked the horses and, after leaving them free to graze, he went and stood in the presence of Rama.

21. GUHA, A CHIEFTAIN OF HUNTERS

Shringiberapura was a place which was ruled by Guha, a chieftain of hunters. It was well known that he was a great friend of Rama. He was a powerful king in his own way with a large army at his command. He heard that Rama had arrived in the neighbourhood and hastened towards the spot where Rama was, with his ministers and other attendants. Rama saw him approaching and went towards him to embrace him. They were good friends and the meeting between them was tender. After a while, Guha spoke to

Rama and said: "Rama, my friend, tell me what I should do to please you. This place is as much yours as Ayodhya. It is not often that one is fortunate enough to entertain a glorious guest like you." Guha had brought with him food and he spread what was a feast in front of Rama and said: "Welcome to you, great one! Please accept my hospitality. This kingdom is yours. Please stay with me and rule this kingdom. At the moment refresh yourselves with the different kinds of food I have brought for you. There is rice, milk and curds, honey, food and sweet dishes cooked in diverse ways. I have brought also mattresses for all of you. Please honour me by using them."

Rama smiled at Guha and said: "You have come all the way walking, to welcome me and you have so much affection for me that I am touched by your gesture." Embracing Guha again and again Rama said: "I am pleased to see you well and happy. I hope your kingdom is thriving and that your subjects are happy. As for this feast which you have spread out before me, I am afraid, Guha, I am not in a position to accept it. I have to refuse to partake of it. I have taken upon myself an oath to live the life of a tapasvin. I must wear tree-bark and deerskin and my food will be fruits and roots gathered by hand. You asked me how best you can please me. I will be immensely grateful to you if you will see to the feeding of these noble horses. They are very dear to my father and I should take good care of them till I need them no more. They should be returned safe."

Rama, with his upper cloth tied round his waist, entered the waters and offered the evening worship to the sun who was setting. He then drank water which had been brought to him by Lakshmana. Rama sat on the bed of dried leaves which had been prepared by Lakshmana and he smiled with affection when Lakshmana washed his feet, wiped them with his cloth and massaged them.

Rama lay down with Sita and soon he was asleep. Sumantra and Lakshmana sat around, watching them. Guha had his bow and arrows in his hand and he thought that he should guard Rama. None of the three slept that night. The very night seemed to keep jealous watch over this noble prince who, till then, had never known what discomfort was, who was the son of a king and who now slept on this bed of dried leaves because of the vagaries of Fate.

Guha was sorry for Lakshmana who was keeping awake and standing guard over Rama. He said: "Child, Lakshmana, here is a bed which I have made for you. Why should you not relax your limbs and rest for a while? You are accustomed to comfort and we will guard Rama tonight and all through the night. You need have no worry. Forget your cares for a while and sleep, my son. In this world there is no one dearer to me than Rama and I swear that in the name of Truth itself. Because of him I have learnt the lesson that in this world the accumulation of Dharma is the only wealth worth earning and not the riches of the earth. With my many followers I will guard my dear friend. Nothing can happen in this place without my knowing about it. I have, at my command, a large army."

Lakshmana said: "Guha, my friend, you are indeed very noble and full of affection for us. I do not have the least worry about the safety of Rama when you are here, you who seem to me to be the very image of Dharma. Tell me, how can I sleep or rest after seeing my beloved brother sleeping on the ground with his wife, Sita? How can I think of hunger or thirst or sleep when my heart is ready to break at the sight of this noblest among men lying like a mendicant on the ground? This warrior who can vanquish Indra himself in war, is now sleeping on a bed made of leaves. Rama has no equal either in the noble qualities which abound in him, or in the wealth of learning, or in the knowledge of the codes of Dharma. My father, the king, will not live very long after his son's departure to the forest. The world will soon lose her lord. That beautiful city Ayodhya will soon look desolate having lost her lord. I am sure of it. The palace will be without any noise since the women would have collapsed in sheer exhaustion after they have cried their eyes out. I doubt very much if the king and our mothers Kausalya and Sumitra, will survive this night. My mother, at least, may perhaps live to see Shatrughna, her other son. But Kausalya, separated from her only son, will die of grief. My poor father, the king, has lost sight of his beloved son who is a divine being so pure and sinless is he. How can life remain in my father's body after all this? Once the king is gone, Kausalya Devi will also die and my mother is also sure to follow them. My father could not realise his desire to crown Rama as Yuvaraja. What has happened, has happened. Nothing can change the course of events and the king will certainly die. Fortunate will be the son who will be able to perform the funeral rites to his father. Do you think the king will survive this calamity? Do you think we will be able to see him after we return from the Dandaka? Will the day ever come when we enter the city of Ayodhya having completed our exile?" Lakshmana was beside himself with grief. Guha shed tears of sympathy and he could not speak a word. He was overcome with sadness and compassion for the young prince who was so devoted to his brother. And the night passed slowly.

The song of the birds woke up Rama and soon they were standing on the banks of the Ganga. Rama said: "Lakshmana, the sun is about to rise. The birds are making such sweet music the heart feels uplifted with joy. I can hear from a distance the raucous sound made by the peacocks. Let us perform the worship of the sun and then cross this sacred river who is rushing towards her lord, the sea."

Lakshmana conveyed the wishes of Rama to Guha and Sumantra, and came back to Rama. Guha summoned his attendants and said: "Get a boat ready. Take good care that she is strong and well-built. She should be able to cross this turbulent Ganga without any effort. Rama and the other two must have a comfortable crossing."

The boat was soon brought to the edge of the river. Guha went to Rama and said: "Rama, my friend, I have got a boat ready for your crossing. Is there anything else I can do for you before you leave?"

"Guha, you have given me all that I asked for," said Rama. "Help Lakshmana load the boat with the weapons." The brothers accompanied by Sita took up their bows and arrows and their swords were strapped to their waists. And they walked towards the river bank where the boat was waiting to take them across.

Sumantra went to the presence of Rama and stood before him. Rama touched him with his right hand and said: "Sumantra, go back to the presence of the King."

Sumantra was weeping and Rama said: "Do not grieve, Sumantra. The king needs you and you must stay by his side. I have no need of a chariot any more. From here onward I must walk into the forest. You should go back to Ayodhya."

Sumantra spoke with pain in his heart. He said: "Rama, it has never happened before in the line of the Ikshvakus. A prince with his wife and brother is planning to live in the forest for the duration of fourteen years. I see now that proficiency in the study of the Vedas, performance of all religious rites, which are meant to please the devas, are all futile when one like you has been made to suffer thus. Fortunate indeed will be the dwellers in the forest who will see the three of you. You will seem to them to be

Narayana Himself who has deigned to descend to the earth to grace her. As for us, we are the most unfortunate of all human beings. We have sinned in our previous births and we are suffering for it." He stopped for a moment and continued: "Because of Kaikeyi we are doomed to suffer eternal sorrow." Contemplating on the separation from Rama, Sumantra could not contain himself and he could not control either his grief or his tears. He washed his eyes with water and still his tears were flowing. Rama spoke to him in a soft gentle voice. "Sumantra, I am yet to see one who is as devoted to the family as you are. It is up to you to take care of my father and help him to bear the pain at parting from me. My old father could not achieve the desire in his heart and he is sorely distressed by it. You know how firm I am in following the dictates of Dharma. Because of the compulsion to please Kaikeyi my father the king had to take recourse to this step and I have to do as I am bid. He will be very unhappy and you should not abandon him at this stage. My father has never suffered like this before. He is aged and he deserves to be honoured by everyone. Please convey this message to him from me: 'Father, I am not in the least unhappy about leaving Ayodhya or about the life in the forest which I have undertaken. Neither Sita nor Lakshmana are unhappy. After the lapse of fourteen years we will return to the city and take the dust of your blessed feet. There is no doubt about the happiness that is in store for us when we will be re-united.' Sumantra, tell him that I spoke these words after saluting him."

After a while Rama spoke again. He said: "Give this message to the king. Then convey my respects to my mother Kausalya and Sumitra and Kaikeyi and all the mothers I have in the palace. Tell them that I am happy and well and so are Sita and Lakshmana, who also send their respects. You should be the one to bring my brother Bharata to the king. You should advise him to conduct himself in a manner which will please the king and make him happy. When Bharata is crowned and the country has a Yuvaraja, this grief in your mind will abate slowly. Tell Bharata that I have asked him to be equally affectionate towards all the wives of the King. Tell him in my words: 'Bharata, you should treat Sumitra with the same affection which you have for Kaikeyi. Even like her, my mother should be the object of your affection. These two women are quite unhappy because of the absence of their sons. You should pay special attention to them. Rule the kingdom righteously and earn a place for yourself in the world to come.' " Sumantra refused to be comforted. He said: "Rama, Ayodhya will now be like a woman who has lost her child. How is it possible for me to enter the city without you? This chariot which had you when it left the city will now be empty and the entire city will set up a wail of woe. The horses will refuse to pull the empty chariot, I can assure you. I will not go back to Ayodhya. Please take me with you. If you do not let me come with you and go away, I will throw myself into fire and kill myself. I will be of help to you, Rama, in the forest. I did not have the good fortune to be the charioteer when you were crowned. Let me at least do that duty in the forest."

Rama's eyes were wet because of the love his charioteer had for him. He said: "Sumantra, you do not have to tell me how much you love me. I know it only too well and I also know that you would like to be with me all the time. But I have to send you back to Ayodhya. I have a reason for it. I will tell you. My young mother Kaikeyi will see you enter the city without me and Sita and Lakshmana. Then, and only then, will she be sure that I have reached the forest. She will cease to doubt the words of my father. Or else she will persist in torturing the king by calling him untruthful. My younger mother will see her son established on the time-honoured throne which my father has graced all these years and she will be happy. That is my only desire. For my sake and for the sake of the king you should go back."

Rama then turned to Guha and said: "My friend, I should no longer dwell in palaces or in places which are frequented by men. I have to take up the life of a dweller in an ashrama and that is the rule set down for me. I must make myself fit to dwell in the midst of tapasvins and I must wear my hair as a 'jata'. Please bring me the milk of the Nyagrodha tree so that I can twist my hair into a tangled mass." Rama and Lakshmana had adopted the tree-bark in the palace itself and now their guise as tapasvins was complete. Seeing them with their 'jata' Sumantra wept loudly. Rama spoke to Guha and said: "It is only too well known that ruling a country is not easy. I wish you well. I take leave of you and Sumantra.

They stood on the banks of the river Ganga and Rama said: "Lakshmana, assist Sita to get into the boat. Hold it firmly until she is seated. Then you should enter the boat." After they had seated themselves in the boat Rama set his foot into the boat. Guha prompted the oarsmen to steer them safely across the river. Rama closed his eyes and prayed for the success of his arduous undertaking. He prayed that he should ever please the Lord by his actions. He prayed that he should win a good name and fame as a righteous man. Rama and Lakshmana touched the water and did Achamana. Again he took farewell of Sumantra and Guha who were standing on the bank of the river with swimming eyes. Rama asked the oarsmen to untie the boat and to set sail. The boat began to move and it moved fast.

When they had reached the middle of the river Sita prayed to Ganga with folded palms. She said: "Devi, Ganga, please grant that this lord of mine, Dasaratha's son, reaches the other bank safe. Please grant that after fourteen years we should, all three of us, return here safe. I will worship you again after we return. I have no doubt that my prayers will be answered since you are ever bountiful with your gifts. You are famed in all the three worlds. You are the favoured queen of the ocean. I prostrate before you and when we come back and when my lord goes back to his city I will give away gifts of gold and cows to brahmins, to please you. Grant that we return safe to Ayodhya."

Soon they reached the southern banks of the Ganga. Rama abandoned the boat and sent it back to Guha. He then spoke to Lakshmana: "You should be alert always, Lakshmana. We should remember to protect Sita. You walk first and Sita will follow you. I will walk behind her and thus we will proceed. This will be the best way to pursue our journey. If something happens in spite of all caution it will then be beyond our power to rectify it. In a mood of affection for me Sita has undertaken this difficult life in the forest. It is not going to be easy for her.

"From here onwards, there will be no habitation and, as such, the paths will be difficult to follow. There will be ups and downs and we must guard her very diligently."

And so they entered the forest–Lakshmana in the lead, Sita in the middle and Rama bringing up the rear.

Sumantra, who was watching them as he stood on the northern bank of Ganga, stood still and watched until they were out of sight. Wiping his tears he turned away from the southern bank his eyes which could see nothing any longer..

22. THE THIRD NIGHT OF THE EXILE

When evening approached, the three travellers, Lakshmana, Sita and Rama reached a big tree whose shade seemed to be large enough to accommodate all three of them. They watched the sun set and then sat down under the tree. Rama said: "Lakshmana, this is the first night we are spending outside the country. We do not have even the company of Sumantra. I can see that your emotions are still beyond your control. That should not be so. Compose yourself. Tonight we can spend here spreading the leaves on the ground."

They lay down on the ground and spent the night conversing about Ayodhya and the king. Rama said: "The king will be sunk in sorrow tonight. As for Kaikeyi, she will be extremely happy since her desire has been achieved. A sudden fear is now frightening me. Once Bharata is made the Yuvaraja, will Kaikeyi leave my father alive? What will my unfortunate father do, alone as he is, without me by his side, old in body, unhappy in mind and entirely in the power of Kaikeyi because of his love for her? Lakshmana, when I think of this change in the mind of the king and his sorrow, I feel that Kama is more powerful than Dharma, Artha and Moksha. Or else how could he have banished me to the forest? For the sake of his wife which father will abandon his son who has ever been obedient and loving towards him? Even an ordinary illiterate man will hesitate to do so. I hope Bharata will be able to rule the great Kosala unassisted by anyone. If, perchance, my father loses his life, because of the sorrow caused by separation from me, Bharata will have to be alone with the burden of ruling the kingdom. King Dasaratha who has sacrificed his Dharma and Artha because of his Kama which held him under its sway will, I am afraid, leave us soon.

"Kaikeyi, who will be deluded by the power which will be hers will, perhaps, banish our mothers and their dependents. Lakshmana, I am worried about them. Why should Sumitra suffer for my sake? I think you should go back to Ayodhya. I will have Sita with me and we will live together in the forest. You should go back and protect your mother and mine from the possible tyranny of Kaikeyi. She hates my mother and she is likely to be cruel enough to do injustice to the two queens. You must go back and see that Bharata does not overstep Dharma. I see the urgency, Lakshmana.

Perhaps, in some previous birth, my mother had separated some mothers from their sons and that is why she is suffering now. At this age when she should be served by me, whom she has brought up with such loving care, she has been separated from me. I am unfortunate since I am not able to serve my parents at this stage of their lives. I have been the cause of immense grief to my mother. I am her only son and it is my duty to be by her side. But I am far away and she is grieving for me. Kausalya, my mother, is the most unfortunate woman. Lakshmana, you know me and my prowess only too well. If I had so desired, I could have, single-handed, made Ayodhya mine and even the entire earth. But one should not misuse one's power. Do you agree? I am afraid of being called an Adharmi and I desire a place in the heavens. That was the sole reason which made me withhold my wrath and renounce the kingdom." Rama was shedding tears at the thought of his mother and his father and the happenings in Ayodhya and so he sat, silent, thoughtful, and to Lakshmana he seemed like a fire which had burnt itself to ashes: like the ocean which had become silent. He spoke in a very soft and comforting voice: "You are right. There will be no joy in the minds of the people of Ayodhya and the city will be sunk in gloom. You are not there and to them it will be like the sky which has no moon to brighten it. Rama, it is not meet that you should grieve so much. You are making Sita and me sad too. Neither Sita nor your servant Lakshmana can live without you even for a moment. Like fish which die when they are taken out of water we will die soon.

"But one thing is certain, brother. I have no desire to see my father, or my brother Shatrughna or my mother. I do not desire even heaven if its gates should be held open for me, unless you are with me, What has happened has happened, and no amount of thought or tears can help us to correct it. Bharata is sure to take good care of our aged father and our mothers too. Do not grieve too much. If you are unhappy so will we be, and who is to comfort us?"

They took shelter under the spreading Nyagrodha tree and spent the night in peace. Rama found great comfort in the words spoken by Lakshmana. He told him: "My beloved Lakshmana, I have shed my grief about my father and my mother. I should not have asked you to go back to Ayodhya. I need you by my side even as you need me. Let us, together, spend the stipulated number of years in the forest happily."

In the midst of that wide land which had no inhabitants except the birds and animals, the two princes slept under the tree and they looked like lions in the caves of a mountain: noble-looking and fearless. So passed their first night in the forest.

23. THE ASHRAMA OF BHARADVAJA

After spending a night peacefully under the shade of the Nyagrodha tree Rama, Sita and Lakshmana rose up early in the morning. There was a feeling of holiness in their minds and silently they worshipped the rising sun chanting the Gayatri. They walked fast entering the very heart of the forest. Sights which they had never seen before confronted their eyes and they walked happily feasting their eyes on the novel scenes and beautiful trees and flowers unknown to city dwellers. Sita was greatly excited at the sight of it all and Rama would smile indulgently whenever she pointed out something new to him.

They travelled towards the sacred region of Sangama, where the river Yamuna entered Ganga. The path was not very difficult and the sun had not reached the high heavens either. Rama was looking around for a place to rest since the sun was now fast climbing in the sky. He said: "Lakshmana, look there, in the distance. Close to the sacred spot Sangama where the golden waters of the Ganga merge with the midnight blue of the Yamuna, I can perceive a plume of smoke. I gather there is an ashrama there and rishis must be living in that ashrama. I am sure we have reached the sacred spot Sangama or Prayaga, since the roar of the impact of the two rivers can be heard. I am almost sure it is the ashrama of the great sage Bharadvaja which we are nearing."

They walked fast unmindful of the heat of the sun which was rising steadily higher and higher in the sky.

All on a sudden a cool breeze set in indicating that the sun was wheeling towards the west and, when it was almost setting they arrived at the ashrama of Bharadvaja.

Rama went to the vicinity of the ashrama. For a moment the birds and the deer in the ashrama were startled by the arrival of strangers. The three of them stood some distance from where the rishi resided. They were eager to meet him and pay their respects. They entered the ashrama, prostrated before Bharadvaja and announced themselves. He was a great rishi, so rich in tapas that he was able to know the past, the present and the future. He was well-read and was greatly respected by all rishis. He was bent on meditation and he had performed all the many types of tapas. He had, in his ashrama, many disciples who were studying the sacred lore and the shastras under his guidance.

Rama said: 'My lord, we are the sons of King Dasaratha who rules over Kosala. This is my brother Lakshmana. She is Sita, my wife, and she is the daughter of Janaka. She has accompanied me to the forest. My father has commanded me to live in the forest and this my brother, in his affection for me, has decided to accompany me. We will have to live like the rishis there in the Dandaka forest to which I am proceeding as per the wishes of my father. We have come to you to ask you for your blessings."

Bharadvaja listened to the words of Rama. He spoke softly and affectionately to them and after their meagre repast he indicated to them a place where they could rest and spend the night. Peopled as it was by deer and birds as well as other rishis, the ashrama welcomed Rama. The great sage was extremely happy to have them as his guests. The young princes were seated before the rishi. Bharadvaja said: "Finally, after waiting a long time, I have been able to see you here, Rama. With my inner eye I have seen that this banishment is for no fault of yours.

"Look at this ashrama and the beautiful spot where it is situated. The kshetra is sacred, this Sangama where the two great rivers mingle. If you so desire, you can spend your time here."

Rama pondered for a moment and said: "I am honoured by your invitation. But my lord, it will not be right. If the people of Ayodhya come to know of the fact that I am here, they will come here often to see me since this ashrama is not too far away from the city. To see me and Sita they will be making frequent journeys to this place and it is not right. This is the sole reason why I have to deny myself the happiness of staying in these glorious surroundings. Please suggest to us a place where we can be away from people, where Sita can pursue her worship of the Lord with no one to disturb her."

Bharadvaja was convinced that Rama spoke the truth when he voiced his fear about the nearness of the city to the ashrama. He said: "Rama, ten krosas from here is a mountain by name Chitrakuta. It is as beautiful as the Gandhamadana mountain. All around this Chitrakuta are trees and waterfalls and lakes which will please the eye. It is inhabited by rishis and it is a hill famed for the number of monkeys dwelling there. Once a man sets his eyes on the peaks of Chitrakuta his mind will never dwell on unholy thoughts and he will be blessed. Several rishis have attained their salvation after performing tapas in Chitrakuta. I consider this hill to be the ideal place for your dwelling, next, of course, to this ashrama where you are welcome to stay."

The rishi entertained them with great gladness in his heart. He knew who Rama really was and it was to him a blessing that Rama had graced his ashrama. After they had conversed on various topics they found that night had set in and Rama with Sita and Lakshmana spent a very happy night there in that sacred place.

In the morning Rama approached the rishi who was like Agni, so radiant was he because of his tapas. He said: "Entertained by your graciousness, we spent the night very happily in your ashrama. Please grant us leave to proceed further on our journey."

All through the night the rishi's thoughts had been with Rama and his proposed stay in Chitrakuta. He said: "I am of opinion that you should proceed to Chitrakuta. It is full of fruit trees and overflowing with honey. It is a blessed mountain and very picturesque. It is famed among the rishis as a spot which has granted them salvation. Elephants and deer are numerous there. Sita and you can wander on the banks of the river, near the waterfalls, on the mountain tops. The caves will be new for Sita and the slopes too. You will always hear the music made by the sparrows and koils. This beautiful Chitrakuta will be the ideal place for you."

The princes were ready to leave. The rishi blessed them by reciting special verses meant for those going on a journey and he went with them a short distance as a father will. Bharadvaja told Rama: "When you reach the Sangama where the two rivers meet, proceed towards the east and walk along the banks of the Yamuna. Walk along the path which is well-worn by constant usage and when you reach a possible place which you think fit, make a raft and cross the river. After crossing the river you must still pursue your course until you come to a Nyagrodha tree. This tree is a sacred tree. It has been worshipped by Siddhas too and it is named "Shyama". You cannot miss it since it is very big and occupies a place which cannot be passed without your seeing it. Let Sita make a Pradakshina to it and offer prayers to the tree. When she has worshipped the tree you can all rest a while or go further into the forest. If you travel a distance of another krosa you will reach a forest filled with Palasa and Badari trees. The forest will be dark because of the bamboos growing along the banks of Yamuna. The path inside the forest is very beautiful. It is kind to the feet and you do not find the hardships of the forest there. I have often walked in that path."

Rama listened to the directions given by Bharadvaja and said: "I will follow the path indicated by you." They took leave of the rishi who bade farewell to them and Bharadvaja went back to his ashrama, his mind still filled with thoughts of Rama and the time he had spent with him.

When the rishi had left Rama said: "Lakshmana, the sage Bharadvaja is very gracious towards us. We are fortunate to have found such a godfather to guide us." Talking of the rishi and the picturesque Chitrakuta which they were impatient to reach, the brothers, with Sita walking between them, walked along the banks of the Yamuna. The waters of the river were flowing rapidly and they were looking for a suitable place where they could cross the river. Soon they reached a spot where the turbulence of the river was not so apparent. They asked Sita to rest under a tree. Together they collected dried wood, bamboos, soft grass and soon they made a raft. They spread grass on it and made it comfortable. Lakshmana collected soft and pliable creepers and weaving them together he made a beautiful seat for Sita. Rama made Sita climb on to the raft and she sat down on the seat made for her. By the side of Sita, Rama and Lakshmana placed their weapons, the basket, the spade and the clothes and jewels which the king had given Sita. They pushed the raft into the water and then got on to it. Slowly they steered it in the waters and Sita prayed to Yamuna even as she did to Ganga at the beginning of their journey.

Soon they reached the opposite bank, the southern bank. Abandoning the raft they walked further along the banks which were known by the name 'Yamunavana'. Very soon they reached the Nyagrodha tree which the rishi had told them about. The shade was extremely cool and pleasant since the tree was dense with green leaves. Sita went towards the tree and made Pradakshina as she had been told by Bharadvaja. She said: "I salute you, O holy tree! Please make my husband succeed in his undertaking. Grant us that we return to Ayodhya safe and see our elders."

Rama was watching her all the while and said: "Come, let us not tarry. Lakshmana, you lead and Sita will walk after you. I will follow her. Remember Lakshmana, if, on the way, Sita admires any flower or fruit, you must at once make haste and get it for her. She should be kept happy."

They decided not to spend any time near the tree but began the last lap of their journey. But one krosa more, and they would reach their destination. Rare flowers and trees and creepers would meet her eyes and Sita would promptly ask Rama about them. Rama would reply her with enthusiasm which was equal to hers and often she would be given a branch with clusters of the flowers by Lakshmana. Sita was thrilled at the sight of the river with its sandy banks, the birds and flowers floating on it and with the music of the birds and the running water.

They covered the distance of a krosa and walked in search of a place to stay. Soon they discerned a spot on the river bank. It was very charmingly located and peacocks and monkeys were sporting there. The long trek had tired them and it was decided that the night should be spent in that lovely spot on the river bank.

24. CHITRAKUTA AT LAST

When they woke up in the morning, for a moment they stood spell-bound, so breath-taking was the beauty of the place. Rama sounded happy and excited. He said: "Lakshmana, listen to the noise made by the inmates of the forest! Come, let us continue our search for the place to live in: the mountain by name Chitrakuta." Lakshmana had already shed the drowsiness of sleep and he was not tired either. They began walking in the path indicated by Bharadvaja. Rama was showing to Sita the beautiful trees and flowers which were all along the way. He said: "Sita, look! the Palasa trees have shed all their leaves during the cold season and now, when the flowers have bloomed on the branches, the trees look as though they are burning with crimson flames. Look at this tree laden with fruit. I am sure I can spend my entire lifetime living on these fruits. They are so luscious. Lakshmana, see there! Every tree has a beehive in it and each is so large! They look like small boats hung from the tree branches.

"This tiny bird is singing and the peacock is answering in its rough voice. The ground is strewn with forest flowers and the scent is intoxicating. We have almost reached Chitrakuta mountain. We are near enough to discern the herds of elephants. I am certain we will be very happy on the hill surrounded by the trees."

Very soon they reached the beautiful mountain Chitrakuta. They ascended the hill slowly and all the while Rama was looking around for a place fit enough for them to built a hermitage. The hill was as Bharadvaja had described: a thousand different types of birds were there. Flowers and fruits could be seen everywhere and waterfalls made music all around them. Rama said: "This is indeed a very beautiful spot and we are fortunate that we were sent here by sage Bharadvaja. I can see the ashramas of rishis scattered round the hill. We can live here without any intruder disturbing our peaceful existence."

They came across the ashrama of Valmiki and they visited him. He welcomed them and he said: "Rama, I know why you have come to the forest. I am glad you have decided to live here where the rishis have made their homes."

"I will do so," said Rama. After spending some time with the rishi they took leave of him and went on their way. Rama told Lakshmana: "My beloved brother, collect some sturdy and straight logs of wood. Make sure that they are not from trees which are forbidden for building an ashrama. I like this particular spot. You must build for me a hermitage here."

Lakshmana hastened to obey his brother's commands. He gathered the wood and very soon he completed the construction of the hermitage. It was built very well and roof had a covering of straw and grass. Lakshmana stood before Rama as though he were asking him to approve. Rama was extremely pleased with the skill with which Lakshmana had built the hut. He said: "We are planning to stay here for a length of time. We have to perform certain religious rites to avert evil from entering our ashrama. An offering has to be made in burning fire. You must get the flesh of a deer and we will make the offering to the God of fire. It is the proper thing to do and we must obey the dictates of custom." Lakshmana brought the flesh of a deer which he killed and at the behest of Rama he cooked it.

Rama knew that it was an auspicious day and that it would be a good day to begin living in the new house. The ritual was called *Vastu Shanti* which Rama was so particular about observing. He bathed and recited all the verses meant for the ritual. He prayed to all the devas and, after offering the flesh of the deer into blazing fire, Rama entered the hermitage. He was very contented. He prayed to the gods Rudra, Narayana and the Vishvedevas. After it was all over Rama bathed again.

Lakshmana had assigned different parts inside the hermitage for different purposes. There was a place for performing the daily puja and there was a sheltered portion where Rama could rest. The three of them entered the ashrama after worshipping all the gods of the forest and the gods who governed the fates of men. Rama was pleased with Lakshmana and he felt that their ashrama was extremely beautiful.

Rama looked like one of the gods in the divine hall by name Sudharma. They were happy there, surrounded as they were by nature on all sides. Food they had in abundance and the river Malyavati, which flowed near their ashrama was ever making a rustling noise which pleased the ear.

They were not unhappy at the thought that they were away from the city and that they were living in the forest: so peaceful was life in Chitrakuta.

25. SUMANTRA RETURNS TO AYODHYA

After the departure of Rama, Guha and Sumantra stood on the banks of the river Ganga for a long time conversing on the tragic events which had taken place with so much suddenness. Guha heard from his men about Rama's proceeding to the ashrama of Bharadvaja and of his going to the mountain by name Chitrakuta where he had decided to stay.

Sumantra took leave of Guha and, after yoking the horses to the chariot, he turned his face towards Ayodhya. He travelled fast and it took him three days to reach the city. Evening had set in when he reached Ayodhya and as he had imagined, there was no activity to be seen in the streets. The city seemed to have been sick and gone to sleep out of exhaustion: so silent were the streets, empty as they were of men. There was a silence which was very frightening and Sumantra entered the city gates and someone heard the chariot. The street was soon filled with men and women and children who rushed towards Sumantra asking him: "Where is Rama? Have you not brought him with you?" "No," said Sumantra. "I left him on the banks of the Ganga and I have been sent back by him."

Without speaking to anyone, with a downcast face, Sumantra drove fast towards the palace of the king. He descended at the doorstep and entered the glorious mansion. The women saw him enter and they knew that he had left Rama in the forest. Tears welled up in their eyes.

Sumantra went to the chambers where the king was and he entered it. He saw the king, approached him and, after prostrating before him, he stood silent. Dasaratha looked at him and his eyes were questioning. Sumantra recounted to him everything about Rama in detail and he ended the recital with the scene when he had to leave them on the banks of the river Ganga. He had to stop since the king had fainted. Kausalya and Sumitra raised up the sorrowing king and tried to make him regain consciousness.

Sumantra looked at the king. Three days had made it impossible to recognise him. Dasaratha was changed. He was a picture of woe and repentance and every sigh which escaped his lips seemed to shatter his entire frame. It was a pathetic sight to see the king grieve thus for his son. He turned his lustreless eyes on Sumantra and asked him: "Tell me once again how my son walked all the way to the forest. How did he sleep? How could he bear the hardness of the ground? Did Rama send me any message? What did Lakshmana say and Sita? Talk to me about Rama and I may find a semblance of peace, of comfort from your words."

Sumantra gave Rama's message to the king and added: "The prince, Lakshmana, however, was angry. He said: 'What was the fault which the king found in my brother that he should have banished him to the Dandaka forest? The king decided to please Kaikeyi Devi and as a result we have been made to suffer. Because of this unjust behaviour of the king I refuse to think of him as my father. Rama is my father, master, brother and the god whom I worship. Rama was dear to everyone. He is righteous and by sending him to the forest the king has alienated everyone from himself. How will he command respect as a king from now on?"

"Sita was looking dazed and stood silent. She never spoke a word but stood looking at her husband. Rama had tears in his eyes when I bade farewell to him. And Sita too looked at me with her eyes filled with tears. They crossed the river Ganga in a boat which Guha placed at their disposal and I stood on the banks of the river watching the boat until they landed on the southern bank. Before they went in the boat the princes who were already dressed in Valkalas asked Guha for the milk of the Nyagrodha and, even as I was watching, they matted their hair into a tangled mass and they looked like young rishis. When they had landed on the other bank, Lakshmana walked first and Sita went after him. Rama walked behind her and thus, in single file, they walked away and I watched until I could see no more. I yoked the horses to the chariot and hurried to your presence, my lord. When I entered the city Ayodhya was dismal. I was not welcomed by anyone since I was the one who took Rama away from the city."

The king was listening and he spoke nothing for a while. His mind was lost in thoughts of his son and he imagined the picture which Sumantra had presented to him so vividly. He spoke at last in a faltering voice: "This greatest of all calamities has befallen the House of the noble kings because of me and my thoughtlessness. Sumantra, take me to Rama. I cannot live without Rama."

Dasaratha was beside himself with grief. And Kausalya sat with tears coursing down her cheeks. She spoke not a word and so they sat, the old king and his wives, Sumitra and Kausalya, the bereaved mothers,

After some time Dasaratha turned his eyes on Kausalya and said: "Kausalya, I ask you to forgive me. I fold my palms thus and ask you again and again to forgive me for this my unjust action. You have always been just, kind and good even to your enemies. You are generous at heart. Do not be angry with me. I am suffering already and do not add to my misery by your displeasure."

Kausalya was shocked by the words of the king. She spoke to him in a kind and gentle voice and said: "Do not do this my lord. A husband should never ask his wife for forgiveness. It is wrong. A woman whose husband does so will be unfit for the next world. I am familiar with the rules of conduct and, if I have said anything to hurt you, it is because of my sorrow at the separation from my child. You know, my lord, sorrow kills one's courage. It destroys the power to think properly. There is no enemy worse than sorrow since it has the power to annihilate all one's good qualities. When your enemies hurt you, you can fight back. But when the gods will that certain events should take place, we are helpless and we cannot alter the course of Fate. Five days have passed, since our child left us and went away and already it seems like five years. And thoughts of him only make sorrow increase more and more and it grows tenfold in the heart."

The sun's rays had lost their heat and they were being slowly withdrawn. The sun was setting and soon night set in. Out of sheer exhaustion King Dasaratha slept for some time.

After a while he woke up. Kausalya was there by his side. It was a tragic sight: the two old people sitting and talking about their son and crying again and again. Sumitra could not comfort them. Dasaratha was thinking back on the glorious life he had led and about this sad end to it. He was certain in his mind that he would not live after this calamity which had visited him. As he looked back on his eventful life he was able to remember something which had happened when he was a young man. He looked at Kausalya for a long moment. His eyes were sad and tender. He decided to tell her about it.

26. THE CURSE OF A RISHI

As Kausalya had mentioned, it was the sixth night after Rama had departed. Half the night had passed and the king was now wide awake. He called Kausalya and asked her to sit very close to him. He said: 'My queen, when a man does something, whether it is good or bad, he is sure to reap the harvest of his act. A good act will grant him punya while the wrong act will definitely make him suffer for it. If this is not realised, then man is foolish. An action performed with no thought of the consequences will, if it is wrong, make the man realise the truth about it and by that time it is too late: he is unable to stem the tide of retribution which is sure to follow a wrong act. I have to relate to you an incident which took place when I was a young prince.

"I had learnt a difficult trick in archery. I could, by listening to the sound made by an animal, kill it with an arrow aimed from a distance. This is called 'Shabdavedhi," and I was very good at it. It was of great use to me during hunting and I was quite proud of my achievement.

"It was the rainy season. Then sun had burnt the earth with his fierce rays during summer and the skies had now assumed a darkness because of the rain clouds. The noise made by the frogs was welcome since it was an indication that rain would follow soon. I remember everything very clearly. The birds were drenched with the rain which had begun to pour suddenly and the trees were the only shelters they could find. The mountains were covered by the rainfall and the earth looked like the sea, so full of water was it. Water was flowing from the mountains like snakes winding down its slopes. It was exciting to go out in the rain and, armed with my bow and arrows, I went to the banks of the Sarayu to hunt.

"I stood still and, to my ears, came the noise made by the elephant drinking water with its trunk. Familiar as I was with 'Shabdavedhi' I took up an arrow and shot it in the direction from which the noise came.

"A moment passed and, to my dismay, I heard the cry of a human being in pain. I heard someone say: 'Why should I, an ascetic, be hunted like an animal? Who is this sinful man who has done me to death? Who is this shameless man? Who is he?" I rushed to the spot and there I saw a young ascetic. His body was covered with dust and blood and by his side was a pot from which water had flowed out. He looked at me and said: 'A prince! And yet you have done something unforgivable. How have I offended you that you should punish me like this? I came to the river to take water for my old parents who are blind. They will be helpless without me. They will also die since they cannot exist without me. They were thirsty and so I came here to fetch water for them. They do not know that I am dying.' He was getting tired and I fell at his feet and told him about the mistake which had been committed by me. He could not be pacified but, after a while, he said: 'O Prince! go at once to my father and tell him what you have done. This footpath leads to our ashrama and if you go along this

THE CURSE OF A RISHI

you will reach him. Try and pacify him and avert a curse which he is likely to pronounce. Take this pot, fill it with water and take it with you. And, do me a favour. This arrow is hurting me abominably and my life is ebbing away too slowly. Be kind and remove the arrow from the wound.'

"I was hesitant but he assured me that I would not be dogged by the sin of killing a brahmin. I removed the arrow and almost immediately he died.

"Like a sinner I walked to the ashrama of the old people with the pot of water in my hands. I saw them, the old couple. They were sitting near the doorway waiting for their son. They heard my footsteps and said: 'Have you brought water for us?' I did not know how to approach them. I stood still and the old man said: 'Why are you standing so far away? Come closer and give the pot of water. We cannot see you and you know you are everything to us. Do not sport with us but give the water. Your mother is very thirsty. Why are you so silent?' I plucked up enough courage to go near them. I said: 'I am not your son. I am a prince by name Dasaratha. I belong to the race of the sun. I have, unwittingly, caused great pain for both of you. The act is not to be forgiven easily and yet, I beseech you to forgive me since I did not mean it.'

"They were impatient to know what had happened and I told them what I had done. 'The sound of the pot being filled,' I said, 'seemed to me to be the noise made by the elephant while drinking water with his trunk and I aimed my arrow at the source of the sound. It was only when he cried out that I realised I had hit a human being and that he was moaning in pain. I hurried to his presence and he told me who he was. I have killed your son. He has left you alone and helpless and it was because of me. I stand here before you asking you to forgive me for my thoughtless action.'

For a moment they were speechless and then the old man said: 'If you had not come of your own accord and told me, your head would have split into a thousand fragments because of my anger. Be good enough to lead us to where our child lies. We would like to touch him.' I led them to the spot where their son lay dead. It was painful to see them mourning him. The father performed the last rites for the son according to the shastras. He offered water as a tarpana for the son. The father then turned to me and said: 'I am suffering extreme sorrow because of the separation from my son. I am now cursing you who has caused this suffering for us. Your death will also be similar to mine: you will die as a result of separation from your son.'

"After cursing me the old couple entered the fire." The king and queen were silent for a long time. Poor Kausalya was stunned when she heard the story. She had not known that such a curse had been pronounced on her lord. She held his hand firmly in hers and wept hot tears which fell on his hands and seemed to scorch him.

Dasaratha said: "Kausalya, this incident comes back to my mind now. The words of a brahmin will never be untrure. I am sure I will die very soon. My eyes are no longer able to see you. Everything looks dark to me. Kausalya, touch me with your hands and comfort me with your presence. I cannot see you."

He said musingly: "What I did to Rama is a grave injustice and it does not befit me and the name I have earned so long in this world. But Rama's attitude towards me is worthy of him. Which father will send away his son even if the son is ill-natured or even if he is a sinner? No father can treat his son as I have treated mine. My senses, Kausalya, are getting numb and I am certain that the messengers of death have already been sent to fetch me. I am dying and my eyes are not able to have one last look at my beloved child. My life is draining away slowly from my body and it is because my son is not with me. Those who will see Rama after fourteen years will be fortunate. They will see his face charming like the moon, with eyes like lotus petals. Because of the sin I have committed knowingly, death is fast approaching me. I am not able to perceive anything with my senses. My eyes, my ears, my touch, have all ceased to function. I can see that, one by one, they are being withdrawn into the departing breath like a lamp which has no more oil to feed it. Rama, you are away from me at the moment when I need you most. Kausalya, my dear Sumitra, I have been deceived by Kaikeyi. She has proved to be my death."

The king was moaning for a long time. Often the name of Rama would escape his lips. The queens were beside him on the couch and they were exhausted too and leaning against the couch they slept the sleep of exhaustion.

27. THE DEATH OF DASARATHA

Day dawning, the Vandhis and Magadhis came to the palace of the king and, as was the custom, they stood at the doorway and began to sing the praises of the king and to rouse him from his sleep. They sang in tunes befitting the morning and the rise of the sun and the music was pleasing to the ear. Women from inside the apartments brought water and other necessary articles for the king's morning ablutions. They were outside the chambers where the king was, and stood waiting for the king to wake up.

The women who were around him woke up from their sleep and they tried to wake up their lord. When he would not get up, even then the women did not realise that the king was dead. The unfortunate king Dasaratha had died during the middle of the night and on one knew about it. Suddenly, by the lack of movement in his limbs and by the general posture of the sleeping king they guessed what had happened. It was not sleep and they trembled with fear and shock at the calamity.

Neither Kausalya nor Sumitra had woken up yet. The women in the palace knew now that the king had died some time during the night and that the queens did not know it yet. Their hearts went out to them and a wail rose from their throats, a wail fraught with anguish since they had lost their master, their lord, their king. The sound roused the sleeping queens and it did not take them long to realise that they had lost everything. They fell on the ground and wept tears of sorrow and it was not possible for them to realise that their beloved husband was lost to them for ever. Dasaratha who had been such a glorious king, such a just ruler, such a noble soul, such a famed warrior, now lay dead and it was tragic since Rama's banishment was the cause of his death. For five nights the king had lived after Rama had left Ayodhya. On the sixth night he could not bear the pain any longer and had died quietly. He had waited for Sumantra, perhaps, to tell him about Rama. When he realised that Rama had gone, that he would not come back for many a long year to come, the noble heart cracked and his breath left his body without anyone knowing: like water leaking silently from a cracked pot.

He had been a friend of Indra, the lord of the heavens and when he was ruling, the earth was like heaven. The people loved him as though he were their father and such a king had come to his tragic end because of the ambition of one woman. He was the king whom Lord Narayana chose as the one worthy to be his father and, grieving for his son, the unfortunate died of a broken heart and condemned by the world for his unjust act.

He was dead and he looked like a fire which had died down, like the ocean which had dried up, like the sun devoid of his brilliance.

Kausalya took his head and placed it on her lap. She wept with an abandon which was painful to watch. She had lost Rama and now her lord was dead and she repeated that she had nothing left to live for and that she would ascend the funeral pyre with the king. With great difficulty the other women in the palace took her away and comforted her with empty words, words which meant nothing at all.

Soon the city learnt the terrible truth that their king was dead. Ministers hurried to the palace and the people were now crowding the doorway of the palace and the streets. One calamity following another was something they could not take and there was a shocked silence. People did not know what was to happen. And so they stood, all of them, outside the palace, waiting for an indication of what would take place.

Blessed as he was with four sons, yet the king's death occurred when not one of them was by his side. The courtiers with Vasishtha conferred and decided that Bharata should be sent for and that the king's body should be preserved in oil.

The painful day came to an end and night set in. The city which had been mourning the absence of Rama now found this sorrow to be unbearable. They had loved their king and everyone talked only about Kaikeyi and her cruelty which had caused all this unhappiness to all of them. No one slept and all through the night could be heard the sobs and wails: and so the night passed.

Everyone woke up to another day and it seemed to the wise men of the court that panic would set in unless someone took the initiative and did something. There assembled in the council hall all the wise men who had been advisers to the king and they were led by Vasishtha, the preceptor. And they said: "The king died because of the terrible unhappiness caused by the separation from his beloved son Rama. And the night was, to us, a terrible night, lost as we are without a father. The palace is empty. Rama has gone and with him went Lakshmana. Bharata is in Kekaya with his brother Shatrughna. The kingdom will be orphaned unless we take some decision. A kingless country is vulnerable and there should be no aggression by enemy kings when we are in this plight. As for the people there will be no control over them and so very soon Dharma will disappear and that will indeed be a sad state of affairs. There must be someone to rule the country. The king's son will have to be crowned as early as possible. We depend on your wisdom, great sage, to do the needful and save the country from destruction."

Vasishtha addressed the ministers and the rishis who had assembled there and he said: "Bharata has been living Rajagriha and we will despatch messengers to Kekaya to fetch him as early as possible. There is no cause for us to be alarmed unnecessarily."

Vasishtha called Siddharatha, Vijaya, Ashoka and Nandana and said : "I will tell you what should be done. You must shed this grief first and get interested in action. Take the fastest horses in the stable and go to the city of Rajagriha in Kekaya. You must meet Bharata and repeat this my message to him. 'Your preceptor sends you his blessings and wishes you well. Since there is some work which you have to perform at once, return to Ayodhya immediately.' You should not tell him either about the banishment of Rama or about the end of the king. Carry with you the usual silks and gems which one king should take when he greets another king."

Very soon the messengers were on their way. They travelled northwards, crossing a river by name Malini. They passed Hastina where they crossed the river Ganga and turned westwards. Panchala was soon left behind and they came to the river Ikshumati. They travelled fast and after a long and strenuous journey they reached Girivraja. They did not tarry there but proceeded from there and that very night they reached the city by name Rajagriha. This city was the capital of Kekaya and the young sons of Dasaratha had been spending some time with the old king Ashvapati and his son Yudhajit.

28. BHARATA HAS BAD DREAMS

On the night when the messengers reached Rajagriha, the prince Bharata had bad dreams. The dream was early in the morning, just before sunrise and he knew that such dreams are said to come true. He was greatly worried and his face was not cheerful and smiling as was usual with him. His companions tried to cheer him with light words and they tried to engage him in pleasing sports. But he would not be comforted. His mind was filled with strange misgivings and one of the young men who was very close to him asked him: "Bharata, tell me what bothers you so much that you are not able to share any fun with us? If you talk about it, perhaps you can lessen your worry."

Bharata said: "I will tell you. Last night I dreamed of my father and the horror of the dream is still haunting me. My father, the king, was dressed in soiled clothes and his hair was flying in the breeze. I saw him fall from a mountain peak into a pit filled with dirt. I saw him drink oil with his palms cupped together. I saw his body smeared with oil and he was drowned in oil. I also dreamed that the sea was dried up, that the moon had fallen on the ground. I saw darkness all around me and I saw an elephant with his tusk broken. My father was sitting on a seat made of iron and his clothes were black. He was wearing a garland made of crimson flowers and red sandalwood paste was smeared over his arms. He was riding in a cart drawn by donkeys and it was going fast towards the south. This was the dreadful nightmare which is still vivid in my mind and, try as I might, I am not able to shed this terror which seems to envelop me. I fear some calamity. It is not possible for the king or Rama or, for that matter, Lakshmana to have come to grief. I have been told that if, in a dream, a man is seen riding in a cart pulled by donkeys very soon smoke will plump skywards from his funeral pyre. I am afraid, my friend. My throat is dry and a strange restlessness is making me feel ill. I do not know what I should fear. My voice seems to be choked and my eyes seem to have lost their lustre. I am not able to find the reason for it but it seems to me I dislike myself suddenly. I am suffering from the dread of the unknown and this dread is painful."

The messengers from Ayodhya had arrived late in the night and they were at the outskirts of the city. Early in the morning they entered the gateway of the palace riding on their tired horses. They were welcomed by the old king and his son. They paid their respects to them and they approached the young prince Bharata who was with Shatrughna. They saluted him and repeated the message of their guru Vasishtha and added: "These silks and gems have been sent for your uncle. Please give them to him and these gold pieces. They are to be accepted by the king and his son.

This is a gift from Ayodhya." Bharata took them with him and offered them to his grandfather and his uncle. They accepted them with smiles of pleasure.

Bharata asked the messengers: "I hope my beloved and revered father is well and happy. I hope Rama and my brother Lakshmana are well and happy too. Is my saintly mother Kausalya without any ill health? Wise Sumitra the mother of Lakshmana is well too, I hope. Has my wilful mother Kaikeyi sent any message for me."

The messengers were extremely careful in answering the questions of Bharata. "They are all well, young prince. Goddess Lakshmi, born of the lotus, is waiting for you with open arms. Do not have any worry. Please make haste and ask your chariot to be ready. You are needed in Ayodhya."

Still suffering from the uneasiness following his dream the prince went to his grandfather and told him about the summons from Ayodhya. He said: "I do not know why I have been sent for. But it is my guru's command and I must obey it. I will come again to see you whenever you want me and send for me."

The old man was disappointed that the departure of his grandson was so abrupt and he said: "Fortunate is my daughter to have such a noble son like you. Convey my blessings to her and to your father. Convey my regards and respects to your guru, the great Vasishtha and also my blessings to your brothers."

Accompanied by the many gifts from his grandfather and his uncle Bharata left for Ayodhya. The gifts were many and rare but Bharata's mind was elsewhere. He could not even notice the excellent horses and elephants and the soft silks which had been given to him and to Shatrughna. His thoughts were already in Ayodhya. His dream during the night, and the arrival of the messengers early in the morning with their vague message from his guru had unnerved Bharata. He took leave of his uncle and his grandfather. Bharata and Shatrughna took their places in the chariot and the journey began. Out of the immense gateway of the palace of the Kekayas the princes entered the royal path in their chariot, on their way to Ayodhya.

29. BHARATA IN AYODHYA

They passed several beautiful cities, picturesque forests and rivers which snaked their way along. And Bharata's eyes were unseeing. He did not notice anything on the way and his face was grave and thoughtful. A premonition that something dreadful was in store for him, filled his mind and he could not shed it. Seven days and seven nights had to pass before they could reach the promontory of Kosala. Early in the morning of the eighth day they could see, from the distance, the golden turrets of the city of Ayodhya. Bharata spoke to his charioteer and said: "Even from this distance the sight of my beloved Ayodhya makes my heart swell with joy and pride. Ayodhya with its many gardens, with its white sands, with the music of the Vedas recited by the holy men and ruled by the best of men, is ever beautiful like Indra's Amaravati."

They came nearer and nearer and soon they reached the gates of the city. Bharata seemed to be nonplussed by its unusual appearance. He said: "Strange! There seems to be no noise coming from the city! As though there are no people! The gardens seem as though they have not been used since a long time. There is not to be heard the noise made by chariots of passers-by in the streets. It looks more like a desolate forest than a city to me. The perfume of the city would always greet one who entered it and I miss it now. What about the music of the trumpets, bugles, veena and other instruments?"

Bharata looked around him in puzzled wonder and said: 'Bad omens greet me when I enter the city. I am afraid, very much afraid that something terrible has happened to me."

Bharata entered the city by the beautiful gateway by name Vaijayanta. The doorkeepers stood up and greeted him with the usual 'Jaya Vijayee Bhava'. Bharata looked around and it seemed to him that the people were weeping and that the entire city was sunk in sorrow. He hurried towards the palace of the king. Jumping down from the chariot he rushed inside.

The king was not in his chamber. Bharata was disappointed that he could not meet him as soon as he arrived in Ayodhya. He decided that his father was certain to be found in the apartments of his mother Kaikeyi. He went there.

Kaikeyi heard him coming and, rising gladly up from her couch, she rushed to meet him and welcome him. In a moment Bharata was able to perceive that the usual decorations were absent there. He prostrated before his mother and clasped her feet in his hands. She raised him and after embracing him, asked him about the welfare of her father and brother. Bharata replied that they were in the best of health. He added: "Mother, messengers came from Ayodhya to Rajagriha and told me that I was wanted here. To obey the king's behest and the command of my guru I hurried here. From the moment I arrived in Ayodhya there seems to be sadness and nothing but sadness which greets me. Wherever I look, the people seem to be unhappy. And, as for this chamber of yours, why is your couch so empty? Father is usually to be found here, in your chamber on that couch. I am eager and impatient to fall at his feet. I want to see his face which I have been missing all these days. Is he, perhaps, with mother Kausalya? Tell me where my father is. I want to go to him and take the dust of his feet."

With her mind still deluded in her love for the throne, Kaikeyi could not grasp the extent of the misfortune which had befallen her. She spoke in a flat and unemotional voice: "Your father, the righteous Dasaratha, the refuge and solace of everyone who was in trouble, father of the country, has attained that state which all living beings should attain one day."

The suddenness of it, the abrupt manner in which she broke the news to him, made Bharata reel with the shock and he fell unconscious to the floor. After a few moments he recovered and still rolling on the ground he said: "Everything is lost! I am killed, I have nothing to live for." Bharata could not be comforted. He had been anticipating some bad news but this was something which took him unawares and he could not bear it. He wailed aloud and said: "I have always seen my father on that couch and ever since I can remember, it had been thus. Today, like the sky without the moon, the couch seems empty, so empty. My father is not there any longer." He covered his face with his upper cloth and wept for a long time. Kaikeyi was looking on while he mourned the death of his father. She went near him and stroked him with loving hands. She raised him up and said: "Come, rouse yourself. Wise men do not give way to grief like this."

After the first shock had abated somewhat, Bharata, in between sobs, asked his mother: "Mother, when the messengers came and insisted that I should leave for Ayodhya at once, I was hoping that I was being summoned for the coronation of Rama as Yuvaraja. I was very happy at the thought and, all the way during my journey, to here, I was imagining the celebrations that would be arranged here. And all my happiness has been destroyed by this one word from you. My mind is shattered. I will not see my father again. Mother, tell me, what caused his sudden demise? When I left for Rajagriha he was quite well and I never dreamed that this calamity would befall me. Fortunate indeed is Rama who was here by his side to perform the funeral rites for our father. I have come back from Kekaya and my father does not know it. I would have fallen at his feet and he would have lifted me up and embraced me again and again. He would have stroked me and my arms with loving hands and smiled at me with love. Announce me to Rama, mother. I have to go to Rama. I need him since he is my brother, my father and my mother. He is everything to me. I will clasp his feet in my hands and find solace in it. Mother, how did my father die? He was the very image of Dharma and he was famed for his prowess and his love for his subjects. Tell me, what were his last words? Unfortunate son that I am, I was denied even the privilege of staying by his side when he left us for the world above. What were his last injunctions to me? I am eager to hear them."

Without a qualm Kaikeyi spoke: "That lion among men, your father, was wailing all the time and he spoke only three names: 'Rama! Lakshmana! Sita!' And wailing thus he shed his body. Like a big elephant is helpless when tied with ropes, even so, your father, bound as he was by the noose of death, spoke this one sentence: 'Fortunate will be the people who will see Rama, that handsome son of mine with Sita and Lakshmana, returning to Ayodhya.' These were the last words spoken by your father, the king."

Bharata was taken aback by her words. He was surprised at the news that Rama was not in Ayodhya, when his father died. He asked her with a perturbed look: "Rama not here when the king died! What a strange situation! With Rama, I know Lakshmana would have gone too. But why Sita? What strange absence is this mother? How was it possible that they went somewhere and that, when the king was indisposed? Or did the king leave us suddenly? Where is Rama?"

Kaikeyi was just waiting for that question and she spoke as though the banishment of Rama were a common occurrence. She said: "Bharata, my child, the son of the king, Rama, has left for the forest Dandaka dressed in tree-bark. And with him have gone Lakshmana and Sita."

Bharata covered his ears with both his palms and he was trembling all over. He dreaded some misbehaviour on the part of Rama which led to his banishment. He thought of the glory and prestige of the line of kings of whom Rama was a descendant and now, this banishment. His mind was sorely troubled. He asked his mother: "Rama in the Dandaka forest? But why? Why, mother? Why was he sent to the forest by my father? Did he annex the wealth which belonged to someone else? Did Rama punish anyone who was guiltless? Did he, by any chance, look at another man's wife with lust? What was the reason for the banishment?"

Kaikeyi knew that the moment had come: the moment for which she had been dreaming of, all these days.

With feminine cupidity she had worked havoc in the house of the Ikshvakus and unaware of the monstrosity of her crime she spoke: "No, Bharata. Rama did not commit any of the sins you have enumerated. It is true that these are the crimes for which your father would have decided that banishment was the only punishment. But Rama's banishment was for a different cause altogether. Bharata, my child, the king had made all arrangements for the coronation of Rama as the Yuvaraja. When I heard about it, I did not like it. I made the king grant that Rama should be banished and that you should be crowned as the Yuvaraja.

"Years back, once during the fight with the devas against the asuras, your father had been summoned to the heavens by Indra to assist him. I had gone with him and I was able to save his life on one occasion. Pleased with me he had granted me two boons which I had told him I would ask for if and when the occasion arose. I asked for those now to serve my purpose.

"I wanted you to be crowned and I wanted Rama to be sent to the Dandaka. Because he could not break his word the king, your father, had to agree to it and Rama was asked to go and live in the Dandaka forest. This exile has to last for the duration of fourteen years. Lakshmana insisted on accompanying Rama and so did Sita.

"As for the king, you know how much he loved Rama. He could not bear the separation from Rama. He could not live without Rama and his end came.

"Come now, all that is in the past. I did it all for your sake and to see you king. Accept the kingdom which has been won for you by your mother. Do not grieve for what has happened. The city of Ayodhya is now yours and so is the entire kingdom. There is no obstacle in your path. Obey the instructions of Vasishtha and perform the funeral rites for your father. When he has reached the land of the Pitris, you will be crowned as king."

30. THE WRATH AND SORROW OF BHARATA

To Bharata the words of Kaikeyi seemed so unreal at first he could not grasp them. It seemed to him as though one lightning after another were striking him and that he was standing helpless when they descended on him. He tried to shut out the terrible words by closing his ears with his hands but her clear calm voice went on droning and the words were like hot lead being poured into his ears. He could not bear to hear any more. Nature, which is ever kind, allowed him a respite of a few moments by letting him faint. He lay motionless on the floor and Kaikeyi stood watching him till he became aware of her. "Rama!" he wailed. "Rama! my god, my lord!" he moaned. Words would not come to his lips. He could only repeat Rama's name and he could say nothing else. Finally he stood up.

For a long moment he looked at his mother and said: "I have been ruined. My good name is gone for ever. The king is dead and the world has come to an end. Woman! Who was the evil mentor who taught you to behave thus? Tell me, who did this mischief? The king has become just a lifeless body and Rama is now a dweller in the forest, dressed in tree-bark and deerskin. All this had to happen because you wanted the kingdom! God, what can I do? I have become an outcast overnight. You banished Rama to the forest and you have been the death of your husband and, to my lasting shame, I have to remember that I am your son, born of you.

"There is no way to gauge the extent of your wickedness. Why did you not kill yourself by putting a noose round your neck or by drinking poison? Go, drown in the sea or fall into the blazing fire.

"I will willingly kill you myself. I would have done so too, but then my revered brother Rama will not look at me since he will attribute the sin of matricide to me. That is the only reason why I hesitate to draw my sword and kill you."

Kaikeyi stood with her eyes trained on him. She spoke no word and Bharata continued: "How have I wronged you that you should have caused this infamy to besmirch my name?" Kaikeyi said: "I am your mother and I had your interest at heart. I desired to see you king of Kosala. You speak such harsh words to me. I do not deserve them. I have not wronged you. Why do you talk like this? Your father is dead and your brothers have both been sent to the forest. What is the use of your anger against me? It serves no purpose. Listen to the words of your mother and accept the throne I have got for you with so much trouble."

Bharata said: "My father is gone and Rama, who is like a father to me, is also away. What is left for me in this world? You have caused me this misery and you have poisoned my entire life. Because of you the great House of the Ikshvakus has been ruined. My unfortunate father took you into his bosom not realising that you were but a spark of fire. You betrayed him to Yama, the god of death. What hold did you have over my father that he had to agree to your infamous proposal? How could you do this to Rama? He loved you so much. He loved you as much as he loved Kausalya Devi. You have said so often, yourself. As for mother Kausalya, she has treated you like a younger sister and has always loved you. And how is it possible for you not to be unhappy when this same Rama is wandering in the forest like a mendicant? You have sent him far away from all of us and you do not seem to regret it. Your avarice has blinded you and prevented you from seeing me as I really am. That is why you engineered this.

"Did you think, even for a moment, that I would accept the kingdom? With my father dead, with my brother banished, did you think I would dare to sit on the sacred throne which has been graced by my father? I would rather die than contemplate such a sinful act. It is well known that in the line of the sun, the eldest son always inherits the kingdom, and the younger brothers serve him all the time. This is the time-honoured custom which has been followed for years on end. And you did not respect this precedent. How could you forget such an important fact?

"Your ancestry too has been faultless. Your father is noble and so is your brother. You father's ancestors have all been famed for their righteousness. How is it possible for such a daughter to be born to that great man? You can be sure of one thing. I will never agree to do what you want me to. I prefer to kill myself. I will, this very moment, go to the forest and bring back my beloved brother Rama: Rama the sinless, Rama the favoured prince of Ayodhya. I will bring him back, make him king and serve him as a servant all my life and try to expiate the sins of the monster who bore me."

The noble prince Bharata was unable to grasp the truth and he was still reeling under the dreadful shock of the many happenings in Ayodhya. He had gone away for a short time and during that short time his father had died and his brother had been sent away to the forest. All because of his mother who wanted to see him king. What could he do about it? "Why do you stay in this country? Go away from here. You will see me dead very soon. Unconcerned as you seem to be about the rudiments of Dharma, that is the only punishment for you: being sent away from the city. Tell me, what did Rama do that you should have done this to him? He is as sinless as my father and that noble monarch met his end at your hands. I am certain there is a special hell waiting for you. This is no ordinary sin you have committed. You have lost your name and men in aftertimes will talk ill of you and they will remember you for this act of yours as long as the sun and moon move in the orbits assigned for them. As for me, because I am unfortunate enough to be called your son, this stigma will always be attached to my name. I refuse to recognise you as my mother any more. Those other hapless mothers of mine, Kausalya and Sumitra are suffering untold misery. I have been forsaken by my brothers. My father has left me for ever. The people of the city do not look on me with love since they consider me to be a usurper. What avarice is this which has blinded you to the noble qualities of Rama who is like my very life to me? How could you think even for a moment that I would accept the throne which has been forcibly snatched from him? For which my father has paid with his precious life? Because of you that gentle lady Kausalya is undergoing this suffering. As a punishment for that you will suffer in this life and in the next.

"I cannot rest until I bring Rama back from the forest and make him accept the throne which is his. This is the only way in which I can bring a semblance of peace to the bruised heart of my mother Kausalya. I can, to an extent, vindicate my honour also."

Bharata was overcome with emotion. He fell down again on the floor. His limbs were not able to bear him up. After a while he rose up. With his eyes red with anger and the copious tears he had shed, with his clothes all dusty and disarrayed, with his golden ornaments thrown on the ground in disgust, Bharata, the young prince, strode out of the chambers of Kaikeyi and the earth trembled under his footsteps: so angry was he.

31. BHARATA'S OATH

Bharata went to meet the ministers and others who were waiting to see him when they heard that he had returned from Rjagriha. He said: "Believe me, I have no desire for the kingdom. I do not have any affection left for this woman who was my mother. I knew nothing of the coronation which the king was contemplating. I was far away in Kekaya with my brother Shatrughna. All of you are aware of it. As for the forest life which has been meted out to my noble brother Rama and to Sita with Lakshmana, I knew it not." Bharata was sobbing as though his heart would break. Kausalya heard the voice of Bharata and told Sumitra: "Bharata, the son of cruel Kaikeyi has come back from Kekaya. I would like to see him: I would like to see this prince who has been blessed with so much forethought."

Sorrow had made Kausalya bitter and her words had a sharpness which they did not have before. Her face had lost its glow and her silks were soiled and uncared for. Her form trembled often and her steps were faltering. She had grown old overnight when she lost her lord and her son.

Bharata, eager to meet Kausalya was walking fast towards her apartments and she had come out too. They met half way. Bharata embraced the thin emaciated figure of Kausalya. The queen looked at Bharata and she spoke words which were extremely wounding. She said: "How easily has the kingdom been won for you by your mother Kaikeyi! Child, you have now no obstacles in your path and you can ascend the throne immediately. Fortunate are you to have such a capable woman for mother. As for my son, Kaikeyi has managed to send him far away, dressed in tree-barks. She seems to be exceptionally happy ever since she did this to my son. I only wish to ask a favour of her. If only she will be good enough to send me where Rama is, she will be the kindest person I have ever known. Or else, why should I wait for her to send me? Accompanied by Sumitra I will go myself to the forest. I will stay there, since I have nothing left to live for, in Ayodhya. If there is any compassion left in your heart for a grieving old woman you can help me to reach my son's hermitage. I will take with me the household fire and tend it with care in the forest. Your mother has won for you the kingdom flowing with wealth, overflowing with prosperity. Enjoy it to your heart's content with your mother. Only let me find peace in the company of my child."

Kausalya's words were sharp and hurting and to Bharata it was like a needle probing a wound which was still bleeding. He was sinless and he suffered under the lashing. He could not bear it and he fell senseless on the floor. He recovered, and then he prostrated before her and he clasped her feet in his hands. His tears washed them and he stood up. With folded palms he stood before her. She could see that he was suffering intensely. He said: "Mother, I am innocent and it is not right that you should blame me for something which happened in my absence. You know only too well my devotion to Rama. He is like a god to me and I worship him. A great and noble soul is Rama and to him Truth is the only religion to be followed. He has been sent to the forest. But mother, do not, even for a moment, think that I had been party to this dreadful act of my mother's. If I really had done it, then all the punishments which are described in the Vedas will be meted out to me. The sin of kicking a sleeping cow, of a master making a servant work and then refusing to pay him: of a king who takes money from the subjects and does not govern them properly: of a man who does not honour the rishis who have performed a yaga for him: of a man who talks ill of his elders: who eats all alone when his wife and children are starving: who kills a king, a woman, an old man or a child instead of protecting them. I will suffer like a beggar with a *kapala* in my hand and with tattered clothes covering me.

"Mother, there are a million other punishments and they will all visit me if what you think of me is true: if I had really tried to get the throne after having my brother banished and my father killed. I must have sinned in some other life or else how can my mother, you, who has known me and my love for Rama all these years: how can you believe this of me?" Kausalya was overcome with self-reproach for having spoken so sharply. She gathered sorrowing Bharata in her arms and said: "Do not weep, child, do not be sad. I have been very unhappy these days and that has blinded me to such an extent that I spoke thus to you. You must forgive me. With your sorrow you are only making mine increase. May the gods be praised that your firm mind has not been moved by the temptation of a throne dangled in front of you. You are a noble prince and there is a special place for you in heaven; for a selfless man like you."

Kausalya's tears mingled with his and, to an extent, he was comforted by the words of Kausalya. He was happy that she believed his words and his sincere devotion to Rama.

He spent the night in the apartment of Kausalya and they spent the night in talking of Rama and about the king and the dire happenings in the city when he was away.

32. THE LAST RITES FOR THE KING

Vasishtha, the wise, came to Bharata early in the morning. He said: "Shed this grief, my son, and do the needful. We have taken great care to preserve the earthly remains of your noble father. You must now perform the last rites considering that Rama, the eldest, who should have been the one to do it, is absent in the forest."

Perhaps Bharata detected a sneer, a touch of sneer in the last words of his guru or perhaps he imagined it. If he did, he did not reveal that he was aware of it. He wiped his eyes and silently followed his guru to where his father was, and Shatrughna accompanied him. Bharata saw his father.

Because of the soaking in oil for a week or more, the king's skin looked slightly yellow. He had been placed on the ground where darbha grass had been spread and it seemed to Bharata that his father was sleeping. There was an expression of infinite peace on the face of the king and to Bharata, who had not seen the king in agony and pain, the sight was all the more heart-rending. He wept like a child and said "Father, king, emperor, how could this happen? What thoughts were lodged in your mind when our beloved Rama left you and went away? I was away and knew nothing of this. Father, separated from Rama, where have you gone? How can you live even in the heavens when Rama is not by your side? Who will rule the country without you on the throne and with Rama, the rightful heir, away in the forest? The city has the appearance of a beautiful woman who has been widowed and, like the night without the moon, it is dark and frightening."

Vasishtha tried to help Bharata recover from the fit of gloom into which he had fallen. He said: "Come, Bharata, compose yourself. Get up and perform all the rites calmly and bravely. You are a prince and you are brave and firm. Do not give way to extreme sorrow. It is weakening to the mind. You must cast off this sadness."

The *kulaguru* Vasishtha had already collected the articles necessary for the rites. Ritviks and priests had assembled in the hall of the great palace. The home-fire which the king was wont to worship daily was brought from the place where it was always kept and it was now worshipped with oblations poured into it. All the rites were performed by Bharata with Shatrughna standing by his side. The young prince spoke not a word and did not shed a tear. He said nothing and did everything which he was asked to do.

The last moment had come. In a palanquin decorated with flowers and with silks, the servants of the king with their throats choked with unshed tears carried him to the ground where he had to be cremated. Ayodhya was there, everyone of the citizens. Death had vindicated the king from the censure of the people and their anger was all against Kaikeyi and the king was pitied and mourned by all.

The pyre had been prepared with sandalwood and other woods which gave forth fragrance when burnt. The woods were Sandal, Sararsa, Padmaka and Devadaru. The fire which was said to transport him to the other world was properly worshipped by the ritviks. Sama Veda was recited and, as was the custom, the funeral cortege left the palace. The queens went with it in their palanquins. The king was placed on the pyre and Bharata touched it with the sacred fire. Dasaratha soon became one with the elements and, after they had bathed in the Sarayu, the royal family and the others returned to the palace.

The nights were spent on the bare ground by the queens, Bharata and Shatrughna. On the twelfth day the Shraddha was performed and on the thirteenth day gifts were given away to the poor and brahmins as was the custom. Cows, houses, goats, clothing for them were all given away and the prince was bountiful in his gifts even as his father was.

THE LAST RITES FOR THE KING

On the thirteenth day early in the morning, the prince had to go to the burnt out pyre to collect the bones of his father and that was when Bharata broke down. He thought of his father, his imposing figure, tall and dignified, with a noble look on his face, with a smile on his lips when he was with his sons, with a stern eye when he was in the council hall engaged in the affairs of the state, a look of love in his eyes when he entered the apartments of Kaikeyi. All that was nothing but a handful of ashes and a few bones. Bharata was inconsolable. He said: "Father, we have never known what suffering is. You had been such an affectionate father and you have now abandoned us and gone, where?

"When we were eating, when we were being dressed, when we went out to play, all the time your loving eyes would rest on us with infinite love and we would bask under that warmth. Who will bother about us now, father? This earth should have split when she saw you leave her and go. She did not, why? As for me, my father has abandoned me and gone to the abode of the gods and my beloved brother who is like a father to me, has also left me and gone away to the Dandaka. What is there left to live for in this Ayodhya? I will throw myself into the fire and join my father. This desolate city is not beautiful any longer, since the two whom I love, have left it. I will die or I will become a tapasvin like my other brothers and live in the forest. I will not come back to the city." Vasishtha had again to come and talk to him. He said: "Bharata, I thought you were an intelligent human being. You should do your duty and not play the woman when, already, the women are sorrowing for their lord. Come, collect the bones which are still remaining on the pyre. Bharata, three pairs visit every man. They are, hunger and thirst, sorrow and delusion, birth and death. No man can escape these unless he is wise enough to know them for what they are: that they are transient and inevitable. If man is prepared for them and can tackle them properly then they will fail to take firm hold of his power of thinking. Man should know that this world is beset with these and similar opposites and life is an eternal warfare between these and intelligence which should be prepared to subdue them whenever they threaten to gain ascendancy over man. Death can never be averted. A man who is born has to die and that is the law of nature. It is true that your father, the king, died under tragic circumstances but then, that is again the work of Fate. No one can withstand Fate. Do not give in to grief. We know how much you are made to suffer. I know that the shock of your father's death has been too much to bear. Still, man that you are, you must abandon this excessive grief and comfort the women who are helpless in their sorrow."

Sumantra spoke words of comfort too. He had been very dear to the king and his grief was immense. He had gone through the harrowing experience of taking Rama to the forest and, after leaving him there, he had come back to the king with Rama's words of farewell. That was the last he had seen of the king. He comforted the youngsters.

The two brothers, with their eyes cast down, with tears still streaming from their eyes, pursued their painful duty and collected the bones of their father to be cast into the river at a particular spot designated by their guru. They then offered the *Anjali* to the departed soul and came back to the palace.

33. MANTHARA AGAIN

Shatrughna and Bharata were alone after the painful fortnight spent in performing the obsequies to the king. Shatrughna said: "Rama, our dear Rama who was the home of all noble qualities, who was the refuge of all those who were in trouble, who was the only star in our sky, that Rama has been driven away to the forest because of the sinful whim of a woman." He stood for a while and his face was flushed and his brows were knit. He was the twin of Lakshmana and his thoughts were the same as those of Lakshmana. He said : "I am intrigued about the behaviour of my brother Lakshmana. He is valiant and efficient too. How is it he did not control this madness in our father? Why did he not take action against this injustice to Rama and avert the calamity? He should have stopped the exile. If a king, known for his righteousness, becomes suddenly bereft of it because of his infatuation for a woman, and, in the process, loses sight of Dharma and does wrong things, then it is up to others to interfere, consider what is right and what is wrong, and prevent the injustice from taking shape and coming to pass. I do not know what stayed the hand of my brother."

As they were talking to each other, there appeared at the doorway, Manthara, the hunchback. She had smeared red sandal paste all over her arms. She was wearing costly silks and several golden and gem-set ornaments were "decorating" her figure. A girdle of gold was set with many precious stones and it was strapped round her crooked waist. Her hair was intertwined with pearls strung together in wreaths.

By now the entire palace knew the attitude of Bharata towards his mother. The doorkeeper now saw Manthara and he was furious with her. He caught hold of her and dragging her to the presence of Shatrughna, said: "Prince, this woman is the cause of everything. If you want to know why our beloved king died and Rama was banished to the forest, it is because of this sinful creature. Because of her mind which is as crooked as her back, she contrived to bring about all this tragedy in the city of Ayodhya. Do what you will with her. Nothing is punishment enough."

Shatrughna stared at the woman standing in front of him trembling in every limb and staring stupidly at him. All his pent up fury burst forth and addressing the inmates of the palace who had been dreaming of the time when she would be punished, he said: "This woman has caused immense suffering to our father and to our dear brothers and to us. I will make her reap the reward for her actions."

He dragged her about and she screamed with fear and terror. She tried to cling to the other maids but she was so unpopular with all of them that no one would come near her. Even the one or two who were friendly with her ran away from there when they saw the fury in the eyes of Shatrughna. They were scared that he would punish them also since they were friends of Manthara.

Shatrughna dragged Manthara on the ground and her jewels, the ornaments which she was wearing, were now scattered all over the place. The ground was almost like the sky during autumn, the sky which is studded with stars.

Kaikeyi heard the commotion and came towards them but the prince paid no heed to her. He was dragging the wretched hunchback to and fro and Kaikeyi went to Bharata and asked him to intervene.

Bharata saw how angry his brother was and he said: "My dear brother, women should not be punished even if they deserve to be. They should be forgiven. If you would like me to tell you the truth, the only reason why I have not killed this Kaikeyi yet is because I am afraid of Rama. He is noble and he will be displeased with me if he knows that I have killed a woman and a mother, at that. He will never talk to me or even look at me. Even so with this sinful creature. She is the cause of all the unhappiness which has visited us. But we should do what Rama would have done: forgive her and not punish her."

Shatrughna let her go and, bleating like a sheep, she fell at the feet of Kaikeyi and cried her eyes out. Kaikeyi led her away from there speaking words of comfort to her.

34. THE THRONE IS YOURS

On the next day, when the sun had risen and when Bharata and Shatrughna had completed their morning worship of the sun, the ministers of the state came to Bharata and said: "Prince Bharata, King Dasaratha who was like a father to us, has now been gathered to his forefathers. Rama with Lakshmana has gone to the Dandaka to dwell there for the duration of fourteen years. This land of Kosala should not be without a king. It is now up to you to take up the reins of the kingdom in your hands and rule it. The articles for the coronation are all ready and waiting for you. The people are also expecting to see your coronation. Please accept the throne and rule us as your father did."

Bharata walked with them to the spot where the many accessories for the coronation were assembled. Silently he made a Pradakshina to the myriads of pots containing holy water and to the chamaras and the white umbrella. He then came and stood on a raised dais so that the people could see him, and hear him. He said: "My beloved brothers in woe, together we are suffering this great calamity which has been visited on us. It is not right that you should talk like this to me asking me to take up the ruling of the land into my hands. Since time immemorial the throne of the Ikshvakus has been reserved only for the eldest son of the king. Rama is the eldest son of the king. He will be king. I will, instead, go to the forest and spent the fourteen years. I have decided to go to the forest and bring my dear brother back to Ayodhya. Please help me to do this. Assemble the army and as for me, I will carry all these articles meant for the coronation with me and crown Rama in the forest itself. I will bring him back as the king of Kosala. Rama will certainly be the king. I will not let this woman have her dream realised. I will remain in the forest and expiate her sin. Now make the paths to the forest wide enough and good enough for the army. Send people immediately so that we can leave as early as we can." The citizens were thrilled with the words of this prince who was selfless.

The next morning Vandhis and Magadhis sang the praises of the prince and the sky resounded with the noise set up by the drums and bugles and other instruments. Bharata's sorrow was intensified by these which were tributes to a king and not to him. Bharata had woken up because of these and he came out of his chamber and said: "Please stop this. I am not the king."

He then told Shatrughna: "Look, Shatrughna, look at the extent of my mother's crime! The king has left Ayodhya in my hands and gone. That image of Dharma has left the country an orphan and, like a boat without anyone to steer it, it is tottering in the grip of uncertainty. Rama, who would have taken it up as easily as he handles the bow, has been sent away to the forest. What a situation!"

Poor unfortunate Bharata was sorely tired. He was worried about many things and the journey to the forest was now uppermost in his mind. If only Rama could be brought back everything would be alright.

In the meantime, while he was conferring with his brother, Vasishtha entered the council hall. Resplendent as the divine sabha "Sudharma," the king's council hall was a glorious sight. The rishi seated himself on a seat which he was in the habit of occupying. He asked for his counsellors and other officials to assemble there. He said: "We have to make some important decisions. Ask Sumantra to bring the young prince Bharata to the council hall."

The hall was soon filled with the people whom Vasishtha had summoned. People were already filling the streets and the rooftops even. Bharata entered the hall filled with the men who had been the advisers of his father. They were all there but the king was not. Both the princes stood still after they had saluted the elders.

Vasishtha then said: "Child, Bharata, your father, the king, has left this land for you to rule. He was a righteous man and he acted thus because he did not want to be called an Adharmi. As for the reason your brother Rama left for the Dandaka with his wife and Lakshmana, it was the same. Rama did not want his father to be called untruthful. This throne of the Ikshvakus is yours. Accept it and allow yourself to be crowned. Rule this large expanse of land, this Kosala which has been the heritage of your ancestors."

Bharata listened to the words without any expression on his face. His mind was far away in the forest, with Rama. He looked at his guru with pained eyes and said: "My lord, you are the person who has taught me what Dharma is, ever since I was a child. Having sat at your feet and listened to the nuances of Dharma as expounded by you, how is it possible for me to accept the throne? I am the son of King Dasaratha and from him I have inherited a sense of justice also. How can a son of Dasaratha take what does not belong to him?

"The kingdom as well as myself are Rama's to do what he will. Please do not ask me to remind you of the rule of the line of the Ikshvakus: that the eldest son has the right to the throne and none other. If I now do something which has not been done before, it will be a blot on the name of the Ikshvakus. It will be a sin. It is unbecoming to one like me, born in a noble house and it will unfit me to claim a place in the next world. I do not approve of the sinful act of my mother. From here I salute Rama the king who is, at the moment, dwelling in the forest. I am bent on but one thing: that Rama should rule the kingdom. He is the rightful heir to the throne and he is the person who is capable of ruling the country and not my unfortunate self."

The hall was silent. Everyone was touched by the love Bharata had for his brother and they were pleased with his adherence to Dharma. Bharata continued: "I will go to the forest and bring Rama back from there and I will offer the kingdom to him. If I am unable to bring him back, if I do not succeed, I will remain with him and serve him like my brother Lakshmana is doing. I will try my best to instal Rama on the throne. I have already asked for the roads to be made ready for the march of the army to the forest."

The young prince asked Sumantra to collect the army. Everything was got ready very soon and there was a thrill of anticipation in the mind of everyone. They were sure that Rama would come back with Bharata and that they would be able to forget the loss of their father Dasaratha in the happiness of being ruled by Rama.

Bharata took the blessings of Vasishtha who was by his side during all the painful days when the preparations were being made. He admired this young pupil of his who seemed to be as great as, if not greater than, Rama in the observance of Dharma. He smiled to himself softly when he remembered telling Kaikeyi the same thing on that memorable day when Rama left for the forest. He had told her in the presence of everyone that Bharata would never accept the throne and that he would, most probably, wear tree-bark and remain with Rama in the forest. Vasishtha was proud of his pupils.

Bharata called for his chariot and it was at the doorway in no time. Bharata who had hopes of bringing Rama back to Ayodhya spoke to Sumantra: "Sumantra, let us hasten towards the forest with the army. The country should not be without a king for long. Let us go."

Bharata and Shatrughna were seated in the chariot driven by Sumantra. The ministers and others came in chariots, on horsebacks and on elephants. The queens went with him too: Kausalya, Sumitra and Kaikeyi. Many of the people of Ayodhya also went with Bharata.

35. BHARATA ON HIS WAY

After travelling some distance they reached the river Tamasa and after that they continued the journey. Sumantra who had gone that way before went straight towards the city Shringiberapura and the army followed him. Guha was the ruler of the city. The entire army came to a halt on the banks of the river Ganga. Bharata told his ministers: "Let the army camp on the banks of the river. After rest tonight we can pursue the journey tomorrow. We can cross the sacred river Ganga and reach the opposite bank in the morning. I will also offer *Anjali* for my departed father with the waters of the Ganga."

Guha came to know of the army which had camped on the banks of the river. And he spoke to his men: "This army is as big as the sea. When I look at the chariot I can see the Kovidara flag on it. The banner indicates that Bharata, the evil-minded, has arrived in person. The son of Kaikeyi may have intentions of fighting with us or imprisoning us. Or perhaps, he has designs on Rama. He is now the king and, perhaps, to stabilise his position he means to kill Rama. Rama is my friend and I am ready to lay down my life for him. Get the army ready and wait for my instructions. Guard the river banks also. If Bharata has evil designs we should not let him cross the river."

Guha then took offerings which a vassal king takes to his emperor and decided to go and meet Bharata. Sumantra spied the hunter king from a distance and told Bharata: "This man who is approaching us is the king of this land. He knows all about the forest Dandaka. He is also a great friend of Rama. If you talk to him he will be able to tell you about the whereabouts of Rama."

Guha approached Bharata and paid his respects to him. And he said: "This land is but the garden belonging to your country. I have a request and that is, you should honour me by accepting our hospitality. You can spend the night here in peace and proceed in the morning." Bharata replied in a suitable manner and added: "I am told that you are a good friend of my lord Rama. I will be grateful to you if you can tell me the way to the ashrama of rishi Bharadvaja. This part of the country seems to be impregnable and the river Ganga is difficult to cross on foot." Guha spoke very respectfully. He said: "Please have no worry about the way. Faithful men I have who will steer you across and I will come with them to take you to the ashrama of Bharadvaja. But I hope no evil is meant for Rama. This large army makes me worried. I love Rama and cannot bear to think of evil befalling him and that is why I ask this of you." Bharata heard these words of Guha who did not mean to insult him but, nevertheless, his words hurt Bharata. He said: "You should not doubt my intentions. I consider Rama as my father. I am going to the forest to make Rama come back to the city with me. I promise you that is the only wish in my mind. He is my elder brother and the rightful heir to the throne."

Guha's face was all smiles when he heard the assurance of Bharata and he said: "Indeed, I am amazed at the nobility of a man such as you. You were offered the kingdom and you have refused it. I am yet to see a more selfless man than you. You are great. You have made up your mind to bring Rama back with you. I know that your fame will last for ever in the world of men in aftertimes."

Bharata's thoughts were directed towards Rama and the heart of the noble youth was filled with sorrow at the misfortune that had befallen Rama because of his mother Kaikeyi. He was the food of unseen fire: like a forest tree which burns and dries up because of the hidden fires inside it. Like the great Himalaya which has its snow flowing in rivulets after being melted by the rising sun, even so, the sorrow inside him made Bharata melt into tears all the time. He spent a sleepless night and Guha was trying to pacify him even as he did Lakshmana several nights back when they were with him.

He talked about Lakshmana to Bharata. He said: "Rama and Sita spent that memorable night here and Lakshmana, armed with a bow and arrows, stood guard over them all through the night. I told him that I had a bed ready for him and that he could rest, while I would take over from him the task of guarding Rama. I said: 'My dear young prince, every one of my men is used to hardships and you have been brought up in the lap of luxury. We will keep awake the whole night and you can sleep.' There is no one dearer to me than Rama. I promise to you that I will see that he will come to no harm.'

Lakshmana replied: 'My friend, it is not because of my lack of faith in you that I am standing thus, sleepless and armed. When I see my beloved brother on a bed made up of leaves and when Sita and he sleep thus, how can I sleep? I am neither hungry nor sleepy.' He then spoke of the king's love for his son and he had fears of the king's end coming soon. His fears were, I see, justified. He thought of the city of Ayodhya and of the people there, about their grief. He spent the entire night in thoughts like these. Early in the morning, in a boat which they asked for, they crossed this river Ganga and reached the southern bank. Looking like king elephants, these valiant brothers, wearing tree-bark and with their hair matted like rishis, with the bows in their hands, quivers strapped to their shoulders and swords hanging from their waists, they walked along there, on that side, with Sita between them."

Bharata was listening to the words of Guha and he could not bear to hear any more. He looked at Shatrughna and both of them cried out in pain thinking of their brothers dressed like rishis and walking with Sita along the banks of Ganga. Kausalya walked to them and comforted Bharata as a mother would her child. "Listen child," she said. "It is not right that you should grieve like this. With the king dead and with Rama far away, you are the one to take care of us old people.'

Bharata brought a semblance of control to his thoughts and he turned to Guha and asked him: "How did my brother spend the night? Where did he stay? Where did he sleep? What did he eat? What did dear Lakshmana do? Tell me everything. The only words which are kind to my ears are those which talk of Rama." Guha told him about the many eatables which he had brought for Rama and about his refusal: about the water from the river which Lakshmana brought from the Ganga and which was the only food they had that night. He told them about the darbha grass which made up the bed of Rama for the night: the bed prepared with loving hands by Lakshmana, and Guha took them to the *Ingudi* tree under whose shade the exiles had spent the night. He indicated the exact spot where Lakshmana and Sumantra spent the night talking with him.

Bharata led Kausalya to the tree and told her: "Look, mother, this is where the great man spent a night. Descended from the line of the sun, the son of Dasaratha the emperor, he spent the night on a bed made up of leaves and darbha grass." Bharata walked round the tree and spoke again: "I can see the signs of his having spent the night here. There are some spikes of darbha grass still left on the ground. How could he sleep on the bare ground, accustomed as he is to the softest of beds made of swansdown? It is not possible to believe it. I have not yet begun to believe that such a thing has happened to us. It still has the semblance of a dream and I feel that I may wake up and find everything perfectly safe in Ayodhya: that my father is there in his palace and that Rama with Sita is sitting on the couch made of gold where he usually sits. When I think of Rama sleeping on the ground I am fully convinced that even God is not as powerful as Kaala, Fate, which governs the course of the path of man on this earth. Look, mother, there are several strands of white silk caught in the darbha. It shows that Sita slept here that night. When I think that I am the cause of all these happenings my heart is ready to break into a thousand flinders. Lakshmana is fortunate since he is with Rama serving him all the time. Mother, I have made up my mind. From now on, from this very moment, I will live on fruits and roots even as my brother is now doing. And I will also mat my hair into a tangled mass and wear the tree-bark which Rama and Lakshmana are wearing. The floor will be my bed. I will spend fourteen years in the forest instead of Rama. Shatrughna will be with me. Rama will rule the kingdom with Lakshmana to assist him. Will the gods grant me my desire? I will fall at the feet of Rama and I will beseech him to accept the kingdom. If, however, he refuses, I will then remain with him in the forest. He cannot refuse me that privilege."

Bemoaning his fate in a thousand different ways, the poor unfortunate prince spent the night without being able to sleep. Early in the morning he woke up from his short sleep and told Shatrughna: "Get up, Shatrughna. Fetch Guha, the king of the hunters. He will help us cross the river" "I know you did not sleep and I did not sleep either," said Shatrughna. "I saw you tossing about and I lay silent and thought of Rama and Lakshmana." Before he could proceed towards him Guha came on his own accord and said: "Bharata, did you sleep well?" Bharata made a suitable reply and added: "I will be grateful to you if you can arrange to ferry my army across the river Ganga."

Guha collected all his boats and soon the ferrys were ready to transport the entire crowd across. There was one boat by name "Swastika" and into that were seated Bharata, the queens, Kausalya, Sumitra and Kaikeyi, Shatrughna, the preceptor Vasishtha and his group of rishis.

The army and the citizens of Ayodhya crossed the river Ganga with Bharata and the royal household. After they had abandoned the boats they proceeded further and soon arrived at Sangama, the place where the river Yamuna meets the river Ganga.

From a distance Bharata saw the ashrama of Bharadvaja. Accompanied by Shatrughna he walked towards the ashrama of the great rishi Bharadvaja.

The army was placed a krosa away from the ashrama. The ministers went with Bharata and, with his preceptor Vasishtha leading the small group, Bharata went towards the rishi's dwelling on foot. When he was very near the hermitage he left his ministers also behind and went only with his guru Vasishtha as his companion.

36. BHARATA MEETS BHARADVAJA

Bharadvaja saw Vasishtha and he rose up from his seat with great excitement and called out for the proper articles of welcome. He went to the rishi and welcomed him with the respect due to him. Bharata fell at his feet and Bharadvaja knew who he was. He welcomed all the guests and enquired after the welfare of all in the conventional language. He did not, however, speak a word about the King Dasaratha and about his welfare. Courtesies were exchanged and Bharadvaja said: "Bharata, you are the king in Ayodhya. What brings you to the forest? I am puzzled as to what the reason is, for your coming to the forest now."

The old rishi continued: "Kausalya's son has been commanded by his father Dasaratha to dwell in the forest for fourteen years. He could ascribe no fault to Rama but the exile was executed because the king was bound by a promise to his wife. The innocent prince, his wife and his brother left the city and came away to Dandaka. The way is now quite clear of all obstacles for you. I hope you are pleased."

His words hurt Bharata abominably and with tears in his eyes and with his voice faltering because of the suffering caused by the words spoken by Bharadvaja, he said: "I have never sinned. I was, till now, proud of the fact that I have committed no wrong. But the words spoken by you now have killed me. It is not right that you should punish me thus. What my mother did in my absence is neither pleasing to me nor do I accept what she thinks she has won for me by her machinations. It is against all codes of Dharma and I am greatly distressed by the course of events. I have come to the forest to search for Rama, to fall at his blessed feet, to offer the kingdom to him and to take him back to Ayodhya where he should be crowned as emperor. I beg of you to believe me and to consider me a devotee of Rama. Can you help me by telling me where the king of Kosala is? I am eager to see him."

Bharadvaja was sorry to have hurt the sensitive prince. He said: "It is but right that a son of the line of Raghu should have this devotion to his elders, a horror of Adharma and a desire to honour the elders. I know your thoughts. I spoke as I did only to make your selflessness known to the world." Bharata stood with his arms locked across his chest and his face was downcast. He raised his eyes when the rishi spoke: "As for the dwelling place of Rama, I will tell you. With Sita and Lakshmana your brother is living on the mountain by name Chitrakuta. Child, spend tonight here and tomorrow you can go there to meet Rama." "I will obey your commands," said Bharata and agreed to stay the night in the ashrama of Bharadvaja.

The rishi wanted to entertain the guests. Bharata spoke humbly and said: "You have already given us everything, my lord. I need nothing more." Bharadvaja smiled gently and said: "I know that you are satisfied with very little. Tell me, why have you left your army so far away from the ashrama?" Bharata said: "I have been taught that it is against all rules of behaviour to disturb the peace of an ashrama and its tranquil atmosphere by bringing an alien note into it. It is not right to bring a large crowd here, to the vicinity of an ashrama as sanctified as yours. A king or a prince should be very careful in his behaviour towards the inmates of the ashramas. There is always the danger of the army destroying the trees and the flowering shrubs here and they will also, most probably, frighten the tame deer and other animals in the ashrama. That was the reason for my leaving them behind."

"Let the army be brought here," said the rishi and the prince obeyed him. The rishi then touched water and invoked Vishvakarma and when he came told him: "I want to entertain this army and it is up to you to see that they are satisfied by my hospitality."

The heavenly host arrived with the apsaras from the court of Indra and a divine feast was spread out for the army from Ayodhya. Music and dancing by the apsaras accompanied the feast and every one of them was satiated with pleasure.

When the sun had risen Bharata went to the presence of Bharadvaja and said: "We have been very happy and we spent a comfortable night. My army will not be able to forget this ashrama at any time. They have all been happy, extremely happy. Please grant me leave to go in search of my brother. You must wish me well. You must also be kind enough to indicate the path I should follow to reach the hermitage of Rama."

Bharadvaja described the path even as he had done to Rama and added: "On the banks of the river Mandakini, Rama has built an ashrama and you will find him there."

Before leaving the ashrama, the queens of Dasaratha came to Bharadvaja and prostrated before him. They made Pradakshina to him and stood silent. The rishi asked Bharata: "Child, I can see that these are your mothers. Tell me whose son is who." Kausalya had come first and, with her, Sumitra, while Kaikeyi, the queen, whose desire was frustrated and who was disliked by all, had come last.

Bharata said: "My lord, look at this gentle lady with the sad eyes, thin because of fasting and looking divine because of her spiritual greatness. She is the eldest queen of my father and she bore the lion among men, Rama, even as Aditi bore Upendra as her son. She is named Kausalya. The other lady who is holding on to her left hand, who looks like the branch of Karnikara tree whose flowers have fallen off, this lady whose face shows the suffering she has undergone, is the mother of the heavenly twins, Lakshmana and Shatrughna. Her name is Sumitra.

"My father lost his life because of a woman. He thought it better to die than to live with her. He was parted from his beloved son and found nothing left to live for. The woman who forced it on him is an arrogant woman, avaricious, heartless, sinful and deceptively gentle to look at. Look on that woman, my lord, who is standing here beside me. She is Kaikeyi, my mother."

Even talking of the sin committed by his mother was enough to make Bharata angry and he sighed. His words came haltingly and his eyes filled up once again. Bharadvaja looked at him kindly and said: "Do not condemn your mother, Bharata. I can look into the future and I can see that this exile of Rama is for the good of the world. It is going to benefit the rishis of the forest, the devas and all the divine host. Forbear from your censure of this woman."

Bharata took leave of the rishi and, after collecting his army around him, left for the ashrama of Rama. It took some time for them to get ready, lost, as they were still, in the intoxication of the previous night. Finally the journey began. They travelled as fast as they could in the southwesterly direction and they covered a large distance. They passed forests, the rivers and hills. Because of the disturbance the inmates of the forest were frightened. They ran out of their caves and holes where they had made their homes and rushed in panic to other spots seeking shelter. Elephants and deer were to be found everywhere and the trees were almost laden with monkeys of different types.

After some distance had been covered along the southern bank of the Yamuna Bharata said: "It seems to me, we are nearing the place which was indicated by the sage Bharadvaja. This river must be Mandakini and this dense forest must be the one he mentioned. It looks like a dark cloud. I can see the hill clearly. Shatrughna, look at the abundance of flowers here! The slopes are covered by the flowers shed by the trees: like rain clouds showering rain. The breeze is so pleasant it seems to caress me. The place is very like heaven. My brother has chosen well. There is peace here, peace which the tapasvins strive for. Ask men who are well versed in tracking to go in advance and to look for the hermitage of Rama."

37. LAKSHMANA IS WORRIED

Rama, Lakshmana and Sita were very happy in the ashrama on Mount Chitrakuta. Nature was lavish in her bounty here, and Sita, who had ever been fond of flowers and birds and deer, was very happy here. Everyday, something new would be discovered by them and they would talk about it and they succeeded in forgetting the fact that they were exiles and that they were denied the comforts of the city. The river Mandakini was beautiful and, sitting on its banks, Rama would spend hours together with Sita watching the peacocks dance and they would listen to the birds singing in glee. The flow of the river made music and Rama was extremely happy in these pleasant surroundings.

On that particular day when they were seated, they found a herd of elephants running around as though in panic. Rama looked at this strange scene and heard an unusual noise from a distance. He said: "Look, Lakshmana, there is a noise resembling that of an earthquake. The very earth is trembling under the shock, sudden as it seems to be. In this spot there was nothing but peace reigning and now there seems to have appeared some alien element which is frightening the animals. Look at the deer which are terrified beyond measure. Even the wild animals seem to be scared. It seems to me, some king or prince has entered the forest with a desire to hunt. Just try and see what is happening."

Lakshmana ascended a tall Sala tree and from its top he looked all around. His eyes finally came to rest in the east. He saw there a large army made up of chariots, horses, and pedestrians. He looked carefully and saw the banner. He spoke from the top of the tree to Rama. His voice was excited and worried. He said: "My dear brother, please extinguish the fire at once. Take Sita some place which cannot be perceived easily. Hide her from prying eyes. As for you, take up your bow and string it. Please hurry and put on your armour. Danger is approaching us fast."

Rama was more amused than impressed by the flurry in the voice of Lakshmana. He said: "Lakshmana, did you make out whose army it is? Take a good look and tell me."

Lakshmana was looking like fire incarnate. He would have burnt the entire army if it had been possible for him to do so. He said: "Kaikeyi's son Bharata has been crowned king. He wants to stabilise his throne and he has come here to get rid of you and me. There is no doubt about it. I can see the chariot and the Kovidara banner which is only too well known to me. I can even see a look of joy on the face of everyone. Come, let us go to the slope and welcome them with our arrows. Or, we will wait for them here, armed with our bows. Let us capture the banner, my lord. Do you think I will be able to look at that Bharata who has been the cause of the sufferings of you and Sita? Because of him you have been banished from the kingdom which is rightly yours and my hands are impatient to kill him. I do not see anything sinful in this decision of mine. He has taken the initiative now to kill us and he has come here with that purpose. I will defend you and your life. I will kill him and the rightful king will rule Kosala once again. Kaikeyi will fall to the ground like a tree uprooted by an elephant and that will be great joy for me. I will kill her too and her attendants, every one of them. Because you had commanded me I had been keeping quiet all these days: keeping this anger of mine under control and I have been meek since you had asked me to be. But now my anger will blaze like burning fire touching a pile of dried leaves. I will pierce every heart in that army with my sharp arrows and the mountain will flow with rivers of blood. The wild animals will find food for a long time because of the bodies of the men I am going to slay. My arrows are getting rusty. I will use them on Bharata and I will be happy after his death."

Rama was greatly distressed by the violence of the anger of Lakshmana. He tried to pacify him with his soft and gentle words. He said:

"Lakshmana, if Bharata is coming here where is the need for us to take up arms against him? You know only too well my promise to my father. Now you suggest the killing of Bharata. Breaking my promise to my father and taking upon myself the sin of killing my brother, I will become the king of Kosala. Do you think such a thought is welcome to me? Wealth which one wins at the cost of the life of a kinsman or friend, is like food which has been poisoned. I will not even look at it. Lakshmana, do you remember my telling you something on the day the throne was promised to me by our father? I said: 'I am glad for you, my brother. We will rule this kingdom together. I am happy for you.' I assure you, I wish to be king only because I wish to share it with my brothers. I have but their happiness and welfare at heart. It is not as though I cannot conquer this entire world girt but by the sea. I do not desire to get it the way you suggest. Even the position of Indra, obtained by unrighteousness, is not desirable. If it is the only kind of happiness meant for me at the cost of losing my brothers, let that happiness burn to ashes. It is not welcome to me."

Lakshmana stood silent and Rama stroked him on the back with love and said: "My beloved brother, I know you are angry for my sake and that is the reason why you want to kill Bharata. I will tell you why Bharata has come. Bharata is extremely fond of his brothers. I love him more than my very life and he knows it. Bharata must have come back from Rajagriha. He must have heard about you and me with Sita living in the forest dressed in tree-bark and with our hair matted like rishis. He must have been grieved at the painful happenings at Ayodhya when he was away. He has great respect for the prestige of our royal line and does not want to transgress it. With pain in his heart, with affection for me he has come to the forest to see you and me. I am certain that he has come just for that. That saintly brother of mine would have, I am sure, chastised his mother Kaikeyi for what she has done. He has made my father give me the kingdom and Bharata is coming here to coax me to go back to Ayodhya. This journey of Bharata to the forest is but natural for him and I assure you, he means no harm to me. How has poor Bharata offended you, Lakshmana, that you should be so angry with him? furious? Why do you doubt him? It is not right that you should speak ill of Bharata. It displeases me. If you hurt Bharata I will think that you have hurt me.

"Lakshmana, even when some crisis occurs, will sons kill their father? Will a brother kill his brother? Perhaps you want the kingdom and that is the cause of this your rancour against Bharata. If that is so, your wish will be granted soon. The moment Bharata comes to me I will tell him: 'Bharata, let the kingdom be given to Lakshmana.' The moment I say so Bharata will say: 'As you say,' and you can be happy."

When he heard the words spoken by Rama Lakshmana shrank within himself, so ashamed was he of the idea which had been suggested by Rama. He realised that his behaviour was unpardonable as far as his brother was concerned. What hurt him most was the fact Rama ascribed to him the fault for which he said Bharata was to be punished. He stood still without speaking and with his eyes down-cast. He then roused himself and quickly changing the subject he said: "I think it is our father who is coming with his entire retinue to see you. He cannot bear to be without you." Rama saw how small Lakshmana was feeling and so he pretended to ignore it. Rama said: "Perhaps you are right. Perhaps the king had second thoughts. He cannot bear to think of us living in the forest. He remembers the luxury in which he has brought us up and he has decided to take us back with him. Father must be particularly concerned about this Sita who has been brought up so tenderly and who is too delicate to live the rough life which she has adopted for my sake. Look, Lakshmana our father's two favourite horses are there and the noble Shatrunjaya, my favourite elephant, is walking in state in the van of the army. I am not able to see my father's white umbrella, though."

The brothers watched the army come to a halt and they did not know that Bharata, in deference to his brother, had forbidden the army to proceed further.

38. BHARATA'S QUEST

The trackers whom Bharata had sent came back to him after a while with great excitement and they said: "At some distance from here on a spot where the ground is fairly level, where there is no habitation as far as the eye can see, we found smoke rising up to the skies. We are almost sure the prince must be there. Perhaps some tapasvins are there, but our instinct is that it is the ashrama of Rama."

Bharata was trembling with excitement. He told the army men: "You should not proceed any further into the forest. Remain here and wait for my instructions. Let Sumantra and Dhriti come with us." The army halted and Bharata with Shatrughna and the two others walked in the path which was indicated by the guides. He looked hard at the sky where smoke was spiralling up. There was in the heart of everyone the feeling that the journey had ended and that Rama had been seen. Bharata could not contain himself.

He walked towards the slope of the hill from where the smoke was snaking its way upwards. He said: "Shatrughna, you should, with these men, search all over the place for the ashrama. Guha will also do so with his men. I will go with some of the men and search. Unless and until I set my eyes on Rama, I can find no peace. I will not rest until I place him on the throne and leave the kingdom in his hands. I am eager to place my head on his dear feet and wash them with my tears. I am jealous of Lakshmana who has the good fortune to be with him always. This Chitrakuta is blessed since Rama dwells in it. It is like the Nandana garden of Indra. The very trees and animals here are more fortunate than me since Rama's eyes have rested on them often." Bharata passed a Sala tree and climbing to its top he found that the ashrama was very near: he could see the smoke very clearly now. He was thrilled and he looked like one who had found the other shore of an ocean which seemed, till now, to stretch far into the horizon.

Bharata beckoned to Guha and with him, walked fast towards the ashrama. He walked to where his brother Shatrughna had been sent and recalled him. All of them walked together now. Bharata's call had convinced Shatrughna that the ashrama had been found and he told Vasishtha: "Please be good enough to come with our mothers along the path we have taken. I will rush to my brother."

Sumantra walked with Shatrughna. He was just as eager as Bharata was to see Rama.

39. BHARATA MEETS RAMA

They spoke not a word. They walked fast and Bharata's heart was ready to burst with happiness. He had found his brother. In a few moments he would return to Rama the kingdom which had been stolen from him by his mother. Rama would come back with him to Ayodhya and there would be nothing but joy everywhere from now on. Thoughts like these chased each other across his mind like white fleecy clouds racing in the sky. They had come very near the ashrama. Bharata saw that it was beautifully built. He saw firewood which had been collected and placed nearby, for use daily. He saw flowers which had been gathered, probably for the worship of the gods to be performed by his brother. He saw the cicatrices on the tree branches where the clothing of the brothers had been tied daily for drying. He saw the cow-dung cakes which had been piled up in pits to keep the cold away when night sets in.

Bharata said: "I am quite sure that we have arrived at the place indicated by sage Bharadvaja. There are signs of habitation here. The smoke from the household fire is dense here. My brother Rama is living in this ashrama, like a tapasvin and soon I will feast my eyes on him."

They walked for a while longer along the banks of the river Mandakini. They ascended a slight slope and all on a sudden they were near the ashrama of Rama. Sala trees, palm and Ashvakarna trees had been used to build it and the roof was covered with a thatch of leaves. The entrance had soft darbha grass spread on it so that it would be soft under the tread.

Beyond the doorway could be seen bows inlaid with gold. There were quivers which were filled with arrows lustrous as the rays of the sun. There were swords inside scabbards made of gold and encrusted with gems. Shields and finger-guards were to be seen and it seemed to them like the cave of the king of the forest.

Bharata perceived a platform on which was burning the fire which had led them to the spot. He looked again and he saw his brother Rama seated in front of the fire, Rama with his hair all matted and tangled, with his noble figure covered by tree-bark and deerskin. Looking like a flame himself, Rama sat facing the fire. With his wide shoulders looking like those of a lion, with his magnificent arms bare of the ornaments which were wont to adorn them, with his eyes like lotus petals, Rama sat in front of the fire worshipping it. The prince who should have ruled the world which had the sea as its boundary now sat like Brahma on darbha grass, spread on the floor and with Sita by his side. Lakshmana was standing near him with his arms locked across his chest.

Bharata stood still for a long moment. His limbs refused to bear him. He then rushed towards Rama. He could not see properly since tears were clouding his eyes. His sorrow was like the sea which had burst its boundary. He stood thus for a while and then spoke in a voice that shook with tears:

"My brother who should be seated in the court served by his myriad attendants and courtiers is now seated on the floor covered by darbha grass and attended by the animals of the forest as his subjects. This great prince who should wear nothing but the softest of silks is wearing tree-bark since he is righteous. How is it possible for him to live with this matted hair? I have seen sandal paste covering those glorious arms and that wide chest and I now see dust from the air clinging to his body and covering him. He has been accustomed only to comforts and such a man is undergoing this rigorous life. All these things have happened because of me. The censure of the world is on me and I should have died before seeing this sight." Bharata, with his face drenched in tears, advanced towards Rama but fell down even before reaching his feet. He looked at Rama and could just say: "Rama!" "My beloved brother!" and could say no more. Shatrughna who was with Bharata all the while fell along with Bharata at the feet of Rama.

Rama raised them up and embracing them, shed tears. It was a very tender meeting of the four brothers. They looked like the sun and the moon with Sukra and Brihaspati beside them. That was the thought in the mind of Sumantra when he came there along with Guha.

Rama wiped his tears and looked at Bharata again and again. He saw Bharata wearing tree-bark and he had also matted his hair. He could not be easily recognised, so thin had he become. Covered with dust and dimmed with the coarse cloth he was wearing, Bharata looked like the sun which had fallen on the earth at the end of the Yuga. Rama embraced him again and again. He placed him on his lap as he would a child and asked him: "Child, it is not right that you should come to the forest thus, since our father is alive and ruling the country. I have not seen you for quite a while since you had gone to the city of your grandfather. And now it seems to me, you look travel-stained and worn-out. Why did you come to the forest? You should not have left father alone at home. I hope he is bearing bravely the separation from all of us. He is so full of love for all of us. Tell me how is my father, that saintly king who has won for himself the other world by his righteous deeds. How are my mothers? Kausalya, Sumitra and Kaikeyi? How is Vasishtha, our guru? I remember Sudhanva, our instructor in the use of weapons. How is he? Tell me all about everyone in Ayodhya and tell me why you have come to the forest."

Bharata looked with his red eyes at Rama and said: "Rama, I am an outcast from Dharma and the observance of it. I have therefore adopted this tree-bark. My lord, emperor of the world, no younger brother inherits the throne when his elder brother is alive. This has been the code of the Ikshvakus. If you wish to bless Ayodhya please come back with me. For the good of the country and of all of us, please come back and be crowned. You have to rule the kingdom which is now an orphan."

Bharata paused for a moment not knowing how to proceed. Rama noted the hesitant voice and he also noted the word 'Orphan.' In a voice full of concern he asked Bharata: "Orphan? Why do you call the country by that name? Our father is ruling the kingdom and with him as father how can Kosala be called 'orphaned'?"

Bharata sobbed out: "It is orphaned, my lord. When I was away in Kekaya, when you left for the forest with Sita and Lakshmana, our father, that saint among men, was gathered to his forefathers. He was not able to bear the separation from you and he died mourning your absence. He lived for just five days after you left. When Sumantra came back to Ayodhya and told him that you had gone beyond the river Ganga, the king's heart broke and died that night.

"Rama, please offer tarpana to him. I paid him the homage of an Anjali and so has Shatrughna. But the soul of a departed person is satisfied only when the Anjali is offered by one dear to him. And, brother, you have ever been dear to our father. You were his favourite. Father thought only of you. He would look only at you. And when you left him and went away, he was sorely distressed. His eyes which were ever resting on your beloved face could not see anything else. His mind which was always set on you could not be withdrawn from thoughts of you and sorrow was the disease which killed our father, the king."

Rama fell down senseless when he heard the news. He was a shattered man. He loved his father just as much as Dasaratha loved him and this tragic death of the king was terrible. When he realised that it was because of him that the king had died, Rama's grief knew no bounds. Trained as he was in controlling all his feelings, this sorrow, however, proved to be too much for him to bear. The news hit him like a thunderbolt hurled by Indra and Rama reeled under it. The brothers and Sita sprinkled water on him and tried to revive him.

After a while Rama woke up from his faint and wept like a child. "I had hopes of finishing this exile of mine and coming back to Ayodhya to grasp the feet of my beloved father in my hands. Now there is nothing left for me in Ayodhya. You tell me that the king died as a result of the sorrow caused by me. I was not fortunate enough even to perform the funeral rites to my father even though I am his eldest son. What is the use of my being alive? You and Shatrughna are fortunate since you could do your duty to your father and perform the samskaras. Kosala is indeed orphaned. You spoke right. I have no desire to come back to Ayodhya even after the termination of the fourteen years. My father will not be there. Will I never set my eyes on him again? Will I never call him 'father!'? Will I never hear him calling me 'Rama!' in that extremely loving voice of his?"

Rama wept for a while and turning to Sita said: "Sita, did you hear what Bharata said? Your father-in-law is dead. Lakshmana, you have lost your father." There was not a single person there whose eyes remained dry at the sight of Rama whose sorrow was inconsolable.

The brothers finally led him to the banks of the river for him to offer tarpana to his dead father. Rama told Lakshmana: "I am going to offer tarpana to my father. Bring me my upper cloth. Bring also the dried cake made of the Ingudi fruit. Let Sita walk in the forefront. You follow her and I will walk behind you. This is the proper way to do it." When they reached the river Sumantra who was devoted to the family comforted Rama, and he held him while he entered the waters to have a bath. The brothers bathed in the river Mandakini and with their cupped palms holding water they said: "This is the Anjali we offer to our father."

Rama lifted his arms with his face turned towards the south and said: "King of kings! You are in the land of the Pitrus. May this water offered to you by me be acceptable to you." Rama came out of the waters and made the offering of the 'Pinda' for his father. He mixed the Ingudi cake with the flesh of the Badari fruit and, after spreading darbha on the ground, he placed the Pinda on it. With great pain in his mind Rama said: "A man's gods should accept the food which he eats. We now eat this and be gracious and accept this offering and be satisfied."

Rama walked away from the water and ascended the slope. After coming back to his ashrama he embraced his brothers. Their grief was great and the men around stood silent while the great man gave vent to his grief.

40. BHARATA'S APPEAL

By this time the army had realised that Bharata had reached his brother's ashrama and so they decided to advance further into the forest and join Bharata. They were eager to see Rama who seemed to have been away from Ayodhya for a very long time, though it was not so. To them, ages seemed to have passed since they last saw him and they could not stay back any longer.

Vasishtha came first with the queens. They walked along the path traced out on the banks of the river Mandakini. They knew that this was the river which had been favoured by Rama for his daily bath and his other rituals. Sumitra and Kausalya were walking slowly and some distance was covered by them. Kausalya said: "Sister, this seems to be the path along which your son Lakshmana walks daily bearing on his manly shoulders the pots of water for the ashrama where my son stays. He has taken upon himself the task of serving Rama and he is doing it well as I can see".

As they were walking their eyes lighted on the darbha grass on which were placed the Pindas. Kausalya exclaimed: "Look on this Pinda which has been offered by the great prince Rama for his dead father. King Dasaratha who was like a god to us, and who lived like a god, who had tasted of all the joys this world had to offer, will now be satisfied by this Pinda made up of Ingudi and Badari since it has been offered by his beloved son. Can anything be more pathetic than this sight?"

They reached the ashrama of Rama. The sight of Rama with his Jata was shocking to the mothers. Rama came forward to meet them and prostrated before all of them. They stroked him with loving hands and Lakshmana followed Rama and then Sita. Kausalya took Sita in her arms and caressed her as she would a daughter born of her.

Rama saluted his guru Vasishtha and so did Lakshmana. Like Indra greeting Brihaspati Rama grasped his guru's feet in his hands and placed his head on them. The first flush of grief had abated and when Vasishtha asked him to be seated Rama did so and by his side sat Bharata, Lakshmana and the youngest brother, Shatrughna. The ministers had come and so had the priests.

Silence, a long silence, pervaded the entire place. Everyone was looking at Bharata and wondering what he would say. Glowing like flames from the same fire, the brothers sat around their guru and it was a glorious sight. Rama spoke first. He looked at Bharata and asked him:

"I am eager to know why you have come here to me dressed in tree-bark and with your hair matted like ours. Give me some plausible reason for this behavior of yours."

Bharata stood up. He folded his palms and suddenly he prostrated before Rama. He then said: "Our father, who was a saint among men, who was renowned the world over for his valour and for his righteousness strayed away from the path of Dharma and performed an unforgivable act. And because of that, he was separated from you and not being able to bear it, he lost his life. Our father gained for himself this blemish in an otherwise blameless life because of a woman who happens to be my mother: Kaikeyi. Because of his promise to this sinful woman he did what he did. Neither has she gained the kingdom which she wanted, nor is she happy now since her lord is dead, her king who loved her to distraction. Her future is terrible to contemplate since it will be a special hell meant for sinners like her.

"Rama, I appeal to you to absolve me of this sin. Please be gracious enough to come back to Ayodhya and accept the kingdom which is yours by right. We want you to be crowned. All these people have come to you to join me in appealing to you. You have always granted the wishes of everyone. It is up to you to keep up the reputation you have earned and grant me my wish. Let the clouds be cleared from the skies and let the moon shine in all his splendour as he does in the autumnal sky. You should not refuse the desire of all of us. Return to the city and rule the people even as our father did. The orphaned city will find a father in you who would make them all happy."

Bharata found great difficulty to talk clearly. He had suffered so much during the past few days. Constant weeping, his anger against his mother, and, in addition, the fear of the censure of the world had worked havoc in this young prince and he was a sad young man trying to voice his eagerness to make Rama go back with him. Rama embraced his beloved brother warmly and spoke to him. "Child, Bharata, you have been born in a noble house. You are blessed with qualities which are not human but divine. My glorious Bharata, how can one like you, walking in the path of Dharma, ever be accused of doing a sinful act with the desire to rule the kingdom? You are of those rare souls who have their senses under control. I am yet to find fault with you for anything. You do not know all the facts and that is why you blame your mother. Do not do so. Fathers have every right to command their sons to act according to their wish and this applies to their wives also. You should not blame our revered father for his actions. He is the ruler of the land. He has right to crown me king of the land or to make me dwell in the forest dressed as I am now. Righteous men should respect their mothers just as much as they do their fathers. When such is the case, when *both* my father and my mother told me: 'Go to the forest', how could I act otherwise? You have been commanded to rule the kingdom and I have been commanded to live in the Dandaka forest for fourteen years. The great emperor Dasaratha has so commanded us and he has reached the land of the forefathers. It is your duty to act according to his wishes, whether you like it or not. The kingdom has been forced on you, I know. But you cannot escape the responsibility. I will rule over the Dandaka for these few years. My father has said so and so will it be. My only aim in life is to obey my father; and the three worlds, even if they are offered to me, hold no charm for me." Night was drawing near and, after the worship of the sun, they returned to the ashrama. The night seemed interminably long for everyone, particularly to Bharata and none of them slept that night.

The sun had risen and they reassembled in the same spot as on the previous evening. No one spoke and they sat silent for a while. Bharata broke the silence and said: "I will recast my words, Rama. My mother has been granted the kingdom which she had desired for my sake. And I own it. I accept the fact. Permit me now to make an offering of the kingdom at your blessed feet. Make it yours. This kingdom is now like a dam which has burst its banks because of the floods caused by heavy rains. Only you can gather up the broken fragments and make it whole. My trying to do what you should will be like a donkey trying to imitate a high-born horse, like a sparrow trying to soar into the heavens like Garuda. It is a happy state of affairs if one is protected by another and is allowed to live without care. On the contrary to protect someone is indeed a hard task. I will look like a dwarf reaching out to the fruits and flowers on a branch well beyond his reach. Please have pity on me and on the citizens of Ayodhya who are waiting with eagerness for your word of assent to this prayer."

Rama was very unhappy. But he had no intention of making any compromise with the code of Dharma which he followed implicitly. Pure of heart and firm in his decision, Rama would not be moved.

He said: "Bharata, do not think that I have no sympathy for you in this your predicament. I understand it fully. But, then, my child, no man is allowed to do as he pleases. Man has no freedom. Fate tosses him about in all directions. The game which Fate plays is unpredictable. Nothing lasts in this world. What has been gathered is scattered about. What was once at the top soon reaches the lowest position. Meetings only end in separations and, as for life, it only ends in death. Ripe fruits have but one fear, that of falling down. And even so, man has no fear other than death. Think of a house built sturdily with strong pillars. Even that, in course of time, becomes weak and ancient. Men too become old, lose their power of thinking and death claims them. The night which passes will never come back and the waters of the Yamuna which flow fast, when in flood, towards the sea, will never return. In this world, Bharata, just as the waters on the surface of the earth get less and less, dried constantly by the rays of the sun, man's life also gets lessened day by day. Your life and mine are fast ebbing away. Think on the Lord, my child. Do not spend your time in the contemplation of another's life. Death walks with us: and he accompanies us on the longest journey we undertake. The skin gets wrinkled. Hair grows white. Old age makes man weak and helpless. Man delights at the sight of the sun rising and again, the setting sun is pleasing to the eye. But man forgets that every sunrise and every sunset has lessened one's life on earth by another day. The seasons come and go and each season has a charm of its own. But they come and when they go, they take with them large slices of our lives every time.

"On the large expanse of the sea two pieces of wood come together. They float together for a while and then they are parted. Even so it is with man and his relationship with life, child, kinsmen, wealth and other possessions. Meetings end only in separation. It is the law of nature. No one is capable of altering the course of Fate. Weeping for one who is dead will not bring him back to life. Like a flood which will never return to the spot it came from, the part of one's life which has gone by, will not come back. Man should take heed of this and set his mind on the attainment of the next world. He should perform his duties and fit himself for the heavens which he will surely inherit then. Our father lived a blameless life and he has reached the heavens which he has earned by the many righteous acts he has performed. He lived a long and happy life and he is now one with the gods. It is not meet that we should mourn his death. He has shed his old and serene body and is now in the *loka* belonging to Brahma. We should not weep any more for our father. A brave man should, under all circumstances, avoid weaknesses like shedding tears or sorrowing for the inevitable.

"Such a father has wished that you should rule the world and that I should live in the forest. Try and calm your mind which is given to this agitation. Go back to Ayodhya and take up the reins of the kingdom. You know me and my determination. I will not give up this forest life because you request me to. It is against all Dharma to disobey one's guru. We should both abide by his command. This is the only path to the heavens. Walk in the path of Dharma which you have been following all these years and do what our father has asked you to do. I will do the same."

Rama ceased to talk and no one spoke for a while. His words were so full of wisdom and at the same time, so compassionate that Bharata was at a loss for words. Bharata tried again and said: "Who can be like you, in this world, Rama, with all your senses under control? Nothing can hurt you. What is considered to be difficult for others is not so for you. And what pleases the ordinary man is not a source of pleasure for a great soul like you. In this ashrama, banished as you are from all comfort and easy living, from the kingdom which should have been yours, you live like a hermit and you look contented, unruffled and calm. Which other man is capable of such wisdom? Unaffected as you are by the reverses of fortune, you should make a gesture to make others happy. Please save me and my mother from the sin which has been committed. In your affection for me, it should be done. My hands are tied by Dharma and that is why I am not able to punish her for what she has done. Born of that righteous king Dasaratha who walked in the path indicated by his predecessors, how can I pursue a course which will win for me nothing but infamy and censure? My father is my guru and he is dead. For these reasons I am not able to pass judgement on his action. Or else I would say: 'Which man who is so well-versed in Dharma will, at the insistence of a woman, do something which is wrong? Which is harmful to all?' There is a proverb that a man, when his end is near, will lose his power of thinking and that has been proved true in the case of my father. Because of thoughtlessness, a lack of vision or some other reason, father has committed a sinful act. It is up to you to save father's name by setting it right and averting the calamity following it. A son's duty is to be jealous of his father's good name. You must take it upon yourself to rectify the wrong done to the kingdom by the king and redeem his name.

'Where is the comparison between the forest and the city? Between the Dharma of a Kshatriya and these matted locks? Between this apparel of yours and the ruling of a kingdom? You should adopt the right course, abandon this way of life which is fit only for sanyasis and rule the world. It is the first duty of a Kshatriya to protect his subjects. This life should be taken up by you later when you have renounced the kingdom at the sunset of your life. I am inferior to you in every way and I am not fit to rule the country. You should do it: only you.

"All the articles necessary for the coronation are here with me. Please allow our guru Vasishtha and the ritviks to crown you, to perform the coronation and make us all happy. That is why the entire population of Ayodhya is here: to witness the coronation. They were cheated once of it and it is up to you to make it up to them. Accept the throne and come back to Ayodhya. We will be your servants standing around you to obey your slightest wish. I fall at your feet and beg you. Do not refuse our desire. If you refuse, I will not go back to Ayodhya. Like my brother Lakshmana I will also remain in the forest serving you all the time."

Rama would not agree. He was firm and the people realised that nothing would move him. His decision made them unhappy and yet, they could not help admiring the greatness of this god among men whom nothing could tempt. Rama tried to soften it for Bharata and he stroked his bent head with loving hands. "My child, only such words will be spoken by the son of a king like my father was. Let me tell you something which you may know or may not. Once, long ago, when our father was wedded to your mother he had promised to the father of the bride, King Ashvapati, that the son born of Kaikeyi would be crowned king. This was the *Kanya Sulka* promised to Kekaya. And again, during the war in the heavens our father's life had been saved by your mother and she had been granted the two boons. She had every right to ask the king to grant them to her. And so, my younger mother asked the king for them: they were not expected by the king of course and still, they were not to be ignored: the kingdom for you and banishment for me. The king was bound by his oath. He has not been unrighteous at all. On the other hand, much against his will he had to comform to the words of your mother. I will certainly obey his wishes and those of my mother. I came to this forest at their behest. You can make my father truthful only if you go back to Ayodhya and rule the country. Our father's promise will be kept only if you go back. We must save father from the sin of Adharma and this is the only way to do it. I have Lakshmana to keep me company and you have Shatrughna with you. Let us, all four of us, do what our father asked us to do and save his name. We will have the satisfaction that we have obeyed father and there is no danger of Adharma if we do so. In fact, it is the only path open to us."

Vasishtha intervened on behalf of Bharata and said: 'Rama, I am your guru and I wish to tell you about the race of which you are a worthy descendant. Every one of the heirs has been the eldest son. This has been the rule and it is not right that you should transgress it. A man has to obey three gurus. One is father, one is the mother and the third is the guru, the one who has initiated him into the mysteries of learning and who has taught him the sacred Gayatri. The third is superior to the other two since the father and mother are but the life-givers while the guru shows man the path to the world, the world of spirituality. You owe me something and you should obey me. For the sake of all these people who have assembled here, for the sake of the antecedents of your family, for the sake of Bharata, and to honour my words you should come back to Ayodhya and be crowned. Your Dharma will not in any way be tainted if you do what I ask you to do. Come back to Ayodhya."

Rama was sorely distressed by all this. He was embarrassed by the words of Vasishtha. He knew the old man's affection for him and he could not obey him. He spoke in a voice full of respect. "The debt I owe to my parents is infinite. They made me what I am. They brought me up with love. They have denied me nothing. They have bathed me, fed me when I was a child and their words steeped in love have made me what I am. It is not possible to return the love of one's parents. Such a man was Dasaratha, my father, and I will not disobey him."

Bharata was desperate. He looked at Sumantra and said:

"Sumantra. spread darbha grass on the ground for me. Unless and until my brother changes his mind and agrees to my proposal I will sit here without moving. If he will not come back with me, I will not go back to Ayodhya. I will sit here, I will lie down without food, without sleep, without water and that is certain."

Sumantra was unhappy too and he brought the darbha grass and stood with it in his hand hoping for a word from Rama. Bharata saw his

BHARATA'S APPEAL

hesitation and talking the darbha from his hands he spread it on the ground himself.

Rama spoke in a firm voice: "Bharata, why do you compel me like this? According to the dictates of Dharma, only a brahmin is allowed to sit in Prayopavesha. This type of compulsion is not allowed to kshatriyas. Abandon this desperate resolve and return to Ayodhya."

Bharata addressed the people of Ayodhya and said: "Why do you all stand silent? Make him come with us." He saw their discomfiture. Rama understood it. They had agreed with him that he was doing only what he thought was right and they had, by now, realised that it was not possible for them to influence him. He said: "Bharata, get up. Come, rise up, touch water and say that you have given up this madness." Bharata stood up and, after touching water, said: "Let the world listen to my words. I have never once spoken to my father about the kingdom. I have never wanted it. I did not instigate my mother to ask for the kingdom on my behalf. I will not allow Rama to dwell in the forest. If he insists on the letter of the law, I suggest that he should rule the kingdom and I will, instead, spend the stipulated number of years in the forest." Rama was astounded by the words of Bharata. He said: "What was sold and what was bought by my father during his lifetime can be altered neither by Bharata nor by me. Devi Kaikeyi's wish that I should spend these few years in the forest is neither wrong nor is it against Dharma. My father's words are right too. I know Bharata. I know what a noble man he is. I know the wealth of affection he has for me. He has great respect for those who are elder to him and he is always truthful. Never once has he uttered a lie nor have his thoughts ever been inclined towards Adharma. There is nothing but good in store for him.

"When my banishment is concluded I will accede to his request and rule the land of my forefathers. Bharata, my child, our father was bound by his promise to Kaikeyi and I accepted the conditions imposed on him by her. You must co-operate with me by obeying me and him too and thus make his words come true." The rishis around were listening spellbound to the conversation between these noble brothers. It thrilled everyone around to see how each was vying with the other in selflessness. "Fortunate is Dasaratha to have such glorious sons," said all of them. They spoke to Bharata in pacifying tones and said : "Noble Bharata, you are a worthy scion of a great race of kings. You are wise and have been brought up to learn early in your life the many nuances of Dharma. Rama is right. If you should desire to vindicate your father's honour, you should listen to the words of Rama. King Dasaratha died without seeing his words come true. We approve of the words spoken by Rama and you should also listen to his advice."

Rama was extremely happy to hear the words of the rishis since this was the first sign of approval he had seen during the long painful hours of discussion with his beloved brother, Bharata. His face was lit up by a smile of gladness and he thanked them silently.

41. BHARATA ASKS FOR THE PADUKAS

Still Bharata maintained his stand. He asked Rama to change his mind. Rama raised him up from the floor where he was prostrating before him and, placing him on his lap, he said : " Do not say that you will not be able to rule the kingdom and do not advance that as a reason for asking me to come back with you. I know how wise you are and I know only too well the path of Dharma which you have ever followed. You are capable of ruling the entire earth and the three worlds too. There is no need for you to worry about it. The ministers who were the advisers in our father's court are with you and they will help you. But you must give up this hope of taking me back with you.

"Bharata, the radiance may be separated from the moon : the mountain Himavan may, perhaps, be seen bereft of its snowy cloak : the ocean may overstep the bourne set for it but I will not break the promise I gave to my father. Child, whether your mother did what she did because of her love for you, or because of her avarice, is immaterial. Your duty is to obey the command of our father and rule the kingdom."

Bharata's face was a picture of unhappiness. He now realised that he would have to go back to the city without Rama. He wiped his brimming eyes with his forearm and said :

"You have commanded me. You are now like a father to me and I should do what you ask me to. But one thing is certain. I will not accept the kingdom for myself."

From among the many articles he had brought for the coronation of Rama in the forest, Bharata hunted out a pair of sandals inlaid with gold.

He had, evidently, hoped to make Rama wear them during the ceremony. He said: "Here are sandals inlaid with gold. I beseech you to stand on them for a moment. Blessed by the touch of your sacred feet these sandals will become sanctified and they will bear the burden of ruling the world." Rama smiled at Bharata and stood for a moment wearing the golden sandals as desired by Bharata. He gave them to him after that. Bharata prostrated before the sandals and said: "My beloved brother, remember I will live wearing these coarse tree-bark and deerskin for the next fourteen years and I will retain these matted locks until you remove yours. I will wait for you to come back and I will live outside the city of Ayodhya. My food will be fruits and roots. I will enthrone these sandals and they will rule the kingdom as your symbols. I will rule the kingdom as your representative. The day your banishment is concluded I must see you or else, I will fall into the blazing fire and end my life. You must keep this in mind." "I will," said Rama.

He embraced Bharata and Shatrughna and said : "Bharata, remember, you must treat your mother with respect. Do not pursue this anger and displeasure. I want you to swear in my name and in the name of Sita that you will do so." Tears were flowing freely from the eyes of Rama as he bade farewell to the noble Bharata. Bharata took the sandals in his hands and placed them with reverence on his head and he made a Pradakshina to Rama. Three times he went round him and then stood still.

Rama went to each one of the many who had come to see him and spoke to them with affection. Finally he bade farewell to his mothers and to Sumantra with tears in his eyes.

The moment had come when they had to leave and the leave-taking was painful on either side.

When they had left Rama tottered into the ashrama unable to bear the parting from his dear and beloved people and kinsfolk.

42. BHARATA'S RETURN

To an extent, Bharata was happy. He had not been able to take Rama back with him, it was true. But he was able to avoid the sin of accepting the throne. Rama's sandals would rule the country and he was but a servant of the king. Still carrying the Padukas on his head Bharata ascended the chariot and Shatrughna followed him. The *kulaguru* Vasishtha and the ministers preceded him. They went round the Chitrakuta mountain after crossing the river Mandakini and travelled eastwards. After covering a large area of land they reached the ashrama of the sage Bharadvaja. Bharata decided to halt there for the rest of the day and he got down from the chariot. He went to the rishi and saluted him. Bharadvaja asked him: "My dear child, did you meet Rama? Were you successful in your mission?" Bharata's face was downcast. He replied: "Rama, my revered brother, was requested by me again and again but it was in vain. Guru Vasishtha asked him to come back to Ayodhya and to him also Rama said: 'I am firm in my resolve to obey the commands of my father. After the termination of the fourteen years I will return to the city and rule it as per your wish, but not till then.' Our guru then suggested that he should give me permission to place the sandals touched and sanctified by Rama's feet to be placed on the throne and Rama agreed to it. Rama stood facing the east and he stood for a moment on these Padukas and then he gave them to me. I have got a semblance of peace, my lord, after noble Rama gave me these and I am going back to perform the coronation for the Padukas."

Bharadvaja was thrilled to listen to the events which took place at Chitrakuta. He was full of admiration for the sons of Dasaratha, each vying with the other in loyalty and selflessness.

He said: "Child Bharata, I am not surprised that you are the home of all good, great and noble qualities like a deep lake is full of clear sweet water. When he has you for son the king Dasaratha has been made immortal." Bharata took leave of him in a humble manner and continued his journey to Ayodhya. They passed the river Yamuna and they came again to the banks of Ganga. The river was crossed as before and Guha went back to Shringiberapura.

After that the journey to Ayodhya did not take very long. Bharata saw before him the golden turrets of his father's city. He realised that the city would be empty of his father's presence and that of Rama, for a long time. He spoke to Sumantra sadly and said: "Look at the city — which seems to me to be in ruins since my dear ones are absent from there."

As he was talking they entered the gates. Soon they reached the palace of the king. Bharata descended from the chariot and entered the palace. It was empty and to Bharata it resembled a 'durdina', a day cursed by the gods: a day without the sun to brighten it. Tears welled up into his eyes and he let them fall unheeded.

He helped his mothers to go back to their apartments and he then called a council of the elders of the court. He said: "I have made up my mind to go to Nandigrama now. I want to take leave of all of you. I will live there and try to bear this separation from my brother with fortitude. My father, the king has been gathered to his forefathers, and my brother who should have succeeded him now rules the animals in the forest. He is the king and I will await his return: the Padukas will rule the country till then."

Vasishtha and the others listened to his words with approval and said: "May your fame live long in this world of men as a symbol of nobility. Your devotion to your brother has made you the best among men. May you be blessed with a good name and great fame in aftertimes."

Bharata called for his chariot. He took tender leave of his mothers and accompanied by his brother he ascended the chariot. The royal court accompanied him. Vasishtha, as usual, preceded him to Nandigrama which was situated east of Ayodhya. The people of Ayodhya were also travelling to the little village since they knew that the coronation of the Padukas would be taking place there.

They reached the place. Bharata addressed the elders and said: "I have been appointed as the guardian of the country by my revered brother. These sandals will rule the kingdom." He saluted the sandals and spoke again : "To me these are the blessed feet of my brother. The white umbrella will be held above them and they will inspire me to walk in the right path and never to swerve from it. I will guard them as my very life. Soon, very soon, I will see them decorating the feet of my brother and I will find peace of mind. I can then serve him as a servant all the time. I will then redeem my name from the stigma which my mother earned for me. I will be relieved of a great burden when my brother comes back and begins his rule."

Dressed in tree-bark and deerskin, Bharata lived in Nandigrama. He would talk to the sandals and report to them about the happenings in the kingdom as though they were human. There was nothing he did without consulting them! Dedicating it to the Padukas he ruled the kingdom, the noble Bharata who was devoted to Rama.

ARANYA KANDA

1. RAMA ABANDONS CHITRAKUTA

Bharata had come and gone. There was an aura of sadness in the ashrama of Rama. All three of them were unable to forget the painful episode and Rama was grieved that he had to be so firm with Bharata and his tear-stained face was always in the mind of Rama. He could not erase it from his mind. They would sit and talk about it often and finally they would conclude that Fate was more powerful than all the other forces. And so several days passed.

Rama noticed something strange in the behaviour of the rishis who were residing in the several ashramas on the mountain. They seemed to be conversing together in secret and they would not even speak. Rama felt that this unrest in their minds concerned him in some way. Rama decided to ask them. He went to their *kulapati* and asked: "My lord, I am worried about some strange happenings in the ashramas. It seems to me the rishis are different in their attitude towards me. They seem to be ill-at-ease. Have I, by any chance, offended any of them? I hope my behaviour has not in any way been responsible for this. Perhaps my brother Lakshmana has been at fault by some inadvertence. Or is Sita to be blamed for any lack of respect towards them? I am very unhappy about it and I would like you to tell me the reason for this unrest in the minds of the rishis in Chitrakuta. Please enlighten me."

The old *kulapati* smiled kindly at Rama and said: "Child, all three of you are not to be blamed at all. How can anyone ascribe carelessness in your serving us? The rishis are afraid of a new threat to their peaceful living. Rakshasas have begun to harass us. That is the subject of their conversation. There is a rakshasa by name Khara. He is a brother of Ravana, the rakshasa monarch. Khara resides in Janasthana and he is killing all the rishis who reside in Janasthana. He is cruel, shameless and he eats human flesh. He is arrogant because no one has, so far, been able to defeat him in battle. He has now heard about you and he is jealous of your reputation as a valiant man. And so, perhaps, you are the indirect cause of the trouble brought about by the rakshasas to the rishis.

"The henchmen of Khara have begun to visit the ashramas in Chitrakuta only after you began to dwell here. They are well-versed in Maya tactics too and so, unseen by us, they cause a lot of trouble to every one of us in many ways. The yajnas are disturbed: the sacrificial fire is extinguished all on a sudden: the utensils disappear for no reason at all. There is nothing but cruelty in their hearts and the rishis have begun to dread the coming of these miscreants. They have made up their minds to abandon this spot and they are asking me to suggest a safer place. Before they are killed they want to go away from here. We have now decided to go to a forest which is not far away from here. The ashrama of Kanva is located there and we will be welcomed there. It is situated on the banks of the river Malini. The rakshasas may try to harm you and Sita also. If you so desire, you can also come with us. However careful you may be, there is always danger for you and Sita here."

Rama was very unhappy to hear about the predicament of the rishis. He was not able to prevent them from leaving the ashramas which had been safe for them until now and which had become dangerous because of the rakshasas. He accompanied the host of rishis to a short distance and after bidding them farewell he came back to the ashrama.

After some days Rama felt that he was not happy any longer in Chitrakuta. Several reasons prompted him to think of moving away from there. He thought: "Bharata came here and saw me. My mothers came with him and their sad faces are etched in my memory. Look where I will, there are signs of Bharata's visit and it hurts me all the time."

He spoke to Lakshmana and Sita about it and they were also of the same mind. The ashrama which had once been a haven of peace had now become full of painful memories and they were willing to abandon that beautiful mountain.

Collecting all their belongings which were but few in number, the three began their journey again. They descended from Chitrakuta.

2. ATRI AND ANASUYA

After travelling some distance Rama, Sita and Lakshmana came to the ashrama of the renowned rishi Atri. They entered the ashrama and stood still after saluting the grand old man. He considered Rama and his brother as his own sons, so affectionate was his welcome. He entertained his young guests with fruits and he was pleased to see Sita. Noble-minded Anasuya was the wife of Atri and the old rishi was very proud of her, and her tapas.

He told Sita: "Go inside the ashrama and pay your respects to Anasuya, my wife. She is a great tapasvini and an emancipated soul. You will be fortunate to have her blessings. He told Rama about her.

"Once, when the world was suffering from a drought for a duration of ten years, Anasuya created fruits and roots for the good of humanity. She made the river Ganga overflow so that the land could become fertile. She has performed severe tapas for a thousand years. She is famed in all the three worlds for her tapas, its severity and for the Vratas she has observed. She is like a mother to you. Let Sita go to her presence and prostrate before this great lady who is worshipped by everyone."

Rama spoke to Sita and said: "Sita, you have heard the words spoken by the great sage. Go at once to the lady and take her blessings." Sita hastened towards the inner parts of the ashrama where Anasuya was.

She saw Anasuya. She was weak because of her age: her frame was shrunk and her hair was white. She was so weak that her body trembled always like a plantain tree shaken by a strong breeze. Sita went to the venerable old woman and prostrated before her and announced herself to her.

Anasuya was extremely pleased to see Sita and her humility. She said: "It is good that you are righteous by nature. A beautiful young woman like you, brought up in luxury, will find it hard to adopt this forest life. But you have followed Rama to the forest and you have given up all thoughts of comforts and ease because you wanted to be with your lord. It is a great thing you have done. There will surely be a place in heaven for women like you to whom a husband is worthy of honour, whether he is a king or a mendicant, a saint or a sinner. For a pure-minded woman her husband is her lord and god and he is the only god whom she worships. I am very happy to see you. You are a Pativrata. You will attain great fame and a great name because of your devotion to Rama." Sita was feeling embarrassed by the praise which was being lavished upon her and she spoke with befitting words.

"I have been taught the lesson that the husband is the only god for a woman. Your praise of me because I am doing only what is right is superfluous. There is nothing here to be surprised about, mother. Even if my husband had been devoid of good qualities which are expected in a man, still, it would have been my duty to follow him wherever he went. But then, this my lord is the home of all great and noble qualities. He is compassionate. He has never been a slave to the senses. He is steadfast in his affections. He has always tried to please his mother and he is his father's favourite. The affection he has for his mother Kausalya has been given to his other mothers also. When such a man is my husband, is it strange that I should be devoted to him and that I have come to the forest with him?"

Anasuya was listening to the young girl with a smile on her wrinkled face. She was pleased with her.

Sita continued: "When I was given away in marriage, my mother taught me these lessons before I left for Ayodhya. And Rama's mother spoke the same words too when I left for the Dandaka with Rama. I have locked the advice safe in my heart and I have tried to follow it as well as I can. I am grateful to you since you have approved of my behaviour."

Anasuya said: "Sita, I have accumulated a wealth of tapas and I am able to grant you any boon you desire, and I wish you would ask me for something which can be granted by me. I want to give you something."

Sita was surprised at her words. This was the first time she had heard of a woman who had accumulated enough tapas to be able to grant boons to others. She smiled softly and said: "Mother, all the desires in my heart have been fulfilled. What need have I for boons ?" Anasuya was not surprised at the answer from Sita. She did not think that the wife of Rama would have any desires which had to be gratified by her. She said: "I bless you with all my heart. May you be fortunate in every way."

The old lady then brought several articles with her and said: "Sita, accept these clothes, garlands and ornaments. I also want to give you these specially prepared perfumes and scented water which will make you look and feel fresh always. Take them and wear them to please your husband even as Lakshmi will please Narayana."

Sita accepted the gifts with humility and she saluted the old lady. Anasuya was an old and revered saint and she made Sita sit by her side. Anasuya stroked her with her old and twisted fingers and said: "Sita, I have heard that Rama won you in a Swayamvara. I would like to hear about it in detail. Tell me everything: about how it happened. I am very eager to hear it from your lips."

Sita smiled happily and said: "Nothing will excite me more than recounting that incident. You must have heard about my father. He is Janaka and he has won a name as a very good and righteous king. He is called a Rajarshi. He is ruling the country of Videha and Mithila is the capital for the land. Once he wanted to perform a yajna and for that purpose he ploughed the ground meant for it as had been ordained by the priests. I have been told by him that when he was doing so, the earth had split and there he found a small child. He was wonder-struck at the sight of me. He was childless and he took me in his arms and said: 'This is my daughter.' He was very fond of me.

"I have also been told that a voice from the sky said: 'O king! She is your daughter according to Dharma.' My father brought me up with great affection. When I had grown up and was considered to have reached an age when I should be married, my father was worried about me. No father will consider anyone good enough to be the husband of his daughter even if it be Indra himself. He wanted to give me to one who would be fit enough to take my hand in marriage.

"He finally decided to have a Swayamvara for me. He had with him a divine bow given to him by Varuna and two quivers which were inexhaustible. It was a powerful bow and it was not easy for anyone to lift it. My father had that bow brought before the kings who had assembled and said: 'My daughter will be the wife of the man who will lift the bow and string it. My word is given and I will not go back on it.'

"The kings tried and they all failed. No one could even lift it. They all saluted the bow and went away.

"After a long time, this Rama came to Mithila with the rishi Vishvamitra on the occasion of a yaga and Lakshmana had come with him. My father welcomed the rishi with great excitement and he was told about the young men who were with Vishvamitra. The rishi said: 'These young men are the sons of Dasaratha. They have come to see your bow. Show the divine bow to them.''

"My father at once asked for the bow to be brought. The valiant prince Rama lifted the bow without any effort, strung it and twanged the string. Because of his strength the bow which was held in his left hand broke in two and the sound was like the clap of thunder. My father was very happy. He had water in a gold vessel brought and wanted to give me to Rama at once. But Rama would not agree to it. He wanted to have his father's approval before he could accept me.

"My father sent messengers to Ayodhya and it was only after king Dasaratha came to the city that I was given in marriage to Rama. My sister Urmila was given to Lakshmana. This is the story of my marriage to Rama."

Anasuya listened eagerly to the words of Sita watching the happy face of Sita as she recounted the story of her wedding. She embraced the girl and said: "For a long time I have been wanting to know the details of this your wedding and it was good to hear it from your lips. You speak very softly and your voice is very beautiful."

The evening faded into night and they could hear the noises made by the birds which were returning to their nests. Rishis were coming back to their ashramas after bathing in the rivers and bringing water in the Kamandalus in their hands. The red flames from the evening fires could be seen crimson like the breast of a dove. The forest was dense all around and it was dark. The tame animals in the ashramas had already gone to sleep and there was a hushed silence everywhere.

Anasuya said: "Sita, look, the sky is studded with stars and the night is far advanced. The moon has risen brightening the heavens. Sita, go and join your husband. I want to see you dressed in the ornaments and perfumes given by me. Wear them."

Sita did as she was bid and she touched the feet of the revered Anasuya. She then walked towards Rama with shy steps. Rama looked at her with a smile and knew that Anasuya had made a gift of them to her. Sita told him about her conversation with the old lady and about the gifts. Rama knew that this was a happening which was unique in the life of a human being: the love of a noble and saintly lady which made her make Sita wear ornaments which she had possessed.

Rama spent the night in the ashrama of Atri. In the morning they asked the rishi for permission to leave. The rishis dwelling in the forest spoke to them about the dangers in the forest. They said: "Rama, this forest is infested with many rakshasas who are fond of human flesh and human blood. Never for a moment should you be careless. Be on your guard always. Follow this path. This is frequented by rishis who go in search of fruits and darbha daily. It will be easy for you to penetrate into the forest if you do not stray away from this path."

Rama listened to their words carefully and, after being blessed by them, he walked with Sita and Lakshmana along the path indicated by the rishis. He entered the dense forest and the rishis who were watching their progress lost sight of them. Rama had entered the forest like the sun enters a mass of dense dark clouds. They had entered the Dandaka forest.

3. THE DANDAKA FOREST

When Rama entered the Dandaka forest his eyes lighted on a group of ashramas belonging to the rishis there. Wherever he turned his eyes, they were greeted with the sight of tree-bark garments hanging from tree branches. Darbha grass was abundant there. He could perceive the spiritual glow. The impact was almost physical. There was this spiritual glow pervading the entire atmosphere. It was very much like trying to look at the noonday sun with naked eyes. The place was the refuge of all animals. Deer were there and birds. Almost everywhere could be seen platforms erected for the performance of Agnihotra and the floor was literally strewn with darbha, deerskin, samith, pots to hold water which was sanctified with incantations, and all the many things to be found in the ashramas of rishis. The forest was full of trees favoured by the holy men and they bore fruits and flowers which were needed by the dwellers there. The air was filled with the solemn music of the recitation of the Vedas.

There were rivulets there scattered around the place and lakes too and all of them had lotuses blooming on their surfaces. And the rishis who lived on fruits and roots, who had their senses under control, who wore nothing but tree-bark and deerskin, were resplendent with the spiritual glory which was equalled only by the sun and Agni. The sacred spot was like the *Brahmaloka,* the abode of the Lord of Creation and Rama walked softly and hesitantly into this realm of the ancient rishis who were rich in the wealth of tapas.

Rama and Lakshmana took up their bows in their hands and quietly unstrung them. After they had done so, the brothers walked towards the ashramas. The inmates of the ashramas had already divined the coming of Rama and they welcomed their guests with great excitement. They recited verses blessing the noble brothers and Sita while they stood with humble looks embarrassed by the words of the rishis. All of them looked at the glorious brothers, their handsomeness, their powerful arms and their broad chests, their fingers which had become scarred with their constant use of the bow and arrows. They saw with sadness the tapasic dress they were wearing and they were very pleased to have the scions of the Ikshvaku line in their midst. They made them accept their hospitality.

They said: "Your fame has travelled faster than you, O prince! You are the protector of the world. You are to be worshipped by us since we are your subjects. You are our emperor who will punish the wicked and keep the good from being harmed. Rama, it has been said that a king is an amsha of Indra, the lord of the heavens. He rules the world of men and is meant to enjoy the pleasures of the world. We are dwellers in the world ruled by you. This is true whether you live in the city or in the forest. You are our king. We have given up the power to curse, we have given up anger and we have no fear of the senses gaining ascendancy in our minds. We are like your children who need the love and care of a father."

They spent a night there and proceeded on their journey. The further they progressed, the more apparent became the fierceness of the forest. There were wild animals everywhere: tigers, wolves, and wild buffaloes. The trees were strange to them. They had not seen the likes of them before. Some had creepers clinging to them and these creepers were sucking the lives out of the trees. There were lakes which were so deep that the water looked dark and fearful. The birds did not sound as happy as they did in Chitrakuta. They seemed scared, silent and the travellers were feeling uneasy.

They had a premonition that something dreadful was waiting to happen. They felt it in their bones.

While they proceeded cautiously Rama saw a stupendous figure appear before him. He was immense like the peak of a mountain. His voice was loud and coarse and his deep-set eyes were fearful. He was dreadful to look at and he was wearing the skin of a tiger. In his hand he held a trident which had the carcasses of several wild animals impaled on its prongs. He came before them suddenly and they were taken aback by the terrible rakshasa.

4. THE KILLING OF VIRADHA

The rakshasa rushed towards them and, before they could grasp what was happening, he snatched Sita in his vile hand and held her to him. And he asked them: "Evidently Fate has decreed that you should be short-lived. Or else how could you have been foolish enough to enter the Dandaka forest? Who are you? Strange is your apparel! You are attired like tapasvins but your weapons contradict your garments. I am yet to see a rishi walking with a beautiful woman like you are doing. Evidently you are not rishis. Or else, you are depraved rishis who take a woman with you. You are insulting the garments you are wearing. Who are you? As for me, I am a rakshasa as you can see and they call me Viradha. This forest, which is difficult to penetrate, is where I live and my food is the bodies of the foolish rishis who dwell here. I have decided to make this woman my wife and I will kill you both and drink your blood."

Sita was trembling like a leaf, caught as she was in his forceful grip. Rama was extremely distressed and he spoke to Lakshmana as though he had no hopes of rescuing Sita. He said: "Lakshmana, this princess, this beautiful Sita who had been happy till now, has been carried away by a rakshasa, and that under my very eyes. Look at her frightened face.

Lakshmana, Kaikeyi's wishes have been fulfilled. And how soon! She desired the kingdom for herself and that was not enough for her. She did not want me in the land and she banished me from my father's city. Lakshmana, I have touched the very depths of despair. This calamity which has befallen Sita is much greater than my losing my dear father or losing the kingdom."

Rama's face was drenched in tears and he was despondent. Lakshmana, however, was spitting anger like a cobra which had been trodden and he said: "Rama, how can you mourn thus? You, who is equal to Indra in valour, who is the Lord of lords and who has me by your side? Come, shake off this sadness, brother. This earth will soon be soaked with the blood of this sinner whom I will kill with my sharp arrows. My anger which has been smouldering against Bharata will now find an outlet against this Viradha. I will fell him even as Indra did the mountains with his Vajra. I will pierce his enormous chest and watch him fall to the ground and die in agony."

Lakshmana accosted Viradha and said: "Indeed you are stupid if you think that you can go back alive once you have appeared before us! Tell me about yourself. I would like to know more." Viradha shouted at him and asked: "Who are you both? You have not told me. Where have you been planning to go?"

Rama, ever courteous, replied softly: "We belong to the race of the Ikshvakus. We are well-behaved righteous men, kshatriyas who have come to the forest. We would like to know more about you. Tell us."

Viradha said: "I will tell you. I am the son of Jaya and my mother is Shatahrada. My name is Viradha. Brahma has granted me a boon. I am immune to the weapons which may be used against me. I cannot be killed by any of them. I cannot be cut up nor can you cleave my body. You can abandon all hopes of killing me. Leave this woman to be my wife and I will be gracious enough to let you escape alive."

Rama was very angry with him for his arrogance and he said: "Do not be too hopeful. You have asked for death and, believe me, you will attain your desire in a fight with us. Only, do not run away like a coward."

He suited the action to the word and sent sharp arrows to hurt the rakshasa. Golden-tipped, decorated with the feathers of the eagle, the seven arrows of Rama were like scorching fire and they pierced the chest of Viradha and fell on the ground. He dropped Sita and rushed towards Rama with his trident uplifted. They rained arrows on him but he stood firm and laughed at them. Again he rushed towards them. Rama broke his trident into two with his arrows and it fell to the ground. They tried to fight with their swords and Viradha lifted them off the ground and carrying them, ran into the forest.

Rama said: "Lakshmana, let him have his way. Let him carry us as far into the forest as he wants to. He is taking the path which we were pursuing and it will save us the trouble of cutting our way into the forest."

Viradha entered the dense forest. Sita wailed and sobbed as though her heart would break. With her arms lifted to the skies she said: "This dreadful rakshasa is carrying my very life away from me. O rakshasa! kill me and eat me, but leave him alone. Do not kill the princes. I am alone here and instead of tigers and panthers or wolves eating me, you can do so and let them live."

He paid no heed to her words. The brothers decided to kill him. Lakshmana cut off his left arm and Rama, his right arm. Viradha fell to the ground. They wrestled with him, maimed him and he was bleeding. He had told them that he could not be killed by weapons and this was the only way they could hope to get rid of him. It was not possible to kill him. Hurt as he was, still life would not leave his body. Finally Rama said: "Lakshmana, let us dig a pit and bury him after strangling him. That is the only course open to us."

The moment he heard the words of Rama, Viradha said: "Lord of lords, now I know who you are. I have been defeated by you and in my ignorance I did not realise who you are. You are Rama, the son of Kausalya and you are the protector of the entire world. This is Lakshmana your valiant and noble brother. It was your pure and chaste wife whom I tried to carry away. Forgive me for my ignorance. I will tell you who I am, really.

"I am a gandharva by name Tumburu and I had been cursed by my lord Kubera to assume this form. Asked to recall the curse by me, he could not do so. He said: 'Rama, the son of Dasaratha, will defeat you in a fight. Then you will be able to shed this cursed body and come back to the heavens.' May you be blessed, Rama. I have reached the end of my life which I have been cursed to live through, all these years, since ever so long.

"At a distance of a yojana and a half from here, is located the ashrama of the great rishi Sharabhanga. He is famed for his tapas and you must go now to him and take his blessings. As for me, please bury me in the pit and put an end to my misery. I knew that this is the best end for a rakshasa. If he is buried as you suggested, he becomes heir to the heavens. I have been told so."

After strangling him Rama and Lakshmana buried him in a pit. Viradha abandoned the rakshasa's body and regained the form of a gandharva. He saluted Rama and Lakshmana with Sita and reached the heavens.

Rama took Sita with him and they entered the Dandaka forest, their destination being the ashrama of Sharabhanga. Rama said: "Very soon we will try to cover the distance and reach the ashrama of sage Sharabhanga. We are not in the least familiar with this forest and it will be wise if we reach a shelter before nightfall."

The anticipation of seeing a rishi about whom he had heard so much made Rama forget the fatigue in his body because of the fight with Viradha. Sita too was happy so much so that she did not mind the long distance they had to cover before reaching the ashrama.

5. THE SAGE SHARABHANGA

They had reached the vicinity of the ashrama of the sage Sharabhanga. While they were very near, Rama saw something very unusual. He saw a chariot and the chariot wheels did not touch the ground. They were poised in the air. Four green horses were yoked to it. Out of the chariot descended a glorious form, bright like the rising sun or the flames of a sacrificial fire. He did not touch the earth, either, and his feet were above the ground. Rama saw that it was Indra, the lord of the heavens. He was wearing ornaments which were resplendent in the light of the sun and his silks were flying in the breeze. He was with several devas who had accompanied him. Indra entered the ashrama of Sharabhanga.

Rama with Sita and Lakshmana stood some distance away from the ashrama. He indicated the chariot to the other two and said: "Look at that fascinating sight! The glorious chariot is staying poised in the air! Green horses are yoked to it: This must be Indra's chariot and the group of men who went inside are divine beings. They were all looking young and their garments and their bearing was in accordance with those of the dwellers in the realm of Indra. I have been given the description of the chariot of Indra and the green horses yoked to it. This must be Indra. Wait for me here a while, Lakshmana. I will go near and find out who it was who went inside just now."

As he was proceeding towards the ashrama, Rama saw Indra emerging from it. He had already taken leave of the rishi and he told his attendants: "Look! This is Rama who is approaching the ashrama of Sharabhanga. He should not meet me until the purpose of his Avatara is achieved. I should talk to him only later. He has to perform an act which no one else will be able to. A great task is ahead of him and I will see the completion of it very soon. Let us go away from here before he meets us."

Indra hurried to his chariot and went back to the heavens.

Rama stood as one under a spell. He watched the chariot until it was out of sight and he went back to Lakshmana and Sita. He took them with him and entered the ashrama of the great Sharabhanga. The welcome which they had at the ashrama was heart-warming and they were made to seat themselves on the darbhasanas provided for them. Rama asked the rishi about the divine-looking person who had just gone out of the ashrama.

Sharabhanga said: "That was Indra. Rama, Indra had come to take me to *Brahmaloka* which can be attained only by those who have realised the Brahman. I have earned it by my tapas. But then Rama, I had heard that you have come to the forest, that you are already in the Dandaka forest, and that I would soon be able to see you. I refused to go to *Brahmaloka* now since I was keen on entertaining a noble guest like you. Noble Rama, after spending some time with you, I will go to the heavens. Rama, I have performed tapas and the wealth of my tapas is enormous. I have gained all the heavenly abodes for myself. Take my tapas from me as a gift. I wish to give it all to you. I will then be happy."

Rama, who was well-versed in all the shastras, said: "I will have to earn them all for myself on my own, my lord! At the moment, I do not seek the other worlds but a spot here in Dandaka where I can dwell with Lakshmana and Sita."

Sharabhanga smiled gently at the sweet manner in which Rama had evaded the issue and said: "Not very far from here is the ashrama of Sutheekshna, a rishi rich in the wealth of tapas. If you go to him he will be able to help you find a place for your living. Go to the spot where his ashrama is situated. Go in a direction opposite the flow of this river Mandakini. You will come across rivers and flower-laden trees and boats filled with flowers. You will reach Sutheekshna's ashrama.

"Do me a favour, Rama. I know who you are. Rest your eyes with love on me and I will shed this body of mine as a snake sheds its skin."

He asked for a fire to be built and he poured oblations into it. He then entered it.

Even as they were watching, tongues of flames were licking the old and serene form which was once Sharabhanga. The fire died down and a young and handsome form rose out of it. He looked as though he had been made out of light itself, so glowing was he. He ascended into the sky and reached the abode of Brahma and was welcomed by Brahma.

After the ascension of Sharabhanga to *Brahmaloka*, the rishis in the forest came to visit Rama. They were a large group and Rama saluted them all. They said:

"You are, we have been told, a very valiant prince. Like Indra to the devas you are, to us, the protector. Born in the line of the Ikshvakus you are endowed with all the qualities of the kings of that line. There is no one in the three worlds to equal you, in fame, in valour or in righteousness. You are devoted to your father and, to you, truth is the religion ultimate. We have come to you to ask a favour of you. Since you are born to see that Dharma is established and followed wherever you go, we ask this of you. We do not have to remind you of the duties of a king. One who does not give succour to his subjects is tainted with sin. But the king who treats his people like his own children, like his very life, will be famed as a just king and his fame will last for ever. He will win the acclaim of the gods in the heavens, and in *Brahmaloka* he will be honoured as a good king.

"Rama, we are very unhappy. We have you as our king and yet fear is the predominant feeling in the minds of all of us. Rakshasas harass us and we are helpless against them. Come with us and we will show you a sight you have never seen before."

They led Rama to a spot nearby and said: "Look, Rama! Look at that little white mountain. Can you guess it for what it is?"

Rama could not. And they said: "That is made up of the bones of the myriads of rishis and their disciples who have been killed and eaten up by these rakshasas. The dwellers in the ashramas built on the banks of the Pampa, on the slopes of Chitrakuta and on the banks of the river Mandakini are greatly oppressed by them. We can no longer bear the many atrocities of the rakshasas. Rama, when we heard of your arrival we thanked the gods above and rushed to you for succour. We have no one else to guard us. You are our only refuge. We consider you to have come here to help us."

The pathetic story recounted by the rishis made Rama extremely concerned about their welfare. He said: "It is not right that you should address me thus. I am but your servant and you should command me. It is my duty to enter the great Dandaka forest and to rid you of this menace. It is my personal responsibility. I have been sent by my father, the emperor, to this forest. I will take up the duty assigned to me by all of you. My life in the forest will be worthwhile if I can help you. I will fight with the rakshasas and try to destroy their entire clan. Please have my assurance. Aided by my brother I will rid this forest of the rakshasas."

The visiting rishis returned to their ashramas with light hearts and Rama proceeded towards the ashrama of Sutheekshna. Some of the rishis accompained them to show them the way and for the pleasure of their company. They indicated several spots in the several places where some strange tree or flower was to be found and so they walked along the banks of the river Mandakini.

After they had traversed some distance there came to view a big mountain which looked like a large, black cloud. Rama and the other two were now on the fringe of a thick forest; the trees were all dense and it was frightening: the darkness there. After they had penetrated into the forest they came upon an ashrama. It was lonely and many fruit trees were surrounding it. Flowers there were in plenty and the atmosphere was soothing and peaceful.

6. THE SAGE SUTHEEKSHNA

Rama approached the ashrama and they entered it with soft and reverent steps. They saw Sutheekshna seated there. Rama announced himself and prostrated before him and Lakshmana and Sita followed him.

Rama said: "Lord, I am Rama. I have come to the ashrama to pay my respects to you and take your blessings." The rishi rose up from where he sat, embraced Rama and said: "I am pleased with your coming. I should have reached the heavens long ago. But I heard that you were here, in the hill by name Chitrakuta. I knew that you would come down later, to Dandaka and that was the sole reason for my remaining on the earth. I have been wanting to see you. Indra came to fetch me to the *Brahmaloka*. He told me that I had won all the *lokas* because of my tapas. Rama, accept all the worlds from me and you with your brother and with your wife can live in these worlds. I will be only happy to give the results of my tapas to you."

Rama smiled his gentle smile and said: "The worlds you mention, my lord, have to be won by me on my own accord. I want you to help me find a place where I can dwell in comfort with my brother and my wife. Sage Sharabhanga asked me to approach you about this. He told me that you will be able to advise me."

The sage said: " You can stay here, Rama. There are fruits and you can get enough roots to feed the three of you! There are any number of flowers to please your wife and the river with her constant music will be pleasing to the ear. Herds of deer come to the ashrama, unafraid of anyone and they are the sole visitors to this place, far away as it is from other ashramas."

Rama listened to him and replied: "My lord, perhaps, in spite of me, my kshatriya blood may prove to be my undoing. I may kill one of the deer and pollute this sacred spot. I do not think it is right on my part to dwell for long on this ashrama."

Evening had set in and the brothers accepted the hospitality of Sutheekshna. They joined the rishis in the prayer to the setting sun. The rishi plied his guests with luscious fruits and the night passed peacefully for them.

Rama woke up very early in the morning. He bathed in the waters of the river which was very cold and which had the perfume of the lotuses in it. He then approached the great Sutheekshna and said: "We spent a happy night after being entertained by you. We have been honoured by your hospitality. May we take leave of you? We desire to visit the dwellers in the forest Dandaka. We want to get to know all the rishis, get acquainted with them. We will try to visit all the ashramas here. Grant us leave to go further into the forest. The sun has just risen. Before he assumes his full glory and rides high in the heavens we would like to cover some distance."

The brothers saluted him and Sutheekshna, after embracing them, said: "May you have a good journey with your brother and this Sita who is following you like the shadow follows the body. Go and visit all the saints in this forest. Their ashramas will abound in fruits and roots, and they will be peopled by gentle deer, herds of them, birds which are tame and sweet. There will be many lakes and ponds full of lotuses and water-birds. There will be small waterfalls here and there, and often, you will hear the voice of the peacock which dances with sheer joy. Visit me again after you have completed your pilgrimage."

"I will do so," said Rama and bade him farewell. Sita brought their bows, quivers and swords. They strapped them on and came to the doorway of the ashrama. They set out once again bound for the many ashramas in the Dandaka forest.

7. SITA'S ADMONITION

While they were walking and talking about different impressions of Dandaka, Sita spoke a few words. She spoke with great diffidence, with great affection, but with a desire to express her opinion on something which happened.

Sita said: "Rama, the word Dharma has such subtle shades of meaning. It is couched in no uncertain terms and yet it is not always easy to know what one's Dharma is. To act rightly without swerving even a hair's breadth from it is possible only for one who has no desires in his mind. I am wondering about it since some time now.

"There are three attitudes towards the observance of Dharma: am I right? These three should be avoided if one should be righteous. Uttering a falsehood is the first of these three. It is a great sin. A greater sin is desiring to possess the wife of another man, the third, which is said to be worse than even these two, is hurting someone who has not offended one in any manner.

"Rama, you have never been guilty of speaking an untruth. You have not done it so far and you will not do it in the future. That is certain. As for the second sin, you are not guilty of that either. Never once have you looked at anyone other than me."

Sita paused and Rama smiled at her as if to say: "Go on. Tell me what you want to. I will listen. Do not be hesitant."

Sita spoke softly and said: "I am afraid that the third sin may taint you. In your partiality towards the inmates of the forest you have decided to fight with the rakshasas who have not offended you in any way. Was this why you came to Dandaka, bow in hand? Is the bow an indication of future sorrow in store for us? I am scared, my lord, of the possible consequences. Ever since you gave them your word to the rishis that you would fight with the rakshasas and rid the forest of them, I have been worried. I am against your proceeding into the forest any further. I will give you my reason. The moment your eyes light on a rakshasa, your fingers will itch to kill him and to you, to think is to act. Fire increases in strength when fed by firewood and the glory of a kshatriya is enhanced by the bow in his hand. The touch of a weapon, I am told, is like the touch of fire. It is not because I do not respect you that I am talking like this, Rama. I do not want to teach you Dharma. Far from it. But because of the privilege of love which is there between you and me, I am asking you if you have done right. Unless provoked to do so, it is not right for you to kill anyone even if he is a rakshasa. You have adopted the garb of a tapasvin. Then you should also live in accordance with it. When we go back to Ayodhya, you can go back to the kshatriya dharma which you should follow there. This entire world is the essence of Dharma. Dharma grants one all the four Arthas and man is granted peace if he observes Dharma. Man obtains everything he desires if he is strict in his observance of Dharma.

"Forgive me, Rama, for trying to tell you what you should do. A woman's natural fear of the unknown has prompted me to say these things.

You are the image of Dharma and it is not pertinent to talk to you about it. Consider what I have said with your brother, think it over and come to a decision."

Rama was pleased with the concern of Sita about him. He knew what was worrying her and he said: "Sita, I will never swerve from the path of Dharma, you know that. You are the daughter of Janaka, the greatest of saints, and it is not surprising that you should know all the nuances of Dharma. But I am sorry for these rishis.

"Consider these rishis, Sita. They have donned the garbs of mendicants. They have abandoned all the pleasures and all comforts of life with but one view: tapas. They are now distressed because of the rakshasas and they have come to me asking me to save them. They have lost their peace of mind which is essential for meditation. And such good people are tortured and eaten up by the rakshasas. These men have come to me and they asked me to protect them. When I heard them the only words I could speak were the ones you heard. They called me their only refuge and I have assured them that I will do what they have asked me to. Tapas is very difficult to undertake and they have done it. I consider it my duty to help them pursue their tapas. I cannot go back on my promise.

"I may give up my life, Lakshmana or even you. But I have to keep my promise to the rishis. Even if they had not asked me for it, I should have, on my own accord, offered to protect them since I am a kshatriya.

"I am charmed by your concern for me, Sita. I know that advice is given only to those in whom one is interested and you are interested in my welfare. It befits your birth and it is but right that Rama's wife should be jealous of his Dharma. Sita, you are my *Sahadharmachari*, are you not? You should be concerned about my Dharma. But I have made up my mind to kill the rakshasas in Dandaka and make it a happy and safe place for the dwellers there."

8. THE GREATNESS OF AGASTYA

Rama walked fast and Sita walked behind him. Lakshmana followed them bow in hand, and so they walked. They passed several peaks, coppices, rivulets and sandy banks where Sarasa birds and Chakravaka birds were numerous. They passed ponds with lotuses blowing on their faces and they saw herds of deer and also wild bulls and hogs. Because of the dense trees, the sun did not much worry them and when evening drew near, they reached a pleasant lake full of sweet and cold water. The water-birds were numerous there.

After a while they reached the dwelling of the rishis in Dandaka. There were numerous ashramas and great was the joy in the minds of the rishis when they saw their royal guests.

Rama spent happy days in the company of these simple-minded rishis. Sorely tried as he was by the happenings in Ayodhya, and by the death of his father, followed by the distressing scenes with Bharata, Rama was in search of peace and he found it in Dandaka.

Rama was welcomed everywhere and he would spend several days together in one ashrama and then go to another and come back to the ones he had visited before and thus they spent their days happily. In some places they spent ten months and in some, a year. Several ashramas hosted him for four months and thus in different places he spent nearly ten years.

Ten years had passed by and Rama, remembering the injunctions of Sutheekshna, returned to his ashrama. He spent some time there and once Rama asked the rishis: "I have been told that the great and revered Agastya is living in this forest. The forest is so large and so intricate are the paths in it that I have not been able to know where his ashrama is located. Where does this great man live? I want to go there and pay my respects to him. I have had this desire in my mind for a long time now and with your help my wish should be granted."

Sutheekshna said: "Rama, I have always been wanting to tell you this: 'Go and visit Agastya,' and you have asked me the way to his ashrama. I will tell you how to reach the ashrama of Agastya. Go southwards from here for a distance of four yojanas. There you will find the beautiful ashrama of Agastya's brother. Spend a night there in those sylvan surroundings.

Agastya's brother will be happy to have you with him as his guests.

"After spending a night there you can proceed in the morning to the ashrama of Agastya. You should continue southwards and after you cover a distance of one yojana you will find yourself in Agastya's ashrama. Since you are eager to visit the famed rishi I think you should leave as early as possible."

Rama was only too happy to begin his journey. Sita and Lakshmana were ready to leave at once and soon they were on their way. They pursued the path which had been indicated by Sutheekshna and the view was picturesque. Rama was enjoying himself and told his brother: "Lakshmana, look, there is an ashrama set in the midst of trees and that should be the ashrama of Agastya's brother. Look at the trees with their heads drooping as though they are unable to bear the weight of the flowers. I can see *samith* here and there, gathered for the kindling of the sacred fire. Darbha grass with the dew drops still on the tips look like they are set with gems. I can see smoke rising from the ashrama. Look at the dense smoke like a cloud! Did you know that this entire south was made safe for the rishis dwelling here by the power of Agastya's tapas?

"Once there were two cruel rakshasas, brothers, and their names were Ilvala and Vatapi. They were always engaged in killing the brahmins who were here. Their method was novel. Ilvala would assume the garb of a brahmin. He would talk the purest language and he would accost a brahmin passing by and tell him that it was his father's *shraddha* and that he would be honoured if the brahmin agreed to accept his hospitality. The deluded brahmin would agree. Ilvala would ask his brother to become a goat. The goat would be killed and a feast would be prepared for the guest by Ilvala. After he had consumed the entire food the brahmin would be ready to get up. Ilvala would shout: "Vatapi! Come out!" As soon as he was called the brother would bleat like a goat and, tearing the entrails of the guest, he would jump out. They would then make a meal of the dead guest. This went on for a long time. The devas were not able to do anything about it. Finally they went to Agastya and asked him to help the poor unfortunate inmates of the forest. He agreed.

"On a particular day he went past the place where Ilvala was said to wait for a possible victim. Agastya walked slowly past, and sure enough Ilvala was there and the request was made as was usual with him. Agastya agreed to be the guest at the *shraddha*. Vatapi in the form of a goat was killed and it was consumed after it had been cooked. When the meal was over Ilvala gave the offering of water in the outstretched palm of Agastya and cried out: "Vatapi! Come out!"

"Nothing happened. The rakshasa called again and still Vatapi did not appear. Agastya laughed at the discomfiture of Ilvala and said: 'Vatapi, in the form of a goat, had been consumed by me and he has been well digested by me. It is of no use calling him. He is not there to respond to your summons.' Ilvala was dumbfounded and he was furious with the sage. He sprang at Agastya with the desire to kill him. Agastya looked at him in anger and he was burnt to ashes. This ashrama is that of his brother. Come, let us go there. We have reached the hermitage, I think."

It was evening when they entered the ashrama of Agastya's brother. They went to the presence of the rishi who welcomed them with great excitement. They spent the night there.

In the morning Rama went to the rishi and said: "Salutations to you. We spent a happy night here. We want you to grant us leave to go and visit your illustrious brother."

After taking leave of him Rama and Sita with Lakshmana went in search of the ashrama.

What impressed them most was the picturesqueness of the Dandaka forest. Wherever they looked, nothing but beauty met their eyes. It was the sight of the magnificent trees, some of them rich with dense green leaves, some with edible fruits and some with flowers whose perfume was exceedingly sweet. Everywhere, there were animals: monkeys, elephants, and flocks of birds and they flew in the sky making patterns as they flew in groups.

Rama was walking fast and he was excited at the thought of meeting the great Agastya. The yojana had been covered and Rama said: "Lakshmana, the trees look well cared for and the deer are tame. Even the birds here are flying without any fear. We must have come very near our destination. See, the clothes of the ashrama dwellers are hanging out in the sun to dry. I can smell the ghee which has been poured as an oblation into the fire. Come, I can see the ashrama which is very near now. Let us hurry.

"We will be meeting the great Agastya at whose command the mountain Vindhya stopped growing. I have held him in great regard and I am very happy that we are able to see him in person now. He is worshipped by men and gods alike. He will give us his blessings.

"Lakshmana, I will wait here with Sita. Go to the presence of the rishi and tell him that I am waiting to pay my respects to him."

9. AGASTYA'S ASHRAMA

Lakshmana entered the ashrama of Agastya and he saw a disciple of the rishi. He said: "There was an emperor by name Dasaratha. His son Rama has come here with his wife Sita. He wants to take the dust of the feet of the great Agastya. I am Lakshmana, his younger brother. I am devoted to him and I serve him. You must be knowing all about my brother. Because of the commands of our father we have entered this fierce forest Daṇḍaka and we have been spending our time visiting all the great and good men living here. We want to see the rishi at his convenience."

The disciple agreed to announce the arrival of the princes and he entered the *agnihotrashala*. This was where the sacred fire was placed and worshipped daily. He stood before the rishi who was glowing with the radiance of his tapas and standing with his arms locked across his chest the disciple gave him the message of Lakshmana.

"Two sons of Dasaratha have come to visit your gracious self. The elder son has brought his wife with him. They await your convenience."

Hearing about the coming of Rama Agastya said: "I am very pleased that Rama has come to see me. I was thinking of him and wishing him to come to me for some time now. Why did you not bring them at once? Go and ask them to be with me. Welcome them with great honour and bring them to me." The disciple went out in a flurry, approached Lakshmana and said: "Our guru is impatient to meet Rama, his wife and you. Please enter and I will take you to him."

He went with Lakshmana to where Rama was waiting and after he had repeated the words of Agastya to him, he took all three of them to the presence of Agastya.

Rama and Sita walked into the ashrama followed by Lakshmana and they looked around them to see the many shrines which had been built for the different gods. Agastya himself had come forward to meet them and to receive Rama. Rama was thrilled at the sight of the great man about whom he had heard so much.

He said: "Look, Lakshmana, the great Agastya is coming towards us. Does he not seem as though nobility and tapas have taken a single form and that is Agastya?"

Rama approached him and prostrated at his feet. His heart was full of happiness since he had seen Agastya. All three of them stood humbly before him waiting for him to speak. The rishi asked Rama about his welfare and said: "Take your seats and let us converse."

They sat and watched while he performed the homa to the fire. He then made them take their food. After they had partaken of the food Agastya spoke to Rama.

"Rama, you are a great prince and you are the image of Dharma, so I have been told. I am happy to have you as my guest and with your wife and your brother you are welcome to spend some time with me."

Agastya was very happy to have Rama with him. He showed a magnificent bow to him and said: "This divine bow inlaid with gold and encrusted with gems has been designed by Vishvakarma and it was Vishnu's *dhanus*. It is spoken of as *Brahmadatta* since it was given to Narayana by Brahma. I have with me two quivers which are inexhaustible and they were given to me by Indra. I have with me a sword with a silver scabbard. In ancient times Narayana used this bow to fight with the asuras during a war in the heavens. I am giving all these to you. Accept them and wear them as Indra does his Vajra. Indra also gave me an armour which cannot be pierced. Use that also. I wish you well. You will ever be victorious.

"When the time comes, when you need a chariot, Matali the charioteer of Indra will bring you the chariot of Indra and you will use it. But that is not now. That will be after some more time. You will know when."

With great humility Rama accepted the wonderful gifts from Agastya. The rishi continued: "Rama, evening is drawing near. The sun has just set. Rest here, all of you, happily. Look at the owls on the treetops. Birds and animals have quietly gone back to their nests and lairs. The sky is dark and unlit by the moon."

Rama woke up early in the morning and waited for Agastya to complete his morning ablutions. He then went to him and Agastya welcomed him with a smile and asked him: "Did you spend a comfortable night with your wife and your brother?"

Rama replied: "We were honoured, my lord. We felt that we were back in Ayodhya, in our father's mansion. So well and with so much affection were we taken care of."

They seated themselves with the other rishis and disciples of Agastya and the great man said: "Rama, the time which you have been asked to spend in the forest by your father, Dasaratha, is almost coming to an end. When your promise is kept, when the time is fully spent here, you will go back covered with glory. Fortunate indeed is your father to have a son like you who has undertaken such a strenuous task to save him from ignominy."

Rama replied humbly: "I have not been unhappy at all, my lord. I have actually enjoyed these few years wandering from ashrama to ashrama and being with the noble men of the forest. And now, your words full of affection make me feel that I am blessed. I am very fortunate since you think so kindly of me. As for my father, he has, on his own, won a place for himself in the heavens. It is not that I have saved him from Adharma. He has performed so many yajnas and so many charitable deeds and the heavens have been earned by him." He was silent for a moment. Perhaps, to his mind came the face of his father as he last saw him.

Rama shed these sad thoughts away and said: "I have a favour to ask of you, my lord. Can you suggest a place for me where I can dwell in peace and spend the rest of my exile? It should be convenient in every way and, at the same time, it should not be too crowded with people. I am eager to find such a place and make a home there for a while till my return to Ayodhya."

Agastya said: "Rama, I wonder if you know the story of this place called Dandaka forest. In ancient days, Dandaka, the brother of your ancestor Ikshvaku, had to abandon this place because of the curse of Bhargava. It then became uninhabited even by animals. Stretching five hundred yojanas up to Vindhya mountains, this place became a dreadful forest filled with wild trees and wild creepers. No rishi had the courage to build an ashrama here. The clouds would not gather and shed rain and the wind would not blow here. It was a place wholly occupied by rakshasas. Gandharvas and rishis did not think of using this place and for many long years it was without any habitation.

"After some time, from the heights of the Himavan, which was my dwelling place, I came here, by chance. With me came the rains and suddenly there was copious rain here. Diseases, which are the messengers of Yama, were here in abundance and, with the power of my tapas, I destroyed them. I made the trees from Himavan to grow in this place. The rivers were filled again and lotuses bloomed on their faces. Ponds were formed and lakes. Seeing the country changed in appearance, the rishis came here to build their ashramas. The place became prosperous with trees which yielded fruits.

"But then, in spite of all this, because of the curse of Bhargava, the place is still frightful. Rakshasas have made their home here. Ever since you came to Chitrakuta the rakshasas have begun to harass the rishis here more often than they used to.

"Rama, you are a valiant kshatriya, and it is up to you to grant them succour. Evidently Fate has decreed that you should come down to Dandaka for this sole purpose: to destroy these rakshasas and save us, poor hermits. You are capable of protecting the three worlds. It is not going to be hard for you to perform this small task for us. Ikshvaku's kinsman Dandaka had to abandon this place, as I told you, because of the curse of a rishi. But as a result of your coming and since your eyes have lighted on it, Dandaka is now freed from the curse under which it was labouring all these many years. Make no delay in destroying the rakshasas."

Rama was fascinated by the narration of Agastya. He said as much to the rishi who continued to talk. Agastya said: "I am gratified to know that both of you with Sita came here to see me and to take my blessings. Perhaps you are both tired after the long trek you had yesterday. I am certain this delicate princess Sita will be extremely fatigued. She is very tender and she has not known what discomfort is, till now. Because of her devotion to you she has walked all this distance beset, as it is, with so many hardships.

"Rama, remember she has done something which is not easy. She has accompanied you to the Dandaka. You should try to keep her happy always. Women, generally, shower love on their husbands when fortune favours them and, when the men are poor, are robbed of their wealth, or when misfortune visits them, then women will shrink away from them and abandon them even. This has been the habit of ordinary illiterate women. Again, the poets compare the mind of a woman, her fickleness, to lightning. The sharpness of a sword's edge is used as an example for their cruel words and the eagle and the wind are the examples for the swiftness of their actions. But this your wife is innocent of all these faults. She is like Arundhati among the divine women. She is a Pativrata. The place where you are going to dwell with Lakshmana and Sita will indeed be a holy spot."

Sita was feeling embarrassed by his praises of her and Rama spoke very humbly: "It is gracious of you to look on us with so much affection. I am honoured by you. If you will indicate to me a place where I can spend the remaining years of my exile I will be immensely grateful. There should be a river by the side of my ashrama and there should be trees and flowering shrubs so that Sita can be happy there."

Agastya thought for a while and then said: "Rama, child, about two yojanas from here is a place which is known as Panchavati. There are fruits and roots in plenty for you there. Water can be found very near to the place and there are deer which will please Sita. You can build an ashrama there and spend your time happily without any worry till the time comes when you can go back to your Ayodhya. I know all about the happenings in Ayodhya. With the power of my tapas I have been able to know the past, the present and the future. It is this knowledge of the future which is prompting me to ask you to go to Panchavati. This is inspite of my desire to ask you to spend all your time here, with me. Great events are waiting to be born and it is essential that you should go and stay in Panchavati.

"The place I have suggested is beautiful and very pleasing. The river Godavari flows by the side of this Panchavati and you will find peace there. It is a lonely place and not many people frequent it. But it is not very far from here. I suggest you remain there and protect the tapasvins. Rama, look on this coppice full of Madhuka trees. When you pass through it, you will reach a Nyagrodha tree. From there, you can ascend that slope, and ascend to a raised land if you go northwards. When you ascend that land, you will find, near the mountain, the famed place by name Panchavati. It is the ideal spot for building an ashrama."

Rama stood up and with him, Lakshmana and Sita. They took from him the great bow, the armour, the sword and the quivers which were inexhaustible and made Pradakshina to the divine weapons which had been graciously given to them by the great man.

They prostrated before him and sought his permission to leave. After prostrating before him and taking the dust of his feet they travelled in the direction which he had indicated and their destination was Panchavati.

10. PANCHAVATI

While they were walking towards Panchavati Rama saw, on the way, an immense eagle, which was perched on the very Nyagrodha tree which Agastya has mentioned. The brothers were almost sure that it was a rakshasa who had assumed this form and was waiting for them.

Rama asked the bird: "Who are you?"

The bird was greatly excited at the sight of the princes. He said: "Children, I am a great friend of your father."

When Rama heard that he was his father's friend, he was extremely happy. He wanted to know more about him and about how the friendship between the two had begun. The bird told them about himself. This was his story.

"Kashyapa Prajapati had several daughters, one of whom was known as Shyeni. You must have heard of Vinata, who has two sons. One is Aruna, the charioteer of the sun and the other is Garuda, the vehicle of Narayana Himself. Aruna married Shyeni and he had two sons, both eagles, taking after their mother. I am the younger of the two and my elder brother is Sampati. My name is Jatayu. This forest is very fierce and dangerous. If you so desire, I will live with you and be your companion. When you have to go out with Lakshmana I will be with Sita and guard her."

Rama embraced Jatayu with affection since he was his father's friend and thanked him for his offer which he accepted gratefully.

The four of them travelled towards Panchavati. Guided by Jatayu they reached it very soon and Rama thought to himself: "It is fortunate that we have found a friend in Jatayu. I can leave Sita in safe hands and destroy the rakshasas like fire burns up moths."

They had arrived at Panchavati. Rama looked around and said: "Lakshmana, this is the place which was indicated by the sage Agastya. Look at those trees laden with flowers and the river which is so near! This must be Panchavati. Look around, Lakshmana. You know only too well the kind of place I would like. Look for a place where there is enough water for us to perform our daily worship of the gods. Sita should be happy and we should have peace. Trees should be around and Samith, darbha grass and flowers should be within reach. Build for us an ashrama in such a place."

Lakshmana said: "I am but your servant, Rama. I will build the ashrama but the choice of the location should be yours. I will not presume to know where it should be." Rama smiled at the words of Lakshmana and together they looked around for a suitable site. After some rambling around they found the ideal place. Rama took Lakshmana's hand in his and said: "Look, this place seems to me to be best suited for our purpose. The ground is level and it is surrounded by trees in abundance. Build an ashrama here for us. Close by is a small stream and the perfume of lotuses floating on its surface reaches us here. And just across, some distance from here is the river Godavari which the rishi told us about. There are mountains and the herds of deer are roaming on the slopes. Peacocks are dancing everywhere and the mountains have several minerals that glow red, white and yellow. The green of the trees together with these colours present the appearance of a painted picture. The elephants stand out against this colourful background as though they are etched in space. I like this picturesque Panchavati. Let us live here."

Lakshmana built an ashrama there on the site indicated by Rama. He brought lotuses from the river Godavari after bathing in it. He made an offering of the flowers to the gods that guarded the forest and spoke words prescribed for averting evil. He went to Rama and Sita. He told them that the ashrama was ready for them.

Rama saw how well-planned it was and how sturdily built. He was enchanted with it. He embraced him warmly and said: "Lakshmana, I am very pleased with you. You have done me a very good service and the only way I can thank you for it is to embrace you. You are wise, you are righteous, and, even without being told about it, you know what my wishes are. My father, I think, is not dead but is here, before me in the form of my brother." Rama was shedding tears of joy and Lakshmana stood with an embarrassed smile on his face.

They lived happily in that ashrama for a long while without any disturbance, without any worry. Sita enjoyed herself collecting flowers and stringing them, making friends with the birds, the deer and the peacocks. Rama was like Indra in his Amaravati. He was happy.

Once during the season *Hemanta* when the waters were chilly and the river was bitter cold in the morning, they had entered the river Godavari. Lakshmana at once thought of Bharata and said: "Bharata will also be bathing in the cold waters of the Sarayu now. He is performing tapas because of his devotion to you, my brother. He has now abandoned all the comforts of a palace, the power which was given to him to rule the kingdom, and, like a tapasvin, he wears coarse cloth and sleeps on the floor. He must have risen before sunrise and proceeded to the river Sarayu even as we are doing now.

"I do not know how he is able to bear the cold. What a noble brother you have, Rama. Dark like you, he is so handsome and he will never act in a manner distasteful to anyone. Always smiling when he talks he has been very dear to all. He has won for himself the heavens because of his devotion to you.

"Rama, they say that, generally, men inherit the qualities of the mother and not the father. In the case of Bharata, our dear brother, the saying has been falsified.

"I still cannot understand how Kaikeyi, the queen of such a noble king and the mother of noble Bharata, could have been so evil-minded."

Rama was listening to his words and said: "Child, my dear Lakshmana, do not talk ill of our mother. Keep on talking of Bharata. It is pleasing to my ears. When you speak his name my mind has become sad and greatly distressed, thinking of my beloved brother. I have also thought often of him and his pleasing ways. I cannot forget the tragic manner in which we parted when in Chitrakuta I refused to go back with him to Ayodhya. He was so disappointed and his tear-stained face, when he finally had to accept my words as final, is ever before my eyes and I cannot sleep at times thinking of him. I see him walking with the Padukas placed on his head, and his eyes streaming with unheeded tears. Bharata, my beloved Bharata, how much he loves me! I wonder when we will all be re-united! When will I go back to our beloved Ayodhya and when will four of us be together again, happy as we once were?"

They spent their time in talking about old days, about their mothers, their dear departed father and so time passed them by unheeded. They spent very happy and peaceful days at Panchavati.

11. SHURPANAKHA

Rama spent many happy days in the ashrama at Panchavati. They would bathe daily in the river Godavari, worship the sun and recite verses in praise of the gods whom they worshipped. Rama would walk back to the ashrama with Sita and Lakshmana would follow with the pot filled with water from the river. And so they spent their time adhering to a routine and wandering in the nearby forest and they were happy. Rama with Sita by his side would look like the moon with his favourite star Chitra by his side.

Once, when they were seated thus, Sita by the side of Rama and Lakshmana some distance away, a rakshasi, Shurpanakha by name, came there by chance. Shurpanakha was the sister of the famed Ravana. She stopped in her tracks and looked again and again at Rama. She saw his wide chest, his long arms, his eyes long and beautiful like the petals of a lotus, and his face glowing with a beauty which was not earthly and she stood rooted to the spot. She had not seen so much beauty. This man was wearing his hair in a tangled mass as though he were a rishi and yet he looked like a king. He was dark like a blue lotus and his looks, his handsomeness was that of Manmata, the god of love. Shurpanakha realised that she was in love with him and wanted him for her lord.

This ugly woman wanted the handsome man: she was enormous and her eyes had lighted on this slim and lissom figure. Her eyes were red and cruel and his eyes were soft and gentle. She was red-haired and his hair was dark and soft in spite of the matting. One could not bear the sight of her since she was so fearful and, as for him, the eyes which had lighted on him once refused to look at other things. Her voice was like thunder and his was pleasing to the ear. She was old and he was young. She was crooked in her thinking and he was straight.

Shurpanakha could not resist the charm which was Rama and she went to him. She asked him: "You seem to be a stranger in these places. You are wearing tree-bark and deerskin and your hair is matted like that of a rishi but your arms belie your appearance. A bow, arrows and a sword are not used by rishis. This is the dwelling place of rakshasas. How did you come here? Tell me the truth."

Rama said: "There was a famous king by name Dasaratha. I am his eldest son and they call me Rama. The young man standing there is my younger brother and his name is Lakshmana. This is Sita, my wife and she is the daughter of Janaka, the king of Videha. Because I was commanded by my father I have come to live in forest. I would like to know who you are. To whom do you belong? Let us know about you. Looking at you and your appearance it seems to me you are a rakshasi. Tell me truly, why have you come here?

Shurpanakha, afflicted with love for this godly man, said: "Rama, I will tell you all about myself. I am called Shurpanakha. I am a rakshasi and I can assume any form I desire. I move about in this forest frightening everyone who lives here. You might have heard of the powerful and famous rakshasa king by name Ravana. I am his sister. He is the son of Vishravas. Ravana has a brother by name Kumbhakarna and this brother of mine is afflicted with a dreadful inclination to sleep all the time. He is very brave and a very great fighter but he loves sleep. I have another brother. He is Vibhishana. He is alien to the qualities of rakshasa. He is very righteous in his thinking and in his acts too. Khara and Dushana, the famed fighters, are also my brothers, They live here.

"Be that as it may, I came here by chance, and I saw you. Ever since I saw you my mind has no other desire but one: to be your wife. I have chosen you as my lord. I am very powerful and I can go where I please.

Be my husband. What can this Sita do? She is not fit to be the wife of a man like you. I am the perfect mate for you. She is ugly and ill-formed. Look at her. She is fit only to be my food. I will eat her up and your brother too. Then, free of them, you can live with me happily in this Dandaka forest."

Laughing loudly she stood with her hands on her immense waist looking at all three of them. Rama would not take her words seriously. He decided to make a sport of it and get rid of her easily. He smiled slightly and said: "I am a married man. I also happen to love this woman who is my wife. For one like you, it will not be easy to be the second wife to a man. Sharing a husband with another woman will not be possible for the likes of you. This Lakshmana who is my younger brother is handsome and he is valiant like me. He is not married and he is the ideal mate for you. Accept him as your husband and you will have him all for yourself."

Shurpanakha, obsessed as she was with lust, thought that he spoke the truth and she went to Lakshmana. She said: "I am good-looking enough to be your wife. You are very handsome and so am I. Marry me and we will be happy here in the Dandaka forest."

Lakshmana decided to play up to Rama's joke. He smiled too and said: "I am the servant of this Rama. How will it be possible for you to be the wife of a servant? I have no independence. I am but his vassal. Able as you are to assume any form you please, you should press your love-suit more vehemently and be the second wife of my brother. He will be so charmed by your looks that he will give up this ugly ill-looking wife of his and live with you. Which sensible man will let go of this chance to marry a beautiful woman like you and be attached to a human being?"

Shurpanakha could not perceive that the brothers were making fun of her. She went near Rama and said: "Because you have this woman by your side you refuse to look at me. I will, this very moment, eat her up even as you are looking and then I will have you as my husband."

Her eyes were red like embers and she rushed towards Sita whose eyes were wide with fear. Rama could not bear to see Sita frightened of the dreadful rakshasi. He held her back and said: "Child, Lakshmana, I realise that it is wrong to sport with wicked people. Take care that Sita is not harmed. This rakshasi has got to be punished. Maim her and send her away."

Lakshmana promptly took his sword and he snipped of the tips of the nose and ears of Shurpanakha. Screaming with pain Shurpanakha ran into the forest. To them her screams sounded like the rumblings of the rain clouds.

She reached Janasthana soon: Janasthana which was the place where the rakshasas lived. She fell at the feet of her brother Khara and her fall made a sound like thunder.

Khara saw her drenched in blood and he saw that she was in great pain. He did not know what had happened. He was furious with the persons who had hurt her and he asked her: "Rouse yourself, my dear sister! Tell me what happened. Who has to be punished for this outrage? It seems to me this person is as foolish as a man who teases with his finger-tips a poisonous cobra which is sleeping. He has taken the noose of death and has placed it on his neck thinking it is a garland of flowers. He has not been wise. He has neared his end, evidently, or else he would not have done this to you. How did this happen? Does he not know what it is to antagonise me and my clan? Even Indra is powerless in my presence. I will, this very moment, drink his life with my arrows. I will spill his blood on this thirsty earth. The eagles and the hawks will have fresh food to eat today. Tell me which gandharva or deva or danava had the foolishness to lay hands on you."

Shurpanakha was very unhappy. Her tears were flowing freely, and her love for Rama had turned to hatred and a desire for revenge. But her words betrayed her real feelings. She said: "My dear brother, how is it you have not heard about the newcomers to Dandaka! I saw them today. There are two of them. They are young, handsome, and strong too. They seem to have been accustomed to luxury and their limbs are tender. They are extremely powerful, though. Their eyes are long and more beautiful than the petals of a lotus. They are dressed like ascetics. They seem to be extremely righteous and they live like hermits. But they are princes. They are the sons of a king named Dasaratha and they are called Rama and Lakshmana. As archers they seem to be unequalled in the world and they seem as though they are very good, kind and compassionate. Their beauty is like that of gandharvas. All the glory of the kshatriyas seems to have found a home in these two brothers. It is difficult to believe that they are human beings: so divine is their appearance.

"By their side was a young woman. She was very beautiful. Unlike them she seemed to have decked herself in ornaments of gold and she was dressed in fine silks. Because of this woman, these two men who seemed to be righteous, hurt me and maimed me thus. I wish to see them dead in battle and I wish to drink their blood. If you cannot help me to have my revenge I will myself go and fight with them."

Khara was naturally angry with these strangers to Dandaka who had the audacity to touch his sister. He called for fourteen of his men and instructed them: "Go into the forest Dandaka. There are, I am told, two men dressed in tree-bark and deerskin like ascetics. They have a woman with them and they are dwelling in the Dandaka forest. They are armed with bows and arrows which belie their garb. Go immediately to their ashrama, kill all three of them and come back. My sister wishes to drink their blood."

They bowed in acquiescence and Shurpanakha led them to the ashrama of Rama. They appeared like rain-bearing clouds driven by the wind. They were there led by Shurpanakha. They saw Rama and Sita and with them was Lakshmana. Rama saw them and said: "It looks like we have to do some fighting. Lakshmana, take care of Sita for a moment. I will kill these who have come with that woman."

Rama took up his bow and arrows and asked them: "We are two princes from Ayodhya and we are living the lives of ascetics and we have not harmed anyone. Why do you come here and try to fight with us? I have been told that you bother all the rishis here with your cruelties. I have taken up my bow and arrows to punish the likes of you. If you have courage enough stay and fight with me. If, however, you want to live, then leave this spot at once and run as fast as you can."

12. KHARA, DUSHANA AND TRISHIRAS

The servants of Khara could not brook the insulting manner of speech adopted by Rama. They did not realise that he really meant well when he said that he would spare their lives. They taunted him with their bravery and, suiting the action to the word, they flung their tridents at Rama. Rama broke all of them and he sent the arrows by name Narachas and each one of them was killed by his arrows. It was like a game for Rama and he saw all fourteen of them dead and on the ground.

Shurpanakha was amazed at the prowess of Rama and, at the same time, frightened. She ran back to Khara and stood silent in front of him. She could not speak and Khara became impatient with her silence. He said: "I have done what you wanted me to do. I have sent my men to kill the men who insulted you. What more is expected of me? Why do you still stand before me with tears in your eyes and with a woebegone face?"

She said: "My dear brother, I know you always try to please me and, to avenge my disfigurement, you sent your men to kill the human beings. But Rama has killed all of them. They are lying there in a large pool of blood. I am frightened. You should see to it that these men are destroyed. You should kill them or else I will kill them myself. From the manner in which you seem to hesitate, it seems to me you are afraid to encounter him. You realise, perhaps, that you are quite powerless in the presence of Rama. You are a disgrace to our House. If you have any pride or valour in you, go at once and fight with this Rama and kill him. Or else abandon this Janasthana with all your kinsfolk. You are of no use to anyone by staying here, afraid as you are, of just two ordinary human beings."

Khara was mad with anger at the insults which she was hurling at him. He said: "Stop talking like this. My anger is trying to burst its bonds like a sea in stormy weather. Who says I am scared of Rama? How dare you insult me like this? I will, this very moment, go and despatch the two of them to Yama's land."

Shurpanakha was glad to see that he was going to fight with Rama. She began to praise him and Khara called his commander Dushana and said: "Collect our army. Let the fourteen thousand warriors who are extremely powerful, brave and fearless, get ready to fight with this unknown man who seems to have killed fourteen of our best men. Hasten to collect the weapons and bring me my chariot yoked with the best horses. I have decided to fight with this small man and kill him today."

Khara's chariot had arrived. It was beautifully made: covered with gold and set with gems, the chariot gleamed like the sun. The inlay work was wonderful and it was a work of art. Fully equipped with all the weapons needed for fighting, Khara entered the chariot and he was surrounded by the entire army and Dushana was with him. The army set out on its march. Fourteen thousand of the rakshasas led by Khara to kill two human beings. Out of Janasthana streamed out the immense army and the noise rose to the skies. Led by the footmen the army advanced fast and in the midst of that sea of warriors gleamed the chariot of Khara like the sun in the midst of rain clouds filled with hailstones.

Everywhere, evil omens could be seen. Suddenly there appeared a crimson cloud in the sky and there rained a ghastly rain of blood on the army. While they were in the royal path the horse tripped and fell down. There was a circle of black round the rim of the sun and on the pillar which carried the banner sat an eagle. Several other omens all indicating some great calamity were seen by all of them. But Khara paid no heed to them.

"I am not affected by these manifestations of nature," he said. "It is only weak and cowardly men who will attach any importance to such things. I have no fear. With my arrows I can fell the stars from the sky. I will make even death enter his own city. Unless and until I kill that arrogant Rama and his brother I will not return to my city. It is well known that there has not been anyone so far, who has been able to meet me in fight. Indra, riding on his Airavata, cannot face me. What then should be the fate of these mere men?"

The army was infused with enthusiasm by the words of the master and they did not heed the omens any longer.

Rishis, devas, siddhas, and charanas with the gandharvas filled the sky to watch the encounter. They spoke among themselves: "Narayana has taken upon Himself the task of ridding the world of these sinners and we are fortunate to witness the killing of this huge army by Rama. Let us wish him to be victorious and let us pray that the same fate will be met by the grandson of Pulastya. Rama has been born for the sole purpose of killing Ravana and this fight is but the forerunner of the great achievement of his in the near future."

Twelve of his chief fighters surrounded Khara. Four more, Mahakapala, Sthulaksha, Pramathi and Trishiras brought up the rear of the army. Dushana was at the forefront. Like evil planets hurrying towards the sun and moon to harass them, these rakshasas rushed towards Rama and Lakshmana.

Rama, in the meantime, was in his ashrama and he too saw the evil omens which spelt misfortune to the rakshasas. He told Lakshmana: "Look on these omens. It is a sure indication that the rakshasas will all be destroyed. As for my bow it seems to throb as though impatient to be used. My arrows are already fuming and I can almost see the smoke coming from them! From what the shastras say, these evil omens indicate that the rakshasas will all be destroyed. A dreadful war is in the offing, a number of lives will be lost. My right hand is throbbing and that means that I will be the victor. I can hear the noise made by the army which is approaching us. Evidently that woman has not been idle. It has been said by the wise that a man who desires to be victorious should anticipate danger and be ready to face it. He should make all the preparations beforehand. Take your bow and arrow, Lakshmana, and, with Sita, go to a cave whose entrance is hidden by the trees and which is not easily accessible to anyone. I know that I am denying you the pleasure of using your arms but the safety of Sita is just essential. That sinful sister of Ravana may cause her harm when we are both engaged in fighting. You will have to obey me, I am afraid. I know that you, unassisted, will be able to destroy this army of rakshasas. But I want to do it myself since it is a promise to the rishis. You must guard Sita very carefully."

Lakshmana took up his bow and arrows and, as Rama had instructed him, he led Sita to a safe cave. Rama waited to see them enter the cave and sighed with relief. He put on his armour and he strung his bow, strapped his quiver to his shoulder and stood there looking as glorious as fire which burns without smoke. The rishis in the forest thought that Lord Mahadeva was there before them, with his famed Pinaka in his hand: the anger on the brow of Rama was like the third eye of the Lord.

Rama waited and the noise of the army came louder to his ears. He pulled the string of his bow and the noise of the twang was frightening. The army was approaching him and very soon it was close at hand. Even the *vanadevatas* were not able to look at Rama who was looking like an image of fury and they thought too that this was how Mahadeva must have looked when he destroyed the yagna of Daksha.

Khara had now come very near the ashrama. He saw Rama who stood bow in hand. He asked his chariot to be brought before Rama. Khara began to shoot arrows at Rama and his army did the same thing. Hundreds of arrows, thousands of arrows looking like the rays of the sun were rushing towards Rama. The rakshasas hurled their weapons at Rama: tridents, sickles, axes and several other different weapons. The arrows looked like the rain which falls in the mountain Himavan. Even as the sea lets all the rivers drain into it and is unaffected by it, Rama stood, unmoved by the onslaught of the warriors of Khara, of the army of Khara and the arrows of Khara. Rama's body was hurt in several places but he fought calmly. He looked like the rain cloud lit up by the setting sun. Rama's bow was now bent almost to a circle. Arrow on arrow left his hand and each arrow claimed a life. The devas who stood in the skies could not see when he took up his arrow, when he fixed it to the string, when he pulled the string and when he released it. The dexterity with which he was handling the bow and arrows was a source of wonder to all of them. The rakshasas died in tens, in hundreds, in thousands. Horses which were yoked to the chariots, elephants, with the mahouts, were all strewn on the ground, rendered lifeless by the arrows of Rama. Arrows by name Nalika, Naracha and Vikarni were specially fierce and painful and the army screamed with fear and pain when hurt by them. Panic set in and they all rushed to Khara.

He could see the devastation in the group of brave and valiant rakshasas who had made up his immense army. He was furious with Rama and collecting all of them together he went to the presence of Rama. Emboldened by the nearness of their chief they began to fight again with vigour. Rama took up the astra by name 'Gaandharva' and after invoking it he sent it towards the army of Khara. Myriads of arrows were emerging from the single bow which he held and the quarters were darkened because the arrows filled them. The arrows were now changed to five-headed serpents and they killed the rakshasas. A large portion of Khara's army had been destroyed completely and it was a really large slice.

Dushana came to the forefront and began to fight with Rama. Five thousand men surrounded him. Rama warded off all the weapons and stones and trees which were being hurled at him and his arrows replied the onslaught. Dushana fought valiantly. His arrows were like thunderbolts. Rama killed his four horses with four arrows and with the fifth, the charioteer. He hurt Dushana with three arrows. Dushana was mad with pain and taking up his gada, he rushed towards Rama. Rama cut off his two arms with two of his arrows. He was mad with pain and fell down to the ground and the bow slipped out of his severed arm as his life ebbed away.

The rakshasas who were at the rear of the army now came to the front to attack Rama only to be killed one by one by him. Khara saw how terrible the devastation was in his army and he was grieved that Dushana had been killed. Sorrounded as he was by several of his men Khara attacked Rama. The men fell one by one like miniature mountains felled by the Vajra of Indra. The entire army was gone and only Khara and Trishiras were left.

Trishiras went to Khara who was even then trying to approach Rama and said: "Let me go. I will put an end to this man who has caused so much havoc in our ranks. I will be the death of him. If, by some strange chance, I should die, you can then avenge my death and that of all the others."

Trishiras, spurred by death, approached Rama in a chariot. Rama received him with a rain of arrows. The fight between these two was glorious to watch. Trishiras was fighter of no mean order and he hurt Rama on the forehead with three arrows. Rama thought: "He seems to be an excellent archer. He has managed to hurt me." Rama decided to put an end to Trishiras. He sent fourteen arrows at the chest of the Rakshasa. The horses were killed and the banner which was fluttering on top of the chariot was now on the ground. The chariot was broken and when Trishiras rose out of the broken chariot Rama killed him by cutting off his three heads.

For the first time Khara was worried lest he should also be killed. He had seen all his warriors lying on the ground which was strewn with their bodies. Like Namuchi approached Indra, Khara came to fight with Rama. Both were good archers and this duel, like that between Rama and Trishiras, was fascinating to watch. Some arrows of Khara were able to pierce the armour of Rama. Khara was elated at his achievement and he laughed loudly. Rama took up his bow. He was as calm as ever and he took up an arrow and fixed it in his bow, a new one since the old one was broken by the enemy. The one he had now was the bow given to him by Agastya.

Rama broke off the flagstaff of the banner of Khara and with thirteen arrows he wounded Khara. Khara stood on the ground and Rama spoke to him: "No one who has always been perpetrating cruel deeds and hurting innocent animals and men, can go unpunished for his crimes. He should be killed like a snake which is poisonous and which bites without reason. In this Dandaka you have been killing all the people who have done you no harm. Your sinful acts will bear fruits even as the eating of poisoned food will take one's life away. I have been authorised to punish evil-doers like you who have been doing nothing but harm to the world. My arrows will enter your chest like snakes will the anthills where they dwell. You will now follow the several innocent people whom you have killed in the Dandaka. Prepare yourself to die, Khara."

Khara was not impressed by Rama's words. He said: "Rama, just because you have been able to kill a handful of weak and powerless soldiers you talk about it like an ordinary braggart. Wise men do not talk about their valour. Only kshatriyas like you are in the habit of talking about themselves. I am standing here with my mace in my hand. Can you not see that I am firm as a mountain which cannot be shaken by the severest of storms? Remember I am Yama with the noose of death in my hand. I could talk to you about so many things but it is not wise. The sun is about to set and I do not want this fight to stop in the middle. I want to put an end to you and your arrogance and then sleep in peace". Khara flung his mace at Rama. Rama split it into a thousand fragments even as it was travelling towards him in the air. Rama smiled a little and said: "With that gada has fallen all your hopes of defeating me. You will now find a permanent place of rest on the ground. You will embrace the earth as you would a woman whom you have been wanting for a long time. You said you wanted to sleep in peace. Do not worry, I will grant you the sleep. As for the peace it is not for you. You have lost all right to it. After your death the inmates of Dandaka will wander around without fear in their hearts and that is my mission: to rid this forest of you."

Khara was wild with anger. He uprooted a big Sala tree and flung it at Rama. Rama warded it off easily and he now showered arrows at his opponent. Khara, with pain all over his body, with blood pouring from his wounds, rushed towards Rama. Looking at his unsightly form, Rama was overcome with disgust and he went back a step or two. He adjusted his bow and, taking up a terrible arrow and invoking Indra, he sent it towards Khara. It entered the chest of Khara and the rakshasa fell down dead, looking like Antaka who was burnt by Mahadeva in the Shvetaranya.

Flowers rained on Rama from the heavens and the ground was strewn with dead horses, dead rakshasas, dead elephants, broken chariots, and thousands and thousands of weapons of the rakshasas, even as a yagnasala is strewn with darbha grass.

Lakshmana had been watching the war and he now came out of the cave with Sita. He entered the ashrama and his face was glowing with happiness. He was proud of his brother. Rama entered the ashrama and Lakshmana saluted him by taking the dust of his feet. Sita saw her lord entering with a triumphant smile lighting up his face and she rushed to him and embraced him spontaneously. Again and again she embraced him and tears of joy were in her eyes.

13. RAVANA IS TOLD ABOUT JANASTHANA

There was a rakshasa by name Akampana. He had somehow managed to escape unscathed, and he rushed to Lanka. He went straight to the rakshasa monarch Ravana and said: "My lord, almost all the rakshasa in Janasthana have been killed. Khara is dead, as also Dushana and Trishiras. I managed to escape alive from there."

Hearing these terse sentences from Akampana, words which spelt the devastation of his entire outpost in the forest, Ravana looked hard at Akampana who stood trembling. Ravana's eyes were red with anger and he asked: 'Which foolish person has destroyed my favourite Janasthana? Evidently his death is very near. He will not be able to escape death at my hands even if he tries to find succour in the celestial places. Having wronged me and displeased me he cannot enter the land of Indra since Indra is afraid of me. So is Kubera and so is Yama, the god of death. I am death to death himself and I can burn up Agni with my wrath. I can send even Brahma to his death. Tell me who did it?"

Akampana, seeing the wrath of his master, was talking words which faltered so much that he had to say it twice before he could make himself understood. He spoke just one word: "A man: a man did it."

"A man?" asked Ravana. "A human being? I never heard of any army marching into Janasthana. None of the spies have reported any such progress to me. And you say a man destroyed our Khara and his army. How did it happen?"

"Not an army, my lord," said Akampana. "It was a man, just one single man with a bow and arrows."

Ravana stared at him and he thought that Akampana had lost his reason. Akampana continued in his wavering voice: "Please listen to me patiently, my lord. It is unbelievable, but true. I hear there was a king by name Dasaratha and he belonged to the race of the sun. He has a son by name Rama. This Rama has come to the Dandaka forest. He is as strong as a lion. He is young and he has wide shoulders like a wild bull. His arms are round and long. He is dark and his fame has spread far and wide. He is valiant and he is a great archer. Single-handed he killed fourteen thousand rakshasas and Khara, Dushana and Trishiras have all been killed by him."

Ravana still would not believe that such a thing was possible. He said: "Perhaps, Indra has sent a host of his army to assist this man. Tell me the truth."

"No, my king," said Akampana. "No one came to his aid. He is unbelievably powerful. He is a great archer. He seems to be conversant with all astras. He made me think of Indra while he was fighting. He is so glorious. He has a very valiant brother by name Lakshmana. He is equally powerful though he did not take part in this war. He is just as handsome as Rama and he is charming like the moon. Every arrow sent by Rama became a serpent with five heads and killed a rakshasa. The handful of Rakshasas left alive are unable even to sleep since Rama haunts their dreams. Janasthana is a wasteland now."

Ravana said: "I will go at once to Janasthana and kill these two brothers Rama and Lakshmana."

Akampana said: "I would not advise you to do so, lord. I will tell you more about Rama. His fame as a warrior is known in all the three worlds. He can stop the flow of a river with his arrows. He can destroy the heavens with the stars, the planets, the sun and the moon, if need be. He can, if he so desires, raise the earth out of the ocean if it gets submerged. He can plunge the world into the sea by breaking its bounds if he wants to. He can destroy the Universe and create a new one entirely. He cannot be conquered by anyone, not even you. It will be like a sinner desiring to enter the heavens. In fair war you cannot defeat Rama. I can suggest a method by which you can punish Rama.

"Rama has a wife and her name is Sita. She is young and she is beautiful. They say that her beauty is unequalled in all the three worlds. Her limbs are tender and delicately made. Her waist is slim. She is a jewel among women. No woman, whether she is divine, or a gandharva, or apsara, or danavi, can equal her in beauty. Need I say anything about human beings then? I suggest that you go to Dandaka and steal this woman from Rama. He is so devoted to her that once she is gone, he will take thought and die, unable to live without her."

Ravana considered the words of Akampana and said: "I like your suggestion. I am quite pleased with the idea. Tomorrow when the sun rises I will go alone to the Dandaka in my chariot. I will capture Sita and bring her to Lanka."

Ravana called for his chariot and the golden chariot which had donkeys yoked to it came and waited for him at the doorway. This chariot could fly in the sky and it could travel far. Ravana went in it to the ashrama of Maricha, the son of Tataka. Maricha was now an ascetic and he had built for himself an ashrama. He was supposed to have spurned the comforts of a palace and preferred the simple life of an ashrama. He was excited at the thought of the emperor paying a visit to him and he entertained him as best as he could with fruits and such like forest fare. He placed a seat for Ravana and made him comfortable.

Maricha then said: "I hope you are well. And I am certain that some important reason lies behind this gracious visit of yours to my humble abode. Please tell me and if I can, I will do what you command me to do."

Ravana, the great warrior, Ravana who had learnt the art of talking pleasingly and convincingly, smiled at Maricha and said: "You are right. I have a reason for coming to your ashrama asking you for assistance. Uncle, did you know that the entire army in Janasthana has been wiped out?"

"Janasthana wiped out!" repeated Maricha. He was filled with wonder. "But how, my lord? Our army is invincible. Khara is there and how can this have happened?"

"By a mere man named Rama," said Ravana. He saw the rakshasa trembling as he heard the name of Rama. Maricha was scared out of his wits and sweat was pouring down his face. Ravana paid no attention to his reaction and went on talking:

"Evidently Rama seems to possess some kind of power or else this could not have happened. I wish to capture the wife of this Rama and bring her away to Lanka. I need your help in this. That is the only way to punish Rama."

Maricha said: "Ravana, someone evidently wants to see you dead or else he would not have spoken to you about Sita. Someone pretending to be your friend is really your enemy and he has done this mischief. Have you insulted anyone and is he trying to seek revenge thus? You are the lord of the world of rakshasas and someone is jealous of you and wants to make you lose everything you possess.

"The one who suggested this evil deed is indeed your enemy. It is like trying to extract the fangs from the mouth of a poisonous snake: your attempt to steal Sita. Rama is not to be approached by anyone in warfare. There is no one like him. He is like a wild elephant which will crush you if you taunt it. He is like a lion which is sleeping. Do not try to rouse him. He is like a sea which is full of sharks and whales. Do not jump into it unwarily.

"Listen to my words of advice. I mean well. I have your well-being in mind when I speak thus. Go back to Lanka and go back to your beloved wives. Leave this Sita alone. Let Rama live happily in the forest. Do not have anything to do with him. He is a dangerous antagonist."

Ravana was not frightened of the prowess of Rama which they all seemed to talk about. He listened with unconcern when Maricha spoke for his well-being. But he valued the words of Maricha and considered them to be those of a wise old man. He, therefore, went back to his palace and decided to give up the thought of Sita.

14. SHURPANAKHA AND HER TALE OF WOE

Shurpanakha was desperate. Her brothers were all killed and their army destroyed. The Janasthana was now empty of her kinsmen and she was frightened of the valour of Rama. She decided to go to Lanka and tell Ravana about the entire happenings in Janasthana. When she went to Lanka her brother Ravana was in the council hall and she went there.

Ravana was glowing like Indra in the midst of the devas. His throne was made of gold and silver and there were pearls, corals and gems which gleamed in it. Ravana was like fire which was burning on a golden shrine. Invincible by all the devas and danavas, this Ravana was a warrior who was extremely noble-looking. His chest was scarred because once the elephant Airavata, Indra's mount, had gored him.

Ravana also bore the signs of Indra's Vajra having scorched his immense chest. His broad chest was beautiful and there was something exceedingly magnificent about this great warrior. Dark and handsome, he was the favourite of Lord Mahadeva. He was the great-grandson of Brahma. Ravana was a hater of the devas and he was unrighteous. He did not hesitate to take the wives of others if he so desired. He did not hesitate to disturb the yagnas performed by the rishis and the ascetics in the forests.

Ravana was proficient in the use of all the weapons. He knew the astras and their incantations. Once he had gone down to the nether world and fought with Vasuki, the king of the serpents. He had defeated Kubera, his half-brother, in a fight and had captured for himself the vimana by name Pushpaka which could fly in the air. He played havoc in Kubera's pleasure garden by name Chaitra and in Indra's garden, Nandana. He had quelled all the devas and they were considered by him to be his vassals. He had performed a severe tapas and had pleased Brahma. He had obtained boons from him. He had asked for immunity from death at the hands of devas, danavas, gandharvas, pichachas, and every living being he could think of. He had forgotten to include the names of men and monkeys since they were too insignificant and negligible to be considered even and he did not think of them. He had once lifted the mount Kailasa and he had pleased Lord Mahadeva with his singing of the Sama with the veena as an accompaniment.

In thinking of the unrighteousness of Ravana, one should not forget the greatness of this personage. He was great. There was no doubt about it. There was no one to equal him in beauty, in prowess, in valour, in generosity, in the skill in fine arts, in his power to capture the minds of women, in his learning, in his mastery of the sacred lore. He was a personage in whose presence the devas were all made to pale into insignificance. There was no one like Ravana.

Shurpanakha stood for a long moment looking at the heap of glory that was Ravana. She knew that this son of Vishravas, this great hero, would avenge the insult which had been rankling in her bosom like a thorn which could not be removed. She went near him and began to talk. For a moment Ravana could not recognise her. Her face was disfigured and her voice was also sounding different.

She said: "A king indeed! You are ever lost in the pleasures of the harem and you do not think of anything else. You do what you please and you have no thought for others. You have forgotten what is happening outside in the world, drunk as you are with your power. But there are some truths which have to be known by you. There is a danger which is nearing you and you are ignorant of it. When a king indulges in lust excessively people will lose their respect for him. A king who forgets his duties and refuses to perform them at the proper times will be destroyed in course of time because of his carelessness: and with him, his kingdom also will be lost. You have no efficient spies evidently nor have you been interested in seeing about the welfare of your subjects. Your enemies, the devas, will surely be planning your destruction and you should be very careful. But you have not paid enough attention to the ruling of your kingdom. I have come to tell you something.

"Janasthana is destroyed, wiped out. Khara, Dushana and Trishiras with all the others have all been killed and nothing is left in Janasthana to tell people that it is your stronghold in Dandaka. A man, mere man, by the name of Rama has done this and he has made Dandaka a happy place for the rishis who were dwelling there.

"My dear brother, you are too careless to be a good ruler. You think there is no one like you, that you know all that is to be known, that you are inaccessible, invincible. You are too arrogant and such a king as you will be sure to earn the contempt of others since you are too indifferent. You are complacent and that is why this has happened.

"Once you lose your position as king you will be like clothes which are soiled, like flowers which have been used and thrown away. It is only if you are alert all the time with your senses under control, well-informed about all the many things which go on in your kingdom, that you will last on the throne. Though asleep, such a king will be considered to be awake since his sense of justice will never go to sleep and he will be loved by all.

"In your ignorance about the tragedy at Janasthana, you have proved that you are unfit to be a king. You will soon be without a kingdom."

Ravana, who was proud of his wealth, his prowess and his popularity, had been listening to the tirade by his sister. He considered the words she had used, and, without losing his temper, he let her complete her talk. Slowly his anger mounted and he glared at her. He said: "Who is this Rama? How powerful is he? What is he like in appearance? Is he really all that powerful? Have you found out why he has come to the Dandaka? You say that he killed my army and my chief men single-handed. What are his weapons like?"

The mention of Rama made her angry once again and she remembered him and his scathing smile which she had not understood then. She could not help dwelling on the beauty of Rama which had captured her.

"Rama is the son of an emperor named Dasaratha," she said. "He has long arms and his eyes are long and liquid. He wears tree-bark and deerskin and he is handsome like Manmata. He has a bow which is inlaid with gold and this bow he strings and out of it shoot forth arrows which are called Narachas. I stood there nearby when he was fighting. I saw Rama.

"I could not see when he bent his bow, when he fixed the arrow to the string and when it left his bow. All I saw was the incessant stream of arrows and the army devastated like a field of corn after a hailstorm. In a muhurta and a half, this Rama destroyed the army, fourteen thousand strong, and, with it, Khara, Dushana and Trishiras and other leaders in the army. The rishis in Dandaka are now moving about without the fear of rakshasas. Rama would have killed me. But he is not desirous of killing a woman and so he maimed me and left me alive. Rama has a brother who is his right hand.

"It seems to me it is Rama's very life which has taken a form and a name and moves about by the name Lakshmana. They are so dear to each other. He is just as valiant as his brother. He is devoted to Rama. He is efficient and he is invincible. He will never fail in a task he has undertaken. Lakshmana is wise and he is strong.

"Rama has a wife and her name is Sita. She is the daughter of Janaka, the king of Videha. My dear brother, she is very beautiful. Her eyes are long and large and her face is as charming as the moon. She is very dear to

Rama and she loves him. She is bent on serving him.

"Her hair is long, her nose is very finely chiselled and the tip is tilted up provocatively. Her thighs are so well sculptured, it is unbelievable. I have never seen the like of her. She has the perfection mentioned in treatises on beauty. She is famed for her beauty all the world over and for her devotion to Rama. She is like a maid from the heavens. The forest seems to boast of a second Lakshmi by her presence there. Her complexion is that of molten gold. I saw that her slender fingers had pink and rounded nails. Her waist is slim and her figure is quite the most captivating figure I have ever seen. No yaksha woman, or a gandharva maid or one from the heavens can equal her in beauty. There has not been born a woman as beautiful as Sita in this world. I am certain of that.

"This perfection, I thought, would be the ideal wife for you and you, the perfect mate for her. Your wide chest is where her beautiful arms should find refuge. I tried to capture her and bring her to you as my gift and that was when Lakshmana did this to me and maimed me for life. If you set your eyes on this charming woman you will be stricken with the arrows of the god of love. If you think you can take her for wife, set about it immediately. Let your subjects be reassured that they have a king who will protect them. Kill that Rama and bring away his wife with you to Lanka.

"Brother, your prowess is well known. It will be an easy task for you to capture Sita after killing those two princes with your sharp arrows. You can be happy and the rakshasas will be without fear after you render this service to them. If you consider my advice to be worthy of execution, then, do not waste time. Hesitation is not necessary. You have to avenge the death of the thousands of rakshasas in Janasthana and the death of Khara, Dushana and Trishiras."

15. TO MARICHA'S ASHRAMA AGAIN

Ravana was lost in thought. The court was asked to retire. For a long time he sat alone in his chambers pondering on the words of Shurpanakha. His mind was dwelling on the description of Sita. Shurpanakha knew how to use her words and Ravana was impressed by the plan suggested by her. He considered plan after plan and, after weighing each one carefully, he rejected it. He was not foolish enough to treat the valour of Rama with contempt since he knew the story of his fight with Khara and his army. Ravana made up his mind to pursue a certain plan of action.

He went to his stables and commanded his charioteer to get his chariot ready. It was the same chariot with the donkeys yoked to it: the chariot which could travel in air. Ravana ascended the chariot and crossed the sea which was raging underneath. Ravana was glorious to look at. He was glowing like a gem and he was wearing ear-rings made of gold. He was wearing the softest of silks and his eyes were full of thought as he considered how he should talk to Maricha. He had gone once before and the rakshasa had convinced him that his act would be an act of folly. But now the added spur was the thought of Sita and he had to make Maricha listen to his words.

Ravana had to traverse a long distance and the journey was interesting since he had to cross many beautiful and picturesque places. Ravana's eyes were seeing them without his being moved by their beauty. His thoughts were elsewhere.

Finally he arrived at the neighbourhood of the Nyagrodha tree which had been considered sacred since the bird Garuda was said to have rested once on its branches. The tree was named Subhadra. Not far from that tree Ravana came to the ashrama which was where Maricha lived.

Maricha, clad in tree-bark and deerskin, saw the chariot of Ravana. He was full of misgivings since he knew that some great event was bothering Ravana or else he would not have undertaken this long journey to the ashrama. He hoped that it would not be a repetition of the previous visit. Not displaying his emotions and his concern on his face, Maricha welcomed the emperor in the proper manner and stood humbly before him. When Ravana had made a pretence of partaking of the simple fare placed before him, Maricha asked him: "I hope all is well with you in Lanka. May I know what has made you undertake this journey and grace again this humble hermitage of this slave of yours?"

Ravana was extremely well-read and he knew the art of conversing and the art of persuasion with words. He looked at Maricha and said: "I had to come to you, uncle, because I am sorely distressed in mind and I want a word of comfort from the likes of you.

"I am suffering and only you seem to me to be capable of sympathising with me. You must already have known about the happenings at Janasthana. I told you briefly last time I came here. My brother Khara, Dushana and Trishiras with the fourteen thousand rakshasas who dwelt there have all been killed. My sister Shurpanakha has been insulted. Her nose and ears have been mutilated mercilessly and all this has been caused by that one man, Rama.

"I am told that even while fighting Rama was unruffled. His arrows were spouting anger but he was placid. This one man stood on the ground and he has achieved something I am still unable to believe it has happened. Listen to the story of Rama, this intruder into my territory.

"Evidently he is a sinner or else his father would not have banished him from the kingdom. He is an insult to the clan of kshatriyas and evidently he is doomed to be short-lived since he has courted my enmity. He is very crude, and he is foolish, obstinate, characterless and cruel. He must be an Adharmi and his mind does not dwell in the realm of Dharma. He is bent on doing evil to others. For no cause at all my poor unfortunate sister has been insulted by him. The only way to punish him is to capture his wife Sita."

Maricha who had been worried about the coming of the king had his fears justified. He was unhappy since the king, who had seemed to be convinced by his arguments the previous time, had suddenly changed his mind and had gone back to the old scheme, the dangerous task of stealing Sita.

Ravana knew the turmoil in the mind of Maricha but he pretended not to notice it and went on talking. He said: "Uncle, you must help me in this strategy of mine. With you by my side I will not be afraid to face even the devas in warfare. My brothers and you are my sole supporters. I am yet to see one like you. You are so strong and so efficient. You are intelligent enough to think up plans by means of which the enemy can be baffled. You are at home in Maya tactics and, therefore, I have come to you. Listen to my words and you can tell me if you can do what I wish."

Maricha had begun to tremble. He knew that he had no chance of living once he accepted the plans of Ravana. He was not able to talk. To antagonise Rama was the worst thing that could happen to him but then, he was in the presence of his master, his emperor. Tossed as he was on the horns of a dilemma, the poor unfortunate Maricha spoke not a word. Ravana continued: "Uncle Maricha, I want to tell you my plan. I want you to take up the guise of a deer, a golden deer. Your spots should glitter like silver. You must go near the ashrama of Rama and wander around until Sita's eyes light on you. If I know women right — and I know all about women and their caprices! — I know that Sita will at once ask her husband and Lakshmana to get the deer for her. They will try to capture you. This is where your cleverness should come into play. Stay near them and when they are near run further and thus you must lure them both away from the ashrama. When Sita is alone, unprotected, I will enter the ashrama and like Rahu captures the glow of the moon, I will steal her and come away.

"Rama will be heart-broken because of the loss of his wife and when he is sunk in despondency it will be easy for me to kill him and avenge the death of my men."

Ravana looked triumphantly at Maricha. He had not said a word about the beauty of Sita and about his desire to possess her. He spoke as though revenge were the only motive behind this subterfuge of his.

Maricha's mouth had gone dry at the mention of the name of Rama. He was terribly frightened. Licking his lips which had gone dry, he stood staring at Ravana. His eyelids has ceased to function. He was still staring at Ravana with wide and frightened eyes. His mind was not in the task that was assigned to him since he knew only too well the prowess of Rama. He said: "Ravana, my child, you told me that you need someone to comfort you in your hour of need. I am that person. I am your well-wisher and my words are essential to you. You must listen to me."

With his palms folded he stood humbly before his emperor and continued: "You are the emperor and you are surrounded by sycophants. They will speak words which are pleasing to the ear and which will flatter you. It is rare to find a courtier who will tell you what is good for you and who will speak the truth. It is also rare to find a man who will listen to such words. Evidently your spies have not done their work properly or else they would, long ago, have told you about the coming of Rama to Dandaka and about his valour. Rama is a great warrior. He is more powerful than Indra or Varuna. He is the home of all good qualities. How could you expect him to leave the rakshasas alone in the forest without destroying them? I am telling you now. If you want to live, abandon this aimless plan of yours. It is foolish. Sita will become your death. Because of her you will go through untold suffering. You have been wilful and there is no one to control you or to advise you. I am certain that Lanka will be destroyed: and, with Lanka, you and all your rakshasas. You are not able to think far ahead and that is why you have come to this decision.

"You have not heard about Rama, not correctly. Someone has been telling you lies. He is not an Adharmi. His father was deceived and because of his desire to save the reputation of his father Rama came to the Dandaka forest. He is Dharma personified and it is not right to cast aspersions on his name. How can you possibly think of stealing his wife? It is like falling into blazing fire without realising that it will burn you up. Sure as Fate, you will be killed. Do not attempt this foolishness. Sita cannot be separated from Rama. She is dear to him. And he is her very life. She is the wife of a great warrior and she is like the flame from a sacrificial fire. Do not try to touch her. When you encounter Rama in a fight that will be the end of you. You are now the happy emperor of the rakshasa world and there is peace in your mind. If you want it to last, do not antagonise Rama. Go back to Lanka and put the proposal before good ministers like Vibhishana. They will tell you what I have told you.

"I will tell you about Rama. There was a time when I was a wild youngster. I had the strength of a thousand elephants and I would wander at will eating human flesh and causing havoc in the ashramas of the rishis. Once the sage Vishvamitra was performing a yaga and I was bent on disturbing it. He went to king Dasaratha and asked him to lend Rama to him. Rama, the son of Dasaratha, was then hardly sixteen years old. Vishvamitra went back to his ashrama accompanied by Rama.

"I went to the yagnasala and there I saw this young man. I still remember vividly the picture he presented. He was handsome and he was unbelievably young. He held this huge bow in his left hand and he looked like the young crescent of the moon rising in the east on the third day after the new moon. He saw me and calmly he fixed an arrow to his bow. I treated him with contempt and went on with my act of polluting the yagnasala. Rama despatched an arrow at me. It pierced my chest and lifting me in the air it carried me a distance of a hundred yojanas and flung me into the sea. Being a kind boy he did not have the heart to kill me and he left me alive. Slowly I returned to Lanka after I had recovered my senses.

This was years ago when he was a boy. Now he is a man and there is no one in this world or in the other worlds who can stand and fight against him. Listen to my words and abandon this foolish plan of abducting Sita. If you do so, you will only be courting the destruction of everything. It will mean death: death for yourself and for the entire city of Lanka and for the rakshasa clan."

Maricha paused to see if his words had any effect on the king. Ravana was silent. "Perhaps he is becoming convinced," thought Maricha and tried to use further arguments.

"Again, I will tell you something else which happened to me," continued Maricha. "You know how we have all been in the habit of eating the rishis in the Dandaka. My favourite guise is, as you know, that of a deer. With two more rakshasas I entered the Dandaka once and went into several of the ashramas and made a meal of the rishis living there. On one such occasion I saw Rama and Lakshmana in the garb of ascetics and I told myself: "This Rama is now a tapasvin. I will punish him for what he did to me once." I went to them and with my sharp horns attacked them. Rama took up his bow and with three arrows fixed to it, he turned towards us. He shot the arrows and my two companions died. But I managed to escape. My life had been spared twice by this prince. But I gave up all my rakshasic nature since then and I have begun to dwell in this ashrama. I have become a Sanyasi and, believe me, even now, when I set my eyes on a distant tree I see Rama there in his garb of an ascetic. Everything seems to me to be like Rama. Words even, which begin with the letter 'Ra', frighten me. I know about Rama and his valour. It is not good for you to make an enemy of Rama. Avoid him at all costs. If I listen to you, I will be killed. You will also meet with death at his hands.

"As for the tragedy at Janasthana, something tells me Shurpanakha is the cause of it. She must have taunted the brothers and must have been punished for it. To avenge that, Khara must have been incited by her to fight with Rama. I see no wrong in the behaviour of Rama. Ravana, I am talking to you as an uncle and not as a subject. I want to see you live long with your wife and with your sons. If you do not listen to me, I assure you, it will be the end of you and all those who are yours."

When a man is doomed to die, he does not relish the medicine which is good for him. Even so, the words of Maricha were not welcomed by

Ravana. His tact and his diplomatic approach were gone now and Ravana was very angry. Prodded by Fate, Ravana spoke harsh words to his uncle. He said: "It is no use, Maricha; your words will have no effect on me, even as seeds will not sprout in barren land. You can never convince me about the prowess or valour of that sinful and stupid human being. I am not afraid. Think of the banishment of this Rama to the forest. An old man listens to the words of a woman and because of that this Rama of yours is ready to give up his kingdom, his mother, his father and all those who are near and dear to him. He comes to this dreadful forest and lives here. He has not the courage to defy the woman who wanted him banished. Such a man, you tell me, is a hero and you want me to believe it. I will not do so. I still wonder how Khara could have been killed with his immense host of rakshasas.

"Maricha, I have made up my mind. Sita has to be abducted and you have to help me to carry her away. No one can make me change my decision. If I had asked your counsel as to the wisdom of my action then you could have come out with all these arguments which you have advanced. But you are here only to obey me. You seem to have forgotten that I am your king and that you should talk to me humbly. Instead, because you are older than me, and because I treat you with respect considering you are my uncle, you are overstepping the privilege I have granted you. I do not need your concern about my well-being. I can take care of myself. All I want from you is implicit obedience.

"As I said before, you must assume the form of a golden deer and wander around in the vicinity of Rama's ashrama. After Sita is captivated by you, you are at liberty to go anywhere you please. She will do the needful. She will coax Rama and his brother to chase you, capture you and to bring you to her. If, however, Lakshmana stays behind, you should lure Rama to a great distance from the ashrama and from there, imitating the voice of Rama you should shout: "Ha! Sita! Ha! Lakshmana!" The two remaining in the ashrama are sure to be frightened and Lakshmana will go in search of his brother anxious to help him.

"That short interval will be enough for me to go to the ashrama, capture Sita and carry her away with me. Once you have achieved this, you can go wherever you please. I will be so pleased with you, I will give you half my kingdom. Go to the Dandaka taking an easy and quick path with me. We will go in my chariot. My intention is to avoid a war which is unnecessary. I will deceive the brothers and go back to Lanka with Sita as my captive. If you still refuse to obey me, I will, this very moment, send you to the abode of Yama. A king's command should be honoured or else death is the punishment. If you do this, you may live after the incident. But if you do not, death is certain."

Maricha would not give up. He said: "Someone is desirous of your destruction or else you would not have been advised to be so rash. You were living happily with your wives and your valiant sons and you have now been led to the gates of death and, strangely enough, you seem to be eager to enter it soon. You do not seem to have any wellwishers as ministers. On the other hand, they are leading you astray.

"A king who is wilful and who has chosen to follow the wrong path should be advised against it by good men who claim to be his ministers. Because of this decision of yours, your subjects are going to suffer, your city is going to suffer, your wives, your children will all suffer. I promise you, there will not be a single person left alive in Lanka once Rama turns his angry eyes on you. It is not possible for a cruel king to rule his kingdom well. The good of his people is not important to him and he is thinking only of himself and the gratification of his senses. The evil mentors you have will lead you to destruction even as horses yoked to a chariot will rush to ruin driven, as they will be, on ground which is not levelled, and bring death to themselves as well as to the rider in the chariot.

"Do not think that I will come out alive after this encounter with Rama. He will kill me and, later, he will kill you. If I am killed by that noble soul, I will at least be sure to inherit the heavens. The instant I see Rama, it means that my death has appeared before me.

"You may capture Sita from the ashrama now. But remember, you would have captured death in your arms. You refuse to listen to my words which mean well, and you are doomed. Your entire family is doomed. Lanka with all her inmates is doomed. I know it."

16. THE GOLDEN DEER

Ravana did not care for the words of Maricha. As soon as he agreed to do his bidding Ravana stood up and Maricha said: "Come, let us go." They came to the doorway of the ashrama which Maricha had built for himself. He took one last look at the spot which had granted him refuge all these days. Ravana was walking fast and he waited impatiently while Maricha said: "Once Rama's eyes light on me, that means I am dead. No one who has incurred his displeasure has escaped the arrows of Rama. I realise today that you are extremely wicked and I know that Rama will punish you for it. You will certainly be dead very soon."

Ravana did not hear a word of what he was saying. His mind was far away. But he embraced Maricha and said: "I am now very pleased with you. Come with me. My chariot pulled by the magical donkey is waiting at the door. Let us go soon. I am impatient to reach Dandaka."

The chariot travelled fast in the air and very soon they had reached the neighbourhood of Rama's ashrama. Ravana saw it from a distance. They descended from the chariot and Ravana took Maricha by the hand and said: "See, that is Rama's dwelling place. Come, make haste."

Maricha changed himself into a deer. The deer was golden in hue as though it had been made out of molten gold. The face was white and dark, and there were silver spots on the body of the deer. They gleamed in the light of the sun. The neck was long and bent at a charming angle. The horns gleamed and they seemed to have gems set in them. The deer was wandering about on the grass-covered frontage of the ashrama. It walked, it ran, it frisked and it jumped around. It danced around, almost, all over the place. At times it would step softly and at other times it would be bent on eating the grass. It walked about near the Karnikara trees which surrounded the ashrama and it wandered around with the sole purpose of tempting Sita. Deer which were grazing around knew by instinct that this was no deer and they ran away in panic from him. Maricha would have loved to eat one of the many deer which were there but he knew he could not do so.

Sita came out of the ashrama to gather flowers for worship. She came near the shrubs which were laden with flowers. She walked round the Karnikara trees and the Ashoka trees. These were her favourite flowers and she came to pluck them for herself. The deer which was prancing around till now, came very near where she was and stood still, grazing.

Suddenly Sita saw the deer. Her eyes were filled with amazement at the beautiful picture in front of her. The deer was unbelievably beautiful. While she gathered her flowers her eyes were trained only on the deer which was frisking around and which wandered here, there and everywhere, remembering to be within her neighbourhood all the time.

Sita called out Rama and Lakshmana. They came out and they saw the deer. Lakshmana looked at the deer for a long moment and said: "Rama, my dear brother, I am sure this is not a deer. As a matter of fact, I am sure this is our old friend Maricha whom you left alive long ago and who escaped again from us, very recently. He had assumed the form of a deer then, do you remember? An ordinary deer though, not one as fascinating as this specimen here. But this deer is Maricha. Several rishis in the forest have been killed by him while he has donned this guise. This glowing skin which covers him, this glister like that of a rainbow are all like the gandharva nagari we see in the sky: a mirage, a deceptive appearance which seems to be real but is not. Rama, have you ever heard of a deer with the skin of gold, with silver spots and jewelled horns? This is the Maya of that rakshasa. I am sure of it."

Sita smiled at Lakshmana. There was disbelief in her eyes. She said: "Rama, this deer has stolen my heart. Please, please capture it for me, I will have a playmate. I have seen herds of deer in the forest and several of them come to us in the ashrama. They are tame and gentle. But then, I am yet to see a deer as beautiful as the one before me. It seems to me the moon has come down to the earth. It is perfect. I am fascinated by it. If you can capture it alive it will be great. After we go back to Ayodhya it will be an object of wonder to all the inmates of the palace. If, however, you cannot take it alive, its skin at least, can be taken. It is unique in its beauty. Rama, I have never felt like this before. Never before have I been so vehement in any desire to possess something. It is unwomanly and I feel it is against my nature to behave like this. But this deer is captivating, there is no doubt about it." Rama was standing there, smiling at the excitement of Sita. She had never been so excited before. He looked at the deer and he had to agree with Sita. Its beauty was unworldly. Even he fell a victim to the Maya of Maricha.

He said: "Lakshmana, Sita wants this deer. I have not seen such a deer before either, and this eagerness of Sita to possess it is understandable. Even Indra's garden Nandana or Kubera's Chaitra will not have such a deer, I am sure. Look at its tongue when it licks up the grass! Does it not seem like a streak of lightning? or a tongue of flame? When even a man like me is falling a victim to the charms of this animal, what then of a young woman who is accustomed to play with animals like this? I will try to get it for her.

"Lakshmana, you suspect that it is not a deer but our old Maricha. In which case it is my duty to chase it and kill it to save the Dandaka from his mischief. Once, do you remember my telling you about Vatapi who would assume the form of a goat to deceive the victims, and was later killed by Agastya? When I think of Agastya I remember him telling me that I should take care to please Sita in every way. Lakshmana, you must remain here and guard Sita. I will chase this deer and kill it most probably unless I manage to capture it alive. Slowly I am also getting the feeling that this is not a deer at all. Lakshmana, be very careful in taking care of Sita. With a single arrow I will kill this deer and bring it with me. Jatayu is also here and he will help you to take care of Sita. You must be extremely alert. Be on the look out for danger. I smell danger. I am afraid some danger is awaiting us and Sita is mainly involved in it. Clasp your bow firmly in your hand and be ready to tackle danger. It seems to be very close.

"I am not able to define it but I am getting a feeling that some crisis is imminent in our lives. Guard Sita and I will return with the deer, dead or alive as the case may be."

17. THE KILLING OF MARICHA

After giving the instructions to Lakshmana, Rama set out to get the deer for Sita. He strapped the sword to his waist. The quiver was on his shoulder and his bow with the three beautiful bends in it was in his hand. He looked at Sita and she was smiling with happiness. Her Rama would get the deer for her. She was sure of it.

Rama looked around and the deer was just beyond his reach. It began to prance about and Rama followed it with casual steps. After some distance had been covered the deer seemed again to come within his grasp but in the end it eluded him. It was an exasperating chase since the deer was playing a game with Rama, a most tantalising game. Suddenly like a streak of lightning it would appear before him and turning its beautiful neck it would look at him with terror in its eyes. At other times it would come near enough as though exhausted by running about so much. It would disappear into the dense forest and appear again and the glimpse made Rama impatient. Like the moon which is seen in the sky and is hidden by the clouds scuttling across the sky the deer was seen and unseen by Rama. Before long Rama realised that he had come a great distance from the ashrama. He was now getting angry. His impatience had turned into anger. He stood for a while on the grassy land and the deer appeared suddenly in front of him. He rushed towards it and the animal fled in panic. Rama decided to kill it as soon as it came within his sight once again.

Rama's anger knew no bounds now. He took an arrow out of his quiver and fixed it to his bowstring. He pulled the string to the utmost stretch and, invoking the astra of Brahma, he despatched it towards the deer. Spitting fire like a shooting star the astra entered the body of the deer and split it in two. Maricha made a hideous noise and fell to the ground. No longer able to keep up his guise, he fell on the ground and Rama saw his hideous form. He told himself: "So Lakshmana was right! This is Maricha and my brother was astute enough to recognise him at once. I was not able to do so." Maricha in the meantime was dead. While his life was fast ebbing away from him, as per the instructions given to him by Ravana he shouted: "Ha! Sita! Ha! Lakshmana!" in a voice very like Rama's and the next moment he was dead.

Rama was intrigued by his dying words. He was worried about the safety of Sita. He was certain that some mischief was afoot. Again and again he praised the insight of his Lakshmana and he feared that something terrible was about to happen. He saw now that he had been deliberately lured away far, very far, from the ashrama. But Lakshmana was there to guard Sita. That was the comforting thought. But still his mind was full of misgivings. He thought: "Maricha had some reason for shouting out like that. He made it sound as though I was calling out in agony. Sita must have heard it and she will be distraught with grief thinking that I am in danger. I do not know what Lakshmana will do now. I hope they are not taken in by this deceptive cry of Maricha."

Try as he might, Rama could not shed the uneasiness which was troubling him. He walked back towards Janasthana in a hurry. He tried to walk as fast as he could, and he realised that he was quite far away from the ashrama.

Sita heard the pathetic shout which Maricha had set up and she was convinced that Rama was in danger: that he was in need of help. She turned her agonised eyes to Lakshmana and said: "Did you hear the cry for help which my lord has set up? My mind is full of fear and I want you to go immediately to the assistance of your brother. He is in great trouble or else he would not have cried out like that. I am certain he is surrounded by rakshasas and that his life is in danger. Please hurry to his assistance at once. Save him, Lakshmana. He needs you."

She was trembling with fear and her eyes were filled with tears. Lakshmana heard her but he made no attempt to leave. He was determined to stay by her side and carry out the wishes of his brother. Sita asked him again and still he would not move from there.

Sita was angry with him and said: "Why do you stand like this? Why do you stay still when I am asking you to go? Evidently you do not love your brother: or else, to remain unmoved by that cry of distress is not possible. You are not a real brother to Rama but you are really his enemy. I now feel that you wish him dead. Your intentions about me must be evil. You are hoping to make me your wife and with Rama out of the way you can achieve this sinful end. I am sure that is the reason for your indifference. You are happy that this incident has taken place. You do not love your brother. I am sure of it. You are not affected at all by his call for help. How can that be possible? You must have some ulterior motive which is making you deaf to your brother's call for help."

Lakshmana looked at her and spoke in a pained voice: "Sita, have you not been made aware of the prowess of Rama? No deva, danava, pannaga, yaksha or rakshasa can harm that god among men. There is no one in any of the many worlds to hurt him. Rama cannot be killed in a fight. You should not talk thus. My brother has commanded me to stay by your side and guard you. I will not leave you alone here, in the ashrama. Hardly a few days back you saw with your own eyes how Rama, my brother, stood alone on the ground and, single-handed, destroyed the army of Khara and killed him too with his chief commanders. Even as my eyes lighted on that deer I knew that it was a rakshasa and I am afraid some mischief is afoot. Rama has been lured away and it has been so contrived that we should be alarmed by the cry for help supposedly from my brother. There is, I am sure, some deep scheme and I am afraid, very much afraid, to leave you alone here in the ashrama.

"Rama will be back very soon, I can assure you of that. No rakshasa can kill him, least of all Maricha. Please possess your soul in patience and wait for your lord. This voice we heard is the voice of that Maricha who is all Maya. He has been killed, I am sure, by Rama, and with his Maya he has faked this cry for help to confuse you. Rama has asked me not to leave you alone. He has asked me not to move away from this place and I have been asked to guard you very carefully. I cannot disobey Rama. I will not leave you alone. After the killing of Khara and his men, several rakshasas must be wanting to avenge his death. I am sure this is one of their plans. Please do not be upset by these. Rama will be here very soon and you will realise the truth of my guesses."

Sita was very angry with Lakshmana. Her sorrow had made her lose all sense of proportion and she said: "You are an Anarya. You are not fit to be called the brother of Rama. You are without any compassion and you have decided to commit sin. You are a blot on the name of the Ikshvakus. You know that Rama is in trouble and yet you are unconcerned. I do not set any store by your words of assurance. All these years you have managed to conceal your evil intentions, and you have pretended to be devoted to Rama. Either with a desire to take me, or because of Bharata's designs on the life of Rama you have followed us into the forest. Let me assure you, none of your wishes will come true: neither yours nor those of the son of Kaikeyi. I will, this very moment, give up my life. I will not let you touch me."

Lakshmana folded his palms and stood before her in a suppliant frame of mind. He said: "You are like a mother to me since I consider Rama to be my father. You are my goddess and I dare not talk back when you speak such sharp and wounding words. Women are prone to talk words which wound abominably. But it is born with them and I do not set great store by it. Your words are like Narachas which leave the bow only to kill. You are attributing sin to me and I am sinless. I am standing firm in your presence because of the commands of my elder brother and you think of me as a sinner. It is your womanliness which makes you talk like this. I have never known you to talk like this before. It is painful to hear your words suspecting me of the most heinous of sins: lusting after a brother's wife. I cannot bear them any longer. I will go where my brother is. May you be safe. I beseech the *vanadevatas* to guard you from mishaps. The omens do not seem to be good. I fear some calamity is threatening you and I still feel that I should stay back and guard you."

"If you do not go, I will kill myself," said Sita. "I will swallow poison or I will throw myself into blazing fire. I will make a noose and hang myself or I will fling myself into the waters of the Godavari and kill myself. I will not let you touch me."

Lakshmana was on the verge of tears. He said: "I am sure I do not know what to do. You are obstinate and I am helpless. When I come back with Rama I hope I will see you. I am hoping that no evil will befall you."

Sita would not be convinced. She was like one demented. In her distraction Sita was behaving like a country-bred woman, unacquainted with decorum. She screamed at Lakshmana and she beat her stomach like one who had lost everything. Lakshmana could bear it no longer. He stood for a while looking at her and she would not talk to him or look at him. Finally with great hesitation, he saluted her, and looking back often he turned his unwilling steps away from the ashrama and walked in the direction where the cry of distress came from.

18. RAVANA IN OCHRE ROBES

Unable to bear the harsh words spoken by Sita, Lakshmana left her and went in search of Rama. He was extremely angry and his breath was coming in gasps. He could hardly control himself or his anger. He had been unwilling to go but he was forced to do so.

Ravana had been waiting in a spot not far away from there. He had been waiting for Lakshmana to leave the ashrama. Ever since the dying voice of Maricha reached him, Ravana knew that the poor rakshasa had been killed by Rama. He felt no compunction at all about the mishap to his uncle. Maricha had served the purpose and it was no matter if he died now. For a while Ravana was worried lest Lakshmana should remain in the ashrama. He was greatly relieved when he saw him leaving.

Promptly he assumed the garb of a Parivrajaka, a mendicant, and walked towards the ashrama of Rama. He was now wearing robes which were ochre-coloured and he had an umbrella in his hand. His hair was matted and there were wooden sandals on his feet. He bore a staff on his shoulder and in his hand he held a Kamandalu. He walked fast towards Sita.

Sita was alone without the protection of the brothers and he now approached her. It was like the dark night nearing the evening when it is bereft of the sun and the moon. Ravana came to the doorway of the ashrama and he saw Sita. He looked at Sita as Angaraka would the star Rohini. His eyes were hungry and impatient.

The very trees in Janasthana held their breath. The air did not move: so appalling was the crime which he was now contemplating that nature held her breath and wept in silence. Ravana was not able to conceal the redness in his eyes and the river Godavari flowed softly, scared of his angry looks. Ravana stood at the doorway waiting for Sita to appear. Slowly he walked nearer and stood very near the entrance of the ashrama. Like a well, deceptive because it is covered with grass, Ravana, dressed in the garb of a Sanyasi, stood at the doorway of the ashrama and then he saw Sita.

He stood as though he were paralysed: so bewitching was her beauty. Her face was like the moon in its charm and her teeth could be seen gleaming white, between her lips. Wide and large, her eyes were like the petals of a lotus, a white lotus, and her beauty was unearthly. Dressed in yellow silk she stood alone in the ashrama and Ravana feasted his eyes on this woman who was much more lovely and captivating than he had imagined. He thought that she was the most beautiful woman in all the three worlds. He thought her to be Lakshmi who had abandoned the lotus and come down to the earth to beautify it. She was beautiful, unbelievably beautiful and, stricken as he was by the arrows of the god of love, still Ravana composed himself and, reciting verses from the Vedas, announced his presence to her. Hearing someone at the doorway, Sita came out and saw the Sanyasi and saluted him. He saw that she was alone and he asked her:

"Who may you be? who lives alone in the forest, alone in this ashrama? You are very beautiful. Fair, like molten gold, your gold coloured silk enhances your charm. Your charm makes me think of a lotus pond filled with lotuses. Are you Parvati, by any chance, who has thought of wandering at will in the forest? Are you Shachi Devi? Lakshmi? Are you the earth who has assumed a form? Are you Rati? The bride of god of love or do you happen to be an apsara? Your teeth are captivating. They are like pearls strung together and they glisten like pearls. What lovely eyes! Your dark eyes hold magic in them and they are so guileless and bewitching. As for your form, it is perfectly made. What divine hands sculptured your lovely breasts. Your smile, your teeth, your eyes, your face are all so beautiful; they have captivated me. I am like a river whose banks are eaten up by the flood in the river. Your waist which is so slim I can hold it in one hand! What long and beautiful hair you have! You are not a woman from the heavens nor are you a gandharva damsel. I have never seen the like of you before. I am dumbfounded by so much beauty. Your youth and your dwelling in this forest are intriguing.

"This place is infested with rakshasas and it is not meet that you should live here, alone. Go back to where you came from. You should grace the palace of a prince and peacocks and parrots should keep you company on the terraces of the palace gardens. Tell me who you are. This is not a favourite place of the celestials. You are not one of them. How is it possible for you to dwell in the midst of cruel animals in this forest without being afraid of them? Who are you? To whom do you belong? Why have you come here? This fearful Dandaka is not the place for you. Why have you come here? I am full of curiosity."

Ravana's words were embarrassing to Sita. But she thought that he was an elderly man, a Sanyasi, who was genuinely concerned about her and she entertained him in the usual way a guest should be. She offered a darbha seat to him and asked him to sit down. She had no doubt that he was one of the passing Sanyasi who had lost his way. He was, to her, a brahmin, a Sanyasi who had come as a wanderer and had come upon their ashrama by chance.

Ravana was watching her every movement with hungry eyes and he decided to abduct her at once and he made up his mind to bring about his own ruin. Again and again Sita would look towards the doorway waiting for the coming of her Rama with Lakshmana. But they did not come.

She thought to herself : "When I am eaten up with worry about Rama this guest has come here. It is my duty to pay him respect and to entertain him or else, who knows, he may curse me. I will have to answer his questions."

She said : "I am the daughter of Janaka, the king of Mithila. I am the wife of Rama and my name is Sita. I lived with my husband in the midst of comfort while I was in Ayodhya, the city of the Ikshvakus. The king Dasaratha, my husband's father, decided to crown him as Yuvaraja. But his other mother, Kaikeyi by name, did not approve, and she wanted her son to be crowned and she desired that my husband should be banished to Dandaka. The king had to agree and my husband has come to Dandaka. The name Rama is well-known in all the three worlds. He is the image of Dharma and, to him, truth is the utmost religion. With him came his brother Lakshmana who is an equally powerful warrior. I accompanied Rama since I cannot live without him nor he without me. We have been living in this forest for a long time now. If you are so inclined, please wait for Rama. He will come back soon. Please let me know your name and the gotra to which your honoured self belongs." She stood respectfully before him.

Ravana said : "Sita, you must have heard about a rakshasa by name Ravana. The three worlds live in fear of him. His name spells terror for them all. I am that Ravana.

"O you lovely woman! ever since I set my eyes on you, ever since they lighted on your beautiful face, I have not been able to think of anything else. I have forgotten that I have other wives. Come with me Sita, and be my wife. My city is named Lanka. It is surrounded on all sides by the sea and it is situated on top of a hill. Come with me and you can be happy wandering around in the beautiful gardens which are many in my palace. Cast away this forest life and come with me and be happy."

Sita was more angry than frightened. She was horrified by the words of Ravana and said : "Listen to me. I love my husband. Rama is everything to me. He is the noblest of all beings and you do not know anything about him. He is as firm as the Himavan and as deep and calm as the ocean. He is the home of all virtues and he is purity itself. How can you have the audacity to ask me to be your wife? I am like a lioness and you are a jackal desiring me. I am unattainable even as the glory of the sun. Do not dare to talk like this to me. You do not realise what a dangerous desire this is. It is like trying to pull the fangs from the mouth of a dread snake with your bare hands : like trying to live after having quaffed a draught of Kalakuta. You are trying to touch your eyes with a needle point : touch the edge of a sword with your tongue. Do not dream of sin of such magnitude. If you say that you want to possess me it is like trying to gather fire in your upper cloth and to imagine that it will not burn the cloth. Give up these sinful thoughts and go away from here before my husband comes and kills you."

She spoke valiantly but her mind was full of fear. She was trembling like a plantain tree caught in a strong gale and she stood staring at the ground. Ravana, who was like Yama himself, saw her fear and spoke to her about how strong he was and he bragged about his prowess. He told her that he was far superior to Rama in strength and in wealth and in beauty: in short, in every way, he was better than Rama. He said : "You know nothing about me. I am the son of the noble Vishravas and my brother is Kubera whom I defeated in a duel. He has given up his city and he had to go and live on top of the Kailasa peak because of me. I have with me his chariot by name Pushpaka which will fly in the air. The devas led by Indra run away if they hear that I am in the vicinity of the heavens. The God of Wind, Vayu, dares not blow hard when I am around and the sun becomes cool lest I should be offended by his hot rays. The very trees do not move even a leaf because of their fear of me. The rivers halt in their course if I so desire.

"My Lanka is beautiful as the city Amaravati, the city of Indra. Come with me and live happily in this city of mine. Forget this mere man who is called Rama. Celestial pleasures will be yours if you come with me. You will be queen of my entire harem. Look how your Rama has come to the forest. If his father does an unjust act, the son does not have to obey him. Your Rama has not courage enough to defy his father but agrees to do as he is told. Do you call that valour? I do not. What is the use of being the spouse of one who has lost his kingdom and lives in the forest like a Sanyasi? You are too beautiful to be wasted on that man. Do not refuse me and my love for you. Consider that it is your good fortune that I have come here to rescue you from a life of hardihood in the forest with Rama who is not fit enough to fight with me."

Sita was unconscious of the danger that was threatening her. She only knew that her Rama was being insulted by this rakshasa and she said: "You say that Kubera is your brother. You are born in the great family of Vishravas and so you should be righteous. How can a son born of a noble man behave as you do? How can you talk to Rama's wife thus? You are thoughtless and you will be destroyed if you pursue this sinfulness. You may be able to live after taking Shachi as captive but not if you do so with Rama's wife. I am warning you that Rama's arrows will split your chest if he sees you now. You cannot escape death at his hands."

Ravana clapped his hands together in anger. He shed the guise of a Sanyasi which he had donned and his eyes had now become tawny with anger. He stood staring at Sita for a moment and said : "Once again I am telling you. Listen to my words and be my wife willingly. Accept my love and I promise you, I will never once displease you. Forget this man and turn your eyes to me. He is far inferior to me. He does not claim the respect of the world. Because his father asked him to, he has given up his chance of ruling a kingdom. I am sure he is stupid. He has nothing to boast of : neither a kingdom, nor friends, nor any hope of regaining his land. Such a frustrated man is not good enough for you, and still you persist in this foolish love for this undeserving man."

She spoke not a word and her fear became greater. She saw the rakshasa Ravana in his true form and he was fearful to look at. Ravana knew that time was running short and he also realised that Sita was not listening to his words.

Spurred by Fate, by Death, Ravana approached Sita and he dragged her towards himself. With his left hand he caught hold of her long hair and, with his right, he lifted her up, placing his hands under her thighs.

The *vanadevatas* trembled at the sight of Ravana who was like death incarnate. No one dared to stay near him. The chariot endowed with magic powers appeared from nowhere and Ravana entered the chariot placing Sita on his lap. Sita, the beloved wife of Rama, was being carried away by Ravana.

She called out : "Rama ! Rama !" in vain. Rama did not hear her.

The chariot rose up in the sky and she was wriggling in his grasp but he would not let her go. Sita was like one demented. She screamed out:

"Lakshmana, you pure-hearted, noble brother of my Rama, this savage rakshasa is carrying me away and you know nothing about it. Rama, I am being separated from you and I do not know what is going to happen to me." She turned to Ravana and said : "At Fate's behest you have perpetrated this crime and you will be punished for it by Rama. If you are not killed at once it is again because of Fate. Fate is like time. Even as it takes time for a field of grains to be ready for harvest, your sins have to accumulate before Rama can kill you."

Sita looked at the land which was falling away from her. She saw dense areas and these were the trees she knew and they were studded with flowers : Karnikaras. She called out to them and said : 'My beloved flowers, my dear Janasthana, please tell Rama that Ravana is carrying Sita away. I take leave of you."

She spoke to the *vanadevatas*. She was like one demented and Ravana paid no heed to her pleadings.

19. JATAYU'S DEATH

Ravana was jubilant since his plans had been carried out without a hitch and he did not spare a thought for Maricha who had died for his sake. He was trying to go as fast as he could.

While the chariot was speeding away from Janasthana, Sita saw Jatayu perched on top of a tree. She called out to him in desperation: "Jatayu! Revered sir? This rakshasa king is carrying me away. He pretends that he is valiant but he is a coward. He entered our ashrama when Rama and Lakshmana were not there and he had captured me. He is armed and no one can accost him. Please tell Rama that Ravana has carried away his Sita." Sobs stopped her from speaking further.

Jatayu who had gone to sleep on top of the tree woke up when he heard her piteous cry. He tried to talk to Ravana. He said : "Ravana, I am Jatayu and I am extremely powerful. I have been called righteous by everyone. I am telling you this Rama is a great man and a dangerous opponent. He is the lord of the world. You are trying to steal his wife. This is a wrong act which you are contemplating. You are a famous king and you should try to follow the right path which is indicated by the shastras. If the king does something wrong how can he win the respect of his subjects? You should protect women as you would your sister or your mother. Do not be impulsive and court infamy and death. Rama has not wronged you in any way and you should not do this to him. If you think of the episode in Janasthana, it is because of Shurpanakha. She incited Khara to fight with Rama and he had to die because of his foolishness. Tell me truly, why are you acting like this? Give up this madness. Else, you will regret it later. A man can carry only so much burden which he is capable of carrying and he can eat only as much as he can digest. If either of these is in excess then the man suffers for it. Ravana, I am old and you are young. You have a chariot and you are armed while I have none of these things. And yet, let me assure you, I will not let you take her away and watch without interfering. If you will take my advice and leave her, you will be forgiven. If, on the other hand, you insist on persisting with your sinfulness, you must fight with me first. I challenge you to fight with me first. I will, this very moment, make you lose your chariot and later, your life."

Ravana had not bargained for this unforeseen obstacle in his path. He was furious with the old bird which tried to bar his way. He began to fight with Jatayu and the encounter between the rakshasa and the bird was a glorious sight. Ravana hurt the bird with his arrows and Jatayu was able to fight with his claws, his wings and his beak. He hurt Ravana and blood was pouring from his wounds. Jatayu was able to withstand all the arrows of Ravana. He broke the jewelled bow which Ravana held in his hand and, later, his armour also. The donkeys which were yoked to Ravana's chariot were killed and the chariot was crushed to powder. All this the bird was able to achieve with the help of his beak, wings and claws.

Ravana held Sita firmly in his arm and came down to the earth. He saw that Jatayu was now tired and weak. Ravana rose up into the skies once again and so did Jatayu. He went near Ravana. He hurt him in several places. He tried to talk to him also. Ravana was now desperate. The valour of the old bird was amazing. He took up his sword and flashing it at Jatayu he cut off both the wings of the bird. Jatayu had no more fight left in him and he fell to the ground. Sita was sorely distressed at the happenings. The old bird had died and it was because of her. She wept loudly for the old friend of Dasaratha.

She extricated herself from the grip of Ravana and, running to the old bird, she covered him with her arms and wept for him. Ravana came near her and pulled her with a rough hand. She screamed : "Rama! Rama!" and he would not leave her. Again he took her in his arms and placed her on his thigh. He then rose up in the sky.

Nature stood still when this outrage happened. The day was now dark as night. The sun lost his lustre and the wind stood still. There was only one happy person and that was Brahma, the creator. He said : "What had to happen, has now happened." The rishis were unhappy at the plight of Sita.

Decked with glittering ornaments and draped in yellow silk, Sita looked like a streak of lightning against a dense dark cloud, held as she was against the chest of the mighty Ravana. She was wearing lotuses in her hair and they lay scattered about after falling on Ravana. Her face had lost all its glow and was like the lotus during the season when frost kills the flower. Against the dark hue of Ravana her face was like the moon breaking through the clouds enveloping it. The flowers from her hair were falling on the ground and they seemed to ask her to take them again, so forlorn they looked. Her anklet fell down on the earth while she was sailing in the sky held in the arms of Ravana.

The fish in the rivers seemed to sigh with sadness when Sita was carried away. The wild animals followed the shadow cast by the rakshasa and they were growling with anger. The deer in the forest which had played with her so often were now shedding tears. The *vanadevatas* were terrified of Ravana and they could not help Sita.

"Rama, Lakshmana, can you not hear me? Can you not come to my rescue?" shouted Sita as loudly as she could but they were not able to hear her. They were far away.

Ravana was pleased with himself. He was carrying Sita in his arms and he did not know that he had sought out his death and was even then carrying it in his arms thinking that it would be but a source of happiness to him.

She tried to beg him to let her go. She tried to convince him that her lord would kill him if he carried her away thus. She spoke scathing words and she uttered angry threats but all in vain. Ravana paid no heed to anything she said and so they moved in the sky.

She looked down and they were passing a mountain. She could discern five monkeys sitting on top of it. A sudden thought came to her. She quickly removed her ornaments, several of them, and she took a piece out of her upper garment. Sita tied up the jewels in the piece of silk and threw it at the monkeys and hoped that somehow, somewhere, Rama would meet them and they would tell him about her. Ravana had not noticed this and he sailed happily along without a care. The monkeys saw the beautiful woman in the arms of a rakshasa and they saw that he was travelling southwards. They heard her crying out : "Rama! Rama! Lakshmana!" and they wondered who she was.

Ravana went fast, like an arrow released from a taut string and he travelled straight and fast towards Lanka. He crossed the sea and still he held her firmly in his left hand knowing that she might prefer to kill herself by falling into the sea.

Sita was death incarnate for him and he knew it not. He carried her into Lanka. He arrived in the city and entered his *antahpura*. He kept her a captive there and he surrounded her with rakshasis. He instructed them : "Without my knowing, this woman by name Sita should not be allowed to see anyone : nor should anyone see her. Give her anything she asks for, whether it is silks, or food or jewels. She has only to ask and it should be hers."

He then called for eight of his henchmen and said : "You must have, by now, heard about the death of Khara and the end of the others at Janasthana. This was caused by a man named Rama. My only desire now is to avenge the death of these. Go at once to Janasthana and go armed. You should remain there and spy on the movements of Rama. I must get frequent reports as to what he is doing. Attempts should be made by you to kill him, if possible. I know how valiant you are and that is why I am sending you to Janasthana."

The eight warriors left at once for Janasthana and Ravana was happy since he had punished Rama and he had got for himself the most beautiful woman in the three worlds.

20. SITA IN RAVANA'S CITY

After he had despatched the spies to Janasthana, Ravana decided to go and talk to Sita. He had known many women and they had all been willing to become his paramours. They would resist him in the beginning, perhaps, but his beguiling words would win them over and they would become his in the end. This was his experience with women and he did not think that Sita would be an exception to this rule.

And again, though he had set out with a view to punish Rama by abducting Sita, Ravana had become a slave to Sita's charms. He fell in love with her and this love was burning him like a fire. He could not rest even for a moment without thinking of her.

He could not be without her and he hurried to where he had kept her as captive. He saw her. She was surrounded by the rakshasis whom he had placed there as her keepers. Sita was sunk in woe and her face was tear-stained. She was helpless and she looked like a small boat caught in a storm in a vast sea. She was like a stricken deer, hunted by a pack of dogs. Her eyes were cast down and they were veiled by her long lashes. Ravana approached her and she did not raise her head.

Ravana spoke to her about the magnificent palace which would be hers if only she decided to use it. He made her look all about her. He showed her the several pillars which were beautifully wrought and terraces which decorated his palace. There were lakes there in the garden and beautiful trees. And he said : "Sita, ten crores of rakshasas and twenty-two more, is the number of subjects whom I rule. I have a thousand just to attend to my wants. I leave all this at your dear feet. You have become more dear to me than my very life. There are thousands of beautiful women in my harem but not one of them is fit enough even to touch your feet. Listen to my plea of love and accept me. This city of mine is inaccessible even to Indra. It is surrounded by the sea which is a hundred yojanas in width. When you compare my wealth and my greatness with that of Rama who is an exile, a victim of the whims of a woman, a tapasvin dressed in coarse cloth, a mere man whose life is so short, when you think on us both, surely you cannot still think of him! He is feeble and he is lacking in prowess. Do not waste your youth but accept me and my love. Rama can never come here and take you with him. It will be as futile as trying to tie up the wind with silken strands or like holding a smokeless flame in the naked hand. I am yet to see one who can face me in battle. Be my queen. I lay the world at your feet. I have a *vimana* by name Pushpaka and it can wander in the sky. Let us go in that *vimana* and travel wherever you wish and be happy. Your face like a lotus should not look faded and downcast."

Sita covered her face with her dress and cried as though her heart would break. Ravana stood by and watched her for a while. He then continued : "You do not seem to realise the enormous love I have for you. I have laid the world at your feet and you do not welcome it. I have placed my head at your two feet and you do not seem to see that I am your slave. Come, Sita, accept me and my love. Have you heard of Ravana placing his head at the feet of anyone, least of all, a woman? And yet, I am doing it since I love you. Consider me as your slave. You will be mine very soon."

Ravana was assured that some day Sita would become his. He had to wait and convince her and that was all.

She had been listening to his words and she spoke to him. "You know nothing about my Rama and that is why you dare to talk so disparagingly of him. He is the image of Dharma and he is truth personified. He has a brother by name Lakshmana and these two will, one day, come to this city you are bragging about, and kill you. Even as Khara was killed you will also be slain. You have touched me with your sinful hands and Rama will punish you for it. The best of warriors is like a snake in the presence of my husband who will be Garuda to them. His arrows will one day drink your blood and the earth will be drenched with it. You tell me that you are more powerful than the devas and the danavas. But that is nothing to me. My Rama is sure to destroy you and your entire city along with you. You call yourself brave and yet you have taken me away from the ashrama when Rama was not there. You are a thief and that is why I am here. You are not a hero. I think you are the greatest coward that ever has been born since you are a thief. Considering how you have behaved with me, how can you think so highly of yourself? Your end has come and that is the reason why you have dared to steal me and bring me here."

Ravana, naturally, was nettled by the sneer in her voice and her words. He said : "I am not impressed in the least by your words. I will give you twelve months to consider my proposal. If, within that time you agree to be mine, you will be queen of the entire world. If you refuse, my kitchen will take care of you. Your delicate flesh will be cut up into small pieces and will be served to me for my morning meal."

Ravana stormed out of the place and his lips were throbbing with anger and humiliation.

21. RAMA'S LAMENT

Rama had killed Maricha and was hurrying towards the ashrama. He suspected some serious scheming on the part of the rakshasas. This guise of Maricha's was too much of a coincidence. Maricha knew how deadly were the arrows of Rama and yet he had accepted the commission to lure Rama away from the ashrama. He knew that he would be killed. Surely something stupendous was at stake if Maricha had been instigated to risk his life and lose it, if necessary, for achieving this end. Lost in thought Rama walked fast. He saw ill omens all along the way. A jackal howled fearfully and Rama was startled. "Some danger is awaiting me, I am sure of it," said Rama to himself. "I think the rakshasas are even now, eating up my Sita. Maricha called out to Sita and Lakshmana in my voice when he was dying. Perhaps Lakshmana believed it and thinking it was genuine, and leaving Sita alone, perhaps he is coming to my aid. I am convinced that the plan is to kill Sita or else why this guise of Maricha? Why should he call Lakshmana's name and Sita's while dying? I am certain that Lakshmana has left her alone and is coming to me. I am, at the moment, the object of the hatred of the rakshasas at Janasthana and the only manner in which they can hurt me is to kill Sita. I feel they have planned it. I must hurry."

Several other bad omens greeted Rama and he walked with worried steps. His mind was full of the two whom he had left behind in the ashrama. When he was approaching the famed Janasthana, he saw Lakshmana. His face was greatly troubled and Rama waited for him to come near. The eyes of Lakshmana were red since he had been shedding tears and Rama held him in his arms. He then held him by his left hand and spoke in a voice sweeter than honey to his brother. "Lakshmana, my dear Lakshmana, you have left Sita alone in the ashrama and have come away here. It should never have been done by you. I did not expect you here. I do not know what has happened to her. I hope she is well. I hope she is safe. I have been seeing nothing but a series of evil omens and my mind is full of misgivings. Either Sita has been carried away by force or she has been eaten up by the many inmates of this place. Lakshmana, my child, will we see Sita alive? You were right, Lakshmana. The golden deer which deceived Sita and even me, *was* Maricha and you found him out even by looking at him. I should have listened to you and killed him even then. But Fate willed it otherwise. He had been sent to lure me away from here and he succeeded in doing that though he paid for it with his life later. He had to go back to the form of a rakshasa before dying. When he cried out Sita's name and yours I knew there was some mischief which had been planned and that Sita was somehow involved in it as the victim. Lakshmana, my left eye is throbbing and the birds are all flying in the wrong direction. I do know for certain that we will not find Sita in the ashrama. Either she is dead or she is abducted by the rakshasa. I wonder if my beloved Sita is alive?"

Lakshmana was feeling very unhappy at the thought of Sita staying all alone in the ashrama. Rama said : "She came with me to the Dandaka since she could not live without me. I was a mendicant without a kingdom and a wanderer in the forest and yet she preferred that life with me to the comforts of the palace since she loved me. I cannot live without her even for a moment. She is more precious to me than the three worlds. Will my Sita be alive? I wonder if my exile will be fruitless, finally. If Sita dies so will I and when you go back to Ayodhya you may see Kaikeyi happy in the thought that her desire has been fulfilled. My mother will die of a broken heart when she hears of this. Lakshmana, I can assure you of one thing : if Sita is alive, I will remain in the ashrama or else I shall give up my life.

"Tell me, Lakshmana, why did you leave her alone and come here? When that sinful Maricha called out to you it must have worried you and Sita must have been really concerned and she must have sent you to assist me. I guess this is what must have happened. By listening to her you have done something which is harmful to her. The rakshasas have been able to take her away. What am I to do now?"

They had almost reached the ashrama by now and Rama, unhappy and sorely tried, torn by the certainty that Sita was dead, tired, thirsty, hungry because of the long chase after the golden deer, came to the vicinity of the ashrama. He was sighing and he looked everywhere for Sita. He searched in all her favourite haunts and he called out : "What I dreaded has happened. Sita is gone." He was sunk in woe and he sat on the ground as though his limbs could not bear him up any longer. Lakshmana stood silently by the side of Rama and except for the tears which were flowing all the time he spoke not a word.

Rama asked him : " Lakshmana, with the assurance that you will be taking care of my Sita I went out chasing that deer. Why did you come away leaving her alone ?"

Lakshmana could not talk. Sobs choked him and finally he said: "I did not abandon her willingly. She spoke such harsh words, Rama, it was unbearable, I had to come. When we heard the names of both of us calling out to us piteously, Sita heard it and at once she became greatly upset and asked me to go to you for help. I tried to convince her that no one could hurt you : that no evil could befall you and that it was an Aasuri Maya which made the voice sound like yours. But she insisted on my going. I told her that no one in the three worlds can hurt you. But she would not listen. She said : 'You have cast your lustful eyes on me and you wish to see your brother dead. But you will never have your wishes granted. You refuse to go to the aid of Rama in spite of his calling for you. He is evidently, not loved by you. You have conspired with Bharata and that is why you came with Rama to the forest. Your intentions have been evil right through. You are Rama's enemy.' Rama, my beloved brother, I was not able to bear the words spoken by her and yet I did not move from there. But she threatened to kill herself if I did not come to your assistance. In a fit of anger, with my eyes filled with tears I left the ashrama and walked towards you. This is what happened." Lakshmana sobbed like a child.

Rama, who was like one demented, heard Lakshmana and said : "You know me and my prowess. And yet, because Sita spoke words which were sharp and wounding, you left her and came away. It is wrong, child, what you did. When a woman is angry, she will talk without paying any attention to the sense of what she is saying. She will not be aware of what she is saying. Sita was worried and she was angry because of that. You should not have paid any heed to her words. You disobeyed me, Lakshmana, and now look what has happened! You gave way to your emotions and forgot to do my bidding. As for that Maricha, he took me very far from here. Since he was a rakshasa his voice could reach you at this distance and he has accomplished what he set out to."

Rama was saying the same thing again and again : "Sita must be dead. I am sure she has been eaten up by a rakshasa." They had now reached the ashrama. It looked desolate and Rama entered it with eager steps. He walked all over the place and he did not find her. The ashrama appeared like a lotus pond during the cold season. The trees appeared as though they were weeping. The flowers were faded and the birds and the deer were looking sad too. Rama saw the seat made of darbha grass to have been pulled here and there and the deerskin was thrown on the ground. Like an ordinary man, Rama was now lamenting his wife's death.

"Perhaps she has been taken away by force or, perhaps, she has been killed. Is she a captive or is she still in the forest? May be, she has gone to collect fruits for me or to pluck flowers to make a garland. The river! Perhaps that is where she has gone, to bring water." He searched everywhere and he did not see her. He wandered from tree to tree; from shrub to shrub asking them if they had seen his Sita. He asked the Kadamba tree if it had seen Sita. He went near her favourite trees, the Tilaka, Ashoka, Karnikara, Kritamala and several others and said : "She must have bade you farewell when she went away. Will you not tell me where she is?" He looked at the deer and said : "She has eyes like yours. She was very fond of you. Will you tell me where she is?"

Rama was inconsolable and Lakshmana could do nothing to pacify him. The brothers ran around all over the vicinity of the ashrama and could not find Sita. Rama saw the confusion inside the ashrama and concluded that she had been taken away from there forcibly. Rama cried out : "Lakshmana, I cannot live without Sita. When I am dead my father will not look at me with love since I have not been able to take care of my wife."

Lakshmana spoke softly to him. He said : "Rama, my brother, do not give way to grief like this. This forest is so large and there are many caves and so many hiding places here. She may be hidden somewhere by someone. Let us make an attempt to look for her methodically. She loved the trees and the river bank was her favourite place. Let us go and search everywhere. Rouse yourself from this despondency and let us look for her."

Rama tried to do so but could not. With a very great effort he controlled himself and together, they began to search for Sita all over again. Lakshmana was the greatest source of comfort to Rama then. He argued that she could not have gone far since Lakshmana had just left the ashrama when he encountered Rama. She must have been kept somewhere very near. They did not bargain for the Maya of Ravana which helped him to fly in the air and carry her far away from Janasthana. Lakshmana tried to help Rama to regain his mental poise and it was not easy.

The search was over and they did not find her. Rama was spent with sorrow and fatigue and he was silent for a muhurta.

He did not know what to do. His limbs were all limp and his face had lost its lustre, its habitual calmness.

Lakshmana spoke words of comfort to him but it was of no avail. Rama said : "I do not think there is a greater sinner than me in this world. That is why misfortune after misfortune visit me and they have made me lose my reason. My mind and my thinking have all been shattered by this series of calamities. I must have committed several sins which are unforgivable. The punishment for them is meted out to me in this birth. Lakshmana, I lost my kingdom : I lost my kinsmen and I lost my beloved father. I remember these and that makes me unhappy. I am wandering around in the forest like a beggar and my unhappiness had become assuaged and made bearable because of this peaceful life in the forest. My pain was no longer fresh and painful but was like a heap of dead and dried leaves. But now, with the loss of Sita, the unhappiness has been kindled again and it is burning me up. Sita, my queen, has been captured by a low-born rakshasa and is in great danger. I am certain of that. Lakshmana, look at this slab of stone. This is where we once sat and talked for long about many things. Sita could not have gone alone to the river bank or to gather flowers all by herself. She is a very timid woman. This sun will know where she has gone and he will not tell me; this wind which is present everywhere will know where Sita has been taken but will not tell me." Again and again Rama would call out to Sita and Lakshmana was unhappy. He had never seen his brother give way to grief thus and it was painful.

He took Rama to a place nearby and made him sit down. Without overstepping the decorum of a younger man talking to his elder brother, Lakshmana said : "My dear brother, abandon this grief and let me see your fortitude. Let us set about searching for her in a thorough manner. It is only men with firmness who will be able to achieve their desires. They will not give in to frustration even if their attempts are not fruitful in the beginning."

His words fell on deaf ears. Rama sat as one bemused and there was no way of comforting him. He sent Lakshmana to the banks of the Godavari to look for Sita and, to please him, Lakshmana went there and came back to say that she was not there. Lakshmana's grief was intensified since he felt that because of him and his anger, Sita had been abducted. Rama went himself to Godavari and asked her : "Tell me, where is my Sita? You must be knowing where she is."

Afraid of Ravana, the river would not tell him though Sita had asked her to! All the animals and trees stood silent though they knew and had been asked by Sita to tell Rama that she was being carried away by Ravana. Rama said :

"Who will comfort me now and make me forget my misfortunes? I lost my kingdom, my father, and I was forced to live the life of a Sanyasi. Sita was here and I did not mind any of these happenings, but now Sita is gone and I am the most wretched of human beings. Lakshmana, how can I live without her? Come, let us search this Janasthana once again and this hill. She may still be found. Lakshmana, look at the deer. They seem to be trying to tell me something. Their eyes are eloquent. They look at me and then somewhere else. I am sure they know." And turning to the deer Rama asked them : "Where is Sita?" They all turned their eyes towards the south and with their heads they indicated the sky and ran in the direction they had shown, as if to say : "She was carried away fast in the air and towards the south." Again and again they showed as though in pantomime, the manner in which she had been taken away. Lakshmana was extremely astute and he said : "These deer are telling us something. They are indicating the south and the sky. It means that she must have gone that way. Let us go south, Rama, and perhaps, we may get a clue as to where she has been kept captive."

22. THE FRUITLESS SEARCH

The brothers walked southwards with slow steps and they looked all around hoping to see Sita somewhere. As they were on their way they saw, on the ground, petals of flowers. Rama looked at them and said :

"Lakshmana, I know these flowers. I gathered them and gave them to Sita and she was wearing them in her hair. I think the god of wind is kind and has left this undisturbed so that I will know where she is gone."

Rama's sorrow was turning into anger. He looked at the mountain and said : "I will crush you with a single arrow from my quiver. Tell me where Sita is concealed, or else be prepared for my anger." Rama was almost losing his reason. He said : "Lakshmana, I will burn up the waters of this river and I will crush this mountain to dust. I will destroy the entire world. I am like the god of death at the end of the Yuga."

Silently Lakshmana showed something to Rama and the unfortunate prince brought his eyes to the ground. They saw large and deep dents made in the earth by the feet of Ravana, and also the footprints of Sita who ran hither and thither to escape from his grasp. Rama saw too the broken bow, the two quivers full of arrows and the chariot which had been broken up. He could not make out the message of the mute earth. He said : "Look Lakshmana, these are Sita's jewels and they are scattered about. Her flowers have been stamped down into the earth. There are signs of blood having been spilt here. Look at the stains in the mud. The rakshasas have been more than one in number and they have killed her and they have eaten her here." They walked around trying to guess what had happened. Rama said : "I wonder who held this bow with the gold inlay work beautifying it! It is a very good bow and only a great warrior can handle such a bow. There is a jewelled armour also which has been split and it has fallen down. How richly decorated it is, with all the gems on the earth! There is also a white umbrella. This is the insignia of a king. Which king could have come here and committed this atrocity? There are two donkeys which are lying dead. I am intrigued and I cannot, for the life of me, guess what took place here. The charioteer is dead too and obviously he is a rakshasa. So our conjectures are true. Sita has been carried away by a rakshasa.

"If their intention had been to avenge the death of Khara and his army, they have succeeded only too well. They have planned the end of my life also. How can I live without her? They will be happy now to see me dead."

Rama stood silent for a moment and then said : "Lakshmana, it seems to me, what you once said is true. When we were in the apartments of my mother immediately after I had been asked by Kaikeyi to go to the forest." He paused and asked : "Do you remember?" Lakshmana said : "Remember? Of course, I remember. I have not forgotten it and, in fact, I have forgotten everything else. Only that one day stands out in my mind like a dark tree etched against a bright sky."

Rama said : "Lakshmana, you said that I was too soft : that gentle-minded people are always overlooked. You are right, child. My devotion to Dharma and my kindliness towards all living beings has been misunderstood to be a lack of courage, of bravery, of this fighting spirit. Because of their ignorance they are indifferent to me and my power to rule the world. I have kept my senses under control and I have accepted this role of a Sanyasi willingly for the good of mankind and the gods do not seem to understand me! I am a changed man today, my dear Lakshmana. I will be the death of all the rakshasas. Even as the moonlight vanishes to give its place to the scorching rays of the sun, my kindliness, compassion, will all be cast aside and my unforgiving nature will become uppermost from now. Yakshas, gandharvas, rakshasas, and even human beings will all be destroyed. You just stand and watch and I will make the three worlds empty of all beings. My arrows will burn up the entire universe. I will dislodge the planets, the moon. Fire and air will be burnt by a bigger fire which is my anger and the devas who are silently watching my suffering will regret it. I will drain the sea of all water and my bow will be bent into a circle till everything is destroyed in the entire universe."

Rama was looking like Mahadeva when he went to fight with the Tripuras. He took the bow in his hand and pulled out an arrow from his quiver.

Lakshmana had never seen Rama like this and he was frightened. He prostrated before Rama and with his palms folded and with tears in his eyes, he said : "Rama, my beloved brother, it is not befitting your nature to be angry like this. You have ever been gentle and kind even towards animals and it is unbelievable that you should give way to anger like this. You have always held your senses under control and you have had but one thought in your mind : the good of the world. Such a man should not give way to anger, my lord. The charm of the moon, the radiance of the sun, the universality of the god of wind, the patience of mother earth, have all been found in you and it is not meet that you should allow anger to gain the upper hand in your mind. You should not destroy the entire universe. Adharma will never win in the long run. Sita and you have been images of Dharma and no evil can befall either of you. Let us be calm and try to guess what might have happened. It is evident that there has been a fight here. Some warrior has taken part in it and has not fared well since his chariot, his bow and quivers and his armour too, are all scattered on the ground. These footprints are all fresh, evidently. They have not lost their shape yet.

"Kings, my brother, should convoke their anger, and should try and find out who the culprit is, and punish him for his misdemeanour. Because of the crime of one man, a single individual, the world should not be punished. Rama, consider your ancestors and think of our father. You should remember who you are and forget this desire to vent your fury on the innocent world. Let us devote all our time to discovering the whereabouts of Sita. We will not rest until we find out about her fate. We will search in the three worlds and if, in spite of all that, we do not find her, then you can destroy the world of gods but not till then. Your arrows like thunderbolts are always there to do your bidding. Please wait and let us contain ourselves."

Again Lakshmana fell at the feet of Rama and said : "Our father once showered love on you and he was lavish in his favours. And, by a freak of Fate, the same father condemned you to a life in the forest. When you could bear these reverses in your fortune with serene fortitude, how is it you are losing faith in yourself now? This misfortune has been added to your burden of pain. If you are unable to show courage in this situation, how then will an ordinary man react? If you should allow yourself to be swayed by emotions so easily, how will your subjects find comfort in you? How will they trust you and consider you to be a father to them and help them out of their troubles?

"As for troubles visiting men, Nahusha had been raised to the status of Indra and was hurled to the earth and had to be a python for thousands of years. Yayati was thrown out of heaven since he was proud. Our guru Vasishtha lost his hundred sons in a single day. He has not lost his equanimity. Even mother earth is not immune to suffering. There are earthquakes which torment her often. The two eyes of the universe, the sun and the moon which are established in Dharma, even they are eclipsed by Rahu. When such is the fate of the devas, what of mere human beings? No one can escape Fate. You should not allow sorrow to gain ascendancy ever in your mind. Even if Sita is abducted, we should not lose our powers of reasoning. People like you never lose their moral and mental strength even when confronted with the most terrible of misfortunes. Forget your emotions and give place to your intellect in your mind. It is then and only then that men will know what should be done and what should not be. Lesser men can give way to their feelings but not you, Rama. All this I learnt from you. You have often taught me these lessons. And, even Brihaspati is not wise enough to teach you the definition of Dharma. As for me, how can I delve deep into the secret recesses of your heart and know your thoughts when the gods themselves are not able to do so? The god in you is sleeping because of this sorrow. Wake up, my lord. Display your valour which is unearthly and destroy the one who has wronged you. How does it profit you if you destroy the world because of the misdeed of one? You must search him out wherever he is and punish him and only him."

Rama listened to the sweetly spoken words of Lakshmana and after stroking his beloved brother with his right hand, he unstrung the great bow which he held in his hand and said : "Child, you have shown me the way to bear sorrow. I will follow your advice. You must tell me what we should do now. What shall we do? Where do we go from here? How will I be able to find Sita? Think it over and tell me. I am oppressed by this sorrow and my mind refuses to function properly. You are the one who should think for both of us."

Lakshmana said : "Let us, once again, search this Janasthana thoroughly and if we do not find her here we will proceed southwards. Only, remember, Rama, wise men like you should stand firm like the mountain stands undaunted in the face of storms."

23. MEETING WITH JATAYU

Rama was still labouring under the anger which threatened the world. Together they looked for Sita in the Janasthana and it was a vain search. And while they were looking about, suddenly, they came upon Jatayu. He was on the ground, like a small hillock and his body was soaked in blood. Rama said : "Lakshmana, it must be a rakshasa who has assumed the guise of an eagle. He has eaten Sita. His body is covered with blood which is hers. I am going to kill him now." With his bow clasped in his hand Rama approached the fallen eagle. Jatayu was dying and he was spitting blood. With great difficulty he spoke:

"Rama, do not waste your time wandering around here. I know you are searching for Sita. My life as well as Sita have both been taken by Ravana. When she was alone in the ashrama Sita was abducted by Ravana. I saw him carrying her away. I tried my best to rescue her from him. I fought with him. I broke his bow and his chariot and killed his charioteer. He fell to the ground. But I could not fight for long. I had caused as much havoc as I could with my beak and my claws, and my wings. Ravana took up his sword and cut off my wings. When he knew that I was helpless he lifted her again and flew up into the skies and speeded away from here. I am not a rakshasa, my son."

Rama's woe was great. This eagle, this friend of his father and their guardian, had been true to his word and had tried to save Sita from the clutches of Ravana and he could not do so. Rama fell on the ground and embracing the dying eagle he cried like a child. "Lakshmana," he said. "We were banished from our country. We were made to live in the forest Dandaka. We have lost our Sita and now Jatayu, who was like a father to us, has been killed. Misfortune like this is more virulent than poison. It is so intense it will burn up even the god of fire. If I should now touch the waters of the sea, my misfortune will dry it up. In this entire world there is no one more unfortunate than me. I have been pushed into this deep pit of pain by Fate and because of my ill-luck this great soul is dying."

Rama sat there, shedding tears and stroking the dying eagle with loving hands. And so they sat for a while. Rama said : "Lakshmana, life is fast ebbing from the body of noble Jatayu. His movements are stilled and only his breath remains and that will leave him very soon. He has turned his sad eyes on us." Rama turned to the dying bird and asked : "Tell me, if you can, more about what happened and how it happened. What prompted Ravana to take away my beloved Sita from me? How have I offended him that he should do this to me?

"I have done him no wrong. What does he look like? How strong is he? How does he act? Where does he live? If you can talk please tell me about him."

Jatayu was sorry to see Rama unhappy. He was finding it hard even to breathe. And yet, with great effort, he spoke : "She was carried away by him. He was like a whirlwind and she was dazed. He travelled southwards. Child, my life is fast slipping by. I am not able to see. Hold me in your arms. Let me find release from the bondage called life when I am held by you. But one thing I can tell you. The time when Ravana carried her away is named 'Vinda' or 'Vijaya'. It is a certainty that a lost thing will be found if it is lost or stolen during that time. Ravana did not know it or was careless about it. He is sure to die at your hands and you will get Sita back. I am sure of it. Be without sorrow, Rama, and get Sita back after killing Ravana." Jatayu was gasping and blood was spurting from his mouth and he said : "The son of Vishravas, the brother of Kubera............" He could speak no more and Jatayu was dead.

Rama was heart-broken. He said : "Lakshmana, remember when we came back from Agastya's ashrama we met Jatayu? He said he would guard Sita when we should both be absent from the ashrama and he did what he promised to do. But Fate is so powerful and it wins every time. For many years Jatayu had been living in this Dandaka and he is gone. Nothing can equal the sorrow I am suffering because of the death of Jatayu. He died for me. He was so much like our father in his love for us. Lakshmana, collect wood. I will rub the *Arani* and out of the twigs cause a fire. Jatayu died for my sake and I will cremate him myself."

Rama carried the dead Jatayu in his arms and walked towards the banks of the Godavari. Darbha was placed on the ground and he placed Jatayu on it. Lakshmana brought dry wood and made a pyre. Rama placed his foster father on the pyre and said : "King of birds, may you reach the heavens meant for those who have performed tapas, yagnas, who have accumulated punya by performing good deeds. I grant you permission to dwell in these worlds." Rama touched the pyre with the fire he had himself kindled with the *Arani* twigs. He offered *Anjali* to the dead bird and made offerings of *Pinda* to pacify the Pitris. Rama recited the verses meant for performing *Shradha* for the dead. The princes came to the river Godavari and bathed there. They then performed the *Tarpana* for Jatayu according to the rules prescribed in the shastras. Jatayu reached the heavens meant for the rishis.

24. AYOMUKHI AND KABANDHA

The cremation of Jatayu was, in a way, a happening which blunted the edge of the sorrow caused by the disappearance of Sita. They were unhappy but there was a semblance of determination in the manner in which Rama accepted the inevitable and thought seriously of the task ahead of him. The first flush of grief had passed and Lakshmana breathed a sigh of relief. He had never seen Rama angry and it had frightened him lest the world should be destroyed by Rama. He had looked like the fire at the end of the Yuga when the entire universe is burnt up in a single conflagration.

The brothers now walked towards the south since Jatayu was definite about the direction which Ravana had taken. It was a sad journey. Sita was not there to ask a hundred questions about the trees and the birds and the flowers which were never to be seen in cities. Rama spoke not a word and Lakshmana walked silently by his side. Both were busy with thoughts of Sita and they did not want to talk about it : and again, the tragic death of Jatayu had driven even the sorrow of Sita's separation out of their minds for a while. They had loved him so much.

They were wandering in the denseness of the Dandaka forest. They had walked a distance of about three krosas from the Janasthana. They were now in a forest by name Krauncharanya. It was frightening, inhabited as it was, by wild animals. The darkness was palpable and resting often on the fallen branches, or on slabs of stones, they pursued their journey. They covered another three krosas and passed the forest Krauncha. They came upon a cave which was dark and seemed to be very deep since it appeared black to the eye. Near the mouth of the cave they saw a rakshasi.

She was immense in size and fearful to look at. Even as Shurpanakha approached Rama, this rakshasi approached Lakshmana and said : "Come, let us be together. My name is Ayomukhi and I have fallen in love with you. You must be fortunate indeed since I have chosen you as my lord. Come with me and we will haunt the slopes of the mountains and this dark and fearful forest together."

Lakshmana's patience was sorely tried. Racked as he was by the feeling that he had been careless about the safety of Sita, overcome with fear when he saw the anger of Rama, and distressed beyond measure by the death of Jatayu, the prince Lakshmana did not even stop to talk to her.

He took his sword and severed her nose, her ears and also her breasts. The dreadful rakshasi, making the forest resound with her cries, ran away from there and they walked on.

Another forest was ahead of them. Lakshmana turned towards Rama and spoke in a respectful manner: "Rama, my left arm is throbbing and my mind seems to be full of evil forebodings. I feel that some danger is awaiting us. The omens are not good either. Please pay heed to my words and be alert. Be prepared for any danger. But then, even though danger is indicated, the cry of this bird Vanjulaka convinces me that we will overcome the danger."

While they were walking ahead, there came to their ears the fierce noise as though the entire forest was being felled to the ground. The noise filled the surroundings and reached the skies. Rama and Lakshmana looked about to see where the noise came from and, in the middle of the forest, they saw a rakshasa whose chest was exceedingly wide and whose form was immense. They saw something wrong with him and when they looked again, they found that he had no head. His mouth was in his stomach. There was one eye which was looking at them who were approaching him and that eye was situated in his chest! His tongue was coming in and out of his cavernous mouth which had huge teeth as ridges along the edge. What was most frightening about him was the pair of arms he had. Each arm was a yojana in length. They could not pass him since he was standing or, rather, placed in their way and his arms prevented them from going away from him or around him.

The name of the rakshasa was Kabandha. He caught them both in his two arms and steadily he pulled them towards his mouth. Lakshmana was helpless in the terrible grip of Kabandha. Rama was unaffected by the danger which was now threatening both of them. Lakshmana said: "Rama I am prepared to die at the hands of this rakshasa. Save yourself and pursue the search for Sita. Go back to the kingdom and live happily there with Sita. Think of me sometimes. I do not think I will escape this iron grip."

Rama replied: "Do not despair, Lakshmana. There is always a way out of any kind of trouble. You should not give up so easily." Pulling them steadily towards himself Kabandha asked them who they were and why they came to the fearful forest. "I seem to be lucky today," said Kabandha. "I have got two human beings as my food. It is a long time since I ate human flesh. I have caught hold of you and it will not be possible for you to escape from me."

Rama turned to Lakshmana and said : "Sorrow has been heaped upon sorrow for us and now, finally, we are at a stage when we may be eaten up by a rakshasa. Fate is the one enemy whom no one can conquer."

Even as he was saying this Rama thought of making some attempt to save himself and his brother. Lakshmana had also been thinking of some way to circumvent the danger. He said : "Rama, let us sever the hands of this rakshasa which are pulling us towards his dreadful mouth." Kabandha heard their words and tried to open his mouth and swallow them at once. Rama and Lakshmana cut off his arms. Rama's share was the right arm while Lakshmana cut the left. Kabandha fell on the ground and the noise was terrible. He asked them again : "Who are you?" Lakshmana told him about themselves and asked him who he was.

Kabandha said : "It is my good fortune that you came to the forest. I am a rakshasa as a result of a curse. Once I was as handsome as the moon. I was fond of poking fun at the rishis and I would assume dreadful forms and scare the rishis in the forest. One of the rishis was very angry with my pranks and he cursed me : 'You will be permanently ugly. The form you have assumed will be yours for ever.' I begged him to recall the curse and he said : 'Rama, the son of Dasaratha, will come to the forest with his brother and they will cut off your hands. If you are cremated by them you will regain your old handsomeness.'

"My name is Dhanu, and I had also offended Indra and his curse was added to that of the rishi. Indra has maimed me with his Vajra and my legs are broken. Brahma said that these long arms of mine would help me to live as long as I had to. I was told by Indra that you would release me from this condition. Rama, please cremate me and release me from this dreadful existence."

Rama said : "My wife has been captured by a rakshasa named Ravana. We know nothing else about him. We do not know where he lives nor what his nature is. You have been here since a very long time. Surely, you know about him. Tell us all about this Ravana and about some method by which we can rescue Sita from him. We will certainly cremate you as you wish. Only tell us all you know about Ravana." Kabandha said : " I have lost the power to know everything, the power I had before the curse. However, once I am cremated, I will get my old form back and also my old powers and I am sure I can help you in your quest for Sita. I can tell you if there is anyone to help you find your wife. Please dig a pit and, after placing me in it, cover it with wood and set fire to the pyre. I will tell you later how you can find your wife. I will be able, I am sure, to tell you the name of the person who will help you. Vague things are coming back to my mind already. The person I am telling you about has travelled all over the world and there is no place which he does not know about. I want to remember it all perfectly."

25. A RAY OF HOPE

Rama and Lakshmana prepared a very large pit, and a deep one as indicated by Kabandha and filled it half with wood and, after placing Kadandha in it, they covered it with more wood along with his severed hands. They set fire to it and it took a long time to burn fully. Lakshmana said : " Rama, after Sita was carried away we prepared a pyre for Jatayu and burnt him. Now we are doing it again for Kabandha. I wonder if there will be a third cremation to be undertaken !"

When the body had been consumed fully there arose out of the fire Dhanu, the divine being. He was as handsome as he said he was and dressed in divine ornaments and silks he was a rare sight. A chariot had arrived to take him.

Dhanu told Rama: "I will tell you how to set about your quest for Sita. There are six different factors which are needed to know the truth about anything. These six lead you to the truth. They are *Pratyaksha,* that is, what has been seen actually. The next is *Anumana,* conjecture : meaning, arriving at some conclusions on the basis of what one has seen. The third is *Upamana :* comparison to something which is similar and so, guessing by comparison. The fourth is *Shabda* which evidently means trying to get at the truth by means of noises made and such like. The fifth is *Anuphalaprati* which means : making certain that it is not there because it is not found. And the sixth is *Arthaprapti* : guessing and arriving at the truth with the help of the other five and the knowledge obtained by the other five.

"A man who is in some kind of trouble will find a sympathetic friend in another who has had similar sufferings. Lakshmana and you are going through a difficult time. Rama, you have lost your wife. I know of one whose friendship should be sought by you. I have thought about it and this is the best way. You will achieve your end if you follow my advice and meet this person. I will tell you all about him.

"There is a monkey chieftain and his name is Sugriva. He is the brother of Vali, the son of Indra. Vali has been harassing Sugriva and has driven him out of his kingdom. Sugriva is a good soul and he has a fear of Adharma. With four monkeys as companions he is living now in the mountain by name Rishyamooka. The mountain is on the banks of the lake Pampa which is very picturesque. Sugriva is quite a good-looking monkey, brave, powerful and he is true to his word. He is highly intelligent and skilful in many fields. His strength is proverbial and he is the person who must be sought out by you to help you in your hour of need. He will be a good friend and he will help you. Rama, do not indulge in grief but proceed towards Pampa and Rishyamooka. You know only too well that on one can alter the course of Fate. No one has been able to conquer Fate and what Fate wills will have to be suffered by everyone. Rama, go at once and meet Sugriva. Make friends with him. Let the fire be witness to your oath of friendship. Do not ignore him, but, on the other hand, he has to be cherished by you. He has a desire which can be achieved only by you and for the sake of returning the favour done by you, he will help you. His father was a hero by name Riksharajas. He is actually the son of Surya, the sun. He is conversant with all the haunts of the rakshasas who eat human flesh. Like the sun, there is nothing on the earth which he does not know. He will seek Sita everywhere to please you." Dhanu paused and continued: 'This path leading towards the west is the path you should follow. It leads to Rishyamooka. The path is lined with beautiful trees which bear fruits and flowers like those in the heavens. The path ends in a garden which is like Nandana or Chaitra. Very soon you will reach the lake by name Pampa. It is the most beautiful lake that has ever been seen by human eyes. There are lotuses blowing on its surface and the bottom of the lake is sandy. The water is so clear you can see the sandy bed. Swans and cranes and other water-birds will make music. They have never seen human beings and they will not fly away when they see you. Fish leap about in the water. The water from the lake is sweeter than the Amrita they talk about. Go to Pampasaras. Your sorrow will be assuaged by the beautiful sorroundings in Pampa. The flowers there never dry up and the fruits do not get spoilt. The disciples of the rishi Matanga were dwelling there once and their presence has made the spot unique in this respect.

"Rama, even now, there dwells an old ascetic by name Shabari who was serving the rishis. She is very old. Several times has she been asked to go to heaven. But she heard that the Lord in the form of Rama has come to the Dandaka and she is waiting to serve you before leaving for the heavens which have been granted her. So Rama, when you arrive at the western bank of the lake Pampa you will see an ashrama which is situated in a lonely place. The forest surrounding it is named Matangavana. This is because the rishi created it. You can spend some time there and rest your bruised heart. The Pampasaras is at the foot of the Rishyamooka. There is a story attached to the mountain that no sinner is allowed to ascend the mountain. On the mountain are many large and deep caves and Sugriva lives in some of them, at times, and on top of the hill at other times. Go to him Rama, and you will succeed in your search. Now it is time for me to go. Please grant me leave. " Rama and Lakshmana looked kindly at him who was seated in the celestial chariot and said : "Farewell, go back to where you came from. " He in turn said : " May your search be fruitful," and the chariot vanished.

26. SHABARI'S ASHRAMA

The two princes were in a happy frame of mind since Kabandha had given them some kind of assistance by asking them to meet the chief of the monkeys. They talked about it as they travelled towards the west along the path indicated by Kabandha. They looked around and saw the trees and flowers which were to be found everywhere. But they paid no heed to them. Their only thought was to reach Rishyamooka as early as possible and to meet Sugriva. At the foot of the hill they saw a place which seemed to them safe enough from the wild animals and, since the sun had set, they deemed it wise not to go any further in the dark.

They spent the night there and early in the morning they made preparations to continue their journey. They saw that they had covered quite some distance now. They had reached the western banks of the lake Pampa which had been mentioned by Kabandha. From there they could see a small ashrama. Rama had been looking for this ashrama since he had been told that Shabari, an old woman, was waiting for his coming. This was, to him, more important than even meeting Sugriva. They walked towards the ashrama. It was surrounded on all sides by trees and shrubs and they entered the ashrama of Shabari.

Shabari stood up with great excitement and she prostrated before Rama and then before Lakshmana. Rama spoke to her in his sweet and pleasant voice : "You are rich in tapas. Have you shed all the desires of the world? Is your tapas increasing day by day? Have you conquered anger? Have you learnt to live on meagre fare? How are your Vratas helping you in finding peace? Has your service to the great been fruitful? Have you realised that you are ready to leave?"

The old woman Shabari stood humbly before Rama and said : "My tapas has been fruitful now, at this moment, since my eyes have lighted on you. The rishis have been served by me faithfully and it has granted me the reward : I have seen you. My life has not been lived in vain since you have graced me with your presence and I have earned a place in heaven. I have been purified since your eyes have rested on this body of mine and I will certainly attain salvation.

"The rishis whom I served went to the heavens in the many chariots sent for them by the celestials. I was asked by them to stay on here. They told me : 'Rama will visit this sacred ashrama of yours and with him will come Lakshmana, his brother. Honour these guests and then you can enter the heavenly abode meant for you.' Rama, my lord, for entertaining you, I have been collecting fruits from the trees on the banks of the Pampa this many a day. I have kept them carefully." Rama looked at Shabari whose birth was that of a huntress and he said : "You have, by your tapas, won a place for yourself in the heavens : what is more, you have been able to reach the Brahmi state. From Dhanu, who was cursed to be a Kabandha, I heard about the greatness of your tapas. I would like to spend some time here and look at the surroundings of your ashrama."

Shabari said: "This place is famed by the name Matangavana. Rishis have made it a sanctified spot because of the tapas and the yagas they have performed here. They were so old that their hands would tremble while offering the flowers on the Vedi. Because of the tapas of these rishis this Vedi which is called *Pratyaksthali* glows like sunlight and illumines all the quarters. They were thin and weak and old and they could not go out and gather the waters for the yaga and so the waters from the ocean reached them on their own accord. They bathed here and the tree-bark which they were wearing is still on the trees and they are not dry. The blue lotuses and other flowers are as fresh as they were on the day they were used for worship. The place has this special quality."

They went round the ashrama and Rama partook of the fruits which Shabari had saved up for him. She asked him: "My desire has been fulfilled. I have entertained you and I am now ready to depart for the other world. Please grant me leave to do so."

Rama said: "You are holy and with a pure heart you have worshipped the rishis. I have been worshipped by you. May your desires be granted and may you reach the heavens where the rishis are, the rishis whom you served faithfully when they were here."

Shabari, who was a Brahma Gnani who had shed all attachments and desires, meditated on the God of fire, after touching water with her hand. She was consumed by fire created by herself and became a mass of flames. Out of it she rose up and she looked like a celestial damsel. She prostrated before Rama and she ascended to the heavens while the brothers stood watching.

27. THE LAKE BY NAME PAMPA

They resumed their journey and they talked of the huntress Shabari and her devotion to Rama. Rama was amazed at the glory of the rishis who could summon the waters of the ocean at will to serve them and he said: "Lakshmana, I am chastened by this experience. Look how the tigers and the deer are playing together! What a hallowed spot this is! The seven seas have flowed here and it is a very pure ashrama. I have found peace here. My mind is now rid of the agitation which had been troubling me till now. I have found strength which will help me bear the separation from Sita. Something tells me that we are on the brink of discovering something which will be of great benefit to us. Come, let us hurry towards Rishyamooka hill and let us locate the lake Pampa which is said to cling to the foot of the mountain. Kabandha told us that Sugriva is there and that he is in constant fear of his brother Vali. Our destination is Rishyamooka and we should meet Sugriva as early as possible and forge a friendship with him as we have been advised to. Sugriva will organise a search for Sita and I am sure she will be found."

Lakshmana was equally impatient and together they hurried onwards. They passed many trees and small forests and soon they were near the lake which was named Matangasaras.

They bathed in its cool waters and went further. After they had gone some distance they were greeted by the fragrance which was part of the famed lake Pampa. There seemed to be an exhilaration in the air and they forgot their fatigue and walked on. They reached the banks of the beautiful lake Pampa.

It was a magnificent sight. On the banks were flowering trees of all types : Ashoka, Tilaka, Punnaga, Bakula and the perfume was overpowering. There were lotuses everywhere and the water in the lake was clear as crystal. The lake seemed to have been the haunt of even the celestials. The grassy banks were strewn with flowers of all hues and it seemed as though a rich carpet had been laid there. The mango trees were many and the birds were making music. Peacocks were dancing and the lake Pampa was exceedingly beautiful.

Rama looked at the lavishness with which nature had adorned the lake and he was overcome with sorrow. He said : "Lakshmana, child, as Kabandha said, there, at some distance, is the mountain Rishyamoooka where Sugriva dwells. You go and meet him."

28. RAMA'S GRIEF

Lakshmana heard Rama and stopped in his tracks and looked at Rama with wonder in his eyes. Rama said : "Lakshmana, I cannot live without

Sita. I have given my very life to her and I am finding it hard to be without her. This Pampa and its exquisite beauty would have made her happy. This place makes me think of her and only her. Lakshmana, I cannot find peace anywhere at any time unless I see Sita. I will not be able to meet Sugriva. You must take it upon yourself to go to Rishyamooka. I will remain here and I will not be able to forget my Sita. I cannot help these tears which are drenching me." Rama sat and wept there and Lakshmana tried to comfort him.

Rama had found some comfort in the ashrama of Matanga and Lakshmana had heard him say that he was able to bear the grief which was burning him up. But the sight of Pampa was painful. It was painful for Rama to be in the midst of so much beauty and to be parted from Sita. He gave way to his grief and his love for Sita had grown tenfold. He was sorely tried by the pangs of separation. He said : "Look at the beauty of this lake, Lakshmana. It has beautiful trees growing on its banks and on its face are blooming lotuses, red and blue. The trees are so dark and dense, they seem to be hillocks. This beauty is overpowering. And it makes me sad. It makes me think of Bharata and his devotion to me.

"I am unhappy at the thought that we are parted. It makes me think of Sita and this season Vasanta makes me long for her.

"This Pampa with clear pellucid water makes me sad. Sita would have been happy to see this grassy bank strewn with flowers of all hues. The entire earth seems to be made of flowers. The creepers have twined themselves about the branches of the trees and they are laden with clusters of flowers.

"Lakshmana, this month Madhu is the first month of Vasanta and it increases love in the mind of man. I have been told that Manmata is always accompanied by Vasanta and my mind is distraught with pain, by the arrows of Manmata. The wind is scattering flowers all over the place and the air is laden with the perfume of flowers. He seems to be playing with the flowers, this god of wind. The bees are making sweet music to accompany his sport. The koils from the trees around sing and the wind is dancing to the music. The branches of the trees seem to be embracing each other, so deeply entwined are they. The breeze is so pleasing : it is neither too strong nor is it stagnant. The scent of sandalwood is borne by the wind and it is refreshing to my tired body. Look at the Karnikara tree in full bloom! How can I look at it and not think of Sita who loved it?

"I am drowned in sorrow and no one can comfort me except Sita and she is far away, I know not where. This water-fowl is making a noise which amused Sita. I remember once she heard it and, excited by the strange noise it made, took me by the hand and led me to where it was. She was so happy that day. I cannot forget her happy laughter.

"There are so many types of birds here. I have never seen so many birds all together like I am doing now. Even the birds fly only in pairs. The music of the koils intensify my love for Sita and I am longing for her presence. This Vasanta is like fire to my body. I feel a burning all over me since I am aching for Sita. I miss her large black eyes, her sweet voice and her gentle touch. I cannot live without her. Vasanta was her favourite season. I do not know how I am going to live, separated as I am from my beloved. The peacocks are strutting around with their tails spread out and the hens are watching them. If only she had not been carried away, Sita would have been thrilled by the coming of Vasanta and the touch of the breeze which is soft, gentle and laden with perfume. This same Vasanta will be where she is and she will be pining for me even as I am, for her. How can she live without me? My mind is racked with worry about her and about her safety. Lakshmana, she will most probably kill herself unable to live without me. She will not be able to bear the torture she may be made to undergo. My life is in her keeping and hers, in mine. We cannot live without each other. Everything about this Pampa, from the flowers to the birds, the trees, the breeze and the murmuring bees make me long for Sita and I am not able to bear this pain. Lakshmana, I cannot live without her."

Lakshmana was looking at Rama and was listening to his words. He said : "Rama, I can see how unhappy you are. I know what a jewel Sita is, and it is not possible to find another woman like her. Her qualities are incomparable. But you should not give way to sorrow like this. Remember, we have a duty to perform. Rama, there is nothing which is greater than Dharma. If a man is devoted to the observance of Dharma nothing is impossible for him. Steadfastness and firmness are needed for it. A man of intelligence will know how to overcome sorrow with the help of his Dharma. A man, an ordinary man, who does not know the secret of living will be unable to bear the reverses of fortune. But a man like you will know that it is the result of Fate : this misfortune, and he will bear his unhappiness bravely.

"Without a second thought, you have given up the kingdom and the many comforts to which you were accustomed. Like a mountain which stands firm and unmoved by the lashings of storm after storm, you have stood, serene and unmoved, unaffected by them all. Remember who you are, my dear brother. Even you are becoming blinded by this ignorance of your Atman, and you are allowing yourself to be deluded by it. Even as a charioteer knows how to pull the reins skilfully so that the horses go in the right direction, the path which he has chosen, you should control happiness and sorrow with the help of your intellect. You should not succumb to sorrow like this. Your courage is as great as that of the turbulent ocean. You will fulfil the promise you made to our father and go back to Ayodhya. You will rule the kingdom and you will earn the praise of the gods and the world of men. You will find peace and happiness. You are certain to be happy soon.

"Let us not sit helplessly like weaklings. We must try and find the miscreant who stole Sita. He has not realised that he has chosen death when he chose to steal Sita. You will kill him and be with Sita very soon. I am sure of it.

"Please resume your old self. Be firm and strong. Let there not be any more sorrow in your mind. The pain of separation from Sita has been renewed by your dwelling on it again and again. Abandon this grief. The wick of a lamp, even if it is wet, will burn when soaked in oil.

"Let us set about the search for Sita. Ravana may have imprisoned her in the nether world, or in the next world, it is no matter. We will not let him escape alive. He will have to encounter us. He will either release Sita and run away or meet his death at your hands. He must return Sita and fall at your feet and ask you to pardon him or else, even if he hides in the womb of Aditi, I will kill him. Do not let me see you grieving. It is unbecoming. You look like a man who does not know what his duty is. Come, shed this pain and be your real self. Undaunted, firm and serene under any circumstance. Without effort no man can achieve what he desires. Enthusiasm, repeated efforts, will grant you anything you ask for. There is nothing as great as constant striving.

"We will certainly find Sita because of our efforts and we will not let anything deter us and make us hesitant. Realise that you are a great personage and, forgetting this meaningless sorrow, make up your mind to fight the enemy whom we must hunt out as soon as we can."

Rama found great comfort in the words of his brother and with an effort he shed his despondency. He gathered his scattered thoughts once again and, with a firm step, began to proceed towards the mountain called Rishyamooka. They passed the lake Pampa and walked towards their destination. Rama's eyes rested constantly on the beautiful waterfalls which flowed in great tumult all over the slopes of the mountain and, with set lips, he walked with Lakshmana. They walked together, and they looked like two elephants which had come to the Pampa for sport. Very soon they reached Rishyamooka and they walked slowly on the slopes, eager to meet Sugriva.

KISHKINDHA KANDA

1. SUGRIVA SENDS HANUMAN TO RAMA

Sugriva was seated on one of the peaks of the hill and he had four monkeys with him. From this vantage point he could see everything, everywhere, and his roving eyes rested on Rama and Lakshmana who had arrived at the foot of the hill. They were walking slowly, with halting steps. Their eyes were questioning and seemed to be looking for something. They were eager to find out where Sugriva was and, seeing them and their searching looks, Sugriva's mind was alerted and fear crept into his heart. From a distance he discerned the two stangers in the vicinity of his hiding place and Sugriva, though brave by nature, was sorely perplexed by the sight of strangers on the hill. He was afraid of them and he did not know what to do. They were all scared of the coming of the two strangers and quickly they hid themselves in a cave which was nearby.

Sugriva was afraid since these tapasvins were armed. His eyes were wandering all over the place and his fear was excessive. He was only too well aware of the strength of his brother Vali and his own inefficiency as far as Vali was concerned. With his voice trembling with fear he said : "These two are sent by Vali : I am sure of it. Or else how could they have passed the forest which is considered to be impenetrable? They are dressed as Sanyasins but that is only a guise since they carry bows and arrows and I can see the gleam of swords at their waists. No tapasvin will attire himself thus. Let us choose a safe place where we can hide ourselves."

Sugriva's ministers were with him and the chief of them was Hanuman. He knew the dread which was in the heart of Sugriva. Hanuman, who was well-versed in the art of conversing, spoke with humility : "Forget this fear of Vali, my lord. This mountain is safe from the attack of Vali since he is forbidden by the rishi's curse to set foot on it. I do not see Vali anywhere. Be firm in your faith as far as the safety of this Rishyamooka is concerned."

Sugriva said : "Look at these two persons coming this way, Hanuman. They look like divine beings. They are handsome and they seem to be extremely strong. They are armed and I am frightened : and so will you be, if you had been oppressed as I have been. I suspect them to have been sent by Vali to kill me. I am sure of it.

"Kings have different people to aid them in their rule. It is essential for us to know who they are before we dismiss them as harmless wanderers. Vali is very clever and is capable of using human beings as his aids. Hanuman, I want you to go to them. Talk to them cleverly and get all the information about them. Try and see if you can find out the reason for their coming here. You are wise and you will be able to find out all about them, I know. If they are guileless, win them over with flattering words and make them reveal their real purpose in coming to this mountain. Go to these men who are armed with bows and arrows and find out about them. It will be easy for you to find out if they are good men. If they are, make friends with them."

Hanuman, who was the son of Vayu, agreed to obey the commands of his master and proceeded to where Rama and his dear Lakshmana were wandering. To appear in the guise of a brahmachari seemed to him to be a wise decision since he did not know who the two strangers were. From the top of the mountain he reached the neighbourhood of the princes very soon since he leaped from tree to tree and from rock to rock. He went to the presence of Rama and Lakshmana and welcomed them to the mountain with very sweet words and in a charming manner.

Hanuman said : "You seem to be Rajarshis and you appear to be divine beings. I have been watching you and you are looking for something on the slopes of this mountain. You are watching the trees and the herds of deer which pass you by and you are, to my mind, observing strict penance. I am intrigued as to who you may be. You appear to be Sanyasins but your weapons and the fact that you are both armed seem to belie it.

"I can see eagerness in your steps and a semblance of impatience as though you are seeking something. Bravery seems to have taken a form in the two of you. Serene as the surface of a lake, your faces express courage in the face of misfortunes. Your radiance is like that of molten gold and your sighs express some sorrow which is lodged in your minds. Your gaits like that of lions, your wide chests and your powerful arms, your bows which are as glorious as the bow of Indra, make me eager to know who you may be.

"Your handsomeness is captivating. I am convinced that you are royal personages though your garbs are those of mendicants. This mountain, the river which flows here, the waters of Pampa, have gained an added glow because of your presence. You resemble each other so much that I can easily guess you are brothers. With your eyes like the petals of the lotus, with your divine looks, you make me wonder. It seems to me as though the sun and moon have abandoned the heavens and have come down to the earth for some heavenly purpose. What is the reason behind your wandering in this place which is devoid of human beings? Your arms are bare but it is apparent that they should be wearing ornaments made of gold. Perhaps you have come here to guard this beautiful mountain which is even more lovely than the Vindhya or the Meru. Your bows which are looking so powerful and these arrows like flames are never at rest, I am sure, once your anger is roused. These swords look like serpents which are asleep. They gleam like serpents which have just shed their skins.

"I will tell you who I am. There is a good and powerful monkey chief by name Sugriva. He has been driven out of his kingdom by his brother and this Sugriva has been wandering about on the slopes of this Rishyamooka. My name is Hanuman and I have been sent by him to find out about you. Sugriva desires friendship with you. I am a monkey and I can assume any form I wish. To find out about you I assumed this guise of a brahmachari. As I told you, I am a monkey and I am the son of Vayu. I am one of the faithful servants of Sugriva and one of his mentors."

Hanuman said nothing more and stood waiting for them to reply. Rama was thrilled by the words of Hanuman. He turned to Lakshmana and said : "Lakshmana, we have been looking for Sugriva and this messenger from him is his mentor. He has approached me with a desire to be friends with me. This Hanuman speaks beautifully. He seems to be a very sincere person and pure in mind. I want you to talk to him. I am sure he is well-versed in the Vedas or else he would not have been able to talk so well. He knows all the three Vedas.

"He is a master of grammar and, while he spoke, I could not find a single mistake in the formation of his sentences. His entire personality is very attractive and his voice is very pleasing and attractive too. Pitched low in the Madhyama, his voice is musical to the ears. He spoke well too. His manner of talking was convincing, short and spontaneous. It was genuine, straight from his heart and I could detect no deception in him. His words were so well formed, scholarly, clearly spoken, that they are to be praised to the utmost. With his words which rose from the heart, neck and head, which are bewitching, how can even an enemy resist him? Fortunate is Sugriva to have such a gem as his minister. All his desires and plans will succeed if Hanuman is the mentor for him. His deeds will all be accomplished by the messenger himself, so capable is he."

Lakshmana turned to Hanuman and said : "We have already been told about your master Sugriva and about the misfortune which has been visited on him. We have been wandering here on the slopes of this mountain in search of this same Sugriva. We were asked to meet him and forge a friendship with him. Please think about our desire and the commands of your master and do what you think is best under the circumstances. We will do anything you deem is wise."

Hanuman was extremely pleased with his words. He was happy about the success of his mission. He decided to take them to the presence of Sugriva and wished that the friendship between the two should be formed at once. He thought to himself :

"They have also come to the forest with some task where they need assistance. It seems as though the troubles of my master will soon be things of the past because of these two men. He may regain his kingdom." Hanuman asked Rama : "Can you tell me why you are wandering in these fearful forests on the banks of Pampa? It is ridden with fierce animals and there is not a single human being here. I am curious to know."

Again Rama looked at Lakshmana as if to say : "Answer him." Lakshmana said : "There was an emperor named Dasaratha who ruled the world. He was a righteous man and never once has he swerved from the path of Dharma. He had no enemies since he did not consider anyone to be such. He had performed many yagnas and he was a devotee of the Lord. This is his eldest son and he is called Rama. The word of his father is sacred to him. Rama is a great soul. He has conquered his senses and he is famed for his prowess. He was asked by his father to spend fourteen years in the Dandaka forest and I accompanied him. I am his younger brother. To me, the only god is my brother and my only religion is to obey him in everything. Lakshmana is my name.

"Even as the glory of the sun cannot exist without the sun, Sita, the wife of Rama, came with him to the forest. When she happened to be alone in the ashrama Sita was captured by a rakshasa and we do not know where he dwells. While we were wandering in search of my brother's wife we came across Dhanu, a celestial being, who had been pushed down to the earth because of a curse. He told us that there is a chieftain of the monkeys by name Sugriva and that we should seek him out. We were told that he would help us in our search. He said : 'Sugriva is a great hero and he will certainly help you to find your wife. He will find out who stole her and find where she is.' Dhanu went back to the heavens after telling us about your king. Here is where he is supposed to live. Rama and I are on this hill Rishyamooka for the sole purpose of meeting Sugriva, your master. We seek his help. My brother wants him to help him in his quest for his wife.

"It is indeed the vagaries of Fate which have made a plaything of this noble Rama, the son of Dasaratha, the refuge of all those who are in trouble, the home of Dharma and truth, the sole hope of the entire populace of Kosala, the honoured prince of the country, the eldest son of an emperor, a hero whose prowess and valour are known to all the world. This Rama is now reduced to a state when he has to seek the help of others to achieve his end. Rama is sunk in sorrow and your master should help him."

Overcome with emotion Lakshmana was talking while tears poured down his face. Hanuman watched him and said : "It is the good fortune of my master Sugriva that such a noble soul who is without anger, who has the senses under control, who is like a god among human beings, should desire friendship with him. His troubles are over and my master will be happy once he makes friendship with you." They stood silent for a moment and Hanuamn continued : "I will take you to Sugriva. He has had his share of misfortunes. He was driven out of his kingdom and his wife was taken from him by his brother Vali. He has been treated ill by his brother and, believe me, my master will do his utmost to find Sita for you." Lakshmana turned to Rama and said : "Rama, I feel that our task will be accomplished with the help of the chief of the monkeys. This son of Vayu seems to be a truthful person : in fact, he seems to me to be incapable of ever uttering a falsehood."

Hanuman took both of them on his broad back and went to the presence of Sugriva.

The peak where Sugriva was dwelling was named Malaya and it was part of Rishyamooka. Hanuman went to the presence of Sugriva with the brothers and told him : "This is Rama. He is very wise man and a great warrior. He has his brother with him and I met them when they were wandering about." Hanuman told Sugriva about the circumstances which had brought them to Dandaka and now to Rishyamooka. "He has been asked to meet you," said Hanuman. "He was told that he should seek your aid in searching for Sita. These two brothers are valiant and powerful and it is but meet that you should honour them accordingly."

2. A FRIENDSHIP IS FORGED

Sugriva was greatly relieved when he heard that they were not emissaries from Vali. His fear vanished and he welcomed Rama with a great show of affection. He said : "Hanuman, the son of Vayu, told me all about you and your greatness. You are a terror to your enemies and you are righteous. The fact that you desire friendship with me is a great honour you are bestowing on me. I consider it my good fortune that you should have come to me seeking my hand in friendship. Here is my hand which I hold out to you with affection. Please accept my gesture of love. Let there form between you and me a kinship which nothing can break." Rama took his outstretched hand in his and embraced Sugriva. Hanuman had shed the guise of a brahmachari which he had put on when he went out to meet Rama. He now kindled a fire with two twigs of *Arani*. He worshipped the fire with offerings of flowers and brought the fire and placed it in front of them. Rama and Sugriva went round the fire and took the oath that they would remain friends for ever. They were very happy at this new friendship which had been formed. They felt that something momentous had been achieved. They were now like long lost friends : so well did each welcome the other's affection.

"You have become my good friend. From now on, everything will be shared by us, whether it is happiness or sorrow" : thus they spoke to each other. Sugriva broke a branch from a Sala tree which was nearby and placed it on the ground. He made Rama sit on it and he sat beside him. Hanuman, the wise, at once broke a branch from a sandalwood tree and offered it to Lakshmana as a seat.

Sugriva spoke with tears in his eyes and told Rama about his misfortunes. He said : "Rama, I am a very unhappy person. I was insulted by my brother and driven away from my land and kingdom. My wife was stolen from me and I have found refuge in this mountain which is the only place where any enemy cannot touch me. I want you to protect me from Vali, my brother. You are my refuge."

Rama was touched by the sufferings of Sugriva. He said : "I know that the meaning of friendship is to help each other. I will, this very moment, kill Vali. My arrows, sharp and keen, radiant as the rays of the sun, with their ends beautified by the feathers of the eagle, which are as fearful as the Vajra of Indra, will hiss like angry snakes and find a home in the chest of Vali. I assure you that Vali will fall on the ground with my arrow lodged in his chest." His words made Sugriva happy. He spoke with a great show of gratitude." "With your grace I will get the kingdom back and my wife too. I will see my enemy destroyed and I will live without the fear which has been haunting me all these years. I will sleep in peace from now onwards." When they were talking thus Sita's left eye which was like a lotus petal throbbed suddenly. And so did the tawny left eye of Vali and Ravana was puzzled since his left eye, crimson like blood, throbbed all on a sudden.

Sugriva continued talking. He said : "This Hanuman who is my minister told me all about you and the many mishaps which have been visited on you. I am sure your sorrow will soon disappear. The Vedas had once been stolen by the rakshasas Madhu and Kaitabha and they were rescued by Narayana. Even so, you will find that I will institute a search for your beloved wife and bring her to you. Whether she is concealed in the nether regions or in the heavenly haunts, I will find her for you. You can depend on my word. I want to tell you about a recent occurrence.

"The five of us were sitting on the top of this peak as is our custom and we suddenly saw something in the sky. We saw a rakshasa dark as a rain cloud, and just as huge. And in his left arm he held a beautiful woman who was glowing golden like a streak of lightning. She was wriggling like a queen serpent and he held her fast. She was crying out : "Rama! Lakshmana!" From what you say, it must have been your wife who was carried away. We saw her. While we were wondering about them there dropped in our midst a small bundle tied up in yellow silk. She had taken off some of her ornaments and had hastily tied them up in a piece of silk torn from her mantle. It was a quick gesture and she hoped, perhaps, that somehow you would get to know of it. We have kept the bundle very carefully and I will bring it to you. See if the jewels belong to Sita."

Rama was greatly excited and exclaimed : "Why do you tarry, my friend? Bring them to me at once and let me see them." Sugriva leaped from his seat and ran to a cave which was nearby. In a moment he was back with a small bundle tied up in yellow silk. He placed it before Rama. Rama knew the silk. It was Sita's favourite mantle. With trembling hands he took up the jewels tied up in the scrap of yellow silk and his face, drenched as it was with tears, seemed like the moon in winter, pale and lifeless. "Sita!" he cried out and fell down in a faint. They revived him and, holding the bundle to his heart, he sighed for a while and looked piteously at Lakshmana.

He said : "Lakshmana, look at this scrap of silk thrown by my beloved while she was being taken away. Look at these jewels. They have not lost their shape and that is because they must have landed on the grassy slopes. My eyes are blurred with tears, my child. Tell me, are they Sita's jewels? I am overcome with grief which has been renewed by the sight of these. Tell me which ornaments she has thrown." Lakshmana cried too and said : "I have never looked at her face nor at her hands. I cannot recognise the bangles nor can I, her earrings. But these anklets I know, since every morning I would fall at her feet and take her blessings."

Rama turned to Sugriva and said : "Tell me more about how you saw my beloved Sita. Where were you when you saw her?" He continued : "That sinner who has stolen my wife will soon realise that the gates of the City of Death are wide open to receive him. I am angry with him and that means that he will not live very long. Tell me where he lives, and I will, this moment go and end his sinful life."

Sugriva was very affectionate by nature and tears sprang to his eyes when he saw the distress of Rama. He said : "I know nothing about him, Rama. I only know that he is a rakshasa. I do not know who he is, what his ancestry is, what his valour is like nor where he lives. I saw them flash past and in that one moment I could gather that he was a rakshasa. I remember her calling out your name and that of Lakshmana and though I knew nothing of you then, I gather now that it was your wife whom he was carrying away. But do not be unhappy. I swear I will make every attempt to get her back and make you happy. Very soon you will be rid of this grief which is killing you and you will find Sita by your side. It is not right that you should be so despondent. Wipe those tears and regain your poise which is natural to you. It is not proper for me to tell you the truths which you must know already. But then, when one is unhappy one is apt to forget what one has been taught and observed all the time. A man who is contented will not give way to grief whether he is in grave trouble or when he has lost all his wealth, or even when his life is in danger. He will remain placid, calm and unaffected by these buffetings of Fate. It is only a man who is lacking in courage who lets grief get the better of him. I ask you on my bended knees, please abandon this grief. It robs you of your naturalness and you will lose your peace of mind and that is a terrible state of affairs. Extreme grief will make you dislike even the thought of being alive. Abandon this state of mind. Be brave and be hopeful. I have been accepted as a friend by you and because of that privilege which you have granted me, I am talking to you like this. Do not be swayed by emotions."

Rama was touched by the concern of Sugriva and his words had a soothing effect on his troubled mind. Till now he had only Lakshmana to share his grief but now he had found a friend and to him he could unburden his heart. He regained a semblance of composure and said : "My friend, Sugriva, you are indeed a good friend since you know the right words to say when I am unhappy. Your affection for me has, to a large extent, comforted me and I will soon regain the peace of mind which I was almost losing. It is rare to find a friend, particularly when one is in trouble. I depend on you to look for this Ravana and find out where he has concealed my wife. Tell me what I should do for you. Like seeds sown on good fertile soil during the rainy season your words will be fruitful and you will reap the benefit very soon. Remember that these words of mine which are spoken out of my affection should be considered as words of promise. I will never go back on my word once it is given. I have never before uttered an untruth and I will not do so hereafter. I swear to you in the name of Truth that I will do what you want me to do, to make you happy."

Sugriva was thrilled by the solemn promise of Rama. Rama had sworn that he would help him achieve his dream. He had been suffering all these years and now he had found a saviour. The best among men and the wise monkey were friends and Sugriva was convinced that his troubles were at an end. He said :

"The moment you accepted me as your friend, I am sure the gods have let their kind eyes rest on me. With your help one can attain the heavens and reign supreme there. What, then, of a mere earthly kingdom belonging to monkeys. I have been honoured since such a great man like you should have taken my hand and, in front of sacred fire, said that you are my friend. You may be sure that I will not forget this in a hurry. It is not right to talk about one's own self and one's prowess but I will be able to do what seems impossible. Once a friendship is formed between two, then other feelings vanish except the love for each other. It is immaterial whether the friend is rich or poor, unhappy or contented, good or evil. These qualities should not stand in the way of friendship. For the sake of a friend a man should be ready to give up anything : his wealth, his comforts, and, if need be, his life itself. I will follow rules since I am your friend and I will help you in every way. I swear."

3. VALI AND SUGRIVA

They had been talking for a while and Rama had regained his composure. The sight of Sita's jewels had upset him but he was now his old self and he waited for Sugriva to tell him about the quarrel he had with his brother. Lakshmana, Rama, Sugriva and Hanuman were all seated on branches of trees which had been felled on the ground.

"Rama," began Sugriva. "I have been spending my days in constant fear of my brother. I have been ill-treated by him and he has been trying to kill me. I have eluded death thus far and I am afraid of him all the time and of his threat to kill me. It is up to you to help me... I must be rid of this fear of Vali for ever. I want peace of mind."

Rama smiled softly at him and said : "As you rightly observed, a friend considers the grief of his friend as his own and tries to help him. To hurt is second nature to an enemy and I will kill Vali who has stolen your wife. Look at these arrows of mine. These feathered friends of mine, inlaid with gold have the power to kill even as Indra's Vajra. They are like angry serpents and they have never failed me. Your brother, who is a brother but in name, has become your enemy. I assure you that you will see him fallen on the ground like a mountain split by a thunderbolt."

Sugriva embraced Rama for the warmth of his affection and said : "I will unburden my unhappiness to you. I was driven away from my country by my arrogant brother. Those who were dear to me were imprisoned. He has sent several monkeys to kill me but they have been killed by me. I thought that you were also sent by him. Such is my fear of him that I would not welcome you to Rishyamooka. I was certain that you were here to hurt me. Your bows and arrows made me more suspicious than ever. A man in danger and dread is afraid of the passing breeze even. These four are my only faithful friends and because of their words of comfort I am alive. I will tell you the story of our enmity.

"Vali is my elder brother. He was my father's favourite and he was very dear to me. I was devoted to him. After the death of my father he was crowned king since he was the elder son. I was his subject and I obeyed him in everything he said. We were very happy together.

"There was an asura by name Mayavi and he was the eldest son of Dundubhi. It has been said that there was some enmity between him and Vali over some woman. One night, when everyone was asleep, Mayavi came to Kishkindha, where Vali was ruling. He roared at the gateway and called out to Vali to fight with him. My brother was sleeping soundly and he was roused from his sleep. He rushed to answer the challenge of the asura. His wives and myself requested him not to be impulsive and asked him to think twice before rushing to the fight. But he would not be stopped. Because of my love for him I went with him. Mayavi, who challenged Vali, saw the two of us emerging from the gateway and he was suddenly afraid. He began to run. We pursued him and we covered a considerable distance. It was not a very dark night since the moon was shining and lighted our way. Suddenly the asura vanished from our sight. He had entered a cave whose mouth was well hidden by grass and creepers which were growing there. We went there too and waited for him to come out. Vali knew that he had entered the cave since he saw him do so. His anger knew no bounds and he told me : "Sugriva, I will enter the cave and kill that asura. Till I come back you should wait here right at the mouth of this cave. Guard it very carefully." Prostrating before him, I told him that I would do so. Vali entered the cave.

"Believe me, Rama, one year passed since he entered the cave and I stood waiting for him..... I was afraid to leave the spot and, at the same time, afraid of the happenings inside the cave. I did not know what was taking place. I was afraid that my brother was faring poorly in the fight with the asura. I was unhappy and yet I stayed on since Vali had told me that I should.

"After a long time, out of the cave flowed blood. I was horrified to see so much blood frothing out of the mouth of the cave. I thought I heard the roar of the asura and I thought I heard the voice of my brother weak and helpless in the grip of death. I assumed that my brother was dead and I was very sad. But I was afraid of the asura. I was sure he would come out and kill me too. Therefore, I took a large boulder and closed the mouth of the cave with it and, after offering *Tarpana* to my brother, came back to Kishkindha. I did not tell anyone about the happenings at the cave. But they pressed me and forced the truth out of me.

"After due consideration the ministers decided to crown me as the king. I was ruling the kingdom and, suddenly, one day, Vali came! He saw that I had been made king and his eyes grew red with anger. He imprisoned the ministers who had crowned me and spoke harshly to me. He spoke words which hurt like arrows. Still I did not talk back since he was my elder brother. I fell at his feet the moment he came to the city. He did not heed me and my humble love.

"I said : 'It is fortunate that you are alive and that you have come back to us. You are our lord and please take this white umbrella which is rightfully yours. For a whole year I waited at the mouth of the cave and you did not come out. Later I saw blood gushing out of it and I was grieved. I was certain that you had been killed. I was scared lest the asura should now attack me. When such a powerful fighter like you had been vanquished, I did not have hopes of being able to withstand his strength. I therefore closed the mouth of the cave to prevent his coming out and came back to our Kishkindha. I never asked to be made king. The citizens and the ministers thought that the country needed a king and, since I am the younger brother of their king, they crowned me. But all that is over, my brother. Now that you have come back, please take back what is yours. I will, as before, be your devoted slave. I have guarded the kingdom carefully and please be seated on the throne. Do not be angry with me. I stand as a suppliant before you. Do not spurn me since I meant you no harm.'"

"Vali would not listen to my words. He would not look at me and he spoke insultingly in the midst of the entire court. The elders were there and the ministers and in their midst he said : 'This sinner has told you only the first half of the story. After I had entered the cave I was able to kill Mayavi after a long interval of more than a year. It was his blood which flooded the cave and flowed out. When I tried to come out I found that the mouth of the cave had been closed up. I could not find the opening at all.'

"'I called out : Sugriva! several times and there was no response. It was all to no purpose. I was only wasting my breath. Finally I broke the rock into bits with my fist and I came out and hurried to Kishkinda.

"'And what do I find? This brother of mine is seated on the throne. I know that he grabbed the chance that came his way and his intention was to get rid of me.'"

"I tried to tell him that his death was the last thing I desired but it was of no avail. He threw me out of the city. I had no place to call mine. I wandered all over the world and finally came to Rishyamooka. Vali cannot come here because of a curse and so I feel secure only here. I have told you everything, Rama, and it is a painful story. Even at this distance of time, when I remember the incidents, they come back fresh to my mind and I can never forget the pain and the humiliation to which I have been subjected by my brother whom I once worshipped like a father."

He was crying openly now and it was Rama's turn to pacify him and assure him that Vali would soon be dead.

4. THE VALOUR OF VALI

Sugriva said : "Rama, I have no doubt that your arrows will find a home in the chest of my enemy. But let me tell you something about the valour of my brother. He is brave, firm and valiant. He could leap across from the western sea to the eastern easily when the sun had not yet risen. He could span the distance between the south and the north with a single leap. From the top of a mountain he could pull out a peak and fling it far, all in sport. In the exuberance of spirits he would pull out trees along the path he found in the forests and laugh when they fell down.

"There was an asura by name Dundubhi who was as strong as a thousand elephants. He was very fond of assuming the form of a buffalo. He had been fortunate to have obtained some boons and, because of that, he felt there was no one to equal him. He went to the sea and addressed Varuna, the lord of the seas : 'I want to fight with you. I challenge you to give me fight.' Varuna replied : 'You are too mighty for me! I am certain that I will not be able to fight with you. But I know that your arms are itching to fight, to wrestle with someone and I know just the right person for it. In the north, the quarter of the gods, there is a mountain by name Himavan. He is known as the king of all mountains. He is the dwelling place of many tapasvins. The mountain is full of waterfalls and it has many caves where wild animals have made their homes. Himavan has been chosen as his father-in-law by lord Mahadeva Himself. Himavan will offer you resistance and you can wrestle with him to your heart's content.'"

"The asura thought that the sea was too much of a coward to be a worthy opponent and, like an arrow shot by a good archer, went straight and fast to the mountain Himavan. There he played havoc among the peaks and the forest trees and shouted at the mountain. A white form very much like a cloud was assumed by Himavan. He stood at the top of a peak and said : 'Dundubhi, you are a righteous asura and I am a tapasvi unacquainted with the skill you possess. The art of fighting is something I have not learnt. I am your suppliant. Do not oppress me since I am not able to withstand your valour.'"

"Dundubhi stopped in his tracks and said : 'You will have to oblige me, irrespective of your ability or inability to fight. Or else, tell me of someone who will dare to fight with me.'"

"Himavan said : 'There is a beautiful city by name Kishkindha. A powerful monkey by name Vali dwells there. He is the ruler of the city. He is the son of Indra and he is reputed to be extremely powerful. Even as Indra fought with Namuchi, this Vali might fight with you since he is a fighter and you can have some kind of opposition if you fight with him. There is no use in your challenging water and rocks or the trees. I assure you, Vali will make you happy.'"

"Dundubhi in the form of a buffalo flew in the sky looking like an immense rain cloud and reached Kishkindha. He stood at the gateway of the city and, pawing the ground with his great hooves, he let out a war cry summoning Vali to fight. His roar was like the sound made by the instrument by name Dundubhi. Vali was in his harem and he came out, angry with his challenger. He came to the gates of Kishkindha and said : 'Why do you make so much noise here? I know who you are. You are Dundubhi. If you have any desire to stay alive, get away from here and do not incense me.'"

"Dundubhi would not go. He wanted to fight with Vali. He said: 'Do not brag about your valour in the presence of your women. If you so desire, I will wait till morning so that you can have a happy night which will be your last night on the earth. I have been told that you will be able to give me a good fight and this was said by none other than that cowardly mountain Himavan. I am very eager to fight with you. I have come specially to challenge you for a good fight with me.'"

"Vali smiled at the women who surrounded him and sent them back to the harem. He then spoke to Dundubhi : 'Come, let us fight. I am neither drunk nor am I immersed in the pleasures of the harem as you seem to imply.' Vali placed around his neck the garland of gold given to him by Indra and came out to fight with Dundubhi.

"There was a fierce fight between the two. Both were very powerful but, as the duel continued, the asura was losing ground. Vali lifted him and flung him on the ground. So violently was he thrown that he lost his life in that very moment. Blood gushed forth out of his torn limbs and out of his mouth. Vali's anger had not abated. He lifted the dead asura as he would a clod of mud, and flung him far into the distance. It fell a yojana away from the gates of Kishkindha.

"While it was travelling in the air, drops of blood from the body were wafted by the passing breeze and they fell on the ground where the rishi

Matanga had his ashrama. The rishi was very angry since the spot became polluted by the falling of the drops of blood from the dead form of an asura. He was very angry.

"He said: 'Evidently the person guilty of this misdemeanour is wicked, evil-minded and wilful.' He came out to see who it was and found the body of Dundubhi coursing through the air and he saw that Vali had done this. He cursed Vali. 'This ashrama of mine has become unclean because of Vali. If, at any time, he sets foot in this vicinity he will die.'"

Sugriva continued: "Rama, a yojana around the ashrama was forbidden ground for him. The rishi said: 'A yojana around should be avoided by Vali. It should not be used by his friends either. My trees and shrubs and flowering creepers have been uprooted by the dead body of Dundubhi and Vali is responsible for this. I cannot forgive him for this atrocity.'"

"Hearing his words the monkeys near the ashrama went away from there. Vali wanted to know why they had all come away from Matanga's ashrama and he was told by them about the curse of the rishi.

"Vali rushed to the presence of the rishi and prostrated before him. He stood humbly before him and sought his forgiveness. But the rishi ignored him and entered his ashrama without even looking at him. Vali returned to his city in a dejected frame of mind. Ever since then he has not dared to set foot on this lovely mountain by name Rishyamooka. I am living here in comparative peace since I know for certain that he will not come here. Rama, come with me and I will show you something."

Sugriva led Rama to a place nearby and there was the immense skeleton of Dundubhi. Sugriva said: "My brother is very strong and powerful. Look, for instance, at these Sala trees. Vali can, with his strong fist, denude the tree of all its leaves. I have told you about my brother and about his valour. How can you kill him in a fight and that, single-handed? I am worried about the encounter."

Lakshmana was amused by the words of Sugriva. He smiled and asked: "Evidently you are in two minds as to whether my brother will be able to keep his word or not. Tell me, what should my brother do, to convince you that he is more powerful than your brother and that he can kill him? Rama wants to please you and he will prove his strength to you. Tell us what act of Rama's will set your mind at rest and make you have faith in him? How can Rama prove to you that he can kill Vali?"

5. SUGRIVA HAS DOUBTS

Sugriva had a shame-faced look on his face. He did not know that his words were so transparent nor did he realise till he spoke how astute Lakshmana was. He was certainly afraid of Vali and he did want to make sure that Rama was strong enough to fulfil his promise to Sugriva. He said: "You should not misunderstand me. Please do not think that I have no faith in Rama and his prowess or in his words. I have, but then the fear I have of Vali is so great, so terrible that I am dubious about the success of the task Rama has undertaken.

"Once, my brother pierced these seven Sala trees with seven arrows, one by one. Just one arrow was enough to pierce one tree. I have thought up two tests for Rama. If he can also pierce each of these trees with an arrow and if he can lift up the skeleton of Dundubhi with one foot and fling it to a distance of a hundred bows, I will be certain that Rama is more powerful than Vali and I can be sure that Vali is as good as dead."

Sugriva stood still for a few moments and turning to Rama he said : "Rama, as I told you before, my brother is very powerful. Asuras are afraid to meet him in single encounters and he has never been defeated in any fight as yet. Even the devas have been amazed at his feats. And all these many successes have made him arrogant and constant fear of him has made me unhappy. I have found a good friend in you and I have come to you for succour. Please do not, for a moment, think that I am testing your strength or that I am trying to insult you by asking you to display your ability. I have not seen you before and it is my fear which makes me act thus."

Rama listened to the words of Sugriva and, with a sweet smile, he said : "It is but natural for you to be doubtful about my accomplishments: that is, as far as fighting is concerned. I will try to convince you."

Rama walked up to the skeleton of Dundubhi and, lifting it with his toe, he threw it to a distance of ten yojanas. Sugriva was quite impressed but not enough.

His doubting mind said : "Rama, when Vali threw this body away it was much heavier, filled as it was with blood and flesh. Now it is just a framework of bones. And again, he did it when he was tired and as for you, you are fresh and full of great enthusiasm. Even this feat, amazing as it is, does not make me quite sure of my future. If only you can pierce one of these Sala trees with a single arrow I can be certain of your ascendancy over Vali. Please have pity on me and forgive me for my doubting nature. But I must make sure of everything. Please, Rama, string your bow and, with an arrow, pierce one of these seven Sala trees. I will be satisfied. I will know then that you are the best among men : that you are, among archers, what the sun is among the luminaries : what Himavan is among the mountains : what the lion is among the animals."

Rama took up his bow in his hand. He strung it and then he fixed an arrow to it. He pulled it far and then released it. He had aimed at a Sala tree.

The arrow glittering with its tip of gold, streaked through the air, pierced all the seven Sala trees and entered the earth. After splitting the ground, it came back to the quiver of Rama and rested there.

The five monkeys were amazed at the feat and they were jumping in the air because of the excitement. Sugriva was jubilant. He spoke again and again about the certainty of the death of Vali. His doubts had been cleared and to make up for his impertinence in doubting Rama he praised him in glowing terms.

He could not contain himself. He said : "Rama, let us not waste time. You must kill Vali today and rid my heart of the thorn which has been lodged there for so many years."

Rama embraced Sugriva and with a smile at Lakshmana he said: "Let us go to Kishkindha now. Sugriva, you go first and summon your brother to fight with you."

They went fast towards Kishkindha. In the dense forest Rama and Lakshmana concealed themselves behind some trees and stood waiting.

Sugriva was dressed to fight. He went to the gateway of Kishkindha and summoned Vali with a terrible roar.

6. THE KILLING OF VALI

At first Vali could not believe his ears. He had never thought that his brother could summon up courage enough to fight with him. But here he was, and obviously, he wanted to fight! Vali laughed at first and anger gave place to amusement. He laughed for a long while and said : "How dare this Sugriva challenge me? Has he gone mad?" He thought for a while and he decided that Sugriva had to be taught a lesson. He had the audacity to call out to him and it was obvious that the roar was a war cry.

Vali came out of the city and he looked like the sun poised on the western hill just before sunset. He rushed towards Sugriva and there was a terrible fight which ensued between the two brothers. Sugriva was no mean fighter and Vali was powerful. The duel was fearful. It was like the two planets Budha and Angaraka (Mercury and Mars) which were confronting each other. The brothers used their fists and each was like the Vajra of Indra. Rama fixed an arrow to his bow and turned it towards the fighting pair. But they were so much alike he did not know who was who. They were like the Ashvini twins and Rama could not distinguish between the two.

Sugriva found that he was weakening and Vali had hit him all over the body. He was bleeding and not finding Rama anywhere he ran towards Rishyamooka. Vali was pursuing him and he had to stop when Sugriva entered the forest near the ashrama of Matanga. Vali shouted after him : "You have managed to escape alive. Do not taunt me again."

Rama, Lakshmana and Hanuman went to where Sugriva was. His face was cast down and he spoke in a piteous voice : "You displayed your valour to me. You asked me to summon Vali to a duel. When I did it, you stood watching me being beaten up, and you did not kill Vali. Why? If you had told me at the beginning that you had no wish to do so, I would not have gone near my brother and asked for trouble. Look at me now."

He was on the point of weeping and Rama said : "My dear friend, please do not be angry with me. Listen to me when I tell why I did not shoot my arrow to kill Vali. In form and feature, face and limb, in gait and in the method of fighting, you are both so much alike that it was not possible for me to distinguish between the two of you. Your valour was equal to that of your brother and even your voices were alike. I was not able to shoot because of this similarity between you both. I did not want to kill the wrong brother and kill the friendship which has sprung up between you and me. I did not dare make a mistake. My arrow will never return without drinking the life of the one it is aimed at and I would have committed a tragic mistake if it had hurt you instead of your brother. It is a most heinous crime to kill one who has asked for succour and that might have happened if I had been hasty. Come, shake off this depression and go again to fight. You will certainly see Vali dead. Lakshmana, pull out that creeper *Gajapushpi* and place it round the neck of Sugriva. I will then be able to make out who Vali is."

Lakshmana took the creeper which was full of flowers and twisting it into a semblance of a garland, he placed it round the neck of Sugriva. Reassured by the words of Rama Sugriva walked again towards Kishkindha. He walked ahead while Lakshmana and Rama followed, with Hanuman to accompany him. Behind them walked the other three monkeys : Nala, Neela and Thara, the commander-in-chief.

They went back to the same place where they had concealed themselves and Sugriva summoned Vali once again to fight. Before he went to the gates of the city Rama had assured Sugriva that he would certainly kill Vali this time.

Vali heard Sugriva and naturally he was furious. He could not bear to hear the voice of Sugriva calling out to him again. He jumped out of his seat and with long strides began to walk towards where the call came from.

His beloved wife Tara felt very nervous.

She said : "My lord, give up this anger against your brother. If you wish to, fight with him tomorrow. I feel afraid of this hurry with which you have set out to fight with him. Just a while back he came and fought with you. He was well punished by you and sent back. He has come again which is surprising. It worries me. You should not be indifferent to the cause of this sudden courage of Sugriva. Something tells me that he has someone to assist him or else he will never be able to face you alone. He is very clever and he would not have come unless he is sure of victory."

"Angada told me something which comes to my mind now.

"He had been to the forest and his spies told him that two princes, Rama and Lakshmana, the sons of Dasaratha, have come to the forest and that they have made friendship with Sugriva. I feel that Sugriva is assisted by Rama and I know how great a warrior Rama is. If he is against you, no one can save you. Sugriva has found refuge in him and Rama is famed for helping those who seek his aid. He is famed in all the three worlds. His prowess is unparalleled. He will destroy his enemies. He is like the fire at the end of the Yuga when he is angry. He is the protector of the helpless. He is the home of all virtues and he is wise. I think it is inadvisable on your part to antagonise Rama. Please listen to me and take my advice. Do not fight with your brother. Go to him, make friends with him and take him into your heart. Crown him as the Yuvaraja. You will thus make friends with Rama too. Cast away this hatred and give place to affection in your heart. Your quarrel has lasted long enough and you should now make it up with him. He is your brother. He is valiant and it is good for you to do as I say. Take my advice and do not seek enmity with Rama. I am afraid for you."

Her words fell on deaf ears. Vali was too angry with Sugriva to think of him as his brother. He looked at Tara and said : "How can I bear to hear this arrogant call of that coward? When I am challenged it is not befitting that a hero like me should avoid fighting and make friends with the enemy. I will be called a coward. As for your worry about Rama, there is no need for it, Tara. Rama is famed for ever following the path of righteousness and he had never once swerved from the path of Dharma. He will never act contrary to it. Go back to the inner chambers, Tara. I will punish this audacious brother of mine and come back to you. I will only punish him and, I assure you, I will not kill him. After some more beatings from my fist he will run away and I do not think he will come back to fight."

Tara embraced Vali with tears in her eyes. Praying for his victory she entered her chambers with slow and dragging steps. Vali waited for her to go and then he came out to fight with Sugriva the second time.

He stepped out and looked around for a sight of his brother. Sugriva was there and they were locked in a duel. Each beat the other with his fists. Vali was using his fists while Sugriva uprooted a Sala tree and beat up Vali with it.

The fight between the two was fierce and for a while there was only the sound of their groans, their angry words and their deep sighs. Sugriva, however, was gradually showing signs of weakening. The weariness was visible. He persisted, however, and did not run away as he did the previous time.

Rama was watching the fight. Perhaps he hoped that Sugriva would be able to defeat Vali. He was holding the bow in his left hand and it had been strung already. Rama now saw that Sugriva was not faring well : that he was losing and Rama took up an arrow out of his quiver. He held it in his hand for a long moment. Perhaps, he was thinking of the stigma which would cling to his name because of the act he was planning. He fixed the arrow to the bowstring. He pulled the string and despatched the arrow towards Vali.

The noise made by the bowstring was frightening. Even as it was vibrating, the arrow, glowing like a streak of lightning, sudden like a thunderbolt, entered the chest of Vali and stayed there. Vali fell to the ground, hurt by Rama's arrow. He fell like the Indradhanus on Paurnima day in the month of Ashvayuja when it is pulled to the ground after the festival of Indra.

7. VALI'S CENSURE

With a single arrow Rama had hurt Vali and he was on the ground and he looked like a fallen god. The moment he fell, the kingdom was as forlorn and helpless as the night sky without the moon. He was not looking fatigued nor was there any sign of death in him. His splendour had not faded. His golden garland was brilliant and he was looking glorious with this gift of Indra. He was as beautiful as he was before the fight and the garland made him look like the sunset cloud with an edge of gold. So he lay on the ground.

VALI'S CENSURE

Rama, accompanied by Lakshmana, came out of the screen of trees and walked towards Vali who was like a flame without smoke, like king Yayati who fell to the earth when his punya was all exhausted: like the sun which had fallen on the ground at the end of the Yuga : Vali was lying on the ground; Vali, who was the son of Indra, was as proud as Indra and as powerful.

Rama approached him and with him went Lakshmana. Vali had regained consciousness and he looked at the approaching figure of the two brothers. He waited for them to come near. Rama stood there, one hand loosely clasping the bow and the other, unstringing it. Vali said: "I was fighting with my brother. When I was absorbed in the fight, I was hit in the chest by an arrow coming from out of nowhere. Tell me, how does it benefit you to fight with an opponent who did not offer you any fight? I had no quarrel with you and yet hiding behind the trees, you have killed me. To what purpose? What did you gain by it?

"You are the son of an emperor, born in a noble family. You are said to have great, good, and noble qualities. They say you are valiant, generous, righteous. I have heard praises of you. You are indeed a famous personage. You are said to be compassionate and you are the home of kindliness and mercy. Your valour is not of this world. You are well acquainted with the rules of conduct and you are said to have observed all the rules of Dharma all these years.

"A king should be afraid of committing sinful acts, and he should have the senses under control. He should have patience and manliness; truthfulness and valour should be his ornaments. He should punish only those who have offended him. When Sugriva called me the second time, Tara warned me about you and I laughed at her fears since I had great faith in your noble birth and your great qualities. I was fighting with someone else and I had not encountered you. I told her that you would never agree to fight me thus.

"My belief is all wrong. I see now you are an Adharmi, you are like a well, covered with grass and, therefore, is more treacherous than an open well. You are a sinner in the guise of a good man and you are like fire covered by ashes. I have done you no wrong. I did not come to your country and offend you. I have not insulted you in any manner. Why then did you kill me? I am a monkey dwelling in the forest and so is Sugriva. We were fighting our personal fight and you were not in any way challenged by me. You took it upon yourself to aim your arrow at me and kill me. WHY? You are a kshatriya and you are well-versed in all the nuances of Dharma. You are called the image of Dharma and I was deceived by your reputation. Your righteousness is just a pretence. You are a prince, Rama, and we are animals dwelling in the forest. Fighting over trivial things like a piece of land or a few pieces of gold or a woman, are all natural to us. How does our quarrel affect you? Kings have the power to punish or to pardon. But they are not expected to misuse their power.

"As for you, it seems to me, you act only according to your wish and you are prone to be affected by anger. You have not followed the rules of conduct set down for a prince, a kshatriya. Irrespective of whether it is right or wrong you have become addicted to the use of the bow and arrow. You are not completely righteous nor are you firm in your thinking. You are easily swayed by your emotions.

"Rama, today you have killed me who is innocent. This act of yours is cruel and unforgivable. When the wise question you about it, what will be your explanation? I have also been taught the rules of Dharma.

"I have been told that one who kills a king, one who kills a brahmin, a cow, one who steals wealth belonging to another, one who enjoys hurting animals, who does not believe in God, who marries when his elder brother is still unmarried, who reveals a secret to the world, who is avaricious, who betrays a trusted friend, who lusts after the wife of his preceptor : all these will be doomed to dwell in the hell meant for great sinners.

"You may say that a prince has a right to kill an animal as a hunter does. But I am a monkey. My skin is not of any use as an apparel like the skin of the deer. My bones and my hair are not of any use to anyone. My flesh is not eaten by men. Brahmins and kshatriyas are allowed to eat the flesh of animals which have five nails. I do not belong to that group.

"If I had listened to the words of warning spoken by my beloved Tara, I would not have come to this sad end. It is a pity that a righteous king like Dasaratha should have a son like you. This act of yours is against all codes of Dharma, and I have become the victim of an unrighteous man.

"If you had challenged me and fought with me, you would certainly have been defeated by me. But, like a serpent which creeps under the grass and crawls up to a sleeping man and bites him, you have attacked me. I know why you have killed me. You wished to please Sugriva by this act of yours and, in return, he is to find your lost wife for you. If you had approached me first, I would certainly have brought her from where she is imprisoned and, that, in a single day. I would have put a noose round the neck of that sinful Ravana and dragged him to your presence.

"After I am dead Sugriva will ascend the throne. That is lawful. But your killing of me is unlawful. I ask you, nay demand of you, that you justify your act and convince me that what you did is right. I am quite willing to listen."

The brave Vali, the son of Indra, was in great pain and his voice was growing faint as he spoke to Rama. His words had now ceased and he looked at Rama.

Rama listened patiently to the accusations of Vali. The monkey king spoke words which were true to Dharma, which were just and which were spoken quite softly. There was no harshness in the voice of Vali when he said these things. Rama looked at Vali for a long moment. He was like the sun whose glory had been dimmed : like a rain cloud which had been emptied of its waters : like fire which had died down.

8. RAMA JUSTIFIES HIS ACTION

After a long pause Rama spoke deliberately and with words chosen very carefully. He said : "You do not seem to know all about Dharma, Artha and Kama. You do not know the nuances of Dharma. You are not fully conversant with the word Dharma and yet, you dare to accuse me of overstepping the bounds of Dharma. Without consulting men who have expert knowledge of Dharma, without hearing the views of great preceptors, you accuse me of being an Adharmi.

"This world, this forest with its mountains, its rivers and lakes, are all ruled by the kings of the race of the sun. To punish the inmates of the cities or the forests is the right of the kings of our House. My brother, Bharata who is highly righteous, truthful and straight is ruling this kingdom. We have also followed the path of Dharma and we have been wandering in these forests to see that right is established everywhere. When Bharata is the ruler of a country where is the chance for Adharma to raise its head? We are assisting Bharata to rule the world. And we have taken it on ourselves the task of punishing those who are in the wrong. You are an Adharmi, you are sinful in behaviour and you are given to satiating your lust. Anyone who follows the path of Dharma knows that the father, the preceptor and the elder brother are to be considered as fathers.

"Your younger brother who is a good-natured person should have been treated as a son by you. It is not easy for beings like you to understand the subtleties of the word Dharma and its application as understood by us. Only the Atman inside knows what is right and what is not. Like a fool, when he is associated with other fools, is incapable of learning anything, you have, with your companions, failed to learn anything about the code of behaviour. Do not accuse me because you are angry with me. I will tell you why I killed you.

"You ill-treated this brother of yours and captured his wife, Ruma. You have transgressed the rules of Dharma, of behaviour, by taking your brother's wife and I have punished you for it. For one who has overstepped the code of behaviour according to Dharma as stipulated by the elders, the only punishment is death. Your sin is unforgivable. It has been said that one who looks with lust at his daughter, his sister or the wife of his brother, must be punished and the punishment is death. Bharata is the monarch and we are his brothers who have been walking in the path of Dharma. You are outside the pale of Dharma. How can I overlook your misdemeanour? However we look at it, you are in the wrong and your behaviour is punishable.

"Sugriva is as dear to me as Lakshmana. I have sworn to be his life-long friend and I have done this since he is a good soul and I have decided to restore his lost kingdom and his wife to him. I have promised to do this for him and how can I go back on my promise?

"You must realise that I did not wrong you in any way. My friend has been quite righteous and this is a duty I owed him. You would have acted the same way if you had been placed similarly.

"O king, enough of this self-pity. My action is within the law. We are not prone to act as we please. I will give you another explanation for my action. You object to my hiding behind the trees and shooting an arrow at you. Remember, you are an animal and we, Rajarshis, will always kill wild animals which are harmful to the safety of society, of humanity, by trapping them in pits, by spreading nets for them, with several types of traps, and with bows and arrows shot from behind trees, or from the tops of trees. Whether you stood in front of me or not, I consider you as one of the wild animals and I treated you as such. I do not think I acted wrongly."

Vali thought of the words spoken by Rama defending his action and he was convinced that Rama had done no wrong. He stopped finding fault with Rama and he realised the truth underlying Rama's arguments. He folded his palms together and said : "Lord of lords, I abide by what you say. It is not meet for a lowly being like me to argue with one like you. Because of my ignorance as to your true nature harsh words were spoken by me. I pray that you will forgive me for them. You are well-versed in Dharma and its many nuances and, as you say, I know very little. You are bent on doing good to the world. The act and the reason prompting that act are both known to you and they are always right. They should not be questioned. Bless me before I go, Rama, and forgive me."

Vali's voice was choked with tears and he looked at Rama with eloquent eyes. He then said : "I am not worried about myself, Rama. You must know only too well that I have the welfare of my Angada at heart. He is my only concern and not any of the others, not even Tara. He has been brought up by me with great affection and when I die, he will pine for me and my loving hands. He is young and has still a lot to learn. He is my only son and he has never once displeased me. I appeal to you to protect him. Love him as you love Sugriva. You are the protector of the world and you should take him under your care. He should be as dear to you as Bharata, or Lakshmana. This is my only request. Please do not let my beloved Tara be insulted by Sugriva. You should see to it also. One who is loved by you, who has been left in your care, who will please you in every way will rule the kingdom well, and he will be able to rule the entire world. He can conquer the heavens too. It was because I had to meet my death at your hands that I accepted the call of Sugriva in spite of Tara's misgivings. Fate is more powerful than anything else."

Rama tried to comfort the dying Vali and he spoke many words full of affection. He said : "Abandon this ignorance and pain in your heart. Do not be upset by these thoughts. Nothing can avert Fate and every one of us has to do what Fate wills us to do. I promise you that your son Angada will be dear to me and he will be as dear to Sugriva as he was to you. I will take good care of him. You can rest assured that it will be so."

Vali was comforted by the words of Rama. He spoke again : "You are the emperor and you are like Indra in valour. I still regret the hasty words I spoke when I was in pain and when I was angry. You must forgive them." Vali lost consciousness and he lay gasping on the ground.

Tara heard that her lord had been killed by Rama. Clasping her son with trembling steps she emerged from the city. There was panic in the city and all the monkeys were feeling scared and they were fleeing from the spot where Vali was. They were so frightened that they looked Tara with her son in fear and asked her to go away from there and hide herself lest her son should be harmed. Tara smiled scathingly at them and said : "My beloved husband is lying dead and where is the need for me to protect myself? Of what use is life when he is gone? I do not want the kingdom and I am not worried about my son. I want to go to my husband and stay by his side. I want nothing else."

She rushed out of the city Kishkindha and ran to where Vali was lying. He was dying and she saw him.

9. TARA'S GRIEF

Vali had never before been defeated by anyone. He had killed so many asuras. Even as Indra hurls his Vajra, Vali would hurl huge rocks at his opponents and his prowess was known in all the three worlds. His voice was like the rumbling of a thunder cloud and his valour was greater than that of Indra. Such a great hero was now lying on the ground and she looked around. She saw Rama who stood with the bow in his hand, at Lakshmana and at Sugriva, her husband's brother. She looked down at the ground and saw the unconscious form of Vali. Tara fell on the ground and, clasping him in her arms, set up a wail of woe which was heart-rending.

Angada was sobbing along with his mother and Sugriva was sorely grieved at the sight of them.

Tara saw the arrow which had lodged in her husband's chest and again and again she embraced him.

"I am Tara, my lord!" She cried. "I am your dear wife and when I am calling you why do you not answer me? Come with me and we will go back to the palace. This hard bed is unbecoming to you. Evidently you are more in love with the earth or else you would have heard my piteous appeal. There is now another city like Kishkindha which has been prepared for you in the heavens and it seems to me, you prefer that. My heart is very hard or else how can it still beat and not break into a thousand pieces after seeing you on the ground, with your life ebbing away? Why did you not listen to me when I asked you not to fight with Sugriva? If you had only paid heed to my words of warning, you would not have been dead. It was Fate which made you a victim to the guiles of your brother. Your son Angada, who has never known what hardship is, will now be a dependent on Sugriva and I wonder how he will be treated. I am afraid.

"Child, Angada, take a last look at your valiant father. You will never see him again. Rama has kept his promise to his friend and has despatched your father to the heavens. Sugriva, the kingdom is yours. Your enemy is killed and you will be re-united with Ruma. All your desires will now be fulfilled. I hope you are happy.

"Vali, my lord, how is it you are deaf to my pleadings and my voice? Have you forgotten me so soon?"

She wept bitter tears and her piteous weeping was painful to watch. Again and again she called out to Vali and asked him not to leave her and her son and go away. Finally she decided to cast off her life by fasting unto death. Hanuman came to her and tried to comfort her. He said : "A man reaps the fruits of the actions he has performed : actions whether good or bad, and death grants him these fruits. No man's action depends on those of another. This human body is like a bubble on the surface of water. No one need mourn for another since we are all to be pitied. You are in a pitiable state and you feel sorry for Vali who is dead. You are drowned in misfortune and you feel that Vali is unfortunate. There is no cause for grief in this world where everything is transient. It is not right that you should think of giving up your life. You have a son and it is your duty to protect him. Think of his future and make up your mind to act in such a way as to ensure his safety and good. You are a wise lady and you know only too well what the ultimate truth is; birth and death are inevitable and life on earth is not permanent. That is the reason why a man should try and perform as many good acts as he can when he is alive.

"This Vali who was a great king and on whom depended all his subjects, is now dead. He knew the codes of behaviour. He was sweet-spoken, generous, and he was very patient. He had attained the world meant for good people and so he should not be mourned. You are the queen of this kingdom and your son, young Angada, looks to you for comfort. All the subjects look to you for assurance. Abandon this grief and this decision to lay down your life. Angada will surely be king. Let him be prepared to perform the duties which a son has to. The Vedas say that it is for this purpose that a son is born to man. Angada should perform the final rites for his father. After he has done his duty Angada will be crowned as Yuvaraja. Your thoughts must now be only for the welfare of your son."

Tara refused to be comforted and she would not give up the thought of death. Vali had recovered from his faint and with great difficulty he tried to breathe and his eyes lighted on Sugriva. He called him affectionately by name and called him to his side. He said : "Sugriva, I am sad that I wronged you because of my pride and arrogance. Evidently Fate was against your sharing the affection which brothers normally should. That happiness was denied to us. No one can alter the decrees of Fate. You know only too well that I am dying. Accept this kingdom from me. I am giving up my life, my son, the immense wealth which was mine, and the great fame which I had earned. You must now listen to my last wishes. You must fulfil them.

"Look at this son of mine, Angada, who stands numb with the pain of separation from me. I love him to distraction and I have taken very good care of him. He is dearer to me than my very life and, bereaved as he is, it is up to you to treat him as your son and take good care of him. I am certain that you will do so. He is valiant and in the fight that is to ensue with the rakshasa Ravana, Angada will be at the forefront. He will display his prowess and make a name for himself. This Tara, the dear daughter of Sushena, is a very wise woman. She knows the subtleties of statecraft.

She knows how to react to any unforeseen situation. Take her advice in everything. If she approves of a thing then it is certain to be correct. You have taken up the responsibility of helping Rama. You must do it properly. Sin will cling to you if you fail in your duty. Also, Rama can be very angry if he wants to. He will punish you. Sugriva, lastly, take this golden garland from me. It is divine and you must wear it. Once I am dead the effect will go. So take it before my life ebbs out."

Listening to the words of Vali, Sugriva's pleasure at having got the kingdom was all gone. With sobs he took the garland from Vali and placed it round his neck.

Vali had no regrets now. He called Angada to his side and said: "Child, Angada, remember to be aware of the altered circumstances and the situation which you are now facing. Do not pay much attention to things which please you and things which are apt to displease you. Accept happiness and sorrow as they come and do not be moved by them. You must please Sugriva in every way. Perhaps you may not be petted and loved as much by him as you were by me. Do not mind it. Remember to avoid those who are his enemies. Be neither too attached to any one nor should you be completely indifferent. Adopt the middle course and try to find comfort in the guardianship of Sugriva."

Vali's end was fast approaching. When he had spoken to his son he struggled in pain because of the arrow which was lodged inside him and a moment later, he died.

Tara was inconsolable. Neela, one of the chiefs, approached the body of Vali and gently he pulled out the arrow. Tara made Angada prostrate before the dead form of Vali. Sugriva was shedding tears and he went to the presence of Rama and said : "Rama, you kept your word and Vali is dead. But now, I have lost all interest in the worldly things which once seemed unattainable. The death of Vali, my brother, the sorrow of his queen, the helpless look in the eyes of Angada have all made me averse to the thought of becoming the king. I wished for the death of Vali and it was because of my anger and wickedness. I am full of repentance. I will continue to live on top of Rishyamooka. I will find peace there. During all the many fights we had, Vali could have killed me. But he would say : 'I do not have the heart to kill you. Go and stay out of my sight.' That meant that he loved me and I did not realise it. I should never have wished for his death. It was my greed for wealth and the kingdom which made me wish for it. I am a sinner. I am not fit to rule a kingdom. My servants will do my bidding and search for Sita. I will not break my promise to you. But I do not want to live any more. I will fall into the fire and burn to death."

Rama was, by nature, very compassionate, and he was very unhappy to see this grief. Tara was made to rise up from the side of Vali and she looked at Rama. She went to him and said : "I have heard about you and your good nature. You should take pity on me and use the same arrow on me with which you killed my husband. I will be united with him and he will be happy. He cannot be without me. You have been separated from your wife and you know how painful it is and, surely, you will not want Vali to suffer as you do. He needs me. I assure you, the sin of killing a woman will not cling to you. Please do me this one favour."

Rama was sorely distressed by her sorrow. He spoke words of comfort to her. He said : "You are the wife of a hero and you should not give way to despair. Fate rules the world and the Vedas say that everything functions according to the will of Brahma. All the three worlds have to obey his wishes and you cannot overrule the dictates of Fate. Your son Angada will be the Yuvaraja and, seeing him, you will forget your sorrow. No woman who has a hero for husband and a hero for son will give in to grief. Abandon this despair." He comforted all of them with his gentle words and he then asked them to perform the last rites for Vali. He spoke again about the power of Fate over everyone and everything. He said : "No one can circumvent Fate. In this world Fate is the only powerful cause for every happening. No man does anything on his own : nor is he free to command anyone to do anything. Fate is the sole Power which rules the actions of man. No one can escape the rulings of Fate. Fate is neither partial nor has it any personal gain or loss to sustain. Fate makes man suffer or enjoy pleasure and man is helpless in the hands of Fate. Vali has been the plaything of Fate and he has now reached the heavens which he has earned. Rouse up yourselves from this despondency and perform the last rites for Vali."

Lakshmana spoke to Sugriva to do the needful. He organised the entire proceedings and soon the palanquin, richly decorated, was ready. Vali was placed in it and carried to the pyre which had been prepared with sandal and other scented woods. They placed Vali on it and Angada touched it with fire. They bathed later in the cool waters of the river which flowed nearby and after offering Tarpana to the departed soul they returned to the city Kishkindha.

10. THE CORONATION OF SUGRIVA AND ANGADA

They all stood around Rama with their palms folded. No one knew what should be done and they looked to Rama to command them. Hanuman spoke on behalf of all them and said : "My lord, with your help Sugriva has now been given the kingdom which had been ruled by his ancestors. Please enter the city and command us to proceed further in the matter. Please guide our king as to how he should manage his affairs. Our king would like to honour you. Please enter the cave which leads into the city Kishkindha."

Rama looked at Hanuman and said : "Hanuman, according to the commands of my father I will not enter a village nor a city until the fourteen years of exile are completed. Let Sugriva be taken into the city and be crowned." He turned to Sugriva and said : "Go and take up the ruling of the kingdom. Crown this young prince as the Yuvaraja. Angada is the very image of his father and he will bring fame and glory to his father's name." Rama paused for a moment.

He then looked around at everyone and at Lakshmana and said: "Sugriva, the month is Shravana, the first month of the rainy season. I will spend some time with Lakshmana in this mountain during the four months when rain will fall continuously. I will be happy in the caves of this mountain. Go to the city. When the month Kartika comes round, when the rains cease, you can set about your task of fulfilling your promise to me. Go now to Kishkindha and accept the throne."

Sugriva went into the city and was crowned as king. At the same time he crowned Angada as the Yuvaraja and he embraced him with affection. Sugriva was re-united with his wife and he spent many happy days as the king in Kishkindha.

11. RAMA AND LAKSHMANA IN PRASRAVANA

After he had sent Sugriva and the others to Kishkindha, Rama went to the hill by name Prasravana. The brothers searched all over and finally located a cave which was very spacious and comfortable. They decided to make it their home for the time being, during the rainy season.

Rama spent the rainy months in Prasravana, with Lakshmana to keep him company. He was very pleased with the location of the cave which they had chosen as their dwelling place. They were surrounded on all sides by beautiful trees and flowering creepers which were entwined round their trunks. Nature had been lavish in her bounty and wherever their eyes were cast, they encountered nothing but beauty. Rama was ecstatic in his praise of the spot and he waited impatiently for the rainy days to come to an end. He spent sleepless nights thinking of Sita and he had no peace of mind. Lakshmana would try to comfort his brother who was ever full of sorrow. The days seemed very long and the incessant rain did not, in any way, assuage the pain in the sad heart of Rama.

Once the moon had risen and Rama saw the moonlit peak of Prasravana from the mouth of the cave where they were staying. His thoughts flew to Sita and he broke down. Lakshmana was his sole comfort. He said : "Rama, my dear brother, you must be brave. You should not be unhappy. You have told me that one who loses his mental equipoise will cause all his actions to go waste. You are powerful and you will win back Sita from that rakshasa after killing him. Do not give way to despair. You are able to make or break this entire universe. Why then should we worry about this sole enemy? Let the rainy days pass and soon the season Sharad will be here. We will then be able to locate Sita. Ravana will be killed. It is not as though you do not know your strength. Like fire which is covered with ashes needs an *ahuti* of ghee to make it glow again, I am trying to remind you of your prowess."

Rama was touched by the tenderness with which Lakshmana was taking care of him. He said : "Child, Lakshmana, you have ever been devoted to me and your love for me is infinite. You speak the right words at the right time. I realise the enervating effect sorrow has on one. I will try and shed it. I will wait for the coming of Sharad. I will wait for Sugriva's aid when the rains cease. It is hard to be patient but I will wait."

Lakshmana said : "Rama, Sugriva will do the needful and he will organise the search for Sita. These days will pass and soon we can act. This inaction is making me impatient too and we will soon see the end of it."

The four months had come to an end and the skies were regaining their blue. Hanuman saw that the time had come when Sugriva should set about his task : the search for Sita. But he found that Sugriva, after many years of exile had come back to luxury and in this state of mind, had forgotten himself and the duty he owed to Rama. He was busy enjoying himself with wine and women.

Hanuman who knew the nuances of Dharma, who was ever wise, saw that the time had come when the king should be shaken out of his complacency. The skies were clear and there was no longer the sound of thunder or the flash of lightning. Moonlight was chaste and white and the moon shed its soft radiance on the terraces of the king's palace and still he had not woken up to the fact that the time had come when he should remember his promise. Sugriva was spending his days and nights in tasting the joys which had been denied him so long. He had left the affairs of the kingdom in the hands of the ministers and was, himself, always in the harem.

Hanuman went to the presence of Sugriva and spoke to him words full of wisdom. They were words of advice but spoken very humbly. He said : "My lord, this kingdom has been restored to you and also your dear wife. There is still something undone. You should return the favour done to you by your friend. It is not for me to tell you what your duty is. But, since your have accepted me as your mentor, I have assumed that you will follow my advice. I need not tell you what you should do now. When a man knows how to act as befits the nobility of his character and keeps his word which was given solemnly to a friend, his fame will be lasting and his kingdom will spread far and wide. He will be honoured by everyone.

"I know your good nature and it is up to you to help Rama who was responsible for your becoming king. You should now set aside your other interests and devote yourself entirely to the task undertaken by you. No man should prove unfaithful to a friend. My lord, please make all arrangements for the search for Sita. We have promised Rama that we will do this. Even though he is impatient to learn about her, Rama is too noble to trouble you and remind you of your duty.

"Shravana is long past, and the four months are over. The rains have ceased and the time has come when you should act. Collect the Vanaras to go in search of Sita. It should not seem as though you are indifferent about Rama once you have gained what you desired. You should not wait to be reminded of your duty by Rama. Rama can easily destroy the three worlds. He is very much upset by this delay, I am sure. But he is attached to you and he expects to remain your friend. He is still patient and he is waiting for some kind of communication from you telling him that you are keeping your promise in mind and that you have not forgotten it.

"If Rama becomes angry no one can save you from his anger. Commanded by you, hordes of Vanaras should search for Sita everywhere. After finding out the hiding place where Ravana has imprisoned her, we will be able to say that we have returned the favour done to us by Rama. Please make arrangements for the host of Vanaras to assemble in Kishkindha as early as possible.

Sugriva listened to the words spoken by the wise Hanuman. He thought for a while and then he sent for Neela and told him : "Neela, see that my entire army led by the different chiefs assembles in Kishkindha from all over the world. Let them all come as fast as they can to our city. They must be here within fifteen days from today. If anyone dares to treat this command casually, he will be executed. Ask Angada to represent me and arrange about the collection of the army." After this Sugriva went back to his harem.

12. RAMA'S IMPATIENCE

The rainy season was over. The sky was clear and the moonlit nights were increasing the unhappiness of Rama. He realised that the time stipulated had expired long ago. The sky and the soft air blowing across the Prasravana enhanced his ache for Sita who was not by his side and Rama gave way to despair. He fainted and had recovered and was in a depressed state of mind when Lakshmana, who had gone out to collect fruits, came back to the cave. He looked at Rama and his tear-stained face. He was sorry he had left Rama alone with his grief.

He said: "Rama, my beloved brother, it does not become you to give way to despair like this. I have known a different Rama who could never be affected by the sway of the emotions. Rama, please do not let go of your composure. Do not torture your mind with memories. It is not helping you in any way. Do not let your energy get frittered away by constant dwelling on the tragic happenings. Sugriva will now begin his search for Sita and we can once more be active. Sita would not have come to grief since she is your wife and she is like a flame which will burn anything which dares to touch it. Forget your sorrow and let us think of the future when, with the help of Sugriva, we will find her and bring her back."

Rama was impressed by the words of Lakshmana and he said: "Child, without doubt, a task has to be contemplated. Efforts have to be made to accomplish it and again, thoughts of the result should not interfere with the performance of the task, lest it should detract from its efficacy. I have told you that I would not lose my poise and give way to my grief. But the season and its beauty bring to my mind thoughts of Sita and I cannot but help ache for her and worry about the possible danger to her.

"Lakshmana, with rare patience, I have waited for the rains to cease. Sharadritu has made its appearance but evidently Sugriva has forgotten all about his promise to me. I have not seen him nor have I heard from him. These four months have been like a hundred years to me. My Sita came to the dreadful Dandaka with me since she loved me and she could not live without me. I am not able to spend even a moment without thinking of her and her devotion. She must be unhappy too, without me by her side. How long is this torture to last? Sugriva is indifferent.

"You say that I should not indulge in self-pity. But look at me, Lakshmana. I am helpless. I have lost my kingdom and because of Ravana and his deceit I have lost my wife. I find that my hands are tied and I seem to have become different and I am unhappy.

"Choked with the fumes of lust the king of the Vanaras has forgotten us completely. I have been made to bear the insult of this Sugriva. He promised to help me find Sita and now, when his kingdom has been restored to him, he has become indifferent to my grief and his promise to me. Lakshmana, I cannot bear this any longer. I want you to go to Sugriva with this message: 'The lowliest man in the world is the one who has forgotten the benefits he has derived from a friend and who, having promised something to that friend, does not keep his word. He is the best of men who keeps his word, and pursues the task he has undertaken, irrespective of whether it is easy or difficult. A man who forgets his friends and the good fortune which is his because of his friends, is the most contemptible of men.' Lakshmana, perhaps he wants to see my bow bent and my arrow aimed at his chest. Ask him, if he wishes to hear the twang of my bow which resembles thunder. Lakshmana, how is it possible for him to have forgotten about me even after he has seen my power and valour?

"Remind him of the death of Vali and of the debt he owes me because of that. Ask him if he has forgotten his promises. The rains have ceased and he has not woken up from his dream of pleasure. Drowned in the sea of enjoyment he does not know that the waking up will be frightful if I decide to string my bow and fight with him. Go, my child, and acquaint Sugriva with my anger. Repeat these words to him :

'The gateway through which Vali entered the other world has not been closed up yet. It is essential that you should remember to keep your word. Else, you will have to follow Vali. With a single arrow of mine Vali was killed. If you disappoint me by forgetting your promise, you and all those who are dear to you will be killed by me. Sugriva, it is not too late. You are still dear to me. Time is passing quickly and I have waited long enough. Make haste.' Lakshmana, go to Kishkindha and act as my messenger."

Rama, the scion of the race of the sun, had become angry and Lakshmana who was already reputed for his short temper saw the anger of his brother and he was furious with Sugriva who had incensed his brother so much. Lakshmana said : "I am sure the king of the Vanaras will never follow the path of good people. He does not realise the truth that he owes all his present happiness to you. He will not enjoy this royal status for long. That is why his mind has turned away from the path of duty and righteousness. Rama, he does not deserve to be king. With his mind bemused, he has lost the power to think, drunk as he is with the pleasures of the body. Let him follow his brother Vali. My anger has reached the limit. I will kill Sugriva. Let Angada, the son of Vali, search for Sita."

Lakshmana took up his bow and strapped the quiver to his shoulder. Rama's anger had abated to an extent. He saw that Lakshmana's anger boded Sugriva no good. He said : "Lakshmana, I wish I had not expressed my anger to you. Do not do anything in a hurry. Be generous and give him a chance to justify the delay. Do not make up your mind to kill him until you are convinced that he deserves to die.

"He and I are friends and we made a Pact in the presence of fire that we would be friends for life : that we would share happiness and sorrow. Talk to him about that and tell him that my affection for him has not decreased at all. Do not repeat what I said in a fit of anger. Remind Sugriva gently about the passage of time and do not speak harshly to him. He may have some reason for the delay."

Lakshmana listened to the words of advice which Rama spoke and, after saluting his brother, he went fast towards Kishkindha. Lakshmana was angry. He had to obey his brother and so he told himself that he would give Sugriva a chance to vindicate himself. If he failed to do so, then he would not wait for Rama to string his bow and honour Sugriva with an arrow from that mighty bow. With these thoughts in mind Lakshmana walked towards the city where Sugriva ruled. His face had lost its soft and gentle look and his bows were knit in fury. He loved Rama and he could not bear to see him so unhappy. He had never seen Rama lose his poise and these four months in Prasravana had been hard for both of them. Lakshmana had spent hours on end trying to comfort Rama and had been asking him to wait till the seasons changed. He was certain that Sugriva would do the needful. But he had failed them and the accumulated anger of these four months had worked havoc in the mind of Lakshmana. Holding the bow firmly in his hand, the bow which gleamed like a rainbow with its gold and gems, he walked towards Kishkindha and his stride was shaking the earth. He passed many trees and peaks and with his feet he kicked the pebbles that were in his path and walked fast.

13. THE FURY OF LAKSHMANA

Situated between two peaks could be seen the city by name Kishkindha. The entrance to the city was through a cave and it was inaccessible to anyone, guarded as it was, by the Vanaras who had been posted at the mouth of the cave. Lakshmana saw these monkeys and his lips throbbed in anger when he thought of their master. The Vanaras saw him approaching and, ignorant as they were as to who he was, they made haste to defend the city by taking up trees in their hands and arming themselves with rocks which lay near at hand. The sight of the monkeys and their attempts to attack him, if need be, made Lakshmana doubly angry. Seeing his fury they became frightened and ran away from his presence. He looked like death at the end of the Yuga.

The monkeys hurried to the mansion of the king and announced to Sugriva the arrival of Lakshmana, and they told him about the extreme anger which sat on his brow. Sugriva was drunk and he was lost to the world in the embrace of Tara. He would not attach any importance to the words of the monkeys. The ministers of the king, realizing the danger that was threatening the city, led the army out to accost the intruder. Angada guarded the several entrances to the city.

Lakshmana saw the army marching out of the city gates. He was beside himself with fury. His eyes were now crimson with rage and he sighed when he thought of his brother languishing in the cave and the reception which he was getting at the gates of Kishkindha.

Angada came out of the city to meet him. He saw the angry face of Lakshmana and he thought that Lakshmana was like the king of serpents, Adishesha. The young prince was worried and afraid. He came and stood near the angry brother of Rama. Words would not come out of his lips since his tongue was cleaving to the roof of his mouth. Lakshmana looked at him and said : "Child, Angada, let my arrival be announced to Sugriva. Tell him : 'Rama's brother, the destroyer of enemies, is waiting at your door. He has come as an emissary from your friend Rama who is sunk in sorrow. If there is a shred of Dharma in your king, let him do what has to be done.' Child, Angada, repeat these words to your king and bring me back his reply."

Angada was scared out of his wits by the words of Lakshmana. He rushed to his uncle and told him : "Lakshmana is here." He face was pale and there was nothing but fear in it. He prostrated before Sugriva and his mother. He repeated the words of Lakshmana. The slothful king was still unaware of the danger which was threatening him. He was so drunk he could not open his eyes. The terrified noise made by the monkeys could be heard even inside the palace. Sugriva was roused out of his stupor by their shouting. His ministers who had been told about the arrival of Lakshmana came to the presence of Sugriva. They tried to make him realise the great threat to their security. After he had regained a semblance of wakefulness Sugriva was addressed by Hanuman : "My lord, the Kosala brothers, Rama and Lakshmana, are truthful and righteous. Your friendship was promised to them and they have helped you to regain this kingdom which you had lost. One of them, Lakshmana, the younger, is waiting at the city gate and he is holding his bow in his hand which is causing this panic in the army. Angada, our prince, has been sent to you with a message from Lakshmana reminding you of your duty. Lakshmana is extremely angry and he looks as though he will burn the world with his angry eyes. You should now go and pacify him. When Rama sends him to you it means that you should assure them that you will do the needful about the search for Sita."

Sugriva was wide awake now and he stood up from his couch. He spoke to them : " I have done nothing to offend them. I do not know why Lakshmana should come to me with anger in his eyes. He is finding fault with me when I am not in the wrong. Some enemy of mine has incited him, evidently. I am not afraid of this Lakshmana nor do I fear his brother Rama. I am only distressed that a friend should be angry with me. It is always easy to form a friendship. But to maintain the friendship is not easy. Because of the mind and its fickle nature, the slightest carelessness is apt to spoil friendship. That is why I am afraid. I know that I can never repay the benefit I have derived from Rama. I owe my everything to him."

Hanuman said : "It is but meet that you should speak thus and assure us that you have not forgotten what Rama has done for you. To oblige you he despatched to the city of Yama Vali, who was valiant like Indra. And now, without any obstacles in your path, you have ascended the throne.

"Rama is not seriously angry with you. It is just a slight displeasure he has expressed through his brother. I am sure of it. You have been, to an extent, careless and you have allowed time to lapse. You have not kept track of the seasons. The rainy months have gone and it is now the season Sharad which beautifies the forest with its fresh green look. The sky is rid of the dense clouds and the nights are bright with the stars and the planets which shine in an azure sky. The rivers are no longer filled with turbid water, but we see clearness in every water-spot, in every lake and every river. The time has come when you should remember the promise you made to Rama and that is the reason which brings the brother of Rama to your doorsteps now. Rama has been separated from his wife and he has been counting the days when the pangs of separation will come to an end. Pained in mind and heart he has sent Lakshmana to you. If the words of the messenger are slightly terse and sharp, please do not be offended by them. I feel that the only way to pacify Lakshmana is to go to him with folded palms and ask him for his pardon. I am your well-wisher and so I have made bold to talk to you so frankly so as to what you should do. It is my duty to save you from the wrath of a righteous man who has been sorely tried.

"Remember, my lord, if Rama should be really angry, if he should take the bow in his hand and string it, the three worlds will tremble and he can destroy them all. If Rama should change in his feelings towards you then nothing can save you or us. Please remember the debt you owe him and make certain that he does not give way to anger. You should not be indifferent to these valiant brothers from Ayodhya even in your thoughts. Rama has great affection for you and you should make every attempt to retain that affection."

Hanuman's words had the proper effect. Lakshmana was requested to enter the city and very humbly he was conducted inside Kishkindha. The doorkeepers saluted him with great respect and they were frightened to see the anger on his brow. He walked along the path which led to the mansion of the king. Soon he reached the doorway and he entered it like the sun entering a dark cloud. It was jealously guarded and no one tried to impede his progress.

Lakshmana entered the palace and passed several sections and terraces which were richly decorated. He reached the antahpura of Sugriva and paused at the doorway. Music could be heard from inside and the twanging of the strings of the Veena. Beautiful women were to be found everywhere. Unused as he was to the company of women, Lakshmana was feeling quite shy and embarrassed by them. The music, the sound of their anklets, and the fragrance which was all over the place, were making him feel uncomfortable. He could not bear it and to shut out the music of them, he twanged the bowstring. Lakshmana stood apart in a corner of the hall, not wishing to be part of the crowd of women.

14. LAKSHMANA IS PACIFIED

Sugriva heard the sound of the bow and he trembled. He rose up from his couch. He thought to himself: "Lakshmana has come as announced by Angada. I dare not face him and his anger." He turned to Tara and said: "Tara, Lakshmana is very gentle by nature and easily pacified. But his anger frightens me. Rama will never be angry without a cause. Why then has he sent Lakshmana who has come with such an angry look on his face? He seems to be prepared to destroy the entire city. What do you think of it? Tara, go to him and find out from him what has caused this displeasure in the brothers' hearts regarding me. Speak to him in such a way that his anger may be appeased. He will not be able to display his anger in your presence. Great people will never behave in a manner harmful to woman. I want you to go first and make him shed his rage. I will follow you and talk to him after a while."

Tara left his apartments and walked towards the hall where Lakshmana was waiting for Sugriva. Her gait was halting and her eyes were half closed with intoxication. Her clothes were all awry and with her body doubled up because of fear she went to Lakshmana with a desire to pacify him.

That noble-minded prince looked at the queen of the Vanara king and noticed the condition she was in, and he was trying to ignore her. He could not display his feelings in front of a woman and he bent down his head to avoid looking at her. Tara, however, went towards him and began to talk to him. Her words were bold, and they were spoken with a genuine attempt to make him quit his anger.

She said: "Welcome to you, prince. Tell me what is the cause for your anger? Who has displeased you to such an extent that your anger should blaze forth thus? Who has been foolish enough to touch fire which has been kindled in a forest abounding in dried trees?"

Lakshmana heard her placating words and without being affected by them he spoke courteously to her. He said: "You seem to be eager to do good to your husband and so you have come to me asking me why I am angry. I will tell you. Your husband is lost in the morass caused by indulgence in the pleasures of the senses and, as a consequence, he has lost count of Dharma, his duty. How is it you have not understood him properly? After he was crowned king he has forgotten all about us. And he seems to be lost to the world living only for his wine and women. Rama has not slept all these many months since he is suffering the pangs of separation.

"My brother set these four months as a time of respite for Sugriva after which he was to remember his promise to us. Instead of which he is lost in the world of pleasure. He has not realised that the four months have passed by long ago. This addiction to drinking has never been of help to anyone in winning the rewards of Dharma. It leads only to the loss of wealth, of Dharma, and of pleasure itself which is one of the result of Dharma. Ingratitude leads to the destruction of the best of men. Sugriva has, I feel, forgotten what Dharma is. A friend is one who does not forget to aid his friend by keeping his word given long ago. He should act according to the dictates of duty. Sugriva has forgotten both of them. When such is the case is it any wonder that Rama is incensed? Tell us what we should do now. We have been betrayed by one whom we considered as a friend."

Tara listened to his words and replied in a soft voice. Her manner was gentle and her words were chosen carefully. She said : "This is not the time for anger, O Prince! Sugriva is dear to you. Do not be angry with him. You must be tolerant and forgive his lapse. He is your devoted slave. A noble-minded person will never display his rage against one who is inferior to him in every way. Rama, the home of patience, should not indulge in this emotion. I can understand the impatience of your brother and I am also aware of the passing of time. I know the extent of his indebtedness to you. I am conscious of the task ahead, which Sugriva has undertaken to accomplish.

"Believe me, the power of Kama is great and it is not possible to control it. Sugriva has become a slave to Kama and so he has forgotten several things which he should have remembered. Your grace is not yet brought under the sway of Kama and so you cannot understand him or sympathise with him. A man who is a slave to his passions will not be aware of anything else. Forgive your friend for his apparent indifference. He has been guilty because of his weakness. Even rishis who have performed tapas have strayed from the path of Dharma because of this powerful Kama. Need I say anything about a mere monkey which is fickle by nature and who has been denied these pleasures for so many years?"

She paused for a while and continued : "Let me tell you that Sugriva has already taken the steps which are necessary for the accomplishment of his task. Hundreds and thousands of monkeys have been asked to be present in Kishkindha. They are coming from all over the world and very soon, they will set out on the quest for Sita. Pure as you are in your thinking and your conduct, it will not be any lack of decorum if you enter the antahpura of your friend. Be pleased to come with me."

Led by Tara and desirous of meeting Sugriva, Lakshmana followed her into the inner apartments of the king. Sugriva was there, seated on a golden couch covered with brocade. He was wearing many ornaments and he was surrounded by his women. Lakshmana's anger threatened to come to the surface again when he saw Sugriva with his arms round Ruma. Sugriva saw Lakshmana entering with Tara and he was scared. He was hoping that Tara had, to an extent, placated him. He rose up from his couch and came to Lakshmana who was a picture of wrath. He folded his palms together and stood silent.

Lakshmana said : "A king wins a good name if he is endowed with good qualities, with a heart full of compassion for others, with a heart full of gratefulness for favours received, and who is truthful. If, however, a king dares to be an Adharmi and forgets his promise to his friends, can there be a man more heinous than he? There are said to be *Prayashchittas* for all sins including the sin of killing a brahmin. But there is no redemption for an ungrateful soul. We are forced to conclude that you spoke an untruth when you promised to help us in our search for Sita. You are not worthy of respect. Rama kept his word but you have failed to do so. Rama's arrows are waiting to send you to the abode of death where you can join your brother. The gateway through which Vali entered it is not closed yet and if you so desire, there is still time for you to save yourself. Try and remember the friendship formed in the presence of fire and act accordingly."

Tara tried to talk once again and pacify Lakshmana. She said : "You have come to the wrong conclusion. He is not ungrateful nor is he a wicked and untruthful person. He does not, even for a moment, forget his debt of gratitude to Rama. As I told you before, he has forgotten himself in the many pleasures of the harem. Forgive him for this apparent lapse and show your nobility. Sugriva is not an Adharmi and you must believe it when I tell you so. For the sake of Rama he will give up everything, even the kingdom, me and Ruma. He is devoted to Rama. He will not rest until Rama is united with Sita. He has already made all arrangements for an immense army of monkeys to assemble here. They will be here any day now. It is the command of Sugriva and no one dares disobey him. Shed this anger."

Lakshmana realised that Tara was speaking the truth and he looked at Sugriva. His eyes were soft now and he had forgotten all his anger since she had told him that her lord was devoted to Rama. With a sigh of relief Sugriva shed the fear which had enveloped him as one discards wet clothes. He was sober and was completely awake.

He spoke words steeped in humility. He said : "Lakshmana, can I ever forget that all this is mine because of Rama? Is there anything which can repay the immense debt I owe to that great man? I will do what little I can to help him find his beloved queen and unite him with her. He does not need the assistance of anyone, not the hero who can pierce seven Sala trees with a single arrow, whose bow-string, when sounded, puts fear in the heart of the bravest of men. I will but follow Rama who will set out to kill the rakshasa who is his enemy. Because of the fact that he is my friend he will overlook a small fault in me. I am hopeful that he will be magnanimous enough to do so."

Lakshmana was very pleased with the apology tendered by Sugriva and with a pleased smile he said : "My brother has found a real companion in you. Your devotion to Dharma and your sincerity, your humility, have all endeared you to him. With you by his side Rama is certain to destroy the enemy. Your words are well spoken and they suit your noble nature. Only my brother is capable of speaking so beautifully. You are another who has mastered the art of talking well. You are a gift of the gods to us, to Rama who has, till now, been friendless. Come with me to Prasravana. You must comfort Rama who is extremely unhappy. I spoke so harshly to you because I have been with Rama during these four months of unhappiness and to see him suffer was unbearable. I spoke impulsively. Please forgive me for my impetuous words." Sugriva turned to Hanuman who was standing by his side and gave the orders for the collection of the army. He said : "As I have already said, the army would have begun its march towards Kishkindha. Vanaras from all the mountains like Vindhya, Haimavan, Mahendra and Kailasa and many other places have been asked by me to assemble here. Ask my messenger to hurry and collect the army. Fifteen days was the limit I had set and five days have already passed. They must be here in another ten days."

Even as he was speaking, some of the monkeys arrived and they came to him with fruits and gifts as their offering to the king. He accepted them gracefully and sent them to their homes. Lakshmana and Sugriva left for Prasravana. Sugriva called for his palanquin and entered it with Lakshmana. Accompanied by his guards the king made a triumphal march to the cave in Prasravana where Rama was. He descended from the palanquin and, with Lakshmana, he walked to the cave and went to the presence of Rama. He stood humbly before him, after prostrating on the ground. Rama raised him up and he embraced him warmly. He asked him to sit and the king sat on the ground at the feet of Rama.

Rama smiled indulgently at Sugriva and said : "Sugriva, a king should devote equal attention to Dharma, Artha and Kama. The king who forgets Dharma and Artha in his absorption with Kama is like a man who is sleeping at the tip of a tree branch and who falls as a consequence. He is rudely woken up from his stupor.

"I wanted to remind you of the rules of Dharma which a king should observe and that was the reason for the coming of Lakshmana to you. I hope you are thinking of the quest for Sita which you have promised me."

Sugriva spoke very humbly and said : "You are like a god to me, and it is not possible for me to forget that I owe my everything to you. I know only too well what a sinful person an ungrateful man is. I have asked for my Vanara army to assemble here in Kishkindha. Monkeys from all over the world have already been sent for. They will be here in a short while. They have begun to arrive and some have already come and seen me. Soon, very soon, the entire face of this hillside and my city will be full of monkeys.

"I will despatch them to the four quarters and make them seek for Sita and that sinful Ravana. They will find out the place where he has imprisoned her. You can be sure of it."

Rama was gratified at the perfection of the arrangements made by Sugriva and they waited for the army to assemble on the mountain by name Prasravana.

15. THE BEGINNING OF THE SEARCH

Ten days passed and the army had assembled and was ready to leave. Sugriva went to Rama and said: "Rama, my army is ready and I will send it in the four directions and ask them to look for Sita. They are all as eager as I am to serve you to the end of their lives. Command them to do your bidding." Rama was very happy with Sugriva and said: "My friend, let them find out where Ravana dwells and let them find out if Sita is alive. If they are able to get these two bits of information I will then decide as to what should be done later. In this connection, neither Lakshmana nor I have any right to command this immense army. You should do it. You are their master and you should ask them to do the needful. You are a friend and a wise man. You know how to act in every situation. You are the person to take care of everything."

Sugriva summoned a monkey chief by name Vinata and asked him to take a portion of the army with him and travel eastwards. He said: "Search for Sita in the caves and the slopes of the mountains. Travel across the forests, rivers and rivulets. Cross the rivers Ganga, Yamuna and Saraswati. Sindhu river will be in your path and Sona whose waters glisten like gems. Search for her in the countries which you come across." He gave them a detailed description of the countries which they had to traverse and he stipulated a month as the time limit. He said: "You must achieve your ends by the time the month is over. If you tarry longer you will have to face death. Come back with success crowning your efforts."

Sugriva decided to send Hanuman to the south and the leader of the deputation was Angada. The chosen few were in this group. Sugriva described the south in detail and then he summoned Sushena, the father of Tara. He told Rama who he was and added that Sushena, was one of his most able chiefs. Sugriva paid the respect due to him as the father of Tara and said: "Take a portion of the army and go in the westerly direction to search for Sita." He described in detail the several countries and mountains which had to be crossed and passed. Sushena left with his army. Shathabali, another capable chief, was asked to take his army towards the north.

After he had assigned their tasks to the different chiefs Sugriva asked Hanuman to listen to his special instructions. He said: "Hanuman, in my opinion, there is no one as capable as you are in doing my bidding. There is no place which is inaccessible to you. Nothing on the face of the earth, nor the sky with its myriad clouds nor all the seven seas can impede your progress. You know about the many spots on this earth and in the other world also.

"Your valour, your speed, which is very like that of your father, are all unequalled. I entrust to you the task of discovering the whereabouts of Sita. I consider you to be the ablest of my men and I am certain that you will be able to achieve our aim when the others fail." Sugriva added: "I feel that Sita is somewhere in the south since on that memorable day when she dropped the bundle of jewels on the Rishyamooka the rakshasa was travelling fast in that direction. I am sure he has imprisoned her there."

Rama was listening to the words of Sugriva. He felt that Hanuman would be the one to see Sita. Ever since the day Hanuman came to him on the slopes of Rishyamooka on that unforgettable day, Rama had been greatly impressed by the wisdom of Hanuman, his humility, his valour. Rama felt as though he had already achieved the purpose of this journey and he spoke with great affection: "Hanuman, I agree with your king and I feel that you will be the one to find my Sita." Rama removed his signet ring from his finger and said: "Take this with you and give it to Sita so that she will be convinced that you have been sent by me." Rama felt a deep sense of contentment which was absent from his mind all these days and he knew the Hanuman would bring him news of Sita. Hanuman received the ring with his palms cupped together and holding it above his head he prostrated before Rama.

Hanuman made preparations for the journey. He looked like the moon on a clear sky surrounded by a thousand stars. Rama's parting words were: "Hanuman, remember that I am depending entirely on you. Make every attempt until you succeed in locating the hiding place of Sita."

Sugriva asked the entire army to hurry towards achieving their goal. The army made up of the monkeys covered the earth like fireflies in the forest and they set out on their quest.

16. THE SOUTH-BOUND VANARAS

Before Sugriva left for Kishkindha after sending the armies, Rama asked him : "My friend, you seem to know all there is to know about the entire surface of the world. From your instructions to the different chiefs I could gather as much. How is it possible for you to have so much information about the different countries?"

"I will tell you," said Sugriva. "I have told you already about my brother and his anger when he saw that I was ruling the kingdom which was rightfully his. He tried to kill me. I ran away from him and he chased me. He made me flee down the caves and mountains and I ran while he followed. That was when I became familiar with all the many countries of the world. The entire world has been covered by me when I was pursued by Vali. My faithful ministers whom you met on Rishyamooka were the only companions I had. Hanuman, the wise, remembered the curse of Matanga and he told me about it. We had forgotten about it completely in our panic. Hanuman said : 'We can dwell in peace on the mountain and we will be safe from Vali since he dare not enter the surroundings of Matanga's ashrama.' This is the way I was able to learn all about the countries of the world."

Rama waited for the end of the month which had been stipulated by Sugriva. Prasravana was their dwelling place as before and Lakshmana tried in every way to help his brother to assume a semblance of cheer and they were hopeful about the future.

Vinata who had gone towards the east, Sushena who had been asked to cover the west, and Shathabali from the north searched in vain with their immense army for Sita and Ravana. At the termination of a month they came back to Kishkindha and told Sugriva about their fruitless search. They were dejected about it but they could not achieve their desire.

Sugriva was with Rama on the Prasravana hill. He spoke to Rama and said : "We are certain that Sita is somewhere in the south since we saw Ravana travelling in that direction when he was carrying her away. Hanuman, the son of Vayu, is sure to succeed where the others have failed. He will surely bring us news of Sita and of the place where she is kept as a captive."

Thara, one of the ministers of the king, was with Angada and Hanuman in the group sent to the south. They went to all the places which had been mentioned by Sugriva. The many caves in the great Vindhya mountains, the dense forests, the peaks of the hills, the many waterfalls and the slopes of the mountains were searched thoroughly by them. The place was extremely large and they found it a difficult task indeed to investigate every cave and every forest. There was no habitation at all in the forests and it was a fearful place. They abandoned forest after forest and with every step their depression increased. They came across several interesting places. One of them was a forest full of trees which had neither flowers nor fruits nor even leaves! There were rivers but not a drop of water could be found. No animals were there and no birds were heard singing. There were no creepers clinging to the trees and there was no grass even to soften the harsh look of the landscape. In the midst of it all was a rishi by name Kandu who lived there all alone. Where he was could be found some water and some ponds with flowers in them, some trees with greenery in them and fruits too. The story was that the rishi lost his son who was but sixteen years old and in anger he had cursed the forest to become lifeless.

Crossing all these places they proceeded further south, intent on their quest. All on a sudden they came across a rakshasa. He was huge like a mountain and he was fearful to look at. He was the son of Maricha and he came towards them with a terrible cry. Angada was certain that he was Ravana himself and there was a fight between the two. The young Vanara prince used his fist to beat the rakshasa and in a matter of moments Maricha's son was dead.

They realised that it was not Ravana and went on with their search. Cave after cave they entered and came out with disappointment writ on their faces. They were now completely without hope and, tired out, they gathered under a solitary tree and sat there dejectedly. After a while Angada said : "Do not be discouraged. We should not give up hope. Let us make another attempt. We are now nearing the end of the month during which we had to complete our search. If we go back without Sita we will be severely punished. Let us try once again. Let us set aside the hopelessness and the fatigue, which have crept into our minds and our bodies, and begin all over again. We must think of something which we might have overlooked in our initial enthusiasm. The wise say that firmness of mind under any circumstance and courage will lead to success. We should not despair since we have met only with failure so far. We should not abandon hope. We must remember the wrath of our king and with that in mind if we proceed further, who knows, we may succeed!"

They began their search again and the place they searched was a hill by name Rajata. It was silvery in colour and hence the name. They went to the very top of it and were not able to find any hiding place where Sita could have been concealed. They gave up the search in the mountain and returned to Vindhya. They reached the south-western peak of the mountain. They realised that the time had expired within which they had to return to the city of Sugriva. Desperately they tried once again. Some of them went once again into the caves and made one last attempt. But it was all in vain. They had become exhausted. They had reached a stage where thirst and hunger were torturing them. Tired out and listless they looked around desperately for a sight of water if not fruits. They came upon a cave which they had not seen before.

They looked at the opening of the cave. They tried to enter it but it was crowded with creepers and trees. They stood still and while they were disputing as to what they should do, they saw water-birds flying out of the mouth of the cave and their wings were still wet with water. And a strange perfume assailed their nostrils and they found that it was very pleasant. But to their chagrin, they were not able to enter the cave. Hunger made them desperate and Hanuman said : "We are tired and our search has been vain. This cave seems to have some water since the birds are coming out of it and they have drunk deep of water somewhere. These trees look luxuriant too and we will somehow penetrate into the cave." They decided to make an attempt to enter the cave which was called Rikshabila.

It was extremely dark inside and their eyes could see nothing. No sunlight could enter there and the darkness was palpable. Each monkey held on to the arm of the other and forming a long chain they felt their way inside and proceeded step by step. In spite of the difficulty they went on and they covered some distance in that oppressive darkness.

They suddenly came upon a brightness which was unearthly. They had traversed a yojana inside the cave and when they were desperate for water and for some hope, they saw light. They saw a celestial garden. No other word could describe it. Trees of all types were there. Some were bearing flowers and some, fruits. But these trees were golden in hue and obviously they were not of this earth. There were ponds which were filled with clear water which gleamed like clusters of gems. They saw mansions which were beautiful and lofty with white gleaming fronts and they were like silver castles. Amazed at the sight the Vanaras entered one of the mansions with noiseless steps. There was nothing but brightness everywhere. Gems and gold were to be found all around the place.

While they were wandering around the place they saw a woman. She was an ascetic and she was dressed in tree-bark and deerskin. They stood silent and stared at her without speaking a word. Hanuman was the first to recover himself and folding his palms together he greeted her and said : "We are in the dark as to where we are and we would like to know who you are and what this cave is. We were oppressed with hunger and thirst and we saw the water-birds emerging out of the mouth of the cave. Hoping to find some water we managed to traverse a distance of a yojana and finally we have come across this divine garden and we are perplexed. Whose tapas has wrought this miracle here? You must tell us as we are very curious."

The ascetic replied : "One of the asuras, Maya by name, created this garden with the help of his divine powers. He was the architect of the asuras. He had gained this knowledge by the favour of Brahma who gave him proficiency in architecture which has been the wealth of Ushanas. Maya lived here for a while. Because of a quarrel about a woman Indra killed him with his Vajra. The girl in question, Hema by name, was given these gardens and palaces as a gift by Brahma. I am the daughter of Merusavarni and my name is Swayamprabha. I have been appointed as the guardian of this garden. Hema is my good friend. Now tell me who you are and what reason has prompted you to enter this dreadful forest and this cave which is not meant to be seen by anyone? I will entertain you all lavishly with fruits and wine. Tell me who you are."

Angada led them all to where she indicated. They ate the divine fruits and their fatigue vanished. She plied them with water and wine and said : "Now that you have refreshed yourselves you must tell me about yourselves."

Again Hanuman took it upon himself to tell her everything about Rama and his misfortunes. He told her about the task which had been assigned to them and he concluded: "We have been entertained royally by you and if we can, in any manner, repay your hospitality please tell us and we will try to do it." She refused with a gracious smile and Hanuman asked her: "We have to go back to pursue our search for Sita. Please tell us how we can get out of this cave." Swayamprabha pondered for a while and said: "It is not usually possible for anyone to leave this cave once he has entered it. But, with the power of my Yoga, I will take you back to the world outside. You will have to close your eyes and you should not open them till I allow you to do so." They all closed their eyes with their hands and in a moment they found themselves outside the cave. Swayamprabha said: "There is the sea which is wide and fearful and on this side is the mountain. Take what course you will and I wish you well." She bade farewell to them and returned to her cave.

17. THE DESPAIR OF THE VANARAS

Angada and his followers found themselves on the shore of a sea. Swayamprabha had called it the 'Mahodadhi. They stood on the shore and watched the fearful waves as they dashed against the sandy shore. The limitless sea which was the abode of Varuna was so frightening and, at the same time, there was a majestic beauty about it and the monkeys stood for a long time watching the waves and listening to the roar of the sea.

They were greatly dejected. The month had passed and they had spent a long time in the cave of Swayamprabha without being aware of the world outside. They sat around and thought about the bleak future that awaited them. The trees around indicated that Vasanta would soon be on its way and they trembled at the thought of Sugriva and his wrath. They had achieved nothing and they had not been able to return to Kishkindha either.

Angada presided over the council and he said: "As you all know, we have been sent on this quest by the king. We have neither succeeded in our mission nor have we been able to confine ourselves to the time allotted to us. What are we to do now? You are all the trusted administrators of the king. You are greatly respected by him. It is a pity that I am not able to find a method by which we can circumvent Fate. Each one of you is a hero and you have all been chosen by the king to travel southwards since he was convinced that Sita is somewhere here. I have been asked to lead you all and I have failed in my duty: the duty which had been assigned to me. I am sure that death is the certain punishment for those who have not been able to follow the king's commands. As I said before, the time allotted to us is over and we are under the sentence of execution if we go back to Kishkindha. I know my king. He is of an unforgiving nature and, added to that, is the fact the that he is the master. He will never forgive us when we go back thus. I feel that there is only one way to end this strange adventure. Let us forget our city and our people and let us give up our lives by fasting to death. I would rather die here voluntarily than face punishment from Sugriva, the king. Let me tell you something else. I was not crowned Yuvaraja by Sugriva. Rama, the best among men, was the one who insisted on this. The king has no affection for me and when he gets the chance he is sure to kill me. He will take full advantage of the situation and punish me severely. There will be no one there to help me and my well-wishers will be surely looking on helplessly when I am punished. I have decided to avoid all that and shed my life here on the seashore."

The words spoken by the son of Vali melted the hearts of the Vanaras and they said : "We see that you are speaking wisely. As you say, our king is of an unforgiving nature and as for Rama, since he loves his wife to distraction, our return will cause him great disappointment. Our king, trying to please Rama, will certainly execute us. There is no doubt about it. It is unwise for a culprit to be in the presence of his master. We will try once again to find Sita and if we are successful we will be forgiven. Else, we will die here with our minds bent on the next world."

Thara, one of the leaders said : "It is not fitting that we should give way to despair and lose our lives. Let us go back to Rikshabila, the cave where we spent such a happy time. We will live there for ever. It has been fashioned by Maya and we have enough food there to last us for a lifetime. We can live without being afraid of the king. Why, even Indra or Rama cannot touch us there since it is a magic city."

The others looked at him and then at Angada as if to ask: "If you are agreeable, we would like that kind of life. We can live without fear of punishment."

Hanuman, however, was worried. He knew that Angada, the prince was a wonderful youngster endowed with rare qualities and he did not want him to despair. Angada was like the moon at the beginning of the brighter fortnight, a crescent with promises of becoming a full moon very soon. He was extremely brave and his wisdom was that of Brihaspati. He was like his father in his courage and valour and such a prince was now despondent enough to think of ending his life. Hanuman himself, who was wise beyond words, did not want the prince to adopt the line of least resistance by agreeing to the suggestion of Thara.

Of the four ways of influencing people, Sama, Dama, Bheda and Danda, Hanuman decided to use the third : Bheda. He said : "My dear child, you are as valiant as your father, if not more. You are as capable as your father was of ruling the kingdom. And yet, true to your nature, you are being too trustful. The minds of men, and specially those of monkeys, are well known for their fickleness. These comrades of ours may agree to your suggestion now, about living in the Rikshabila; but soon they will not like to be away from their wives and children. As for the army which we have brought with us, some of them will not be willing to follow the suggestion of Thara. And again, some of us are old faithful servants of Sugriva and nothing can make us disloyal to him. I wish to remind you, prince, that a weak opponent should never try to fight with an enemy who is stronger than himself. Do not listen to the words of Thara. The cave will not be a sanctuary to us. With a single arrow Lakshmana can destroy us along with the magic city. We were told by the ascetic that Indra's Vajra was used to destroy the owner of the cave. When Indra could do it, our Lakshmana will surely find it child's play to pulverise it. There is no doubt about it. When that situation arises all the monkeys will abandon you and run for their lives. You will be more lonely than a sprig tossed in the wind. Lakshmana will spare you out of kindness as far as your life is concerned but I am sure he will not leave you alone. If, however, you return to Kishkindha, we will all go to the king and pray for your life. We will beseech him to be merciful to you. He will be compassionate and he will crown you as king after him.

"You have not understood the true nature of our king. He is very righteous. He is affectionate and he is firm in his decisions and actions. He is a good man and he will never wish you ill. He is extremely fond of your mother and he will never hurt her. And again, he has no children and he has willingly agreed to make you the Yuvaraja. Come, let us go back to the city."

Angada was listening to the words of Hanuman and somehow they failed to convince him. "Hanuman is devoted to my uncle and so he speaks thus and he expects me to believe him", thought Angada to himself and said: "I do not agree with you. I do not credit him with all the noble qualities which you have enumerated. He is a very ordinary fickle-minded monkey, and he is selfish. He is not pure in mind and he is not compassionate. He is not straight nor is he manly or courageous. Consider how he has made his brother's wife to listen to his forcible words and has made her agree to be his wife. Early in his life he has betrayed his brother by closing up the opening of the cave inside which my father was fighting with his enemy. Can you call such a man righteous?

"Take, for instance, the search he has organised. It is known to all of us how he forgot everything about Rama and the debt he owned to Rama. In the presence of fire he had taken a solemn oath that he would do everything he could for Rama and what did he do? As soon as he got the kingdom, the king was lost in the pleasures of the harem and he forgot all about the promise he had given to Rama. It was only out of fear for Lakshmana and the twang of his bowstring that my worthy uncle woke up from his drunken sleep. He rushes to Rama and, out of sheer terror lest he should also be treated as his brother was, he sent us all in search of Sita. How can I have trust in such an ingrate? Perhaps he will spare my life for the sake of my mother but he is sure to imprison me and torture me. I am sure of it.

"I have made up my mind. I will not go back to Kishkindha. Let us sit here on the seashore and cast off our lives. If anyone is willing to join me, you are welcome to do so. As for me, I am prepared to do Prayopavesa here. If you wish to go back you can all go. Please go back and salute the Kosala princes first and then my uncle, the king. Tell them about me. Then tell Rama and after that, my mother, Tara. It is up to all of you to comfort her. She is very unfortunate. She will not be able to bear this news and perhaps she will die when she hears of my death."

Angada was now sobbing openly and the elders looked on with pity at the young prince. He spread darbha grass and wept as he did it. And with tears flowing from his eyes he lay down on it with his mind bent on death. All the monkeys cried with sorrow in their hearts. They all sat down too on the sand and decided to join the prince. They touched water with their hands and sat down to die.

They sat on the sands and they looked back on the many events which had led to their present sad condition. They spoke of Rama, of his exile to the forest, of the death of Dasaratha, of the travels of the princes with Sita in Dandaka, of their abode in Panchavati. They talked of the destruction of the rakshasas in Janasthana and of the abduction of Sita. They were relating to themselves the death of Jatayu, the killing of Vali, Rama's anger and all the many events which finally culminated in their end on the seashore. Their voices were carried by the wind and the story of Rama was echoed from the surroundings.

18. SAMPATI, THE OLD EAGLE

In a cave in the mountain nearby lived a great eagle by name Sampati. He was famed for his age, his early valour when he was a youth. Sampati was the brother of Jatayu. He saw from his cave the monkeys seated on the sands and he was happy. He came out of the cave and approached the monkeys. He told himself: "Instead of my seeking food with great difficulty it seems to me food has sought me out and has come within my reach without my striving for it. After a long period of starvation this food is doubly welcome." He thought he was talking to himself but because of his age he did not realise that he was talking loudly and Angada heard his words. He was sorely tried and he told Hanuman about the intention of the eagle. "Look, this is Yama himself who has assumed the form of an eagle. We are indeed unfortunate. Our quest was fruitless, we have wasted all our time and now this new danger is threatening the monkeys. What an unexpected misfortune!"

"All animals and birds loved Rama. Take, for instance, Jatayu. The sight of this eagle brings to my mind the other eagle, Jatayu. Rama did his duty as far as Jatayu was concerned. Jatayu cared not for his own life but tried to help Rama and in the process lost his life. Even so, we have tried to help Rama and we could not succeed in our attempt and in the process we are also about to lose our lives. Even so, we have the satisfaction of knowing that we have helped him. We are not as fortunate as Jatayu was, however, since he was fortunate enough to be killed by Ravana and he thus escaped the anger of Sugriva. When I try to trace the misfortune of our group to is source, it all goes back to Kaikeyi. It is because of her that all this happened."

Angada was talking disjointedly and the eagle was hearing all the words spoken by him. He could not follow it all and was bewildered by the many names which sprinkled the long narrative of someone named Rama. But he heard several times the name Jatayu and he was eager to hear about him. He called out in a powerful voice : "I want to know who it is who is talking about the death of Jatayu. Have I heard right? My mind is faltering at the news that Jatayu is dead. He is my dear brother. After aeons of time I am hearing the name of my brother spoken by someone. Will you tell me how he died? What is all this about the fight between him and a rakshasa? I am not able to move fast and I am on the slopes of the mountain. Will you help me descend to the ground? I am very happy to hear praises of my brother and want to hear more about him."

The monkeys were suspicious at the beginning. They were not willing to trust the eagle. But the noble-minded prince Angada came to where the eagle was, and spoke to him. He told him about his father and his uncle. He spoke about the coming of Rama and the change in the fortunes of many because of the exile of Rama. He spoke in detail about the eagle by name Jatayu, about how Rama met him in the Dandaka forest and about how valiantly he fought to rescue Sita from Ravana. Sampati told them who he was again and again and his eyes were shedding tears as he listened about his brother. He was told how Jatayu died and how Rama was the one to cremate him and despatch him to the land of the Pitris. The story continued and was brought up to the moment when he and his companions had to give up their quest in sheer despair. "It is as fruitless as searching for the sun's glory during the night," said Angada. Sampati was listening and now tears flowed without restraint from his old eyes.

He said : "My dear Vanaras, I am greatly grieved by the story I have heard. The eagle Jatayu who was killed by Ravana was my younger brother. I would have flown with eagerness to where Ravana is to avenge the death of my brother but I am helpless because of my old age and because I have lost my wings. That is why I am silently weeping for my brother without doing anything about it."

Sampati was sobbing with grief and the monkeys came, all of them, and stood around him, propelled by curiosity. He saw their eager faces and looking at Angada and the leaders like Hanuman he told them the story of his life.

"Long ago," he began. "Long ago, when the powerful Vritra was killed by Indra we were youngsters. We would vie with each other in everything and once we wanted to find out which of us could fly faster towards the sun who was bathed in his glory. We flew fast in the sky and higher still and higher we flew. When the sun had reached the zenith, my brother Jatayu became tired. He was faint with weariness and his tender body could not bear the heat of the sun. I rushed to his assistance and with my wings I covered him up and we descended downwards. I fell on this portion of the Vindhya peak with my wings scorched and broken. I could not move and I did not know what became of my brother : not until now." His sorrow broke out anew and the monkeys stood with their eyes shining with sympathy.

Angada said : "Revered sir, from the way you speak it seems to me you may know where Ravana dwells. You said : 'I would have flown with eagerness where Ravana is and I would have avenged the death of my brother.' Can you tell us where he is? You will be saving the lives of all of us if you do."

Sampati said : "I am an old eagle without his wings. And still I can help Rama with my words. I have seen many great events during my lifetime. I have seen all the three worlds and all the oceans. I have seen the Vamana Avatara of the Lord when he measured the three worlds with his blessed feet. I saw the ocean milked for the purpose of getting nectar out of it.

"I will, at once, help Rama. I am compelled to do so.

"Listen to me very carefully. I saw Sita as she was being carried away by Ravana. The wicked Ravana held her firmly in his arms and she was trying to wriggle out of his grasp. Her limbs were waving about frantically in her attempts to escape from him. Her jewels were falling on the ground and all the time she was calling out : "Rama! Rama! Lakshmana!"

Her yellow silk which draped her seemed to me like a flash of lightning against a dark cloud. Since you talk about Rama and since she spoke the same name, I am certain that it was Sita whom I saw. I will tell you where Ravana dwells. I know it."

A look of astonishment and a sudden flash of hope could be seen in the eyes of each and every one of the monkeys who stood around him. Sampati continued : "Ravana, the brother of Kubera and the son of Vishravas, rules the city by name Lanka. It is exactly a hundred yojanas from here and it is an island. It has the sea surrounding it on all sides. It was built for Ravana by Vishvakarma. It is a beautiful city. There, in that city, in the antahpura of Ravana, Sita is kept as a prisoner. Her heart is full of sorrow and she is surrounded by rakshasis and I can see her.

"On the southern shore of this sea is Lanka located. If you cross the hundred yojanas you will land in the city of Lanka. Ravana is there and Sita is his captive in Lanka. I am keen that you should set about your task as early as possible since I am eager to see the death of my brother avenged.

"I am an eagle by birth and I am related to Garuda. The eyesight of eagles like me is very keen and I can see from here cruel Ravana and gentle Sita. We are gifted with eyes which can scan a distance of a hundred yojanas since we are dependent on our eyes for our food. We can see our victims from a distance and pounce on them.

"Please think up ways of crossing the sea. I assure you that you will be successful in your quest for Sita.

"Lead me to the waters of the sea. I desire to offer Tarpana to my dead brother."

The monkeys were elated at the sudden change in their fortunes and with glad hearts they led the old eagle to the shores of the sea. After offering Tarpana to Jatayu he returned to his old spot and they sat around him to hear more. Sampati said : "I will tell you how I came to know about the incident. As I told you before, I have been living on this peak for thousands of years, helpless, and depending on others for my food. I have a son by name Suparshva and he tends me carefully, as he would a child. He brings me food regularly and so I live. I need not tell you that eagles are well-known for their insatiable hunger. One day, my son did not bring me food even when the sun had reached the western rim. I was waiting impatiently for my food and my son did not bring it to me. Later in the evening he came without any food for me. I was angry with him since hunger held me under its sway. He waited patiently for me to stop talking and then said: 'I went to the Mahendra hill with a view to bring you food and I was planning to capture several creatures after hunting there. I then saw a rakshasa who was dark and he was carrying in his arms a beautiful woman, as beautiful as the sun at dawn. Seeing me blocking the passage in the mountain he spoke to me in a very humble voice and asked me to make way for him. So I stood looking at him. He was not my enemy and I had no quarrel with him. Also, he was polite in his request. So I acceded to his request and he passed me by, and flew into the sky. I was curious as to who he was, and who the woman was, whom he had evidently captured. I was told by the Siddhas in the sky that he was Ravana. The woman's hair was now unfastened and desperately she was calling the names : Rama and Lakshmana. Her jewels and her silk were slipping down. I was told that she was the daughter of Janaka and the wife of Rama. Ravana was stealing her away from her lord and he was taking her to Lanka. This was a strange incident which delayed me near the foot at the hill and it was, by then, too late to catch anything for you.'"

"This was the story related to me by my son Suparshva. If I had been younger I would have rushed to the rescue of the unfortunate captive of Ravana. I now see that you are here set on helping Rama. All of you seem to be brave and very intelligent and I do not have to tell you much. Rama, with his brother, is capable of destroying or protecting the three worlds. I will only indicate to you that Ravana is powerful and it is up to you to find a way of entering the city Lanka and finding Sita.

"There was a rishi on this mountain and he was sorry for me. He has told me that I should not think of committing the sin of killing myself. He said : 'In the distant future, there is the certainty that you will get back your strength and your wings. You will help in the achievement of a great task.' He then told me about the coming of Rama and all the many things which you recounted to me. I was told that I would be telling you about the existence of Lanka and the captivity of Sita. I was told that I would sprout my wings and afterwards be my old self. I have been asked to wait for that moment." Even as he was talking, there happened a miracle. They all saw wings growing out of the old charred body of the eagle. His eyes grew brighter and his voice, more firm. Sampati looked at himself and was beside himself with joy. He became the eagle he was before the calamity happened to him. He spoke to them words of encouragement. He said : "Nothing is impossible for those who strive for it. Everything seems to indicate that you will succeed in your mission. I wish you well." Like all other young eagles Sampati rose in the sky and flew higher and higher until he was lost to their view. They looked at each other in wonder.

19. HOW TO CROSS THE SEA?

The monkeys were now filled with new hope and they had to plan as to how to cross the sea. They were jumping about in sheer joy and to them Sita was as good as seen and in their minds they returned to Kishkindha with the glad news. They descended from the spot where they were talking to Sampati and they arrived on the shores of the sea. They assembled there and stood watching the sea, mutely, since their shouts of joy had decreased gradually and had died altogether when they saw the vast expanse of the sea.

They looked and again they looked at the sea which seemed to have no shore on the southern side and a feeling akin to despair entered their hearts when they contemplated as to how it should be crossed. Huge waves were beating against the shore and each wave was bigger and more fierce than the earlier one. The sight of the majestic sea with its sonorous sound made them feel frightened and the sea seemed as difficult to cross as the sky.

Angada saw the panic which threatened to set in and he spoke words of encouragement to them. He said : "We should not give in to desperation and fear. Fear is the foremost of all evils. Like a snake is able to kill a child, fear which is lodged in the mind will make children of us and will destroy us. This is the time when one should display one's valour and it is not right to feel diffident now. We will achieve nothing by hesitation. Let us spend the night in peace and when day dawns, we will think up a way to surmount this poser."

Long after the army had slept Angada conferred with the chief members of his team and discussed their future plan of action.

Early in the morning he collected the army round him and spoke to them all. He said : "I wish to know which among you is capable of leaping across the sea and win the approbation of the king and Rama. Who is there among you who can leap a hundred yojanas? If it is done we can then be saved from the danger threatening our lives. We would have obeyed our king and we would have pleased Rama and his brother and thus relieved our king of the debt he owes to Rama. Come, let us know who are all willing to undertake this task which is stupendous."

No one spoke. Angada's voice was still echoing from the slopes of the hills and only the sea roared louder as if to mock him! He spoke again and again he got no reply. He then said : "I will ask you in a different way. Let each one announce how much he is capable of. The spirit of competition may whip up some enthusiasm in all of you."

There seemed to be a stir, a ripple of life in the still crowd and slowly they came out with their capability. Gaja said that he could leap a distance of ten yojanas and Gavaksha said he could do twenty. And so it went on : thirty, forty, fifty, sixty. Dvividha could jump up to seventy and another, eighty. Jambavan now broke his silence and said: "Once, when I was much younger, I was more brave and more valiant than can be thought of by the stretch of imagination. But those days are past and I have almost reached the opposite shore in this journey through life. But then, one cannot ignore the gravity of the task we have undertaken. Our king made a pact with Rama and we should all strive to make it true. At this stage of life I am able to leap only ninety yojanas. I have no doubt about it. Actually I do not know my powers now. In the days of the long ago, the Lord was seen by me when he assumed the form of Trivikrama. I had the privilege of making a Pradakshina round him. My strength was unparalleled and I had made a name for myself. But I am old now. I do not think I can negotiate this leap across the sea successfully."

Angada's face was grave and he was worried. What had seemed easy the previous day now seemed to pose problems which were new and it seemed to be an impossible task for them to cross the sea. He spoke words of comfort to the sorrowing Jambavan and then said: "I am sure of leaping this distance of a hundred yojanas. But I am not quite certain if I will be able to come back. I am doubtful about my strength lasting till I come back."

Jambavan said: "Child, Angada, I am certain that you will be able to leap this distance. Why, you are capable of doing more. You can, I know, cross even a thousand yojanas. But, my child, it is not proper that you should do this. You should not undertake such a task. You are our master and you are here to command us. It is not right that you should do it. We should not let you do our work. You are the only fort which is our refuge. The master is the refuge of the army. You should stay here and guard us even as the fort grants protection to those who have come inside it for succour. It is our duty to guard you at all costs. You are our prince. You are like the mother-root of a tree without which the tree cannot bear flowers and fruits. You are valiant, intelligent and brave. You are a model to us. You are the heir to the throne and now you are our master. We exist because of you and you should not risk your life."

Angada was quite embarrassed by the affectionate words spoken by Jambavan. He paused for a moment and said: "If I do not go, who else is there? This task has to be undertaken by someone. Or else we will have to go back to our original decision of Prayopavesha. Please consider the gravity of the situation and, wise as you are, you will be able to arrive at a solution."

Jambavan said: "I will do the needful, Angada, my prince. I will do my best and think of a way to achieve our end."

The entire army was standing still, aware of the crisis which had to be faced somehow. Jambavan went to Hanuman who was sitting alone, apart, lost in thought.

20. THE GREATNESS OF HANUMAN

Jambavan went to Hanuman and said: "Hanuman, why are you sitting thus, alone, silent and dejected? How is it you do not realise that you are as valiant as Sugriva the king, or Rama or Lakshmana? You must have heard of Garuda, the son of Vinata and Arishtanemi. He is famed for his strength, for the speed with which he can fly, for the beauty of his wings which has earned for him the name 'Suparna.' I have seen him fly in the sky, and suddenly swoop down into the sea and pick a water-snake in his beaks. I am telling you that the powerful wings of Garuda are not to be compared with the strength of your arms. Your strength, your wisdom, your valour, and your good nature are superior to those of everyone else in this entire world. Do you not know yourself?

"Your mother is the beautiful apsara who is born as Anjana. The god of wind saw her and desired her. When she was in his embrace she was told that she would be the mother of a glorious son. Vayu promised her that her son would be a very good person, extremely valiant and equal to himself in the power to travel or in leaping across any obstacle. That son is you. Once, when you were a child, you saw the sun who had risen newly and you thought it was a glorious fruit. You leaped up and rushed towards the sun. Three hundred yojanas were crossed and the heat of the sun was strong and yet you were undaunted. Indra was incensed at your valour which he mistook for insolence and he flung the Vajra at you. Your left cheek was slightly hurt by Vajra. That was when you got the name Hanuman. Your father was extremely displeased with the behaviour of Indra and, with a desire to punish him, Vayu refused to waft across the three worlds. The worlds were suffering and the gods finally pacified Vayu. Brahma granted you the boon that you will never meet your end by any weapon. Indra's anger changed to a great affection for you when he saw that his Vajra was powerless against you. He granted the boon that you can summon death to you as and when you desire. You are the son of Vayu and you are just as powerful.

"Hanuman, we are all on the brink of despair and it is up to you to save us. You are able to save us from death. You are our only hope. The entire army is waiting for you to display your valour and please be good enough to shed this weakness and rise up. Come, cross the sea and put life into the sad hearts of all of us. Do not delay. Show us the strength you have and take the leap to Ravana's city. Assume the form the Lord took when he measured the universe with his feet. Do not be indifferent any longer. Help us."

Hanuman heard the words of Jambavan and he stood up. There was a gleam of pride in his eyes when he thought that he would be able to help and he grew larger and larger in size and, even as he was growing, his face assumed a benign look. The army looked on and he had grown to immense proportions. He shook himself like a lion does, and with a deep growl, he prepared himself to cross the sea. The army was thrilled at the sight of Hanuman's gigantic figure standing on the seashore. The praises showered on him by Jambavan had made him extremely happy and still he kept on growing. He looked like an immense lion roaring in a cave of the mountain. He was glowing like a flame without smoke. He saluted the elders in the group and said : "Vayu, the friend of Agni, is very powerful. He cannot be confined in any manner and he pervades the universe. I am the son of that great Vayu and there is no one to equal me in the art of leaping. I am capable of going round the mountain Meru a thousand times. I can push the world with its mountains and forests into the sea with the strength of my arms. I can accompany the sun in his journey round the world from dawn to sunset. I can crash mountains with my bare hands and turn them to dust. I will travel in the sky and it will seem as though I am swallowing up the entire sky. I am Garuda and Vayu. I am yet to see one who is capable of following me in my course in the sky except these two. I will see Rama's queen and bring her back with me. I will cross the sea in a matter of moments. I feel that I will see Sita very soon. Like Garuda I will bring Amrita to the earth after fighting with Indra or even Brahma. I will bring the radiance from the moon and the glow of the sun. I will uproot Lanka and bring Ravana along with it and place him before Rama. My mind is made up. I will go now."

Amazed at the display of strength, the monkeys were jubilant as though they had already seen Sita. Jambavan said : 'Hanuman, a great tragedy has been averted because of you. All of us will pray that your task will be concluded with success. May you cross the sea without any mishap. We will be waiting here for your return. All our lives are in your hands."

Hanuman said : "The earth will not be able to bear the force when I take the leap into the sky. I will ascend this Mahendra mountain which is made of hard rocks. Its peaks are wide and firm. I will begin my journey from there. I have to leap a hundred yojanas and only the rocks of this mountain can bear the impact." Hanuman who was as powerful as Vayu ascended the mountain. His strides were so firm that the mountain seemed to reel under the weight. He had a set purpose in his mind and he was bent on working up a speed even as he began his journey. In his mind he was already in Lanka.

SUNDARA KANDA

1. THE MAGNIFICENT LEAP

Hanuman looked like a wild bull with his powerful neck stretched to the full and looking upwards. He was to achieve what no one had till then. He wandered about the mountain top with his powerful strides and he frightened all the animals there. The snakes and wild animals which had been dwelling in the mountain were startled and rushed out in panic as the mountain shuddered under him. Mahendra which was rich in minerals was of different hues. There seemed to be a carpet under the feet of Hanuman, a carpet woven of different colours, black and white, red, blue, yellow and the blush pink of the lotus. The mountain was also the home of yakshas and kinnaras. Elephants were roaming about in large numbers and Hanuman had disturbed them all from their places which had been secured till then.

He saluted the gods presiding over the quarters — Surya, Indra, Vayu and Brahma. He then turned to the east and he saluted his father, Vayu. With his mind he saluted the valiant brothers Rama and Lakshmana. He made obeisance to the seas and to the rivers.

Hanuman embraced his companions and made up his mind to set out on the memorable journey: the journey in quest of Sita who had been captured by Ravana. The monkeys wished him a safe return and Hanuman walked to the spot which was wide and open. He stood there facing the south. He had now grown enormous in size. He pressed hard on the mountain to gather momentum before he could take the leap. The mountain which is said to be firm in the midst of storms and tempests shook under the impact of his huge feet. The trees were all denuded of their flowers and the entire slope was a glorious sight since there was nothing but flowers covering them. The rocks cracked under his feet and smoke was seen to emanate from the cracks formed in the rocks. The animals were crying out in fear and the sound filled the four quarters. Serpents were spitting virulent poison and the rocks were burning because of the poisons. Even the rishis who were there were afraid to stay on the hill and they left it in a hurry as also the vidyadharas. They flew into the sky and stood watching the great Hanuman while he prepared himself to take the leap.

He shook himself and roared and it was like the rumbling of a thunder cloud. He swung his large tail in the air and the tail looked like an immense snake pulled by Garuda. He placed his two hands on the surface of the rock on which he stood. He shrunk his waist and folded his legs. He then thrust out his neck and so he stood poised for the flight into the air. He looked far and held his breath. He turned to the monkeys and said: "I will go straight to Lanka as an arrow which is released from the bow of Rama. If I do not find Sita there I will go to the heavens and look for her there. If she is not found even there I will return to Lanka and bring Ravana with me, bound hand and foot. I will somehow return with success. I may even uproot the city and bring it with me. I will succeed."

Hanuman was so confident that he had no doubt about his ability to find Sita. Thinking that he was Garuda himself the great Hanuman jumped up with great force. Because of the speed of his course the trees on the mountain were pulled up with their roots. With the flowering trees rushing along with him Hanuman entered the skies. The trees went with him some distance and it seemed as though they were well-wishers who went with him some distance to make the journey fruitful. The sea was now a mass of flowers from the trees which had fallen into it after accompanying the great Hanuman some distance. The sea was like the sky which is lit up by myriads of stars.

Hanuman coursed through the sky like a thunder cloud driven by the air. His arms were like twin snakes and it appeared as though he would drink the sky with his large mouth, and people from the celestial regions collected in the sky to see the magnificent sight. The very sea was in an uproar caused by the speed with which Hanuman was passing by. His shadow was cast on the waters of the sea and the shadow was ten yojanas in breadth and thirty yojanas in length. He seemed to be a mountain which was flying in the air during the days before Indra cut off their wings : only, this mountain had no wings.

He looked like the moon in a clouded sky as he plunged into the clusters of clouds which were trailing in the sky. Flowers rained on him from the heavens. Since the devas were eager to have success attending on the mission of Hanuman the sun did not hurt him with his scorching rays and Vayu caressed him with his soft breeze.

While he was thus storming through the air, the king of the oceans thought of honouring this messenger of Rama. He respected the kings of the race of Ikshvaku and he thought : "I owe my very existence to the

Sagara princes and this Hanuman is trying to help a scion of that race. I must provide a halting place for him. Having rested a while he can easily cover the remaining distance."

He called for the mountain Mainaka which was submerged in the sea. He said : "You are able to grow large or small. I ask you now to grow larger and larger. Hanuman is now flying in the air with a desire to reach Lanka. He is going on a mission to help Rama. You and I are indebted to his ancestors and it is but meet that we should remember it. You must rise up to the surface and provide a resting place for Hanuman. After he has refreshed himself let him go on with his journey." "So be it," said Mainaka and rose out of the sea. Its peak was golden and had earned for the mountain the name 'Hiranyanabha.' Like the sun newly rising out of the clouds the mountain rose out of the waters of the sea and stood up with its golden peak glowing golden in the light of the sun.

When Hanuman saw the mountain emerge thus out of the sea he thought that it was an obstacle in his path and with his immense chest he pushed the mountain aside. The soul of the hill took up a form and stood on the peak of the hill and said : "Noble Hanuman, we are admiring the stupendous task you have undertaken and the manner in which you are executing it. The lord of the seas asked me to rise up and provide a resting place for you. He has a great respect for the kings of the race of the sun. He wanted to help you and thus show his affection for Rama and you. Please relax on top of me for a while and you can go on after a pause. I owe a debt of gratitude to your father. He saved me from the Vajra of Indra by pushing me into the sea. Accept my hospitality."

Hanuman said : "I am touched by your affection for Rama and for me. You have entertained me with your words and that is enough. I am in a hurry and time is of the utmost importance. I must not tarry. I have taken an oath that I will not rest until I accomplish what I have undertaken. I will proceed on my journey and complete my task."

He took leave of the mountain with a smile and went on with his flight across the sea. He was soon high in the heavens and he was pursuing the path of his father. The devas who were watching Hanuman were trying to test if obstacles on the way would deter the course of Hanuman. They summoned Surasa, the mother of the serpents, and said : "Hanuman is trying to cross the sea with a desire to reach Lanka. We want you to assume the shape of a big rakshasi and bar his way. We wish to see how he will tackle this unforeseen situation and how he is going to circumvent it."

She did as she was bid and soon Hanuman found himself accosted by this fierce woman who stood in his path in the air. She said : "Happily I have found a prey for my hunger now. You are the gift of the gods to me, I think. Enter my mouth and be my food." Hanuman folded his palms together and said : "I am going on a vital mission. I cannot do what you ask me to. When I come back from my destination I will certainly oblige you and enter your mouth. Do not stand in my way." She refused him his plea and said : "This is a boon granted me by Brahma that no one can pass me by without first entering my mouth," and suiting the word to the action she opened her mouth very wide. Hanuman lost his patience and said : "Open your mouth as large as you can so that you can accommodate me." As her mouth grew larger he became bigger and larger too and when her mouth grew gradually to the size of hundred yojanas Hanuman contracted his body to the size of a thumb. He entered the mouth of the rakshasi and came out and it all happened within a matter of a moment. He resumed his original form and said : "Farewell to you. I have entered your mouth and I have come out. Your boon from Brahma is not false. Let me go now."

Surasa was pleased with him and said : "May your journey be fruitful. May you achieve your end."

Hanuman continued his journey in the air. He was flying high now. It was the path of the birds and it was full of rain drops. The rishis like Tumburu used the path and the devas would often frequent it. On that heavenly track Hanuman flew and his mind was set on one thing : to reach Ravana's city, Lanka, as soon as he could and to look for Sita, the queen of Rama.

There was a rakshasi by name Simhika who saw him pass by. She desired to eat him up. She grasped his shadow and pulled it towards her. Hanuman felt the pull and looked around to find out what was happening. He saw the dreadful form of Simhika rising out of the sea. He realised that this was the impediment in his path. He grew in size and she opened her mouth at once and it stretched from the waters to the skies. From where he was Hanuman could see into her mouth and, contracting himself suddenly, he leaped into her mouth like the sudden fall of Indra's Vajra. He killed her and quickly returned to where he was. Growing back to his old size he travelled as though nothing had happened. Like Garuda he flew straight and smooth.

He had covered most of the distance. The hundred yojanas had diminished now to a much smaller number. Hanuman cast his eyes around and he saw trees and forest which indicated that he was nearing land. He saw the gardens which grew on the mountain by name Malaya. He passed several small rivers and their tributaries and while nearly at the end of his journey he told himself: "This form of mine is too big. If I land thus in Lanka the rakshasas will be curious about me and it will not be possible for me to enter the city without being noticed." Hanuman made himself small and insignificant. He looked like a gnani who, having shed all Moha, could now realise the Atman. He was now almost a dwarf just three foot in height. He reached the opposite shore of the sea. He landed on the peak of a hill by name Lamba. From there he had the first glimpse of Lanka. Hanuman had crossed the sea which was a hundred yojanas wide and he had reached the other shore.

2. HANUMAN ENTERS LANKA

The impossible had been achieved and Hanuman was not even aware of his magnificent accomplishment. He stood on the peak of the hill on which he had landed and cast his eyes towards Lanka. It was situated on top of the hill by name Trikuta. He decided to get a closer view and he walked through the flowering trees and forests. The ground was soft and green covered with luscious grass and the perfume of flowers was borne by the passing breeze. He looked at Lanka and saw that it was surrounded on all sides by trees of every description. He went nearer and he could see the mansions which were glittering in the evening light. He also saw the guards to the city. Hanuman could see the wide and fearful moat which was surrounding the city on all sides. From where he was Hanuman could see the wide roads which were clean and white and he thought that Lanka would be just as beautiful as Amaravati, the city of Indra. Situated as it was, on top of a hill, the city gave the impression that it was floating in the air.

Hanuman was lost in thought as he walked slowly towards the city. He had reached the northern gates of Lanka and he saw the fierce rakshasa who were guarding it. Hanuman told himself: "The city is so well guarded that it will not be possible to enter it even if all the Vanaras are able to come here. Even the devas will not be able to conquer Lanka. Guarded as it is so well, even Rama, with his powerful arms, will find it hard to enter the city. Rakshasas are not amenable to reason nor will they be moved by soft speeches. All the tactics employed in warfare will be ineffectual in this case. As for the distance I have covered today, only four of my breed can manage it : Angada, the prince, Neela, my king Sugriva and myself. But let me not despair. I will first make sure if Sita is alive or dead. I will search for her first and then decide on my future course of action."

He was absorbed in thought for a while and he thought : "It is not possible for me to enter the city with this big form. The guards are only too alert and they are all strong and powerful. I must enter the city assuming a very small and insignificant size. I must deceive the guards and enter the city with a view to search for Sita."

For a while Hanuman was quite depressed since he did not know how to set about looking for her. "What method am I to adopt?" He asked himself. "Rama's aim should not be futile. How can I find Sita and will it be possible for me to see her alone and give her Rama's message? It has been said that even great tasks get destroyed like darkness before the sun if it is entrusted to one who is lacking in firmness and determination. Even if one is not able to discriminate between what should be done and what should not be, still, if a person is foolish enough to consider himself to be all-knowing, the enterprise will all go wrong. I am now wondering how I am to set about the task I have undertaken. I should act in such a way that nothing goes wrong. Nothing should be spoilt because of my action.

"If I am discovered by the guards then the crossing of the sea will be just a waste and the desire of Rama to kill Ravana will not be accomplished. Even if I don the guise of a rakshasa it will be foolish since they will surely see through my disguise. How can I get through with this body of a monkey? As for this city, even my father is not able to enter it without the permission of the king. If I am seen now it will be the end of me. And, what is more, Rama will have to go back to Ayodhya without Sita. Considering everything I will wait till nightfall and then decide what I should do. It is wise to stay here where I am till then. I will then make myself as small as possible and enter Lanka. The city will be asleep and I will not be seen by anyone. I can search for Sita then."

Hanuman sat on the peak of the hill and waited for the sun to set. When darkness fell, he roused himself and shrunk his body to the size of a small kitten. He went to the gates of Lanka and tried to enter it. He could see the glorious city from outside. It was like the city of gandharvas. Precious stones gleamed everywhere and pearls and corals were used on the pillars which held up the magnificent mansions which were innumerable. Impatiently he waited for the night to advance so that he could enter the city without drawing attention. The sun had set long ago and the moon, as though to help him in his search, appeared in the sky accompanied by myriads of stars. The moon looked just like a swan in a pond filled with lotuses and he was glad that the night had passed two *Jamas*.

Lanka was protected by a high wall and Hanuman hurried towards it. He stared spellbound at the beautiful city spread out like a piece of rich brocade. It only confirmed his earlier thought that the city was impenetrable by the strongest of forces. He considered his warriors and he could count on his fingers those powerful enough to attempt the task of penetrating into Lanka. Kumuda, Angada, Sushena, Mainda, Dvividha, Sugriva, Kusaparva, Jambavan, Ketumala and himself were the only possibilities. They were worthy enough to undertake the task. Rama and Lakshmana were there to be with them and what could a handful of them do against this formidable army?

Hanuman was trying to enter the city when the guardian of the city, a goddess, accosted him. She stood in front of him and asked him : "Who are you? You seem to be a monkey. Why have you come here? Tell me the truth or else you will lose your life. This Lanka is protected on all sides by the guards of Ravana and it is not possible for anyone to enter the city." Hanuman spoke very humbly and said : "I will tell you. But tell me who you are. You are trying to frighten me with your looks and your voice and with your words. Why do you stand at the gateway of the city?"

The goddess was furious with him. She said : "I am here to obey the commands of the rakshasa king Ravana. I am guarding the city and my name is Lankini. You cannot ignore me and enter the gates. I am going to kill you." Unruffled by the apparition which he did not expect, Hanuman said : "The beauty of this city is captivating. I wished to see the city entirely. I have come to see Lanka and its beauties."

She was not mollified by his gentle manner of speaking.

She said : "You stupid little monkey, unless you fight with me and vanquish me you cannot enter Lanka." Hanuman persisted and said : "I will just see the city and go away. I have not come to stay."

She would not listen to him. With her palm she took aim and hit him in the face. Hanuman was really angry now. He closed his eyes and tightened the fingers on his left hand and he hit her with his powerful fist. He did not display all his anger and all his strength since she was a woman. She fell down the moment she was hit.

Overcome with fright and pain and humiliation she said : "I have been vanquished by you. I am the guardian angel of this city. I will tell you about the boon which had been granted me by Brahma. He had told me that I would be invincible. 'But, when a monkey conquers you by his might, then you must realise that the end of the rakshasas has come,' were the words of Brahma. The time he spoke of has come. Because of Sita the end of the rakshasas headed by Ravana is drawing near. You are at liberty to enter Lanka. You can do what you wish to. I know that you have come in search of Sita. I will not stand in your way any more."

Lankini, the guardian angel of the city of Lanka, vanished from there and left the city for ever.

3. LANKA

Hanuman had got rid of the presiding deity of Lanka. He crossed the high wall which surrounded the city. He placed his left foot first when he landed in Lanka. That was the convention : to use the left foot while entering the house of an enemy or his country. Boldly he walked through the streets which were decorated with pearls and flowers. It was a beautiful city. The music made by the drums and bugles on the one hand and the tinkling of bells in the windows of the mansions on the other, was pleasing to the ear. It was well built with an eye to artistic perfection and wherever his eyes were cast Hanuman saw beauty and nothing but beauty. He was greatly impressed by the wealth of Ravana and the tastefully decorated city which was his. Hanuman jumped on to the terraces of the houses and went from one house to the next and each was different from the other. Music reached his ears from everywhere. The tinkle of the anklets, the rustle of silks and the slight noises made by the ornaments worn by the women could be heard everywhere. In between, could be heard the sonorous music made by the recital of the Vedas. He could see the section of Ravana's army which stood guard over the city during the night.

They were carrying weapons of all types and it was frightful to imagine the fate of an intruder if he were caught. Hanuman went from house to house, mansion to mansion, until he finally arrived at what he guessed to be the palace of Ravana, the lord of the land.

It was like a portion of heaven itself which had been placed on the earth for the pleasure of the king of rakshasas. The neighing of the horses, the impatient pawing of their hoofs on the ground, the music made by the instruments, greeted Hanuman who had become smaller than a kitten in size. He was not noticed and quietly he entered the antahpura of Ravana through the doorway which was exquisitely wrought with gold and inlaid with pearls, corals and gems. The scent of incense assailed him as he entered the palace.

The moon had reached the zenith now. He had spread his silvery radiance on the earth below and the sleeping city was bathed in moonlight. Hanuman stood for a moment contemplating the beauty of the moon. He looked like a swan captive in a silver cage : like a glorious lion in his cave on the Mandara mountain : like a warrior seated high on the back of a proud elephant. The moon was casting its rays on the earth, the moon whose beauty was like that of the Mandara mountain, like that of the ocean in the evenings, like the soft beauty of the lotus. The mist did not obscure him and he was shining with all his radiance.

Most of the inmates were under the influence of drugged sleep. They had, evidently, partaken of wine. Their abandon was amusing and, at the same time, pathetic. Many of them had their women by their sides and they seemed to be very beautiful. Hanuman scanned their faces eagerly and even though they were beautiful, all of them, not one of them was Sita. He knew that Sita was more beautiful than all of them and in his mind's eye he had created a picture of her in accordance with the description given by Rama. The women he was seeing now were not like her.

Hanuman went inside the palace of Ravana and he had to be careful not to be seen by anyone. The armed guards were like lions guarding a forest and into that domain entered Hanuman with careful steps.

To him, the palace seemed to be the ornament of the city of Lanka, so exquisitely was it constructed. His fear of being discovered was gone since he had come inside and he had reached the mansion of the king. The king's house was glowing like the sun because of the glow from the gems and gold which were to be found everywhere. The seats, couches, beds, and other articles were all inlaid with gold and set with gems. Ivory and sandalwood were used in making most of them. Hanuman was amazed at the prosperity which was evident from the houses he had visited and the luxury there. As he walked, Hanuman's eyes lighted on the Pushpaka vimana which, he had heard, had been brought by Ravana to Lanka after he had vanquished Kubera. Hanuman went from place to place and from antahpura to antahpura and looked in vain for Sita. All the wealth of Kubera was to be found in the city of Lanka and Hanuman wondered if it was heaven or a city of the gandharvas which he had been seeing all the while.

Hundreds and thousands of beautiful women were sleeping there and he scanned everyone of their faces and he was sure that Sita was not there. The women were all brought by Ravana during his many encounters with gandharvas, and nagas and kinnaras and every one of the women was in love with Ravana. There were some he had brought forcibly but they had succumbed to his charms in course of time. Hanuman was feeling sorry for Ravana who had so many women in his harem and who could have been happy with all of them. He had, instead, courted death by wanting the wife of Rama.

4. HANUMAN SEES MANDODARI

While he was wandering around, Hanuman's eyes rested on a cot made of crystal, ivory, sandal and gold. It was unbelievably beautiful and he stood for a long time savouring the beauty of the workmanship. On one side of it he could see a white umbrella and other insignia of royalty. He went closer and saw Ravana sleeping on the cot. He was dark like a rain cloud. Golden pendants adorned his ears. His arms were long and they were powerful looking. His garments were full of gold lace and the scent of the sandal paste which had been rubbed on his chest and his arms, filled the room. Like a sunset cloud which is streaked with lightning, Ravana was looking magnificent with the ornaments he was wearing. He was extremely good-looking and Hanuman went near him. He then withdrew a few steps as he would from a serpent which was hissing in anger. He looked again at Ravana from a distance. His huge arms lay prone on the white bed and they were mighty. His broad chest was partly covered by the spotless white silk and his breath was even and regular indicating that he was fast asleep. He saw the wives of the king also there. They were all beautiful and each was more beautiful than the other. They surrounded the king and they were fast asleep too.

As he was scanning their faces Hanuman saw a woman sleeping on a separate bed, apart from all of them. His curiosity was kindled. He went near her. She was wearing jewels made of pearls and gems. But her beauty was such that she needed no ornaments to enhance it. She was Mandodari, the queen of Ravana. Hanuman looked at her fair skin, her skin which was golden in hue, her unearthly beauty, and to him, it seemed as though Sita had been found. He clapped his shoulders with joy; kissed his tail, jumped around, ran hither and thither, and climbed the pillars and jumped down. His exuberance was unbearable and Hanuman decided that he had seen Sita.

After a while, however, Hanuman thought about it and he knew that he was in the wrong. He told himself : "That noble lady will not sleep, parted as she is from Rama. She will not eat and her mind will not be interested in wearing jewels or silken garments. She will not touch wine and, as for her being found in Ravana's harem, the very thought is sinful. This beautiful woman is someone else."

Hanuman wandered about in despondence all over the palace and he saw the kitchen and the storehouse of wine. Go where he would, he encountered hundreds of women and he was unhappy because he was looking for Sita and could not find her. He was also unhappy because it seemed to him that he should not be looking at women who were sleeping with so much abandon. He told himself: "It is a sin for me to cast my eyes on the wives of the rakshasa king. I have never once looked at women with lustful eyes." He pondered for a moment and told himself: "I am not moved by the sight of these women and my senses are unaffected. I have seen them in different positions and embarrassing poses but my mind is not dwelling on the sight of them at all. I can see that it is the mind which controls the senses and, for me, the mind is firm and so I have incurred no sin. And again, to look for a woman I have to search only in the midst of women. My mind is not involved and I am unaffected by the beauty of these women." He pursued his search and still Sita was not to be found. He came out of the palace and went again inside to search anew for her. He looked for her in the flowered arbours in the garden and in summer houses. She was not seen anywhere. He was now almost certain that Sita was not alive. He thought: "She is the symbol of chastity and, unable to bear the oppression of the rakshasa, she must have been terrified. She must have preferred to be dead. Or perhaps, Ravana killed her since she had refused his attentions. I have looked everywhere and she is not to be seen. I have failed in my mission. When I go back all the Vanaras will crowd round me and ask me: 'What did you do in Lanka? Tell us what you have achieved?' What am I to say to them? If I fail them they will all die as was decided earlier. They will censure me in their hearts and Angada with Jambavan will not respect me any more. I must not give in to this weakness in the mind. The only way to fight weakness is to stand firm and refuse to be oppressed by depression. It is this firmness which will make a man keep on trying until he succeeds. I will not let my mind lose its firmness. I will pursue the quest until I find her." He went in and out of thousands of mansions, large and small. He searched in the gardens and pleasure houses and in the arbours covered with creepers. In the palace of Ravana there was not an inch of ground which he had not covered and yet Sita could not be seen.

Hanuman was more and more convinced that Sita was dead. He thought: "Sampati told us in no uncertain terms that Sita is here. And yet, I have not found her. There is no place which I have left out. Perhaps, on the way, when Ravana brought her, she slipped from his grasp and fell down dead. Perhaps her heart stopped in sheer terror when she realised the dread fate which awaited her in the shape of Ravana. Horrified at the thought that Ravana had touched her with his filthy hands she has killed herself. Thinking on the charming face of her lord Rama she must have killed herself. Or perhaps she is a captive in some secret cell in Ravana's mansion and is bemoaning her fate. I do not know what I should do now. To go back and tell Rama this piece of news will be unwise and yet, to hold back the truth is also wrong. Wherever I look, there does not seem to be even a single ray of hope." Hanuman was sitting on top of a pillar and he was in the depths of despair.

He thought again : "I must think again and act. I should not go back without knowing the fate of Sita. If I go back with failure writ on my face my companions will be heart-broken. When I acquaint them and then my king and Rama that Sita could not be found what will they say?

"Rama will give up his life. He will not find anything worth living for once Sita is dead. With him will die Lakshmana. This will kill Bharata and also Shatrughna. With their sons dead how can the queen mothers live? They will be dead too. My king will be unhappy at his inability to keep his promise to Rama and that may make him give up his life. With him will Ruma die and Tara too. After the death of Tara, Angada will have no wish to live.

"Because of me so many deaths will take place. I must not allow it. I will not go back to Kishkindha without news of Sita. If I stay here they will live in hopes of some news and that will be better than my going back. I will vanish from here and adopt Sanyasa. I will go far away and throw myself into a blazing fire prepared by myself. Prayopavesa is a better way, perhaps, to cast away one's life. It has been sanctioned by the rishis. But they say it is a sin to kill oneself. I do not know what I should do. I will kill Ravana, irrespective of whether I find Sita or not. Or I will carry him and leave him in the presence of Rama. Let him avenge the death of his wife."

Hanuman was looking around all the time trying to see if he had left out any place which should have been searched.

Hanuman saw a garden at some distance. He said : "There seems to be an Ashokavana nearby and it is full of large trees. I have not looked for her there. I will do so now." Suddenly, some strange feeling of happiness was filling his heart and he felt that he might see her there. He invoked the eight Vasus, the eleven Rudras, the twelve Adityas, the seven Maruts, and with great humility he saluted them. With an effort of the will he suppressed the feelings of depression which had been, till then, crowding his mind. He first saluted Rama and Lakshmana and then Sita. He prayed to Indra, Yama, Vayu, the Sun and moon and he thought of his king Sugriva. He looked for the path which would lead to the Ashokavana. He felt that he might find success there. He went towards it.

He saw the vana and told himself : "This Ashokavana has to be searched now. Even the trees seem to be well cared for. The breeze is soft and gentle and I have decreased the size of my body to the utmost. May the gods be with me in this last attempt of mine. I am desperate. I hope to see the face of that noblest of women, the face as charming as the moon. She is the captive of the cruel rakshasa and it is imperative that I find her." Hanuman thought of Sita in his mind and with a leap ascended the high wall which surrounded the palace of Ravana. Standing on top of the wall he saw the garden and he could discern the many different trees which abounded there. Like an arrow which had been released from a bow he leaped straight towards the Ashokavana. He was there in no time.

It was a very beautiful garden and evidently it was the favourite place of the king since it was maintained with great care. Trees of all types, common trees and rare ones too, were growing there. Flowers of every description and birds of all kinds were there. Deer were there in plenty and other tame animals. Peacocks and koils could be found on the trees and Hanuman saw it all with wonderment. He had never seen the like of it before. The sleeping birds were disturbed by his entrance into the garden. They beat their wings in fear and the flowers on the trees fell to the ground. He seemed like a small hillock covered with flowers. He knew that the night was passing only too soon and he hurried with his search. Trees were shook and creepers were pulled apart. There was a small hill nearby and down the hill flowed a small rivulet. He saw several ponds filled with water which seemed to be cool and clear and lotuses were floating on the surfaces. The ponds had banks covered with white sand and the steps leading to them were carved exquisitely. The garden had been designed by Vishvakarma. He went on with his search. He came to the shade of a Shimshupa tree. Its branches were hanging low and it was surrounded by several creepers and under it was erected a small platform richly carved. Hanuman climbed on to the Shimshupa tree and decided to stay there. It concealed his small frame and from its top he could see quite far. Expecting to see Sita, Hanuman sat on the tree well concealed by the leaves and the branches. His eyes were trained to the ground and he was waiting for Sita to appear. He sat patiently waiting for the night to pass.

5. HANUMAN SEES SITA

Hanuman thought to himself : "Maybe, Sita who has her mind set on Rama and who is mourning this separation from him will come to this garden. This Ashokavana is beautiful. Perhaps Sita's steps will lead her towards this tree. I have been told by Rama that she is extremely fond of trees and flowering shrubs and waterfalls. This garden seems to be made just for her. She is sure to find a kind of comfort in these surroundings. This river has very sweet clear water and most probably Sita will come here to touch the water and worship the sun at dawn. If she is alive I am sure this is the place where she is, and I am certain that she will come to this river bank sooner or later."

The garden was like Indra's Nandana or Kubera's Chaitra. It was more beautiful than any heavenly garden. In the light of the moon the garden looked like the sky and the flowers were like the many stars which pierced the dark night with their bright rays. It was like Gandhamadana laden with intoxicating perfume which was heavenly. He cast his eyes around and nearby was a beautiful temple-like edifice. It had many white pillars which supported it and it was white like the Kailasa peak. The steps leading to it were of coral and the surface was covered with molten gold. The eyes were dazzled by the brilliance of the little temple.

Hanuman was intrigued by it and he looked closer. And then HE SAW HER. He saw a woman who was like the thin crescent at the beginning of the brighter fortnight. She was extremely thin and it was clear that she had been fasting endlessly. Sighs escaped her and several hideous-looking rakshasis surrounded her. She was beautiful and her beauty had been dimmed by her sorrow like fire is hidden by the clouds of smoke enveloping it. She was draped in a crumpled piece of silk, yellow in colour. Dust had found place all over her body and she seemed not to care for it. She had spurned all ornaments. She was white like a lotus stalk which had wilted. She had been grieving for long and she looked like the star Rohini which had been swallowed by Angaraka. Tears were flowing from her eyes and she was a picture of despair, this woman with the sad eyes. Thin and weak due to her incessant fasting she looked frightened, thoughtful and unhappy. Constant sorrow seemed to have worked havoc on her and, surrounded as she was by rakshasis, she could not find a single soul to take pity on her. She had been forcibly parted from her dear ones and like a deer in the midst of hounds, she looked helpless and lonely. Her hair was twisted into a single strand and like a black snake it trailed in her back. Meant only to be surrounded by luxury, this lovely woman had nothing but unhappiness as her constant companion. She had never known what it was to be unhappy till then and her large eyes were still trying to understand why she was made to suffer so.

Hanuman saw her and thought : "This is she. This is Sita who has been stolen from her husband by this low-minded rakshasa. She is all that I had imagined her to be. Her face is like the moon and her eyebrows are etched on her face. She is like a goddess who can make the surroundings glow with her radiance. Her hair is dark and her lips are red and full. Her eyes are like the petals of the lotus and this is Sita born on the sacrificial ground and discovered by her father. Dear to the entire world this beautiful woman is seated on the bare earth like a tapasvini. Her sighs are long and frequent. Her sorrow has dimmed her beauty : like a flame covered by smoke her radiance is hidden by her pain. She is the image of forlorn hope: like a desire which has been frustrated : like an unfulfilled task : like fame which has been lost as a consequence of false rumours. Because she cannot go to her Rama she is sunk in despair. This woman with eyes like those of a frightened deer is weak with fear and her eyes can only fill with tears which drop down constantly. She should be the ornament of a harem. She should wear jewels worthy of a queen and she is denuded of them. Pitiable indeed is she who is like the moon which is hidden behind a bank of clouds."

Hanuman was looking at her and thoughts chased each other in his mind and he was sorely distressed at the sight of Rama's queen. He recognised her with great difficulty since Rama had described a happy woman and this lady was a picture of woe. He was quite sure that he was looking at Sita. Rama had described several of her ornaments and he saw them all placed on the branches of the tree which was near her. Her silk which was now soiled and dusty was still yellow and he knew this was the golden yellow silk which Rama had described. He had seen a piece of it too which had held the jewels which she had thrown down at them at Rishyamooka. She had been forcibly parted from her lord but her mind was filled with his image and this was evident from her grief. This was the woman for whom Rama was pining away. Hanuman could see that she belonged only to Rama and he was all hers. No one else had any right to try and influence her, least of all, Ravana. Hanuman thought : "Rama is meant for Sita and she can belong to him and only him. This love is so strong that it has kept them both alive in spite of their terrible unbearable separation. Indeed Rama has achieved the impossible by being alive though he is away from her. It is not an easy task. Only he can do it. No one can live even a day after being parted from a woman like her."

Hanuman thought of Rama in his mind and he prostrated before him mentally and said : "Lord, I have found Sita."

Hanuman was overcome with sadness at the sight of the princess who was sorrowing for her lord who was so far away. He thought to himself : "Fate is indeed very powerful. I realise it when I see this chaste and pure woman wasting away with sorrow. She was protected by none other than Rama and his valiant brother Lakshmana. Suited to be the wife of Rama in every way, this noble lady is made to suffer by Fate. Because of his love for her, Rama killed Vali. Kabandha who was the equal of Ravana was killed. She was rescued earlier from Viradha by these great heroes. In Janasthana fourteen thousand rakshasas were killed because Shurpanakha threatened this wife of Rama. Khara, Dushana and Trishiras were despatched to the abode of Yama for her sake. It was to get her that Rama made Sugriva the king of Kishkindha. For her sake I crossed the deep sea and came to Lanka. I now feel that it will not be a surprising action if Rama should turn the entire universe upside down for her sake. Nothing in these three worlds can equal the glory that is Sita. She is the devoted wife of Rama. Such a woman is the captive of a rakshasa and she is surrounded by these dreadful women and she is not free even to weep. Because of her love for Rama, she gave up the comforts of the palace and walked with him in the Dandaka. She was happy and contented and such a woman is now drowned in sorrow. Rama will not rest until he gets her back. Alone, unloved, uncared for, she is keeping her life for the sake of Rama whom she hopes to meet sometime. She has no eyes for the beautiful garden where she is captive. Her eyes are with her heart and that is with Rama.

My mind is filled with sadness and anger when I see this unhappy woman. Patient as mother earth Sita who had been guarded by the noble princes is now under the watchful eyes of rakshasis. The season is Sharad and the moon must be making her long for Rama. The season is sure to accentuate her sorrow and anguish."

Hanuman was overcome with sorrow and pity for Sita and he leaned back on the branches of the Shimshupa tree and sat silent for a long while.

6. THE COMING OF RAVANA

The moon passed in procession attended by her starry retinue and the night came to an end. Dawn was heralding its approach. From a distance, borne by the breeze, came to Hanuman the recital of the Vedas. Ravana woke up early in the morning. The first thought which came to his mind after waking up was the thought of Sita. He was impelled by his love for her and he could not contain himself. Dressed in beautiful white silks and wearing ornaments which dispelled the darkness of the remaining night, Ravana hurried to the Ashokavana to have a glimpse of Sita. Like Indra is ever followed by a host of apsaras, there were, with Ravana, a crowd of beautiful women. Some brought torches to light the way for the emperor and others carried the chamaras and the other things which were meant to honour him. He walked purposeful towards the temple where Sita was seated.

Hanuman heard the commotion caused by his arrival. He saw the torches lighting the way for the king and he saw the many women and with them came Ravana. He was magnificent. To Hanuman he looked like Manmata, the god of love, who had not his bow with him. His garment was white as the froth on top of fresh milk and it was thrown carelessly across his shoulders. Hiding himself carefully behind the leaves of the tree Hanuman looked at Ravana.

Hanuman was watching Ravana carefully from the top of the Shimshupa tree. Ravana had been sleeping when Hanuman last saw him and his presence was felt by Hanuman. There was power, glory and greatness emanating from him and Hanuman was unable to resist the charm he exuded.

Ravana walked eagerly towards the spot where Sita was seated. Hearing the powerful strides approaching her Sita knew that Ravana had come and she trembled in fear and sheer terror. She tried to cover her thighs and breasts with her two hands and she sat shrinking into herself unable to bear the piercing looks of Ravana. She was like a forlorn branch of a tree, laden with flowers but cut off from the mother tree. She sat on the bare ground and she looked like a lotus stalk covered with mire. Ravana spoke to her words which expressed his love for her.

Ravana said : "Looking at me you cover yourself and try to hide your beauty from my eyes. Wherever my eyes light they see nothing but the beauty in you. You are so beautiful I am certain there is no one like you. Honour my love and accept me. Do not be afraid of me. You think that my action is unrighteous. But it is well within the code of rakshasas to take another man's wife as captive and even to force her to be his. Still, since my love for you is so intense, I do not wish to take you until you wish it yourself and on your own accord agree to become mine. Do not be afraid that I will force you. Trust me and try to love me. Do not persist in this sorrow. Your lovely hair is matted because of neglect. Your silk is dusty and soiled. You are killing yourself by starving thus and you are not meant to sit on the ground. The ground does not befit your tender beauty. Accept my love. Dress yourself in lovely silks. Wear jewels and perfume yourself with sandal paste and incense. There are so many couches for you to use and musicians are waiting to delight you with their art. Beautiful Sita, why is it you do not care for me and my attentions? Do you not know that youth is but short-lived and like water which has overflown, it will never come back? There is no one to equal you in beauty. Brahma must have given up the task of creation after making the perfect woman and that is you. Which man, after seeing you, will be able to think of anything else, even if it is Brahma Himself? Your face is as beautiful as the moon and my eyes cannot be satiated. Wherever I look my eyes are arrested there, whether it be your eyes, or your face, or your arms or your wide hips and your lips. Be my queen and you can rule over my entire antahpura. You will be my first queen and all the others will serve you as your handmaids. All the rare gems which I have collected from many places will be yours. I am a great warrior and there is no one to equal me. I have defeated the devas and the asuras again and again. Come, shed your grief and accept my love. Dress yourself in silks and gold and let my eyes feast themselves on you.

"This entire kingdom is yours to do what you will. You have seen me and my glory. Why do you still think of that Rama dressed as he is in tree-bark and deerskin? What can he give you? He has no wealth, no kingdom, nothing to speak of. He is wandering in the forest like a nomad and lying on the ground he devotes himself to the observance of Vratas. He will never be able to see you any more. You are like the moon hidden by dark clouds. He is unable to rescue you from my grasp. O Sita! What a beautiful woman you are! Lovely smile! Lovely teeth! Lovely eyes! You are made to fascinate and you have stolen my heart. Even in these soiled and dusty silk, with your sad eyes which refuse to look at me, I find that your attraction is such that I cannot, I am not able to, look at my other wives. Come to my antahpura and rule my other wives. My wives are all beautiful and they will serve you like the apsaras who wait on Lakshmi. The wealth which I snatched from Kubera will all be yours if you become mine. Rama is not equal to me either in wealth or in valour or in fame : not in his tapas or in his prowess. He is not capable of competing with me in anything. Come, make my kingdom yours and accept my love. Let us walk hand in hand in these gardens and being my queen you will be happier than you have ever been before."

Sita was distressed by the words of Ravana. She had been listening silently and with a tremor in her voice and with tears in her eyes Sita picked up a wisp of straw from the ground and dropping it before her she addressed it. It seemed to Ravana that she considered him to be as unimportant as that. She said : "Please give up this sinful thought. Go back to your people and leave me alone. You are not fit to have such thoughts about me. It is like a sinner aspiring to reach the heavens. I have been born in a noble House and I have been married into a noble House too and you are asking me to behave like a woman without morals."

Sita had turned her face away from him and tried to convince him about the wrong path he was pursuing. She said : "Listen to me. I am the wife of another man and it is not meant that you should think of me as your lawfully wedded wife. Protect the Dharma which has been handed down by the elders. Follow in their footsteps and get a good name. Even as you protect your wife from the lustful looks of strangers, even so you should behave towards me. You have so many beautiful women who have entered your harem willingly. Be contented with them. Without any forethought you are courting destruction. This act of yours does not bode any good for you. Have you no mentors in your court to tell you what is right and what is wrong? Have you, by any chance, been ignoring the righteous men? It seems to me it is so, since your behaviour is against all codes of Dharma. Or, perhaps, you have not listened to the words of the elders of your court. Because of the foolishness of the king, his land and his people will suffer. I can assure you this Lanka will soon be destroyed because of your sinfulness. You will be disliked so much that when you die men will not mourn you but, instead, they will rejoice over it. As for me, what you ask will never come to pass. Like the glow is part of the sun and cannot be taken away from it, even so, I am part of Rama and nothing can keep us apart. I have been his wife and you ask me to touch you after having grasped his hand!

"Even now it is not too late. Take me back to my husband and we will bless you and forgive you. Rama is a noble soul. He knows what Dharma is and it is well known that he is ever compassionate towards those who come to him for succour. If you cherish your life make friendship with my Rama. Ask him yourself to forgive you and restore me to him. Thus, and only thus can you avert the calamity which is threatening you. If Rama is angry then nothing can save you. Perhaps the Vajra hurled by Indra can be withdrawn or Yama may change his mind about the noose he has flung round the life he has planned to take. But Rama will not let you live. Soon you will be hearing the twang of his famed bow and it will strike terror in the hearts of all. His arrows spitting fire and poison will be aimed at you and all your men. The entire city will be covered by his arrows, golden, and fitted with the feathers of eagles. He will rescue me from you and he will punish you by killing you. You were a thief and you stole me from Janasthana when I was alone in the ashrama. If they had been present you would not have dared even to look at them. Even if you try to escape to the mountains in the realm of Kubera or in the deeps with Varuna or even with Indra in his sabha, you are doomed and cannot escape the wrath of Rama. I am warning you."

Ravana refused to be impressed by the words of Sita. He sneered at Rama and said: "It is my love for you which is holding the reins of my mind and stopping my anger from bursting forth. It has been said that love makes a man compassionate towards the object of his love. It is true. Or else, looking at you who still refuses to forget that powerless ascetic, I should let my anger get the better of me and kill you. You should be punished for every word you spoke but I have forgiven you since you happen to be loved by me and that to distraction."

He was furious and was trying to control his anger. After a pause he said: "I will give you two months to make up your mind. By then make sure that you accept my love. Or else, I will ask the cooks in the royal kitchen to cut you up into little bits and take you for my morning meal."

The women who had come with Ravana were feeling sorry for Sita. They did not dare to say anything but by their expressions they tried to comfort Sita and to show their sympathy. Sita was not frightened by the threats spoken by Ravana. She tried again to advise him against this unholy desire to make another man's wife respond to his advances. She was now more angry than before and she spoke harshly. She said: "I have warned you and yet you do not seem to realise that your death is imminent. How dare you ask me to be yours? I am the wife of the best of men. Only you will refuse to think so. Rama and I are inseparable like Indra and Shachi. Having entertained such thoughts in your mind do you think you can escape death at the hands of my lord? He is like a wild elephant which roams at will in the forest and you are like a crawling hare by his side. You have the courage, the audacity to call my Rama a powerless ascetic and yet you hope to escape death! You have set your eyes on me and I am surprised that they still have not lost the power to see. How can your tongue utter such foul words and still stay inside your mouth? Soon, very soon, you will be a handful of ashes. I could burn you up myself and because of the power of my Paativratya it is possible for me to do so. But, then, I am the slave of my husband and without his permission I cannot do anything on my own. You stole me from Rama and that was done by you since the Fates are against you, since you are doomed to die soon. Or else you would not have invited death. You call yourself a hero who has defeated the devas and Kubera : and yet, when Rama was lured away from my side you stole me and took me away by force. Is that the way a hero should behave? A hero indeed!"

Ravana's eyes were the colour of the dawn which was fast reddening the east. He looked at her for a long time. He was very angry and in a low voice he said : "Sita, you are foolish to persist in this love for a man who is full of Adharma, who has no wealth and who is a tapasvin. I am at the end of my patience. I am going to kill you now."

Ravana drew his sword from the scabbard and stood for a moment with his arms raised. He decided not to kill her and looking at the rakshasis around her he said : "Remember, you have to obey me, all of you. Try all the many methods to make this stubborn woman bend to my will. Talk to her, coax her, threaten her, do anything so long as you succeed in your attempts."

Dhanyamalini, one of the wives of Ravana, came there and she embraced Ravana with her arms around him. She spoke soft words to placate him and said : "Why do you waste your time with this Sita who is a human being? She cannot make up her mind and she is making you so unhappy. She is making you angry too. Come with me and forget her. Brahma has not ordained that she should have the good fortune of lying in your arms."

Ravana forgot his anger and he turned away from Sita to return to his palace. Ravana left her and there was a silence around Sita for a while. She sat with tears coursing down her face and to Hanuman she seemed to be the most unhappy woman on earth.

7. A RAY OF HOPE

The rakshasis began to harass Sita as commanded by their master. They spoke of the glory that was Ravana and tried to influence her. They spoke gently and then harshly and they then tried to threaten her. Nothing would move her. She said : "Nothing will make me falter in my love for Rama. There is no use in your talk. You can kill me if you wish to, but you cannot make me change my mind."

They persisted in their task and Hanuman was listening to everything. Sita was finding them too oppressive and wiping her eyes with her hands she stood up and walked towards an Ashoka tree which was very near the Shimshupa on which was seated Hanuman. The rakshasis were now shouting at her and they talked among themselves that they could easily kill her, cut her up and eat her. Sita was disgusted with them and, at the same time, she was desperately unhappy. She sobbed as though her heart would break. She told herself: "Death will not approach man or woman until the appointed time which Fate has decreed. Or else, how is it possible for me to be alive in the midst of these cruel and unfeeling rakshasis and in the palace of this sinner, parted from my beloved Rama?" Sita was trembling in every limb and it was pathetic to see her alone with her sorrow. She stood leaning against a branch of the tree and thought of Rama. She wailed: "Rama! Lakshmana! My beloved mothers in Ayodhya! I am caught here helpless like a boat tossed about in the stormy sea. The boat is about to sink. I am ready to die. But death has passed me by. I do not know where Rama is and I am still alive parted as I am from my lord who is like my very life to me. It is a wonder that I am able to live. I must have committed some great and dreadful sin in my previous birth and this suffering is a punishment for it." Sita's grief was painful for Hanuman to watch and still he sat quietly on the top of the Shimshupa tree.

When the rakshasis were debating about killing Sita, a wise and good rakshasa woman, Trijata by name, came to them and said: "Please do not talk like this. If you are hungry you can eat me up. Sita is divine and she should not be touched. I had a dream and I will relate it to you.

"I saw Rama wearing a garland of white flowers and he was wearing white silks. He was seated in a vimana which was made of ivory and the chariot was drawn by a number of swans. Sita was also wearing white and she was with Rama like the glow is united to the sun. Rama was seated on an elephant with four tusks and with him was Lakshmana. They came to Sita riding on an elephant. Sita was placed on the elephant by Rama and I saw them flying in the sky.

"The elephant came and halted before our city. Rama came in a chariot drawn by eight bulls. I then saw the entire world swallowed by Rama and it was a fearful sight. In the midst of the milky ocean could be seen a white mountain rising to the surface. On its top was the elephant and riding that elephant could be seen Rama, Lakshmana and Sita. I saw Rama in another place. He was sitting on a rich and costly couch and he was facing the east. He was being crowned by the rishis and the devas were worshipping him. This Sita was seated by his side dressed in pure white. To me Rama appeared to be Lord Narayana. He was the Parabrahman. The heavenly host was around him and divine music could be heard. I then saw Rama with Sita and his brother seated in the vimana by name Pushpaka and it travelled towards the north. I saw Ravana with oil smeared on his body, wearing red clothes and wearing a garland of Karavira flowers. He fell from the Pushpaka and he now wore black garments and he was being dragged by a woman. I saw him in a chariot drawn by donkeys and it was going towards the south. He was drinking oil and he was laughing loudly. Kumbhakarna too was seen by me sinking in a mire as Ravana did. The sons of the king were all seen by me. I saw Vibhishana with a white umbrella over his head and he was wearing rich silks. He was crowned and he went towards Rama seated on an elephant. I saw this city drowned in the sea. I also saw this Lanka which is dear to Ravana burnt by a monkey sent by Rama. According to what I have learnt about the language of dreams, I do understand my dream to mean that Rama will kill Ravana and all his men. Rama will take Sita with him. Do not talk harshly to her. Be gentle with her so that, later, when Rama takes her back, she will remember to be kind to you and not punish you for your ill-treatment."

Sita, in the meantime, was weeping to her heart's content. She had no more tears to shed and she thought that she would kill herself. She knew that it would be futile to look for a sword or poison in that dreadful place and, coming near the branch of the tree, she clung to it and said : "I will make a noose of this long hair of mine and hang from, this branch." She stood near the tree and thought of her short life which she had spent so happily and which was to have such a tragic end. And she paused since some good omens visited her all of a sudden.

Heart-broken, lonely and extremely unhappy, Sita had reached the limit of endurance and had decided to end her life. Good omens made her pause in surprise. Her beautiful left eye throbbed suddenly and it was the forerunner of good news. Her left shoulder which was leaning on the tree branch throbbed too and along with her shoulder, her left thigh. They indicated that good was in store for her and Sita stood as though she had been carved out of stone. She did not know how to understand the omens. Sunk as she was in the sea of despair how was it possible for anything good to happen to her? Like a seed, which had been left on the ground for a long time, suddenly sprouts tiny leaves, even so, into the desolate heart of Sita entered a ray of hope. There was a semblance of wonderment in her face and her tears did not fall any more.

Hanuman had heard the words of Trijata as she related her dream, He had seen all that was to be seen and he had heard enough to know how much Sita was suffering. He thought :

"I wonder what I should do now. I have seen Sita and I have managed to elude the eyes of the many who guard the city. I have seen the entire city and, to a certain extent, I know the strength of the fortress of Ravana. Now, my immediate duty is to comfort this noble woman who is ready to lay down her life because of her love for Rama. This princess, who has never before known what suffering is, has been immersed in a sea of unhappiness and I must hasten to comfort her with my words. If I go back without speaking these words to Sita, I am certain that no good will come of it. I must do it. I might go back to Rama and tell him that Sita is found. But, in the meantime, she may, out of despair, end her life. And, there is also this to be considered. Rama will not be satisfied with just the fact that I have seen Sita. I will have to tell him that I spoke to her and that I have been of some comfort to her. It is imperative that I should talk to her. How can it be done? I cannot tell her anything in the presence of the rakshasis who are guarding her so jealously. The sun has not risen yet and it seems to me she may kill herself before that. If Rama asks me : 'What message has Sita sent me?', what am I to tell him if I do not talk to her? I should not hurry back after taking so much trouble to arrive in Lanka. Rama will be greatly disappointed if I go back without seeing her. He may burn me with his looks. Sugriva's arrival with his immense army will be of no use if Sita should end her life before that.

"I should bide my time and wait for a proper occasion when I can talk to Sita. I must watch the guards and see if I can accomplish my desire when they are careless. I am a small monkey. I am sure they will think me harmless enough. I will talk to her in a manner which will be pleasing to the ear. If I should talk in a faultless manner, she may have doubts about whether I am genuine or not. She may think that I am Ravana disguised as a monkey. But there is no other way of accosting her. I only fear that this gentle woman who is so easily frightened will be all the more scared if she sees me or hears me. She may scream without knowing that she has done so and all my plans will go wrong. At once the rakshasis will be alerted, and again I would have failed. They will try to surround me and to catch me. I will be able to scare them and they will go to their king with the news that a stranger has entered the city. I will be rendered helpless then and Sita will be ignorant of me and my message from Rama. I fear that she will either be eaten by the devils around her or else she will kill herself. I can avert that only by talking to her. If I should be killed by the rakshasas the joint venture of Rama and Sugriva will never materialise. No one except me can cross the sea and no one will know about Sita unless I go back with the good news.

"What should I do now? I must act after great deliberation. Even tasks which seem to be easy are apt to go wrong and get spoilt if they are entrusted to one who is inefficient. I should make certain as to what should be done and what should be avoided. If I think I am very clever that arrogance is enough to ruin all the projects that have been thought up by us. My task has to be accomplished. I should use my power of thinking to the utmost. My leaping across the sea should not be a wasted effort. I must make her listen to my words. How am I to do it?"

Hanuman was pondering on the problem for a very long time until he came to a decision. He hit upon a method by which he could introduce himself to Sita without her being startled. He told himself : "I will recount the great qualities of Rama about whom she is thinking all the time. I will recite the glory of the House of the Ikshvakus and while I recite them, her interest will be kindled and slowly and very gradually, she will cast off her fear and have faith in me and my words."

The wise Hanuman thought that it was the best course to be adopted and began to act accordingly.

8. HANUMAN MEETS SITA

The branches of the Shimshupa tree, on which Hanuman was seated, were very near those of the Ashoka tree under which Sita was standing. All of a sudden she heard some words which she had never heard there before. Hanuman had begun his recital : "There was once a great king by name Dasaratha. He was a saint among kings and he was famed for his prowess and for his truthfulness. All the three worlds were aware of his might and his wealth. He was a Rajarshi and the king was like a rishi because of his tapas. He was born in the race of the sun and he was like Indra himself in glory. Kind to everyone, the king was very noble and very compassionate towards all. He was a great king and he was greatly honoured by men and gods alike.

"He had four sons, the eldest of whom is known by the name Rama. Rama was very dear to the king, Rama with a face resembling the moon in its charm. Rama is a great archer and he is the best among men. He is the protector of Dharma and of his people. He is the dread of his enemies. Devoted to truth, this Rama, at the behest of his aged father, this hero among men, went to the forest Dandaka to live there and he was accompanied by his wife and his brother. He donned the garb of a tapasvin and wandered in the Dandaka forest. Several rakshasas were killed by him during his wanderings. In the Janasthana he killed Khara, Dushana and Trishiras along with an army of fourteen thousand rakshasas. This he did single-handed.

"When he heard about the destruction of his Janasthana, Ravana arranged to lure Rama away from the ashrama by the help of the appearance of a magic deer. When the brothers were away Ravana entered the ashrama and carried away Sita, the beloved wife of Rama. When he saw that his wife had been stolen Rama wandered around in search of her and, during his wanderings, he made friends with a monkey king by name Sugriva. This friend promised Rama that he would help him in his search for Sita. In return, Rama promised to establish Sugriva on the throne of Kishkindha. Accordingly Rama killed the valiant Vali and gave his kingdom to his friend Sugriva. The monkeys are all servants of Sugriva and they have been sent in all the four directions to search for Sita. I am one of them. An eagle, Sampati by name, who is the brother of Jatayu, told me that Sita is in Lanka. I crossed the wide sea and landed in this city. Sita who has been described to me by Rama has been seen by me." Hanuman sat silent after this.

Sita was overcome with wonder and amazement at this strange happening. She did not know whether it was a vision or a waking dream. She held her long twist of hair in one hand and the other was still clinging to the branch of the tree. Her face was half concealed by her dark hair falling on her forehead and she raised it to look at the Shimshupa tree from which the strange voice was heard. There was astonishment in that face and also fear. Her thoughts, her words and her actions were all dedicated to Rama and she looked around in fear lest someone else had heard the words which were like nectar to her. She saw that the rakshasis had given her up as useless and some of them had gone to Ravana to tell him about the futility of their attempts and others had dozed off under the pillars of the temple where they stayed.

"May it be true." Sita told herself again and again and she searched the denseness of the tree for a sign of life. Hanuman, who was wise and far-seeing, was happy that he had thought of doing the right thing. He climbed to a branch which could be seen by her and Sita saw, on top of the Shimshupa tree, a small monkey clinging to the branch. He was wearing white and he was the colour of the bricks which were used for paving the walks in the garden. She was taken aback and she looked again with fear in her eyes. His eyes were the colour of liquid gold and he was small and very attractive. He was seated humbly on the tree and he seemed harmless. Still, doubts had assailed her mind and she considered the arrival of the monkey as an evil omen. To her his eyes seemed suddenly fearful and she lost all her courage and began to weep helplessly uttering the names of Rama and Lakshmana. She did not look at him again and thought it was all a dream. Hanuman knew exactly what her thoughts would be. She had been frightened at the sight of a monkey and, for a moment, her power of thinking had deserted her. She regained her power of thinking and told herself : "They say that it is an evil omen if a monkey appears in a dream. I can only pray that Rama with Lakshmana is well. I hope that no evil has befallen my father. But then, I wonder now if this is a dream. Suffering as I am because of this sorrow of separation from Rama and the captivity in the garden of this wicked rakshasa, it is not possible for me to have fallen asleep. Since it is not a dream it must be a delusion, a hallucination. I am always repeating Rama's name and thinking of the many happenings in our life together in the past and so it seems to me that someone else is repeating the story of Rama to me. It is not possible. It must be my mind which is deceiving me. What then of the monkey? I do see it and it is not a fabric of my imagination! I surrender myself to the gods. May Indra, Brihaspati, Brahma and Agni take pity on me and make the words of the monkey come true."

Hanuman thought that the proper time had come when he could appear before her without startling her. He descended from the tree and prostrated before her. He placed his two hands high above his head and began talking to her. He said: "Lady, I see you wearing a soiled yellow silk like the light of the sun. Your eyes are like the petals of the lotus. You seem to me to be perfect. Who may you be standing so forlorn, clinging to the branch of a tree? Like water drops spilling out of twin lotuses tears of pain seem to find a home in your eyes. Why? Are you a gandharva woman? Or a naga kanyaka or an asuri? A yaksha princess or a kinnari? You seem to me to be a divine woman. Are you the star Rohini, separated from her beloved moon? Your eyes are so beautiful, and they should not be sad. Who are your people? Why are you alone here? Since you are unhappy, since your feet are resting on the ground, since you sigh and weep, you cannot be a divine being. To my thinking, you are the queen of some kingdom.

"If, by chance, you are Sita who was brought here forcibly by Ravana, then please listen to me. It is evident that you are Rama's queen. Your beauty is far superior to that of ordinary mortals. Your appearance is that of a tapasvini. And your mind has become so filled with suffering that I can see it in your eyes. You are Sita. There is no doubt about it."

Sita heard the words of Hanuman and still clinging to the bough of the tree she spoke with a feeling of great elation and said: "I am the daughter-in-law of the famous king Dasaratha. I am the daughter of Janaka, the king of Videha. They call me Sita. I am the wife of the noble Rama. I was very happy in the mansion of Rama and I was a stranger to the word 'suffering.' The king decided to crown Rama as the Yuvaraja, but, when the preparations were being made Kaikeyi, the younger mother of Rama, asked for the throne to be given to her son Bharata and wished that Rama should be sent to the Dandaka for fourteen years. The king had to keep his word to her and Rama considered the word of his father to be more precious than all the kingdoms of the world and he agreed to go to the forest. He asked me to remain with his mother but I refused to do so. I could not live without him and decided to accompany him. Lakshmana, who is devoted to Rama, also wished to be with Rama and the three of us left the city Ayodhya that very day. We were happy in the forest and while we were in the Dandaka, I was carried away by the wicked rakshasa by name Ravana. I have lived in terror all these many months. I have been granted respite for two months more and after that I will give up my life. I am certain of that."

9. SITA HEARS ABOUT RAMA

Hanuman listened to the words spoken by Sita : words which were so piteous and tearful. He spoke in reply; "Devi, I have been sent here by Rama. I have brought you news of him. Rama is well and he asked me to find out how you are. Lakshmana is always with Rama and he is the only source of comfort to Rama who is grieving for you night and day. He sends his prostrations to you through me."

Thrilled with the words which spoke of Rama she said : "There is a proverb which says : 'If a man lives in hope, happiness will come his way sooner or later. Within the hundred years of a man's life it will surely happen.' This proverb has been proved true for me."

Hanuman and Sita spoke for a while about the person dear to both of them, Rama. Hanuman, when he saw that she began to trust him, went near her. Sita was suddenly doubtful about him. She thought that is was Ravana trying to deceive her. She was suddenly convinced that it was Ravana talking about Rama so that he could approach her. Her limbs failed her and she sat down abandoning the bough she had been clinging to. Hanuman knew that she had lost confidence in him. He prostrated before her and she would not look at him since she was terrified of him. After a while she turned her head and saw him still on the ground, prostrate. Regaining a semblance of courage she said : "If you are Ravana who is steeped in wickedness, if this is one of your many tricks then you are only making me more unhappy. You once assumed the garb of an ascetic in the Janasthana and deceived me. You have now donned the guise of a monkey and it is evident that you are Ravana. Have you no heart? Why do you torment me thus? Have I not suffered enough?"

Sita paused for a while and, with a puzzled look, said ; "Perhaps you are what you are, a messenger from my lord. Looking at you, my mind seems to find some peace. If you are really an emissary from Rama, I bless you. Tell me about Rama. In spite of myself I feel drawn towards you and you seem to be good. Tell me about my lord. Describe him to me. Tell me how he looks."

Torn between doubt and hope Sita was suffering and it was pathetic to see her. She finally decided that it was only Ravana who had come to her in the form of a monkey and she sat silent. Hanuman began to speak words which were meant to reassure her. He said : "Trust me, Devi, when I tell you that I have come from the presence of Rama. I will describe Rama to you. He is glorious like the sun and pleasing like the moon. Like Kubera he is the lord of all the worlds. His power is that of Narayana and his speech is truthful and gentle like that of Brihaspati. He is Manmata who has assumed a human form. He is the home of all that is noble and beautiful. He will be angry only if he must be. He is a terror to his enemies and he is the noblest of men. You will soon see punishment meted out to the villain who brought you away from Rama : stole you when you were alone in the ashrama. Rama will soon shoot arrows like tongues of flame at the sinful Ravana and rescue you. Believe me, I have been sent by him to find you. Rama is in the very depths of misery because of you. Lakshmana sends his pranams to you. The king of the Vanaras, Sugriva, who is the friend of Rama, also sent his prostrations to you through me. It is indeed fortunate that you have been found to be alive in the city of Ravana. Soon, very soon, you will see Rama and Lakshmana enter Lanka with a large army. I am the minister of Sugriva and I have been looking for you all these days. I crossed the sea and came here. My name is Hanuman. I have dared to enter the city of the enemy to see you and my mission is now fulfilled. Please do not mistrust me. I have been sent by Rama."

Sita was now certain that he had come from Rama. Pushing her sorrow aside she spoke eagerly to him and asked him : "When did you meet Rama? Where? How do you know Lakshmana? I am eager to know what happened to Rama after I had been carried away by Ravana. Talk to me about Rama and sorrow will not find a place in my mind. Describe Rama to me and Lakshmana too. I want to be certain that you know them."

Hanuman was only too happy to talk about Rama, his hero. He talked about the Kosala brothers and he related to her about their search for Sita and their coming to Rishyamooka. He described his first meeting with Rama and Lakshmana and about the friendship which was formed between Rama and Sugriva. He related to her about the jewels she had thrown and about their finding them; about Rama's grief which was inconsolable. Rama himself had admired the beautiful manner in which Hanuman talked. And now he made every effort to make his words convincing to Sita and she listened as if spellbound to his recital. He ended with the journey of a group of them towards the south. He said : "Devi, I am the minister of Sugriva and I have been chosen by my king and Rama to convey to you the message that they will soon be here and they will rescue you from Ravana by killing him. We were searching for you in vain on the slopes of the Vindhya mountains and we found that the time which had been stipulated by our king had been exceeded long ago. We were afraid to go back to Kishkindha and we made up our minds to sit on the sands bordering the rough sea and to end our lives by fasting. We were fortunate in finding a great eagle which was sitting in a cave in the mountain. He is the brother of Jatayu and, when we were talking about the death of Jatayu, he overheard us and came to us to find out who we were and how his brother had died. We told him and he, in return, told us about your being a captive in the house of Ravana. Our next problem was the width of the sea.

"The sea was a hundred yojanas wide and we were taken aback at the immense task facing us. I was chosen as the one capable of leaping across it and so I came here. I have spent the entire night in roaming all over the city of Lanka. I saw Ravana too in his sleep and I have seen you now. Please accept my words as the truth and recognise me as the messenger from Rama. The brothers are both well. It is my good fortune that crossing the sea has rewarded me with the sight of you. I will earn great fame because of this. Rama will be here soon and he will take you back with him. You can be sure of that."

Hanuman stood with his palms folded. Sita was convinced that he had come from Rama and her joy was great. Tears of happiness were in her eyes and her face was bright and happy like the full moon after it had been released by Rahu. Hanuman said : "Devi, I have told you all that you wanted to hear. Let your mind forget the agitations of all these months. I will take leave of you. Tell me what I should do."

Sita was not able to talk since her feelings were mixed. She was happy that Rama remembered her and she was sorry to hear about the sufferings of her beloved because of her. Hanuman said : "Rama has sent you the message that he is well and that he will come soon and rescue you. He has also sent his ring so that you will trust me. Please accept this and do not grieve any more."

Hanuman went near her and gave the signet ring of Rama to Sita. She took it in her hands and looked at it. Tears dripped from her eyes as she thought of Rama and to her he seemed very near now. She expressed her gratitude to Hanuman with words which revealed her joy. Her relief was great and there was a newly born hope of better days to come. She said: "Hanuman, you are a very noble and brave person or else how could you, single-handed, thwart the entire host of the rakshasas? It is a great feat which you have performed: crossing this sea which is a hundred yojanas wide. You are fearless and even Ravana and his fame do no seem to impress you. If Rama has so much of confidence in you that he should choose you as the one to convey his message to me, you must certainly be out of the ordinary. I am happy to know that my lord with his brother is well. These two heroes are great enough to mete out punishment even to the devas. How is it, my Rama has not burnt up the entire world and the seas surrounding it with his anger? Possibly my sorrows have to be suffered by me and that is why he has refrained from it. I am happy that distance has not dimmed his love for me. I am certain that he will come to my rescue and take me with him. Very soon I will see Ravana and all his kinsmen dead on the ground and the city of Lanka will be devastated because of the anger of Rama. He has suffered a lot. Banished from the kingdom, he walked about in all the forests and all the while he had to protect me. All those years we spent without fear, without worries and finally, this calamity overtook both of us. I hope he has not lost heart. As for me, not my father, nor my mother, nor any one else is as dear to me as Rama and that is the reason why I am still able to live."

Hanuman said: "If Rama had known where you are, you would have been returned to him long ago. It was essential for him to discover where Ravana had concealed you. As soon as I go back I will tell him all about you and about Lanka. Then Rama, accompanied by an immense army of monkeys and bears, will proceed towards Lanka. Not devas nor asuras can keep him back nor can they obstruct the course of his deadly arrows. Devi, Rama is very unhappy without you by his side. He is living in a cave on a hill by name Prasravana. Rama does not eat properly nor does he sleep. He does not care for the comforts of the body and he is ever lost in thought. He is indifferent to his surroundings and to the people around him. If at any time he gives in to sleep out of sheer exhaustion, he wakes up soon with your name on his lips. If his eyes light on anything which is pleasing he calls out your name and his sorrow is renewed and he is inconsolable."

Sita was thrilled that Rama thought of her all the time and that he thought of nothing else. At the same time she was sad to know that he was so unhappy that he was neglecting himself. She was silent for a while and Hanuman waited for her to talk. She said : "Your words make me happy and unhappy too. When I hear that he thinks of nothing else I am pleased and to think that he is unhappy makes me unhappy too. It is the result of one's actions in a past life which ties a man down and controls his actions. The extreme wealth and happiness of a man or the unbearable sorrow he suffers are all the wages he pays for something good or bad he has done in his previous birth. Fate is something which no one can escape. Take for example, Rama, Lakshmana and me. Rama has to reach the other shore of this immense sea of sorrow and he is like a broken boat which is fighting a futile battle against the elements. He has to destroy the rakshasa army and their king and then take me back.

"Time, again, is against us. I am allowed to stay alive only for two months more. This is the tenth month since I have been brought to this prison. Ravana has a brother by name Vibhishana and he has tried to advise his brother that I should be returned to Rama. But his words are of no avail. Ravana, who has been singled out by death, is waiting for Yama and so words of advice do not seem to please his ears. This was told me by a daughter of the brother of Ravana, and her name is Anala. I am certain that Rama will come to Lanka and punish this sinner. I know Rama's power and it will be like a game for him to destroy the rakshasa host and take me back with him. Misfortunes will not be able to overcome Rama. Rama is beyond the ken of such things."

Hanuman could not bear to think of Sita in the Ashokavana for a duration of another two months. He said : "Devi, Rama will soon be here as I told you with the army of monkeys. If you so desire, I will rescue you now, at once, from Ravana. Please allow me to carry you on my back and I will cross the sea with you. I am capable of lifting this entire city and carrying it on my back. Like Agni, the god of fire, carries the Havis to Indra I will take you to Prasravana hill and leave you with Rama. You can reach him now and he will be pleased. Like Chandra is united to Rohini, like Indra with Indrani, like the Sun with Suvarchala, you will be united to Rama. No one in this city is capable of following me when I fly across the sea. I will return to the other shore of the sea as easily as I came here. I am able to do it. Please consider my suggestion for what it is worth."

Sita was touched with the words of Hanuman. She said with a slight smile of amusement : "Hanuman, I am afraid your natural instincts have made you think of the impossible. You are so small and how will it be possible for you to carry me and to restore me to Rama? How could you be so impulsive?" Hanuman thought to himself : "Sita does not know the peculiarity of my natural instincts and my power. I should let her know that I can assume any shape I will." He grew in size and standing at a distance from her he let her see how large and powerful he could become. He was as huge as Meru. Sita's eyes were large with wonder.

Hanuman said : "Devi, I can assume any size I please. It was because I wanted to enter the city unnoticed that I made myself smaller than a kitten. I can carry Lanka with all its inmates, its mansions and gardens without any effort. Have no fear about it. I will take you to Rama."

Sita spoke to him in a gentle voice and said : "I have seen now what a powerful person you are. I realise today your stature, your speed like that of your father and your radiance is equal only to that of Agni. Only you could have crossed the sea so easily. No one else on this earth is capable of this, I know. I see that you can easily take me and leave me in the presence of Rama. But, Hanuman, we should think of every aspect of the situation. I do not think it will be possible for me to go with you. The speed with which you travel may, most probably, make me feel uneasy and I may lose consciousness. Perhaps, when you fly higher and higher, up in the sky, I may feel frightened and slip off your back and fall into the sea. Also, there is a likelihood of your having extra responsibility because of me. You will be pursued by rakshasas when Ravana comes to know of it and you will have to fight with them as well as protect me. At the same time, you will also have to pursue your journey. Both of us may incur danger because of this thoughtless action. If I should fall off your back and be caught by the rakshasas that will become unbearable for me. I would rather die than try to escape, fall, and be caught again.

"Apart from all these, there is this to be considered : and that is, it will not be a credit to Rama if I should be rescued by you. And again, for a woman like me, it is not possible even to think of the touch of a stranger. I belong to Rama and I cannot willingly touch another person. Ravana did touch me, it is true, but that was forced on me and I did not willingly let myself be carried by him. I was helpless in his grasp. I could do nothing.

"The proper thing will be for Rama to come and, after killing Ravana, to take me back. These rakshasas are sure to find it futile to fight with Rama and he will be the death of them. Rama will be like fire fed by the passing breeze and there will be no one brave enough to stand before him and give him fight. He will be like the sun during the end of the world and who can withstand his radiance? Hanuman, go back to Rama and bring the brothers and your king with the army. Let there be a fight and my sorrow will be at an end."

Hanuman was very happy to hear the words of Sita. "Devi," he said. "Your words are spoken like a true chaste woman. It befits your womanliness and your purity that you should think thus. Your argument against being touched by anyone other than your lord is commendable and I salute you for it. I will go at once to Rama and tell him about you : about the duration of two months within which time he should come to your aid. As for my suggestion that I should take you with me, it was born of my immense devotion to Rama and a desire to make you happy. Your unhappy captivity had added to my distress and so I thought of it. I am ready to go back to Rama. I am impatient to go. Have you any words with which I can assure him that I have seen you?" Hanuman stood eagerly waiting for her to speak.

10. SITA'S MESSAGE TO RAMA

Sita spoke and there were tears in her eyes. Her voice was indistinct since she was overcome with sorrow. She said : "Hanuman, I will ask you to repeat what I have said to Rama. "Lord, on the hill Chitrakuta, there was a spot near the banks of the river Mandakini. Fruits and flowers were growing in abundance there and near the ashrama you were reclining on my lap. A crow came to our presence then. He was bent on eating flesh and he pierced me with his sharp beak. I took a pebble and threw it at the crow. But that crow would not leave me. He kept pecking at me and hovering round me. As I was trying to get rid of it you woke up from your sleep and saw my upper cloth slipping down. You looked at my angry face and saw that a crow had made me angry. You made fun of me. I was feeling very shy about the whole incident.

'You took me on your lap and pacified me. My eyes were filled with tears and you saw that I was extremely angry with the crow. I slept on and later, again you slept on my lap.

'The crow came back from nowhere. It came near me and it pecked at my breast and scratched it. This happened again and again. The drops of blood fell on you and you woke up. You saw what had happened. You said: Who did this to you? Who has the courage, the foolishness, to play with a five-headed serpent? Your eyes were looking around and they sighted the crow and its claws which were stained with blood. The crow was the son of Indra. And, fast as the wind, it vanished out of sight. Your eyes were crimson with anger and you pulled out a blade of grass from the darbha seat which was near and invoked the Brahmastra.

'A ball of fire pursued the crow and followed it wherever it went. The crow went to all the three worlds and neither the rishis nor his father Indra could do anything for him. He came back to you and fell at your feet in despair.

'Though he deserved to die you let him escape alive. You said : "Brahmastra should not go waste. Tell me what I should do." After thinking for a moment he said : "Let my right eye be sacrificed for it." After losing the eye the crow fell at your feet and went back to its abode.

'Rama, for killing a mere crow you invoked an astra as fierce as the Brahmastra. How then can you be patient with one who has stolen me and kept me captive? Have mercy on me and save me. You are famed as the sole refuge of those who are in trouble and you should justify your name. You are a great hero and yet you have not killed this rakshasa with your astras. Why? There is no one to defy you in all the three worlds.' Hanuman, why has he been forgetful of me? Why has he not done anything about it? Why are the brothers so indifferent towards me? If, in spite of their prowess, they are not able to comfort me, it is because of some terrible sins I have committed in my previous births. There is no doubt about it." Hanuman saw her weeping openly and said : "Devi, I swear in the name of truth that Rama is not indifferent to your fate. The brothers are sunk in woe thinking of you. The fates have been kind and I have been able to locate where you have been imprisoned. I will go back and tell Rama everything about Ravana and Lanka.

"Soon he will be here. Your misfortune will be at an end. The city will be turned to ashes and Ravana will be dead very soon. Please shed this unhappiness."

Sita said : "Convey to Rama my prostrations. Give my blessings to Lakshmana, that noble soul who, I think, is far more precious than all the jewels on the face of the earth. He gave up the comforts of the palace, of the royal city, gave up his father and his mother, and followed Rama to the forest since he is devoted to Rama and only to him. He considers me as his mother and to him Rama is the father. He serves us like a son. Unfortunately Lakshmana was not in the ashrama when Ravana carried me away. He is very powerful and easily incensed and no one can withstand his anger. If there is anyone capable of serving Rama better than me, his wife, it is Lakshmana. He is efficient, and he is like a dear friend to Rama. Please convey my blessings to him. Hanuman, you are responsible to arrange everything in such a way that my sorrow is ended early. Tell Rama these words of mine : 'I promise you, Rama, I will stay alive for a month more and not a day longer. You must come soon and take me away from this Ravana.'"

Sita wiped her eyes and she unwrapped the end of her mantle. Out of it she took out her Choodamani, the jewel worn in the hair. She gave it to Hanuman and said : "Give this to Rama." Hanuman accepted it with reverence and, after making Pradakshina to her, he stood with his palms together. He had already reached the presence of Rama in his mind. He was very happy that he had achieved what he had set out to do, and he was thrilled at the thought that he was carrying the jewel from Sita's hair to Rama. Sita spoke again and said : "Rama knows this jewel particularly well. As soon as he sees it he will be reminded of three people : me, my mother and his father, Dasaratha. Once again let me tell you that everything depends on your sagacity. My very life depends on you."

Hanuman bent his head as if to say : "I am fully aware of it." Again and again Sita spoke of Rama and asked Hanuman to convey her pranams to him. Hanuman listened to all her injunctions and comforted her. He told her that Rama would soon be coming to Lanka. Sita said : "Do you have to go back today? Why should you not tarry here for a day longer? Your presence is like a balm to my bruised heart and it is a comfort to hear you talk about Rama. I know that you are going back only to come back soon with Rama, but I am not sure if I will be alive then. Again, I will feel very unhappy once you have left me and gone away. I want to ask you something else. Tell me, how will it be possible for the brothers Rama and Lakshmana with the army of monkeys and bears to come to Lanka? How can they cross the sea? As far as I know, only three people can do it : Vayu, Garuda and now, you. You are extremely powerful and capable and so you could achieve the impossible. But how will it be possible for the others to do what you have done? I am worried about it."

Hanuman realised her diffidence and said : "Devi, the Vanaras who serve the king are all strong and capable. Led by our lord Sugriva, they can achieve miracles. You can be sure of that. Nothing can stop their progress. They have travelled over the entire world with its mountains and rivers. In the army of the king there are many who are my equals and there are those who are far superior to me. Only ordinary men are sent as emissaries and I am but an ordinary server of the king. When even I could manage this crossing of the ocean, need I say anything about the others? You can rest assured that there will be no difficulty about it. As for Rama and Lakshmana, they will be carried on the shoulders of your humble servant and like the sun and the moon they will traverse the sky seated on my back. Please possess your soul in patience for a while and do not give way to despair. Rama will come and there will be an end to your misery."

Sita was unwilling to let him go. She said : "Hanuman, your coming has been the greatest good fortune to me. It is like the rain falling on a field which has its sprouts half-grown. Remind Rama of another event known only to him and me. Once, when we were alone, my *tilaka* had become obliterated. Rama, in a playful mood, took the dust of the stone by name Manasila, and placed the *tilaka* on my cheek. Remind him of that.

"How is Rama able to bear this separation from me? This jewel was a source of comfort to me during the days of pain since it reminded me of those who are dear to me. I have sent it to Rama so that he will now be comforted at the sight of it."

Sita wiped the tears which were flowing incessantly now and Hanuman comforted her with suitable words of cheer. She was unwilling to let him go but she knew that it was dangerous for him and for her to be found together by the rakshasas. Hanuman was happy with the course of events and his mind was turned towards the north, his destination.

11. DESTRUCTION OF THE ASHOKAVANA

Hanuman had taken leave of Sita and was getting ready to leave. He prostrated before her and left her presence. After going some distance he told himself: "I have seen Sita and I have spoken to her. But it seems to me there is something still left undone. I should not go back without letting my presence being known. I should become aggressive and make the rakshasas see my prowess. I should let them realise the power of the army which they will have to face later. A really efficient man is one who does more than what he is expected to do. I was asked to find out Sita's hiding place, to give the ring to her and to assure her that Rama will surely come and rescue her. But then, I should try to collect some information. I must use several methods by which this can be achieved. I must find out about the strength of the army of Ravana and if I go back armed with all the information which I can gather, it will be of great advantage to us later. How am I going to make the rakshasas fight with me? It is essential that I should try to make it come to pass since Ravana will have to get acquainted with our power. I must manoeuvre things in such a way that I can see Ravana and to hear from his lips his views on the matter on hand. I will then go back gladly to Kishkindha.

"This garden which is being tended with special care is, evidently, the favourite garden of the rakshasa king. That Sita has been kept captive here is, in itself, proof that this is a favourite garden of Ravana. I will set about destroying the garden methodically like fire destroys a heap of dried wood. When he hears about it Ravana will become very angry. He will despatch a big army to kill me or to capture me. I will destroy the army easily and that will frighten the rakshasa and their king."

To think was to act and Hanuman began to destroy the Ashokavana. Trees were broken as though they were twigs and creepers were pulled out, tanks were stirred up with so much vigour that the waters spilled over and turned muddy. The small hillocks which beautified the garden were reduced to powder and the beloved garden of Ravana was desolate with the dead trees and the flowering shrubs strewn on the ground. Running all over the garden Hanuman made short work of it and there was nothing left of the Ashokavana and its beauty. He then climbed to the top of the entrance and he sat there waiting for things to happen.

He did not have long to wait. There was a great commotion caused by the havoc wrought by Hanuman. The birds and the beasts which had been living at the garden were screeching and howling piteously and it struck terror into the hearts of the citizens of Lanka. The rakshasis who had slept off when Hanuman met Sita now woke up from their drunken stupor and they saw the author of the mischief. He grew in size and even the rakshasis were frightened to see him. They were vaguely aware that they had seen Sita talking to a monkey. They accosted Sita and asked her: "Who is this? Where has he come from? Why has he come? Tell us everything. We have a vague feeling that we saw you talking to him. What was it about? Is it true that he spoke to you? Tell us the truth. Do not be afraid to tell us. We will not harm you. We want to know who he is." Sita said : "I have nothing to do with him since I think he is a rakshasa who can assume what shape he will. It is up to you to find out about this one. Only a snake will know about the passage of another snake. You can be sure of that. I feel that this is a rakshasa who can take up any guise as he will. I do not know him and I am just as afraid of him as you are."

The rakshasis were not convinced by her words. They rushed to the presence of Ravana and told him everything. They described the actions of the monkey. They told him that they were certain about the monkey talking to Sita though she denied it. They said : "We saw that they were talking. Evidently Sita does not want to betray him and so she is refusing to admit that he spoke to her. Is he a messenger from Kubera? From Indra? Or perhaps he has been sent by Rama to find out all about Sita. But my lord, all that apart, the monkey has not left a single tree alive in your garden. The spot where Sita was seated, however, has been left unharmed. The Shimshupa tree under which she sits is unharmed. It is a fierce-looking monkey and it should be punished. Should you not put to death one who has dared to talk to Sita?"

Ravana was furious when he heard about the fate of his garden. His eyes filled with tears because he loved the Ashokavana. He sent some of his strong rakshasas to subdue the monkey. Eighty thousand rakshasas were sent to fight with the monkey. Hanuman was delighted since he was waiting for just such a happening. The army surrounded him on all sides and tried to beat him up. Hanuman grew in size and very soon he was frighteningly huge. He struck his great shoulders with his palms and the sound was like thunder reverberating in the sky. He shouted : "Rama with his brother Lakshmana is with his friend Sugriva and victory to him. I am Hanuman, the son of Vayu, and I am the slave of Rama. Not a thousand Ravanas are capable of withstanding me and my prowess. I will return only after making Lanka shed tears of frustration."

His war cry was frightful and the rakshasas attacked him all together. Hanuman pulled out a pillar which was supporting the gateway and with it he beat up the host of rakshasas and he killed every one of them. News reached Ravana that the entire army had been destroyed. He could not believe it.

He sent the son of Prahastha, one of his ministers, and with him went a large army. Hanuman pulled down the very beautiful hall by name Chaitya and waited for the next consignment of rakshasas. The guardians of the hall which he had destroyed were on him and it was a matter of moments before they were crushed to death. Again and again he would shout out that he was a messenger from Rama and that Sugriva was waiting to assist Rama in his march towards Lanka.

Jambumali, the son of Prahastha, came to fight with Hanuman. He was handsome, young and arrogant and he was also a good fighter. Hanuman was greatly excited at the thought of fighting with this youngster. His arrows were lodged in the body of Hanuman and a great fight ensued between the two. The stones which were flung at him by Hanuman were broken up by Jambumali with the help of his arrows. After fighting for a while Hanuman revolved the pillar which he held in his hand and after twirling it fast he flung it against the chest of the young fighter. Jambumali was killed and there was great confusion in the army when this happened. The army was also destroyed and when he heard about it Ravana sent another army with the sons of his ministers to lead it. The noise of their march was like the rumbling of rain clouds and they encountered the lone monkey with a very casual attitude. They were punished soon for it and the river of blood was flowing in the streets of Lanka. Not one was left of the third consignment of warriors which Ravana had sent under the leadership of the sons of his ministers. Ravana's anger was mounting.

He now sent five of his army chiefs and they led another army to fight with Hanuman and they suffered the same fate. Hanuman was enjoying himself immensely and he was announcing that there were thousands of monkeys just as powerful as he was, or even more powerful than himself in the army of Sugriva and that they would be coming to Lanka accompanied by Rama and Lakshmana.

Ravana was taken aback at the reports of the valour of this lone monkey who had strayed into his city. He decided to send his son Aksha. This son was very dear to Ravana and he looked with affection at his son, the young man who had dressed himself up for battle. He had a beautiful bow in his hand and he looked like the first tongue of flame leaping out of the fire fed with Havis by the brahmins who worshipped the fire. He was wearing an armour of gold and, glowing like the sun, he ascended the chariot and proceeded towards the place where Hanuman was waiting. He went near him and looked with admiration at the great monkey which was waiting for the next group of rakshasas to accost him. Aksha gauged the valour of Hanuman and he thought of his own ability. It was a terrible encounter between the two. The earth quaked and the sun did not shine as he was wont to do. The wind stopped blowing, the mountains trembled and the sky resounded with the noise. The sea was brimming over and it was fearful to watch the fight between Hanuman and Aksha. Hanuman was greatly impressed by the manner in which the young prince fought. He told himself: "This young man is like the young sun and he fights like a great warrior, with great valour. I do not have the heart to kill him. He is strong and he is undaunted. He seems to be a very noble youth and it is certain the devas will be afraid to face him in battle. And yet, I have to kill him. It is not wise to ignore fire which is raging." Hanuman killed the horses of the chariot of Aksha, and then the chariot was broken. Aksha rose into the sky abandoning the broken chariot and Hanuman caught hold of him as Garuda would a snake, and twirling him around, Hanuman dashed him to the ground. Aksha fell down dead and there was panic in the army. Many were killed and some escaped to tell Ravana about the death of his son.

Ravana was grieved at the unexpected turn of events and it took him a while to compose himself. He summoned Indrajit, his valiant son, and said: "My son, you are familiar with the astras and you are a great warrior. You have been able to vanquish Indra, the lord of the heavens, and you have gratified Brahma with your worship and have obtained the astras from him. You are brave and you are intelligent. You are capable of making quick decisions and there is nothing which is impossible for you. You are as valiant as I am and I want you to succeed where others have failed.

Your dear brother has been killed and also your companions led by Jambumali. Something unusual is happening. Go, my son, and, after assessing the strength of the enemy, fight with him. Evidently it is futile to send an army to subdue this monkey. You should trust your bow to do the needful. It is not pleasing to me at all to send my beloved son to fight as soon as I have lost another. But the situation is such that I have to. Come back with success."

Indrajit was eager to go and fight. He made a Pradakshina to his father and, after taking the blessing of the elders, he set out to fight with Hanuman.

12. THE BRAHMASTRA

Seated in his chariot Indrajit rushed to the neighbourhood of the Ashokavana. It thrilled the heart of Hanuman when he heard the noise made by the approaching chariot. He had assumed the large size which would frighten the rakshasas. Indrajit came near him and he pulled the string of his bow. The challenge was exciting to Hanuman.

There then ensued a great fight between the two. Both were valiant and neither of them could gauge any weakness in the other. Indrajit was however, finding it frustrating since his arrows were all proving futile against this monkey. He pondered as to how he could suppress the enthusiasm of the powerful opponent. He did not seem to be tired nor could anything make him frightened. After great deliberation Indrajit took up an arrow and, invoking the astra presided over by Brahma, sent it towards Hanuman. He realised by now that it was not possible to kill Hanuman and he decided to bind him with the astra. Hanuman, out of respect for Brahma, allowed himself to be bound by the astra and fell to the ground. After a moment of unconsciousness Hanuman was able to regain his senses and he thought to himself : "Brahma has granted me the boon that I will be bound by the astra only for the duration of a moment. This young man has tied me up with the astra and he is under the impression that I cannot escape the bonds. It is necessary for me to remain bound. I am not afraid of the astra and I am protected by Vayu, my father, and Agni, his friend. This is a chance for me to meet the rakshasa king Ravana and it is good that things have happened thus. Let them take me to the presence of Ravana." He lay down on the ground motionless and the rakshasas thought that he was under the power of the astra.

They came near and tied him up with ropes and strips of bark. He was willing to be tied up. The moment ropes touched his body the astra lost its influence since it is well known that no astra will tolerate bonds of another type to interfere with its power. Indrajit saw that the monkey had been tied up with ropes and he knew that the Brahmastra had become ineffectual. He was unhappy at the rashness of his men and regretted the incident. He was sure that there would be no way of stopping the monkey any more. But, to his surprise, Hanuman had allowed himself to be dragged along and he did not let anyone know that he was no longer under the sway of the astra. Soon he was taken to the great hall where Ravana held council and the young prince Indrajit accompanied him with a puzzled look on his face. He could not understand how the monkey could be bound by the astra, when ropes had touched him. He went to his father and told him about the capture of the monkey.

13. HANUMAN IN THE COURT OF RAVANA

Ravana saw Hanuman being dragged to his presence. On his arrival at the palace and in the presence of Ravana, Hanuman opened his eyes. He saw Ravana, the rakshasa, wearing a beautifully made golden crown set with gems and pearls. He was wearing ornaments made of gold and he was wearing the softest of white silks. The perfume of sandal paste which he had used on his chest and arms was filling the entire hall. His eyes were large and beautiful. He was wearing a necklace of pearls round his neck and his arms were beautified by the bracelets placed on them. He was seated on a throne which was magnificent and he was surrounded by his many ministers — Prahastha, Nikumbha and others.

Pulled as he was rudely by the jubilant rakshasas, Hanuman looked with amazement at Ravana and kept on looking. He was dazzled by the glory which was Ravana and told himself : "What a glorious personage! What beauty! What a courageous look! What strength! What radiance ! It is wonderful to see the many glorious qualities which find a home in this king of the rakshasas. If only this powerful king had not been an Adharmi, he can easily be the lord of the devas themselves. It is because of his cruel and heartless acts that the three worlds with the devas and the danavas tremble before him. He is capable of destroying the entire world when he is angry. He is valiant enough."

Ravana, who had earned that name because he was making the world cry out of fear of him, looked in front of him and looked into the tawny eyes of Hanuman. For a moment he was taken aback and an unknown fear gripped him. He asked himself : 'Can this be Nandi, the devotee of Mahadeva? Perhaps he has kept his promise and come here. Years back, when I lifted the Kailasa peak, I insulted Nandi and he cursed me that my defeat will be indicated by himself in the form of a monkey. Can this be Nandi then? Or is it Banasura?" Ravana looked at Hanuman with fury in his eyes and turning his eyes on Prahastha, his minister, he said : "Where has he come from? What is his purpose in coming here? What did he achieve by destroying the garden and frightening the rakshasis there? Ask him why he did all this. Why did he come to our city and indulge in the rare pleasure of destroying the army? Ask him."

Prahastha, in response to Ravana's command, turned to Hanuman and asked him : "Monkey, have no fear to answer us. You will come to no harm. If you have been sent here by Indra tell us the truth, and that, at once. You will be let off without being hurt. You are a henchman either of Vaishravana, or Yama or Kubera and you have come here to spy the land, I guess. Why did you do so? Or perhaps, Narayana has sent you here. It is evident that your appearance like that of a monkey is not real but it is a guise which has been put on by you. Your valour is not that of a monkey. We want the truth from you. A lie will mean death to you. Why have you come to this temple sacred to Ravana?"

Hanuman did not reply him. He would not deign to talk to a mere minister. He turned to Ravana and said : "I have not been sent either by Indra or Yama or Varuna. I have not been acquainted with Kubera. Nor am I the emissary of Narayana. I assure you this is no guise which I have donned but it is my natural self. I am a monkey by birth. I was keen on meeting you, the king of the rakshasas, and with that end in view I destroyed the garden. With a desire for fight several rakshasas came to me and I fought with them only in self-defence. Not the devas nor anyone else is capable of binding me with astras. Brahma has granted me that boon and that privilege. Because I wanted to meet you I allowed myself to be bound by the Brahmastra. When I was tied up by the rakshasas the astra lost its power to bind me. But since I had a reason which is intimately concerned with you, the lord of this island, I allowed myself to be dragged to the presence of you, the king. Let it be clearly understood that I am a messenger from Rama, the invincible. Let me be allowed to talk to you and it will be for your benefit." Hanuman paused for a long moment and allowed his words to be grasped by them all.

He then said : "O king! I have come here, to your presence, by the wish and command of my king Sugriva. He wishes you well and listen to his words which will be beneficial to you in this world and the next. This is the message of my king : 'There was a very noble king in the line of the Ikshvakus. He was a great warrior and his name was Dasaratha. His eldest son is Rama. He is a great warrior too and because of the mandate of his father, he came to the Dandaka forest, accompanied by his wife and his brother, the brave Lakshmana. His wife Sita, who is the daughter of Janaka, was lost in the forest. Prince Rama arrived in the hill Rishyamooka while he wandered in search of his wife. There he met Sugriva, the monkey, and became friends with him. They made a pact and Sugriva promised to organise a search for Sita and in return Rama said that his lost kingdom would be restored to Sugriva. As per his promise Rama killed Vali and gave the kingdom to Sugriva, his brother. As for Vali, your majesty knows him well enough, I think. That Vali has been killed by Rama with a single arrow.' The king Sugriva has sent monkeys in all the four quarters to look for Sita and they are still engaged in the search for the lost princess. They are all powerful and valiant monkeys. Some of them are as powerful as Garuda and others as fleet as Vayu. As for me, I am the son of Vayu and my name is Hanuman. With a desire to locate the hiding place of Sita I leaped across the sea which is a hundred yojanas in width. While I was wandering around, I happened to see Sita in your house. I was surprised at it.

"You are a wise king and you are quite familiar with Dharma and the observance of it. It is not becoming that such a noble person like you should keep another man's wife as captive. It is not fit for men of superior intelligence like you to get involved in acts which are not righteous. Which deva or danava or asura will be able to withstand the sharp arrows which will be shot from the bows of Rama and Lakshmana? No one who has wronged Rama will escape the suffering which is sure to follow it : not in the three worlds. Please consider my words. Make up your mind to act in such a manner that it will be according to the dictates of Dharma and which will benefit your past, your present and your future. Make haste and return Sita to Rama who is a god among men. I have seen Sita and the impossible has been possible for me. The rest is in the hands of Rama.

"I saw Sita immersed in sorrow and I am surprised that you do not recognise her to be a five-headed serpent whom you have kept with you with so much affection and love. Like food which is mixed with poison cannot be digested, this woman will prove to be too much for you.

"This, your life, has been blessed with so much tapas and strict observance of several Vratas which demand a control of the senses. It has been blessed by the gods. Do you think it is right that it should all come to an end because of a woman? You are without any care since your tapas has granted you immunity from death by asuras and the devas. Still, you seem to have forgotten one factor. This Sugriva is neither a deva nor an asura. He is not a rakshasa and he is not a danava. Gandharva he is not, and he is not a yaksha or a pannaga. He is but a monkey and as for Rama, he is a human being, a mere man. O king! Remember this and tell me how you are going to protect yourself. The results of one's righteousness and those of one's trespasses against Dharma do not go together. Even Dharma is eclipsed if Adharma is harboured in the mind. You have, so far, enjoyed the fruits of your Dharma. There is no doubt about it. And it goes without saying that the fruits of your unrighteousness will also be inflicted on you and you cannot escape them. Remember the destruction in Janasthana. Remember the killing of Vali. Take them as a warning and think again of the friendship of Rama and Sugriva. Consider all these and try to think of a method which will help you to guard yourself from the fate which is imminent. My valour, the valour of a single monkey, is enough to destroy the entire city of Lanka. But that is not the way Rama thinks. He has already decided on the fate of the sinner who has the foolishness to steal his wife from him. Monkeys and bears will form the army of Rama and Indra himself cannot escape punishment if he has offended Rama. What then of a mere rakshasa like you? You think of Rama's wife as Sita, a woman whom you have captured and imprisoned. Listen to me and understand that she is like the dark night which will swallow the lustre and glory of Lanka. She is like the noose of death which you have placed on your neck unknowingly. Enough of this foolishness and think of the best course of action. You must realise that Sita is like fire which is certain to burn up this city with its beautiful gardens, and mansions. Rama's anger is deadly. Please protect your friends, your kinsmen, ministers, brothers, children, wealth, your women and all the beauty which is Lanka. Listen to my words and act accordingly. Rama can destroy all the entire universe and create it again. There is no one who can oppose him in the three worlds. Having offended Rama it will not be possible for you to live long. No one can help you : not Indra, nor Brahma nor the three-eyed Rudra."

Ravana's anger was mounting with every word uttered by Hanuman. He was beside himself with anger and he promptly ordered that the monkey should be put to death.

Vibhishana, the brother of Ravana, felt that this was not the right action on the part of Ravana. He was a rakshasa who was righteous-minded and he thought about how to dissuade Ravana from taking this wrong decision. The king was very angry and it was not easy to talk to an angry person, more so when he is the king. Vibhishana was wise and he could use words which had the proper effect. He spoke softly to the king. He said : "Be calm, O king. Do not give way to anger. Listen to my words. It is a convention among kings that no messenger should be put to death. Your orders that this monkey should be executed is against all codes of Dharma which a king should observe. It does not become a king like you, a great emperor known the world over, to do this to a mere messenger. I do not have to teach you the nuances of Dharma nor about the code of behaviour. You are at home in all the rules of kingship and you know the intricacies of it. When a wise man like you gives in to the sway of anger the proficiency in the shastras, which you have attained, will all go waste. You are the undaunted lord of all of us and it is not right that you should be carried away by anger. You should consider the situation calmly and punish the monkey properly."

Ravana was not willing to listen to Vibhishana. His anger had not abated yet. He said : "Death as a punishment is not wrong when it is meted out to wicked ones like this monkey. He is a menace and a sinner and I see nothing wrong in putting him to death."

Vibhishana pursued his arguments and said : "No, you should not do so, my lord. On no account should a messenger be put to death. The rules are very clear about it. The wise have declared it to be so. No doubt he is an enemy. He has caused untold harm to us. Good people have prescribed different types of punishment to different people. Except death, you can pronounce any other form of punishment. That is allowed. Whipping, maiming, shaving off their heads or marking them with scars are all punishments allowed for a messenger. But not death. A righteous king like you should not lose your name because of the anger in your mind. And again, there is not particular gain in killing this monkey. The punishment should, actually, be given to those who have sent him. Whether he is docile, or wicked or aggressive, is immaterial. He is here only to convey the message sent by the enemy. He is doing his duty and, by himself, he is guiltless. Therefore, he should not be killed. Taint will besmirch your name and it should not be courted. You gain nothing by the judgment you have pronounced except the censure of the wise and infamy.

"Attempts should be made to attack the princes who have despatched the monkey. You have any number of brave and good warriors who can fight for you to the end. To destroy these two human beings a small army can be sent and your wishes will be done. Only, do not kill this monkey. It is not the right thing to do."

Ravana was convinced now that Vibhishana spoke the truth. He was not willing to court the censure of the wise and the discerning and he accepted the advice of his brother with good grace. Ravana was still worried about Hanuman. He told himself : "I am certain that it is Narayana's glory which has assumed the form of a monkey with the purpose of killing me. Is it His Radiance? Is he Brahma Himself? Or is it the Brahman itself? I wonder."

Ravana held back his anger with great effort and spoke to Vibhishana.

14. CONFLAGRATION IN LANKA

Ravana said : "Vibhishana, you are right. It is wrong to kill a messenger from the enemy. I must think of some other punishment for him. I have it.

Nothing is dearer to a monkey than its tail. He is extremely proud of his tail. Let the tail of this impertinent monkey be set on fire and let him go back to where he came from without his tail. His friends and those who sent him will see his desolate condition and that will be punishment enough for him and a warning to the others. Let his tail be lighted and let him be dragged through the streets of the city. Let every one of the citizens see him and jeer at him."

The rakshasas were only too happy to do his bidding. They brought cloth woven out of cotton and placed it round the tail. They wrapped it tightly and Hanuman grew in size. They dipped his tail in oil and set fire to it. It was an immense tail and the sight of it catching fire made them happy. Many of the citizens of Lanka came there to see the monkey and the burning of its tail. Women, children, and old men also came from their houses to see the wonder.

Hanuman was now well and truly angry. He hit the rakshasas with his tail and they caught hold of him and tied him up. Hanuman thought: "It will be very easy for me to break these bonds and rush at them to kill them. No one can touch me. But then, my task will remain unfulfilled and I will be failing in my duty. I will bear the indignity and humiliation of being insulted by these people. I saw the city during the night. I can now get a chance to see it in daylight and I can supplement the knowledge I have already gained. They will be dragging me through all the streets and that suits me to perfection. My mind is unaffected by their jubilation."

The rakshasas tied him up firmly and they dragged him through the streets of Lanka and his tail was blazing all the while. They made a lot of noise and Hanuman walked very quietly with them as though he had decided to be docile, finding their might to be superior. He had a good view of Lanka and he walked silently with them. People scoffed at him and he heeded them not.

Some of the rakshasis rushed to Sita and said : "Sita, do you remember that red-faced monkey with whom you were talking this morning? He is being dragged through the streets of the city and the king has ordered that his tail should be burnt. They have set fire to it and it is blazing."

Sita was horrified at the fate of Hanuman. Pain was writ on her face and tears welled up into her eyes. She invoked Agni, the god of fire, in her mind and, with a view to helping Hanuman, she said : "If it is true that I have served my lord and husband, if it is true that I have considered my husband as my only god, if it is true that I have observed all the Vratas and performed tapas with a pure mind, then let not Hanuman feel your heat. If it is true that Rama has any affection for me, if there is at least a small amount of good fortune which is due to me, let Hanuman be unaffected by you. If it is true that my only prayer is to be with Rama once again, let Hanuman be free of your fiery touch." Agni was prompt to obey her injunctions. He was cool like the paste of sandalwood and the wind Vayu blew softly on his son. Hanuman was, in the meantime, amazed at the fact that fire had not hurt him at all. He asked himself : "Though my tail is burning so bright I do not feel the heat at all and my tail is not being burnt up. I feel a coolness as though sandal paste has been applied to my tail. There is no doubt about it. This is as amazing as the appearance of a mountain in the middle of the sea when I was coming here. When the lord of the seas was filled with respect for Rama so much so he sent Mainaka to greet me, is it a wonder then that the god of fire has decided to leave me unhurt? Sita's compassion and the glory of Rama and the friendship of my father must have made Agni refrain from hurting me."

Hanuman had seen all that was to be seen. Suddenly he roared and sprang into the air. He gave them all a jolt. He grew to an enormous size and he reached the top of a roof which was not easily accessible to the captors who were dragging him along. He made himself small enough to make the bonds slip from him and grew again to enormous proportions. He grasped a pillar in his hands and beat up all those who dared to approach him. He sat for a moment thinking on his further course of action. "What remains for me to do?" He asked himself. "What can I do now to hurt Ravana further? His garden is destroyed. Several of his good fighters are gone. I have killed one of his sons. I should now set about on the task of destroying his fort. This fire which was used to punish me has been denied its food since he does not hurt me. It is but right that I should feed him. I will set fire to the mansions in the city."

Hanuman was like a cloud lit by lightning as he leaped from house top to housetop. Active to an unbelievable degree, assisted by Vayu, Hanuman was busy setting fire to house after house, mansion after mansion, palace after palace. It was a terrible fire which rose to the skies, plied with the food supplied by Hanuman. The houses of all the important courtiers of the king were burnt up. All the rich brocades and silks and precious articles in the mansions and palaces were reduced to ashes. Hanuman finally landed in the house of Ravana and he touched it also with fire and soon it grew into a blaze. The city was aflame and the leaping flames made one think of the conflagration at the end of the Yuga. The citizens who were so full of exuberance a while ago were now panic-stricken. Screams could be heard everywhere and there were innumerable deaths as people jumped down from the terraces of the burning houses and Hanuman was unaffected by the havoc he had caused. The flames were licking everything they touched. Perhaps, thought the people, when Lord Mahadeva burnt the three worlds, it must have looked like this. The sound made by the buildings tumbling down and the cries of distress from the people added to the crackle of fire and they were all together making a terrible noise and it seemed to reach the sky.

Hanuman seemed to be a being from another world. They could not believe that a mere monkey could be capable of so much valour. It was, evidently, not born of this earth. Fright was writ large on the faces of the people in Lanka.

Hanuman had completed his self-appointed task of destroying the city and he now stood on top of the hill by name Trikuta. His tail was still burning and he thought of Rama. The heavenly host praised Hanuman for his great achievement and his anger was appeased to an extent when he thought of Rama. He reached the sea and dipping his tail in it, he extinguished the fire which had burnt up the city of Lanka.

He was suddenly struck with a dread fear. He felt that he had been too impulsive in setting fire to the city. He told himself : "I should not have done it. The really wise and great people will be able to control surging anger and hold it back. Like water which quenches fire which is burning they should use their intelligence to control their anger. Only such men are considered to be wise, great and to be the best among men. Man is easily prone to commit sins when he is angry. No one is exempt from this law. An angry man may kill even those who are to be respected. He will talk to good people with a lack of respect which is unforgivable. One who is a slave to anger will not be able to discriminate between what should be spoken and what should not be. There is nothing he will not do. The really great man will shed anger like a snake sheds his skin. I now censure myself for this act of mine which was impulsive and thoughtless.

"When I set fire to the city I forgot that Sita is in the city. When the entire city has been burnt it stands to reason that she has been burnt also. Foolish, senseless traitor that I am, I have betrayed my master. I have ruined the future for Rama. I have seen Sita and yet, because of this fire she has been killed by me. I have not taken her safety into consideration. I have struck at the root of happiness for Rama and killed it. There is no place in Lanka which has been left untouched by fire and it follows that Sita has been burnt to death. Because of my stupidity I have brought ruin on everyone. The only course open to me is to lose my life. I should drown myself or become a victim to fire. It is the curse of monkeys that to them fickleness is second nature. My rajasic quality which is not controlled by the mind should be condemned. Even I who should be above the sway of emotions became a slave to anger." Hanuman was sunk in the depths of despair. Even as he was standing thus, desolate, on the shores of the sea, he thought again : "Perhaps her glory and her divinity would have prevented fire from approaching her. Her chastity would have held it at bay and fire is incapable of touching her. She is herself a heap of fire. It is Rama's glory and her purity that prevented the fire from hurting me. When such an insignificant monkey like me could be spared how then can she be burnt?"

Hanuman convinced himself that she was safe. He was still pondering on it when some charanas who were passing by in the sky spoke some words within his hearing. They said : "It was indeed a miracle which happened in Lanka. Hanuman had set fire to the entire city and nothing is left of it. And yet, there is one person who is not harmed at all and that is Sita." Hanuman was thrilled to hear the words of the charanas and he prostrated before the great Rama in his mind. Though he was sure now of her safety Hanuman wanted to see Sita once again before he left Lanka. "I will salute the Devi under the Shimshupa tree and I will express my relief at her safety and then proceed to the north on my journey back."

He went to where Sita was. She was overjoyed to see him and said: "I am convinced that you can, alone, destroy this entire rakshasa host. There is no limit to your power. Go back to Rama and give him the message of mine that I am waiting impatiently for his coming." Hanuman said : "Rama will soon be here surrounded by his army of monkeys and bears. You can be without any worry." He prostrated before her and took leave of her.

Hanuman was eager to go back to Rama and give him the great news and he hurried to the top of the hill by name Arishta. He strode on the surface of the top and the rocks were crushed by him and his heavy steps. As he did on the top of the Mahendra mountain Hanuman grew in size. He took one look at the sea surging under him and he sprang into the air his face towards the north. The mountain was pressed down by his weight and it was pushed down into the earth. The trees were like broken twigs and there was a great crashing noise made as they fell to the ground accompanied by the rocks which had been dislodged in profusion. Serpents and lions left their hiding places and came out in terror. The rocks were covered by the poisons which the serpents were spitting out of their fear.

Hanuman was in the air after shaking the mountain away from his great feet.

Spurred by his eagerness to reach Rama, and pleased with himself since he had achieved his objective, Hanuman was finding it very easy to cross the sea. It seemed as though he were swallowing the sky with his immense frame. He seemed to touch the moon and he seemed to pass very close to the sun and the region of the stars. The clouds were pulled along with him because of his speed. He passed through the sky where the clouds were tinted in myriad hues. Some were white, some red, and others were blue and yellow. There were some which were tinted green and red and it was beautiful to see Hanuman streaking like lightning through them. Roaring like a rain cloud he coursed through the sky like an arrow shot from a bow. He met the mountain Mainaka and he set up such a roar when he went near it. After stroking it with affection he went on his way. Soon he was nearing the Mahendra mountain and here could be heard the roar which he set up. The four quarters resounded with the echo of his roar. As he neared the spot where his friends were awaiting him he shouted to them and shook his long tail. The triumphant cry of Hanuman was heard everywhere.

The Vanara host which was waiting for him eagerly and with great anxiety heard his war cry. They waited for him to land. Jambavan called them all together and said : "It is evident that Hanuman has been successful in his adventure. Or else he would not have sounded so jubilant."

The entire army was dancing with joy in anticipation of the good news which Hanuman was sure to bring them.

15. THE RETURN OF HANUMAN

They ran hither and thither in excitement and pulling out flowering branches from the trees nearby they waved them about in ecstasy. Hanuman could be heard approaching and they stood with their palms folded together while he landed on the mountain Mahendra. The monkeys rushed to him and stood around him. They were greatly relieved to see him come back without any mishap. They tried to serve him with fruits and roots and asked him to refresh himself. Hanuman approached Jambavan and Angada and saluted them. They welcomed him with great affection and Hanuman said: "In the pleasure garden of Ravana, in a garden by name Ashokavana, I saw her. She was surrounded by rakshasis who had been placed to keep watch on her. She was thinking only of Rama and it was sad to see her covered with dust, thin because of her eternal fast, with her hair twisted into a single strand and lying on her back like a dark serpent."

The monkeys, as soon as they heard the words : "Sita has been found," jumped in the air and showed their happiness by various demonstrations. Angada said : "In this entire world, there is no one like you. No one can equal you in valour and might. You have crossed the sea, and you have come back safe after succeeding in your task. Your devotion to our master is great. Your achievement is indeed incomparable. The noble queen of Rama has been seen by you because of our great and good fortune. Rama will soon be rid of his sorrow."

They all stood around looking at Hanuman eager to hear in detail about his journey to Lanka and about Sita. Mahendra mountain was looking glorious with Hanuman and Angada and all the others crowding on it.

Jambavan made them all sit down and he asked Hanuman : "Tell us how Sita was found by you. How is she? How does Ravana behave towards her? We are all eager to know all about everything. Relate to us the happenings in Lanka. We will listen to you and later we will decide as to what should be done. There may be some facts which can be told now, and some which may have to be suppressed. You are wise enough to know all about it. Tell us everything now. We are eager and impatient to know."

Hanuman made obeisance to Sita by prostrating towards the south and then began his recital. He told them about the Mainaka hill and about Surasa. He told them how he had to outwit her and then he came to the incident of Simhika whom he had to kill. Then followed his landing in Lanka and his encounter with Lankini, the guardian of the city. He spoke in detail about going into the antahpura of Ravana in search of Sita. They listened as though they were spellbound and they suffered with him as he told them of his frustration which he met with everywhere. He told them how he felt that he would never reach the end of the sea of sorrow. Then came the visit to the Ashokavana which was the only place which he had not scrutinised.

"In the midst of that garden was a Shimshupa tree," said Hanuman. "I sat on that tree and looked all around me. The moon had come up in the heavens and I could see clearly. A short distance from there, in a temple-like shelter I saw her. I saw Sita. In the midst of the rakshasis she was like a stricken deer surrounded by tigresses. She was seated on the ground, the bare ground, and she was weeping all the time." Hanuman here wiped his own eyes and continued his recital. He told them about his shrinking himself to the size of a kitten and hiding himself among the leaves of the trees : about the coming of Ravana and his words to Sita : about his threats and his ultimatum. Hanuman told them everything in great detail and the recital was thrilling to the listeners. What had been abandoned as a hopeless task had been achieved and Hanuman had saved their lives.

He recounted to them the dream which Trijata had spoken of and about the despair of Sita. He then told them how he made himself known to Sita, about her initial distrust and about how he had convinced her that he was from Rama. He was happy when he described in detail the several words he spoke and which Sita had spoken and how she gave him the jewels to be given to Rama in return for the ring.

He came to the destruction of the Ashokavana. The monkeys who were listening were now greatly excited when they heard how Hanuman had killed the many chiefs of the army of Ravana and about the death of a son of the king. This was greatly to their liking and they jumped in the air, waved their tails and embraced each other. Hanuman told them about his getting bound by the Brahmastra and about his encounter with Ravana in his court. When they were told about the death sentence which had been pronounced on him they listened in silence and then with a slight smile on his face Hanuman described graphically the burning of Lanka. The excitement of the monkeys was gratifying to him. Each one of them thought that he has done it himself and they laughed. They screeched and they jumped in the air and kissed their tails again and again. They were astonished at the miracle which made him immune to the effects of the fire which was blazing at the tip of his tail and about Sita being unharmed by the fire which destroyed the rest of Lanka.

Hanuman said : "I went and saw her again to make sure that she was safe. I saw her again and took leave of her and I hurried to your presence. There is a mountain by name Arishta there and from the top of that mountain I leaped on to the air since I was impatient to meet all of you, to bring you the happy tidings that Sita is there in Lanka and to end your worries. I have come back and my service has been rendered to my king and to Rama. My mission has been fruitful because of the grace of Rama, because of the good wishes of all of you and because of the desire to please our king I managed to succeed when I least expected to. I have told you everything that happened in Lanka. Let us now decide on the future course of action."

He paused for a moment and said : "It is our good fortune that Sita has not been harmed in any way by that sinful rakshasa. Rama's sorrows will soon be at an end and our king will be released from the solemn promise he has made.

"When I think of the immensity of Ravana's crime I am surprised that he is still alive. I then realised the tapas he has performed, which is what is protecting him. He is a great man, he has performed intense tapas and has pleased Lord Mahadeva Himself with his devotion and that is what is guarding him. Or else touching fire is not as terrible as touching Sita, the wife of the Lord. She is sitting patiently there, under the tree by name Shimshupa, the very picture of woe and despair. Like the moon hidden by a bank of clouds she is there, hiding her glory. She does not consider Ravana as anyone important enough to talk to. As I told you, she placed a blade of grass between her and Ravana as she spoke to him making him realise that she has as much respect for him as she has for that blade of grass. Her mind is ever set on Rama and she has no other thought in her mind. She is a pathetic figure and we must hasten to her rescue. Rama will find it very easy to kill Ravana and rescue her. She could have killed Ravana with the fire of her Paativratya but she respects Rama so much that she wants him to rescue her."

After listening to the thrilling narrative of Hanuman, Angada, the prince, said : "We should try our utmost to do the needful. Under the leadership of Jambavan we can strive to reach our goal. I can, single-handed, accost Ravana and his army. Is there any doubt of our destroying him and his entire host if we go all together? I can kill him and his kinsmen and his sons. I am familiar with the astras like Brahma, Aindra, Vayavya and many others. I can tackle the astra warfare of Indrajit. Give me permission to go and I will come back crowned with glory. I will rain stones on their army and it will all be crushed beyond any recognition. Hanuman is enough to work havoc in their ranks. If all of us, Panasa, Neela, aided by Dvividha and Mainda who have been granted boons, attack the army of Ravana, we can destroy it completely. Let us go back to Rama with Sita who will be rescued by us. If we go back and say : 'Sita has been found but we have not brought her with us', it will not be pleasing to the ears of our king and those of Rama. We are a powerful army and all the world knows of our valour. It is of such a high order. Hanuman will, single-handed, do the needful and we can go back to our Kishkindha with Sita Devi who has been captive all these many months. Our king will be pleased with what we have done."

Jambavan listened with an indulgent smile to the words of young prince who was very dear to him. When the enthusiastic talk of Angada was ended he said : "You are right, Angada, my prince. It is not an impossible task that you have suggested. We can easily do it.

"Still, I feel that Rama should know the situation and we should leave it to him to decide on the future course of action which should be adopted by us. Sita herself, I gather from Hanuman's words, wants Rama to go to Lanka, punish the miscreant and take her back with him. Let us go back to Kishkindha and relate the entire happenings to Rama and to our king. We will leave the future in their hands."

Angada and Hanuman with the rest of the group accepted the advice of Jambavan, since they considered him to be the wisest of them all and with great joy in their hearts the entire host of monkeys began its march towards Kishkindha.

16. SUGRIVA'S MADHUVANA

Excited as they were by the good news they were carrying and, with the thought of the great fight ahead of them, the monkeys proceeded fast towards their city and soon they reached the outskirts of the city of Kishkindha. On the very edge of the city was a garden, beautiful and exciting. It was almost a forest, in size, but it was a well-tended garden. It was inaccessible to everyone and it was called 'Madhuvana'. It belonged to Sugriva. The king's uncle, Dadhimukha, was in charge of it.

When they saw the garden the monkeys became extremely excited. They went to their prince Angada and asked him for permission to enter it and to taste of the honeyed wines which were to be found there in plenty. Angada consulted with Jambavan and Hanuman and finally decided that they should be granted the thrill of tasting the madhu in the favourite garden of the king.

The entire crowd rushed into the forest and soon each and every one of them was drunk gloriously. The monkeys were already happy and the prospect of tasting the madhu of the king made them jump in joy. They entered the garden and enjoyed themselves to their heart's content.

Some began to sing and some were so drunk that they could not walk steadily. Some were dancing and others were laughing for no reason at all. Some were jumping from tree to tree and others were wandering around aimlessly. They were talking incoherently and some embraced each other. There were small tiffs and arguments typical of the intoxication caused by too much drinking. There was not a single monkey who was not drunk and each had drunk until he was satiated.

Dadhimukha tried to prevent the havoc that they had caused in the garden and the garden was no ordinary garden : it was the king's garden and he had been guarding it so jealously. He talked to some of them, frightened some of them, threatened some and beat up others. Some he tried to coax with sweet words and not one of them would respond either to his appeals or to his threats. He was dragged here and there by the drunken monkeys and they enjoyed themselves immensely in the garden of their king.

Hanuman said : "Drink your fill and do not be afraid of this guard. I will take care of him."

Angada heard the words of Hanuman and approving of them he said: "Let them drink as much as they wish. They have come back from a long journey with gladness in their hearts and they should be allowed this pleasure."

The entire garden was filled with the monkeys in various stages of intoxication. Dadhimukha who tried to avert the damage to the garden found it impossible to do so and he saw that the prince had sanctioned the mischief that was being caused by the monkeys.

There ensued a fight between the guards led by Dadhimukha and the drunken monkeys. But the guards were not able to quell the army. Even Hanuman joined in the fight! Finally Dadhimukha said : "Let them do what they like. Let us go to the king and tell him. He is at the moment on the Prasravana hill with Rama. We will tell him all that has happened here. He is so very fond of this garden he is sure to punish these intruders. Come, let us go."

Soon he was in the presence of Sugriva. He went near his king and prostrated before him. Sugriva looked at him and asked him : "Rise up. What has happened? Why are you so distressed? Tell me everything."

And Dadhimukha told him about the havoc played by the host of monkeys in Madhuvana and about Angada and Hanuman allowing and encouraging this outrage.

Lakshmana was near Sugriva and he was listening to the complaint lodged by Dadhimukha. He asked Sugriva : "Why has this guardian of the forest come here? What is he so grieved about? I am extremely curious."

Sugriva who was famed for his sagacity turned to Lakshmana and said : "He is telling me that the Vanara host led by Angada has entered the Madhuvana, my favourite garden. And the garden, he tells me, has been destroyed completely. Contrary to his expectations, I am going to leave them all unpunished and I will welcome them with open arms and gracious smiles."

Dadhimukha could not believe his ears when his king spoke thus. Lakshmana turned his inquiring eyes at Sugriva and the king said : "It seems to me, the monkeys, whom I had sent down south to search for Sita, have returned. They have dared to enter Madhuvana, my garden, which has been zealously guarded by none less than my valiant uncle here. Considering that they have been so bold, it stands to reason that they have succeeded in their quest. I am almost certain that Hanuman must have met Devi Sita. No one else is capable of such valour. Hanuman is the only person I know, who can achieve the most difficult task.

"Hanuman is always efficient and never once has he failed in any task he has undertaken. The perseverance, wisdom, firmness, valour and the power of the intellect are all to be found in this great Vanara, Hanuman. And again, Jambavan and Angada are both very wise and they have been with him to assist him in his enterprise. These two are excellent in organising and they know what should be done, when. Nothing which Jambavan has planned has ever gone wrong.

"Now this Madhuvana has been ruined by the host of Vanaras who went southwards. It was led by Angada and evidently they are armed with good news and the news must be so dear to my heart that they are sure that the ruin of Madhuvana will not be noticed by me at all. They would never have dared to do so unless they had been sure of my forgiveness. These guards have been hurt because they tried to protect the garden. It is evident that the host of Vanaras is bringing me good news.

"Consider the circumstances, Lakshmana. They are all only too familiar with the fact that this garden of mine should not be entered by anyone else and yet they have wrought so much harm to it. They are enjoying themselves so much that I am led to believe that it is their happiness which has granted them so much courage. If they had failed in the quest for Sita they would have been so depressed they would never have thought of getting drunk and incurring my displeasure."

Rama was listening silently to the words of Sugriva and it was clear to his mind that Sugriva was reasoning well and he and Lakshmana thought that he had guessed right. They respected the high order of Sugriva's intelligence and they knew that he was right.

Sugriva turned to Dadhimukha and said : "My dear uncle, I am extremely pleased that the Madhuvana has been destroyed by the monkeys. They have made a triumphal entry into the kingdom and they deserve this privilege of using my garden. I am eager to meet them all, led by Angada, by Jambavan and Hanuman. With Rama and Lakshmana I am waiting here, impatient to hear the news they have brought."

Dadhimukha went back to the Madhuvana in a state of stupefaction. Such a thing had never happened before. He could not understand how the king could forgive such an outrage. As for Sugriva, he was thrilled that he has been able to keep his word to Rama and that Hanuman and the others had made it possible.

17. THE NARRATION OF HANUMAN

Dadhimukha went back to Madhuvana and he found the monkeys just getting over their intoxication. Some of them were sober and others were just half awake. He went to the presence of Angada, the prince, and, standing with his palms folded, he said : "My dear prince, child, please forgive me and the guards for trying to stop you from enjoying yourself. Please do not be incensed by our foolishness. You are the prince and the master of this garden and it was wrong, nay, highly impertinent, on my part to have behaved as I did. I seek your forgiveness. In my foolish anger I left you all and rushed to the presence of the king and told him about the happenings here. He was extremely happy when he heard about it and I was amazed. He was happy that you had all come back. He sent me to you with the message : 'Ask them to come and see me soon. Rama, Lakshmana and I, are waiting for the news brought by them and we are impatient.' I was asked to give you this message."

Angada, after hearing the words of Dadhimukha, said : "Evidently Rama also knows about our tarrying here. Let us not spend any more time here but let us go back to our king." He addressed the monkeys and said : "You have been allowed to have your fill of the madhu which is precious to my uncle. Let us now hasten to the presence of the king." The army rose up as one man and hurried on the last lap of their journey. Some flew in the air and some leaped from tree to tree and soon they were in the presence of Sugriva.

Sugriva, in the meantime, was talking to Rama about the news which they were sure to hear. He said : "Be of good cheer, my friend. Sita has been discovered, I am sure of it. The time I had stipulated has been overstepped and they would never have had the courage to come back to me without their task being completed. Prince Angada, who led the army, would never have come back to me, I am certain of that. He would have been frightened of the punishment I would have meted out to him and his troupe which might have failed in the mission. Angada would not have had the courage to grant permission to the army to drink the honey and the wines which have been exclusively mine. His great enthusiasm and his assurance that I will not be angry with any of them, proves to me that they are bringing us good tidings about Sita. And I am sure it was Hanuman who has dared to enter the enemy's country and discovered her whereabouts. Forget your misery, Rama. The time has come when sorrow should be shed since it will soon be forgotten."

The monkey host arrived with a great tumultous noise. Each one of the monkeys walked as though he had managed to achieve the impossible and they strutted with pride. Sugriva heard the noise and he was happy. He waited for a while and Hanuman with Angada led them to his presence. Their faces were beaming with joy as they prostrated before their king, Rama and Lakshmana. Hanuman prostrated again and again before Rama and said : "Sita has been seen."

It was heavenly for them to hear the words of Hanuman and he told them briefly first about his finding Sita unharmed by Ravana, but very unhappy because of her captivity, her separation from her lord and because of the hopelessness of her condition. Sugriva was very proud of his men who had helped him to keep his promise. Lakshmana looked with affection at Hanuman and Rama's eyes rested with love and grace on Hanuman who stood humbly before him after telling him about Sita, after giving him a new lease on life.

Hanuman waited for an opportunity to tell Rama in detail about the many happenings in Lanka and the monkeys vied with each other to tell Rama about the captivity of Sita and about the cruelties she had to face. From the graphic manner in which they spoke it would seem as though it was these monkeys and not Hanuman who had seen all these!

Rama asked again : "I am glad to know that Sita is unharmed and still alive. Only tell me, where is she? What does she think of me? Tell me all about Sita."

The monkeys, with slightly ashamed faces, went to Hanuman and stood by his side silently looking at him as if to say : "It is up to you to take up where we left off." Rama was looking on with a smile and Lakshmana hid a broad smile which was dawning on his lips. Sugriva was too happy to see anything comical in the situation.

Hanuman came near to Rama. Solemnly he made a namaskara in the direction where Sita was, and then said : "My lord, Rama, with a desire to see Sita Devi, I leaped across the sea which was a hundred yojanas wide. On the southern shore of the sea is a city by name Lanka which is where Ravana rules. In the antahpura of Ravana, I saw Sita, the purest of women. With her thoughts and hopes centred on you, she is managing to keep alive. She is a captive in a garden which is the pleasure garden of Ravana. When I first saw her, she was surrounded by rakshasis all of whom were trying to bully her into accepting the unholy love of Ravana. This noble lady who has been born to be an heiress to nothing but happiness is, today, the most unhappy of women. I saw her hair which was matted due to neglect and which was lying in a single strand, twisted into a rough plait and hanging on her back like a deadly snake. She was half reclining and half sitting on the bare ground. She is imprisoned in that garden and several fearful rakshasis guard her. Like a lotus drenched in dew she is looking wilted and sad. There is no way for her to escape from Ravana. She had made up her mind to give up her life and I saw her then. Her thoughts are bent on you, Rama, and she is thinking only of you."

Hanuman told Rama about his sitting on top of the tree and reciting the story of the kings of the Ikshvaku race and about how he won the confidence of Sita. He related to him the conversation with Sita and about everything in great detail. He said : "She has sent you the following message: 'Rama, I will stay alive for a month more. I will not be allowed to live longer than that by this Ravana. Save me before the expiry of the month.' When she was given your ring, she was as happy as though she had seen you in person. She has sent you her jewel which she would wear in her hair in the days when she had been with you. She had kept it very carefully and she gave it to me and asked me to give it to you. She asked me to remind you about the incident of the crow and also about the *tilaka* made by the dust of the stone Manasila. She said that only she knew about it and you and she wanted you to remember them."

Rama took the jewel in his hands and tears sprang to his eyes as he clasped it to his bosom. With his voice faltering because of his emotion he told Sugriva : "Seeing this jewel my mind is sorely distressed as a mother cow's will, when it thinks of her calf. This was given to Sita by her father and she was wearing it during our wedding. She was beautiful when this jewel adorned her hair. This had been given by Indra to Janaka when he was pleased with that king. This jewel brings to my mind my father, Sita and her father. I feel that Sita is here by my side when I see this."

He was silent for a while and then said : "Lakshmana, I am seeing this jewel and not Sita who was always wearing it. Can anything be more pathetic than this?" He turned to Hanuman and asked him : "Tell me all about the words which Sita spoke. It will be like water to the parched lips of a thirsty man. If she says she will stay alive for a month more, then her life will be longer than mine. I cannot live for a moment more without Sita. Take me to her, my dear Hanuman. Take me to where Sita is. After knowing where Sita is, I cannot tarry even for a moment more. How is my beloved able to bear the cruel words of the rakshasis who surrounded her? Her face must be without its natural lustre and will be like the moon during the season Sharad when clouds obscure its beauty. Hanuman, tell me once again about her. I am eager to know."

Hanuman spoke humbly and in great detail he related all that had happened in the Ashokavana, and about how he spoke to Sita.

Hanuman began right from the beginning and told Rama about their meeting Sampati and about the certainty with which he had told them that Sita was in the antahpura of Ravana and about how he could see her. Then came their problem as to how the sea was to be crossed. Playing down his own prowess as much as he could, Hanuman told them about the many adventures he had. When he had come back from the city of Lanka he had told his comrades about the happenings at Lanka with great gusto. But here, it was different. He spoke mostly about the incidents which had Sita as the central figure and he went on to relate the conversation he had with Sita in great detail. Hanuman spoke very humbly and related everything which happened in Lanka. He repeated the manner in which Sita had narrated the episode of Kakasura and her lament that Rama, who could be so angry with a mere crow, was silent now that she was abducted by a rakshasa. The words of comfort spoken by himself were also repeated to

Rama. He did not leave out even a single word spoken by her and all the while Rama listened with tears running unheeded down his face. Hanuman concluded: "My lord, I have assured her that you will soon be in Lanka accompanied by our king and his army of monkeys and bears. Her grief is slightly assuaged by my words of encouragement and assurance and Devi is bravely counting the days which will have to pass before she can be reunited with you. She is eagerly waiting for the day when Ravana will be killed by you and when she is assured of the deliverance from the hands of the wicked rakshasa king."

YUDDHA KANDA

1. PREPARATIONS

Hearing the words of Hanuman, words which were extremely pleasing to the ears, Rama spoke to him with affection. He said : "A task which cannot be accomplished by anyone else in this world, a task which is beyond even the concepts of the imagination, has been achieved by Hanuman. With the exception of Vayu and Garuda, and, now, Hanuman, I have never heard of anyone crossing the ocean. With the strength of his will he has entered the city of Lanka, the stronghold of the enemy, and he has come back to us, alive. Not one of the celestials would have been able to do so. The city is inaccessible to everyone and it is so well guarded by Ravana that the very thought of entering it would have made anyone else think twice before attempting it. There is no one to equal Hanuman in courage and in valour. Hanuman has done his utmost to do the bidding of his master Sugriva. He is a real servant who acts in such a way that his master's honour is not besmirched. However hard the task may be, he will act properly and he is called the best among men by the wise. He has done what he had been ordered to do and he has acted in a way which is pleasing to Sugriva. Hanuman, Lakshmana and I have been helped by you since you have discovered Sita for us. There is only one sorrow which is hurting me and that is my inability to reward you in a manner suited to the greatness of your achievement. Poor as I am, I can only embrace you with open arms and express my gratitude to you."

With tears in his eyes Rama embraced Hanuman and the scene touched the hearts of everyone there. After a while, when his emotions were somewhat under control, Rama spoke to him and to Sugriva : "Sita has been found. And yet my mind is not quite at ease since the thought of the sea is frightening. Hanuman could do it but how can all of us, the entire army cross the wide sea? Tell me what you all think of it. How are we going to cross the sea?"

Hanuman said nothing and Rama was lost in thought. Sugriva broke into his reverie and said: "It is not right that you should worry about these things like an ordinary mortal. Forget these worries even as an ungrateful man forgets his erstwhile friendship. Now that Sita's hiding place has been discovered our biggest problem has been solved. There is no need for these small details to worry you and make you despondent. You are learned, well-versed in the shastras. You are known to study a matter deeply. You are wise and you are able to find the best way to tackle any problem. When such is the case, it is not becoming that you should give in to these small worries which tend to rob you of your peace of mind. We will certainly cross the ocean filled with crocodiles and whales. I do not have to tell you that to a man who loses his enthusiasm and allows himself to be drowned in the sea of sorrow, all his tasks become frustrated and also, there is the chance of danger assailing him in his enterprise. As for my men, every one of them is a brave and devoted warrior and fighter and, if necessary, they will jump into the fire to please you. I can see from their faces that I am speaking the truth and only the truth when I say so. It is up to you to command us and to think of ways of punishing that sinful rakshasa and bring Sita back.

"I feel that you should think of building a bridge across the ocean and we can easily reach the city of Lanka. You will soon see that Lanka situated on top of the hill by name Trikuta. The moment your eyes are set on the city, you can rest assured that Ravana is killed. Without a bridge to span the ocean, the domain of Varuna, it will not be possible even for the heavenly host to attack the city of Ravana. If the bridge is built then you can see the valour of the Vanaras who make up my army. They are able to assume what form they will and they are all, every one of them, able to kill the enemy. Rama, my friend, please shed this depression which destroys a task even before it is begun. In this world, it is worry which causes mental unrest in man and dampens his enthusiasm. You must not give in to this weakness. You must show your natural firmness in this context. This is not the time for sorrow. Remember we are all here to help you and make up your mind to rouse us into action. There is no one who will be able to face you once you enter the field of battle with the bow in your hand. No one in all the three worlds can think of opposing you. You have entrusted a duty to us and we will stand by you throughout. Cross the ocean and see Sita soon. Anger is the weapon with which you can frighten the enemy and you should shed this sorrow and adopt anger instead, as your armour. You must think of a plan by which the ocean can be crossed and the rest is in our hands. Once the crossing of the waters is achieved, the rest is easy. You can be sure that my army will be able to destroy the rakshasa army with the help of trees and rocks. I am confident that we will be able to destroy that army.

We are going to cross the ocean and we will soon be seeing Ravana dead. The omens are all good and I am certain that you will court victory in the war with Ravana."

Rama listened to the words of Sugriva and his mind found a semblance of peace. He turned to Hanuman and asked him : "I am sure to think of some method by which the sea can be crossed. My tapas will stand me in good stead or if nothing else works I will drain the sea and make a pathway for the army. Tell me more about the city of Ravana. How many fortresses are there? What is the strength of the army? What are the securities with which the gateways are guarded? How are they constructed? How is the city protected and how is the city built? Tell me in detail and make it graphic enough to make the picture rise before my eyes. You have seen the city in its entirety and I know how intelligent and far-seeing you are. You must have collected all the information necessary for us to attack the city and to assure us of victory."

Hanuman stood humbly before Rama and recounted to him in detail all the many defences which Lanka boasted of. He described in detail the formation of the city, of the architecture, of the strength of the fortress, and all about the army and the gateways which decorated the city. He told Rama about the valiant rakshasas who were part of Ravana's army and who guarded the city so jealously. He spoke then and only then, about his own prowess because of which a part of the army was destroyed. He spoke very wisely. He did not underrate the strength of the enemy and, at the same time, he assured Rama that their own army made up of the mighty Vanaras and led by great fighters like Angada, Dvividha, Mainda, and others was capable of subduing the strength of Ravana's army.

He concluded : "It is a very well-guarded city and well-nigh impossible to enter. But that applies to ordinary men, not for one like you and you are sure to find it easy to bring Sita back after killing Ravana. Please command us as to what should be done now. You should think of an auspicious moment when we should begin our march and as for us, we are willing to set out immediately."

2. THE MARCH SOUTHWARDS

Rama listened to the words of Hanuman with great attention and said : "I assure you I will destroy Lanka. As it happens, the sun has reached the zenith and the time of the day is called Vijaya. It is sure to forebode victory to us if we begin our march now. Sugriva, we can arrange to leave immediately. I have followed your advice and anger has now filled my heart. How can this rakshasa hope to be left alive after he has dared to steal my queen? And where can he go to escape my wrath? When she hears about my arrival in Lanka, Sita will once again want to live and, like a dying man who has been fed with poison will find hope sprouting in his heart when he sights Amrita, she will long to live and abandon all thoughts of death. Today the star is Uttara and tomorrow it will be Hasta. Let us begin our journey. I can see good omens which you spoke about and I am certain that I will kill Ravana and rescue Sita. My right eye is throbbing and it means success in our endeavour." Rama sat for a moment thinking of the future and he added : "Let Neela, with a section of the army, go in advance and lead it through a path which has trees with fruits in them and which are shady and cool. Neela, be on your guard all the time. The rakshasas will come to know of the purpose of our journey and it is quite likely they may poison the fruits and the water ponds which are in your path. Be very careful.

'You should look around all the time and find out if the army of the enemy is stationed anywhere. Gaja, Gavya and Gavaksha should lead some portion of the army. Rishabha should be the leader of another section. Hanuman will carry me and Angada, my brother Lakshmana. We will be like Indra on Airavata and Kubera on the elephant by name Sarvabhauma. Let the army be divided into sections and let each be led by one mighty warrior and let us all proceed towards the sea." Sugriva was happy to obey Rama and the army left the slopes of Prasravana with great shouts and demonstrations of their excitement. They jumped about, leaped from tree to tree and from rock to rock. And so the entire army proceeded southwards and Rama and Lakshmana looked like the sun and moon together. There was joy in the minds of everyone and specially the brothers from Kosala.

It was now evening and the sun had set. Lakshmana said : "Rama, soon you will kill Ravana and bring Sita back from her prison. You will return to Ayodhya with a happy heart. I can see the omens which prophesy nothing but good and success to us. The breeze is blowing softly and with a caress. The birds are happy and with the beasts they are making pleasing noises. The sky is clear in all directions and the sun is glowing with great splendour. The planet Sukra is behind you. The seven rishis who are stationed around the star Dhruva can be seen very clearly and Dhruva too. In the south, the world of Vishvamitra, the heaven created for Trishanku by our guru, can be seen clearly too and I can see the royal sage supporting it. The star Vishakha is shining brightly and that is the star sacred to the House of the Ikshvakus. The waters in the lakes and the brooks are sweet and clear and the trees are full of fruits. The fragrance of the flowers is overpowering. Look around you, my beloved brother, and take heart. We will be seeing the end of our misfortunes."

The Vanara army proceeded with speed and passing many hills, forests, gardens, streams and rivers, with ease, it reached the shores of the sea. They reached the foot of the mountain Mahendra and Rama ascended the peak of the mountain.

He stood there looking around and he saw the broad expanse of the sea which lay unfurled at his feet. He then descended and with Sugriva and his brother Lakshmana, he entered the small forest at the foot of the mountain.

Rama said : "Sugriva, we have arrived at the southern shore of this great sea. I am again tormented with the diffidence which visited me before. This lord of the rivers has his other shore too far away from here. It is not possible to cross the sea unless we hit upon a method soon. Let the army call a halt here now. Let us sit and think up methods of crossing this wide ocean. Now that we have neared the city of the enemy let the warriors be doubly cautious and alert."

The army was made to spread out on the many hill tops and broad expanses of land and the entire earth seemed to be covered with monkeys and more monkeys. It was a glorious sight and it was frightening as well. It was like another sea. All of them had but one thought teasing them : how to cross the sea. It was indeed formidable and they stood staring at the fearful waves and the roar of the sea was maddening.

Rama was alone with Lakshmana and he said : "Lakshmana, my dear brother, it has been said that sorrow gets lessened with the passage of time : that time is a great healer. But believe me, it is not true. The sorrow in my heart born of the separation from my Sita seems to be growing day by day. I am not unhappy because of the distance that separates us, nor by the fact that she has been abducted by a cruel rakshasa. I am worried greatly by the vital factor called time. It is the short time which has been left of her life. She has sent word through Hanuman that she will not be able to live longer than a month." Rama gave way to his grief and he said:

"O Vayu! Go to where my beloved is, and blow there. Touch her and then come back to me and caress me when her touch is still fresh on you. That will make me see her in my mind's eye. She must have called out to me : Rama! My lord!' when he carried her away and the thought is eating into my heart like poison eats into the limbs and destroys them. I am tormented by the thought of her helplessness. This fire of separation is tormenting me, burning me day and night. It is the thought that she is alive, which is keeping me alive. All these days it was this hope that she may be alive somewhere, which kept me hoping and now that I know where she is, I am impatient to see her. I long for her, her smile, her gentle looks, her caressing voice. Though she has me for a husband, beautiful Sita is there, far away, in the midst of those rakshasis, and without any one to rescue her from this fate. How can she sleep when she is surrounded by them? Like the crescent moon which shakes off the dense clouds and emerges in triumph, when will Sita come out of her captivity? She has always been slim and now, the fasting and the sorrow caused by the separation from me must have made her thin and weak. I am aching for the day when I can kill that rakshasa king with my arrows and take her back to my heart. I want to cast off this sorrow like one casts off soiled clothes."

When they were thus engaged in conversation the sun began to withdraw his rays and wheeled towards the west. With a heavy heart Rama worshipped the setting sun on the shores of the southern sea.

3. RAVANA IS WORRIED

Ravana, in the meantime, was engaged in a discussion about Hanuman who had played such havoc in the city. He was quite chagrined at the result of his command that the tail of the monkey should be burnt and he said : "A low-born, small-minded monkey has been able to enter our Lanka, to see Sita and to destroy our beautiful city. The temple of our goddess has been razed to the ground and a large portion of my army has been wiped out. What is to be done now? I invite the opinion of the wise in my court to help me decide the future course of action. It has been said that success lies in following the advice of wise and old people. I want suggestions as to how I should behave towards Rama whose messenger has troubled us to such a large extent.

"In the world of men, people fall into three types. The best among men is he who depends on his wise ministers for guidance : men who are his well-wishers, who are adepts in the art of advising the king. He should also listen to the words of his friends who consider happiness and sorrow as equals, who think only of the good of the king. After listening to their words, if a man acts accordingly, throwing the entire burden of success or failure on the power of Divinity, he is considered to be the best among men.

"One who thinks it all out on his own, who walks in the path of Dharma indicated by his own mind and proceeds in accordance with it, is said to be inferior to the previous type. But one who acts without considering the good or bad results of hasty action, who forgets that there is a divine power which controls the fates of men, who says that he will accomplish an end and is unable to do so, is the lowest type of man. This is said by the wise.

"Even as there are three types of men, there are three types of advisers also. Those who view everything in the light of the shastras and advise accordingly are the best kind. There are those who discuss the course of actions, who do not agree on several things but who, finally, come to the same conclusion are the next type. Those who follow their personal opinions with obstinacy and who do not agree with the views of the others, are the lowest type of advisers.

"I appeal to all of you to come to an agreement about the course of action which should be adopted. I have been told by my spies that Rama, accompanied by an immense army of monkeys and bears, is even now proceeding towards our city with the intent of hurting us. From what I have heard of him it seems to me, Rama is capable of draining the sea or adopt some other ruse which will help him cross the sea. I am certain that he will easily cross the sea. I would like the advice of the wise men of my court regarding the danger threatening our city."

The rakshasas stood humbly before him and said : "My lord, it is only the foolish and the ignorant, those ignorant of their own strength and the weakness of the enemy, who allow their king to worry. Why should you worry when we have an immense army? You are a foe who cannot be vanquished. You once went to Bhogavati, the capital of Varuna, and the serpents which inhabited the city were all killed by you. Kubera who dwells on top of the Kailasa peak was defeated by you and was forced to accept you as the suzerain of the three worlds. He thought that he could not be touched by anyone since he was a friend of Lord Mahadeva. But you humbled his pride and took away from him his Pushpaka. Maya, the lord of the asuras, wanted to be friendly with you and he gave his daughter Mandodari to you in marriage. The demon king Madhu was another who has been subdued by you and brought here as your slave. The inhabitants of Patala have all been made to fear you and your prowess. From them you have learnt the art of fighting in the Maya fashion. Varuna's sons were killed by you since they dared to oppose you. Yama, the god of death, has been defeated by you.

"Do you think Rama can equal any of these opponents of yours? We feel that you do not have to go to the field of battle at all. Your valiant son Indrajit can easily kill all the Vanaras and you need have no fear. He has performed a yaga and has pleased Lord Mahadeva. He has been granted a boon by the Lord. Have you forgotten how he fought with the devas and, when he was victorious, was given the name 'Indrajit'? Indra was brought to Lanka as a captive by your son. It was because Brahma asked you to that you released Indra and allowed him to go back to the heavens. My lord, we suggest that you send your son Indrajit to fight these two men with their army of monkeys. The entire army will be destroyed along with Rama in a matter of moments. This is not important enough for you to worry over. Rama will be killed by you and we are certain about it."

Prahastha, the favourite minister of Ravana, stood up and said : "The devas, asuras, gandharvas, pishachas, have all been conquered by you and why do you pay any attention to this mere man? Why should a hero like you devote so much thought to this Rama? If you are thinking of the incident of the monkey which came here and caused such havoc it is because we were all caught unawares and were deceived. I assure you it will not happen again. Let them see me in battle and Rama cannot escape death at my hands. Allow me to go and fight with them and I will rid the surface of the earth of all monkeys."

Ravana's other ministers spoke in the same strain and their words were comforting to him. All of them were vying with each other in talking about his valour, about their prowess and about the ease with which they would destroy the army of the Vanaras brought by Rama and how they would kill Rama and Lakshmana in a very short time, in a matter of moments. They were making Ravana happy.

Vibhishana stood up and he spoke words of wisdom. He said : "My beloved brother, for a task to be successful one should adopt three methods: Sama, Dana and Bedha. If all three of them fail then and only then should the method Danda be adopted. The punishments meted out by Fate succeed only in the case of one who is arrogant and careless and again, for those who are cautious, very cautious, but are abandoned by the gods. I have heard about Rama. He is reputed to be cautious, ever victorious, and, what is very significant, he has the gods on his side. He has conquered anger and no one can approach him in greatness. How can you contemplate opposing him?

"Consider the feat of Hanuman. He has crossed the sea which we thought was too wide to be tackled by anyone. We should never underrate the valour of the enemy and that of his army. Do not judge them in a hurry. Consider the situation. Has Rama offended you? How? It is you who stole his wife from the Janasthana and you have kept her captive here. Khara had overstepped the rules of behaviour. His cruelties were innumerable. And so Rama decided to kill him and his army. Lusting after another man's wife is the cause of infamy. It lessens your life span and it destroys your right to a place in the other world. It is a virulent poison which kills everything it touches. It is a breeder of further sins. I assure you, this act of yours has not done us any good. Sita will be the cause of untold misery for you and for all those who depend on you. I advise you to take my words for what they are worth and return Sita to Rama. What is the purpose of an act which causes a fight? Rama has not swerved from the path of Dharma and he is a dangerous opponent. It is not right that we should hate him and earn his hatred.

"Trust me to speak words which are meant for your good. Restore Sita to Rama. Or else this beautiful city will be ruined by his arrows. The frightening army of Vanaras will enter the city. If you do not act at once great danger awaits all of us. We will be killed and there will be nothing left of Lanka.

"My king, I have great affection for you. I am taking advantage of the privilege I enjoy as your brother and I have dared to advise you. Accept my words and act accordingly. I wish you well. I want you to live long and that is the reason why I am so outspoken. Please return Sita to Rama. Rama's arrows are known to spit fire and let us not be the ones to be destroyed by them. Anger is to be avoided since it blinds man. It clouds the power to think and it prevents you from knowing what is good for you. Let us have peace and peace has to be sought at any cost. Walk in the path of Dharma and save all of us. We would like to live in peace and comfort with our wives and our children. Grant us our lives. Return Sita to Rama."

Ravana said nothing. He dissolved the council and went to his mansion without speaking a word.

Early next morning when the sun's rim had reddened the east, Vibhishana hurried to the mansion of Ravana. This brother of Ravana was righteous. He knew the nuances of Dharma and the other Purusharthas. He was valiant and powerful. He was unlike his brother in the fact that he believed in controlling the senses. He was not a slave to them and so he was superior to Ravana in that respect. He entered the mansion even as the sun enters a bank of clouds. He listened to the chanting of the mantras which were recited to safeguard the king from evil. Vibhishana walked into the inner chamber and there he saw his brother, the king.

He went near him and prostrated before him. He spoke the conventional words which a subject speaks when he sees his master. Ravana signalled to him to a seat and Vibhishana seated himself. There was silence for a long moment.

Vibhishana was well conversant with the art of talking. He knew what should be spoken when, and where and he could also guess when his words were effective and when they fell on deaf ears. He was happy to find Ravana alone in his apartments and decided to speak words steeped in wisdom to the erring king.

Vibhishana said : "My king, evil omens have been seen in our city from the moment Sita entered it. They presage a great calamity to all of us. For instance, the fire which has been kindled by the incantations does not burn without smoke. It emits sparks and belches smoke which is dark like the night. The Havis which is meant for worship is often polluted by ants. Cows have been giving very little milk and not in profusion as they were wont to. Elephants are listless and they are off their food. Our animals shed tears for no reason at all. Crows are making a raucous noise all the time and they sit on top of the vimanas. Eagles and other birds of prey are wheeling about in the skies. Jackals make mournful music throughout the night. I am afraid for the inmates of our city and for you, my lord. Please send Sita back to Rama. Please do not, for a moment, think that I am saying this to save myself from destruction. I am not worried about myself but I am afraid for you. I am frightened of the fate which awaits you if you persist in this path you are walking in.

"The many ministers who spoke to you last night in the council hall were silent about these omens which have been observed by each and everyone of them. It is the duty of a minister to tell the king everything, whether it is good or bad. It is for the king to decide on the course of action he should adopt. My dear brother, I beseech you, return Sita to Rama and live in peace."

Vibhishana's words were well-meant and they were logical and he had explained the urgency of the act he was suggesting : returning Sita to Rama.

However, Ravana would not listen. Blinded by his intense love for Sita and by anger which was second nature to him, Ravana spoke harshly. He said : "I do not see any danger from the enemy. Rama will never get Sita back. I can assure you of that. Let Rama ask for the assistance of Indra and the entire heavenly host. That will not make me frightened of him. How can he face me in battle? I do not need the advice born of cowardice."

Ravana stood up and signalled to Vibhishana that he was not willing to listen to any more words. The talk was ended and Vibhishana had to go back without achieving anything.

4. RAVANA LOSES VIBHISHANA

Ravana was worried. He thought that another council of war had to be assembled. He called for his golden chariot and went to the council hall. The rakshasas who were his guards went in front of the chariot with their weapons and a small army accompanied the king when he went to the council hall. He passed through the wide streets of the city and bugles and drums announced that the king was passing by. The white umbrella was seen by the citizens as they stood watching their glorious warrior king pass by. They were very fond of their master.

Ravana reached the council hall and he was greeted by words of felicitations and praise by those who stood at the doorway. Ravana walked with kingly strides to the throne. It was a magnificent hall which had been wrought for him by Vishvakarma. It was said to surpass even the great hall of Indra in its beauty and magnificence.

Ravana sat on the throne and near the throne were placed seats which were covered with rich brocade. Ravana spoke to those who were there. He said : "A crisis has arisen and it needs great effort on our part to meet it. Bring all the important citizens to the hall."

The messengers hurried out and soon the hall was filled with the ministers of the king. Vibhishana also came in his chariot. He saluted the king and, along with the other chiefs like Prahastha, he sat on the jewelled seat meant for him. All those who had assembled there were valiant. They had fought with Ravana in several battles which he had waged against the devas and danavas. And the arrogant king sat in their midst like Indra in the midst of the Vasus. He was a great person and that had been accepted by the devas themselves.

Ravana looked around him and he first asked Prahastha to make arrangements for setting aside a portion of the army to guard the city. Prahastha, the commander, agreed to do so. Ravana then spoke to the assembly : "I have summoned all of you since I know that you are all my well-wishers and will advise me properly at this juncture. I have never known you to fail me at any time. I have been wanting to talk about an important matter but I was waiting for my brother Kumbhakarna to wake up from his sleep. He is awake and he is here.

"I wish to tell you all about Sita. She was brought here by me from Dandaka forest. You know only too well that it was the dwelling place of our rakshasas. I find that she refuses to accept my love.

"There is no woman to equal Sita in all the three worlds. She is beautiful. Words cannot be found by even poets to describe her beauty. I have become a slave to this passion which is burning me like fire. She thinks of Rama and she refuses to look at me. I have granted her respite for a year as per her request and it is to end soon.

"I have now been told that Rama has collected an army of Vanaras and is proceeding towards Lanka with a desire to rescue his wife. How can the sons of Dasaratha and the monkeys cross this wide sea? As it happens, a monkey did cross the sea and after coming to our city it caused havoc here. I would like the opinion of the wise people assembled here as to what should be done now. I do not have to tell you about my achievements since you have been with me in several of my encounters with the devas. I am certain that there is absolutely no danger for us from these two men. They have discovered the place where Sita has been imprisoned and they have the assistance of Sugriva, the king of the monkeys and his entire army. They have reached the northern shores of this sea. I want you to consider the problem carefully and tell me what should be done to keep Sita here and kill the two princes from Kosala. I am not afraid of them. I would like to get rid of them easily and it is up to you to suggest a scheme by which this end can be achieved."

Kumbhakarna was listening to the words of his brother who had been obsessed with this passion for Sita. Kumbhakarna was very angry and he said : "This speculation about the correct thing to be done should have been adopted before Sita had been separated from Rama and Lakshmana : before she was brought here. We were not consulted as to the wisdom of this act of yours. A king who does not transgress the rules of conduct set down for a king will have no cause to repent later. But acts, which are not righteous, will certainly lead to misfortune. One who sets such a great store on his own valour and acts without foresight will certainly suffer for it later. This stealing of Sita was an act of yours which has now become like food which is mixed with poison. It chokes you. It is a wonder that Rama has not killed you as yet. Perhaps it is because you have been blessed with a long life! You have set in motion certain events without the consent or the approval of the others. It is up to you to see that no harm befalls those who depend on you for their lives.

"I will kill your enemies and rectify the error committed by you. I will fight with the heavenly host led by Indra even. I will face your enemies and destroy them. Who is there in the three worlds who is not afraid of me? I will suck the life out of them. Do not be worried about anything. You do not have to come to the front at all. I am able to kill all of them single-handed. Once Rama is dead, Sita will have to be yours."

Ravana was not pleased with the frank manner in which his brother Kumbhakarna had expressed his disapproval of his act. He was silent and spoke nothing.

Mahaparshva, one of the ministers, spoke in glowing terms of the certainty of success if there should be a war. He then said : "My lord, why do you have to plead with Sita for her love? Can you not take her forcibly?"

Ravana was slightly mollified by the words of Mahaparshva. He said: "I am glad to know that you are all so sure of destroying the enemies. Mahaparshva, you asked me why I have not taken Sita by force. I will tell you why.

"It happened long ago. Once I saw an apsara by name Punchikasthala. She was going towards the abode of Brahma in the pathway of the stars. I became enamoured of her and I approached her. I forced my attentions on her. She went to the abode of Brahma afterwards and she was like a wilted lotus. He realised what had happened and he was very angry with me. He cursed me and these were his words : 'From now on, if you take any woman by force, your head will break into a thousand pieces."

"Mahaparshva, that is the only reason why I am unable to take Sita by force. My valour is as immense as the sea and I am as powerful as Vayu. Rama does not know this and he has dared to march against me. He is as foolish as one who rouses a lion sleeping in the cave of a mountain and hopes to be left alive. Rama has not seen the sharp and deadly arrows which will be released from my bow. I will burn him up with them. Like the sun absorbs the light of the stars when he rises in the east, even so will I absorb all the power this Rama is reputed to possess. A mere man, with the help of a crowd of monkeys, hopes to oppose me! How foolish and thoughtless!"

Vibhishana had been listening to the talks of his brothers. He said: "My lord, can you not see that Sita whom you love is a poisonous serpent? The nape of her neck is the hood of the serpent and her sorrow is the poison in it. Her smiles are but the fangs of the dread serpent and her five fingers are the five heads. Listen to me. Restore her to Rama before the Vanaras enter our city. Rama's arrows are as deadly as the thunderbolt of Indra and each arrow will claim a life. Your warriors are not powerful enough to withstand the valour of Rama. Why, even you will not be able to face him. Even if the devas offer to protect you it will not be possible for you to escape death at the hands of Rama. You may hide your head in the heavens or in the nether world but you will not escape the wrath of Rama. Prahastha, you are bragging about your valour. Wait till you face the sharp arrows from the bow of Rama." He waited and listened patiently to the words of protest from the warrior and continued: "You are wrong. You are all wrong. The words of the king, those of his brother Kumbhakarna, and the words spoken by you all, are all wrong. You cannot gauge the strength of Rama, never. The certainty with which you and the king and Kumbhakarna speak is as improbable as the thought of an impure man who thinks he can attain the heavens. No one has been born who can kill Rama. Even the gods will not be able to gauge the strength of Rama. None of you will face him in battle.

"This our king, is cruel by birth and by nature. He is impulsive and acts without thinking of the consequences. He does things which are forbidden. He is led to his destruction by people like you who pretend to be his well-wishers but are, really, his enemies. You are all encouraging him in the path of destruction and ruin. A dread serpent is holding him in its coils and it is up to all of you to release him from it. Instead, you are all hurrying him towards his death. You should stop him and use force, if necessary, to save him from himself. He is heading towards the dreadful and dangerous sea by name Rama and you should rescue him from certain death. You should advise him to return the princess Sita to her husband and I repeat that this is the only course open to the king. A minister who has the welfare of his king at heart must consider the strength of the enemy and compare it with that of the king. He should also think of the power of Fate and find out if the gods are against us. After due consideration he should arrive at a decision which will be good for the king and the country."

Indrajit was listening with impatience to the words spoken by Vibhishana. He said: "Father, king, I am surprised at the words of your younger brother. They are ineffectual and they are spoken by a coward. It will taint your name with infamy if you listen to him. In this House, no one will follow such words nor will he speak such words if he is really belonging to our lineage. Your brother is unlike his brothers in everything : in the natural qualities of the family, in valour, in might, in manliness, in the power to be firm in the face of a crisis in the intolerance to any stain on the name of the house. Vibhishana, you are a coward. You praise the two princes from Ayodhya to the skies. What are they? The weakest of rakshasa will be able to kill both of them. Why do you frighten everyone with your talk about Rama and his 'invincibility'? I have had the prowess to bind the lord of the heavens and bring him captive to our city. The heavenly host fled in panic when they saw me. Have you forgotten that or am I saying something which is untrue? I took the Airavata by the tusks and pushed it to the ground. I have made a name as a formidable warrior. Why should you assume that my valour will all vanish when accosted by these two mere men? Why do you underrate my valour?"

Vibhishana listened to the words of his nephew with a calm and placid look. He tried to make him understand the reason for his talk. He said : "Child, Meghanada, you are yet young and your thinking power is not fully awake. You have not learnt the great lesson : to discern between what is right and what is wrong. Your words are meaningless and you are but seeking your destruction by such bravado. Even when you are told about the greatness of Rama you are not able to recognise the danger that is awaiting you and you think you are helping your father. But really you are his enemy because you are encouraging him in his delusions about his own grandeur. I am certain that you will meet your death very soon. The king should not have invited an inexperienced warrior like you to the council chamber. He is also courting death by his behaviour. Child, Indrajit, you are not aware of the path of Dharma. You are not able to realise that there are certain things which will be impossible for you to do. You are not quite disciplined and you do not know how to respect elders, and the words of those older and wiser than you. You are not wise nor are you generous in your thoughts. Your thoughts are ever bent on wickedness. You are talking without any sense. You know nothing of the potent arrows which will be leaving Rama's bow very soon."

Vibhishana turned to the king and said : "My lord, please listen to my advice. Take with you the rarest gems which you have and take Sita with you. Go to the presence of Rama and give her back to him. You can then shed this worry and we can all breathe sighs of relief and live long and happy lives. I entreat you to do as I say."

Spurred by Fate Ravana would not listen to the words of Vibhishana. He turned to his brother and spoke harshly to him. He said : "I realise the truth of the saying that one can live amicably with one's enemy : with a serpent which has been angered. But he should not live with one who appears to be friendly but who, in reality, is devoted to the enemy. I am only too familiar with the nature of Gnatis, (kinsmen), in all the three worlds. Men like you are ever in one's company and they seem to be happy too, and yet, all the while they are whetting their swords which will be raised against their own people in times of danger. They are traitors and are evil-minded. It has been said that all good fortune is to be found in cows : control of the senses is to be found in brahmins : fickleness is ever to be found in women, and danger in the minds of Gnatis. O, it is true.

"I have won honour in the world of men. I am blessed with all the wealth and glory of the three worlds. I have placed my foot on the heads of my enemies. Evidently you do not like it. The water-drops which are cradled in the leaf of the lotus are never attached to the lotus. They are always aloof. It is even so with the affection of low-minded men. They are never attached to those who support them. The bee visits the flower and after it has sucked its fill it does not remain with the flower. You are like the bee. The love of small-minded people is like the roar of the cloud during the season Sharad. It is very noisy but there is not a single drop of rain. Vibhishana, if the words you have spoken had been uttered by anyone else I would have seen to it that he died on the spot. But you are beneath even that anger. You are a traitor to me, you are a disgrace to my family. I have no wish to look at you even."

Vibhishana had been trying to advise him against his own folly and the king had hurt him abominably with his words. Suddenly Vibhishana rose up from the ground and with him, four of his followers. He was furious with Ravana and poised in the sky he spoke to his brother : "O king! You happen to be elder to me and so you can say anything you please. The elder brother has to be treated as a father by the younger ones. But, my lord, you refuse to walk in the path of Dharma. I meant to save you. I had but one thought in my mind and that was your well-being. That love for you prompted me to give to you advice which was not palatable since you are already caught in the noose of death. Men who have no control over their senses or their emotions will not relish words like mine. It is always easy to find myriads who will please you with honeyed words which charm the hearer. But it is not easy to find one who speaks the truth boldly. Truth is not welcome and so the hearer will treat it with disdain. When a house is burning it is not possible to stand still and watch it without making an attempt to save it. I tried to do my duty and when I saw you rushing towards certain death I could not let you destroy yourself. I tried to intervene. I wanted to save you from Rama's arrows. Many of the warriors who sit here boasting of their strength are already seen by me dead on the battlefield. Forgive me for my words, my king. Please try and save this city and yourself. I am going away from here. May you be well. Parted from me you will be rid of the thorn in your side and live happily. I wanted to help you but when his life is drawing to a close the man will be deaf to the words of friends and well-wishers."

5. VIBHISHANA AND RAMA

After speaking out his mind to Ravana the saintly Vibhishana left the city of Lanka and soon he was on the other shore of the sea, where Rama and Lakshmana were. The monkeys who were guarding the army saw Vibhishana and the four rakshasas in the sky. He was glittering with his jewels and his massive gada which he held in his hand. Sugriva was summoned by the lesser monkeys and he saw the five rakshasas poised in the sky. He looked at them for a long moment and at Vibhishana in particular. He then spoke to Hanuman and the others : "This rakshasa is well armed and there are five of them. I am certain that they are here to kill us."

The monkeys around pulled out the trees nearby and armed themselves. While they were preparing for a fight Vibhishana who was seeing everything from above spoke in a voice loud enough for them to hear. He said : "There is a sinful rakshasa by name Ravana. I am his younger brother and my name is Vibhishana. It is this Ravana who stole Sita from Janasthana, who killed Jatayu and who has kept Sita a prisoner in his city. I tried very hard to make him give her back to Rama. I tried to advise him against the sinful path he is pursuing. But he would not listen to me. I have been treated like a slave by him and I have been greatly hurt by his stinging words. I have abandoned my sons and my wives and I have come to Rama for succour. Please do not delay but announce me to Rama who is the refuge of the entire world."

Sugriva heard him and, with his breath coming in gasps, he went and stood in front of Rama and Lakshmana and said : "There is a rakshasa who is accompanied by four more. They flew in the air and they came from Lanka. The leader tells me that he is the brother of Ravana, that his name is Vibhishana and that he has come to you for succour." He paused for breath and continued : "Please consider everything carefully, Rama. Pay attention to the enemy, their views and consider also the dictates of Dharma and the path to be followed. As for these rakshasas, they are able to wander invisible in the skies. They can assume any guise they will. They should never be trusted. Most probably this Vibhishana is a spy sent by Ravana. He may come into our midst and plan something evil. He may win your confidence first, and later, when you are careless, he may cause you some harm. He is by nature a rakshasa and he is the brother of Ravana, as he himself announces. He has obviously been sent by the enemy to spy out our forces. How is it possible to trust him and his sincerity? I feel that you should treat him as an emissary from Ravana and punish him since he deserves to be punished. Like an owl which will wait for the proper moment and destroy the entire clan of crows he will join us and he will destroy us when we have placed all our faith in him."

Sugriva was a politician and he was wise in the study of men. After saying this, he stood silent.

Rama listened to his words and then turned to the other Vanaras led by Hanuman and said : "I have heard the words and you have all heard too, the words of Sugriva, my friend. When a situation like this arises, when different views are possible, it is wise to invite the opinions of several people before coming to a decision. You are all my well-wishers and you can say what comes to your minds."

They all spoke their minds with humility and respect. They said : "There is nothing in the three worlds that you do not know. It is your innate nobility which prompts you to make us feel important by asking for our opinions. To you Truth is the only religion. You are righteous and you are brave. No one can face you when you are angry and you will never arrive at a decision without considering it in all its many aspects. You are famed for your compassion towards those who are dear to you. There are many who are older and wiser than us. Please ask them to talk one by one."

Angada wanted to speak. He came to Rama and said : "At the outset Vibhishana has to be treated with suspicion since he is here from the enemy camp. Hypocrites will always act in such a way that their innermost thoughts are hidden from others. When the opportunity arises they will take advantage of it and hurt those who have trusted them. We should consider the evil and the good which may follow our taking this rakshasa into our fold. If it seems advantageous, then, by all means, let us accept him. If it seems as though it will be injurious then let us not take him. Do not accept him if there is even a shred of doubt about his sincerity. If he seems good and noble we can take him as one of us."

Different Vanaras expressed different opinions. But they were all, more or less, against accepting Vibhishana into their group. Finally Hanuman spoke. He spoke words which were soft, full of meaning, sweet and faultless. He said : "Even Brihaspati is not as wise as you in the art of conversing. Your wisdom is infinite and your choice of words is exquisite. Yet, since you have asked me to talk, I will tell you what I feel. It is not because I want to contradict the words of others or because I want to appear wiser than others that I am talking.

"There was a suggestion that a spy should be sent out to find out about Vibhishana. I do not think it is practicable nor will it be needed. As one adviser said : 'This Vibhishana has come suddenly and his coming is not in conformity with the rules set for visiting.' I feel that the very fact of his coming like this out of the blue, is in favour of him. According to my thinking, he has done this after great deliberation. He has seen the sinfulness of his brother and he has heard of your nobility. He has tried to advise his brother to abandon the path of Adharma and found it to be impossible. He has argued within himself the facts, the future. After a lot of thinking, he has made up his mind to come to you. Abandoning an Adharmi and taking refuge at the feet of a noble soul like you seems to have been the only course open to him and he has acted accordingly.

"I saw him in Lanka when he spoke to the king against Ravana's decision to kill me. His face was calm and he did not seem to me to be deceptive in any way. I do not think he is dangerous to us. A deceiver will not act like he has done. He has announced himself frankly and he can be trusted. The face will always indicate the thoughts in the mind. The greatest of efforts will be insufficient to hide the feelings completely. He has openly renounced his brother and come to you. I feel that you should accept him and his words as genuine. I have spoken my mind and you should do what you think seems to be right."

Rama, the very image of all the wisdom of the Vedas, the abode of compassion, Rama, the invincible, was pleased with the words of Hanuman and he spoke his mind. Rama said : "I have made up my mind about Vibhishana. It is quite in consonance with our welfare. I want the opinion of others also about this. As for me, when anyone approaches me with love which is genuine I will not abandon him on any account. Even if there are faults in him I will not give him up. This is the code set forth for us by the elders. I will follow it."

Sugriva intervened and said : "Rama, this stranger is a rakshasa. It is immaterial whether he is good natured or evil-minded . It does not affect us in any manner. According to me, one who has abandoned his own brother who is in trouble, is not worthy of thought. He is capable of betraying anyone who trusts him."

Rama, the valiant, listened to the words of Sugriva and he turned to Lakshmana who was the personification of Punya. There was a ghost of a smile on the lips of Rama when he said : "It seems to me Vibhishana has no aspirations to the throne. Even in a rakshasa family a righteous man can be born. I feel that he should be accepted. Evidently he found it impossible to stay any longer with his brother and so he has come to me. We should take him at his word. My dear Lakshmana, all brothers will not be like Bharata. A father may not have all good sons like our father had nor will everyone be blessed with a well-wisher like you." Sugriva heard the words which Rama had addressed to his brother. He said : "Rama, you are too noble. I still feel that he is a spy sent here by Ravana. It is safer to kill him." Rama smiled at him and said : "It is of no importance whether he is good or bad.

If he is a wicked rakshasa what does it matter to me? Even if he tries to, he cannot harm me. If I so desire I can destroy the entire world peopled with rakshasas, danavas and pishachas with the tip of my little finger. The code of Dharma says : one who has come seeking refuge should not be abandoned. I have made it a rule in life never to refuse succour to one who has come to me and says that he is mine. I have granted him a place at my feet which is what he wants. Let it be Vibhishana, let it be Ravana himself asking me for it and it will be granted to him. Go and bring him to me."

Sugriva was amazed at the firmness with which Rama spoke and he said : "Rama, you are the image of goodness and you have ever walked in the path of Dharma. Is it a wonder then that you should talk like this? After due consideration my heart has been convinced that Vibhishana is not a spy nor is he here with evil intentions. Without a doubt let him be admitted into our fold and let him be one of us. He will be a friend to us."

Sugriva went to the open space above which was hovering Vibhishana and told him that Rama had accepted his homage. Thrilled beyond words Vibhishana descended to the earth and accompanied by the four rakshasas he went to the presence of Rama. He prostrated before the feet of Rama and held on to them. He then stood up and addressed Rama : " I am your slave. I am the brother of Ravana. Insulted by him and touched to the quick by his harsh words I have come to you for succour. I have left Lanka. I have left my friends and my everything behind in Lanka. You are everything to me. My life is yours and my happiness is in your hands. I have surrendered my joys and my sorrows and my very life at your blessed feet." Rama was touched by his devotion and looked kindly on him.

6. PREPARATIONS FOR THE WAR

Rama lifted him up and smiled at him. Vibhishana was so overcome with happiness his tears would not stop flowing. Rama said : "First, tell me about the strength of the king of the rakshasas. I am curious and you are the right person to give me that information."

Vibhishana told him everything without holding anything back. He spoke of the valour of Ravana and about the boons from Brahma which had made him invincible from the devas, gandharvas and all the celestials. He spoke about Prahastha, the minister of the king, and about Kumbhakarna. Prahastha was the commander of the king's army as well as the adviser to the king. Vibhishana spoke very highly of Indrajit and his power to become invisible while fighting. He was a pastmaster in the Maya tactics. This was a gift he had obtained from Agni, the god of fire, and this was a great asset to him : this Maya warfare. Vibhishana spoke all about the many warriors on the side of Ravana and it was a formidable army which was lined up against the meagre army of Rama made up of monkeys and bears.

Rama listened very carefully to the recital of Vibhishana and said : "I have been made familiar with the prowess of Ravana and his myrmidons. I am telling you that I will kill Ravana and all his men beginning from Prahastha and others. I will make you king of Lanka. I promise you that I will do so. Let Ravana try to escape to the *Rasatala* or *Patala* or the abode of Brahma. I will not let him escape from the fury of my arrows. I will kill him and his sons and his army and his kinsmen. Unless I achieve this object I swear I will not enter Ayodhya. I swear in the name of my three brothers that I will do so."

Vibhishana fell at the feet of Rama and said : "I will try and assist you as much as I can in your attempt to wipe out the city of Lanka. I will be one of your army and fight for you. This I swear in the name of all that is good and great : in the name of Dharma."

Rama embraced him and said : "Lakshmana, bring the waters from the sea." He smiled at everyone around him and said : "I am extremely pleased with this Vibhishana. Lakshmana, perform his coronation in the presence of the Vanaras and our chieftains."

Lakshmana brought the waters as he was bid and Vibhishana was crowned king of the rakshasas. There was great joy and jubilation in the camp of the Vanaras.

Sugriva with Hanuman said : "Vibhishana, tell us how we can cross this immense sea. The entire army has to be transported to the opposite shore. How can it be achieved? We have been thinking on this ever since we came here and we are at a loss as to how we should set about it. Can you suggest a way out of this predicament?"

Vibhishana said : "Our king Rama should ask a favour of the lord of the seas. This sea owes its existence to the Sagara brothers who were the ancestors of Rama and the sea owes its name to them and its waters to Bhagiratha, another of the ancestors of Rama. The lord of the seas should remember the urgency of the task which Rama has undertaken and should assist him in the achievement."

Sugriva went to the presence of Rama and Lakshmana and spoke to them about the suggestion of Vibhishana that Rama should ask a favour of the lord of the oceans. Rama thought that the idea was to his liking. He said : "My dear Lakshmana, I approve of the suggestion of Vibhishana. Tell me if you think so too and Sugriva, are you pleased with the idea? Sugriva, I am asking you since you are extremely intelligent and you are good at advising others. Consider this proposal and tell me if you give your approbation." Lakshmana and Sugriva said : "We feel too, along with you, that the advice of Vibhishana is sound. The sea can never be crossed unless there is a bridge to span it. Not Indra nor the asuras can have any access to the city by name Lanka. It will be of advantage to follow the suggestion of Vibhishana and proceed in the matter. Pray to the lord of the oceans and he is sure to let us cross the sea."

Rama prepared himself and spreading darbha grass on the sands he lay down on it. He looked like the god of fire placed on the Vedi of a yagna. He set his mind firmly on the wish in his heart and contemplated on it.

In the meantime, a rakshasa by name Shardula happened to see the immense army which surrounded Rama and which was manned by Sugriva. He was a spy of Ravana and he paid special attention to the details regarding the army and the management of it. He went back to Lanka and presented himself to his king. He said : "My lord, the army of monkeys is like another sea and it is stationed on the northern shores of the sea. The valiant brothers Rama and Lakshmana have come to know of the hiding place of Sita and they are waiting on the seashore. The army is covering the face of the earth and the trees, hills and land seem to be made up of monkeys and nothing but monkeys. Ten yojanas are covered by the army of Rama. We have brought you the report about the situation there. It is up to you to decide on the future course of action. It is really a formidable sight."

Ravana heard the report of Shardula and he wanted to act immediately. He sent for another rakshasa by name Suka and told him: "Go at once and meet the king of monkeys, Sugriva, and repeat the message I have sent : 'O king of Vanaras, you are born of a brave and noble line. You are the son of Riksharajas. Your strength is well known. You are like a brother to me. I do not see why you should be concerned about the stealing of the wife of the prince of Ayodhya by me. You are not in any way connected to him, and there is neither gain nor loss which will befall you by your involvement. I suggest that you go back to your city. This Lanka is impregnable even for the celestials. How then can Vanaras and men enter this city? Forget all about Lanka and go back to Kishkindha and live there in peace.' Give this message to Sugriva and try to coax him and make him leave the shores of the sea along with his army. We can tackle the two men easily."

Suka went to the spot where Sugriva was stationed with his army and repeated the words of Ravana to him. The Vanaras heard his talk and began to beat him up with their fists. They tied him up and flung him on the ground. In desperation he appealed to Rama and said : "I am but a messenger and I carry the words of my master. He sent word to the king of the Vanaras and I repeated them to him. I should not be killed. Please save me from the anger of these monkeys. I am but an instrument of my master and I should not be punished. If I had spoken on my own accord and given my views then I am fit to be punished but not now."

Rama heard the piteous cry of Suka and he asked the Vanaras to stop harassing him. Suka was allowed to go and he rose to the sky and said: "Noble Rama, you are indeed a hero among men. What am I to say to Ravana?"

Sugriva said : "Repeat the words I say now : 'You can never be a friend to me. Nor will you earn my pity. You have never been a benefactor to me and you are not dear to me. You are the enemy of Rama. You and your kinsmen deserve nothing but death at my hands and to me you are like Vali. I have determined to kill you and all those who are yours. I am arriving soon in your city and with my army will raze your Lanka to the ground. You are a fool, Ravana. You may be protected by the devas, you may hide yourself in the orb of the sun, you may enter Patala and hide there and yet you will never be able to escape Rama. I am not able to think of anyone who can guard you when Rama has made up his mind to kill you. Just because you killed the old and ancient bird Jatayu after a fight, do not rate yourself to be very strong. You were such a coward that you did not dare to face Rama or Lakshmana. When they had been lured away from the ashrama by Maricha at your instigation you stole the helpless queen of Rama. You do not seem to know about the prowess of Rama. No one in the three worlds can equal him in valour.'

Angada intervened and said : "My king, this is not just a messenger. He is a spy. It is not wise to let him go back to Lanka. We will keep him as our captive." No sooner had he said this than the monkeys eagerly tried to tie him up. But Rama prevented him from being tortured. He was just a captive.

7. RAMA'S ANGER

Rama spread darbha grass on the shores of the sea and lay down on it. He placed his head on his beautiful arm and he was lost in meditation. He decided in his mind : "I should either cross the sea or else I will give up my life here." With this thought in mind he lay down on the sands. Three days and three nights passed thus. The lord of the oceans did not seem to notice Rama and his Prayopavesha. Rama's prayers had been unheeded since the lord of the oceans did not appear before him.

When he found that three days and three nights had passed and still there was no response from the sea, Rama became angry. His eyes turned crimson and he looked at his brother and said : "Lakshmana, the lord of the oceans is very proud and that is why he is not appearing before us. Really great people are known for the depth of their goodness, their nobility, their forgiving nature, sweet words, and gentleness. These qualities are not recognised by low-minded people and to them these great and good qualities appear to be signs of weakness. The world honours an arrogant man who praises himself, who is wicked, who is wilful and inconsiderate, who is sinful. Lakshmana, in this world, the method by name Sama which is a gentle and soft persuasiveness, will never be useful. In the battle front fame is not going to be won by Sama and neither is it possible to subdue the enemy with Sama. I am going to punish this lord of the seas. I will drain it of all waters. The sea animals and the fish and the sharks and the whales and the tortoises will lie dead in a matter of moments. Watch me shoot my arrows which will burn up the sea. I have been patient and gentle with this arrogant demigod and he seems to mistake it for helplessness in me. It was foolish of me to have been so patient. Fetch my bow and arrows, Lakshmana. I will drain the vast expanse of the sea and the Vanaras can walk across to Lanka."

Rama took up the bow which Lakshmana had brought. With a face like thunder he strung the bow and fixing an arrow to it began to despatch it towards the sea. Arrow followed arrow and there was a terrible upheaval in the sea. The serpents and whales which were in the waters came to the surface in fear and the world trembled at the anger of Rama. A storm was blowing across the tumultuous ocean and the waves rose higher and higher as though in protest. They were as large as small mountains and soon it seemed as though Vindhya and Mandara peaks had been thrown up by the sea. Lakshmana could not bear to see the anger of Rama. He grasped the bow in his hands and beseeched Rama to forbear. He spoke in placating tones : "Rama, you are a great warrior and you can succeed in your task without this anger against the sea. Men like you should not be carried away by anger. Please follow in the footsteps of our ancestors and abandon this wrath." Voices from the heavens were heard saying : "Rama, refrain from this dreadful decision to drain the sea." It seemed as though Rama did not hear these words. He said : "O Sea! I will drain you and with you I will destroy the Patala. There will be nothing left of you except a great expanse of dust and mud, with the dead animals sprinkled all over you. I will make my army walk across you and reach Lanka. You do not seem to recognise my prowess nor my anger. You have no concept of the ruin I will wreak on you."

Rama took up his bow and taking up an arrow he began to invoke the dreaded Brahmastra. The earth and the sky seemed to be rent in fear when he did it. The mountains trembled like leaves shaken in the wind. The world was enveloped in darkness and the quarters were covered with a pall of gloom. Rivers and lakes were muddy and the heavens were looking strange since the sun and moon were straying from their orbits and the stars could be seen. The sky was not able to let the sun shed his rays on the earth. Torches seemed to fall from the sky and there were incessant noises of thunder. The stormy winds were uprooting the trees and even the tops of the mountains were blown about like wisps of straw. Lightning could be seen in the skies and the hills reverberated with the noise of thunder. The animals on the earth were crying out of panic and they stood without any movement, paralysed with fear. The sea receded by a yojana and Rama's fury had not abated.

Out of the midst of the sea there arose the lord of the seas. Over the waves which were like mountains he arose and it seemed like the sun rising from atop the Meru mountain. He was making the entire sky and air glow with his radiance and he was wearing ornaments made of corals, pearls and gems. His magnificent chest was adorned by a necklace made of pearls and he was wearing beautiful silken garments. He was surrounded by the sea serpents and his consorts, the rivers, rose with him and they surrounded him. He stood on the crest of a wave and with his palms folded in humility he greeted Rama. He approached Rama with his hands held high above his head and after saluting him he said : "Rama, you are reputed to be the abode of peace and tranquillity. This anger of yours is unbecoming. The earth, the winds, the sky, water and fire are all ruled by the laws of nature and they should not be overstepped. I am by nature deep and wide and it is not possible to cross me. That is my nature and it cannot be altered. If the bottom is exposed then it will be against all the laws of creation. It is not for me to tell you this. I am only reminding you of the laws set down by the Lord. It is not possible for me to stop the waves and the whirlpools which are part of me. They cannot be frozen into a state of immobility. Not by any amount of effort, nor an intense desire nor fear can make me attempt it. That is the reason why I was silent when you asked me to let you cross the sea, pass over the waves which are part of me. I will, however, assist you in every way I can. When your army crosses me I will not let the whales or crocodiles harm you in any way. I will make it easy for your Vanaras to cross me."

Rama intervened and asked : "This Brahmastra which has been invoked should not be insulted. How should I pacify it?" Samudra said : "There is, in the north, a place sacred to me. It is named as Drumakulya and its fame is as widespread as yours. Some sinners by name Abhiras live there, and drinking my waters they perpetrate sins innumerable. I have not been able to bear the touch of these sinners all these many years. Grant me that your astra is aimed at them and rid me of the one source of unhappiness which has been making me suffer for long."

Rama despatched the arrow towards Drumakulya and there was great rejoicing in the heavens at the achievement of the arrow sent by

Rama. The earth suffered under the impact of the astra and out of the fissures which had been formed, there welled up waters from the Patala. The place then got the name Vranakoopa. The waters which were filling up the place seemed like those of the ocean and the noise made by the splitting of the earth was frightful. The waters which had collected in the hollows were dried up by the astra and the spot also gained the name Marukantara. Rama granted a boon to the place. It became a sacred spot and it was filled with Oshadhis, with sweet water which was like milk, which had healing herbs in it and it became famed for its healing quality. It became a Tirtha.

Samudra spoke to Rama and said : "I will tell you how you can cross me with your entire army. This Vanara with you, Nala by name, is the son of Vishvakarma, the architect of the devas. He has inherited his father's craftsmanship and he is very clever in the art of building. Let him build a bridge across me and I assure you, I will take good care of it. It will not sink nor will it come apart when this huge army marches on it."

After speaking to Rama, Samudra vanished into the sea. Rama found Nala by his side and Nala said : "I will build a bridge across the sea. I have the skill of my father in me and I assure you, I will make the bridge wide and strong. It is true what Samudra said. I can do it."

8. THE BUILDING OF THE BRIDGE

Nala was standing with a smile on his lips and Rama was curious as to what was amusing the Vanara. He looked at him and Nala said : "My Lord, there is nothing like the method of Danda to get one's work done. That is the most rewarding of all the methods. It is the best rule to be adopted. It is futile to use soft words and patience towards those who are ungrateful. This Samudra was scared into submission. He wanted to protect himself from your wrath and he has assured you that he will keep the bridge afloat. I am like my father and I am sure to make a success of the task which has been assigned to me. I am glad Samudra reminded me of my talent. And again, even if I had been conscious of it, is not good to talk about one's own accomplishments. Commanded by you, I will set about the construction of the bridge immediately. I will summon the other Vanaras to assist me and the bridge will soon be ready."

Rama was pleased with the words of Nala and his modesty. He gave orders for the construction of the bridge. According to the instructions from Nala the monkeys in the army hurried to collect the materials needed for the bridge. All the trees around were uprooted and piled on the shores of the sea. The mountains were denuded of their peaks and their trees. The rocks which were like elephants were carried without any effort by the many Vanaras and there was great excitement and gaiety among them while they worked under the direction and command of Nala. The skies resounded with the noise of the rocks being hurled into the sea.

Hanuman joined the rest of them and he wanted to serve Rama by assisting in the work done by the monkeys. He would fling a large boulder and Nala would catch it with his left hand and so the work proceeded with great speed.

Fourteen yojanas had been built on the first day, twenty on the next. The bridge had been completed in five days and the mountain by name Suvela formed the other end of the bridge.

The bridge built by Nala was beautiful and it was poised in the middle of the sea looking like the milky way which is woven across the sky. The celestials came and watched the bridge as it was being built and when it was completed there was great joy in their hearts. To them, looking from above, the bridge seemed like the parting in the dark hair of a woman. The Vanaras were proud of their handiwork.

The Vanaras were ready to cross the bridge. Sugriva came to the presence of Rama and said: "My lord, Rama, please allow Hanuman to carry you on his shoulders. Angada will bear the precious weight of Lakshmana. These two will take you to the other shore easily and they will fly in the air with you."

Rama went to where the army has assembled and with them he walked to the bridge. Sugriva was with him and Lakshmana. Rama first set foot on the bridge : then Lakshmana and then Sugriva. The army followed. The monkeys jumped around in joy. They would walk some distance and then they would jump into the sea and swim for a while and say: "This is how our Hanuman reached Lanka. We will fly across. We are all able to do so," and they would leap in the air and go there in the sky for a while. The noise made by the army of Rama was so great that it drowned the sound of the waves and the sea seemed to hold its breath in awe until they had all passed by. The celestials with the rishis of the heavens collected in the sky and they mentally drenched Rama with sacred waters and blessed him with the words : "May you conquer your enemy. May you rule the world for many, many years." Many were the words spoken by them and they all seemed to be waiting for the great event, the killing of Ravana.

The army landed on the other shore, the southern shore of the sea. Rama was conversant with the language of the omens and he embraced Lakshmana and said : "Let the army camp here since there are groves and fruit trees in abundance here. I see from the omens that a great calamity is waiting to be born in the Womb of Time. It spells destruction to the rakshasas and also to these Vanaras and the bears. The breeze which blows towards us is full of dust and the earth is shaken by tremors. The mountain-tops are trembling too and trees are falling to the ground. The noise of the clouds is fearful and drops of blood are raining from them. The evening light is crimson and frightening and the sun looks like a ball of fire. Animals are making piteous noises and their faces are turned to the sun. I can see the setting sun and there seems to be a dark spot on the face of the sun. Look at the stars which have begun to appear one by one, Lakshmana. They seem to be covered by dust and this is a foreboding that the world will be destroyed. Crows and eagles are wheeling in the sky and they are making unpleasant sounds. The surface of the earth will soon be covered with the weapons flung by the rakshasas and by the rocks and trees hurled by the Vanaras. We have landed in the territory belonging to the enemy. We should guard our army and see to it that Ravana's watchmen do not harm it in any way. Come, let us set about the task of settling them down."

Rama walked fast in the van of the army and he walked towards Lanka. Vibhishana and Sugriva were certain of their success and there was happiness in their minds. Rama saw the many Vanaras in his army and he saw the excitement on their faces. They had come to help him and they were eager. Rama was touched by their devotion and his heart was brimming with gratitude, happiness and humility at the sight of so much devotion and such selfless love.

9. SPECULATIONS

The sun had set and the moon had just risen. Rama had now arranged the army properly and they were resting in the groves which were to be found on the shores of the sea. The earth could not bear the weight of the Vanara army and they could feel her trembling. The Vanaras heard the music made by the bugles and the drums and they were thrilled at the thought that they had come so near Lanka. The sounds from the city came floating to them in the air and they listened with excitement. And they roared with sheer joy. The noise was heard by the rakshasas who were in Lanka.

Rama was lost in a reverie. He looked at the wonderful city with its flags and banners and turrets made of gold and he thought of her, his beloved Sita, who was imprisoned in this city. He thought : "Sita whose eyes would always resemble those of a frightened deer is now a captive of Ravana in this beautiful city. She is like Rohini eclipsed by the planet Angaraka." Rama sighed with pain and he turned to Lakshmana and said : "Look at the city! Look at Lanka! Stationed on top of the hill it seems to touch the very skies. It was built, I hear, by Vishvakarma for Ravana. The city with its beautiful mansions appears like the sky covered by white clouds. The fragrance of the flowers in the gardens, the music of the many instruments, the noise of the birds all make me think of the garden Chaitra which belongs to Kubera."

Rama stood gazing at Lanka for a long time. He roused himself and turned his thoughts towards the immediate task which had to be completed. He said : "Let the brave prince Angada with Neela take his army and station himself at the heart of the great army. Let Rishabha protect the right wing. Let Gandhamadana, the invincible, be in charge of the left wing. Lakshmana and myself will be at the head. Jambavan and Sushena should guard the van of the army. This, then, should be our plan of attack."

The arrangements were made as per the wishes of Rama and Rama told Sugriva : "The army has been arranged well. It is time to release Suka." The captive rakshasa was released since Rama had asked him to be set free. With a grateful sigh the unfortunate rakshasa rushed to the presence of Ravana. The king had one look at him and laughter took hold of him. Ravana laughed at Suka and asked him : "Why have your two wings been tied up? They also seem to be wounded. You look distressed too. I hope you did not fall into the hands of that fickle crowd."

Suka was still trembling. He had not quite forgotten the treatment meted out to him by the Vanaras. He said : "I went to the northern side of the sea and reached the shores of the sea as you had commanded. I went to Sugriva and spoke the words which you had asked me to say. The monkeys were furious with me and they caught hold of me. They beat me up and tortured me. The Vanaras are, by nature, prone to be angered easily and they are quite ruthless. They are not willing to listen to anyone. It is not possible to reason with them or to talk to them calmly. I saw Rama who had killed Viradha, Kabandha, Khara and the others. I saw him with Sugriva, the king of the Vanaras. He has found out the hiding place of Sita. The sea which has never been crossed by anyone was not a problem to him at all. He has had a bridge built across our sea and the sea has been crossed by the entire Vanara host. They have landed on the southern shore. The land is covered by the monkeys. The army is advancing fast and before it reaches the walls of our city you should decide on the course of action to be adopted by you. Either return Sita to Rama or prepare yourself for a dreadful war to be fought."

Ravana was incensed by the words of Suka. He shouted : "Let the entire world and the other worlds too come and challenge me to fight. Let the devas and the asuras and all the heavenly host come here to fight with me. I will face all of them but I will not return Sita. I am ready to fight. I am eager to see Rama covered with my arrows like a flower-laden tree is covered with bees. I will burn him with my scorching arrows. Like the sun absorbs the light of the lesser luminaries I will take his strength away from him. My valour, limitless, is like the sea : my speed is like that of the winds. Rama is not aware of my greatness and so he has dared to oppose me. He does not know that the arrows in my quiver are like poisonous serpents which will drink life. He has never seen me before. Not Indra, nor Varuna, nor Yama, the god of death, nor Kubera can face me on the battlefield."

Ravana was silent for a long moment. He then addressed Suka and Sarana and said : "The army of Rama has reached our shores. It has achieved what I thought would be impossible. Rama has caused a bridge to be built across the sea. I would not have believed that such a thing was possible and the monkeys have shown that it is possible. I want both of you to go there, enter the camp of the monkeys without being found out and try to learn all about the arrangement of the army, and the weapons used by them. Bring me the information as early as possible. It is necessary for us to know the strength of the enemy before engaging in warfare."

Suka and Sarana assumed the forms of monkeys and entered the army of Rama. It was not possible for them to gauge the beginning and end of the army. While they were engaged in the task assigned to them, Vibhishana saw them and knew at once they were Ravana's spies. He grabbed them and took them to the presence of Rama. Scared out of their wits they fell at the feet of Rama and said : "What he says is true. We have been sent by our king to spy out your secrets. Please do not kill us." Rama was quite amused by their fear and he smiled at them and said : "If you have completed your task, you are welcome to go back armed with your information. If there is anything which you have not studied yet, you can learn that also before going back. If you desire, Vibhishana will take you round and tell you all our secrets. Do not be afraid that you will be put to death by me. You are scared to death, you have no weapons and you are messengers who have been captured. You will not be killed. Vibhishana, release these two pathetic creatures. As for you both, go back to Lanka and repeat my message to your king : 'Depending on your strength you have dared to take my Sita from me. The time has come when you should display that strength to me. Let me see you surrounded by your army and your kinsmen and let me see if they will stand you in good stead. Tomorrow, when the sun brightens the world, you will have an opportunity to see your Lanka destroyed by my arrows. Assemble your army from now since I will be at your doorways tomorrow and like Indra with his Vajra fought with the asuras, I will show you how angry I can be and how unbearable my wrath can be.' "

The rakshasas blessed him and hurried back to Lanka. They went straight to Ravana and said: "My lord, we went there as per your command. We assumed the guises of monkeys and mixed with the Vanaras there. But Vibhishana saw through our disguise and he took us to Rama. But that noble prince released us. Four great warriors are arrayed there against you : Rama, Lakshmana, Sugriva and Vibhishana. They do not even need an army to accomplish their desire. Rama is very handsome and extremely valiant. His weapons are formidable and, single-handed, he is able to destroy you and your city and your entire army. Their army is well-nigh invincible.

"There is great excitement in the army and they are all waiting impatiently for the dawn when Rama plans to begin the war. We feel that this enmity with Rama is unwise. Please return to him his wife and let us all rest in peace."

They repeated the message of Rama to their king. Ravana was furious with them and he went up to the terrace of his palace to see the army of Rama. Sarana and Suka went with him. Ravana's eyes travelled over the vast expanse of land covered by the army of Rama. After looking for a while he asked his spies about the details, as to who was the leader, who was valiant, who was guarding the army and similar questions and they told him. Each one of the valiant monkeys was pointed out to him and the name and the valour of each was recounted to Ravana. Sarana and Suka said : "They are all valiant and you should decide how to tackle this stupendous army made up of heroes."

Ravana had been listening to the spies carefully and as each Vanara was mentioned and indicated he looked at them : Nala, Neela, Angada, Hanuman and many others. His eyes rested on his brother who was standing by the side of Rama. Lakshmana was on the other side of Rama and from him his eyes passed to Sugriva, Hanuman, Jambavan, Sushena, and the many powerful guards who protected the army : Gaja, Gavaksha, Gavaya, Mainda, Dvividha, and many others. For a moment there was a twinge of misgiving in the mind of Ravana but it was soon lost even as it was formed and he trained his angry eyes once more on his spies and spoke : and he spoke harshly. Ravana said : "It is not meet that people like you who depend on a king for your living should speak words which are displeasing to his ears. I can make you or break you and you dare to speak words in praise of my enemy in my presence. Your words are out of place and do you think it is correct to talk in such glowing terms of the enemy host to your king against whom they are arrayed? You do not know even the rudiments of behaviour. It is fortunate that I am king in spite of being surrounded by folks like you. I am the one to command you and you insult me by saying things which displease me. Are you not afraid of death? A tree in the forest may escape the conflagration which is destroying the entire forest but no man who wrongs his king can have hopes of living. You have been loyal to me all these days and that, to a large extent, has softened my anger or else I would have executed you. Go away from my presence before I change my mind. You should be ashamed of yourselves for your disloyalty."

They saluted him with the words "May you be victorious" and disappeared from his presence.

Ravana had his minister Mahodara with him. He asked him to get hold of two efficient spies. When they came Ravana sent them to the enemy camp with injunctions similar to the ones given to the previous ones. They went to the army of Rama and disguising themselves they went to the top of the hill Suvela and viewed the army. They saw Rama with Sugriva, Lakshmana and Vibhishana. The sight of the army filled them with dread and, as they were hesitating as to what they should do to carry out the wishes of their king, Vibhishana spied them out.

The spies, one of whom was Shardula, were captured and the same scenes were repeated. The Vanaras beat them up as much as they could before Rama intervened and they returned to Ravana in a chastened frame of mind. They went back to their king.

10. RAVANA TRIES TO DISTRESS SITA

Ravana called for his council to assemble. He spoke to all his ministers and said : "The time has come when we have to pool our wits and decide on the future course of action. Let all our men be called to duty immediately." After conferring with them he gave orders that he should be obeyed in every way and went back to his mansion.

He summoned Vidyudjihva, one of his men who was skilled in the art of Maya and with him went to where Sita was. On the way he told his henchman : "Let me confuse Sita with the help of your Maya. Prepare for me a head just like that of Rama and also a bow with its arrows."

Ravana entered the Ashokavana. He saw Sita seated on the ground. Her face was as charming as the moon. She had discarded all her jewels except the ones which were essential for a sumangali. She had never been insulted before in her life and she was looking forlorn. Her head was bent and her thoughts were with Rama. Surrounded by the rakshasis she spoke to no one but sat silently with tears filling her eyes often. She was like the thin sliver of the moon covered by the clouds and she was like a wilted creeper which had been uprooted by the breeze. And yet there was a depth and dignity about her and she was like the river Ganga. Sorrow could not drown her completely and she seemed to be above the sway of happiness and sorrow. They seemed but to touch her but they could not go deep inside and hurt her.

Sita was lost in thoughts of Rama and Ravana walked towards her. He paused for a moment to drink in her beauty with his eyes and then he approached her. He called her by name and said: "Sita, it is time for you to forget Rama and turn your thoughts to me. I have tried in vain to convince you about my greatness and you have not paid any attention to my words. But now you have to. You have prided yourself on the fact that your husband is Rama the great. You have often told me that there is no one to equal Rama in valour.

"Well, that Rama who killed Khara, has been killed by me in battle. You have been left all alone and there is no one to help you now. Your pride has been humbled by me. Your Vratas have all been in vain. You must become mine now. Forget Rama who is dead. Come with me to my antahpura. Evidently your punya is not enough or else you would not have lost your husband. You thought that your husband was invincible and yet, I have managed to kill him. Your pride has been humbled and your waiting for Rama has been in vain. It has become fruitless. Abandon the thoughts of Rama from now on. Come to me and I will cherish you. You, foolish woman, listen to me when I recount to you how Rama was destroyed by me even as Vrita was by Indra. Rama came to the shores of the sea with a large army of monkeys. He wanted to fight with me and he was intent on killing me. On the northern shores of the sea, with a large army arrayed with great pomp, he planned to attack us from there. My spies have been busy and they found the followers of Rama asleep with exhaustion after so strenuous a march to the city.

"Prahastha, my commander, led his army and he easily massacred the army of Rama. Rama was sleeping and Prahastha went near him and, with a swift stroke of his sword, he was able to cut off the head of your brave husband. Vibhishana was captured and Lakshmana, with the monkeys, has been made to flee from there. Sugriva is lying with his neck broken and as for Hanuman, your old acquaintance, it is a pity that his jaw was splintered and he was killed by my men. The northern shore of the sea is drenched with the blood of the many dead monkeys. You do not seem to believe me. I anticipated it and so I have brought the head of your beloved Rama to convince you that he is really and truly dead."

Ravana summoned one of the rakshasis and he told her : "Ask Vidyudjihva to bring the head of Rama to me. He is the one who brought me this gift from the battlefield and let him show it to Sita also."

The rakshasa who was waiting for the summons from Ravana bent low before him and stood waiting for the commands of his master. The wicked Ravana said : "Delay not. Place the head of Rama before Sita. Let her have no doubts about the words spoken by me."

Rama's head was placed before her. Ravana took up the magnificent bow of Rama in his hand and he said : "You must be able to recognise this bow which was Rama's! The string has not been loosened yet. Prahastha brought it and I had to bring it to you to show it to you. You have seen the proofs of the death of your master, your lord, your very life, as you are fond of saying. Now that he is dead, make haste to come with me and be my queen."

Sita looked at the head of Rama which seemed to be covered with blood since it had been severed at the neck. She saw the famed Kodanda also and remembered the words of Hanuman who had told her about the friendship which has been forged between Rama and Sugriva. She looked at the lotus eyes of Rama, at the glow on his face, forehead, the locks that were framing it, and she set up a wail of woe. She spoke words filled with pain and despair. Sita said : "Kaikeyi, I hope you are happy now. Your aims have been achieved and the light of the House of the Raghus has been extinguished for ever. The entire family has been ruined because of you. How had my Rama offended you that you should have banished him to the forest clad in tree-bark and deerskin? He has ever been true to Dharma and he was punished for no fault of his." Sita could speak no more and she fell down in a faint. She woke up after a while and taking the head of Rama and caressing it she wept as though her heart would break. "The shastras say that the woman who loses her husband is lacking in punya. I have observed Vratas and I have never knowingly swerved from the path set down for a Pativrata. And yet, this misfortune has befallen me. Our misfortunes were numerous and we had to bear them bravely. I thought that my imprisonment was the last mishap that should have happened to me. I was hoping that the imprisonment by this dread rakshasa was to come to an end soon and that you would come to my rescue. And now you have gone. How will your dear mother Kausalya Devi bear this sorrow?

Our guru had cast your horoscope and he had said that you would be long-lived. How could his words have gone wrong? How is it you were caught unawares and done to death by a mere rakshasa? Fate has so conspired that you should have met your end in this manner. You were an adept in the art of statecraft and yet you have been deceived. How well I remember now, the first time I saw this bow. I have always decorated it with sandal paste and flowers. And it has been held by this sinful Ravana. You are one with the stars and you have forgotten us who belong to the earth. Let me join you soon. I will soon die and poor Lakshmana will be left all alone. He will go to Ayodhya with a face wet with tears and he will recount to those in the city the tragic deaths of you and me. I have been the cause of your death. If it had not been for me, this would never have happened and you would have been alive and well."

Sita was heart-broken and there was no one to comfort her. Her tormentor Ravana was standing by, watching her sorrow with glee and hoping that she would agree to his unholy proposal. He stood by, angry with her, since she did not look at him even once.

When they were in the Ashokavana, a messenger rushed to the presence of Ravana and stood with folded palms. He announced the arrival of Prahastha. Ravana realised that it was an urgency which had prompted Prahastha to announce his coming like this and he left the Ashokavana in a hurry and went to the council chamber. When Ravana left the gardens, the head of Rama vanished from there and the bow too. Sita could not understand what it was all about.

Ravana went to the council hall and discussed the situation with all his men and commanded that the army should be collected immediately. It had to be announced with the help of drums, by the town criers and several other methods. Urgency was the watchword and they agreed to collect the army as early as possible. Sarama was one of the few rakshasis who was sorry for Sita and who was wont to comfort her when she was very depressed. She heard about the deceit practised by the king on her and she hurried to the side of Sita. She saw her lying on the ground and bemoaning her fate. Sarama went by her side and lifting her up she said : "Abandon this grief, Sita. I know all about the schemes of Ravana. How could you ever believe even for a moment that Rama, the noblest of men, could be killed? And that by a rakshasa who is but a servant of Ravana? Not one of the monkeys can be killed and yet the king has told you that Rama was killed while sleeping. Rama is well and so is Lakshmana and the entire army of the Vanaras. Ravana has adopted Maya tactics to deceive you and to make you agree to his evil thoughts.

"Be of good cheer, Sita. It will be but a short while before your sorrows will come to an end. Your star has arisen and your tears will cease to fall. Rama is safe and he has landed on the rakshasa soil accompanied by the Vanara army. News has reached the king that Rama has crossed the ocean and has arrived here and that has upset him no end. He tried to play this trick on you and now he has returned to the council hall to discuss about the course to be adopted by him and the army." Even as she was talking they heard the noise of the drums being beaten, the blare of trumpets and bugles. Sarama said : "It is calling all the men to assemble. The army is being mustered up and soon the fight is to begin. Soon, very soon, your lord will come and take you back with him. Death is imminent to the rakshasas and you will shed your grief like a snake sheds its skin. Pray to the sun to grant victory to your Rama and your prayers will all be answered. You can be certain about it."

Sarama came to Sita again after a while and she said : "Ravana has been advised by his mother and by his aged minister to return you to Rama and to avert the war which is imminent. But he is adamant. He is bent on the war which means that Yama, the god of death, is even now getting ready to receive him. He will rather die than give you up and so the end of the king is evident. Rama will kill him and his kinsmen and his entire army will be gone, destroyed. Be without any worry from now on. Happy days are in store for you. You will see your lord."

11. IN THE COUNCIL HALL AGAIN

Rama's army was approaching the city and they could hear the noise made by the conchs and drums which the Vanaras were sounding. Ravana heard it and was immersed in thought for a while. He looked at his ministers as though he sought their opinions. No one said anything and Ravana laughed at them. He said : "I have heard enough and more about the valour of Rama and about the strength of his army made up of monkeys and bears. All of you are great warriors and yet I see that you are all pale and frightened because of some rumour that Rama is invincible. I am amazed at this fear in all of you. I am at the same time surprised."

As he said this, Malyavan, one of the veterans in the court of the king, spoke. He said: "Child, when a king is righteous and learned he will rule the kingdom for a long time. He will subdue all his enemies. He should use his discretion in deciding when to fight and when to make peace with the enemy. He should always have the welfare of his men in mind. Ravana, my child, you should never underrate the enemy. If you are sure of your superiority then you can fight. If, on the contrary, the enemy is equal to you or is slightly better than you, it is wise to make peace with him and to avert a war. I advise you to make peace with Rama.

"The cause of all this hatred and ill-feeling is Sita. I suggest that you give her back to Rama. The gods and all the celestials are wishing him success and it is wiser to be friendly with him than to fight with him. Do you remember the boon granted to you by Brahma? You have been assured that you need not fear death at the hands of the gods, the devas, danavas, gandharvas, kinnaras, pishachas and all the many dwellers in the heavens. You did not mention human beings and monkeys and the army which is preparing to fight with us is made up of monkeys and it is led by a man, a human being. I think it does not bode any good for you or yours. The omens are all pointing to a dire calamity in store for us. Make peace with Rama and save all of us and yourself also, Ravana. I have been told that Rama is Lord Narayana Himself who has assumed the guise of a human being at the request of the gods. Consider the bridge which has been built by them across the sea. Is it the achievement of an ordinary human being? No one has thought of such a thing before.

"Think of the destruction at Janasthana. Single-handed Rama killed all of them. You should think of all these and pause before you plunge into warfare with him. Sita will certainly be the ruin of you. Forget her and give her back to Rama. We can all live happily ever after."

Ravana paid no heed to his wise words. He spoke harshly to Malyavan and made him feel small. Ravana said: "Evidently you are one of those who praise the enemy and his valour. Your words have fallen on deaf ears. This Rama, this hero, according to you, is a mere man, abandoned by his father, shorn of his wealth, lone and helpless. And he has now collected a crowd of monkeys, if you please, and has dared to accost me in war. What makes you consider him to be all that brave? You must know me and you know the fear in the minds of the devas and the heavenly host when they think of me. How can you compare me with Rama and how can you dare suggest that he is superior?

"Either you are jealous of me or you are extremely fond of the enemies or else you would not have spoken thus. Perhaps you have been instigated by them. Or else no wise man will talk such foolish words in my presence.

"I have taken so much trouble to bring Sita to Lanka and do you think I will give her back to that mendicant on your advice? She is like Lakshmi who has left the lotus and strayed to the earth. I will never think of giving her up. Wait and see my valour. Soon you will see Rama and his army with Sugriva and Lakshmana routed by me and you will regret your hastily spoken words. Can anyone think of Ravana adopting the wise course and making peace with a mere man since he is considered to be more powerful than me by some fools? Are the words of a few dotards to be believed? I may break in two but I will never bend my head to anyone. This is my nature and no one can change one's nature. By some good fortune the bridge has been built for him across the sea. That does not frighten me. Believe me, Rama is not going to return by way of that bridge with the army of monkeys. I promise you that. Not one of them will be left alive."

Malyavan realised that the king was too angry and he spoke nothing in reply. He spoke the conventional words of blessings and went back to his home.

Ravana hastened to guard the city and he appointed strong men who would be his faithful servants. The eastern gateway was guarded by Prahastha. The south was under the guardianship of Mahaparshva and Mahodara. The western gateway was in charge of Indrajit, his favourite son. The northern section was under the aegis of Suka and Sarana and Ravana told his ministers that he would remain there too. Virupaksha was guarding the heart of the city and the fortress. Ravana was certain that he was now completely protected and that Rama could do nothing against his formidable army.

12. RAMA WITH HIS MEN

The army led by Sugriva had many strong and capable Vanaras and they were all seated round Rama and Lakshmana along with Sugriva. They said : "Lanka is clearly visible from here and the guards are indeed many. The fortress is formidable and it is up to you to think of methods by which we can attack the city."

When they were conversing thus, Vibhishana, who spoke words which were full of good sense and meaning, spoke to them all. He said : "Our spies assuming the forms of birds have gone very near the city and have noted all the precautions which have been undertaken by Ravana. I will relate to you what I have been told by my spies. Prahastha has been placed in the gateway which faces the east. Mahaparshva and also Mahodara are guarding the south. Indrajit has been assigned the task of guarding the west while Ravana himself is stationed at the north. Virupaksha has been asked to guard the fortress in the heart of the city."

Vibhishana told them about the strength of the army of Ravana. He recounted to them the valour of Ravana and about his fight with Kubera and the devas. He concluded with the words: "No doubt Ravana is powerful and an enemy to be reckoned with. But Rama, my lord, it is not a formidable task for you to accost him and to come out of it with victory crowning your efforts. We will so arrange our army that they will tackle the defence easily."

Rama spoke his words of command. He said : "Let Neela proceed towards the east and accost Prahastha's army. Angada and his army can easily take care of the south where there are two of the enemy's men. Let Hanuman go to the west and as for the north which is guarded by that wicked rakshasa who is arrogant because of the boons he has been blessed with, I will face him and fight with him. He is the lowest of the rakshasas. He has been harassing rishis for ages together and he has been tormenting the world. With Lakshmana to assist me, I will enter the northern gate while Sugriva will remain in the middle of the army guarding it along with Jambavan and Vibhishana.

"No Vanara should assume the guise of a human being during the fight. That should be the rule to be followed by all of us. Also it will be easy to recognise who belongs to our army if the natural form of a monkey is maintained by all of you. Lakshmana, Vibhishana and his four friends and also myself will be the only seven human figures on the field."

After giving these detailed instructions to his men Rama expressed a desire to go to the top of the mountain by name Suvela. He asked Lakshmana and Sugriva and Vibhishana to be with him while he ascended the hill. He said: "Let us spend the night on top of this beautiful hill. From atop the hill let us have a look at the city of Ravana, the thief who stole my Sita from me. The very thought of that rakshasa makes my anger rise in me and I cannot hold it back. He knows not the path of Dharma nor the code of behaviour. He has insulted the name of the noble family in which he has been born. His action is so heinous that it has earned for him the censure of the good and the wise. Because of him the entire rakshasa clan is to be destroyed by me. One who has been caught in the noose of Yama performs an act of sin: and, because of the trespass of this sole individual, the entire family is ruined."

Rama's anger against Ravana was still fuming inside him while he ascended Suvela. Lakshmana followed him, bow in hand. His face was calm and unruffled. Then went Sugriva and his chief men along with Vibhishana. Several of the other Vanaras also went with them to the top of the hill.

When viewed from there the city of Lanka appeared as though it had been built in the sky. At a single glance they could see the beauty of the city. They saw the strong fortifications and the high walls which surrounded the city. Even as they were conversing about Lanka, the sun sank in the west and moon rose in all his glory. Rama felt an exhilaration and he spent a very happy night on the Suvela peak surrounded by his friends and his chiefs.

When they woke up in the morning the city with its lovely gardens was a riot of colour and the fragrance of the flowers wafted to them by the breeze was intoxicating. The city was like Amaravati. The garden was like Chaitra, the garden of Kubera or Indra's Nandana. The flowers which bloom during the different seasons were blooming all together there. They could hear the music made by the koils and the water-birds which frequented the lakes in the gardens. The peak of Trikuta rose high from the seashore. It seemed to pierce the sky. Flowers covered its top and it was a hundred yojanas in width. It was sheer and beautiful. The city was built on top of that hill. Its white mansions and high walls made it seem to float on air. Rama was viewing it with amazement and his eyes rested on a palace which was more beautiful than the others. It was like the peak of Kailasa and Rama guessed that it must be the palace of Ravana. It seemed to be an ornament to the entire city. As he was looking Rama saw that there was someone on the terrace of the palace. A white umbrella was held over him and Rama knew that it was Ravana who was standing there. The jewels on his chest were gleaming in the morning light and he was dark as a rain cloud. His chest had the markings made by Airavata and he was wearing a red silk interwoven with gold which glistened in the sunlight.

13. SUGRIVA'S IMPULSIVENESS

Rama turned aside to say something and he found that Sugriva was not by his side. Sugriva had jumped into the air and was flying towards Lanka. A sudden spurt of anger against Ravana made him act impulsively. He was very angry and in that mood he rushed towards the terrace where Ravana was.

Sugriva went very near the rakshasa monarch and said : "I am the servant of the noble Rama who is the lord of the world. Your days are numbered. You will not be able to escape the wrath of Rama."

Before Ravana could recover from the surprise of his visit Sugriva sprang at him. He pulled his crown down and threw it on the ground. Ravana guessed who he was and said : "Your name is Sugriva and very soon you will lose the beautiful neck which has earned that name for you." He grasped Sugriva in his mighty hands and pushed him to the ground. Sugriva was not bothered. He caught hold of Ravana and threw him as though he were a ball made of flowers. The two heroes were locked in a close wrestling match and soon they were wounding each other. The fist fight went on for a while. When he saw that the Vanara was not to be subdued easily Ravana adopted his Maya tactics, and began to fight that way.

Sugriva knew his limitations and guessing the intentions of the rakshasa he jumped into the air and deceived Ravana by flying back to the Suvela hill. He landed beside Rama.

The many monkeys who were watching this encounter of their master with Ravana were thrilled with Sugriva and there were cries of joy from them. Rama embraced him and said : "What a thoughtless act was this of yours, my friend! Why did you not ask me for permission before you ventured on this dangerous mission? Kings should not give in to dictates of impulse like this. We were so worried for you and you should not have done this. I want you to promise that you will not do like this any more. If you had been killed, what would I have done after that ? When once my friend is gone, there is nothing left for me in this world. Not Sita, nor Lakshmana or Bharata or Shatrughna nor my very life will have any meaning once you are lost to me. I am fully aware of your strength : that you are like Varuna and yet, my mind was sunk in the depths of despair when you went off like that to fight with Ravana. I had at once made up my mind to fight with Ravana, kill him, and then, after crowning Vibhishana as the monarch I had decided to kill myself. I promise you these were the thoughts in my mind when I found that you were not there by my side."

Sugriva stood with a shamefaced look on his face and said : "Rama, when I saw Ravana who had stolen your wife, who has caused you untold misery, my anger knew no bounds and how could I hold back?" Rama smiled and turning to Lakshmana said : "Let us make our preparations, Lakshmana. The omens indicate that it will be a great war which is to be fought between us and the rakshasas. Let us make haste and enter the city of Lanka."

Rama descended from the top of the Suvela hill. Preparations were brisk in the army of Rama and, after studying the time and the position of the sun in the heavens, Rama chose the proper moment and began his march towards Lanka.

Vibhishana, Sugriva, Hanuman, Jambavan, Nala, Neela and Lakshmana went with him. The Vanaras armed themselves with stones, rocks and trees and proceeded with great excitement. Very soon they reached the neighbourhood of Lanka. They took up the positions which had been assigned to them by Rama. Rama went towards the northern gate where Ravana was said to have stationed himself. It was protected by an immense army of rakshasas. Rama glanced at their weapons and their armours. The trees and gardens were slowly covered by the army made up of Vanaras. The rakshasas found that the army was indeed formidable and not small and insignificant as they thought it would be.

14. ANGADA'S MISSION

Rama was ready to begin the fight. And yet he decided to follow the rules of fighting very strictly. A messenger has to be sent to try finally for peace and to avert the war if possible. Accordingly, after discussing with friends, Rama decided to send Angada to Ravana. He summoned the young prince and said : "Child, you are fearless and you are capable of obeying me, of conveying my message intelligently. So I have decided to send you to Ravana. Go into the city and go to the presence of Ravana. Give him this message : 'Your glory will soon be lost and your kingdom too. Your death is very near since you are lacking in wisdom. You are a thief. Your pursuit of sinfulness against rishis, against the devas, and against all god-fearing men, will finally yield fruit. You will reap the reward for all your foul deeds. It is inevitable that you should suffer for your sins. I have come to punish you for stealing my wife. The boons you have obtained from Brahma are of no use to you now. Your pride will soon be humbled. You were very brave when you separated me from my wife and stole her when I was absent. It is time for you to show me your prowess and let me see how brave you are when you face me in battle.

'If, however, you agree to return Sita to me and ask forgiveness of me, I will stop this fight. Else, you will have to fight. I assure you, this world will then be rid of all rakshasas because of the sharpness of my arrows and the deadliness of my anger. Vibhishana is a good soul and he came to me seeking refuge at my feet. I will make him the monarch of Lanka after killing you. You have been unfortunate in your ministers since there is no one there to advise you properly and so, you cannot be king for long, steeped in sin as you are. Summon up enough courage to fight. If you meet your death at my hands you will be cleansed of all your sins and you will find a place in the heavens. Take one last look at your beloved Lanka and come to the battlefield.' Tell him this and bring me back his reply."

Angada jumped into the sky and very soon he reached the great hall where Ravana was closeted with his ministers. Angada with his golden bracelet gleaming in the sunlight went to the presence of Ravana and he looked like a tongue of flame. He announced himself to Ravana. He said : "I am the messenger from Rama. I am the son of Vali and my name is Angada. I have brought you a message from Rama." He then repeated the words of Rama and waited for Ravana to speak.

The anger of Ravana knew no bounds. He told his ministers : "Capture this monkey which is bereft of reason. Torture him for his audacity."

Four rakshasas caught hold of Angada who allowed them to do so. When they were tying him up he jumped into the air along with them and landed on the terrace of the mansion. He flung them from him and saw them fall to the ground. He then broke the turret of the mansion to splinters and, with a roar of triumph, he returned to the presence of Rama.

Ravana was furious with him for what he had done but he could do nothing about it. Rama felt that he had given every chance to Ravana and since he did not accept his words, war was now inevitable. That was certain.

The rakshasas who were guarding the gates were watching the progress of the Vanara army. Most of them were not afraid but some were frightened. Everyone on either side was eager to see the beginnings of the war. The Vanaras were particularly jubilant and the rakshasas were equally impatient. They were complacent and they were sure of destroying the army made up of monkeys and they were not worried. Word was conveyed to Ravana about the latest developments : that Rama had begun his march towards the city and that his army had reached the four gateways. Ravana made haste to ensure the safety of the city and in a fit of anger he went up to the terrace of his palace. From there he saw the sea of monkeys which was surrounding his city. For a moment he was worried as to how that army was to be destroyed. But his natural arrogance asserted itself and he looked very intently at Rama and the army he had brought.

Rama was greatly excited now that he had decided on war. He saw too that Lanka was overflowing with rakshasas who had been placed there to guard the city. Rama's thoughts at once went to Sita and be thought : "It is here that my dear beloved Sita is imprisoned. She is wasting away because of sorrow and seated on the ground, she mourns the fact that she is parted from me."

The thought of Sita was enough to spur him to activity. He commanded his army to begin their task of destruction. The moment they heard his words the monkeys vied with each other to rush towards the gates and began to fight. Their shouts resounded everywhere and it was frightening to the weak-minded. The Vanaras had armed themselves with huge boulders and trees which had been uprooted from the hill which was nearby.

15. THE NAGAPASA

Rama's army rushed towards Lanka. They began to attack the gateways and to destroy them. The Vanaras shouted and occupied the high wall surrounding the city and their shouts were echoed from the surrounding hills. The wall was broken and the eastern gate was also broken. Very soon the south was attacked and also the west. The Vanaras occupied the spots which had been indicated by their commanders and Rama, with Lakshmana, went towards the northern gate and attacked it. Nothing could be seen except the many Vanaras leaping from place to place and the destruction following in the wake of their progress. Ravana hastened to send his army to oppose the onrush of the Vanaras.

With the noise of trumpets and drums the army of Ravana came out of the city to defend it. They were ready to fight with the Vanara army led by Rama. They were like the waves of the ocean and they kept on advancing towards the monkeys. The earth trembled at the steps of the rakshasas as they marched towards the Vanaras. The encounter between the two armies was terrible and it was like that between the devas and the asuras in the olden days when they fought for the Amrita on the shores of the ocean of milk. The river of blood began to flow and soon the field presented a gory sight. Several duels were fought.

Indrajit, the son of Ravana, fought with Angada and it was a glorious fight to watch. Hanuman encountered Jambumali. Neela fought with Nikumbha, Lakshmana, with Virupaksha and Rama fought with four at the same time. Indrajit hit Angada powerfully with his gada and in return the prince of Kishkindha broke his chariot and his horses as well as his charioteer. By and large, the army of Rama was gaining the upper hand. Virupaksha was killed by a single arrow from the bow of Lakshmana. All the chariots were crushed by the Vanaras to powder and the fights were really intense and interesting to watch. The field of battle was covered by the many weapons of the rakshasas, with the trees and the rocks used by the Vanaras and the setting sun was welcome to all of them. Even as they were fighting the sun had set and night set in swiftly.

But they did not pay any attention to it. The fight continued and during the night, when they could not see each other properly the incensed rakshasas and the Vanaras fought with fury. The rakshasas found their strength increasing with the advent of the night and they made full use of it. The Vanaras, however, were undaunted. And so the fight went on all through the night.

Rama and Lakshmana were fighting with their bows and each arrow was claiming a life. The noise was like that of the seven seas during the great deluge at the end of the yuga. Ravana's army could not withstand the arrows of Rama and Lakshmana and they fled from their presence.

Indrajit vanished from there and fought with his Maya tactics. Indrajit had been treated very roughly by Angada and he was furious with him. Rama said : "I want you all to assemble in one place. This son of Ravana has been blessed with boons from Brahma and he is bent on harassing the three worlds. It is the prodding of Yama which has made him come to us and fight with us. Please do not be worried about him. I will fight him."

In the meantime, Indrajit disappeared into the sky and from there he showered arrows on Rama and Lakshmana. He wounded them with several arrows. Unseen by them he managed to send arrow after arrow and finally with his arrows he bound the two brothers. The Vanaras were watching and they found the noble brothers tied up by the poisonous bonds which went by the name 'Nagapasa.'

The valiant Indrajit had adopted his Maya tactics and while unseen by them he had managed to send the dread astra and they were caught in its coils. While fighting he said : "Indra the lord of the heavens has not been able to withstand my valour. He is afraid to come near me. How then can you dare to accost me in battle?"

Rama and Lakshmana were bound by the Nagapasa and it was not possible for them to open their eyes. They were also wounded badly by the arrows of Indrajit and they were like twin Palasa trees crimson with flowers. Rama dropped to the ground in a faint and soon his brother lay beside him. The glorious bow slipped from his hand and lay by his side.

Panic set in the army. Sugriva, Hanuman and the others were helpless and they did not know what they should do faced with this calamity. Vibhishana knew the potency of the bonds which held the princes in its grip and he could do nothing. The Vanaras looked hard at the sky but they could not see Indrajit. Vibhishana was the only one who could see through his guise and discern him.

The prince Indrajit said : "Look on this great hero who was the death of Khara and Dushana! He and his valiant brother are now lying on the ground, caught helplessly in the coils of the serpents. Not all the rishis nor all the devas can release them. My dear father will now be rid of the one thorn which was hurting him. All the noise made by this army and its leaders is like the noise made by the clouds in the season Sharad when there is no rain but just noise."

He went on with his work of destruction and there was not one chief among the Vanaras who had not been hurt by him. He was now certain that the Kosala brothers were dead and, followed by a jubilant crowd, he entered Lanka in triumph.

Sugriva was extremely worried for Rama and Lakshmana. Vibhishana said : "Do not weep, Sugriva. I can see that they have fainted and they are not dead. If we have ever performed any good acts at any time they will wake up from this faint and let us comfort each other with hopes of seeing them get up. Truth and righteousness will have to win in the end." Vibhishana recited some verses and sprinkled water on the eyes of Sugriva. He then said : "This is not the time to despair. The army is panic-stricken and it is up to you to bring a semblance of order in the ranks. Your excessive affection for your friends will be enough to weaken you. Do not give in to weakness. Rouse up your sleeping valour and try to act. We will have to guard these two very carefully and when they regain consciousness they will bring joy to our hearts. I can see that they are not dead. Their faces have not lost the glow which is sure to leave them once life abandons the body. I assure you there is nothing to worry. No harm will befall them. You must take care of your army or else it will be wiped out completely. Can you not see the terror in the eyes of the Vanaras? You should comfort them and tell them that nothing untoward has happened and that they should be of good cheer."

Together, Vibhishana and Sugriva undertook the task of reassuring the army and making them shed the excessive fear which had gripped their hearts.

16. SITA SEES RAMA ON THE FIELD

Indrajit, in the meantime, entered the city of Lanka followed by his army. He went to his father and told him what had happened. Ravana rushed to him from his throne and embraced him warmly again and again. He wanted to know the details. His son was only too happy to recount how he had tied them up with the Nagapasa and that they were dead. Ravana's joy knew no bounds and he was very proud of his son who had done such a great service to him. There was nothing but peace in the mansion of Ravana that night.

The fear in the hearts of the Vanaras had not been set aside. They stood around their leader Rama, who looked as though he would never get up again and every noise and every whisper of the trees made them jump in fear since they had become so scared of Indrajit and his Maya warfare.

Ravana at once sent word to the rakshasis who were guarding Sita. They came and with them came Trijata. With a smile on his face Ravana said : "Go at once and tell Sita that her dear husband Rama and his brother Lakshmana have both been killed by Indrajit. Place her in the Pushpaka vimana and let her see for herself the dead forms of the Kosala princes. Depending on him and his valour she refused my love and now he is lying dead on the battlefield. Let her now forget him and come to me. Let her shed her sorrow and become mine. If she sees Rama dead she will know that she has no other course open to her except to accept my love and please me. She will do it on her own." The rakshasis went to Sita and they placed her in the Pushpaka. They forced her to sit in it and Trijata was also with her as the vimana rose up in the sky.

Sita now saw the field of battle and saw the devastation caused in the army of the Vanaras. She saw that the rakshasas were jubilant and there was despair writ on the faces of her Rama's men. Her eyes then lighted on Rama and Lakshmana. She saw the wounds which were bleeding and she saw the arrows which had lodged in their bodies. They were hurt very badly. They were lying on the beds of arrows and they were still. Tears flowed unheeded from her eyes and she gazed with love and despair on the face of her beloved Rama. She saw Lakshmana and her sorrow broke out in wails. She said : "all the words of the wise that I would be a sumangali have been proved false. It was said that my Rama would perform the Ashvamedha and win fame as great as that of any other king of the race of the sun. That is a false prophecy since he has died before even the coronation. How could the words of our guru Vasishtha prove false? My feet also have the sign called the Padma Rekha which assures one that she will never lose her lord and yet, I see him dead. Rama who killed the rakshasas effortlessly in the Janasthana is now lying dead, killed by the son of Ravana. Rama who is the master of all the astras could not summon even one of them to counteract the effect of this astra hurled by that sinner. His Maya tactics have deceived my lord. Or else, how can one escape from my husband's anger? I realise now that Fate is more powerful than all other forces in this world. Even Yama is rendered helpless before Fate."

Trijata was listening to the lament of Sita and she was very sorry for the princess she was very fond of. She said : "Devi, do not weep. Your lord is not dead. Both of them are alive. I will tell you how I am so sure. If they had been killed then this divine vimana by name Pushpaka would not have taken you in and flown in the sky. You are a sumangali and that is why you have been carried by Pushpaka.

"I can see that several of the heroes are guarding Rama and his brother and it seems to me they are waiting for them to recover from the deep trance into which they have fallen. Believe me when I say these words. Take a good look at this dear face of your beloved lord since it is a long time since you last saw him. Look at him and his brother with a calm frame of mind since I know that they are alive. I have never seen a dead man look so alive! Never once have I spoken an untruth, my Devi, and I will not do so hereafter. Look at their faces. There is a glow about them which would have been absent if they had been dead. Forget this sorrow. It is not necessary. It is needless. Rama and Lakshmana cannot die: not at the hands of Indrajit."

Sita was convinced by the words of Trijata and she placed her palms together as a gesture of salutation to Rama. The vimana turned towards Lanka and Sita was taken back to Ashokavana.

17. THE RECOVERY OF THE PRINCES

The heads of the Vanara army stood around Rama and the brave Lakshmana and they were feeling afraid lest they should die without regaining consciousness. While they were watching Rama moved slowly and it could be seen that slowly his consciousness was coming back to him. He looked at once at his brother and he thought that he was dead. He saw his brother lying there, wounded, with blood covering his beautiful body and Rama was inconsolable. He lamented the death of Lakshmana. He wailed : "I have seen my beloved brother dead and what is the purpose of my living any more? What is Sita to me when Lakshmana is gone? What should I live for once he is dead? If one looks diligently enough in this world, there can easily be found a woman like Sita but will I ever find a brother like Lakshmana? Can there be another warrior like him? I am going to kill myself since I have lost my brother. How can I face Kausalya Devi and Sumitra when I go back to Ayodhya alone? How can I comfort them who will weep like mother deer who have been parted from their young? What will Bharata think of me and what about Shatrughna, his twin?

"He came to the forest with me and his mother Sumitra asked him to think of me as his father. Is it like a father that I have taken care of him? I have been the cause of his death. I have no desire to live any longer. I am a sinner and I deserve to die. Lakshmana, when I was unhappy, you were the one to comfort me and now you are dead and I have no one to comfort me. I will follow him to the city of Yama and be with him. He followed me when I left Ayodhya and it is but meet that I should go with him now. We can never be parted. Never once has he spoken harshly to me and he has ever followed the path of Dharma. He was easily roused : but never once against me.

"Sugriva, go back to Kishkindha with what is left of your army. Now that we will both be dead Ravana will harass you and I do not want that to happen. Cross the sea and go back as quickly as you can. You did your best for my sake and I will never forget the love you have for me. But the time has come when you should return to Kishkindha."

Rama fainted again. The Vanaras stood with tears in their eyes. Vibhishana who had been busy trying to bring order in the scattered ranks came there with his gada in his hand and the army fled from him thinking that he was a rakshasa from the enemy camp. After a while Jambavan assured them that it was Vibhishana and they came back and abandoned their fear. Vibhishana sat and mourned the death of the Kosala brothers. And so they sat, hopelessly.

Sushena, the physician, came near them and said : "Once during the war between the devas and the asuras several of the devas were floored even thus and they appeared to be dead. Brihaspati, the divine preceptor, asked for some herbs to be brought from the ocean of milk and he revived them. Let some of the Vanaras bring two herbs by names Sanjivakarani and Vishalyakarani. In the ocean of milk are found the hills Drona and Chandra. They are located in the spot where the Amrita was churned from. These two herbs can be found there. The devas had placed them on these hills. Let Hanuman, the son of Vayu, go there and bring them."

Even as he was speaking, there was a strong breeze blowing from the sea. The sea was in tumult and the mountains were shaking because of the strong wind. Wings seemed to beat in the air and trees were uprooted by the force of the wings. The serpents which formed the bounds and which were choking Rama and Lakshmana were now trembling in fear and the Vanaras looked up to see the great eagle Garuda approaching the fallen princes. When he came near the serpents fled from the bodies of Rama and Lakshmana. Garuda stroked the faces of Rama and Lakshmana with his two hands and their wounds vanished as though by the touch of a magic hand. They were again as glorious as ever and their limbs lost their weakness. They woke up from their stupor. Garuda embraced them and Rama said : "Because of your grace we have both been saved from the danger caused by Indrajit. We feel strong and our fatigue is vanished. I feel that I have been caressed by my father when your hands touched me. You are so handsome and you are wearing garlands which are said to be used by the celestials. You are wearing beautiful ornaments. I do not know who you are."

Garuda said : "Rama, I am Garuthman, or Garuda, and I am your constant companion. I am your very life which has a separate form and which is wandering about. I came here to aid you. No one, not any deva or gandharva nor danava or anyone for that matter is able to loosen the knots formed by the snakes which form the Nagapasa. These serpents are all the sons of Kadru and they had taken up the guise of arrows and they have wound themselves around you. I am their ancient enemy and they are afraid of me. Rama, you are righteous and you are a true hero. You and your brother are destined to destroy all your enemies and you have been released from the Nagapasa. When I heard about this incident I came here with all speed to release you.

"Your Dharma is your strength and you will be victorious even though the rakshasas fight with treachery in their hearts. Give me leave to go back to where I came from. Do not be curious as to how I call myself your friend and how I am your alter ego. When you have achieved what you have to, you will understand my words. Soon you will kill Ravana and Sita will come back to you." Taking leave of the brothers Garuda flew into the sky.

18. RAVANA SENDS PRAHASTHA

The joy which pervaded the army of Rama was indescribable. The noise of their bugles and drums and their shouting filled the four quarters. They clapped their hands and they kissed their tails. They rushed to the gates of Lanka and displayed their eagerness to continue the war. The rumbling of rain clouds during a night in the rainy season was brought to mind when they shouted in happiness.

Ravana heard the tumult of the monkeys. It seemed strange to him that they should be happy and he said : "The sound is startling and it seems to me they are shouting with joy. There is no doubt about it. The brothers Rama and Lakshmana have been tied up by the Nagapasa and yet the monkeys sound as though they are happy. I am wondering what could have happened to cause this sudden joy and sudden noise." He added : "Send someone to find out what is happening in the camp of the enemy." The messengers went and found out all that had taken place and they returned to the king.

They told their master : "The Kosala brothers who were tied up by the Nagapasa despatched by our prince are free of it and they are looking as though nothing has hurt them. There is not even a trace of the many wounds which had been inflicted on them. They are like two elephants wandering happily in a lotus pond."

Ravana heard their words. Amazement and worry were the mixed feelings which visited him. He had never known anyone who had escaped the Nagapasa and its dread bondage. He said : "Indrajit was certain about tying them up with his astra. I am dubious about my strength when I hear of this miraculous escape of these brothers."

He summoned the rakshasa by name Dhumraksha and sent him with a fresh army to fight with the Vanaras. Dhumraksha was happy to obey the commands of his king and soon he left the city in a hurry. A terrible army left Lanka with Dhumraksha to lead it and proceeded towards the field of battle. He went straight to where Hanuman was stationed and there was a smile of confidence on his face. Evil omens were seen by him and his men but he heeded them not, though for a moment, they did frighten him. A furious fight was on between him with his rakshasas on the one side and the Vanaras on the other. The Vanaras used their teeth and nails as well as trees and stones as their weapons and they succeeded in destroying a large portion of the army of the rakshasas. There was great loss on both sides and Hanuman found his army to be suffering a great loss at the hands of Dhumraksha's men. Hanuman raised aloft a big boulder and threw it at the chariot of the chief. Dhumraksha leaped out of the chariot just before it fell to the earth splintered to bits. A duel was fought between the two in which Hanuman killed Dhumraksha. It was a rock which crushed the life out of him.

News reached Ravana that Dhumraksha was dead and he sent Vajradamshtra, who was proficient in Maya warfare. This rakshasa, after he had displayed his valour for a short while, was killed by Angada and after his death, Akampana, who was a Maharathika led the army and he was killed by Hanuman. Ravana was depressed to know that three of his great warriors were dead. He needed to think for a while. He bent his head down and his eyes were trained on the floor. After a while he lifted up his face and he looked at his ministers and said : "I will go now and inspect the army and make sure that the city is guarded well."

He made a tour of all the vital places and found that they were all guarded very well. His anger had not abated and he approached his chief minister and the commander-in-chief of his army, Prahastha, and said :

"Prahastha, things have come to such a pass that it needs me or Kumbhakarna, or Indrajit, or Nikumbha or you to lead the men into battle. There seems to be a kind of fear instilled in the minds of our men because of the successive deaths of three of our men. I want you to go at once and quell this upstart once and for all. When they hear your victorious progress the Vanaras will flee from the place and you can defeat them easily. It is not an army at all, which is trained in the art of fighting. They are wild, fickle-minded monkeys collected from the tree-tops. How can they face you? How can they tackle a disciplined army which marches ruthlessly under the guidance of a master like you? Rama and Lakshmana are sure to be captured by you. Never once have you been defeated in any fight and so often have you fought by my side. Together we have gone to the heavens and the devas have been afraid of you. I have implicit faith in your success."

Prahastha was touched by the affection of the king and his faith in his prowess and he said : "You have always been good to me. I have received many honours from you and several favours have been granted me by you. My life is yours and let me assure you that I am prepared to lay it down for you."

Prahastha went to the front. Rama saw him advancing and asked Vibhishana with a smile : "Who is this rakshasa who seems to be a great warrior?" Vibhishana said : "This is Prahastha, the commander-in-chief of the army of Ravana. He is very brave and he has earned the reputation that he is a great fighter. He is familiar with the astras and he has been to the heavens when Ravana fought with the devas. He is fairly formidable."

The Vanara army was waiting for the coming of the army of Prahastha. They armed themselves with their weapons made up of trees and rocks and soon the fight was on. There was killing on either side and great was the loss to both of them. Neela was watching from a distance and he saw the disaster which was being caused by Prahastha in his army. Neela came to the forefront and he stood facing the commander of the army of Ravana.

Prahastha saw him and went towards Neela in his chariot which was golden. They fought a terrible duel and the rest of the army stopped fighting and stood watching the glorious spectacle. Very soon Neela had destroyed the chariot of Prahastha and he had killed his horses and the charioteer too. He broke the bow of Prahastha who jumped down from the terrace of his chariot which had been broken. Prahastha and Neela were engaged in a duel. Finally Neela took up an immense piece of rock in his two hands and hurled it with all his might at Prahastha. The commander of Ravana's army, the valiant Prahastha, fell down dead with his head split into several fragments.

The army rushed back to the city with fear chasing every one of them. It was like a river which had brimmed its banks and finally broken them.

Rama was thrilled with the valour shown by Neela and there was great joy in the camp of Rama. Ravana was told that Prahastha had been killed by Neela, the son of Agni. He was shocked and grieved to hear the news. Very soon anger was uppermost in his mind and he said : "Prahastha has always stood by me and he has destroyed a large portion of the army of Indra in the days of old. Such a valiant fighter has been killed and that by a mere monkey! His death has to be avenged. We should no longer ignore the valour of the enemy. I will go myself to the battlefield and avenge the death of my dear Prahastha, who was like a brother to me. I will kill the enemies and win the war. Like a forest fire will burn up a forest full of dried trees I will burn them all up with my scorching arrows and make them all lie dead on the field."

19. RAVANA ON THE FIELD OF BATTLE

Ravana called for his chariot and soon it was at his door. He ascended the chariot which was like fire and set out for the field of battle. Surrounded by his rakshasas he looked like Lord Mahadeva surrounded by his Pramathaganas. He went fast towards the field of battle and he saw the army made up of monkeys. He smiled in derision.

Rama saw the huge army advancing and he turned to Vibhishana and asked him : "Who is the hero leading this mighty army? Everyone seems to be enthusiastic about fighting and the chariot which gleams golden has their chief. I can see his bow and it seems to be a mighy bow. I am intrigued as to who he is."

Vibhishana looked at the army and the chariot and said :

"On the elephant which is like Airavata is seated a great fighter by name Akampana. The chariot with the banner decorated with a lion holds Indrajit. The other warrior who is making the earth quake with fear by the noise of his bowstring is Atikaya. He has by his side another of the favourite warriors of Ravana and his name is Mahodara. Along with him can be seen Kumbha whose banner is a serpent. Nikumbha is the leader of this army. I can see Narantaka who is famed for his valour against the devas when he fought with them along with Ravana.

"You can see approaching you a white umbrella which is whiter than the moon. Under that umbrella is seated Ravana, the lord of the rakshasas. He looks like Lord Mahadeva surrounded by his Bhoothaganas. Look at his golden earrings and his crown. He is like the Vindhya and the Himavan in his magnificent physique. He has subdued Indra and Yama in the days of old when he fought with the devas. He glows like the noonday sun."

Rama looked at him for a long, long moment. He said : "The lord of the rakshasas is indeed glorious to look at! What radiance! He seems like the sun which cannot be seen with the naked eyes, so full of splendour is this Ravana. I am certain that he is the home of all that is mighty and valiant. What valour! What courage! What might! What splendour! This lord of the rakshasas is endowed with all the qualities of a great hero. I am amazed at the sight of him. No deva or asura can equal him in might, I am sure. His warriors are all brave and valiant and they seem to be excellent fighters. In the midst of these Ravana looks like Yama, the god of destruction with his Kinkaras."

Rama's lotus eyes turned crimson and he said : "And when I think of my Sita who has been stolen by him I am reminded that he is a sinner. Fortunately he has come within my sight. I will vent my anger on him, anger born of the heinousness of his action."

Rama fixed a sharp arrow to his bow and stood waiting.

Ravana in the meantime, arranged his army in such a way that they could guard the city gates as well as aid him in the fight with Rama. He then plunged into the sea of Vanaras even as the shark enters the sea. Sugriva was the first to encounter him. He hurled rocks at Ravana which were splintered by the arrows from the golden bow of Ravana. Ravana took up an arrow which was like a snake and he despatched it towards Sugriva. It was like Indra's Vajra and it hurt Sugriva. He fell down in a faint and the sight was pleasing to the rakshasas. Several of the Vanara chiefs tried to accost Ravana but in vain. They could not face the arrows from his bow. He soon filled the field of battle with his arrows and nothing could be seen. Everyone rushed to Rama and he saw their distress.

Rama took up his bow and Lakshmana said : "It is not necessary for you to strain yourself. I am capable of killing this wicked sinner. Permit me, Rama."

Rama looked kindly at him and said : "Lakshmana, if you are so eager, then you can go and fight with Ravana. Be very careful. He is no mean fighter and valour like his has not been seen by anyone anywhere before. He is highly incensed and no one in the three worlds can subdue him. I am certain about that. Make a note of his weakness and remember your weakness also. Be calm and unruffled and protect yourself with effort. With your alertness and with the help of your bow you will be able to face Ravana."

Lakshmana touched the feet of his brother and placing the dust of his feet on his head he went to fight with the monarch of the rakshasas. Lakshmana then looked at Ravana who had caused such fear in the minds of the Vanaras.

Hanuman, in the meantime, rushed towards Ravana with a rock in his hands. He shielded himself from the rain of arrows emerging from Ravana's bow. He went very near the chariot of Ravana. He said : "You have been granted a boon that you cannot be killed by devas, danavas or any of the celestials or yakshas and rakshasas. But remember, there is always danger for you at the hands of monkeys alone! This my right hand will teach you a lesson." Ravana was furious with Hanuman and he said : "Let me see you try and hit me. Do it once and you will win lasting fame. I will kill you after that."

Hanuman said : "Remember your son Aksha who was killed by me." Ravana was reminded of his son and his anger grew tenfold and he hit Hanuman on the chest. Hanuman reeled under the blow and for a few moments he stood as though he have been stunned. He fretted under the insult and, spurred by anger and humiliation, he beat Ravana with the palm of his hand. It was now Ravana's turn to reel under the blow. He recovered from the shock and said : "Well done! I admire your strength and valour. You are equal to me in both. You deserve praise for this."

Hanuman said : "Fie on my strength which finds you still alive after my blow. Once more and my fist will send you to the abode of Yama."

Ravana doubled his fist and hit Hanuman on the chest and again Hanuman was staggering under the blow. Before he could resume his fight Ravana went away from there and led his chariot towards Neela. He fought with Neela with his arrows and Hanuman joined Neela. A fierce encounter followed and Neela was teasing Ravana to the utmost. Neela had made himself very small and he jumped on to the banner of Ravana's chariot. Aggravated by this the rakshasa took up the astra Agneya and sent it towards Neela, the commander of the army of Rama. Neela fell on the ground hit hard by the arrow. He did not die, however, since he was the son of Agni.

Ravana went to where Lakshmana was, and he twanged the string of his bow to announce that he was ready to fight.

Lakshmana challenged him to fight and Ravana heard his words as well as the twang of Lakshmana's bowstring. He was furious. He said : 'Foolishly you have come before me and you have the audacity to challenge me to fight with you. Fortunately you have come within sight of me. I will despatch you to Yama's city whose doors are kept open for you and the likes of you."

"You brag too much," said Lakshmana. "Let me see some action and let me see if you can follow up your words with arrows which are equally sharp. I have heard of your valour and you do not have to talk about it yourself. I am here with my bow and show me how you can answer me."

There ensued a memorable battle between Ravana and Lakshmana. Ravana could not bear the valour of Lakshmana who was cutting up every arrow of his into pieces and they fell on the ground like snakes with their bodies severed. He was a true fighter and he admired the glorious fighting of Lakshmana. He now took up an astra presided over by Brahma and with it he hurt Lakshmana on the forehead. Though he was taken aback for a moment Lakshmana did not lose his senses and he broke Ravana's bow into splinters. Arrow followed arrow and it was Ravana's turn to be hurt by his antagonist. He took up the Shakti which had been given him by Brahma. It was hurled at Lakshmana and spitting fire and smoke it travelled towards Lakshmana. Lakshmana tried in vain to stop its progress with his arrows. The Shakti went straight at the chest of Lakshmana and piercing it the Shakti came to a stop. Lakshmana became unconscious and fell down.

With a smile Ravana came near him and tried to lift him up. But he was not able to do so. He was once able to lift up the mountain Kailasa with his hands but he was not able to lift up the brother of Rama. Ravana was amazed at it. Lakshmana had been hit by the Shakti but he was not killed. Lakshmana was the amsha of Narayana Himself and the Shakti could not kill him.

Hanuman came there and again he began to fight with Ravana using his fists. Ravana was unable to bear the impact of it and fell on the terrace of his chariot. Blood spurted from his mouth. Hanuman quickly lifted up Lakshmana and carried him to the presence of Rama. The Shakti left the chest of Lakshmana and went back to Ravana. Lakshmana was his old self once again and there was not a trace of the wound made by the Shakti.

Ravana had recovered and was bent on fighting with fury. The Vanara army was suffering and they rushed once again to Rama in despair. Rama quickly took up his bow and looked at Ravana who was at some distance. He went near him with the intention of offering him fight. Hanuman said: "My lord, he is in a chariot and it is not right that you should stand on the ground and fight. Please be seated on my shoulder and I will carry you."

Rama was touched by the offer of Hanuman and he agreed to be seated on the back of Hanuman.

The king of men accosted the king of the rakshasas. The twang of his bow was loud and it was frightening. He spoke to Ravana : "You are too sure of your valour. You consider yourself to be a great hero. You have offended me in a manner which cannot be forgiven. Be prepared to accept punishment for it at my hands. You are now in front of me and we are going to fight. Let me tell you that neither Indra not Yama and Surya, nor even Brahma, Agni or Lord Mahadeva will be able to save you from my wrath. You may try to hide yourself in the four quarters or anywhere else and yet, you will not be able to escape from me and my anger. My brother whom you hurt with your Shakti will prove to be the death of you and your wives and your sons. Perhaps you have been told about it or you may not.

I destroyed the entire place by name Janasthana and not one of your men could escape the arrows from my bow. I will show you how I achieved it."

Ravana could not brook the words of Rama. He took up his bow and his arrows were aimed at Hanuman who was carrying Rama. But, contrary to his expectations, the glory of Hanuman did but increase with the onslaught. Rama was terribly angry with the behaviour of Ravana. He broke his chariot and the horses were killed and the charioteer was hurt with the sharp and feathered arrows he despatched. Another arrow, powerful like Vajra was aimed at the chest of Ravana and he, who had stood unruffled in the presence of Indra and his Vajra now staggered under the impact of Rama's arrow and his bow slipped from his hand. Rama saw him reeling and quickly he took another arrow which had a crescent-shaped head and with it he hit the golden crown of Ravana which fell down, broken. Rama looked at the king of the rakshasas who was without his bow, who had lost his splendour, who had been insulted because of the broken crown, who had suffered indignities at the hands of Rama.

Rama said : "You acted in an unforgivable manner and you have hurt many of my warriors. And yet, since you are extremely tired I have refrained from killing you with my arrows. I have allowed you to live. Go home, rest your tired limbs and come back with another bow and another chariot. The fight has exhausted you, O king! Go back to Lanka with my leave. When you come back after your rest, refreshed and ready to fight, I will then show you what I am capable of."

Ravana's bow was broken : his chariot, and his horses with the charioteer had been destroyed : his famed crown had been splintered by a single arrow of Rama's. He had been hurt abominably by the many arrows and his pride had been humbled. His enthusiasm had all gone and he returned crestfallen to Lanka. The celestials who had been watching from the skies were pleased with Rama.

20. KUMBHAKARNA IS WOKEN UP

Ravana was very unhappy. He had never before been so insulted as he had been today by Rama. And Rama's chivalry in asking him to come back refreshed and with another bow and another chariot was too galling to his pride. The sensitive monarch was full of humiliation and anger and he could do nothing about it. Like an elephant by a lion, or a serpent by Garuda, Ravana had been quelled by Rama and it was very painful to him. Again and again he thought of the sharp arrows of Rama which were swift and straight and Ravana sat as though he had been stricken with an ague. He sat on his golden throne and addressed his rakshasas:

"You have all seen how I was defeated by a mere man on the battlefield today. All my penance and my everything seem to me to be futile, worthless, and unprofitable when I think of the humiliation of today. After the boon had been granted to me assuring me of immunity from death at the hands of the devas and others Brahma had said : 'Beware of man.' I did not pay any attention to it then and I dismissed man as too much of an insignificant factor to be reckoned with. I remember an incident which took place many years ago.

"There was a king of the Ikshvakus by name Anaranya, and he had said : 'You are a wicked rakshasa who is a blot on the name of your family. Remember, some time there will be born someone in my House and he will be the death of you along with your kinsmen.' I wonder if Dasaratha's son Rama is the man he meant.' And again, there was a woman by name Vedavati and when I assaulted her she cursed me. Perhaps this Sita is that same Vedavati born again to destroy me. Several wise people have cursed me: Parvati, Nandikeshvara, Varuna's daughter. They have been harassed by me and they have cursed me in the days of yore. The words of the learned will never prove false."

Ravana sat silent for a while. He then shook himself out of his despondency and said : "All that is neither here nor there. Let the guards of the city be doubly careful. An emergency has arisen and I am afraid we will have to wake up my brother Kumbhakarna. He has been afflicted by the dread disease, sleep, and that is the curse of Brahma. He has to be woken up."

Finding himself worried by the prowess of Rama, Ravana decided to summon Kumbhakarna whose valour was proverbial. He ordered the army: "Guard the gates and the wall around the city. Make haste and wake my brother."

Kumbhakarna had sat with him in the council hall just nine days back and he had gone back to sleep. Ravana was certain that Kumbhakarna would succeed where Prahastha had failed. He would kill the Kosala princes and the Vanara army would be routed. Ravana was convinced that Rama would meet his end at the hands of Kumbhakarna. He told himself : "Rama seems to me to be as valiant as Indra himself and it is not possible for me to fight him and his army alone. I have to have the aid of my brother."

The rakshasas who had been told that they should wake up Kumbhakarna went to his palace. They carried with them perfumes and flowers and food in abundance with barrels of wine to wash it down. They reached the main entrance. It was large and passing it they entered the hall where Kumbhakarna was sleeping. They could not stand there since the breathing of the rakshasa was so strong that it threatened to make them fall down. The hall was decorated richly and there was gold and silver with gems in great profusion. In the midst of it all was found the prince enormous like a small hillock. They began to try and wake him up. It was no easy task.

They surrounded him with food since he would be hungry as soon as he got up. Huge vessels of wine were placed near him. They decorated his huge body with sandal paste and garlands of flowers and they made loud noises like the roar of clouds and they recited stanzas in praise of him. Nothing could make him get up. They blew on conchs and trumpets and bugles and shouted all together, and yet he could not be roused. They had to use several sticks and rods to prod him and hurt him enough to wake him.

Finally, after a great deal of endeavour and efforts which were persistent, they found that he was disturbed in his sleep. They made a great deal of noise now and that roused him up.

Angry at the fact that he had been disturbed from his sleep Kumbhakarna sat yawning and looked at all of them. He stood up and glared at all of them. His red eyes were frightening and they silently indicated the food which was placed before him. He finished his repast and quaffed the pots of wine which were placed near him. They saw that his anger was somewhat lessened, since his hunger and thirst had been appeased.

They came near him and saluted him. He looked at them inquiringly and asked them : "Why have I been woken up at the beginning of my long sleep? Has any crisis arisen which needs me to handle it? I hope everyone is well and happy. I have my own doubts about it. The fact that I have been waken up from my sleep shows that some great danger is awaiting all of us. It is clearly indicated even by your looks! I am sure of the danger. I will at once go and rid the king of his worry. I am not worried whether it is Indra or Agni who has come to frighten our city.

"I will tackle them easily. My brother would never have asked for me to be woken up unless he is desperate. Tell me truly why he has asked you to fetch me."

Yupaksha, one of the ministers of the king, said : "My lord, there is no danger for us from the heavens. The trouble is caused by a mere man. This evil which has befallen the rakshasas because of one man has never happened before. No asura or deva has caused us any worry so far. The entire city is surrounded by monkeys and each is as large as a mountain. Rama, who is full of wrath because of the stealing of his wife by our king, is causing great havoc in our ranks. Some time back one of the monkeys had come to our Lanka and he had killed our prince Aksha and he also burnt the beautiful city."

They then spoke of the fight which has caused the death of some of the warriors, Prahastha being one of the dead. They then spoke of the fight between Rama and Ravana and the humiliation under which Ravana was still smarting.

They said : "This has never happened before to our king. Till now, no deva or danava has been able to treat the king thus in all these years. Rama allowed him to come back to the city alive since our king was too tired to fight and since he had lost his bow and his chariot. Our king has not been able to live this down and he decided to call you to his aid and to punish the human beings who have waged war on him : the Kosala brothers."

Kumbhakarna was listening to the words of Yupaksha and he said : "I will go this very moment. I will kill Rama and Lakshmana and the host of the Vanaras and then go and see my brother. I am thirsty for the blood of these men. I want to see them dead as soon as I can."

Mahodara, one of the valiant warriors in the rakshasa army, intervened and said : "If I may make bold to say so it will be better if you meet the king first and, after discussing the strength and weakness of the enemy with him, then you can proceed to the field of battle. The king is eager to meet you. Please go and see him. He wants someone, who is affectionate towards him, by his side now. Please hasten to his presence. He needs you now."

Kumbhakarna who was extremely fond of his brother nodded in agreement and Yupaksha and Mahodara went to the palace of the king. They told him : "Your brother has been roused from his sleep and will you be going to see him or should we bring him to you?"

Ravana was very happy to know that Kumbhakarna had been woken up and he said : "Let him be brought here."

They went to the valiant Kumbhakarna and said : "The king desires to see you immediately. Make him happy by talking to him." Kumbhakarna rose up from his bed and, after he had dressed himself in beautiful white silks and decorated his ears with golden earrings, his magnificent chest with necklaces of gold, he walked with noble strides to the presence of Ravana. He looked like Yama at the time when the Yuga ends. The earth trembled under his firm tread and he walked towards Ravana's palace like Indra going to see Brahma.

When he was walking in the streets of the city the monkeys, which had seated themselves on the walls, saw him and fled out of sheer terror. He was radiant like the sun during the middle of the day and the glow was unearthly. No one could look at him with the naked eyes.

At a glance Kumbhakarna saw that his brother's face was devoid of the expression of the pride which was habitual to him. He now saw that worry sat on the brow of the king. Ravana got up from his seat and went towards his brother. Taking his two hands in his he made him sit on the couch placed beside his. Kumbhakarna prostrated before Ravana and was then embraced warmly by Ravana.

When he had seated himself Kumbhakarna asked : "Why was I asked to come to your presence in such a hurry? I was woken up from a deep sleep and I knew that you needed me. Tell me, which sinner is causing you trouble? Who is desirous of meeting death at my hands? Whether the danger is from Indra or even from our great-grandsire Brahma, let it not worry you. There is no one to equal me in valour or in strength. Not one in the three worlds can face me and escape me and my power. Tell me."

Ravana was still smarting under the experiences on the battlefield. He said : "My brave brother, while you were asleep several things have happened. While you were happy and dead to the world, you have not been aware of the crisis that has arisen because of Rama. The son of Dasaratha has collected an army which is led by Sugriva. The army is made up of monkeys and Rama with his army has managed to cross the sea and is desirous of cutting up the entire rakshasa clan with a grim determination. If you turn your eyes about you, you will see the devastation caused to our forests and to our gardens. It is dreadful to see wasteland after wasteland wherever the monkeys have set foot. Many of my brave warriors have been killed and Lanka is inhabited now mostly by old men and children. I am at a loss as to how I am going to destroy these monkeys.

"They have not been vanquished, not even once. A great danger has arisen. You are the only person who can destroy their entire army. That was why I asked that you should be woken up. My city is surrounded on all sides by the enemy. My helpmates are all dead. My treasury is empty. Save the city and save me from complete destruction. Undertake this impossible task for me. My dear brother, never before have I asked such a favour of you. I have great affection for you and I respect you and your valour immensely. I have often seen your valour in the wars we have fought with the devas. I do not think there is anyone like you in all the three worlds. You love me and you hold me in high esteem. I know it. Help me now in my hour of need and, like a strong wind scattering the clouds which have gathered in the sky, reduce the army of Rama to dust and come back victorious."

Kumbhakarna laughed when he heard the words of Ravana. He said: "This was exactly what we all warned you about when we had a council meeting hardly ten days back. You would not listen to the words of wisdom spoken and now, you are faced with the dire problem. One who has committed a grave sin cannot escape the special hell meant for him and your evil deed has rewarded you only too soon. Then, when you were proud of your valour, when arrogance blinded you, this solution was not thought of, nor did you think of the consequence of your deeds. One who is blinded by his wealth and glory, who does not act properly, who does the later things first and who postpones his immediate duties to a later date, does not know the difference between the right path and the wrong path. Actions which have been performed without any attention being paid to the proper time and place, which are unnatural, will be tainted with sin and will be ineffectual even as the yaga performed by a man who has no faith. A king who honours the advice of his wise ministers and adopts the different rules of governing, of statecraft, will ever be following the right path. The king who follow the rules prescribed by the shastras, who listens to advisers and well-wishers and acts according to their advice, who uses his own discrimination, will respect the wise men of his court and reap the rewards of Dharma, Artha and Kama.

"If, however, he does not understand the teachings which have been instilled in him it means that he has not utilised his learning in the proper manner. Sama, Dana, Bedha and Danda should be used at the proper times. The distinction between right and wrong should be discussed with his counsellors and a king should then decide on his action. Such a wise king will never be assailed by danger at any time. He should realise that some things can be done and some should be avoided since it is sinful to do so.

"A king should be careful to have wise and good men as his counsellors. A man who considers wrong to be right and advises accordingly should be shunned and such a man is as good as a traitor. If one acts without considering the consequences of his actions, he will surely suffer later. A king who knows his enemies and yet does nothing to guard himself will fall into danger and he will be pushed down from his state of power.

"Once your brother advised you wisely and you did not take his advice. It will be better if you take that advice at least now. If you do so it will be beneficial to you and to those whom you call yours. Please consider my words and do as you please."

Ravana was listening to his brother's words and his anger was rising. His lips were throbbing and the frown on his brow deepened. He said : "An elder brother has to be honoured like one's own father or guru. And you dare to give me advice! Do not strain yourself unnecessarily. Do what you think fit now and act accordingly. Because of the fumes of lust, because of a deluded power of thinking, because of my arrogance born of power and valour, some events have taken place, perhaps. It is futile to discuss them now. Consider what is to be done now, at the present moment, and tell me what should be done. What has happened has happened and the wise do not waste time regretting over what is past. If you ever did hold me dear in your heart, if you are certain about your own valour, if you think that this task is essential, then wipe out the evil which has happened as a result of my wrong actions. Correct the results of my past indiscretions. One who aids a man who is helpless because all his efforts have been frustrated, is a real comfort. One who helps even a sinner is indeed noble, a real kinsman."

Kumbhakarna saw that his brother was angry as well as very unhappy and he spoke soft and sweet words. He said : "My lord, my king, enough of this sorrow. Shed this anger and summon peace of mind. When I am alive this despondency does not become you. I will kill him who is the cause of your pain and unhappiness. I felt it my duty to tell you what is good for you and because of the affection I have for you I thought I could take advantage of that privilege and give you this advice. I wished you well and so I spoke as I did. If you think I should go and fight I will certainly do so. A well-wisher will act in such a manner as to please his dear kinsman. I will destroy your enemy. Soon you will see Rama and Lakshmana killed in the war. I will bring his head and lay it at your feet. I will be the death of Sugriva. Rama can never approach you, not as long as I am alive. I am not sorry for myself. Send me at once to the battlefield. When I enter the field with the trident in my hand I will set up such a roar that Indra will tremble in his abode in heaven. No one will dare to come near me. I need no weapons. With my bare hands I will kill the enemy. If Rama is able to withstand the power of my fist I will then use arrows against the brothers. My arrows also have been left dry since a very long time. I will go now and bring fame to you. The danger you spoke of will be removed by me like darkness by the sun. Shed all your worries. Go to your antahpura and spend your time with your women and with a flagon of wine. I will go to the field of battle and destroy your enemies. Once Rama is dead, Sita will become yours in course of time."

Ravana was very pleased with Kumbhakarna and his words of encouragement and confidence. He said : "With the trident in hand you will enter the battlefield and they will all think that Yama himself has come to fight with them. Destroy them all and come back to me. Their hearts will tremble with fear when they hear your roar."

Ravana was certain that he had won the war and that the end of Rama was very near. Kumbhakarna left for the battlefield with great enthusiasm and in his hand he held the trident which was very like Indra's thunderbolt or like the great Pinaka of Lord Mahadeva. He turned to Ravana and said : "I do not need an army with me. I will go alone and do the needful."

The king said : "It will be better if an army accompanies you. You do not know the viciousness of those dreadful monkeys. A moment of carelessness will make them bite you with their sharp teeth and torture you with their nails and with the boulders and trees which seem to be their weapons. You should be careful with them."

Ravana stood up and taking up a beautiful necklace which had a pendant set with gems, he placed it on the neck of Kumbhakarna. He placed several ornaments on his chest and arms and fingers. He made him wear a necklace of pearls which gleamed beautifully and softly like the moon. He made him wear an armour which was impenetrable and the noble rakshasa looked like Himavan.

Ravana embraced his brother again and again and the great Kumbhakarna prostrated before Ravana before he left for the battlefield. Ravana went with him to the doorway and spoke words of blessing and then sent him on his mission.

21. KUMBHAKARNA ON THE FIELD

Kumbhakarna who was a Maharathika was followed by several of the warriors in his brother's army and there was a mammoth procession towards the army of Rama. He spoke with smiles and loud laughter about how he would kill the army made up of monkeys. He told his companions : "Rama and his brother Lakshmana are the sole causes for this confusion in the minds of you people and in that of my brother. If they are killed peace will reign once more in Lanka."

Evil omens were seen as he left the city and he did not think of them at all. He was so sure of success that he would not let any other thought enter his mind. He crossed the city wall and he saw that there was an immense army made up of monkeys. When they saw him the monkeys were greatly frightened and they ran away in all the four directions looking like clouds scattered by a strong breeze. He set up such a roar that it struck terror into the hearts of the monkeys. Several of them fainted away even at the sound of his roar. He held his trident aloft and looked like Yama bent on the destruction of the world. The Vanara army saw the terrible aspect he presented and they fled in panic from his presence.

Rama saw the confusion in his army and he saw the cause of it. He saw the stupendous figure striding along with a trident in his hand. He was amazed at the sight and he asked Vibhishana : "Who is he? He is wearing a crown and he is like a mountain. His eyes are tawny red and he is indeed fearful to look at. Tell me, who is he? Is he an asura or a rakshasa? I have never seen the likes of him before."

Vibhishana said : "He is the son of Vishravas and his name is Kumbhakarna. He is the brother of Ravana. Yama and Indra have been defeated easily by him. There is no rakshasa to equal him in size or in valour. He is considered to be invincible. The devas were so scared of him they thought that he was Rudra who was bent on the task of annihilating the universe. He is, by birth, valiant. Others are valiant because of the boons granted to them. As soon as he was born Kumbhakarna was oppressed by a dreadful hunger and he ate all that he could lay hands on. The world of men went to Indra for succour. Angry with him Indra took up his Vajra and hit Kumbhakarna with it. The brother of our Ravana set up such a roar that the world trembled in fear. He was angry with pain and he pulled out a tusk of the great Airavata and he hit Indra on the chest. Those in the heavens saw Indra suffering and they were sorry for him. Indra went to Brahma and told him about the mishap which had visited him.

"Brahma sent for Kumbhakarna and frightened of the possible harm to the world because of his ravenous hunger he cursed him : 'You have been born in the House of Pulastya for the sole purpose of destroying the world. I curse you to sleep as though you are dead.'".

"Kumbhakarna at once fell down there sunk in a deep sleep. Ravana, who is very fond of his brother, became greatly concerned and made a plea to Brahma. He said : 'Your curse is like letting a Champaka tree grow fully and then cutting it down. He is your great-grandson and you should not be so cruel. You should modify your words and stipulate a certain time for his sleep and for his waking up.'"

"Brahma said : 'He will sleep for six months, then wake up for one single day and will go back to sleep and he will sleep for another six months. During that one day he will eat up as many animals as he can find and he will be like a forest fire when he is hungry."

Rama was listening with wonder and Vibhishana said : "When Ravana was defeated by you he must have become worried and he has woken up Kumbhakarna to help him in his hour of need. Kumbhakarna has come with the intention of killing as many of the Vanaras as he can. Our men have fled even at the sight of him. I wonder how they will have the courage to face him and give him fight."

Rama called Neela and said : "Go with your army and guard the fortress of Ravana, the gateways and the moat. Ask our men to collect rocks and trees and to be ready to fight. Let them station themselves on all sides of the field." Neela did as he was bid. Gavaksha, Sharabha, Hanuman and Angada collected the rocks from the mountaintops and began to attack the army brought by Kumbhakarna. Angada called his chiefs and the army and said : "Why do you behave like ordinary monkeys and run away from here? Why are you afraid? What is coming towards us is a machine, a contrivance which is mechanical and the noise from it is arranged to put fright into you. Let us join together and destroy this contraption."

After some hesitation the monkeys returned to the field armed with their usual weapons : trees and rocks. They hurled them at Kumbhakarna who was unaffected by their onslaught. The rocks were powdered and the trees broken into splinters by the impact against his body. He advanced towards them and began to destroy the army methodically. He was like a forest fire bent on burning up the entire wood. There was just one emotion prevailing in the field and that was fear, terror. Some of the monkeys rushed up to the bridge which had brought them to Lanka and they wanted to go back the same way. Angada spoke to them and tried to encourage them to fight. He appealed to their honour and their courage and their pride. He said : "It is shameful not to fight. It is shameful to run away. You spoke so highly of yourselves when we set out. Where is it all gone? Cowardice is the lowest of all virtues. Avoid it and come back here to fight. Let us die on the battlefield. Death here will grant us a place in the abode of Brahma. Come, let us court fame and die on the field. We will wait and see what happens when this monster approaches Rama. Like a moth which encounters a flame he will reach his end when he sees Rama. We should not behave like this now. It is shameful."

They were quite unwilling to come back. Life seemed so much sweeter than the promised rewards of a place in the heavens after death. Finally, with great reluctance and trepidation, they came back to the field and that was not because they were brave-but because they did not dare disobey their beloved prince.

They found their courage coming back in their veins and they fought with enthusiasm. Ravana's brother was harassing them. Hundreds and hundreds of Vanaras were on the ground killed or wounded or maimed by him. He was eating many of them and he strode the field of battle with loud cries of triumph. Dvividha fought him bravely. He hurled a large section of the mountain at Kumbhakarna. The rock missed him but fell on the army and crushed several horses, elephants, chariots and several hundreds of rakshasas. He threw another rock and continued his work of destruction. Hanuman joined Dvividha and the fight went on. Kumbhakarna's trident was enough to whisk away the rocks and trees which were thrown at him and he laughed loudly again and again. Hanuman came near him and smote him. Kumbhakarna was hurt and he was bleeding. He thrust his trident towards the chest of Hanuman and he was hurt.

All the monkey leaders joined together and came to the assistance of Hanuman and Dvividha. But nothing could harm the dreadful rakshasa or his army. Every one of them in the Vanara army was beaten up by him and fell down either in a faint or hurt. The monkeys went in a group and falling on him began to bite him with their sharp teeth. He was unaffected and began to pluck them one by one and eat them up. Angada was the only one who could harass Kumbhakarna again and again. He escaped his trident which was flung at him in anger. He hit the rakshasa on the chest which made him faint for a moment. A moment later, of course, he regained his strength and felled Angada with a blow from his fist.

Kumbhakarna went now in search of Sugriva. He defied the brother of Ravana bravely. Sugriva jumped into the sky and with a rock held in his hand he said : "You are very valiant. Several of my heroes have been defeated by you and have fallen. You have accomplished what no one else has been able to, so far. You are swallowing up my army. You have won fame too. But tell me what you gain by this show of your strength against weak opponents like my poor monkeys? Can you not do something better? Come, fight with me. Let me see if you can bear a hit from this rock which I am going to throw at you."

Kumbhakarna said : 'O monkey! You are the grandson of Brahma, and you are the son of Riksharajas. I know that. Why do you brag unnecessarily? Show some action."

Sugriva hurled the rock at Kumbhakarna and the rock was broken into a thousand pieces and nothing happened to the intended victim. Hanuman came to the aid of his king. He grabbed the trident which Kumbhakarna was sporting and he broke it into two. Sugriva had been thrown to the ground in a faint after a hit from a stone hurled by Kumbhakarna, who now took up Sugriva in his huge hands and walked away from there. He had made up his mind to imprison him. That would throw a scare into the army of Rama. Hanuman was trying to think of a way of saving his master : some way by which he could be released from the clutches of Kumbhakarna. He decided against it knowing that Sugriva was clever enough to extricate himself somehow.

Kumbhakarna entered the city and was walking in the streets of Lanka. He had Sugriva in his arms and the king of the monkeys was slowly regaining consciousness. He realised what was happening and reaching out his head he forcibly bit into the ear and nose of the rakshasa. Pain made him drop Sugriva and to drag him on the ground. Sugriva jumped into the sky and soon he had gone back to the field and was standing beside Rama.

Kumbhakarna returned to the field. He looked like a cloud lit up by the rays of the setting sun. He was like death personified and the number of Vanaras he had killed and eaten was countless. Lakshmana accosted him and used his arrows to hurt him. But they were ineffective against him. Lakshmana was furious. He persisted with his rain of arrows and Kumbhakarna spoke in a voice resembling the rumbling of thunder. He said: "I am impressed by your valour. Yama was not able to withstand my prowess and yet, you seem to be brave enough to stand against me and fight well.

"Indra, mounted on his Airavata and aided by all his devas, has never once stood in front of me as firmly as you are doing now. Lakshmana, though you are a child your bravery is praiseworthy. I am pleased with you. Let me go. I am eager to meet Rama. Though I am pleased with your valour, your courage and your enthusiasm, I am bent on meeting Rama by killing whom I would have achieved the purpose of my life. Once Rama is dead then the rest of the army can be wiped out by my men."

Lakshmana smiled scathingly at him and said : "It is quite true that you have vanquished Indra and Yama. I have seen it with my eyes too. You want Rama. Here he is, firm as a rock waiting for you."

Even as he was saying it, Kumbhakarna did not wait for him to finish his words but went fast towards Rama.

The fight for which he had been waiting and which Rama was waiting for too, began abruptly. Rama sent arrows which had been invoked and they hurt Kumbhakarna. He was spitting fire and the pain caused by the arrows only added to his wrath. Arrows with the feathers of the peacock adorning them were shot by Rama and they lodged in the immense chest of Kumbhakarna. His huge gada fell from his hands and his weapons too. He realised that he had lost his weapons and so he used his arms and legs to cause as much havoc as he could. He was covered with blood and he fought with his arms. He took up a huge boulder from the ground and hurled it at Rama. Rama stopped its progress with seven arrows. His arrows tipped with gold broke open the armour of Kumbhakarna. Glowing like the peak of Meru it fell to the ground. Lakshmana said : "Rama, he is drunk with blood. He has been killing monkeys and rakshasas too indiscriminately. Let all the monkeys climb on him and prevent him from causing further harm." The monkeys scrambled on him and with a shake he shook them off. Rama grasped his bow firmly in his hand and advanced towards him.

Kumbhakarna looked like one of the elephants which hold up the earth. He was as huge and noble-looking as the peak of the Vindhya mountain or Meru. Golden bracelets gleamed on his arms and he was like the fire with seven tongues.

22. THE DEATH OF KUMBHAKARNA

Rama was also like fire which burns without smoke. He stood in front of Kumbhakarna and there was an unruffled expression on his face. He pulled the string of his bow and said : "Brave rakshasa, do not tire yourself. I am waiting for you with my bow. I am Rama whom you have been searching for. You said that you wanted to meet me and here I am. Look at me well and for the last time since you will soon lose consciousness and will not be able to see me. I have decided to kill you."

Kumbhakarna laughed loudly and said : "Do not confuse me with Viradha or Kabandha, nor am I to be mistaken for Khara or Vali. I am not Maricha either. I am Kumbhakarna and I am not like the others. Look at this Mudgara with which I once defeated the asuras and the devas. Let me see your valour. I have heard so much about it."

Rama sent arrows at Kumbhakarna and they did not seem to hurt him. Rama raised a single eyebrow as though to ask : "The arrow which pierced the seven Salas, the arrow which had killed Vali seems to prove ineffective against this Kumbhakarna!" Rama was as calm and Kumbhakarna was as unaffected as a mountain when rain drops fall on it.

Rama invoked Vayu and sent the astra against the enemy. He cut off the arm which held the Mudgara. Kumbhakarna screamed in pain. With his other arm he pulled out a tree and threw it at Rama. Then Rama invoked Indra and sent that astra towards Kumbhakarna and the other arm was now severed and fell on the earth. With two more arrows Rama cut off his legs. He now took up another arrow and very solemnly he pronounced the incantations for the Aindrastra and sent the astra towards Kumbhakarna.

The astra resembled the Vajra of Indra and went hurtling towards Kumbhakarna. It severed his head from his body even as Vajra once severed the body and head of Vritra apart in the days of the long ago.

Kumbhakarna's head fell on the ground. His body slipped down and half fell into the sea.

Kumbhakarna, the great hero, the terror of the world of the devas, the sole hope of Ravana, now lay dead on the field of battle and there was great commotion everywhere. The skies resounded with the cries of : "Well done! Well done!" uttered by the divine watchers from the heavens.

The rakshasas were heart-broken. They cried out in anguish when their chief lay dead. The Vanara army, however, was like the sun released from the mouth of Rahu and Rama stood triumphant in their midst. He was as pleased as Indra when he had killed Vritra.

23. THE YOUNG HEROES

Messengers hurried to the court of Ravana. For a long time they stood without talking and then, hesitantly, they began to speak. They said: "My lord, your valiant brother Kumbhakarna tormented the army of the Vanaras even as a storm worries the sea and the forest trees. He was making a meal of them and there was panic and nothing but panic in the army. He accosted several of the Vanara chiefs and came out victorious in every one of the many encounters. He met Lakshmana and, after fighting with him for a while, he left him and went to Rama."

They paused here and Ravana, with a proud and happy look on his face, smiled and asked them to continue, saying: "I knew that I could depend on my beloved brother to rid me of that meddlesome enemy. Tell me, how did he kill Rama? Did he use his trident or was it with his bare hands?"

They trembled when they heard the hopeful words of their king. They said: "My lord, a great fight ensued between Rama and Kumbhakarna. The limbs of Kumbhakarna were severed by Rama and, finally, his head was cut off from his body and he fell like a tree burnt in the forest fire."

When he was told about it Ravana fell down in a faint. His sorrow was unbearable. Devantaka, Narantaka, Trishiras and Atikaya cried openly when they heard about the death of their uncle. Mahodara and Mahaparshva were sunk in woe.

After a long time, with great difficulty, Ravana came out of his faint and he gave vent to his grief which was immense. He wailed: "O my beloved brother! Where has it all gone? Your valour, your bravery and your indomitable spirit? Leaving me alone here you have reached the abode of

Yama. You have gone giving unbearable pain to me and to the entire rakshasa clan. You were the sole support I had when I fought with the devas and the asuras. I see no purpose in living any longer. How could a great hero like you find his death at the hands of Rama? Indra's Vajra was ineffectual as far as you were concerned and yet you have succumbed to Rama's arrows! How could it have happened? I cannot believe it.

"I can see the celestials dancing and singing in joy at your death. There is no way of controlling the Vanaras who will be filled with ecstasy. Without Kumbhakarna I have no wish to rule the kingdom nor is this life dear to me any more. I am alive only to complete one task. I must avenge the death of my beloved brother, Kumbhakarna. If I do not do so, I will be the lowest of the low. After that I will even be happy. But now, either I fight to avenge his death or I too will die. I will join my brother in the other world. I do not see anything left which is pleasing to me. The devas will laugh at me now that my brother is dead. I can almost see them.

"Vibhishana seems to have spoken the truth when he told me that Rama is valiant. Foolishly I refused to listen to his advice and I have now lost my precious brother. Kumbhakarna and Prahastha were both very dear to me and they are both dead. It is shameful that I should have sent them to their deaths. Vibhishana was righteous and I drove him away from my presence. I am reaping the reward for that act of mine."

Ravana's grief was burning him up and he was indeed a pathetic figure. He was extremely fond of Kumbhakarna and his mind could not grasp the truth that he was dead.

When he was thus immersed in woe Trishiras, one of his sons, said : "Father, our valiant uncle is dead. He is lying on the field of battle, his limbs severed and his head illuminating the entire field. The wise should not give in to grief like this. You are lord of the three worlds and it is not right that you should be unhappy and forget your prowess. You should not lose heart like any ordinary person. You have the Shakti given to you by Brahma and you have an armour which is unbreakable and you have a magnificent bow with quivers full of arrows. There is that glorious chariot of yours and you have won the name that you defeated the devas and the asuras many times without the use of weapons! You should take all your weapons and kill Rama in battle. But that is to come later. At the present moment, allow me to go and I will kill all of them. I will go to the forefront, and like Garuda destroys the serpents I will be the death of every one of them. Permit me, my lord."

Ravana, whose death was drawing near, heard the words of Trishiras and thought that he would agree to his suggestion.

Devantaka, Narantaka, and Atikaya, the other sons of Ravana, were excited by the words of Trishiras and they were eager to fight. These young sons of Ravana vied with each other in their enthusiasm to fight.

They were all great fighters, Maharathikas and they were conversant with Maya tactics also. They had faced the devas with courage and had been victorious in their wars. All were heroes and all were strong and valiant. They had been blessed with boons and they were well versed in everything. The proud young sons of Ravana wanted to be sent to the forefront.

24. THE VALOUR OF THE PRINCES

Ravana felt proud of his sons and he felt that they might win where others had failed. He embraced them with great affection. He blessed them and allowed them to go out into the field of battle. They prostrated before him and prepared themselves to go. Yuddhonmatta and Matha went with them. Mounted on elephants and in their chariots they went out of the gateways of the city and there was great excitement in the ranks of the rakshasas when they were seen. A large army went with them and they reached the field of battle. Their war cry was loud and the Vanaras heard it.

The encounter between the two armies was terrible. There was a rain of arrows and javelins and tridents from the enemy side. The killing of Kumbhakarna had made the Vanaras very happy and certain that they were superior to the rakshasas : and the latter were furious because of the death of their greatest hero, Kumbhakarna, and they fought as though they had been inspired.

Narantaka was wreaking havoc and Sugriva came to the rescue of his army. He called Angada and said : "You must go and fight with this

Narantaka. He seems to be extremely young and he is wreaking havoc among our ranks."

Angada challenged Narantaka and they fought a terrible duel at the end of which the son of Ravana was killed. Yuddhonmatta, Devantaka and Trishiras saw the killing of Narantaka and went to fight with Angada, who was later joined by Hanuman and Neela. A glorious fight ensued in which Hanuman killed Devantaka; Yuddhonmatta was killed by Neela and Trishiras also by Hanuman. Matha was then killed by Rishabha. It was indeed a terrible debacle as far as the army of the rakshasas was concerned.

Atikaya came to the forefront to avenge the death of his brothers and his uncles. He was huge like Kumbhakarna and several of the Vanaras fled from him thinking that it was Kumbhakarna came back to life. They rushed to Rama and Rama asked Vibhishana who he was.

"He is as huge as a mountain and his eyes are tawny. His chariot is large and excellent horses are yoked to it. Fierce weapons have been placed in it and he looks like Rudra with the Pramathaganas. He is really noble looking and seems to be a Maharathika. His bow is beautiful too and he must be a great warrior on the side of Ravana. Tell me, who is he?"

Vibhishana said : "He is the son of Ravana. He is like his father in valour and he is conversant with astras. He has been well-trained. He can fight from an elephant or a horse or from a chariot. He is a great fighter. He is the son of Dhanyamalini, one of the wives of Ravana. Brahma has granted him divine astras and the chariot was also given to him by Brahma. He has defeated the heavenly host. Indra's Vajra and Varuna's Pasha are not frightful to this young hero. He is a dangerous opponent. He is angry at the thought of the death of his brothers and you should put an end to his valour soon."

Atikaya was wading through the army like a farmer walks through a field with a scythe in hand. He brushed aside the many Vanara chiefs who accosted him and he came straight to Rama and said : "I do not want to fight with any ordinary antagonist. Let someone worthwhile come and dare to fight with me."

Lakshmana could not brook his arrogance and he went to fight with Atikaya. He twanged his bowstring and the young prince took up a sharp arrow in his hand and said : "Lakshmana, you are yet a child in the art of fighting and you should go back. Do you dare to face Yama? No one, not Himavan on the earth nor the heavens can bear the power of my arrows. Do not rouse the fire which glows at the end of the Yuga. Do not lose your life at my hands. If you still persist and want to fight, then you will see the speed with which my arrows travel and soon you will be finding a bed on this ground strewn with the arrows and javelins and stones. You can be sure of that."

Atikaya fought with his deadly arrows and the fight was terrible and Lakshmana sent the astra presided over by Agni and Atikaya replied with Suryastra. The two flames destroyed each other and the sight was glorious. Each sent an astra and the other, the one to nullify it.

While the fight was going on Vayu, the god of wind, came near Lakshmana and whispered in his ear : "He has been favoured by Brahma. His armour cannot be broken by anyone. He can be killed only by the Brahmastra. He is immune to the other astras."

Lakshmana listened to his advice. He took up an arrow and, invoking the great Brahmastra he recited the incantations. The four quarters, the moon, the sun and the planets, the sky and the earth trembled with fear. He sent it after he had aimed it at Atikaya's chest.

Atikaya tried to defend himself against it but he could not. His head with its jewelled crown fell to the ground. There was great jubilation in the Vanara camp and intense dismay in that of the rakshasas.

25. INDRAJIT

News reached Ravana that the entire army with the young stalwarts was wiped out. They were all dead, the heroes who had set out with so much enthusiasm and so much of assurance. Ravana was angry with the Kosala brothers and, at the same time, he was extremely worried. Much against his wish he had to admit that they were enemies to be reckoned with. He thought : "Great fighters like Dhumraksha, Akampana, Prahastha, and Kumbhakarna have been killed. They were heroes of no mean order and they have all been annihilated by these men and monkeys."

"My son Indrajit bound them up with his Nagapasha which is well-nigh impossible to escape and yet they shook them off as one would wet garments. All my men have been vanquished by these brothers and their army. I wonder if there is any truth in the words which were spoken to me once about Rama : that he is Narayana Himself born on the earth. I wonder who is capable of fighting with Rama and his army led by Sugriva."

Ravana decided to double and treble the guards who were stationed at the gateways of the city and also at the Ashokavana where Sita was kept captive. Ravana was greatly shocked and grieved that all the young men had been killed. He fainted with sorrow and pain. He woke up with tears in his eyes. There was no way of consoling him. Indrajit, the great hero, the son of Mandodari, went to him and said : "Father, emperor, my beloved king, do not be distressed. So long as Indrajit is alive there should be no cause for despondency in your heart. Your enemies will lose their lives, their bodies split by the arrows of your son. There is no one who has claimed to have won a victory over me. No one has escaped alive once he has been made to face me. Lakshmana and Rama will soon lie on the ground with their lives snatched away by my arrows. Listen to my oath, my father.

"I will, this moment, go to the field of battle and fight with them until they scream in terror. Let the world watch and let the heavens with all its denizens look on when I summon them to fight with me and make them lie on the ground in eternal sleep."

Indrajit took leave of his father and ascended his chariot which was glorious like that of Surya which is driven by Aruna. In the excitement of accompanying Indrajit the army forgot the death of the other heroes and there was hope and eagerness in their steps as they went fast towards the battlefield. The umbrella of Indrajit was white like a conch or like the full moon. It could be seen from a distance and when he reached the field of battle he called a halt. He descended from the chariot and he kindled fire. He poured oblations into it according to the rituals prescribed in the rules of war. He worshipped fire with flowers and incense and fried rice. He performed sacrifices and the fire which burned without smoke surrounding it indicated that he would succeed in his enterprise.

Agni emerged out of the sacred spot and received the Havis with his own hands. Indrajit then summoned the Brahmastra and he worshipped his chariot, his bow and arrows with incantations. The heavens and the planets trembled in awe when he performed these rituals. When he had concluded the worship of the fire Indrajit vanished into the sky along with his bow and arrows and his chariot with the charioteer. The army of Vanaras was now assaulted by his army. Indrajit incited them to fight well and they were inspired warriors. Indrajit had appeared before them and the Vanaras appeared before him prepared to fight with him. He began to kill them in tens and hundreds and in a matter of moments there were innumerable bodies of the Vanaras strewn on the ground.

His arrows were like scorching fire and they claimed a life each. The Vanaras could not withstand his valour. The rain of rocks and trees was futile against the rain of arrows which emerged from his bow.

Gandhamadana, Nala, Neela, Mainda, Gaja, Jambavan, Rishabha, Sugriva and even Angada with Dvividha were not left alone. They were all wounded by him. Indrajit was like the fire which devours the universe during the end of the world. His skill was worthy of admiration. No one saw when he placed the arrow to the bowstring. They only saw an incessant stream of arrows emerging from his bow and it was a beautiful sight.

Suddenly he vanished from their midst and then only arrows were seen and not he. All the great and valiant Vanaras were harassed by Indrajit. He passed them by and approached Rama and Lakshmana. He sent several arrows against them. Rama ignored them and said : "My dear Lakshmana, this son of Ravana has the astra of Brahma in his possession and he is harassing our army with it. And he has come to our presence now. He is blessed with the boons from Brahma and he is a great warrior. He hides himself in the skies and it is not possible to see where he is. How is it possible for him to be seen? Brahma is the strength behind him. Bear this onslaught without being affected by it. Our army is reeling under this devastating attack. His desire is to see us tired out, to see us on the ground and to clasp victory in his arms and return to the city."

The Kosala brothers were suffering the rain of arrows and Indrajit shouted in triumph. He was sure that he has vanquished them all and with a glad cry he went back to Lanka along with his men.

The army of the Vanaras was completely stupefied. They were all on the ground in a faint like death. Sugriva and Angada were in the same predicament and so were the other leaders. Vibhishana saw what had happened and he was trying to be normal and sensible and to bring a semblance of order in the shattered ranks with words of encouragement.

He said : 'Do not be afraid. This is not the time for grief or fear. These two heroes have decided to honour Brahma, who is the presiding deity of the astra aimed at all of you by Indrajit and that is why they have succumbed to it."

Vibhishana looked around and saw that Hanuman was not affected by the astra and that he was his usual self. He said : "This powerful astra was given to Indrajit by Brahma himself. That has been sent by him against the army and the princes."

Hanuman worshipped the astra mentally and said : "Let us see who has survived the virulence of the astra and let us try and see who have all succumbed to it."

They carried torches in their hands and wandered in the field looking for some signs of life there. The ground was strewn with weapons, with rocks which had been splintered or without being broken, thrown on the ground, trees with their branches, arrows which were like darbha grass strewn on the grounds of yagnasala and javelins and broken pieces of chariots.

Vibhishana looked for Jambavan. Finally he located him and he was wincing with pain and torture caused by the astra. He was like a fire which was about to be extinguished. And Vibhishana said : "Revered one, I hope your life is not in danger because of the astra."

Jambavan said : "I can guess it is Vibhishana talking since I am familiar with your voice. I cannot see you. Tell me, is Hanuman alive?"

Vibhishana was amazed at the question and he said : "How is it you are not asking about your master and his welfare, nor about Rama but you ask me if Hanuman is alive? You are not concerned about Sugriva or about the prince and evidently you have greater love for Hanuman than for these or even Rama, or all of them put together. I am intrigued."

26. THE SANJIVINI

Jambavan said : "I will tell you why I asked for Hanuman before I asked after the welfare of the others. If he is alive, then you can take it from me that the entire army has escaped death. If he had died then it would have been the end of all of us. Hanuman is like the god of fire in prowess. I have hopes of life returning to all of us."

Hanuman went near him and prostrated before him, taking his feet in his two hands. Hanuman had very great respect for Jambavan. The old man Jambavan said : "Come near to me, Hanuman. The lives of all the Vanaras is in your hands now. There is no one else as powerful as you. You are our only succour. You can relieve Lakshmana and Rama of the death-like trance into which they have fallen. You must save our king and our prince. Hanuman, you should cross the sea and go towards the mountain by name Himavan. There you will find a peak by name 'Rishabha' which will be golden in colour. Kailasa will be by its side. Between these two peaks you will find a third peak which goes by the name 'Oshadhiparvata.' It is rich in Oshadhis, the healing herbs. There are herbs there which glow in the dark and which illuminate the surroundings. They are four in number. Mritasanjivi, which brings the dead back to life, Vishalyakarani, which will heal all wounds, Savarnyakarani and Santanakarani. Hurry and get these herbs from the peak and come back here soon. You will be giving them all back their lives which they appear to have lost and which they are sure to lose if something is not done about it soon."

Hanuman heard the words of Jambavan and he grew in size as he once did when he crossed the sea at the instigation of this same Jambavan. That was when he found Sita. Hanuman climbed the hill Malaya and even as he did before, he flew into the sky and he turned his face towards the north, the direction of the devas. He went fast towards Meru and Kailasa. He went as fast as his father and he was not fatigued by the effort. Very soon he reached the Himavan. Rivers, rivulets, mountain streams, and many waterfalls decorated the mountain and the top was scintillating with its covering of snow.

Hanuman saw several ashramas and graceful trees which he had never seen before. He reached Kailasa and Meru and he saw the peak which had been mentioned by Jambavan. The herbs were glowing like tongues of flame and it was so very beautiful to see.

Hanuman searched for the particular herbs which had been mentioned by Jambavan and he kept on looking for them. The herbs, realising that someone had come to take them, concealed themselves and he could not find them. Hanuman realised the trick played on him by the hill and he said: "You do not seem to wish for the welfare of Rama. Is this your decision? I will, this moment, destroy you and powder you to dust." In a fit of fury Hanuman shook the hill and easily he lifted it up.

Hanuman lifted the entire mountain and held it in his hand and when he did this there was amazement in the heavens. He flew faster than Garuda and glowing like a flame he rushed into the sky. He was back in Lanka very soon.

Hanuman placed the mountain in the midst of the army of Vanaras. He saluted the elders and Vibhishana. The air was suffused with the scent of the Oshadhis and Rama was awake and Lakshmana too. The Vanara chiefs woke up one after another and the entire army of Vanaras was awake and not one of them bore any trace of the hundreds of wounds which had been inflicted on him. To them it was like waking up after a long restful night of sleep. The Oshadhis, however, did not bring back a single rakshasa to life for the simple reason there was not a single rakshasa dead on the field. Ravana had commanded that any rakshasa who had been killed or wounded fatally should be thrown into the sea and this, he thought, was the only way to prevent his reputation from suffering.

After the resurrection of the army, Hanuman took the mountain back to Himavan and came back to the presence of Rama. Sugriva told him: "Hanuman, Kumbhakarna is dead and the sons of Ravana are dead. It is certain that Ravana will not come to the field now. Let some of our agile Vanaras go to Lanka with torches in their hands."

Twilight had faded into night and several torches moving in the air frightened the guardians of the city. The Vanaras chased them and then made them flee in panic. The Vanaras set fire to the city by igniting different places which were accessible to them. The city had caught fire and this was the second time it had happened. Mansions and the Ayudhasalas were burnt up in no time and since it was night when everyone was asleep the inmates were caught unawares and there was great loss of lives. When the wail of woe reached the ears of Rama and Lakshmana they took up their bows and twanged the strings. The noise drowned all other noises and was heard in Lanka. Rama looked like Mahadeva with the Pinaka in his hand. The army of Ravana prepared itself to meet Rama in battle. They roared like lions and set out to fight with fearful noise.

27. KUMBHA AND NIKUMBHA

Ravana was roused from his sleep by the several noises and finally by the twang of the bow of Rama as well as the cries of distress set up by his citizens. He summoned the sons of Kumbhakarna and sent them to fight with the army of Rama. They were Kumbha and Nikumbha and they were accompanied by several other warriors and again, there was a triumphal march from Lanka of the great army bent on destroying the Vanaras. The moon was still high in the heavens and the stars were shedding their feeble light on the field below. The jewels worn by the rakshasa princes were gleaming like stars and the field of battle was like the sky with the myriad stars which were the gems worn by the princes. The light from the moon and the stars, the glow of the gems worn by the princes, and the redness caused by the tongues of flame licking the city all combined to give an eerie and unnatural light and it was fearful.

The army of the Vanaras was greatly excited at the thought of war. Since they had recovered from the effects of the Brahmastra they felt that they could not be harmed by anyone at any time. There was an exchange of words in different parts of the field and the exchange, again, of blows and of wounding with weapons as well as with rocks and trees. Angada opposed Akampana, one of the heroes who had accompanied Kumbha and Nikumbha. With a large piece of rock the Vanara prince managed to kill him. Three more rakshasas came and accosted Angada who was now joined by Mainda and Dvividha. A fierce fight went on between these two groups. They were killed one after another by the Vanara heroes. The rakshasa army rushed to Kumbha for succour. He came to Angada and asked him for a fight. He wanted to avenge the death of his friends.

Kumbha was a fighter of no mean order. His arrows were like flashes of lightning and they streaked through the air and in the darkness of the late night they gleamed with a beautiful lustre. Dvividha who was with Angada was hurt by the arrows. Mainda was also hurt by Kumbha and he fell to the ground. Angada came to the rescue of his friends and after a long time, he was also made to fall down on the ground in faint.

The Vanara army rushed to Rama and told him of the mishaps. Jambavan was sent to fight with Kumbha. Sushena went with him and the two were joined by Sugriva himself.

In a short while Sugriva realised that Kumbha was an extremely capable archer. In admiration he said : "I am amazed at your proficiency with the bow and arrows. You are like your uncle Ravana in the art of fighting with the bow. You are like Prahlada, Bali, Indra, Kubera, Varuna in your valour. In strength and in your characteristics you are like your father. Indeed I am all admiration for you. Not all the devas can stand bravely in front of you. But then, you have met your match in me. Your uncle is great because of the boons he has obtained from Brahma. Kumbhakarna, your father, was frightening the entire world of the devas by the sheer power of his physical strength. Your valour is a combination of both. You are like Indrajit in the dexterity with which you handle the bow and arrows and in prowess you are like Ravana himself. You are a jewel among your race. The fight between you and me will be like that between Indra and Shambara. Come, let us fight. I do not want to kill you since you seem to be such a worthy warrior and it will be a loss to the rakshasa clan if you should die. And yet, since we are on opposite sides we will have to fight and that, to a finish."

Kumbha was quite pleased with the chivalry of Sugriva and the words he spoke and yet, the words which suggested that Sugriva was superior to him made him angry and he caught hold of Sugriva with both his hands. They wrestled with each other and the world stood still watching them fight. The earth seemed to sink under the impact of their powerful footwork and the sea was in tumult, the waves were tossing high and the sea serpents were flung to the surface. Finally, with a powerful hit of his mighty fist Sugriva felled Kumbha to the ground and the son of Kumbhakarna died. As he fell, there was panic in the ranks of the rakshasas since they had not considered him to be capable of being vanquished even and he was now dead.

Nikumbha saw the death of his brother. He knew that this was not the time of grieve and anger gave place to sorrow. He rushed at the Vanara army and the large weapon in his hand shaped like a pestle, was whirled and it seemed to be a wheel of fire and with this he began to destroy the Vanaras in great numbers. They could not come near him and seeing their plight Hanuman came to the forefront and stood in front of Nikumbha. The pestle was whirled and was thrown at the chest of Hanuman. When it hit him the entire field was watching him expecting him to fall down in a faint. But the pestle was shattered to a thousand pieces and he stood unmoved. Hanuman shook for a moment like a mountain during an earthquake and composed himself in a matter of moments. He gathered up his fist, bunched his fingers and he hit Nikumbha on the chest. The armour of the young prince was split and blood flowed in rivulets. The two were now locked in a close grip and they wrestled even as Kumbha and the Vanara king did. After a while Hanuman pushed him to the ground and sat on his chest. Nikumbha was strangled to death and his head was wrenched off his body.

28. INDRAJIT TO THE RESCUE

The Vanaras, when they saw Nikumbha killed, set up such a roar of joy that the quarters were filled with the noise and the rakshasa army was struck with a fear which was almost superstitious. They were made to realise that all their bravery was as nothing before this crowd of monkeys which was armed only with rocks and trees. Not one of them knew how to use the bow and arrow or even a sword and yet, every time, they seemed to be gaining the upper hand. Makaraksha, another of the good warriors on the side of Ravana, was killed by Rama after he had invoked the astra Agneya. When he heard about the massacre in the army caused by the Vanaras and by Rama and his brother, Ravana was at a loss as to what he should do. He sent for his son Indrajit. He asked him to go to front immediately. He told his son about the killing of Kumbha and Nikumbha and Ravana added : "Go and use your Maya tactics if you must. You are extremely valiant and you should be able to vanquish the brothers Rama and Lakshmana. You have defeated Indra and why should I be worried that you cannot kill these two men?"

Indrajit was eager to go. As was usual with him, he performed a yaga and poured oblations into the fire. He offered sacrifice to it and he was greeted with good omens. Agni also, as was usual with him, emerged out of the Homa and glowing like molten gold, accepted the Havis offered to him. After pacifying the devas, the danavas and the asuras Indrajit approached the chariot which was capable of appearing or disappearing at will. Pure high-born steeds were yoked to it and the bows and arrows were placed there in readiness. The top of the chariot was glistening with golden turrets and his banner was tipped with gold. Indrajit was protected by Brahma's astra and the chariot itself had divine powers. Indrajit was not susceptible to harm from anyone : not even from the astras which were in the possession of Rama and Lakshmana. After completing the incantations Indrajit finished his worship of the fire and he told himself :

"I will court victory in the field today. I will kill these false ascetics who have been wandering around in Dandaka and I will lay my victory at the feet of my father as my tribute to him. I will rid the world of all monkeys. Rama and Lakshmana will be dead."

For a while he concealed himself. Suddenly he appeared on the battlefield with his chariot bristling with weapons of every type but mostly bows and arrows. He approached the two brothers who were raining arrows on his army and he became a cloud which pours rain made up of arrows instead of raindrops. He rose up into the sky and hiding himself behind the clouds he begin to harass the brothers. They despatched astras. These astras were as bright as the sun and were many in number and still they were not able to see their assailant. Still unseen by anyone, Indrajit made the sky to be darkened by smoke. Mist and darkness enveloped the quarters. He could not be seen but his progress could, by the arrows from his bow. No one heard the noise of the horses' hoofs nor the twang of his bow. The arrows by name Narachas were sent by him incessantly and he hurt Rama in his limbs. Like twin mountains drenched in rain they stood, the Kosala brothers, and they sent their arrows towards where they guessed Indrajit was. They touched him and fell down on the ground, their tips red with his blood. The arrows which were shot by Indrajit were cut up by those of the princes and their astras were still gauging the spot where he stood hidden. He was going all over the sky with the speed of wind and he was harassing them. With their bodies covered with blood they looked like Palasa trees in bloom. He could not be seen nor his bow or arrows. Like the sun is concealed behind a bank of dense clouds he was concealed by his Maya. Vanaras were falling in numbers and it was depressing to see them fall one by one and now all together. Lakshmana was greatly incensed and he said: "Rama, this is too hard a task for our Vanaras. I will take up the Brahmastra and send it towards this Indrajit." Rama said : "Lakshmana, Brahmastra will claim a number of lives if it is sent now. It is not righteous on our part to destroy any number of rakshasas because of our wrath against one. The rules of fighting say that one who is not fighting, one who has surrendered himself, one who is running away and one who is careless should not be killed. Let us use our astras which are more powerful than those we have been using all this while. Indrajit may conceal himself inside the earth or in the nether world or in the skies. Still he cannot escape the fury of my astras."

Rama made up his mind to kill the son of Ravana soon since he was causing great havoc in the army of the Vanaras. Indrajit knew exactly what was passing in the mind of Rama and he promptly returned to the city of Lanka.

29. MAYA SITA SLAIN

Indrajit remembered the devastation caused in his own army by the Vanara chiefs and the Kosala brothers and he was very angry. He came out of the western gateway of the city. He saw from a distance the gallant brothers and their readiness to fight. He decided to use his Maya to his advantage. He made up his mind to create a figure which would be the very image of Sita. He thought of taking this Sita with him to the battlefield and there, in the presence of everyone, he would kill her with his sword.

To think was to act, and Indrajit emerged from the gates of the city with Sita in his chariot. He was seen by the Vanaras and they armed themselves with the usual boulders and stood prepared for his coming. Hanuman was leading the army and Indrajit saw him. The rakshasa prince went straight towards Hanuman and in his chariot was seen Sita. She was wearing the soiled yellow silk which Hanuman had seen before and she was beautiful like the moon under eclipse. She was sitting forlorn as though she did not care about what was happening around her. Her long hair was twisted in a single plait and it hung like a black serpent on her back. Her face was tired since she had been fasting continuously and there were not many jewels on her. Hanuman knew her only too well and he stood spellbound when he saw her in the chariot of Indrajit. He looked again and again and seeing the tear-stained face of the Devi, Hanuman was full of sadness. He saw that she was now a captive of Indrajit and he thought: "What are his plans? What is to happen now?"

Hanuman went towards the chariot of Indrajit and began to assail him. Indrajit looked very angry and he took his sword out of his scabbard. He caught hold of Sita by her hair and she wailed: "Rama!" Rama!" in a piteous voice. Even as they were watching, Indrajit began to beat her up. Hanuman saw her caught by her hair and his grief and anger were unbearable. Tears flowed from his eyes and he said: "You are a sinner. Born in the race of Brahma, you do not seem to have inherited any gentleness from your ancestor. You have grabbed the hair of Devi, and remember it is because your end is near: or else you would not have dared to do so. You are fit for the worst kind of punishment. Cruel, sinful, small-minded, and proud of your sinfulness this act of yours is against all codes of Dharma. You have a heart of stone and there is not even a vestige of pity in your cruel heart. She was expelled from her palace, and then she was without a kingdom. She was parted from Rama and, now, you want to kill her. Why do you do it? How has she offended you? After killing Sita you will not live very long. You are now in my power and you will meet your death at my hands. I will despatch you to the world meant for sinners of the worst type."

Hanuman rushed towards Indrajit surrounded by his army. The rakshasas were prepared for his onslaught and Indrajit began his task of destruction. He saw that Hanuman was very unhappy and he said: "Sita was the reason why your king Sugriva, you and Rama with his brother came to Lanka. While you are looking on, I will, this very moment, kill her. After killing her I will kill the others, Rama, Lakshmana, Sugriva, that low-minded Vibhishana and, finally, you. You seem to be fond of teaching Dharma to others: that women should not be killed. I am telling you that anything done with a desire to hurt the enemy is right." Indrajit laughed loudly and with a sharp sword he slashed at the weeping Sita. She fell on the terrace of the chariot and she was cut into two across the chest. Indrajit said:

"Monkey! Look at the wife of your master who has been killed by me. Sita is dead and all your efforts have gone waste." Indrajit was roaring with triumph.

The Vanara army was filled with pain and they did not have the enthusiasm to fight with Indrajit. They ran in all directions unable to withstand the valour of the many rakshasas. Hanuman tried to make them come back and fight. He led them and tried to continue the fight. With anger born of sorrow Hanuman fought with great vigour and Indrajit, seeing the confusion in his army caused by Hanuman, came near and began to harass them.

Hanuman was despondent and said : "Come, let us go back. There is no use in fighting any longer. To please Rama we have been fighting and Sita, the sole cause of this war, has been killed. We will hasten to the presence of our king and Rama and tell them about what happened. We will wait for their instructions and proceed accordingly." Hanuman, the fearless, walked slowly and with halting steps towards the presence of Rama and, seeing him go away from his presence, Indrajit left the field of battle.

30. YAGA AT NIKUMBHILA

Indrajit wanted to perform an important yaga at a place called Nikumbhila and he wanted to set about it as early as possible. He reached Nikumbhila and he kindled the sacred fire. He fed it with ghee purified by incantations. He acted strictly according to the rules prescribed and the fire burned brightly. Fed by the oblations the fire burned, nay, glowed like the sun during the evening. Indrajit knew the rituals well and he fed the fire with Havis and the rakshasas sat round him and they watched him while he sat absorbed in the performance of the yaga.

In the meantime, Rama and Lakshmana heard the tumult in the field where Hanuman was fighting with Indrajit. Rama spoke to Jambavan and said : "It seems to me the Vanaras are in need of help. I suggest that you go with an army." Jambavan went fast towards the western gateway where the fight was going on. He encountered Hanuman on the way and saw the grief that was writ on the face of his friends. The entire army was depressed and there were tears in the eyes of Hanuman. He stopped Jambavan on the way and said : "Let us hasten to the spot where Rama is seated with our king."

They went to Rama and Hanuman said : "Indrajit, the son of Ravana, brought Sita in his chariot and, even as I was looking on, he killed her with his sword. I saw her being killed and, drowned in sorrow, I have hurried to you to give you the terrible news."

Hearing the words of Hanuman Rama fell down in a dead faint. The Vanaras surrounded him and tried to revive him with water and flowers dipped in water. Lakshmana, whose grief was greater than that of his brother if that were possible, took his brother in his arms and mourned with him the death of Sita. He said : "Rama, evidently Dharma is not meant to win. Tell me how it has helped us! You have ever walked in the path of Dharma and you have had your senses under control. Selflessly you have worked in the world of men and this is the manner in which Fate rewards you. Dharma is, evidently, unable to protect us from evil. I am certain that Dharma exists but then it is not perceived by the world around us or by the senses. Men like you who are unmoved under the shock of the greatest of calamities are proofs enough that Dharma is there. If Dharma should be victorious in the end then Ravana should have been despatched to the nether regions and you would never have been made to undergo such untold sufferings. When I see the number of misfortunes which have been visited on you one after another I have come to think that the two words Dharma and Adharma have changed their meanings. Dharma is said to be the breeder of further Dharma and, likewise, Adharma that of Adharma.

"Those who have been Adharmis are said to come to grief in the end. Whoever is attached to righteousness will never be enamoured of Adharma and he will be rewarded in the end. Adharma is the breeder of greed and similar sins. Wicked people suffer for their sins. Rama, I have ever felt that might is right and you should try to think on matters like me now. Because of your adherence to Dharma you were banished to the forest. You did not try to subdue our father with your valour. The time has come when action is needed. Your dear beloved wife had been abducted first and is now killed by these sinners. I will avenge the ills meted out to you. Come, rouse up. How is it you do not remember that you are all powerful and capable of destroying the entire universe? I have been born only to serve you and my anger is now uncontrollable. When I think of the killing of Sita my very breath is fuming. I will go and destroy the city of Lanka with all the citizens there."

While he was thus comforting his brother, Vibhishana who had been looking after the army, came there. He came near and saw Rama faint with sorrow and everyone in tears. Rama had not recovered from his faint and he was lying with his head cradled on the lap of his brother. Vibhishana did not know why Rama was so unhappy that he had fainted and he looked at everyone. Lakshmana looked at Vibhishana and said : "My dear friend, Rama is unhappy and he has lost all hopes of living ever since Hanuman came with the news that Indrajit has killed Sita. When he heard the words of Hanuman my brother went into a faint and he has not recovered yet from it." Vibhishana signed for him to stop and said : "Rama! Lord of the world! I feel that the words of Hanuman which have plunged you in sorrow are not to be believed completely. I know full well the feelings of Ravana towards Sita. He would never have allowed her to be killed. How often have I asked him to give her up and seek for peace with you! He has never once listened to me. She will never become his by any of the four ways of persuasion : not by Sama, or by Dana, Bedha or Danda. He would never have thought of Danda as far as she is concerned. That is certain.

"I have it! The wily Indrajit has deceived the Vanaras including the wise Hanuman and has gone to Nikumbhila to perform a yaga. If he succeeds in concluding the yaga he will be invincible. Not Indra nor any of the gods can touch him. He must have anticipated some kind of obstacle to the proper performance of the yaga by the Vanaras and that was why he has thought up this ruse to keep them away from Nikumbhila. That is certain. Do not be unhappy at the killing of Sita. It is not true. It is one of the many Maya tactics of Indrajit. Let us go soon to the spot by name Nikumbhila where he is busy with the yaga. Let us take a large army with us and go to stop the completion of the yaga. Rama, get up. The army is plunged in grief because of your sorrow. Be at peace and send Lakshmana with me and a portion of the army. This great hero will disturb the yaga and Indrajit will leave it undone. He will then be easy to kill. Lakshmana's arrows will soon drink his blood. Grant permission to Lakshmana to achieve the great task of killing Indrajit. There is no time to be lost. You must hurry. If Indrajit completes the yaga nothing can hurt him : not even you or

Lakshmana. He will be a dangerous antagonist and let us tackle him as early as possible. Time is of the utmost importance."

Rama did not hear even a word of what he was saying since he was sunk in stupor. After a while he regained his senses and the words of Vibhishana were slowly understood by him. He said : "Vibhishana, tell me once more what you have been saying. I want to know what happened." Vibhishana told him once again about Indrajit and his Maya : that Sita was safe in the Ashokavana, and he added : "Please send Lakshmana with me with a portion of the army. Indrajit has, in his possession, the astra by name Brahmashirsha and that was the gift of Brahma. His horses were also given him by Brahma. If, in addition to this, he completes the yaga at Nikumbhila, then, remember he will be able to kill all of us. If the enemy is attacked before this happens, it has been said by Brahma that the one who disturbs the yaga will be able to kill Indrajit. His death has already been destined. Command your brother to set out with me now. If Indrajit is dead that means Ravana is dead too."

Rama said : "I know about the Maya tactics he adopts while fighting. He is conversant with the astras and also the Brahmastra as we know only too well! The gods will be helpless before his valour. When he is in the sky no one can follow his movements."

Then Rama told Lakshmana : "Child, go at once to the spot indicated by Vibhishana. Take as many Vanaras with you as you can and Jambavan also. Kill Indrajit and rid the army of the Mayavi opponent. Vibhishana will lead you to the spot where the yaga is being performed. Go to Nikumbhila and after killing Indrajit come back to me."

31. LAKSHMANA ACCOSTS INDRAJIT

Lakshmana took up his bow in his hand. He put on his armour and he prostrated before his brother with reverence. He said : "Rama, my god, my arrows will leave my bow and rush towards Indrajit. They will pierce his chest and drink his blood." Taking leave of Rama Lakshmana went eagerly towards the place by name Nikumbhila where the yaga was being performed by Indrajit. Vibhishana went with Lakshmana. He was joined by Jambavan and his army made up of bears. Soon they reached Nikumbhila and he saw the army of rakshasas surrounding the place. Bow in hand Lakshmana went with resolute steps and his mind was bent on killing Indrajit.

Vibhishana said : "Lakshmana, let our army assail this army of rakshasa with their weapons made of trees and rocks. Let them concentrate on the destruction of the army. When his army is in trouble Indrajit will come out and his task will be incomplete. You must begin to fight with him and do so before his yaga is completed. He is wicked and an Adharmi. He has been harassing all the three worlds and you should be the one to kill him."

Lakshmana took the advice of Vibhishana. The army of Indrajit was attacked fiercely by the Vanaras and soon they were at the mercy of the Vanaras. Indrajit heard the commotion and he had to come out before he could complete the yaga.

With his breath coming in gasps, the angry prince emerged from the solitary spot Nikumbhila and ascended the chariot which was waiting for him. He took his bow in his hand and with anger on his brow he looked like the god of death who had come to kill everyone who came within sight of him. Vibhishana told Lakshmana : "Indrajit is so angry that he looks like he is ready to kill everyone."

The rakshasa army rushed to Indrajit and he saw Hanuman rushing towards them with a huge tree in his uplifted hand. Alone he was handling a small army and not one of them was left alive once he hit them with the tree. Indrajit went towards Hanuman and began to fight with him. Vibhishana told Lakshmana : "Indrajit is bent on killing Hanuman. Now is the time for you to accost the son of Ravana."

Vibhishana went with Lakshmana to where Indrajit was. He entered the forest where the yaga was being performed in secret and Vibhishana showed it all to Lakshmana. He displayed the huge Nyagrodha tree and said : "Indrajit performs the sacrifices here and begins the fight after that every time. He becomes invisible to everyone before the beginning of the fight and he attacks the enemy from a place of hiding whether it is from above the earth or from behind a bank of clouds. Now is the time for you to display your valour and kill him."

Lakshmana twanged the string of his bow as if to say "Yes." Indrajit came to the presence of Lakshmana and he was well equipped with all the accoutrements for a fight.

Lakshmana called out to him and said: "I am challenging you to fight with me. I am waiting for you."

Indrajit had no option but to accept the challenge. He could not complete the yaga at Nikumbhila. His eyes were crimson with wrath and they were fixed on Vibhishana and he said: "You were born here in Lanka and you have eaten the salt of Lanka. You are the brother of the king, my father. You happen to be my uncle and you have dared to betray me to the enemy. How could you do it? You are a killer of Dharma. You are evil-minded. You have no sense of loyalty. You have no goodness in you and your kinsfolk mean nothing to you. Your brother is not dear to you. Foolish as you are, you have abandoned your people and you have found refuge in the enemy's camp. You have become the bonded slave of the enemy. I feel sorry for you since you have won the censure of the world of men. People in aftertimes will condemn you for your actions.

"Being true to one's own clan is one thing and to be friendly with a small-minded stranger is quite another. You are not just friendly with them. You have become a slave to him. Your shattered mind does not seem to grasp the difference between the two. The enemy may be superior, and one's own people may be in the wrong. But loyalty to one's own kith and kin is far better than being faithful to the enemy. One who abandons one's own people and adopts the other as his will certainly be destroyed once the enemy is victorious.

"My dear uncle, you are a blot on the name of our House. Listen to me. That Rama is pretending to be friendly with you since it serves his purpose to do so. He wants to know all the secrets of our army and conquer us if he can. If he manages to do so, he will then kill you. You are the brother of Ravana and it follows that you will be considered to be his enemy by Rama. This heartlessness which I find in you is possible only for you. It is cruel and it is part of you. I can say nothing more."

Vibhishana spoke back: "You are the wicked son of a king who is wicked. You do not know anything about me and about my behaviour. You think you are wiser than the wisest and you rant at will. Shed this arrogance.

I grant that I have been born in the home of rakshasas. But my instincts have never been in conformity with those of a rakshasa. They are more akin to those of a human being. I am never pleased with violence and Adharma has never attracted me. My brother behaved in a sinful manner and why did he send me away from him? A righteous man should avoid one who is an Adharmi even as one flings away a serpent which has coiled itself around one's wrist. Violence, stealing the wife of another, stealing what belongs to another, lusting after other women, are all to be shunned like one runs away from a house on fire. The wise have said so. These sins are but the forerunners of one's destruction.

"All these many years, my brother has revelled in sin. He has enjoyed killing rishis and he has fought with the devas. His anger and his arrogance are proverbial. He has never followed the path of Dharma and all these are certain to drain him of his wealth, his fame and his very life. Like the clouds obscure the top of a mountain these faults have eclipsed whatever good qualities he might have had. I abandoned my brother, your father, for the simple reason that I could not live with his unrighteousness. I am telling you that this Lanka will not be here any more nor you nor your father. You are young, proud and full of conceit. You revel in performing wicked deeds and the noose of death is on your neck already. Say what you wish to me. I am unconcerned.

"Danger has approached you and you will never reach the vicinity of the Nyagrodha tree. You will not escape death at the hands of Lakshmana. Come, fight with him and if you are killed you will reach the heavens meant for heroes who die on the battlefield. Let us see your valour and let me see you try all the weapons you have and your bow and arrows. Once the arrow of Lakshmana is aimed at you, not all your army will be able to save you from certain death. You are not going back to the city alive. I am certain of that."

32. THE KILLING OF INDRAJIT

Indrajit was highly incensed by the words of Vibhishana. He took up his mighty bow in his hand and he took his stance in the chariot which was famed the world over. The horses which were yoked to it were given to him by Brahma.

He saw Lakshmana who was carried on the shoulders of Hanuman. He twanged the string of his bow and said : "Just wait till you see the arrows which will flow from my bow. They will destroy this army even as fire will a heap of cotton. I will send all of you to the city of Yama and you should prepare yourself for it. Who is there brave enough to withstand my prowess? Lakshmana, do you remember? Hardly a few days ago, during the fight in the night you and your heroic brother were made to sleep on the ground. You were then unable to withstand my arrows. Evidently you do not remember it or else you would not have dared to come here and challenge me now. I am hissing like an angry serpent and I will spit venom and kill you."

Lakshmana was unruffled by his words and he said : "You have told me about your valour. It is up to you to prove it now. Words should be followed up with action which suits the words. You think a task is achieved because you wish it to be so. You adopted Maya tactics and such warfare is not approved of by righteous men. Enough of this empty talk. Let us see what you can do now with me in front of you."

Indrajit sent sharp arrows which wounded Lakshmana. They hurt him and there was blood all over his body. Lakshmana pulled the string of the bow to the utmost and sent several arrows called Narachas to hurt Indrajit. He was able to make them lodge in the chest of the prince of Lanka.

The duel went on. Both were valiant and both were excellent archers. Both were proficient in the art of warfare and both were heroes. They were both conversant with the use of all the many weapons used in fighting and they were at home in the handling of astras. They were like two planets attacking each other in the sky : like two lions fighting for supremacy in a forest. Both were drenched with blood and both of them had arrows lodged in their bodies. Again and again could be heard the twanging of bowstrings and the army around stopped fighting and was watching this duel with bated breath.

Indrajit seemed to be slightly tired and Lakshmana did not lessen his onslaught. For a while the rakshasa was unconscious and he recovered soon and began to fight again. He sent arrows to hurt Lakshmana, Hanuman and Vibhishana. With a gesture of disdain Vibhishana plucked the arrows and threw them down. After a while Indrajit's arrows split the armour of Lakshmana and it fell to the ground and his own armour had already been broken by Lakshmana.

Neither was tired out and again, both were tired. Astra was met by astra and weapon by weapon. Vibhishana joined in the fight and several of the great fighters on the side of Indrajit who were in the rakshasa army, were harassed by him and by the Vanara army which he encouraged to join in the fight. Indrajit was angry with him and the Vanaras. Vibhishana told himself: "It is not right for me to kill the son of my brother. I am waiting for Lakshmana to do it. The others can join in the fight."

Lakshmana and Indrajit were deaf and blind to the rest of the world. Their fight had reached the most fierce stage. The arrows flew so fast from their bows it was not possible to follow their flights. The sky was not seen and the air was thick with the arrows. It looked as though the sun had set since it was so dark all around. Beasts and birds made dreadful noises and the very air stood still with fear. Fire would not burn and the rishis in the heavens wished that the world should be saved from the wrath of these two fighters. They were both determined to fight to a finish.

Lakshmana hurt the horses of the chariot of Indrajit and he killed the charioteer also. Indrajit took the reins of the horses in his hand and drove the chariot himself and, at the same time, he fought with Lakshmana. It was indeed a glorious sight. The Vanara army jumped on the horses and killed them and soon the chariot was also broken.

Indrajit abandoned the chariot and stood on the ground. The man and the rakshasa fought as though nothing had happened during their fight. Indrajit spoke to his men and said: "It is so dark that nothing is discernible. No one can recognise his neighbour. Keep on fighting and I will go back to the city and return with another chariot. See that my absence is not noticed by these stupid monkeys."

Ravana's son deceived all of them and went into the city. Quickly he took a chariot which was provided with all the weapons and he came back to the field.

Lakshmana and Vibhishana were wonder-struck at the swiftness with which he had accomplished his desire. They were all admiration for him.

With renewed vigour Indrajit fought and it seemed as though the fight would never end. Lakshmana saw his army being destroyed and he took an arrow quickly and broke the bow of Indrajit. He took another bow and that was also broken. Hurt by several arrows from Lakshmana Indrajit took another bow. The duel went on and the anger of the prince had not abated : his anger against Vibhishana. Again and again he aimed some of his arrows at his uncle and also at Hanuman.

The second chariot of Indrajit was also broken and the horses killed. Indrajit aimed the astra presided over by Yama at Lakshmana and he replied with the astra of Kubera. It had been given by Kubera himself and that, in a dream. The two astras met in mid-air and there was fire and smoke emitted by both. Each destroyed the other and they fell to the ground in splinters. Lakshmana thought of sending the Varunastra and it was destroyed by Raudra sent by his enemy. Indrajit now sent the astra of Agni and Suryastra was able to nullify it. Asurastra was fierce when sent by Indrajit but Lakshmana knew that Maheshvara would soon put it to shame. Rishis and Pitris were now in the sky and they blessed Lakshmana from there.

Aindra was the astra which Lakshmana took in his hand now. It was presided over by Indra and it was a deadly astra. It was like death at the time of the great deluge and Lakshmana bent his bow and pulled the string to the utmost. While he did so he said : "If it is true that Rama is unequalled in prowess, if it is true that he has ever been righteous, if it is true that he has ever been truthful, then may this arrow kill Indrajit, the son of Ravana."

Lakshmana spoke the incantations with reverence and sent the arrow towards Indrajit. It travelled like a streak of lightning and it severed the beautiful head of Indrajit from his body and it fell to the ground. It was like a golden lotus which had grown on the earth.

Indrajit was dead and there was a roar from the Vanara army which reached the skies. There was a great commotion in the skies and the army of rakshasas fled in all four directions when it saw their master fallen. Their weapons fell from their nerveless hands and they ran as fast as they could towards Lanka.

Indrajit who had been a thorn in the side of Rama, who had fought as no one else had, who had been the favoured great-great-grandson of Brahma, who was an adept in every kind of warfare, who was a master of all the astras which the Kosala brothers possessed, who was so full of bravery and valour, who had commanded the loyalty of every one of his men, who was the sole hope of Ravana, who was the beloved son of Mandodari, was now dead and his head illumined the field of battle like the sun which had fallen to the earth because of a curse. He was like the moon who had been cursed by Daksha and who had lost his brilliance. Indrajit who had captured Indra and brought him to his father's city as a captive was dead, was killed by the astra which was, ironically enough, presided over by Indra.

33. RAMA'S JOY

Vibhishana and Hanuman with Jambavan were thrilled with the achievement of Lakshmana. It was no mean task he had performed and the heavens were raining flowers on him. He stood with his body covered by blood and the string of his bow was still vibrating after the arrow had left it. The entire army stood around him and there were shouts of joy from everywhere. The heavens were filled up with all the celestials and they knew that the task of Rama had been almost accomplished. Ravana was the only one left and Rama would soon kill him. This was the feeling in the mind of every one of those in the heavens and a feeling of relief was to be found everywhere.

Drenched with blood Lakshmana stood in the field of battle and Hanuman with Vibhishana and Jambavan stood beside him. There was a look of triumph on the face of each one of them. And thus they went to the presence of Rama and the entire army went with them. Hanuman led Lakshmana holding his hand and they went to Rama. Lakshmana fell at the feet of Rama and stood by his side even as Indra would beside Brihaspati. His breath was still coming in gasps and he told Rama about the killing of Indrajit. Vibhishana went to Rama and he told Rama that Indrajit was dead.

Rama's joy knew no bounds. He was thrilled that his beloved Lakshmana had achieved what had seemed to be an impossible task. He embraced his brother and said : "Child, Lakshmana, what you have done today is the greatest thing that could ever be achieved by anyone in battle. I am pleased with you. With the death of Indrajit, victory which was somewhere in the dim future had come suddenly within easy reach of us." The noble-minded Rama took Lakshmana on his lap and embraced him much to his embarrassment. He treated him as he would a young child which had done something exceedingly clever! He looked again and again at the body of his brother and stroked him with loving hands. He shed tears at the sight of the many wounds on the body of Lakshmana and he was greatly affected by it. He embraced him again and again and said : "It was a very hard task which I had set you and you have come out victorious. Ravana, when he hears about the death of his son, will be as good as dead. I have already tasted victory because of your valour. To Ravana the death of Indrajit will be like losing his right arm. He was Ravana's greatest strength. Hanuman and Vibhishana have done so much for you and helped you to be successful in your endeavour.

"Three days and three nights have been spent in opposing this Indrajit. He was so powerful, it was unbelievable. Ravana is at the moment getting ready to come out to fight with me, I think.

"He will come out to the field of battle. He will be heart-broken at the death of his son. Ravana is a powerful opponent. I know that. But his spirit is gone along with Indrajit and he will easily be killed by me. Sita will come back to me soon and I will again be lord of the world."

Rama was greatly excited and his words spoke of his gladness and his unusual expressions of joy. He sent for Sushena, the physician and told him : "Sushena, my beloved brother Lakshmana, as you can see, has been wounded. Use your physic and help him to be rid of the discomfort and pain arising from his many wounds. Vibhishana has also been hurt and so is Hanuman. Several of the Vanaras in our army have to be attended to."

Sushena used herbs to assuage the pain which Lakshmana was suffering and very soon the pain disappeared and Lakshmana was his usual self.

Rama breathed a sigh of relief after seeing Lakshmana well and full of his usual enthusiasm and they spoke in detail about the fight with Indrajit. They spoke about the valour of the dead hero, Indrajit, and about Lakshmana and his calm manner of fighting. Rama listened as though it were the story of someone else and Lakshmana smiled with embarrassment. Rama embraced him again and again and there was great happiness in the army of Rama.

34. RAVANA'S GRIEF

Ravana's ministers came to know of the death of Indrajit. They went to Ravana and told him: "Lord, under our very eyes when we were all looking, Indrajit, your valiant son, fought gloriously with Lakshmana who was accompanied by Hanuman and Vibhishana. It was a glorious fight. Your son gave no chance for Lakshmana to rest even for a moment. His body was filled with arrows and each arrow drew blood and very soon Lakshmana was bleeding all over his body. He tormented the brother of Rama abominably and he hurt Hanuman and Vibhishana too." They paused unable to say anything more. Ravana was listening with a pleased expression on his face. They summoned up courage finally and said : "O king! Your son who has never been defeated in any fight was killed by the brave Lakshmana. The fight was intense but in the end Indrajit was killed by Lakshmana. He has been despatched to the world of his forefathers."

Ravana listened as though it were about the death of someone else. He would not, he could not, believe that his Indrajit could die. It was not possible. He heard the news and, after a moment of disbelief, the truth dawned on him that it was true and the rakshasa monarch fell down in a dead faint. The pain was too much for him, and kind nature granted him a few moments of respite by making him faint.

He was roused from his faint and he woke up after a very long time. He said : "Child! My beloved child! You were a great hero and there was no one like you. No one in all the three worlds was able to touch even a hair on your head. You had defeated Indra and how could Lakshmana do this to you? With your anger you would split the Mandara mountain of Lord Mahadeva : and yet you were not able to split this man with your arrows! How can that be possible? Yama has to be praised since he has had the audacity to capture you when I am still here. It has been said that a warrior who dies on the field of battle fighting for his master will reach the heavens meant for heroes and for you, my son, there is a special place there.

"Today all the devas and the danavas as well as the other denizens of the heavens will be without fear since you are dead. Without you, this entire earth seems to be but a blank and empty space. The three worlds have lost all their charm now that you are dead, my child, my Indrajit, Meghanada. Why did you have to leave your kingdom, your beloved Lanka, your mother, me and your wife? Is heaven then more attractive that you should have preferred it to all of us? It is the rule that you should perform the obsequies to me when I am dead but you have altered all the rules and I have to offer Tarpana so that you will reach the land of our dear departed. Sugriva is alive, Rama and Lakshmana are still alive and, when they are there, how could you plunge me in grief and leave me? Indrajit, why did you have to die?"

Ravana was inconsolable and suddenly his grief turned into anger. By nature Ravana was easily angered and this sorrow enhanced it and he was like the summer sun with his rays spouting heat which is unbearable. He frowned and his breath was like the breath of Vritra when he was angry. Ravana was so angry he decided to kill Sita who was the cause of all these calamities. It was not possible to approach him as he stood, angry like Rudra.

Tears which were hot like liquid fire, like drops of hot oil, dripped slowly from his eyes which were crimson with anger. His sorrow was great and great indeed was his anger born of that sorrow. He said : "In the days of the long past, often have I performed tapas and pleased Brahma and, pleased with me, he has granted me several boons. Because of his love for me he has granted that I will not be in danger as far as devas or asuras or danavas or any of the celestials are concerned. Brahma has granted me an armour which is divine. Vajra cannot harm it and during the war with the devas, none of the weapons of the gods could touch me.

"If, wearing that armour, and seated in my divine chariot, I enter the field of battle, no one, not even Indra can face me and escape alive. This bow was given to me by Brahma too and it will grant me my dearest wish, the lives of Rama and Lakshmana when I go to fight with them. Let my weapons and chariot be brought to me immediately." Ravana was like one demented with sorrow at the death of Indrajit. He made up his mind to kill Sita. Those around him could see anger on his brow and sorrow in his eyes. It was pathetic. Ravana was trying to drown his pain in a spate of anger and it was a fearful sight. He could not speak clearly since anger made him stutter. He said : "My child Indrajit tried his Maya to deceive the Vanaras and he pretended to kill Sita and that ruse failed. I will now make it come true. I will, this moment, kill that Sita who is devoted to that despicable human being."

Ravana took his sword in his hand. With his mind completely unhinged because of the loss of his beloved Indrajit Ravana took his sword which gleamed blue in the light and rushed to where Sita was. His ministers and his wives went with him and there was nothing but fear in their minds. They had seen Ravana's anger before but they had never seen this kind of anger before. They spoke among themselves : "It is certain that the Kosala brothers will suffer a great sorrow. This emperor of ours has not once been defeated in war. The devas who guard the four quarters are but his slaves. He is the lord of the three worlds and all that is precious or beautiful or rare has been annexed by our king. There is no one like him. None can equal him in valour or in might."

They reached the Ashokavana and Ravana walked with firm strides towards Sita. Some were bold enough to try and pacify his anger but it was of no avail. Like an evil planet rushing towards Rohini he went to Sita.

Sita saw him coming towards her with his sword raised. She saw that he was being prevented by several and that still he was walking towards her. She thought : "He seems to be in a fit of anger since he is coming towards me with a sword. He is sure to kill me who is helpless, who was no one to help me in my predicament. All these days he has been telling me that he thinks nothing of my Rama. He has been forcing me to forget my Rama and to accept his love and since I have been refusing him constantly he is disgusted with me evidently and has made up his mind to kill me. I am sure of it. Perhaps those brave brothers of his have been killed in the war. Perhaps he is unhappy because his son is dead. He is not able to kill Rama and perhaps out of frustration he has decided to kill me. If only I had listened to Hanuman's suggestion and allowed him to take me back to Rama I would have joined my lord long ago. Perhaps Rama is dead. I do not know what has happened."

Sita was ready to die since she was convinced that Rama had been killed and that Ravana was angry with her because she had spurned his love. He must have felt that all his attempts had been futile and in sheer disgust had decided to kill her.

While he was set on killing Sita, Ravana was not able to think properly. His anger had blinded him to all his surroundings and made him deaf to the words of everyone. He would not listen to anyone. However, one of his ministers, by name Suparshva, was very wise and good by nature. He saw

Sita and he approached his king. He said : "My lord, how could you contemplate the death of Sita? It is not according to Dharma. You are well-versed in the sacred lore and you have ever been observing the rites and Vratas which will win a place for you in heaven. Never once have you swerved from the path of Dharma. How could you consider killing a woman? Wait for her to change her mind about you. Turn the stream of your anger against Rama. Today is the fourteenth day after the full moon. Success will be yours if you set out to fight with Rama tomorrow which is the day of the new moon. Wear your armour and, seated in your golden chariot if you set out to fight, you can kill Rama and Sita will surely be yours afterwards."

35. THE MOOLABALA OF RAVANA

Ravana's anger had been appeased somewhat by the words of Suparshva and he deigned to listen to his words. He put up his sword and returned to his palace without speaking a word to anyone. He entered his Council Hall and he strode up and down like a lion which had been newly caged. His sorrow was great and nothing would make him forget the terrible death of his son Indrajit. He greeted his men with a nod here and a look there and no words came.

After pondering for a long time Ravana stood with folded palms before his men and said : "I would like you all to go surround by the army made up of horses, elephants, chariots and footmen. Surround that Rama on all sides and rain arrows on him. He should be killed. If it is not accomplished today I will myself go tomorrow and even as you are all looking, I will split his chest with my sharp arrows and avenge the death of my son."

This was Ravana's Moolabala and it was famed in all the three worlds for its strength and for the valour of each individual warrior who was in the army. Ravana had great faith in this personal army of his and he sent this army to fight with Rama.

Armed with the many terrible weapons the army of Ravana set out to the field. The sun had just risen and the two armies were soon locked in a terrible fight. Dust rose to the skies and nothing could be seen around the field. Blood was flowing like a river and the clash of the weapons with the rocks hurled by the Vanaras was the only sound that could be heard. After a while it was evident that the Vanaras were being destroyed in hundreds and thousands by Ravana's army. The poor Vanaras rushed to Rama for succour.

Rama took up his bow and came to face the army which was harassing his men. Arrows began to pour out of his bow like drops of rain out of a thundering cloud. He was deadly like the sun at noonday and no one could approach him. He could not be seen. Only his actions were perceptible and like the wind in the forest he could not be seen. Those who were watching saw the weapons of the rakshasas splintered and burnt and they lay scattered on the ground. The men who made up the army were falling and no one could see Rama except the bow which was bent full circle and from which the arrows were emerging incessantly.

Even as men who are lost in the world of senses cannot perceive the Jivatma inside them, even so, Rama was not visible to the naked eyes of the rakshasas. Shouts were heard : "He is destroying the elephant army. The warriors on the chariots are being killed. The horses are dead with their riders." These were the words which were heard in the field of battle. Rama then took up the astra by name Gaandharva and the entire army went into a kind of delusion. The result was, the rakshasas saw several Ramas all at the same time and again, they saw but one Rama fighting with them. They saw the tips of his arrows but they saw him not. In a muhurta, Rama destroyed the entire army. A handful of them, literally a handful, went back to Lanka and the field of battle was like the playground of Rudra when he was in an angry mood. Celestial shouts of approbation could be heard and Rama, relaxing after the fight, spoke to Sugriva, Hanuman, Jambavan, Vibhishana and others : "This powerful astra is known only to Lord Mahadeva and to me." He was extremely happy that he had been able to destroy the army of Ravana, his Moolabala all by himself like he had done in the Janasthana : only this army was much larger and much better organised.

Great was the cry of mourning in Lanka. The wives of the dead rakshasas were demented with grief. They wailed :

"It was all because of Shurpanakha, the sister of our king, that these things have happened. Why did she have to go to the forest and see Rama? Rama is like another Manmata and she fell in love with him. Why did it have to happen? He was not wishing harm to anyone. He has ever been brave and righteous. This ugly woman, obsessed with her lust, wanted him to take her. The old hag was the cause of our great misfortune. She caused the death of everyone in Janasthana and as though that were not enough, to teach Rama a lesson, she had to come to Ravana with her tale of woe. She is the cause of all this enmity between Rama and Ravana. Sita was brought here and that was ordained by the Fates : the forerunner of the death of our king which is imminent. He will never be able to make her his wife and he is sure to be killed by Rama in the fight which is to ensue soon. The death of Viradha should have warned our king that Rama is not an ordinary human being. And now we are all left lamenting because of the evil doings of one single woman. Khara, Dushana, Trishiras and fourteen thousand men were killed by Rama and yet our king would not accept that Rama is a god among men. Kabandha was killed and then Vali, the great Vanara chief. That should have been proof enough ! The crowning of Sugriva should have told us that Rama is no ordinary opponent. Vibhishana was a good man and he tried to advise our king. But it was of no avail. Our king was blinded by his own ignorance. If he had followed the advice of Vibhishana the king and all of us would have been happy. Lanka would not have become a burning ground.

"Kumbhakarna was killed, Atikaya and Indrajit, who, we thought, was invincible. And yet, the king has not been able to realise the truth. Every house in Lanka is sunk in sorrow and he does not heed it. There is no one to save us and we are desolate."

These were some of the words of woe which were spoken by the women who had lost their husbands, brothers, fathers and sons. Ravana heard the weeping of the women in the city. Lanka, from whose houses and mansions were heard, till now, only the music of the Veena and the music of the anklets of the women, was now sending out nothing else but wails and sobs. Ravana was sighing like a serpent and he was deeply immersed in thought. He caught his lower lip between his teeth and tried to hold back his anger and his sorrow. Ravana never thought that his entire Moolabala would vanish like snow on the face of the desert. He was glowing like the fire at the time of *Pralaya*.

He spoke to his rakshasas who were with him and, for the first time, there was a semblance of fear in his voice which was faltering. He said : "Ask Mahodara and Virupaksha to be here immediately. Let Mahaparshva come." They were trembling and they could not face their angry monarch. They rushed to the commanders and conveyed the order of the king. They were with Ravana soon and with great effort he smiled at them and said : "I will, this moment, send Rama to the city of Yama and his brother will go with him. I am going now to avenge the death of Kumbhakarna, Prahastha and Indrajit. All my men have been killed and I have to avenge their deaths. Because of my arrows with their winged ends the quarters will be covered and the sky will not be seen. The rivers and the sea will not be seen. With my arrows I will kill all the many monkeys who have come with these foolish men. I will comfort the women in the city by wiping their tears. I will make amends for the loss of their men to these women. All those who are still alive and who wish to go with me can do so."

Mahaparshva hurried to obey his wishes. A large army was gathered and very soon they were ready to march with their king. They loved him and they were ready to meet their deaths along with him.

The divine chariot equipped with all the weapons was brought to the gates of the palace and the valiant Ravana stood up in his seat all set to go to the field of battle.

36. RAVANA SETS OUT TO THE FIELD OF BATTLE

Ravana approached the chariot which was drawn by eight horses. It was a very fast-moving chariot and it was gleaming like a thousand suns. It was like fire which had been lit in the sacrifice and Ravana ascended the ratha. Surrounded by the large army Ravana set out to fight with Rama. Mahodara, Mahaparshva and Virupaksha also took their chariots and went with him. Ravana's anger was like that of Yama at the time of the great Pralaya and he went fast towards the battlefield. He emerged out of the city and the sun lost all his brilliance. Evil omens were seen. There was a sudden darkness enveloping the four quarters. The birds were all screaming discordantly and the earth quaked. Clouds were raining drops of blood and the horses tripped and fell. An eagle flew out of nowhere and sat on the banner of Ravana's chariot entirely hiding the Veena which was etched on it. Jackals were howling. Ravana's left hand and left eye throbbed. His face did not have its customary glow and his voice was suddenly hoarse. All the omens were indication of death on the battlefield. He was unconcerned and he proceeded fast.

The Vanara army knew that another army had arrived because of the sound made by the chariots and by the clash of weapons. The fight began in no time. Ravana was fighting like one inspired. His arrows were emerging from his bow like rays from the sun and they were scorching the Vanaras. No one was able to face his fury and his valour. The Vanaras ran away from him like elephants from a forest which had caught fire. He was like a strong wind which scattered clouds. Soon he was facing Rama.

Sugriva was assisted by Sushena in rearranging the army and he was engaged in fighting with the army. The rakshasa army was made to realise the prowess of Sugriva. Virupaksha came to the aid of his men. A duel was fought between him and Sugriva. They fought for a long time and both were great fighters. But finally, with a blow from his open palm, Sugriva killed Virupaksha.

Like the waters of a lake become less and less with the advance of summer, even so, as time went on, the army on both sides was getting diminished in number.

Slowly Ravana began to realise that Fate was siding with Rama : that the gods were favouring him. Or else, how could all this have happened to him and his men? He saw the great warrior Virupaksha killed by a blow from the palm of that monkey Sugriva. This was a thing which had to be seen to be believed. He called Mahodara and asked him to take over where Virupaksha had left.

Like a moth rushing towards a flame Mohodara went towards the army of the Vanaras with a desire to annihilate it. Sugriva was the one who faced him when he saw the harm which Mahodara was causing to his army. They fought for a long time and finally Sugriva caught hold of a sword. Holding it in his powerful hand he cut off the head of Mahodara and it fell on the ground like a ripe fruit which can no longer stay on the tree. Rama heard the triumphant cry and was pleased with the prowess of his friend. Mahaparshva tried to win where his companions had lost. A portion of the Vanara army was attacked by him and, armed as they were with but trees and rocks, they could not brook the arrows and javelins and other dreadful weapons used by him and his associates. He was a great archer and his valour was great. They could not bear it. They were being killed in large numbers.

Angada came to the rescue of his men. Jambavan joined him and he broke the chariot of Mahaparshva. Angada fought valiantly for a long time and so did the rakshasa. Finally Angada killed him with a powerful hit from his fist. Panic set in the army of Ravana and within a moment he realised who had caused it. The very sky resounded with the happy cry of the Vanaras whose king and prince had despatched three of the commanders to the abode of Yama.

Ravana hurried towards Rama in his chariot. He had seen the death of his three warriors who had come with him and he was furious. He spoke to his charioteer: "I will end the misery in my Lanka by killing these brothers who have been wreaking such havoc in my army. Take me soon to where they are."

Ravana was once again in front of Rama. He did not want to remember the previous encounter when he had fared so badly. It was like a bad dream to him, to be forgotten as soon as possible. Ravana despatched an astra by name Tamasa which was enough to frighten the Vanaras. It had been given to him by Brahma and the army was being burnt with it. Rama came to where Ravana was. Ravana saw him with his brother and to him he looked like Narayana with Indra by his side.

Rama was leaning against his glorious bow. He seemed to be towering up to the skies, so powerful was the effect of his stance. His lotus eyes were trained on Ravana and his magnificent arms were strong and powerful. The anger on the brow of Ravana was seen by Rama and he grasped his bow firmly in his hand. The valiant Rama whose fame was known to all the three worlds was seeing the havoc caused by the astra of Ravana. He saw too that Ravana had come to him straight with a desire to challenge him. Rama was very happy that the encounter was sought by Ravana.

Rama strung his bow and he began to send his sharp arrows towards him. The twanging of his bow was heard by all. Ravana replied with his arrows and soon there ensued a serious fight between the two. Ravana was not willing to be disturbed by Lakshmana. He passed him by and went to Rama. Rama was only too happy to meet him. They fought for a long while and the sight was pleasing to those who were watching them. The brightness of the arrows and the speed were like flashes of lightning streaking across the sky during the rainy season. The sky was hidden as though by clouds : so dense was the rain of arrows from their bows. Both were great archers both were well versed in the art of fighting. Both were proficient in the knowledge of astras and the fight was glorious.

Rama invoked the mantra and sent the astra by name Rudra and it could not penetrate the armour of Ravana. Again Rama tried another astra and that again proved futile. They were countered by Ravana and they entered the earth. Ravana now despatched the astra by name Asura and his arrows assumed the forms of wild and dangerous animals and began to harass Rama. Rama sent the Agneyastra which was enough to burn them all up.

The Vanaras had all assembled and they stood watching the duel and cheering whenever the astras of Ravana proved to be ineffectual. An astra which was presided over by Maya was sent by Ravana and this was rendered useless by Rama. The duel went on and neither was able to gain ascendency over the other. Gaandharvastra was used by Rama and this was fought by Ravana sending the Suryastra. The sky and the earth were glowing with the many circlets of light emerging from the bow of Ravana. Each was like a miniature sun and the entire army looked at them in wonder.

Lakshmana was impatient to fight with Ravana and he came with his bow. He sent several arrows with a desire to wound Ravana and the fight began now between Lakshmana and Ravana. Lakshmana was able to fell the banner of Ravana's chariot and Ravana's charioteer also. He broke the bow of Ravana. Vibhishana rushed up and killed the horses of the chariot. Ravana's anger against his brother was unbearable. He jumped down from his chariot and took up a Shakti and hurled it at Vibhishana. Lakshmana stopped it half way. Ravana now took up a Shakti which was endowed with divine powers. It was more powerful than Yama. He twirled it in his mighty arms and Lakshmana rushed towards Vibhishana and stood shielding him from Ravana's Shakti, which he had flung in wrath against his brother. Lakshmana fought with his bow and arrows and Ravana decided that he should put an end to Lakshmana and his prowess. He said : "Vibhishana has, no doubt, been saved by you. But you will not be able to escape the fury of my Shakti. I have now hurled it at you. It will, this moment, suck the life out of you after splitting your chest." Ravana roared with anger and hurled the Shakti at Lakshmana. It had been made by Maya and it had never failed to claim a victim. It came towards Lakshmana and it was fearsome like a thunderbolt. Rama said : "May the Shakti lose its potency. May it leave my brother unhurt."

The Shakti entered the chest of Lakshmana and it was like a dread serpent entering the hole which is its home. Lakshmana was wounded in the chest by it and he fell down senseless. Rama was watching him fall and he was greatly upset by the fall of Lakshmana. Tears sprang to his eyes and he was wild with anger. He knew that it was not the time to be angry and he fought with Ravana, and at the same time, minded his brother whom he loved with a deep intense love. His mind was in a turmoil and he saw blood gushing from the wound in the chest of Lakshmana. The Shakti had pierced Lakshmana and had afterwards entered the earth. Rama could not contain himself. He went and tried to pull the Shakti out and when he pulled it with both his hands it broke in his hands. Ravana was all the while sending arrows at Rama and they hurt him.

Rama was unconcerned about his own pain but he embraced Lakshmana and taking him in his arms, he said : "Hanuman, Sugriva, come here and protect my brother. This wicked Ravana who seems to be the personification of evil has to be killed. Like the Chataka bird, which has been aching for rain during the arid months, is thrilled at the sight of the rain-cloud darkening the sky, my heart leaps up at the sight of this man who will be the cause for the display of my valour. I assure you of one truth : this world will have either Rama or Ravana. Two of us cannot live in the same world. Two swords cannot be placed in the same scabbard. With the death of Ravana all my sorrows will be forgotten. The loss of my kingdom, the life in the forest, the wanderings in the Dandaka, the separation from Sita, the opposition of the rakshasa and now this great sorrow, this pain like torture in hell, will all vanish once Ravana is killed. This Vanara army was collected for the sole aim of killing him. Vali was killed and Sugriva was installed on the throne for the sole purpose of killing Ravana. It is for the killing of this sinner that the bridge was built across the sea. Now that he is here before me and now that he has come within my sight he can never hope to escape from me. I ask you all to assemble on the top of the hill and from there you can watch the fight between me and my dearest enemy. The devas and the gandharvas and all the celestials will see what it is that makes Rama a hero. Till the worlds stand, till the earth stands above the sea, so long as living things inhabit the earth and the three worlds the war between me and Ravana will be talked about. I will complete my task successfully."

Rama began to fight with renewed vigour. The encounter was as fierce as it was before and the spectators heard only the twanging of their bowstrings and the swish of their arrows as they hissed in the air. Ravana was tired and he was tortured by the many arrows which had tips of gold and which hurt like living fire.

Ravana left the field and there was great rejoicing at his discomfiture. Rama was, in a way, relieved that Ravana went away from there since he could devote all his attention to Lakshmana who was still unconscious. His mind had not been fully in the duel and he asked Sushena : "Sushena, as you saw, Lakshmana has been hurt by Ravana's Shakti. He is dear to me and my heart is not in the fight when my brother is suffering. I have neither the will nor the desire to devote all my time and attention on Ravana. If this brother of mine should die what will be the use of my living after that? I have no wish to live nor do I desire any happiness if he should die. My valour has gone to sleep and the bow slips from my nerveless hands. My arrows are scattered all over the place and I cannot even aim properly. Tears dim my eyes and my limbs are beyond control like those of a man still wandering in the world of dreams. My concern is great since Lakshmana has not been able to wake up from his faint. I have made up my mind to kill myself."

37. SANJIVINI AGAIN

Rama was sighing with sorrow and he sat by the side of his brother with his eyes raining tears. Lakshmana was his alter ego and he could not bear this grief. He lamented : "I have seen my beloved Lakshmana on the ground. He has been grievously hurt and his body is covered with the dust of the battlefield. I have no longer any desire to win the war, or to live or even to rescue Sita. These things do not seem to be worth anything now. What is there for me if I win this war when my brother loses his life ? I do not desire the kingdom nor my life. Kinsmen can be found from place to place. Wives can be found everywhere. But a brother, one who is born with me, who has been like a shadow to me, who has been my sole supporter and comfort during my dark days, will I find him anywhere? There is no place where I can find another Lakshmana."

Rama was now sobbing openly and Sushena said : "My lord, Lakshmana is not dead. His face has not lost that glow of life and that makes me realise that he is not dead. His face has not the darkness which is associated with death. His face is like that of one who is in deep sleep. His palms are still as pink and soft as a lotus and his eyes have not lost their flash. This is not the face of a dead man. Lakshmana's face is that of a long-lived man. His face has all the beauty and auspicious signs which indicate a long life. He is not dead. Abandon this grief. Lakshmana, the killer of his foes, is very much alive. There is no doubt about it."

Sushena turned to Hanuman and said : "You are the only refuge for us. You once brought the hill containing the Oshadhis at the request of Jambavan. Can you do it again? The Oshadhi by name Vishalyakarani is enough to bring him back to consciousness and heal his wounds."

Before he could complete his sentence Hanuman was in the air rushing towards Himavan. He went there with the speed which was his heritage. He looked at the earth and soon he was high above and in a matter of moments he was landing on the peak which contained the Oshadhis. He looked at the many creepers and, as before, he did not know which was the Oshashi wanted by Sushena. Once again he lifted the mountain and all the while he thought : "This is the safest thing to do. I may, in my excitement, take the wrong herb and do more harm than good. I will take the Sanjivini mountain itself and Sushena can do what he will with it."

He carried the small mountain in his right hand and he flew back to Lanka. Sushena took the herb which he needed and the army was amazed at the feat of Hanuman.

When he breathed in the healing leaves of the herb which Sushena had crushed and held to his nostrils, the fragrance of the herbs made Lakshmana rise up from the ground and he had shed his weakness. The healing fragrance of the herb had made him lose his fatigue and his wounds had all disappeared. He was his old self.

Rama was shedding tears of joy and rushing to Lakshmana said: "Child, Lakshmana, come here. Come to me and sit by my side." With wet eyes he embraced his beloved brother and said: "I am the most fortunate of all human beings. I see you alive and no one knows the extent of my good fortune. Lakshmana, if you had died, then the world would have had no meaning for me. Sita, my life and the kingdom would all have meant nothing to me. I would have killed myself if you had not been revived."

Lakshmana was overcome with affection and he was also distressed at the words of Rama. He said: "Rama, you have been famed because of the fact that truth is your religion. You should not behave like any ordinary human being and give in to grief like this. The valiant never go back on their words: And you should remember to keep your promise. You should not be despondent for my sake. You must kill Ravana and fulfil your promise to yourself. When he is summoned with your roar of challenge he will not be able to face you and your fury.

"Before the sun sets you should fight with him and kill Ravana. If you really desire to kill Ravana, to keep up your oath, if you really love Sita, then listen to my words and summon him to fight with you. You will certainly kill him today. I know it."

Lakshmana's words made Rama feel proud of him. This brother of his had been the sole source of comfort to him during his days of pain and now he was a source of inspiration to him. Rama called himself fortunate that he had a brother like Lakshmana.

38. THE FINAL ENCOUNTER

Ravana was facing Rama and the words of Lakshmana were still ringing in the ears of Rama. He took up his bow and from the string poured forth a stream of deadly arrows, fearful enough to scorch the world. Ravana had taken another chariot and he was as glorious as the sun in his chariot yoked with the seven horses and steered by Aruna. Ravana's arrows were equally deadly and each was like the Vajra of Indra. Rama's arrows tipped with gold were flowing in a continuous stream and the fight was a glorious sight to watch. The skies were filled with the celestials who had assembled to see the fight for which they had been waiting ever since Narayana had promised them deliverance. They exclaimed : "This is an unequal fight. Ravana is riding in a chariot while Rama is standing on the ground. Rama should have a chariot too."

Indra agreed and summoned Matali, his charioteer. He asked him to take his chariot to the earth and ask Rama to ascend it. All on a sudden the divine chariot was found on the field of battle. It was a chariot wrought with gold. Several bells tinkled at the edge of the roof. Gems of translucent lustre glistered on the pillars of the chariot. There was a profusion of chamaras and the famed green horses were yoked to it : horses which were decorated with garlands of gold.

Matali approached Rama and said : "Rama, Indra, the lord of the heavens, has sent this chariot to be of use to you. It will help you win the war. This bow which is divine and this armour have also been sent to you along with these arrows which are like the rays of the sun. Indra has sent you his Shakti. Valiant one, I will steer the horses as you wish and help you to conquer this Ravana even as Indra did the asuras."

Rama looked at the chariot and then at Lakshmana. They both smiled knowingly. They had seen this chariot years back when they were paying a visit to Sharabhanga. And again, Agastya had told them that Indra would send his chariot to Rama when the need arose. Both the brothers remembered this and to them it was a good omen since the gods were favouring them in their struggle with Ravana.

Rama, who made the entire world glow with his radiance, went towards the chariot and, after making a *Pradakshina* to it, he ascended it with great humility.

Both the chariots stood facing each other and the sight thrilled those who were looking on. The fight was to begin.

Ravana took up the Gaandharvastra and despatched it and Rama took the same astra to counteract its effects. Devastra was used against Devastra. Ravana felt angry and he sent the astra Rakshasa. The arrows, as soon as they left the bow, became poisonous serpents and hissed at Rama. Their faces were like flames and they were spitting poison. They were like Vasuki and their hoods were gleaming and all the quarters were filled with myriads of snakes. Rama leaped with excitement and with a faint smile on his lips, he invoked Garuda and sent the astra towards the Rakshasa astra. The gold-tipped arrows from Rama's bow became each a Garuda and they sought out the serpents and destroyed them. Ravana now shot several sharp arrows at Rama and with some he hurt Matali. The banner of Indra's chariot was felled with a single arrow of Ravana's and he aimed some more of them at the horses. The celestials were unhappy at the turn of events and they could not but admire the valour of Ravana. Rama was also hurt because of some of the arrows of Ravana and this caused consternation and sorrow in the minds of Vibhishana and the others. The heavenly rishis were also unhappy. The sea became turbulent and the waves which rose up from the sea were so high that they seemed to be trying to reach the skies. The sun lost his glow and he seemed oppressed by Dhumaketu. He looked fierce. The planet Mars tried to touch the star Vishakha which was presided over by Indra and Agni, which was the family star of the kings of the Ikshvaku race. Ravana looked like the mountain Mainaka as he stood in his golden chariot.

Rama was finding it difficult to meet the shower of Ravana's arrows with own. He was furious at his own frustration and with his brows knit in anger and his eyes red, he glared at Ravana as though he would burn him with his eyes. The world trembled at the sight of Rama in his anger. The mountains were shaking in fear and the lions and tigers in them were frightened too.

The birds and the beasts wandered around in fear. The sky was filled with evil omens and the sight of them and the frown on Rama's face made even Ravana pause for a while in uncertainty. The gods were watching the encounter with eager faces and the asuras blessed Ravana while the devas were accompanied by the divine rishis when they said "May you be victorious" to Rama.

Ravana, in the meantime, decided to put an end to the life of Rama. He took up a trident in his hand. It was as strong as Vajra. It was a great weapon, capable of killing any enemy of Ravana. It was fearful to took at, with sharp points, and smoke was emerging from it. It was like the personification of the god of fire. No one could go near it and even Yama could not withstand it. The world trembled at the sight of it. Ravana took it and held it firmly in his hand. He roared with excitement and the sound was echoed from everywhere. With the trident in his hand he spoke to Rama : "Rama, I am extremely angry with you. I am sending this trident at you and it will take your life. I will soon kill you and make you one with the rakshasas who have been killed in the battle. Stand firm and receive this Shoola which I am hurling at you."

While the words were flowing from his lips the trident left his hand and went fast towards Rama. Like lightning it streaked across the air and the noise was like thunder. Rama bent his bow and sent arrows to break the trident which was speeding towards him. At the end of the yuga when the great Pralaya occupies the world a great fire will be seen and a great deluge will occur too. Even so, Ravana's trident which was full of fire was met by a rain of arrows from the bow of Rama. The arrows were all burnt up by the trident. Rama saw his arrows turning to ashes and the sight incensed him. He took the Shakti which Indra had sent him with Matali and grasping it firmly in his right hand he hurled it in the air. The skies glowed with the brilliance of the Shakti. The trident and the Shakti met in mid-air. The trident was broken by the Shakti and it fell on the ground, its fire quenched. There was joy in the hearts of the Vanaras in the army.

Rama then aimed his arrows at the horses of Ravana's chariot and he hurt Ravana in the forehead with three arrows. His body was covered with blood and he stood undaunted looking like an Ashoka tree in full bloom. He was very much hurt by Rama's arrows and his anger mounted. Again there were arrows from both their bows aimed at each other and the fight went on.

After some time Rama spoke. He said : "You are a blot on the name of the noble House in which you are born. My wife, when she was alone in Janasthana, was stolen by you. Such a thief can never be classed under the list of heroes. You lured me away from the ashrama and in my absence you carried her away. How can you call yourself a hero? You are very brave in the presence of women who belong to other men and before them you exhibit all your bravery and heroism. You have no code of honour, no shame, and you do not know what decorum is. You are arrogant and you defy Fate and actually, you are courting death.

"You have achieved many great things in the days of yore. But now, you are steeped in sin since you have stooped to an ignoble act and you will reap the reward for it. Soon you will meet your henchman Khara. Now that you are facing me there is no escape for you. I will send you to the abode of Yama. After a long time I will be able to get my heart's desire. My anger will finally be appeased."

Rama continued to send arrows towards Ravana. His valour was undimmed by the length of time which had been spent on the fight. His eagerness, his enthusiasm, his quickness, were the same as they were when the fight began. All the astras were at his command. Ravana was beginning to find himself unnerved by the valour of Rama. He was not able to despatch his arrows as quickly as before. His bow also was not used as often as it ought to have been. His heart was not in the fight and so his weapons were proving futile against the onslaught of Rama. His charioteer saw the condition of his master and quietly he steered the chariot away from the presence of Rama.

When he recovered from his faint Ravana who was spurred by death looked at his charioteer and asked him why he had brought him away from the front. He said : "What have you done? You have caused me to be ridiculed by the world. They will consider that I am lacking in valour, in prowess, in courage. They will certainly censure me as a coward and I will be considered to be a weakling. I am proficient in Maya tactics and I am conversant with all the astras and all this will be forgotten because of this one foolish act of yours which has disgraced me. Why did you bring my chariot to this spot away from my enemy? All the name and fame which I had earned through the years have been lost in a single thoughtless moment. Mine was an enviable name and it has been sullied by this seeming fright on my part. Try and rectify the fault. Take me back to where I was before and let me not be challenged by my enemy."

The charioteer spoke calmly and though he was insulted by his master he did not think much of it and said : "I am not afraid, my lord, nor am I foolish as you seem to think. I have not tried to make you out to be a coward. I only tried to protect you and your good name. In my affection for you I did what you do not relish. I saw that you were very much fatigued and there was a lack of enthusiasm in your fighting. Our horses were also tired because of the excessive heat of the sun's rays. They could not run as fast as they should. And again, I was seeing evil omens all around me, and I did not want anything to happen to you. You know, my king, that it is the duty of a charioteer to guard his master even as it is that of the master to guard his charioteer. The place and the situation should be noticed by him all the time and he should pay attention to everything : whether it is good or not as far as his master is concerned. He should pay proper attention to signs of fatigue in his master and act as the occasion demands. I acted only in accordance to the rules which guide such as me. You must command me and I will obey."

Ravana was mollified by the words of his charioteer and he spoke softly to him and said : "I am pleased with you and your affection for me. I am flattered by your concern for me and your loyalty. Take me to where Rama is and station the chariot in front of him. This Ravana will never return from the battlefield without killing his enemy."

Ravana was so touched by the concern of his charioteer that he took off the bracelet he was wearing and gave it to him as a mark of his appreciation and affection.

The horses which had been rested were now led towards where Ravana wanted to be taken and soon the two combatants were facing each other once again.

Agastya was one of those who was watching the fight from the heavens. He had seen Ravana who was fatigued and he saw the chariot being manoeuvred away from Rama. Agastya now approached Rama and said : "Child, Rama, I suggest that you recite the great mantra by name *Adityahridaya* which will grant you victory over your enemy. It is in praise of your original ancestor, the sun. The recital of the mantra will assure man of victory over all enemies. It is a mantra which is very jealously guarded. It is ancient, pure and the harbinger of victory. It is the holiest of holy mantras. It destroys all sins and no man who recites it will have any worries. It drives away sorrow and it lengthens the span of life. It is in praise of Surya, the god with a thousand rays, who is worshipped by the devas and the asuras alike, who is the source of all light and the lord of the world. Worship him, my child, and you will destroy your enemy."

He taught Rama the great mantra and added : "A man, when he is in trouble, when he is in danger, when he is alone in a forest or when he is oppressed with many worries, should recite this mantra and his troubles will vanish. Concentrate on the form of the sun and worship him. Repeat the mantra three times and you will certainly defeat Ravana. Rama, you are a great hero and there is no one like you in the three worlds. I wish you well." With these words Agastya went away from there.

Rama touched water three times, and purifying himself, he took up his bow and, looking at the sun, he repeated the mantra by name *Adityahridaya*. A sense of peace enveloped him and a strange exhilaration too. He knew that he was certain to kill Ravana and his hands were eager to shoot the arrows at Ravana. He went near to where Ravana was and Ravana had already advanced towards him. Surya was surrounded by the heavenly host and he was extremely pleased with Rama and he blessed Rama so that he could succeed and he spoke the words : "Make haste!"

39. THE KILLING OF RAVANA

Ravana's charioteer whipped the horses and the chariot was rushing towards the spot indicated by Ravana. Rama saw the chariot. He saw the black horses and the glow of the chariot which was like the sun in its radiance. The weapons placed in it could be seen from a distance and the noise of the wheels was sonorous and it was like the rumbling of distant clouds. Rama spoke to Matali: "Matali, look at the chariot of Ravana. Evidently he does not know even the rudiments of the language spoken by the omens : his proceeding in the *Apradakshina* direction which is perhaps dictated by his innermost desire to be killed by me! Go carefully towards him and I will destroy him. Do not tire yourself. Do not be upset by any reverses and steer the chariot with care and concentration with the reins held firmly in your capable hand. You are the charioteer of Indra himself and I do not have to tell you anything about how to steer the chariot. In my enthusiasm about the immediate fight between Ravana and me I am trying to remind you of these things, not telling you anything which you do not know already."

Matali was pleased with he courtesy, the innate chivalry and nobility of Rama. The chariot moved in the right direction, moving towards the right which is Pradaskshina, and soon the vehicle of Ravana was covered with the dust raised by the chariot of Indra. Ravana began his assault with his arrows and the great hero, Rama, took up the bow sent by Indra and the arrows which were like the rays of the sun. A great duel was fought between Rama and Ravana who were like two huge lions attacking each other. As before, the heavens were filled with all the devas, danavas, gandharvas, kinnaras and the maharshis who had been waiting for this encounter since so many years. Evil omens were seen. These spelt misfortune to Ravana and good to Rama. Ravana's chariot was bathed in blood. The breeze was blowing in the wrong direction and eagles were flying in a group and they were wheeling round his chariot. Ravana's men were distressed by these omens. Rama saw, at the same time, the signs which predicted victory for him and he was greatly pleased.

The great encounter began. The army stood still and watched the heroes fighting. The weapons they held in their hands were just there and no one thought of using them. The army was like a painted army on a cloth. Each of the two fighters, Rama and Ravana, had made up his mind that this would be the final victory and they fought intently.

Ravana aimed at the banner of the divine chariot and the arrows proved futile. They could not touch the banner.

Rama bent his bow and he felled the banner of Ravana's chariot. Ravana tried again and again and failed every time to hurt Rama's horses. He sent weapon after weapon at Rama. It was frustrating for him to see that his aim was not reaching the objects. The horses were unhurt. Rama, on the other hand, was smiling slightly and he shot arrows which were, however, cut off in their course in the sky by Ravana. Neither of them seemed to be gaining the upper hand. The fight was, however, fascinating for those who were watching.

Both Rama and Ravana were masters in the art of archery and the movements of their chariots, the deftness with which they bent their bows and shot the arrows were pleasing to the eyes of the lookers on, who stood still with wonder. Ravana's arrows were aimed at Matali. They did not harm him but Rama was incensed. He tried to punish Ravana. During their fight the earth trembled. The sun shone but dimly and the air was not blowing at all. All nature seemed to stand still. The heavenly host seemed to be getting disheartened at the prolonging of the fight. The rishis began to chant verses wishing for peace on earth and the general good of mankind. They said : "May the cows and brahmins be without fear. May the world be without danger. May Rama defeat Ravana in the battle." They stood watching the fight with great concern.

The gandharvas and the apsaras stood spellbound while they watched with astonishment the strange fight between a man and a rakshasa. They saw that the sight was thrilling and they said : "The sky can be compared only to the sky and the sea to the sea. The fight between Rama and Ravana can be compared only to the fight between Rama and Ravana."

Rama now took up a sharp arrow and with great force he pulled the string of his bow and sent the arrow towards Ravana. The three worlds saw the beautiful head of Ravana being severed from his neck by it.

Even as he was watching there arose on the neck of the rakshasa, another head and this head too was cut off by Rama only to be replaced by another, and so it went on! There seemed to be no end to it and the death of Ravana seemed to be an impossible task.

Rama was beginning to feel worried and he thought: "These arrows of mine have never been known to prove false so far. I killed Maricha. Khara was killed and so were Dushana and Trishiras. The entire army of Khara was destroyed by me and my arrows. In the Kraunchavana Viradha was killed when we were entering the Dandaka and later, when we were at the other fringe of it, Kabandha was killed. All of them have been unable to withstand the power of my arrows and yet their power has failed in this vital fight. How is it they are not hurting Ravana?"

His face was quite unruffled though he was worried and the arrows continued to issue from his bow in an unending flow. Ravana would not be hurt. He was undaunted and he was fighting just as well as Rama. They fought all through the night too and there was no sign of fatigue on the face of either of them.

While they were thus engaged, Matali, the divine charioteer spoke to Rama and said : "My lord, I am surprised at your behaving as though you are an ordinary human being. You are fighting with him and it seems to me you are letting him off lightly. He has lived long enough. I know that the moment has come and that his death is near. Despatch the Brahmastra and kill Ravana."

Rama suddenly remembered everything. He remembered too the gift of Agastya. The astra was created by Brahma for the sake of Indra. As its wings it had Vayu. Its tip was Agni. Its body was the sky and it had the Meru for its weight. It was a glowing astra and extremely powerful. Its radiance was that of the sun and it was deadly like fire. In noise it was like the Vajra and as powerful, like a hissing serpent in viciousness.

Rama took it in his powerful hands. The noble and valiant Rama took the Brahmastra, invoked it in the manner which had been prescribed in the sacred texts and placed it on the bowstring. When he did it, the earth trembled with fear and all the animals and birds made frightened noises. With a frown of anger sitting on his brow Rama pulled the string to his ear and released the great Brahmastra. It travelled straight and it entered the magnificent wide chest of Ravana. Blood spurted from his chest and the arrow, drinking the life and blood of Ravana, entered the earth. Like a servant who returns to his master after he has completed the task assigned to him, the astra, drenched with the blood of Ravana, came back to the quiver of Rama and remained there.

Ravana's life was fast ebbing away from his body and his beautiful bow slipped from his dying hands. The powerful king Ravana who had ruled the entire world with the might of his arms, who had been blessed by boons from Brahma, who had pleased Lord Mahadeva by his chanting of the Sama, who had no equal in valour and in might, who had terrified the world and had earned the name Ravana, now lay dead on the field of battle even as Vritra when killed by Indra. Ravana, the son of Vishravas, the grandson of Pulastya, the great-grandson of Brahma was dead and Rama had killed him. He was a great hero and because of his love for Sita he was now lying dead and the entire field glowed with the radiance which was Ravana. He was like the sun which had fallen to the ground at the end of the yuga and he was glorious even in death.

40. WHEN RAVANA DIED

The rakshasa army fled in terror when they saw their king fall. With tears falling from their eyes they rushed to the city and they were pursued by the jubilant cries of the Vanaras who saw the conquest of their lord Rama. The heavens made music and bugles and trumpets were heard from the skies. The wind was laden with sweet perfume and flowers from the heavens were showered on the chariot of Rama.

"Well done! Well done!" were the cries of those who had been watching from the skies. The gods were rid of their sorrow and the quarters were shining clear and bright. The sky was a brilliant blue and the earth was green and sweet with happiness. The sun shone with his old splendour.

Sugriva, Vibhishana and Lakshmana followed by the others went to Rama and stood there before him with joy writ on their faces. Words would not come to their lips. Their eyes were wet with tears of joy and Rama, who had kept his oath that he would kill Ravana, now stood proud and happy surrounded by his men and all his friends and he was like Indra surrounded by the devas.

Vibhishana was suddenly overcome with sorrow. He saw his brother whom he had once worshipped as a father and his sorrow was great. Rama comforted him with the words : "Ravana was valiant. He did not die an ordinary death. He fought with great enthusiasm and without any fear. He wanted to be victorious and, like a kshatriya, he died on the battlefield fighting. Such a hero should not be mourned. Ravana was the source of fear to Indra and all the gods in the heavens and when he is dead it is not meet that you should weep for him. Never has a fight been undecided. Either the one or the other has to be vanquished. This is the path pursued by the heroes of old and this is the right way of living as well as dying for kshatriyas. A hero who dies in battle should not be mourned. Consider all that I have said and shed this sorrow. Think of the next course which has to be adopted and make up your mind to be without sadness."

Vibhishana said : "This my brother could not be defeated by anyone. Indra with his entire host could not face him in battle. Such a hero has been shattered by you like a wave of the sea is broken up into fragments by the relentless shore. He has given away gems in innumerable number as gifts and he has tasted of all the many joys of the earth to the full. His servants have been devoted to him. Riches have been showered on his dependants. His enemies have been, so far, punished by him without fail. He has worshipped fire and he has performed many penances. He was well-versed in the Vedas. He has never once swerved from the proper observance of any rites, religious or otherwise. He was valiant. With your guidance I will do what you ask me to do after his death. I will perform the funeral rites, as per your wish."

Rama, the noble, the valiant, spoke thus : "Vibhishana, all enmity ends with death. Our duties end when death ends the life of the enemy. This Ravana is as much my kinsman as yours. Perform the funeral rites for him."

News had spread like wild fire and the city of Lanka was a city of woe. Myriads of women from the antahpura of the great Ravana rushed to the field and they fell on the ground covered by arrows and with blood. They were calling out to him piteously. These women, whom even the sun had not seen, were now on the battlefield and they sought their lord. They came to near where he was lying and there rose up from their throats a great lament. He was like a fallen giant tree and they clung to him like creepers which had been uprooted along with the tree. One fell on his chest and another at his feet. One clung to his shoulders and another fainted even before she reached his side. One of them took his head and placed it on her lap and spoke endearingly to him. They wailed in despair and it was piteous to watch them. They said : "This our lord had driven Indra away in battle. Yama could not face him. Kubera lost his wealth and his vimana to our king and the many gandharvas and rishis were helpless in the presence of our king. He was a source of danger to every one of them and such a hero is lying on the ground dead. Our lord had been granted immunity from death at the hands of the celestials and he was killed by a man. A mere man who was treated by our lord with supreme contempt has now proved to be the better fighter of the two. He has killed our lord. If only he had listened to the words of his mentors he would not have been lying dead like this.

"Sita has been the death of the entire rakshasa clan and he was warned about it : but he would not listen. If she had been returned to Rama all this could have been averted and we would all have been happy. This tragedy need never have happened to him. Fate has decided that events should take place thus and only thus. Fate has ordained that Ravana, the greatest, the mightiest and the most valiant monarch should come to grief because of a man and an army of monkeys which aided him."

41. THE LAMENT OF MANDODARI

Mandodari, the queen of Ravana, the mother of Indrajit, came to the battlefield. She stood for a moment looking at the dear face to her lord and dropped by his side. Her sorrow was burning her and she spoke in a pained voice. She said : "How could this have happened, my lord? No one has even dared to stand in front of you when you are angry. Indra trembled when he heard your name mentioned and all of them including the rishis in the heavens were in awe of you. And I am told that Rama, a mere man, has been able to kill you! How could it have happened? Your eyes should be spitting fire and your lips should be throbbing with fury and your fingers should, even now, be reaching for an arrow from your quiver to kill your opponent. Instead, you are lying still and anger has no place on your face. This silence does not befit you, my lord! I am not able to believe this.

"It is not possible for a man to kill my lord. This Rama is not a man. He is someone divine. The fact, that, single-handed, he destroyed Khara, Dushana and Trishiras with that immense army of fourteen thousand, should have made us realise that he is not an ordinary human being. We should have taken the warning. When Hanuman entered the city which is inaccessible even to the god of wind, we should have been sensible enough to take the warning. When I heard that a bridge had been built across the sea by the monkeys at the command of Rama, I knew that he was no ordinary human being. Perhaps it is Lord Mahadeva who created Maya in the shape of Sita and Himself has assumed the guise of a man called Rama for this sole purpose of killing you! Destroying you!

" I know who Rama is. He is the Lord of lords, Narayana. The greatest of yogis, the Paramatman, the Ancient, the one Truth which has no beginning and no end nor any middle. He is the Eternal. He is the greatest of the great, He is beyond the darkness called Avidya, ignorance. He is the Creator of the Universe. With the Conch and the Chakra and the Gada in his hands this great Lord has the mole on His chest Srivatsa by name. He is ever accompanied by Sree, Lakshmi. He is eternal and He is never a victim of changes. He is the Lord of all the three worlds. He is Lord Narayana Himself and I have no doubt about it. For the purpose of doing good to the world of men and devas he has assumed the guise of man and these Vanaras are all gods who have come down to the earth in the shape of Vanaras.

"My lord, Narayana has killed you and not a man. Once upon a time, my lord, you performed tapas with all your senses under perfect control and now, strangely enough, it was these very senses which have proved to be your undoing. Because your wealth, kingdom and all your subjects had to be destroyed, you desired Sita. She is a great *Pativrata* who is like Arundhati. She should have been honoured by you and, instead, she has been insulted by you. You should have honoured her and, instead, you asked her for her love. It is because of her tears of grief that you have been killed. A *Pativrata's* tears should not be allowed to fall on the ground. There is nothing but truth in the saying that a sinner will certainly reap the reward for his sinful actions. At the proper time Fate will make certain that it happens. We were so many of us in your antahpura and yet, your mind was set on making Sita respond to your wishes. In birth I am as high-born as Sita. In beauty she is in no way superior to me. And yet, because of the blindness of lust, you could not look into the future. Death comes in some form or other and for you, death came in the shape of Sita. You brought death with your own blessed hands when you brought Sita to Lanka. Sita will now be reunited with Rama and will live happily from today. Unfortunate woman that I am, Fate has plunged me into a sea of misery. My lord, my dear beloved, how can I live without you? Your handsome face has lost all its glory. Your eyes which were like the sun and moon are closed now and I cannot see the look of love which you ever had for me. Where has it gone, my lord? Your beautiful smile? Your face is now covered with the dust from the field and your eyes are closed. I cannot bear this.

"I was a very proud woman. I was certain that nothing would harm my lord. My father is the king of the danavas. My husband is the great Ravana and my son is Indrajit, the hero who had humbled Indra, the lord of the heavens. I was so secure in the thought of all three of you and how could I anticipate this calamity which robbed me of my son and lord? Your magnificent chest and your entire body is covered with arrows fully. I am not able to embrace you even. Is it true or is it a dreadful nightmare which will vanish when one wakes up from sleep? Oh! No! It is true enough. Yama was always afraid of you. How could he have had the courage to approach you and trap you in his noose? My death was heralded when my child Indrajit was killed and I stayed alive for the sake of you and now that you have gone, what is left for me? Evidently you did not love me enough or else how could you have had the heart to leave me and go away? I have offended you perhaps, and to punish me you have abandoned me. This is the curse of the many good women who have lost their husbands because of you. In olden days you killed so many good men and their wives shed tears of blood. They say that the tears shed by a Pativrata will avenge the death of her husband. When I think back on it, this act of yours, stealing Sita, was unbecoming to you. You lured Rama away and then stole Sita. It was unnatural that you should have done that. You have never done such a thing before. This cowardly act is unworthy of your bravery and it is really not at all in keeping with your courage.

"You were not defeated in the war by Rama. It was your own sinfulness which killed you. How can you lie like this on the field while all the enemies and the devas too are looking on in triumph? You have fallen in love with the earth and you relish her embrace and not mine any more."

Mandodari fainted and lay by the side of Ravana. The other women revived her and comforted her. Rama said : "Vibhishana, make these women go back to their antahpura and proceed about the funeral rites for your brother." With great difficulty the women were coaxed to leave the dead form of Ravana and amidst great wailings Mandodari and the others left the field of battle and they had to realise that they would never look on his face again and their hearts were broken. They had no more tears to shed and their voices were hoarse with pain and so they went back to the antahpura of Ravana.

42. THE FUNERAL RITES

Vibhishana now said : "Ravana was an Adharmi, a killer, a liar, a lustful person who cast his eyes on the wives of other men. I have no respect for him and I do not feel like doing Tarpana for him, or offering Anjali for him. An elder brother should command respect and worship from his brother. But Ravana was my enemy and I do not consider him worthy of respect and honour. People in the days to come will censure me as heartless. But, when they come to know of the evil which my brother practised, they will think well of me."

Rama said : "You helped me to win this war and I wish to impress upon you that it is your duty which I am asking you to execute. Thinking on the past does not help. This king was, no doubt, an Adharmi and yet, he was valiant and a great fighter. He made the world cry with fear and earned the name Ravana. He has been powerful and we have heard often that the devas and all the celestials were not able to defeat him in war. Remember, Vibhishana, hatred lasts only as long as life lasts. Our purpose has been fulfilled and it is so with me and it should be so with you. Perform the funeral rites for your brother. You know the rules of Dharma, and you must realise that you are the person who should help him reach the world of the Manes, the Pitris."

Vibhishana hurried to obey Rama's commands and soon his men were busy preparing the funeral pyre. The final rites for the rakshasa monarch Ravana were being executed properly. Vibhishana placed his brother's body on the pyre and touched the earthly remains of the great hero with fire which had been kindled according to the rules of the sacred texts. He paid homage to the departed soul with sesamum and water and the rites were ended.

Vibhishana bathed in cold water and with wet clothes he mixed sesamum seeds, and green blades of grass with water and offered the Anjali for the departed soul. He prostrated facing the south and he then comforted the women who were still there again and again and finally coaxed them to go back to the antahpura.

After sending them away Vibhishana came and stood before Rama with his palms folded. All the heroes were with Rama : Hanuman, Lakshmana, Sugriva, Angada and others. The sky which had been filled with the celestials was slowly emptying itself. They were talking about the valour of Rama, the killing of Ravana, the prowess of the Vanaras, the sagacity of the Vanara king Sugriva, the devotion of Hanuman and Lakshmana, and their great and individual heroism.

Rama prostrated before the chariot of Indra and after worshipping it duly, he bade affectionate farewell to Matali and sent him back to the heavens. Rama's joy knew no bounds and he embraced Sugriva. He then went to the midst of his army and spoke to Lakshmana. He said : "Child, this Vibhishana is devoted to me. He has proved it to us in a thousand ways. He has aided us and his help has been invaluable and it has been responsible for our victory. Take him to the city and crown him as the emperor. This will give me great joy." Lakshmana was very happy to do what he had been asked to do. He took up a vessel made of gold and he asked the brave Vanaras to fill it up with the waters from the sea. Water was soon brought. Lakshmana took Vibhishana into the city, placed him on the throne and drenched him with the waters and he gave him his coronation bath. The holy mantras were recited and Vibhishana was crowned king in the midst of the rakshasas. His four comrades who had left Lanka along with him on that memorable day when, he, Vibhishana, abandoned his everything and surrendered to Rama, were exceedingly happy to see their master crowned king. They had been faithful servants of his.

After the coronation Vibhishana hurried to the presence of Rama. The citizens honoured him with flowers, and fried rice. Vibhishana reached the presence of Rama who was seated surrounded by his friends. Vibhishana offered auspicious gifts to Rama and to please him Rama accepted the offerings.

43. RAMA SENDS HANUMAN TO SITA

Rama turned to Hanuman and said : "Honour Vibhishana who is now lord of Lanka. Take his permission and enter the city. Go to the Ashokavana where Sita has been kept captive and tell her that I am well : that Sugriva and Lakshmana are with me and that they are well. Tell Sita that Ravana has been killed by me. Give her this message and come back to me with her words."

Hanuman did as he was told. He entered the Ashokavana. She was seated under the tree as she was the first time he saw her. She was surrounded by the rakshasis and there was nothing but sorrow and despair writ on her face. Forlorn as the star Rohini which had been parted from the moon, Sita was a picture of woe.

Hanuman went to her and stood by her side with his palms folded. For a moment she did not respond to his arrival. She then recognised him and, with a ray of joy illumining her face, she welcomed him. Hanuman spoke softly and gently and gave her the news about the happenings on the field of battle. He said: "Devi, Rama is well with Lakshmana, with Sugriva, Vibhishana and his army. He has destroyed the enemies and he has achieved the purpose of his coming to Lanka. He has been aided by his army and by Vibhishana in this and Ravana has been killed by your lord. Rama asked me to carry these glad tidings to you and he has sent this message to you: 'Sita, I am speaking what will be pleasing to you. I share my joy with you. Fortunately for me you are alive and rejoice with me over the death of our enemy and my victory. Sita you can now shed your grief and peace will be yours. Ravana is dead and Lanka has been captured. I was bent on but one thought: Your rescue and I spent sleepless nights thinking of you. I built a bridge across the sea with this end in view and now your dark days are over. Vibhishana has been made king of Lanka. It is now the house of your brother where you are living and so you can be without pain! Soon he will come to you and bring you to me."

Sita was full of joy so much so she could not speak. Hanuman said: "Why? What is bothering you, Devi? Why have you become silent?" Sita said: "It is joy, Hanuman, joy at the thought of the success of my lord which has made me tongue-tied. I do not know how to reward you who has brought this good news to me. Nothing is good enough for you."

Hanuman stood still as was his custom with his palms folded and said: "Your noble words befit you and they are full of affection. The mastery of the three worlds or heaps and heaps of gold and gems will not be equal to the affectionate feelings you have for me. I have seen you happy and I have seen Rama victorious and there is nothing I desire more than these. I feel that I have conquered the three worlds." Sita said: "Hanuman, there is no one who can speak as beautifully as you do. Your words are well-chosen and they are sweet and they are full of wisdom. Your devotion to Dharma is praiseworthy. Strength, prowess, valour, innate goodness, bravery, divine strength of mind and body perseverance, firmness under all circumstances, control of the senses and many other great qualities have found a home in you." Hanuman was humility personified and he was embarrassed by the words of Sita. He now said: "Devi, I seek your permission to do something. These rakshasis have been harassing you for the last so many months. I have seen how much you were oppressed by them. Let me have the pleasure of killing every one of them. I want to vent my spleen on them. My hands are itching to punish them."

Sita smiled softly and said : "They were servants, Hanuman. They have to obey their master and they have no right to have feelings of their own. It is not fair to judge them. I have been doomed to spend a few months of my lifetime in captivity and that was because of some sin committed by me in some previous birth and because of my misfortune. After all, one must reap the fruits of one's actions. I have always believed in Fate. What has to be borne is at the behest of Fate and none can escape the sway of Fate. I have no anger against these unfortunate servants of Ravana. Now that he is dead they will not ill-treat me. There is an ancient tale and the moral of the story, if I remember right, is : 'A good man will not harm even the person who has tried to harm him.' The only path to be followed is the path of the good, and good conduct is the only ornament worth wearing. Hanuman, compassion and mercy should be shown to everyone, whether they are sinners, good people or those who deserve to be killed. No one is infallible and erring is human. To my mind, even the rakshasas who enjoy killing, who do nothing but evil, should be allowed to live."

Hanuman stood humbly before her and said : "Devi, I stand corrected. You are a worthy spouse of the greatest of men. Please let me go to him and convey to him the glad tidings that you are happy."

Sita's voice was full of eagerness as she said : "Tell Rama, I am eager to see him." Hanuman replied : "Devi, Rama will soon be seen with you and you will both seem like Indra and Shachi devi."

Hanuman left the queen of Rama and hurried to his presence.

44. RAMA AND SITA

Hanuman came to the presence of Rama and he told him about his seeing Sita and he conveyed to Rama her desire to see Rama. Rama's eyes were filling with tears when he heard the narration of Hanuman.

After that he was sunk in thought for a long time. He sighed and his eyes were trained on the ground. He then turned to Vibhishana and said : "Go to Sita. Ask her to dress herself in good clothes. Let her have a holy bath and let her wear her jewels and then come to me."

Vibhishana went to Sita accompanied by his women and told her that the palanquin was ready to take her and he conveyed Rama's instructions to her. Sita said : "I want to see Rama as I am now. I want to be taken there in this state."

Vibhishana said : "My lord Rama has commanded me to bring you to him dressed in silks and gold. I have always obeyed him and if I act contrary to his wishes he will not be pleased with me."

To Sita, Rama was the god she worshipped and she said : "As he pleases." Vibhishana's women washed her hair and combed out her tangled locks. They made her wear silken garments and now ornaments adorned her. Conducted by the rakshasa women and by Vibhishana, Sita entered the palanquin which was meant for her.

Vibhishana came to Rama and he was sunk in thought. Vibhishana prostrated before Rama and with a glad note he told Rama that Sita had been brought. Rama's eyes were downcast.

Rama's mind was filled with mixed feelings. There was gladness, compassion, and, at the same time, anger. A frown sat on his noble brow and he said : "Vibhishana, my dear friend and well-wisher, bring Sita to me."

There was great excitement in the Vanara army and that of the rakshasas also. Vibhishana asked them all to make way and royal attendants with sticks in their hands were trying to keep back the crowd which was eager to see Sita for whose sake the war had been fought. The crowd was pushed back and the noise made by them was like the roar of the sea. Rama looked up from his reverie and saw what was happening. He spoke to Vibhishana in a voice which had affection as well as anger. He said : "Why are they being treated so harshly by you? These are my people and they should be treated well. Stop this check imposed on them at once. These are all my people, my kinsmen, almost.

"A woman has, as her protection, her chastity and not houses and curtains nor high walls. She does not need this royal treatment. It is no sin if they look at her. Under certain circumstances, a woman of the royal household can be seen by ordinary citizens. That it when there is danger, when she is in trouble, when there is a war, when it is a Swayamvara, during the performance of a yagna or during her wedding. Sita has arrived on the battlefield and she is in trouble. And again, she will be by my side and it is not wrong if she is seen by anyone. Vibhishana, let the people stay where they wish and you must bring Sita to me. Let her see me surrounded by those who helped me win this war."

Vibhishana went to the palanquin and made Sita descend from it. He led her with great deference to Rama. Lakshmana was looking on with puzzlement at Rama. He knew that Rama was not his usual self and his preoccupation was noticed by Sugriva and Hanuman. They were unhappy since they could guess that there was some displeasure in the mind of Rama. This was evident from his tone to Vibhishana. They guessed that he was displeased with Sita. His comments on the appearance of Sita in public led them to this conclusion.

Sita, her limbs shrinking into herself with shyness, walked hesitantly with Vibhishana and came near Rama. She covered her face with her upper cloth and in a faint voice called out : "My lord!" Tears choked her voice and she could speak no more. Sita whose very life was Rama stood by and she looked at the dear face of her lord. There was immense affection in her eyes and there was happiness and a feeling of amazement that this happiness had finally come her way. Her sorrow was at an end and her eyes were drinking in the beauty of Rama with thirsty eyes which had long been aching for a sight of him.

Rama spoke. His voice was harsh and his words were cruel. He sounded angry and he looked at the gentle wife, his loving Sita who stood before him and said : "Devi, you have been rescued from the enemy. I killed him and rescued you. This was done to vindicate my honour and my reputation. It was my duty to fight the enemy and kill him and I did so. I have reached the utmost limit of fury and his offence against me has been punished in a proper manner. My insult and my enemy have both been wiped out together. My valour has been displayed to the world and my efforts have been rewarded. When there is danger to his reputation a man of honour should make every effort to wipe it out. Hanuman's achievement in leaping across the sea and his burning the city of Lanka were great tasks well executed. Vibhishana left his brother and came to me with a heart full of love and his attempts have not been in vain."

Sita was listening to this long recital and she wondered why Rama's voice was lacking in warmth. She was looking like a frightened deer and her eyes were filled with tears.

Rama looked at her and his anger grew, like fire which is fed on ghee poured into it as an oblation. His frown was dreadful and his eyes were strangely devoid of the affection meant for her, and only her.

He said : "Sita, as I said before, unable to bear the insult offered by the enemy Ravana, I took up the task of killing him and I have done so. You have been rescued from him. Sita I wish to impress on you one truth : this war, this killing of Ravana was undertaken by me because I am an upholder of Dharma and because I could not brook the insult to me and to the ancient House of the Ikshvakus. I did not do all this for your sake. Your name has now a stain on it and it hurts me to look at you even as a bright light hurts the eyes of man with a pain in his eyes.

"You are at liberty to take leave of me and go where you will. There is nothing I owe you now that my task has been completed. Which honourable man will, with love, take home with him his wife who has been living in the house of his enemy for several months? I belong to a noble house, a very noble House, and it does not befit me to take you with me. You have been sought after by the sinful Ravana and his lecherous eyes. I have won fame by my actions and by my rescue of you. I am indifferent towards you. You can go away from here wherever you wish. I have explained to you my thoughts and my decision. If you so desire, you can go with Lakshmana or Bharata. You can choose the company of Sugriva, the king of the Vanaras or Vibhishana, the rakshasa king."

Rama turned his angry eyes on her once and turned away. He spoke nothing after that.

Sita had never before heard such words from Rama and, trembling like a creeper caught in the wind, she stood silent with tears streaming from her eyes. In the midst of that large crowd of Vanaras, bears and rakshasas, Sita stood and her heart was breaking with the words of Rama. Her head was bowed. She had shrunk into herself and, hurt by the sharp words of Rama, she bent her eyes on the ground.

45. THE RITUAL OF FIRE

After a while, with a faltering voice, Sita said: "My lord, ordinary men will talk thus to ordinary women. But you are no ordinary being and yet it has pleased you to use such harsh and unkind words to me. It is not befitting you. Why do you talk like this to me? Believe me when I say that I have been chaste and pure during my imprisonment in that garden. I swear in the name of my honour that it is so. Because of the behaviour of some low-minded women you have made up your mind to condemn entire womanhood. If I should be tested for my purity and if the test is successful you will then be able to forget this doubt about me which seems to have entered your mind. If I had been touched by that sinner once, that was when I was helpless. The sin is not mine but it should be ascribed to Fate. My thoughts and my love have ever been yours. When I was carried away my body was weak and could not fight his strength. Surely you do not ascribe that as a sin to me? Evidently all these years of living with me have not been able to make you understand me and I am ruined. When the powerful Hanuman came to Lanka and discovered me, it was you who had sent him. Why did you not abandon me even then? If you had sent word through him that you had no further use for me, I would have given up my life that very moment, even as Hanuman was looking. You need never have undertaken this stupendous task of fighting with Ravana. You risked your life and you took immense trouble to reach Lanka. All that was needless. You need not have done it and your friend also need not have exerted himself so much. It is all so futile.

"You are in no way different from an ordinary man who lets anger gain the upper hand in his mind. In your eyes my womanhood appears to be at fault. In your anger you seem to have forgotten that I come of a noble House too, that of Janaka. I was born of the earth and you, well-versed as you are in Dharma, do not seem to pay any heed to my ancestry though you seem to remember your own very well. You once took my hand in yours and made me your wife. You have forgotten that I have been a good wife to you and I have been devoted to you. You seem to have forgotten that also."

Sita looked at Lakshmana who was looking very sad and dejected and said: "Lakshmana, Saumitri, you have always done what I have asked you to do. There is but one cure for this sorrow of mine. Prepare a fire for me. I do not wish to live after this slur has been cast on my name. My husband has abandoned me in the midst of this large crowd and, displeased with me, he has asked me to go where I please. There is but one place for me and that is the heart of fire which you will kindle for me."

Lakshmana looked at Rama in anger and Rama spoke not a word. He seemed to approve of the suggestion of Sita.

Lakshmana prepared the fire and the entire army was watching. This was a Rama they had never known. Soon the fire was blazing. Sita went round Rama in a *Pradakshina* and he was standing with his face trained on the ground. She went near the fire and stood still for a moment. With folded palms Sita stood near the fire and said : "If it is true that my mind has ever been set on Rama, and never once swerved from thoughts of him, then let Agni, the witness to all the actions in this world, protect me. Rama considers that I am tainted. May Agni announce to the world the purity that is Sita. If it is true that I am conversant with all Dharmas and have been true to Rama in thought, in word and in deed, if the sun, the moon, the god of wind, the four quarters, the day and the night, and the earth, my mother, know the fact that I am sinless, then may Agni protect me."

Sita made a *Pradakshina* to the fire and flung herself into the heart of it. There was a moment of stunned silence when the crowd watched with sorrow the self-immolation of Sita. She was the colour of molten gold and she was wearing ornaments wrought in gold and the golden yellow flames were reaching the sky when she threw herself into it.

The women screamed in sheer compassion. The three worlds and the devas with the danavas and the gandharvas saw her and she looked like a goddess flung into hell because of a curse. There were cries of sadness, consternation and woe which filled the air.

Rama stood with the frown still on his face which was cast down. Rama had heard the exclamations of fear, horror, or consternation and compassion from those around him. His head was bent and his face was cast down. His eyes were full of tears and his mind was in a great turmoil.

46. THE GODS SPEAK

Kubera, Yama, Indra, Varuna, Lord Mahadeva and Brahma with all the celestials came down to the earth and they were riding in their chariots glowing golden. The rishis from the heavens stood with raised hands and said : "How can it be possible for you to watch Sita fall into the fire? You are the Creator of the Universe and the wisest of the wise and you have been famed as the best among men : and yet, you have allowed this. How is it you have not recognised yourself to be the leader of the devas? You are all that is good and gracious. You are the Lord who presides over the work of Creation. You are the Ancient, the Immutable. You are the Past, the Present, and the Future. And yet you behave like a common man and behave like this towards Sita."

Rama heard their words and spoke most humbly and said : "I am Rama, a human being, the son of Dasaratha. It is not possible for me to see anything else. If there is anything to be known as to who I am, to whom I am related, the purpose of my birth, all these are not known to me. If there is any special reason for my birth it is up to Lord Brahma to enlighten me."

Brahma said : "I will tell you the truth about yourself. You are Lord Narayana and your spouse is Lakshmi : Narayana with the conch and the discus as your weapons. You pervade everything. You are the one Truth who assumed the form of Varaha in the days of old. You are the Brahman which has neither a beginning nor an end. You hold the bow by name Sharanga in your hand and you are a master of the indriyas. You pervade the Universe and the Vedas call you the Purushottama. You cause the Universe, you sustain it and you destroy it during the Pralaya which is, again, caused by you. You are the refuge of all the celestials and you are the personification of the Vedas. The three worlds owe their existence to you. You are the Yagna and the Vashatkara is but yourself and the Omkara. No one has yet been able to know you fully. You are perceived everywhere. The animals, the brahmanas, the quarters, the sky, the mountains, and the forests are all pervaded by you. You sustain the entire Universe.

"During Pralaya you are seen as Narayana reclining on the immense snake Adishesha and the sea is all around you. Rama, I am your heart and Saraswati is your tongue. Once your eyelids are closed and opened, it means the passage of a single day and a single night. The Vedas are your breath.

In short, there is nothing which does not have you as its very soul. The worlds are your body and the earth is the patience that is you. Your anger is Agni and the moon, your kindliness.

"When Bali performed the yagna you were the one to beg the three paces of earth from him. Sita is Devi Lakshmi and you were born as a human being on this earth for the sole purpose of killing Ravana. You have accomplished what you were born for."

Rama listened to the words of Brahma and there seemed to be a look of wonderment in his face. At that very moment Agni rose out of the blazing fire and he carried Sita in his arms which were glowing. He walked out of the blaze and placed Sita by the side of Rama. He said : "Rama, your Sita has been given back to you. There is no taint on her name and her character is unsullied. Captured by the sinful Ravana she has been separated from you. She has been all the time thinking of you and pining for you : during all the months of her captivity the one thought that has kept her alive is the hope that she will see you some day. She was tempted in many ways by Ravana who was wily and an adept in the art of winning the hearts of women, but she paid no heed to his words. Please believe me and accept this jewel among women."

Rama stood silent and tears were flowing fast from his eyes which were full of sadness. Rama said : "My lord! Agni! This Sita is pure enough to purify the three worlds. She is as chaste as snow although she has been in the antahpura of Ravana for a long time. If she had not gone through this ordeal by fire which is supposed to purify her, people would have spoken ill of me. They would have said : 'Rama, the son of Dasaratha, was blinded with love, so much so, he was foolish to take back his wife who had lived in the home of another man.' If there is one thing I am afraid of, it is the censure of the world of men. I know full well that Sita is pure, blameless and that her heart is ever mine. Truth, my lord, has been my religion and I am keen on the three worlds knowing that Sita has been tested by fire and to have been found untouched by slander.

"Sita is capable of taking care of herself and Ravana could never have hurt her. It is as impossible as the sea overstepping the bounds set for it by nature. That sinner could not have touched her since she is as fearful as the blazing fire. Sita, to me, is what the splendour is to the sun. Even as a good man can never abandon his fame, even so, Sita cannot be abandoned by me. Sita should see the reason for my acting as I did."

Rama had taken the trouble to justify his action to the celestials who had assembled and he now stood with Sita by his side. Mahadeva said : "Rama, you are a great warrior and you are the best among warriors. This act of yours is indeed great. The darkness which had enveloped the entire world and the heavens too, because of the tyranny of Ravana has been lifted and it has been a great achievement of yours. The world is fortunate that it had you to save it from the constant dread of Ravana. You can go back to Ayodhya and comfort Bharata who is waiting for you. Your mothers will be waiting for your return eagerly. Take the reins of the kingdom in your hands and rule the kingdom wisely and well as your ancestors did. You will perform the yagna by name Ashvamedha and finally you will go back to where you came from. Rama, this vimana holds your beloved Dasaratha. He is now in the worlds of Indra. Come, salute him, both of you."

Rama prostrated before his father and so did Lakshmana. Dasaratha was glowing as though he had been made of light. Dasaratha looked at his son who was dearer to him than his very life. He took Rama on his lap as he was wont to do in the days of yore and embraced him. He then said : "Rama, I tell you truly, I am not happy in heaven separated as I am from you. I have not been able to forget the words spoken by Kaikeyi asking me to banish you. I have seen you with Lakshmana and Sita and I see you well. Now I am free of the sorrow like the sun emerging out of the mist shrouding it. Child, because of you I have earned a place in the heavens. I know now that all these happenings had been but engineered by the devas and the purpose behind it all was the killing of Ravana. Fortunate indeed will Kausalya be since she will see you enter Ayodhya and the palace.

"Fortunate will be the citizens of Ayodhya who will see your coronation and who will be ruled by you. My child, you have spent fourteen years now in the forest with Sita and with Lakshmana. Your exile has come to an end and you have kept your promise to me. The devas have been pleased with your valour. You have won a great name and my blessings will ever be with you. Live long and rule the kingdom with your brothers by your side."

Rama said : "Father, I have a favour to ask of you. You were angry with my mother Kaikeyi and my beloved brother Bharata, since she asked you to banish me. You must forget your anger which has been smouldering in your mind. By forgiving her, please attain peace of mind. You had said that you had abandoned them. Please recall those wrathful words and let not your anger touch Kaikeyi and Bharata."

"So be it," said Dasaratha. He took Lakshmana on his lap and said : "You have pleased me very much by your devotion to Rama and Sita. You have followed the path of Dharma. May your name be remembered as long as Rama's will, and you will attain the heavens."

He then told Sita : "Sita, please do not be angry with my son for the harsh words he spoke just now, and for his seeming indifference to you and your fate. It was to vindicate your name in the eyes of the world that he had to adopt this course. He has always loved you and cherished you. May you both be together as long as this world lasts."

Dasaratha returned to the heavens.

Indra came to Rama with a pleased look and said : "Rama, I remember your curiosity when I visited the ashrama of Sharabhanga. I knew how excited you were to see my chariot and later, me. It was not proper for me to see you then and that was the reason why I went away without seeing you. This is the time I have been waiting for. We are all very pleased with you, extremely pleased. Please ask any boon of me and I will be happy to grant it to you."

Rama was standing with folded palms and by his side were Sita and Lakshmana. He said : "Lord of lords, I am honoured by your presence and by your words of affection. If you will be gracious enough to grant me a boon, grant me this : because of me thousands of these valiant Vanaras have been killed in battle. They laid down their lives for me. Please grant them back their lost lives. They have been parted from their wives or mothers or children. They cared not for their lives but they fought valiantly for my sake. I want them all to be happy. Let them come back to life. They were devoted to me and they suffered with me and they died for me. Let them live. This is the only boon I ask of you. Let them all the their old selves without even a cicatrice of the wounds which they received in the war. Wherever they are, there should be plenty of water and fruits of all seasons."

Indra was happy to grant the boon to Rama. The monkeys rose up from the ground they were lying on and they were looking as though they had just woken up after a long sleep. They went to Rama and stood by his side with reverence.

The devas led by Indra said : "Narayana, go back to Ayodhya. Take leave of the Vanaras. With the saintly Sita and with the great and noble Lakshmana return to the city ruled by your father and comfort Bharata and Shatrughna who are waiting for you with impatience. You will be crowned as king and the people of Kosala will be happy under your rule."

The devas returned to their abodes and Rama stood with folded palms until their chariots were out of sight.

47. HOMEWARD-BOUND

The night passed and, early in the morning, Vibhishana went to the presence of Rama and said : "My lord, I have brought silks and sandal paste and perfumed water for your coronation bath. I beseech you to accept them and make Lanka and me happy." Rama smiled softly and said : "Honour Sugriva with all these auspicious articles. As for me, my thoughts are with my child Bharata. That valiant brother of mine has never once swerved from the path of Dharma and he is aching for my return to Ayodhya. Until I see him I have no thoughts of perfumed baths and silks and ornaments. I want to go back to Ayodhya as early as I can and yet, I know only too well how hard the path is that leads to the city of my father." Rama's face was downcast and Vibhishana said : "My lord, I will help you reach the city in a single day. Please honour me by accepting my offer. When my brother fought with his brother Kubera he took the Pushpaka vimana from Kubera and it was the most prized possession of Ravana. I have it in readiness for your use. Please enter it and you will be taken to Ayodhya very soon. Tarry here longer and make me happy. Please honour me by accepting my homage and then you can go."

Rama was really touched by the devotion of Vibhishana. He said: "You have aided me with your advice and your actions during the war which you helped me to win. I have been more than honoured. You have accepted me as yours long ago. Vibhishana, it is not as though I am unwilling to accept your hospitality. My mind is set on Bharata. When I was in Chitrakuta he came to me and on his bended knees he entreated me to accept the kingdom. I refused since it was not right. I think of Bharata as he was that day, his eyes streaming, with the tree-bark covering his handsomeness. My mothers were there and my Acharya too. The citizens of Ayodhya were all there. My heart is leaping towards Ayodhya and I am dying to see all of them. Vibhishana, please bring the Pushpaka to me. With my mind dwelling on my Bharata how can I spend my time here, happily? You have honoured me and bear with me if I seem too eager to go away from here. It is my love for Bharata which is making me hurry. I hope you will not be offended with me."

Vibhishana brought the vimana to where Rama was. He announced himself to Rama and told him that the Pushpaka was at his disposal. Vibhishana was feeling unhappy at the thought of the separation from Rama.

He said: "Rama, what shall I do now?", and his voice was faltering and faint. Rama thought for a while and said: "As I told you before, honour the army of Sugriva with gifts and chariots and other costly articles which will be liked by them. I owe them a deep debt of gratitude. You will get the name that you are a very generous and warm-hearted person." Vibhishana obeyed Rama.

Finally Rama sat in the vimana with Sita and Lakshmana. He had Sita on his lap and his brother by his side. He looked at Sugriva, Vibhishana and the others and said: "You have been my true friends and you have worked a miracle for me. Please grant me leave to go back to my city where they are waiting for me. You should all go back to where you came from. Sugriva, what shall I say to you? As a devotee, as a friend, as a mentor, you have done me a great service and I cannot forget it in a hurry. Go back to Kishkindha with your army. My blessings will always be with you. Angada, child, can I ever forget your prowess in the war? Can I forget your courage and bravery? Hanuman, you are part of me and words will not express what you mean to me. Vibhishana, this kingdom has been given to you by me who has won it in the war. No one can equal you in prowess, not even Indra. I am going back to my father's city. I ask you to let me go. I am bidding you all a farewell, a long farewell."

Rama's eyes were wet and they stood humbly before him and said : "Rama, we want to be with you in Ayodhya. Take us with you. We will move about very carefully in the streets of the city and in the forests. We promise you, we will not harm even a single tree. We wish to see your coronation and after witnessing it we will salute your mothers and go back to our homes."

Rama was overwhelmed with emotion when he saw their eagerness to go with him. He smiled at their promise to behave themselves and said: "I am delighted at the thought that I will enter the city of my ancestors accompanied by my friends and my well-wishers. Sugriva ascend the vimana with all the Vanaras and Vibhishana, ask your ministers to come with you and we will go together to Ayodhya."

The vimana was divine and it could hold all the Vanaras and yet fly in the air. When they were all seated Rama wished the vimana to rise into the sky and Rama looked around him. He turned to Sita and said : "Sita, look kindly on the city Lanka. It is situated on top of the Trikuta hill which resembles the Kailasa peak. It was built by Vishvakarma, the architect of the gods. Look down on the field of battle where the dead forms are still lying. My beloved, for your sake I killed Ravana who was the emperor of the rakshasas, who had been granted boons by Brahma Himself and who, nevertheless, was a sinner. Look, this is the spot where Kumbhakarna, the brother of Ravana, was killed by me. Look there! That was where Hanuman killed Dhumraksha. Just beside this spot is where Sushena killed Vidyunmali. Look carefully at that spot near a big tree! That was where Lakshmana killed Indrajit, the famous son of Ravana. This was where Ravana fell and where Mandodari wailed for her lord. Sita, we have reached the spot where the seashore is caressed by the waves of the sea. We crossed here and the night we spent there. You can see the bridge we named Nalasetu since Nala built it. He was the architect. Cast your eyes on the sea which is so fearful to see. This was the sea which Hanuman leaped across to find you out. In the midst of it can be seen the mountain Mainaka which has a crest of gold. Look at the place where Vibhishana first met me and told me that he was mine from that moment." The vimana was going fast and even as they were talking they saw below them the entrance to Kishkindha. Rama pointed out to her the spot where Vali was killed. And added : "There is the city Kishkindha where Sugriva rules." Sita saw it with wide open eyes and said : "Rama, I wish to take with us Tara and the other wives of Sugriva as also the wives of the other monkeys. They have devoted their everything to you." Rama stopped there and Sugriva was asked to bring the Vanara women. Very soon they had all assembled at the gateway of Kishkindha and they were seated in the vimana and it pursued the journey which had been interrupted.

Rama pointed out Rishyamooka hill to her and he was all the while telling her about his doings after she had been parted from him. He said : "Sita, this mountain glows like a precious gem since it is full of several minerals embedded in its rocks. This is where I first met Hanuman and later, on that peak I met Sugriva. There it is, the peak where we kindled a fire and made a pact that we would be friends for ever." They passed several picturesque spots and Rama showed her where Jatayu was killed by Ravana. He then waited a while and said : "Look! Look, Sita! Look at our ashrama in Panchavati and the area where Khara and the others were killed! The beautiful and cherished ashrama is there and it is now empty. I abandoned it as soon as I found you to have been lost to me. We went south, my Lakshmana and I, after that." Even remembered pain was too much to bear and Rama was silent for a long moment re-living the pain of those days.

They had almost come to the outskirts of Dandaka and Rama pointed out the ashrama of Agastya to her. Close by was that of Sutheekshna. At the entrance of Dandaka was where Viradha was killed and they saw it from above. Atri's ashrama was seen and from the vimana they saluted the great rishi and his noble spouse Anasuya. Rama's eyes were wet when he came further north. He pointed out Chitrakuta to Sita and said : "Bharata came to me here and asked me to go back to Ayodhya with him." They were able to see the river Yamuna and the grove along the banks of the river where they had walked and then made a raft to cross over. They had come to the ashrama of Bharadvaja. Rama said : "Look at the sacred river Ganga. The waters of this river are gleaming golden in the light of the sun. There can be seen the city Shringiberapura where Guha is ruling." Tears were flowing from Rama's eyes when he said : "Sita, this Sarayu, the river which holds Kosala in its embrace! There! There! That is Ayodhya, the city of my father. Salute it from here." All three of them prostrated to the city and the Vanaras strained their necks to see the city where their Rama was born and which would be ruled by him now.

Rama proceeded to the ashrama of Bharadvaja and it was the day when the exile was completed. He went to the rishi and prostrated before him and said : "My lord, I am eager to know about the welfare of my brother Bharata. Is he well? Are my mothers well? Are the subjects happy?" Bharadvaja received Rama and listened to his questions with a smile. He said : "Bharata wears his hair matted even as you and Lakshmana have done. He wears soiled clothes and sleeps on the ground. The sandals which you gave him are keeping him alive and he is thinking only of you and he is counting the days which should elapse before he can see you. Your mothers are all well. Rama, when I look back and think of the day I saw you last, my eyes fill with tears even now. I saw you with the tree-bark and deerskin draped round you. Lakshmana and Sita were with you. You had lost your kingdom and you were bent on one thing and that was Dharma. Giving away all that had been yours, you came on foot to the fearful forest because you wanted to carry out the commands of your father. You seemed to me like a god who had been sent down to the earth for some slight misdemeanour. Kaikeyi wished you to live in the forest and you took her at her word and came to the forest. When I saw you then I was grieved. Now you are making my heart overflow with joy. You have conquered the enemy and you have many friends with you. I have been keeping track of you and I know the misfortunes which have been visiting you during the last few years. I know about the riddance of the Janasthana of the rakshasas, about your dear wife's abduction by Ravana, your killing of Maricha, Kabandha and your journey to Pampa. I know about your friendship with Sugriva, the killing of Vali, Hanuman's search for Sita and the glorious achievements of this devotee of yours. I heard about the bridge you had built to span the sea and the destruction of Ravana and all his kinsmen. I was told about the boon granted to you by Indra because of which your friends, the Vanaras, are happy. I want to grant you a boon. I want to be your host for today. You can go to Ayodhya tomorrow."

Rama accepted the honour with humility. His mind, however, was set on Bharata and his eyes lighted on Hanuman. He said : "Hanuman, you heard the words of the great sage. I cannot disobey him. I want you to go as fast as you can and find out if all is well in my father's palace. Go to the city Shringiberapura and meet my friend Guha who will indicate to you the way to Ayodhya. He will also tell you about Bharata. Tell him about my return.

"Go to Bharata and tell him in detail all that happened to me during the fourteen years. Watch his face when you tell him that I am coming back victorious after killing Ravana. When he hears of my return his face will reveal his feelings. If you feel that there is even a minute trace of disappointment come and tell me. If you feel that he will be loth to return the kingdom to me, I will not stand in his way. I will let him rule the world. Hanuman, you are wise and you should know how the best of men will, at times, be tempted by the possession of wealth to retain it. Study him and, after making up your mind about it, come to me."

48. HANUMAN IN NANDIGRAMA

Hanuman hurried out on his mission. It was a delicate task which Rama had set and that was because Rama knew that he was the only person capable of handling it with tact. He assumed the guise of a human being and rose into the sky like Garuda soaring into the heavens. He passed the Sangama where the golden waters of the Ganga blend with the midnight blue of the Yamuna and from there he went to the city of Guha, Shringiberapura. He gave the message to Guha and from there he rose once again into the sky and he travelled towards Ayodhya. Nandigrama, he was told, was on the outskirts of Ayodhya.

Hanuman went to Nandigrama which was a krosa away from the city Ayodhya and he went there and he saw Bharata. The prince was wearing tree-bark and deerskin. His hair was matted like that of one who had renounced the many pleasures of the world. He had paid no attention to his body and it was covered with dust and dirt. He was a picture of woe and he was thinking only of his brother. He was thin because of the fasts he was observing and he was eating fruits and roots just to keep body and soul together.

Bharata had undertaken to guard the kingdom till Rama came back and he seemed to have been keeping alive only for that one purpose. He was like an ascetic. His eyes were half closed and he was thinking of Rama.

Hanuman saw him looking like a Brahmarshi and he saw, too, the sandals which had been worshipped by Bharata. Hanuman went near Bharata and said: "Rama, for whose sake you have donned this garb of an ascetic, Rama who is living in the Dandaka and for whom you are waiting, has sent me to you to tell you that soon you will be seeing him. He is well. I am bringing you good tidings from your brother. Soon, very soon, you will be rid of this pain of longing in your heart since you are to be united with Rama and Lakshmana very soon. Rama killed Ravana, the king of the rakshasas, and he is on his way to meet you. He wished me to come to you and announce his coming to you."

Bharata, who had been waiting for this moment for the last so many days, was overwhelmed with joy and he fell down on the ground and fainted. In a moment he woke up and with his face shining with joy he said: "Embrace me, my friend, whoever you may be. I am happy at last and you have made me happy."

Bharata embraced Hanuman and his tears drenched Hanuman. He said: "What can I do to show my joy? You have brought me the life-giving elixir: the news that Rama is coming back! Rama, my Rama, my dear brother is coming back! Tell me what will please you and I will do it."

Hanuman was not able to speak. Here was someone who loved Rama as much as he did and he was crying too, with joy. Bharata asked him: "My brother went away to the forest many, many years back. Is it true what you say? Is it true that he is coming back? There is a common saying which says: 'If a man keeps himself alive for a hundred years happiness will be his at the end: even if it should be delayed.' This had proved true in my case. I am happy, very happy. Tell me what has been happening to my brother all these many years. I want to know."

Hanuman seated himself on the seat of darbha offered to him and he spoke in great detail about the many adventures of Rama and the misfortunes. He ended with the words: "Rama has reached the banks of the river Ganga and he has been asked by sage Bharadvaja to spend the night there. So you will see him tomorrow. It is an auspicious day. It is the fifth day after the new moon and the star is Pushya."

Bharata and Shatrughna made haste to prepare for the coming of Rama. The city was decorated with flowers, with garlands of flowers and with perfumed water. All the mantapas had to be beautified and singers and musicians were asked to prepare themselves for the morning when Rama would arrive. The citizens, the army and everyone in Ayodhya had to receive Rama and the path between Nandigrama and Ayodhya was made level and fit to let the army march. Flowers there had to be in plenty so that the path of Rama could be strewn with them. The royal path had to be decorated with patterns traced with coloured powder and the many servants and ministers were busy preparing the city of the coming of Rama. The army left the city of Ayodhya and began its march towards Nandigrama. Bharata was surrounded by several men with auspicious articles of welcome like pots of water, flowers and incense. The citizens had come and the queen mothers travelled to Nandigrama in the palanquins.

The noise made by the conchs and the trumpets seemed to rend the sky. The white umbrella was carried with reverence and also the chamaras. Bharata placed the sandals of Rama on his head and set out to welcome Rama.

49. THE HOME-COMING OF RAMA

A sudden doubt seemed to assail Bharata. He said : "Hanuman, I do not see Rama anywhere. I am not able to see even a single Vanara and you said that an army of Vanaras was coming with him. I do not see the signs of his coming. Tell me why he has not come."

There was pain in Bharata's voice and Hanuman said : "Rama has been granted a boon by Indra. It says that the forests will always be full of flowers and fruits for the benefit of the Vanaras. The entire army has been hosted by Bharadvaja. I am able to hear the noise made by the Vanaras and I can tell you that they have reached the banks of the river Gomati. Can you not see the cloud of dust rising to the skies? Look there in the sky! Can you see a glorious chariot there, bright like the moon and faster than the wind? That is the chariot created by Brahma and it is divine. It belonged to Ravana and Rama is even now travelling in that vimana to reach you soon. This vimana by name Pushpaka belonged to Kubera and was taken forcibly from him by Ravana. In a matter of moments Rama will be with you."

Even as he was saying so, the Pushpaka vimana reached the sacred village Nandigrama. "Rama! Rama!" was the name which was on the lips of everyone assembled there and it reached the skies and it was heard by Rama who was in the vimana.

Bharata stood with his palms folded and his eyes were raised aloft. He could see Rama in the vimana and from the earth he saluted his brother who was in the skies. The next moment the vimana touched the ground.

Bharata rushed to Rama, fell on the ground and prostrated before him. Again and again he prostrated and Rama took him on his lap and he looked at him with his eyes full of love. It was fourteen years since the brothers had been parted and the reunion was tender. Bharata greeted Lakshmana and saluted Sita speaking the words : "Abhivadaye" announcing himself to them all. He met Sugriva and Jambavan and all the heroes of the Vanara army. Bharata said : "Sugriva, you are also one of us. Friendship is proved by the assistance rendered and you are our greatest friend." He then turned to Vibhishana and said : "My lord Rama was able to accomplish the impossible with your help and we are deeply indebted to you." Shatrughna greeted his brothers even as Bharata did and Rama went to the presence of his mother.

He fell at her feet and clasping them in his hands he placed his head over them, his tears washed her feet. After saluting Sumitra and Kaikeyi Rama went to Vasishtha, his guru and prostrated before him.

All the men of Ayodhya stood watching Rama with Sita and Lakshmana. They were so thrilled that Rama had come back to them and they could not speak for joy.

Bharata took the sandals in his hands and went to Rama. He placed Rama's feet in them and said : "O king! These sandals have been guarded by me for your sake and I have now returned them to you and with them, your kingdom. I feel that I have not lived in vain since my desire has been fulfilled. Please look into the treasury, the granary, the army and the city.

By your grace and blessings I have increased them tenfold."

Those around were thrilled to see so much devotion and Rama, taking Bharata and the others with him, entered the Pushpaka and went to the ashrama of Bharata. He turned his eyes on the vimana and said : "I wish that you go back to Kubera who once owned you. I grant you leave to go." The glorious Pushpaka rose in the sky and travelled fast towards the north, the direction of the home of the devas.

Rama saluted his guru even as Indra his guru Brihaspati and he sat near him. Bharata came to his presence and said : "My mother's name does not bear a taint any longer. This kingdom has been left by you in my charge and I give it back to you. I have guarded it carefully. It was a great burden which I had been asked to bear. I am unable to do it. My trying to rule when you should have, was like a donkey trying to walk like a horse or like a crow trying to imitate the gait of the swan. Please allow us to perform your coronation. Let the world see you glowing like the noonday sun. Rule the earth as long as the sun and moon move in their orbits, so long as there are people living in this world."

Rama accepted the plea of Bharata and agreed to rule the kingdom. Shatrughna and Bharata had made arrangements for the matted locks of Rama to be removed and those of Lakshmana. They got rid of their own tangled locks too and they all bathed in the sacred river. They wore silks and ornaments and smeared sandal paste on their long and beautiful arms. Sita was dressed with loving hands by the mothers of the princes. Kausalya, in her affection for Rama, dressed the hair of the wives of the Vanaras.

Sumantra brought the chariot and placed it near the entrance to the ashrama. Rama ascended the chariot. The Vanara army led by Sugriva and Hanuman accompanied the army from Ayodhya.

50. THE CORONATION OF RAMA

The ministers of the king led by Ashoka and Vijaya went to the presence of Vasishtha and requested him to take charge of the coronation of Rama. The entire crowd began its journey towards Ayodhya. Rama was seated in the chariot and Bharata held the reins of the horses in his hand. Vibhishana held a chamara in his hand. Lakshmana held the other chamara in his hand and Shatrughna held the white umbrella. The grand procession was on its way to Ayodhya. The celestials had assembled in the skies to watch the great event.

Shatrunjaya, the favourite elephant of Rama, came to receive him and Sugriva was asked to seat himself on it. Surrounded by the many noble and great people of the court, Rama appeared like the moon surrounded by the lesser luminaries in the sky. Musicians were there and the path was strewn with flowers. Beautiful cows were led in front of the chariot and Vedic hymns were chanted. Rama was talking to the ministers of the court, the old men who had been with his father. They were with him in the chariot. He told them about the events during the fourteen years and about the friendship which had been formed with Sugriva and with Vibhishana. He spoke of the valour of Hanuman and about his divine attributes. Soon they were in Ayodhya.

Rama was looking at his beloved city as though he had never seen it before. His eyes were filled with tears of joy and soon he arrived at the palace of his father. Rama descended from his chariot and entered the palace. After paying respect to all the elders Rama said : "Child, Bharata, let Sugriva reside in my palace." Bharata took Sugriva to the palace of Rama. Sugriva then sent his Vanaras to the sea to fill up the pots of gold with the waters of the sea.

The preparations for the coronation were completed. Vasishtha made Rama sit on the jewelled throne with Sita by his side. Vasishtha, Vamadeva, Jabali, Kashyapa, Katyayana, Gautama, and Vijaya poured the sacred waters from all the sacred rivers and oceans even as the eight Vasus performed the coronation of Indra. With the help of the ritviks and brahmins the coronation bath was given to Rama. Shatrughna held the beautiful white umbrella and Sugriva held in his hand the chamara. Vibhishana took the other chamara in his hand. Indra had sent a garland of lotuses from the heavens and Vayu brought it. A necklace of pearls was also given by Indra. The devas came down to the earth and the apsaras danced. The earth was smiling with joy and the trees were laden with flowers and fruits. Rama gave away horses and cows as gifts to many brahmins.

THE CORONATION OF RAMA

To Sugriva he gave a golden necklace set with gems and he, with his own hands, decorated the strong arms of Angada with golden bracelets. Sita took out a glorious necklace from her beautiful neck and looked around at the Vanaras and at her Rama. Rama understood what she was thinking and said : "Give it to one whom you consider to be all that a man should be: he should have divine gifts and he should have perseverance, fame, truthfulness, skill, courtesy, forethought, prowess, the capacity to subdue enemies and a good intellect. Look around you Sita, and give the necklace to one who, you think, possesses all these qualities."

Sita promptly gave it to Hanuman and he wore it round his neck looking like a mountain top which has a plume of a white cloud on it. All the Vanaras were given gifts by Rama.

The coronation had come to a glorious end and Sugriva and his army with Hanuman took leave of Rama and went back to Kishkindha. Vibhishana also went back to Lanka after having acquired the wealth of his ancestors.

Rama said : "Lakshmana, rule this ancient kingdom with me. Be my equal and let me crown you as the Yuvaraja." Though he was persuaded in many ways Lakshmana refused to accept it and Rama crowned Bharata as the Yuvaraja. Rama performed the Ashvamedha and several other yagas and he ruled the world even as his father had done before him. He upheld the fame of the Ikshvakus and the race of the sun.

When Rama ruled the earth women were happy since none of them lost their husbands. Wild animals did not trouble the citizens. There was no disease which prevailed during the reign of Rama. There was no theft and no one died an untimely death. Everyone was happy. All were righteous in their thoughts, words and deeds. Ramarajya has ever since then become the word which indicates perfect happiness and absolute happiness for the people. Trees were never barren and Parjanya rained in time to feed the crops. There was no avarice and no discontent when Rama ruled the world. The people were all good, god-fearing and ever inclined to follow the path of Dharma. Everyone was happy and there was nothing but prosperity in the country when Rama ruled the earth : during RAMARAJYA.

PHALASHRUTI

This story was composed by Valmiki the sage in ancient times. It is hallowed and sacred. This is the very first kavya that was ever written. He who reads it will be purified and will not be made to suffer for his sins. It grants long life. The childless will have children after he listens to the story of the coronation of Rama. A poor man will become wealthy. A kshatriya will subdue all his enemies and will be ever victorious. Women will all be as great as Kausalya, the men will be as dear to everyone as Rama was.

One who listens to this story of Rama, the blameless, the sinless, will live long. One who listens with devotion to this ancient kavya composed by Valmiki will be able to conquer anger and will face the greatest of dangers with fortitude. He will be reunited with his kinsfolk from whom he is parted, after a long journey. All his desires will be granted.

The gods are mindful of those who study the kavyas with care. Those who listen to this story will be rewarded by the devas and the obstacles in their lives will vanish on their own accord. The king who listens to this story will ever be victorious. The traveller will have no difficulties. Women will be the mothers of sons. One who worships this kavya and studies it everyday will be absolved from all sins and will live long.

Narayana, the Lord who is all-pervading, who has his abode in the ocean of milk and who is also called Hari, who has no beginning, no middle and no end, who is the Lord of lords, who is the Ancient is Rama, and he will bless the one who studies this Ramayana and the one who listens to the story of Rama. He will have wealth and children and he will have peace and contentment. All his desires will be granted. It grants long life, wealth, health, fame, comradeship with brothers, good intelligence, glory.

The study of Ramayana will grant man all these. Repeat the story of Rama with reverence and may you be blessed. Let the world thrive by the Grace of Lord Narayana. The Pitris are satisfied by the study of Ramayana by their descendants. The devas are pleased. One who studies this

Ramayana composed by Valmiki is certain to have won a place for himself in heaven.

AUM TAT SAT! HARIHI AUM!

AUM! SHANTI! SHANTI! SHANTI!

GLOSSARY

Abhiras	A tribe of people who, living on the banks of lake by name Drumakulya, made the lake impure. At the request of the Lord of the seas, Rama destroyed them and purified the waters of Drumakulya.
Arani	A piece of wood (taken from the Ficus Religiosa or Premna Spinosa) used for kindling fire by attrition.
Asuri Maya	The Maya tactics in warfare adopted by the Asuras.
Abhisheka	Anointing, inaugurating or consecrating (by sprinkling water); inauguration of a king: religious bathing.
Abhivadaye	Addressing or saluting with reverence, presenting oneself with reverence.
Achamana	Sipping water from the palm of the hand (before religious ceremonies, before meals etc.) for purification. It is not the custom to sip the water and spit it out.
Acharya	A spiritual guide or teacher especially one who invests the student with the sacred thread and instructs him in the Vedas, in the law of sacrifice and religious mysteries.
Adharma	Injustice, irreligion, wickedness.
Adharmi	One who is unrighteous, impious, wicked.
Adishesha	Son of Kadru. He is the thousand-headed serpent who is represented as forming the couch of Vishnu and His canopy whilst He sleeps during the intervals of Creation.
Aditi	Daughter of Daksha and the wife of Kashyapa and the mother of the gods. She was the mother of Upendra, otherwise known as Vamana, one of the avataras of Vishnu.
Adityas	The sons of Aditi. This name is specially used to refer to the twelve Adityas: the twelve suns.
Aditya Hridaya	Slokas in praise of the Sun said to have taught to Rama by Agastya on the field of battle before the killing of Ravana.

GLOSSARY

Amrita	The nectar produced at the churning of the ocean of milk: supposed to grant immortality.
Agastya	A rishi, the author of several Vedic hymns; he is said to have been short in stature: to have swallowed the ocean: to have compelled the Vindhya mountains to prostrate themselves before him: to have conquered and made the Dandaka forests habitable.
Agneyastra	The astra presided over by Agni, god of fire.
Agni	The god of fire.
Agnihotra	Oblation to Agni (chiefly of milk and ghee). There are two kinds of Agnihotra, one is Nitya, i.e. of constant oblation and the other is Kamya. i.e. optional.
Agnihotrasala	The place assigned specially for performing Agnihotra.
Ahalya	The wife of Gautama and the mother of Sadananda.
Ahuti	An offering, oblation.
Aindra	Belonging to or sacred to Indra: the astra.
Airavata	Name of the elephant of Indra.
Aja	A king of the solar race. He was the father of Dasaratha.
Ajigarta	A brahmana of the Bhargava clan whose son was sold to the prince Rohita for an immense number of cows. The son's name was Sunashepha.
Akampana	One of the few rakshasas who escaped from the arrows of Rama in Janasthana and who reported to Ravana about the destruction of Khara and his entire army.
Aksha	One of the sons of Ravana. He was killed by Hanuman when the Ashokavana of Ravana was completely destroyed by Hanuman.
Akasha Ganga	Ganga, the daughter of Himavan, was given to the devas and she became a river which flowed in the heavens and she was called Akasha Ganga.
Alakananda	When Ganga descended to the earth at the request of Bhagiratha she was caught up in the matted locks of Lord Mahadeva. He released her drop by drop along a single strand of his Jata, which gave her the name.
Alarka	One of the kings of the solar race.
Amaravati	The city of Indra.

Amrita	The nectar, food of the gods, which they got by churning the ocean of milk. It is said to grant immortality.
Amshuman	The grandson of Sagara, the king of the solar race.
Amsha	One who has some part of the Divinity: who is the Lord manifesting as a human being, endowed with divine qualities.
Anala	The god of fire.
Ananga	Manmatha, the god of love, was burnt to ashes when he aimed his arrows at Mahadeva. Ever since then he has been referred to as Ananga.
Anaranya	A king of the solar race who had cursed Ravana that one of his descendants would be the killer of Ravana.
Anarya	One lacking in the noble qualities of a king: base, mean, not respectable.
Anasuya	Name of the wife of sage Atri, the highest type of chastity and wifely devotion.
Anga	The kingdom which was ruled by Romapada, whose son-in-law was Rishyashringa.
Angaraka	The planet Mars, also called Mangala.
Anjali	A folding of the hands together and raising them to the head in supplication or salutation. Hence, a mark of respect of salutation.
Antahpura	Inner apartments of a palace set apart for women: harem.
Antaka	Yama, the god of death.
Anumana	Inferring: conclusion from given premises: one of the four means of obtaining knowledge according to the Nyaya System.
Anushtup	A class of metre. The Ramayana has been composed in this metre by Valmiki.
Aparadhakshama	Forgiveness of those who have offended against one.
Apsara	Celestial nymph. Apsaras are said to have been born of the milk ocean when it was churned for Amrita.
Arghya	A respectful offering or oblation to a god or a venerable person.

Arishta	Name of the hill in Lanka which was used by Hanuman as a spot from where he could leap back across the ocean to the north.
Arishtanemi	Name of Tarkshya. Also, Aruna, the brother of Garuda and the charioteer of the Sun.
Artha	One of the four Purusharthas: Dharma, Artha, Kama and Moksha. Artha is usually meant the acquisition of wealth by honest means. Also end, aim, purpose, desire.
Arthaprapti	The attainment of one's desires: also the attainment of worldly prosperity, riches. Also Ref. Pratyaksha.
Arthasadhaka	One who manages to attain his desires.
Aruna	The son of Vinata; he was born prematurely before his lower limbs could be developed. He is the charioteer of Surya and the brother of Garuda.
Arundhati	The name of the wife of Vasishtha. She was one of the daughters of Kardama Prajapati and Devahuti. One of the Pleiades. She is regarded as the highest pattern of conjugal excellence and wifely devotion.
Asamanja	The son of king Sagara of the solar race. As a prince he was banished from the kingdom for the many cruelties he perpetrated. His son was Amshuman.
Asana	A seat or stool. It is also made of *darbha* grass and this is used by the rishis in their hermitages.
Ashlesha	A star. The star under which Lakshmana was born.
Ashoka	One of the ministers of Dasaratha. Name of a tree which bears red flowers. The Ashoka has the privilege of being one of the arrows in the quiver of Manmatha.
Ashokavana	The pleasure garden of Ravana where he had kept Sita in captivity.
Ashrama	The hermitage of rishis.
Ashvayuja	The seventh month of the year.
Ashvakarna	A tree whose leaves resemble the ear of a horse.

Ashvapati	The king of Kekaya and the father of Kaikeyi.
Ashvattha	The holy tree Ficus Religiosa.
Ashvini twins	The two physicians of the gods who are represented as the twin sons of the sun and a nymph in the form of a mare.
Astra	A missile, a weapon. This is different from a shastra in the sense that it is presided over by a god, and a mantra has to be repeated in discharging or withdrawing the missile.
Ashvamedha	A horse sacrifice. This is a celebrated ceremony, the antiquity of which reaches back to the Vedic period. In later times its efficacy was so exaggerated that a hundred such sacrifices entitled a king to displace Indra from the dominion of Swarga.
Asura	A general name for the enemies of the gods who were Suras.
Atharva Veda	It is regarded as the fourth Veda containing many forms of imprecations for the destruction of enemies, a great number of prayers for safety, for the averting of mishaps, evils, and also a number of hymns, as in the other Vedas, addressed to the gods with prayers to be used at religious and solemn rites.
Atibala	One of the two mantras taught by Vishvamitra to Rama which had the power to rid the knower of fatigue, thirst or hunger.
Atikaya	One of the gallant sons of Ravana. He was the son of Dhanyamalini.
Atman	The Soul: the individual soul.
Atri	The name of a celebrated sage who was the author of many Vedic hymns. His wife was Anasuya.
AUM	The sacred syllable AUM uttered as a holy exclamation at the beginning and end of a reading of the Vedas, or previous to the commencement of a prayer or a sacred work. It is considered to represent the Brahman.
Avatara	Descent of a deity upon earth. Incarnation.
Avidya	Spiritual ignorance.
Ayodhya	The capital city of the Kosala kingdom ruled by the kings of the solar race.

GLOSSARY

Ayomukhi	One of the rakshasis who accosted Lakshmana and was punished for it.
Badari	The Jujube tree.
Bakula	A tree bearing very small and extremely sweet scented flowers: Mimusops Elengi.
Bala	One of the two incantations taught to Rama. (Ref. Atibala).
Balaka	Son of Puru and grandson of Jahnu.
Bali	One of the famed asuras. He was the grandson of Prahlada and the son of Virochana. Vamana was born to humble his pride and restore their wealth to the gods.
Banasura	Daitya who was the son of Bali.
Beda	One of the four *Upayas* (methods) to get what one wants. Sama, Dana, Beda and Danda are the four. Beda means comparison and thereby influencing the other person.
Bhadra	One of the Diggajas who are supposed to bear the earth on their heads.
Bhaga	Name of one of the twelve Adityas.
Bhagiratha	One of the kings of the solar race. A descendant of Sagara. He brought down the sacred Ganga from the heavens to the earth and led the river to the ocean in order to purify the ashes of his ancestors, the 60,000 sons of Sagara.
Bhagirathi	The name given to Ganga since she was considered to have become the daughter of Bhagiratha.
Bharadvaja	Name of the rishi whom Rama visited first after leaving Ayodhya. He indicated the spot Chitrakuta for Rama to build his ashrama.
Bharata	The second son of Dasaratha and the son of Kaikeyi.
Bharatavarsha	The land which was once ruled by Bharata—a king who became a rishi later—was given the name Bharatavarsha: India.
Bhargava	Sukra's other name is Bhargava and his descendants are all called Bhargavas. Parasurama was a Bhargava.
Bhogavati	Varuna's city.
Bhoota	Evil spirit.

Bhootagana	A group of spirits said to be in attendance when Lord Mahadeva moves around.
Bhrigu	Name of a sage, regarded as the ancestor of the family of the Bhrigus. One of the ten patriarchs created by the first Manu.
Brahma	One of the Trinity: the Creator.
Brahmabala	The spiritual strength of a brahmana against which every other kind of strength fails.
Brahmachari	A brahmin who lives in the first order of life: who lives with his spiritual guide from the investiture with the sacred thread and does the duties belonging to his order till he settles in life: one who vows to lead the life of a celibate.
Brahmajnani	One who has realised the Brahman.
Brahmahatya	The sin of killing a brahmin.
Brahmaloka	Satyaloka, the abode of Brahma.
Brahman	The Supreme Being, regarded as impersonal: the all-pervading soul and spirit of the Universe: the essence from which all created things emanate and to which they return.
Brahmana	A man of the first of the four castes of the Hindus.
Brahmarshi	A brahmanical sage.
Brahmastra	The astra presided over by Brahma.
Brahmatvam	To attain Brahmatva is to become one with the Brahman.
Brahma Vidya	The pursuit of the knowledge of the Truth about the Brahman.
Brahmi state	The same as Brahmatvam.
Brihaspati	The preceptor of the gods: the planet Jupiter.
Budha	The planet Mercury. The father of Pururavas.
Chaitra	The first month of the year.
Chaitra	The name of the garden of Kubera.
Chaitya	A sacrificial shed: a place of religious worship. Also a hall in Lanka which Hanuman destroyed.
Chakra	A sharp circular weapon: usually Chakra stands for Sudarshana, the chakra in the hand of Vishnu.

GLOSSARY

Chakravaka	A mythical bird which is said to be the symbol of despairing love: Viraha.
Chamara	A whisk made of soft silk: an insignia of a king.
Champaka	A flower which is yellowish orange in colour and which has a strong sweet fragrance.
Chandala	A general name for the lowest and most despised of the mixed castes: an outcast.
Chandana	Sandalwood.
Chandra	The moon: the moon as a planet.
Chandrahara	A necklace made of gold which glitters as light plays on it.
Charana	A spy.
Chitra	A star. Chitra is the wife of Chandra and the two were inseparable.
Chitrakuta	Name of a hill or district near Prayaga: this name has become immortal since Rama lived there during the first stage of his exile.
Dadhimukha	The guardian of the favourite garden of Sugriva. The garden was called Madhuvana and was the storehouse of the choicest wines.
Daitya	A son of Diti: a rakshasa.
Daksha	Name of a celebrated Prajapati. He was the father of Sati, the wife of Mahadeva.
Dana	One of the four methods of persuasion. Dana is winning over the other person with gifts.
Danava	A demon, rakshasa.
Danavi	A woman who is a rakshasi.
Dandaka	A king, who was the son of Ikshvaku. His land was laid waste by the curse of Bhargava, whose daughter he had violated. His kingdom, in consequence, became the Dandaka Aranya.
Dandakaranya	The forest to which Rama was exiled. (Ref. above).
Danu	The celestial being who had been cursed by the rishis to assume a fierce form which had to be abandoned once Rama appeared before him and killed him.

Darbha	A tuft or bunch of grass used for sacrificial purposes: especially of Kusa grass.
Dasaratha	A king of the solar race. The son of Aja and the father of Rama. He was a friend of Indra and he was given this name since he could ply his chariot in the eight quarters as well as on the earth and the heavens.
Devas	The gods: the heavenly or shining ones. The word is formed from the root "Div" to glow.
Devadaru	One of the Himalayan trees.
Devantaka	One of the sons of Ravana.
Devarata	Name of Sunashepha after he was received into the family of Vishvamitra.
Devastra	An astra presided over by a deva.
Devi	Addressing a woman with respect is to use the word 'Devi'.
Dhanus	A bow.
Danda	One of the Upayas: Sama, Dana, Beda and Danda. If the first three fail, the fourth, Danda, which means punishment, has to be used.
Dhanyamalini	The wife of Ravana and the mother of Atikaya.
Dharma	Virtue, morality, religious merit, righteousness.
Dharmaranya	Name of a sacred forest in Madhyadesha.
Dharmatma	One who is righteous.
Dhata	The Creator, Brahma.
Dhatu	An ingredient, a mineral.
Dhriti	One of the ministers of Dasaratha.
Dhruva	The pole star: the one constant star round which the seven rishis are said to move.
Dhumaketu	A meteor, a comet, a falling star.
Dhumraksha	One of the first great fighters in the army of Ravana. He was killed on the first day.
Diggajas	The four elephants which are said to hold up the earth: Virupaksha, Mahapadma, Saumanta and Bhadra.
Diksha	Consecration for a religious ceremony: initiation.

Dilipa	The father of Bhagiratha who brought the river Ganga to the earth.
Diti	The sister of Aditi and the mother of daityas.
Dushana	The brother of Khara. These two with Trishiras were harassing the rishis in Janasthana and were all killed by Rama.
Drona	A hill in the Himalaya where the Sanjivini hill was located.
Drumakulya	A lake belonging to the king of the oceans. This was being misused by a tribe by name Abhiras. Rama destroyed them with his Brahmastra and he purified Drumakulya whose waters were pure and sweet again.
Dundubhi	Dundubhi was a rakshasa whom Vali had killed and whose skeleton was flung a hundred yojanas away by Rama with a twist of his toe.
Durdina	A day when the sun is not seen.
Dvividha	One of the chief fighters in the monkey army.
Dyumatsena	The father of Satyavan and the father-in-law of Savitri.
Gaadhi	A king of the Chandravamsha. He was the father of Vishvamitra.
Gada	The mace by name Kaumodaki which is always associated with Vishnu: the other two being Sudarshana, the Chakra, and Panchajanya, the Conch.
Gaja	A powerful vanara in Sugriva's army.
Gajapushpi	A creeper which bears large flowers. The creeper with the flowers was twisted into the semblance of a garland and placed on the neck of Sugriva when he went to fight with his brother Vali by Lakshmana at the command of Rama.
Gandhamadana	Name of a particular mountain to the east of Meru, renowned for its fragrant forests.
Gandharvastra	One of the many astras taught by Vishvamitra to Rama on his way to Siddhashrama.
Gandharva	One of the celestial beings.
Gandharvanagari	An imaginary city in the sky, probably the result of some natural phenomenon such as a mirage. The term is used in Vedanta to illustrate the illusory nature, Maya, of the world around us.

Ganga	The elder daughter of Himavan who was given as a gift to the devas. She was Mandakini in the heavens and was later brought to the earth by Bhagiratha.
Garuda	The younger son of Vinata who is the Vahana of Vishnu.
Garuthman	Another name of Garuda.
Gautama	One of the great sages. His wife was Ahalya and his son, Sadananda, the preceptor of Janaka.
Gavya	One of the vanara chiefs.
Gavaksha	Another famed vanara.
Gayatri	A Vedic metre of 24 syllables. Name of a very sacred verse repeated by every Brahmana at his Sandhya. It was composed by Vishvamitra.
Girivraja	Name of a city in Magadha.
Jnati	A cousin: a kinsman.
Godavari	The river on whose banks was situated Panchavati, the ashrama of Rama where he spent the later days of his exile.
Gomati	A river near Ayodhya.
Gotra	The name of the rishi to whose group of disciples one belongs: like Bharadvaja, Kaushika.
Hanuman	A minister of Sugriva and a devotee of Rama. He was the son of Anjana by the god of wind. He is represented as a monkey of extraordinary strength and prowess. He played an important part in the great war at Lanka.
Hari	One of the many names of Vishnu.
Harishchandra	The son of Trishanku, one of the kings of the solar race.
Hasta	Name of a star.
Hastina	The capital city of the kings of the lunar race.
Havis	An oblation or burnt offering.
Hema	The daughter of Maya, the architect of the asuras. She was the owner of Svayamprabha Bila.
Hemanta	One of the seasons.
Himavan	The pile of mountains which guard the North. He is the father of Ganga and Parvati, the wife of Mahadeva.
Hiranyanabha	The mountain Mainaka.

Humkara	The angry grunt made by rishis which turns the victim into ashes.
Ikshumati	Name of a river whose waters were so sweet that the name Ikshumati was given to it.
Ikshvaku	He was the son of Manu and one of the earliest kings of the solar race.
Ilvala	One of the two brothers who were in the habit of killing all the rishis in the forest. Agastya killed Vatapi and Ilvala later.
Indra	The lord of the devas.
Indradhanus	The rainbow.
Indrajit	The favourite son of Ravana. He was the son of Mandodari. He was named Meghanada and this name was later changed to Indrajit since he conquered Indra in the war with the devas and brought him bound to the presence of his father. Brahma asked him to release Indra and so Indra was freed.
Indrani	The wife of Indra.
Indriyas	The five senses with which we experience the world around us: the sense of touch, smell, sound, sight and taste.
Indrotsava	A festival performed in honour of Indra. The belief was that Indra, pleased with their offering, would send them plenty of rain.
Ingudi tree	The name of a tree. Near the banks of the Ganga, Rama, Lakshmana and Sita spent the first night of their exile under the Ingudi tree.
Jabali	One of the preceptors in the court of Dasaratha.
Jahnu	Name of an ancient king who adopted the river Ganga as his daughter and hence her name Jahnavi.
Jambavan	Name of a king of bears who was of signal service to Rama at the siege of Lanka.
Jambumali	He was the son of Prahastha – the minister of Ravana. He was a fine warrior but Hanuman killed him during the fight following the destruction of the Ashokavana.
Jamadagni	A Brahmana and a descendant of Bhrigu. He was the father of Parasurama. He was the son of Richaka and Satyavati who, incidentally, was the sister of Vishvamitra.

Janaka	The father of Sita. He was a famous king of Videha whose capital was Mithila. He was remarkable for his great knowledge, good work and holiness. The sage Yajnavalkya was his preceptor.
Janasthana	A part of the Dandaka forest. This was the place where Ravana had established a camp of his myrmidons and they were constantly harassing the rishis who were living there.
Jata	The hair matted and twisted together.
Jatakarma	Several rites which have to be performed when a child is born.
Jatayu	A son of Shyeni and Aruna. He was a semi-divine bird. He was an eagle. He was a great friend of Dasaratha. His funeral rites were peformed by Rama.
Jayanta	The name of one of the ministers of Dasaratha. Also the name of Indra's son.
Jaya vijayee bhava	The usual form of address of the people, the servants and all the members of the royal household when the prince appears in their midst.
Jitendriya	One who has conquered all his senses.
Jivatma	The soul which is lodged inside the human body.
Jrumbhanastra	One of the rare astras known to Rama.
Kala	Time in general. The Supreme Spirit regarded as the Destroyer of the Universe, being a personification of the destructive principle.
Kabandha	Name of a mighty demon. He was a heavenly being by name Danu and had been cursed to assume the form of a headless trunk till Rama and Lakshmana killed him and granted him release.
Kadamba	A kind of tree whose flowers thrill into life at the noise of the thunder clouds.
Kadru	Wife of Kashyapa and the mother of the Nagas.
Kaikeyi	The daughter of Ashvapati. The princess of Kekaya and the favoured queen of Dasaratha. She was the mother of Bharata.
Kailasa	A peak in the Himalayas reputed to be the dwelling place of Lord Mahadeva.

Kaitabha	Name of a demon killed by Vishnu. He was a very powerful demon. He and Madhu are said to have tried to devour Brahma when they were killed by Vishnu.
Kakuthstha	A king of Ikshvaku race. Mythology relates that when in their war with the demons the gods were often worsted, they, headed by Indra, went to the king Puranjaya and requested him to be their friend in battle. The king consented to do so, on condition Indra carried him on his shoulder. Indra accordingly assumed the form of a bull, and Puranjaya seated on its hump completely vanquished the demons. Puranjaya is, therefore, called "Kakuthshta" meaning "standing on a hump."
Kalakuta	The poison churned out of the ocean of milk and drunk by Mahadeva giving him the name "Nilakanta."
Kama	Kama is the god of love. He once dared to aim his arrows at Mahadeva to make him fall in love with Parvati. The Lord burnt him down with his third eye. His bow is made of the sugar-cane rod, his bowstring is a row of bees and the arrows, five different flowers: the pink lotus, Ashoka, the flower of the Mango tree, Navamallika and the blue lotus.
Kama	Desire. One of the six enemies which obstruct man from reaching equanimity: Kama, Krodha, Lobha, Moha, Mada and Mastsarya.
Kama	A legitimate love of the sensual enjoyments considered as one of the four ends of life: Purusharthas. They are: Dharma, Artha, Kama and Moksha.
Kamadhenu	A heavenly cow granting all desires. This was born of the ocean of milk when it was churned for Amrita.
Kamandalu	A water-pot (earthen or wooden) used by ascetics.
Kamashrama	The hallowed spot where Mahadeva spent years in tapas after the death of Sati: where Kama aimed his arrows at the Lord and was burnt to ashes by the fiery third eye of Mahadeva.
Kandu	A rishi. Because he had lost his son this rishi had cursed that the entire forest should become lifeless. During their search for Sita, Angada and the others came across this forest.

Kankana	A bracelet.
Kanva	A famed sage of ancient times.
Kanyadana	The giving away of the daughter to the groom by the father of the girl. Strangely enough, this is the one Dana where the giver sits down and the recipient stands and receives the gift.
Kanyasulka	In ancient times the bridegroom had to pay a certain amount of wealth to the father of the bride before he could marry her.
Kapila cow	A cow which is tawny, reddish in colour. It is said to be superior to the other types.
Kapila Vasudeva	Name of a great sage. He reduced to ashes the 60,000 sons of Sagara who, while searching for the sacrificial horse of their father, fell in with him and accused the rishi of stealing it. Kapila Vasudeva is also said to have been the founder of the Sankhya system of philosophy.
Karavira	A kind of tree with flowers blooming on it.
Karkataka	The Lagna in which Sri Rama was born: Cancer, the fourth sign of the Zodiac.
Karnikara	A favourite flower of Sita.
Kartaviryarjuna	A king of the Hehayas who ruled at Mahishmati. Having worshipped Dattatreya he had obtained from him several boons. He was slain by Parasurama for having carried off by violence the Kamadhenu of his revered father Jamadagni.
Kartika	Name of the month in which the full moon is near the Krittika or Pleiades (corresponding to October-November).
Karusha	The name of Tatakavana before it became the home of Tataka. When Indra was smitten with the sin of Brahmahatya after the killing of Vritra he was absolved from it by the efforts of his guru. When he was given the religious bath which was to rid him of the sin the waters flowed to the earth. Indra blessed the land which had been drenched by this water and called them "Malada" and "Karusha." He said that they would always remain fertile and luscious.
Kashyapa	Name of a rishi. The husband of Aditi and Diti, and thus the father of both the gods and the demons. He was the son of

GLOSSARY

	Marichi, the son of Brahma. He bears a very important share in the work of creation. He has the appellation, Kashyapa Prajapati.
Kausalya	The eldest wife of Dasaratha and the mother of Rama.
Kaushambi	The city of one of the ancestors of Vishvamitra.
Kaushika	The name of the son of Gaadhi. He later became famed as Vishvamitra after performing a series of severe penances.
Kaushika Gotra	The Gotra which was initially started by Kaushika.
Kaushiki	Satyavati, the sister of Vishvamitra, was so good and pure that she become a river by name Kaushiki.
Kavya	A poem: poetics, poetry, poetical composition.
Kekaya	The kingdom of which Kaikeyi was a princess.
Kesini	One of the wives of Sagara.
Kritamala	A tree which has clusters of golden yellow flowers which cover the tree after it has shed its leaves. The name is because the tree seems to have garlanded itself. The other name of the tree is Suvarnaka (Cassia Fistula).
Khara	Name of a demon, a half-brother of Ravana, who was killed by Rama in the Janasthana.
Kinnara	One of the celestials.
Kishkindha	The city where Vali ruled and which, later, became the city ruled by Sugriva.
Krauncha	Name of a mountain said to be the grandson of Himavan and said to have been pierced by Kartikeya and Parasurama.
Kodanda	A bow. Since Rama was a great archer it is usual to call him Kodandapani. Kodanda is sometimes mistaken to be the name of Rama's bow.
Kosala	The land ruled by Dasaratha and the descendants of Ikshvaku.
Kovidara	A flower, slightly mauve in colour, which was the Dwaja of the kings of Ayodhya.
Krodha	One of the six enemies of man. Krodha means anger. (Ref. Kama).
Krodhagriha	The sulking room which was used by Kaikeyi when she got into one of her angry moods.

Krosha	A measure of distance which is one-fourth of a yojana.
Kshatriya	The second of the four castes into which society was classified in the ancient days. They were kings and fighters.
Kshetra	A sacred spot, a place of pilgrimage.
Kubera	One of the guardians of the quarters. Kubera is lord of the North. He is the god of wealth and he was half-brother to Ravana who defeated him in a war and took away the Vimana by name Pushpaka from him.
Kumbhakarna	The brave and devoted brother of Ravana.
Kumuda	One of the fighters in the vanara army.
Kusa	Rama's son: also darbha grass.
Kushadhvaja	An ancestor of Vishvamitra.
Kushamba	Another ancestor of Vishvamitra. Also Kushaparva and Kushanabha.
Lagna	The point where the horizon and the ecliptic meet: the point of the ecliptic which, at any time, is at the horizon or on the meridian: The moment of the sun's entrance into a sign of the zodiac. An auspicious moment. A figure of the twelve zodiacal signs.
Lakshmana	The son of Dasaratha. One of the twins who were the sons of Sumitra. The faithful brother of Rama who went with him to the Dandaka.
Lakshmi	The goddess of fortune, prosperity and beauty. She was born in the ocean of milk during the churning of the ocean for Amrita and she chose Vishnu as her Lord.
Lamba	The hill on whose peak Hanuman landed as soon as he crossed the ocean from the Mahendra hill.
Lanka	The beautiful city which was built for Ravana by Vishvakarma, the divine architect.
Lankini	The goddess who protected the city of Lanka.
Lava	The son of Rama: twin of Kusa.
Lobha	One of the six enemies of man's equanimity. (Ref. Kama).
Maa Ruda	When the daityas were conquered by the devas, Diti, their mother, was unhappy and she observed a Vrata and got the boon that she would bear a child which would kill Indra: but there was a condition. She should be very pure and clean during the child's growth in her womb. Indra knew

this. Once she unwittingly made a slight mistake. With this as his chance Indra entered her womb and cut the unborn child into seven pieces. But the child would not die and they were all crying. Indra said: "Maa Ruda" meaning "do not cry." Diti woke up and found out what had happened. She knew that Indra could not be destroyed. She made a gift of the children to him and said: "Let them be your companions. Since you said "Maa Ruda" they will be known as the seven *Maruts*.

Maya (tactics)	The peculiar method of fighting for which the asuras and rakshasas were famed. They would disappear from the sight of the assailant and harass him from the skies. Subahu and Maricha and later, Indrajit were excellent in this art.
Mayavi	Possessing illusionary or magic powers, employing deceit deluding others.
Mada	Refer Kama.
Madhu	Honey supposed to be intoxicating and to be of eight kinds. Any intoxicating liquor.
Madhu	Refer Kaitabha
Madhu	Madhu and Madhava make the first two months of the year when Vasanta rules the world.
Madhuchandas	Sons of Vishvamitra.
Madhuka	The name of a tree.
Madhyama	A low pitch which is supposed to be the ideal pitch to converse. Hanuman spoke in this pitch.
Madhushyanda	A son of Vishvamitra.
Mahadeva	One of the Trinity. He is Siva the destroyer.
Mahapadma	One of the four Diggajas.
Mahodara	The disease known as dropsy. Harishchandra was visited by it because of the anger of Varuna.
Mahodara	One of Ravana's trusted ministers.
Mahaparshva	Another of Ravana's trusted ministers.
Maharathika	A great warrior or hero.
Maharshi	The title given to a rishi who has performed intense tapas.
Mahendra (hill)	The great hill on the northern shore of the ocean from whose top Hanuman sprang into the air to leap across the ocean.

Mahodadhi	The great ocean.
Mainaka	During ancient days mountains had wings and they could fly as they pleased. They would cause great havoc wherever they landed. Indra, therefore, took his Vajra and cut off the wings. The god of wind Vayu took pity on Mainaka and concealed him inside the ocean.
Mainda	One of the vanara chieftains.
Makaraksha	One of the rakshasa warriors.
Malada	Refer Karusha.
Malaya (peak)	A small peak on the Rishyamooka hill where Sugriva stayed with his four companions.
Malini	A river in Chitrakuta. Rama stayed very near it.
Mallika	A small fragrant flower growing in bushes.
Manasa Sarovara	A lake created by Brahma.
Manes	The forefathers: the Pitris.
Manasila	A stone with a mineral embedded in it. The stone is red in colour. Most probably the colouring is due to red arsenic.
Manavastra	The astra used by Rama to take Maricha and to fling him into the ocean a hundred yojanas away.
Madhuka	The name of a tree.
Mandanila	Soft, gentle and perfumed breeze which is a constant companion of Kama and Vasanta.
Mandavi	The daughter of Janaka's brother who was given as a bride to Bharata.
Mandhata	One of the famed kings of the Surya vamsha. He was the son of Yuvanashva. He was such a great king that in later times he was referred to as "The ornament of Krita Yuga."
Mandakini	The name of the river Ganga as she flows in the heavens.
Mandodari	The daughter of Maya, the wife of Ravana and the mother of Indrajit.
Manmatha	Another name for Kama, the god of love.
Mantapa	A small building designed like a temple.
Manthara	A companion of Kaikeyi. She had been with the princess even before her wedding and had come to Ayodhya with her. She had been granted several privileges because of her

GLOSSARY 679

	age and her love for Kaikeyi. She was a short, ugly woman with a hump on her back. When she heard about the coronation of Rama as the Yuvaraja she was displeased and she went to the presence of Kaikeyi and after a lot of persuasion convinced the young queen that Rama should be banished from the kingdom.
Mantra	An incantation.
Manorama	The wife of Himavan and the mother of Parvati, and Ganga. Her other name was Mena.
Mantrapala	One of the ministers of Dasaratha.
Manu	The founder of the solar race and he was the first law giver. The collection of his words is named Manu Smriti.
Maricha	An uncle of Ravana and he was first punished by Rama during the yaga of Vishvamitra. Later, when he had lured Rama away from the hermitage at Panchavati, he was killed by Rama.
Marichi	One of the Prajapatis.
Markandeya	A rishi, a great devotee of Mahadeva, who was granted the boon that he would always remain to be sixteen.
Maruts	Refer Maa Ruda
Matali	The charioteer of Indra.
Matanga	He was a very great rishi held in great veneration by everyone. He was served by Shabari.
Matangasaras	A lake called after the great rishi near which was located the lake Pampa.
Matruhatya	The sin ascribed to one who kills his mother.
Matsarya	Refer Kama
Mattha	One of the last few warriors who fought for Ravana and was killed.
Maya (Architect)	The architect of the asuras. He was the father of Mandodari.
Meena Lagna	The Lagna under which Bharata was born.
Meghanada	The name of the son of Ravana. When he was born his cry was like the roar of thunder and so he was named Meghanada. But this name was forgotten after he had conquered Indra and won the name 'Indrajit'.
Menaka	One of the apsaras of the court of Indra who was responsible for the loss of Vishvamitra's tapas.

Meru	One of the famed peaks of the Himalayas. It is a fabulous mountain round which all the planets are said to revolve.
Meru Savarani	Name of the eleventh Manu.
Mithi	He was a king, an ancestor of Janaka. The city by name Mithila was named after him.
Mithila	The capital city of the country of Videha.
Moha	Refer Kama.
Moksha	Attainment of salvation. The fourth of the Purusharthas: Dharma, Artha, Kama and Moksha.
Mudgara	This is a favourite weapon of the rakshasas.
Muhurta	A period of 48 minutes.
Mulabala	Ravana's personal army which he sends to the battlefield after the death of Indrajit. The entire army was destroyed by Rama and he fought all by himself. He used the Gaandharvastra and the army was razed to the ground.
Mritasanjivini	One of the herbs to be found in the hill by name Sanjivini which was brought to the battlefield by Hanuman.
Nagas	The serpents: the children of Kadru. Also a semi-divine being having the face of a man and the tail of a serpent and said to inhabit Patala.
Nahusha	A king of the lunar race: the father of Yayati.
Nala	The architect among the vanaras since he was the son of Vishvakarma. He was responsible for the building of the bridge across the ocean and the bridge is named Nalasetu after him.
Nalika	A particularly sharp and fatal arrow.
Namuchi	One of the daityas who was killed by Indra during the war which was fought after the churning of the ocean.
Nandana	The garden in the abode of Indra.
Nandi	Nandikeshvara as he is popularly known, is the vahana of Mahadeva and an old enemy of Ravana.
Nandigrama	A small city, almost a hamlet, on the outskirts of Ayodhya where Bharata stayed during the fourteen years of Rama's exile.
Naracha	A type of arrow which Rama used against the army of Khara.
Narantaka	A glorious warrior. He was the son of Ravana.

GLOSSARY

Narayana	Vishnu: one of his many names is Narayana.
Narmada	A river.
Nila	He was the physician in the army of the vanaras. Rama thought highly of his powers of healing.
Nikumbha	One of the sons of Kumbhakarna who was killed after a glorious display of his prowess.
Nikumbhila	A secret spot under a Nyagrodha tree where Indrajit wanted to perform a yaga which, if it had been completed, would have made him invincible.
Nimi	An ancestor of Janaka in whose keeping was placed the great Shivadhanus.
Nirvapanjali	Water held in the cupped palms offered to the dead as an oblation.
Nishadha	A hunter, usually. Also a low-born man.
Nyagrodha	Another name for the sacred Ashvattha tree.
Papa	Sin, crime, guilt.
Pasha	Actually a noose. Like the astras presided over by the gods there are pashas also, Varuna Pasha and Yama Pasha to name two of them.
Padmarekha	An auspicious sign. If this line is found on the sole of a woman she will be a Sumangali.
Padya	Offering of water for the washing of the feet: this specially when someone very great in tapas and such like, arrives as a guest.
Palasa	A tree whose flowers, crimson in colour, will cover the tree completely, giving the impression that the tree is a single big flame glowing in the forest.
Pampa Saras	This was the destination of Rama and Lakshmana after they had taken leave of Shabari. It was an extremely beautiful lake surrounded by the most wonderful flowering trees and birds.
Panasa	A tree whose fruit could be eaten as food.
Panchala	A country in the neighbourhood of Kosala.
Panchavati	This was a spot suggested by Agastya when Rama asked him to name a place for a hermitage to be built. It was on the banks of the river Godavari.
Pannaga	A snake, a serpent.
Parabrahman	The Supreme Soul. (Refer Brahman).

Parasurama	The sixth avatara of Vishnu. He was the son of Jamadagni and he killed Kartaviryarjuna. He was a hater of kshatriyas.
Parivrajaka	A wandering ascetic. This was the disguise used by Ravana when he came to Sita's hermitage.
Parjanya	The god of rain.
Parvati	The daughter of Himavan and the wife of Mahadeva.
Pasupata	The astra presided over by Lord Mahadeva.
Patala	The underworld which is ruled by the Nagas, Asuras.
Pativrata	The ideal wife to whom her husband is the only god.
Pauravas	The descendants of the king Pururavas. They are of the lunar race.
Paurnima	The day of the full moon.
Payasa	The elixir given to Dasaratha to be distributed among his three queens. The payasa was sanctified by the performance of the yaga and it was divine.
Pinaka	The bow of Mahadeva.
Pinda	An offering, usually of rice balls made to the departed souls. The sons are meant to offer Pinda, and Tarpana to the father so that he will reach the land of the Pitris (Manes).
Pishachas	A fiend, a malevolent being.
Pitris (Manes)	The forefathers who are dead.
Pradakshana	Circumambulation.
Prahastha	The chief adviser and the commander-in-chief of Ravana's army.
Prahlada	A danava who was a devotee of Narayana. He was the grandfather of Bali.
Prajapati	The Creator, Brahma.
Pralaya	The great deluge which will make the earth become submerged under the sea. This is supposed to occur at the end of the Yuga.
Pramathagana	The attendants of Mahadeva.
Pranama	Touching the feet of elders and taking the dust of their feet. Salutation to elders.
Prasravana	The hill where Rama spent the four months of the rainy season. The hill was very near Kishkindha.

Pratyaksha	There are six different factors which are needed to know the truth about anything. The six are: Pratyaksha, Anumana, Upamana, Shabda, Anuphalaprapti and the sixth is Arthaprapti. Pratyaksha is what has actually been seen. Anumana is conjecture, meaning arriving at some conclusion on the basis of what one has seen. Upamana is comparison to something which is similar. Shabda means, trying to get at the truth by means of noises made, and such like. Anuphalaprapti means: making certain that it is not there because it is not found. Arthaprapti is guessing and arriving at the truth with the help of the other five and the knowledge obtained by the other five.
Prayaga	The sacred spot where the golden waters of the Ganga mingle with the midnight blue of the Yamuna. This was where the ashrama of Bharadwaja was located.
Prayashchitta	Atonement; expiation, a religious act to atone for the sin.
Prayopavesha	A kind of self-immolation by denying oneself food and even water. Kshatriyas are not allowed to undergo Prayopavesha.
Puja	Worship.
Pulastya	The grandfather of Ravana.
Punarvasu	The star under which Rama was born.
Punnaga	A sweet-smelling flower.
Punjikasthali	An apsara whom Ravana had once molested.
Punya	An accumulation of good deeds. Righteous, meritorious deeds and actions.
Puru	A king of the lunar race. He was the son of Yayati.
Pururavas	The founder of the lunar race.
Purusharthas	Refer Kama.
Purushottama	Usually Vishnu is meant when this name is used.
Pushan	One of the Adityas.
Pushkaratirtha	Name of sacred bathing place.
Pushpaka	A chariot which originally belonged to Kubera but was taken by Ravana. It could fly in the sky.
Pushya	The star under which Bharata was born.
Putrakama	A yajna performed with a desire to get sons.

Putrasneha	Inordinate attachment to one's child or children.
Raghu	One of the famous kings of the solar race. He was the grandfather of Dasaratha.
Raghuvamsa	The race of kings who had Raghu as the ancestor: the solar race.
Rahu	One of the nine planets. Son of Viprachitti and Simhika. He is said to cause the eclipse of the sun and the moon.
Rajagriha	The capital city of Kekaya where Bharata and Shatrughna were spending some time during which the tragic events took place in Ayodhya: the exile of Rama and the death of the king.
Rajarshi	Janaka was called a Rajarshi by everyone. It is defined thus: A royal sage, a saint-like prince, a kshatriya who, by his pious life and devotion, has become a sage or rishi.
Rajata hill	One of the small mountains in the South where the vanaras led by Angada searched for Sita. It is so named because of the silvery sheen emanating from it.
Raksha	An amulet: a piece of silk or thread fastened round the wrist as a protection.
Rakshasa	A demon, an evil spirit, a fiend.
Rakshasi	The feminine of Rakshasa.
Rama	The eldest son of Dasaratha born of Kausalya.
Rambha	One of the apsaras from the court of Indra.
Rama Rajya	When Rama was ruling the country the people were exceedingly happy, and there was nothing but prosperity in the country. Hence, when a country is ruled well and when the people are happy it is called Rama Rajya.
Ramayana	The adventures, or the travels of Rama related by the sage Valmiki. This is the first Kavya ever written.
Rasatala	The underworld.
Rati	The wife of Manmatha or Kama
Ravana	The celebrated king of Lanka. He was the son of Vishravas and the grandson of Pulastya.
Raudra	"Like Rudra": violent, wrathful. The astra by name Raudra is fierce and is presided over by Rudra.
Renuka	The wife of Jamadagni and the mother of Parasurama.

Richaka	He was the husband of Satyavati and the father of Jamadagni whose son was Parasurama.
Rikshabila	This was a cave which the vanaras discovered quite by chance when they were searching for Sita. It was actually a magic city built by Maya for his daughter Hema. At the time when the vanaras visited it, the city was minded by Svayamprabha, Hema's friend.
Riksharajas	The father of Vali and Sugriva.
Rishabha	Name of a mountain.
Rishi	A saint, an ascetic, an anchorite.
Rishyamooka	The hill on which stayed Sugriva. Because of the curse of Matanga Vali could not step on the spot and so Sugriva felt that he was safe there.
Rishyashringa	The son of a great sage by name Vibhandaka. He was brought to the country named Anga where there was a great famine. When Rishyashringa came the rains came too and the king gave his daughter Shanta to him. Rishyashringa was responsible for the yajna by name Putrakama which Dasaratha performed with a desire to be the father of sons.
Ritviks	Priests who officiate at a sacrifice.
Rohini	One of the stars.
Rohita	The son of Harishchandra, the king of the solar race.
Romapada	He was the king of the country Anga which suffered from famine. His daughter Shanta became the wife of Rishyashringa.
Rudras (11)	A group of gods, eleven in number, supposed to be inferior manifestations of Mahadeva or Siva or Shankara who is said to be the head of the group.
Ruma	The wife of Sugriva whom Vali had taken.
Sadananda	The son of Gautama and Ahalya. He was the guru, the preceptor to Janaka, the king of Videha.
Sagara	One of the kings of the solar race.
Sagara	The ocean. This got its name because the 60,000 sons of Sagara had scooped up the entire earth in their search for the sacrificial horse of their father. The cavity thus formed was later filled up by Ganga who was brought to the earth by Bhagiratha one of the descendants of Sagara.

Sagaraputras	The 60,000 sons of Sagara.
Sahadharmacharee	A lawful wife: one who is legally married. One who is a companion to her husband in the observance of his dharma, his duties.
Sala	A tree. The name has become famous because Rama, with a single arrow, pierced seven Sala trees which were all in a row.
Sama (Upaya)	One of the four methods employed to achieve one's ends. Refer Dana or Bedha or Danda.
Samadhi	Profound or abstract meditation, concentrating the mind on the subject, perfect absorption of thought into the one object of meditation, which is the Supreme Spirit. The 8th and last stage of Yoga.
Sama Veda	One of the four Vedas. Ravana is said to have pleased Lord Mahadeva by singing the Sama accompanied by veena.
Samith	Wood, fuel, especially fuel of sacrificial sticks for the sacred fire.
Sampati	The elder son of Aruna and Shyeni. He was the brother of Jatayu.
Samskara	Rites to be performed, specially funeral rites.
Samudra	The sea, the ocean. The king of the seas.
Sanatkumara	One of the four sons of Brahma, born of his mind.
Sandhya	The time when there is a juncture of day and night, morning or evening twilight. Juncture of the three divisions of the day (morning, noon and evening). The religious acts performed by the twice-borns at these times.
Sangama	Refer Prayaga.
Sanjivakarani	The life-giving herb which is said to grow on a hill by name Oshadhiparvata.
Santanakarani	This is also found in the Oshadhiparvata.
Sanyasi	One who renounces the world completely: an ascetic.
Sarama	The daughter of Vibhishana who was full of pity and compassion towards Sita during her captivity.
Sarasa	A bird, the Indian crane.
Sarana	One of the Rakshasa spies sent by Ravana to the camp of the vanaras to find out the strength of Rama's army.

Saraswati (river)	The sacred river on whose banks was located the ashrama of Vyasa. At Prayaga, the Sangama is said to be of the three sacred rivers: Ganga, Yamuna and Saraswati and the Sangama is named Triveni Sangama.
Sarayu	The river which flows on the outskirts of Ayodhya.
Sarvabhauma	The elephant belonging to Kubera.
Sati	The daughter of Daksha and the wife of Mahadeva. She immolated herself at the yajna performed by her father and was born again as Parvati to be reunited with her lord.
Satyavati	Vishvamitra's sister. She was the wife of Richaka and the mother of Jamadagni.
Savitri	The wife of Satyavan, the king of Salva. She is regarded as the 'beau ideal' or highest pattern of conjugal fidelity. She restored life back to her husband after following Yama to the nether regions and imploring him to grant her husband's life to her.
Shabari	A Kirata woman who was an ardent devotee of Rama.
Shabda	Refer Pratyaksha.
Shabdavedi	An astra which Dasaratha knew. This would help the hunter to kill an animal with the help of the noise produced by it. Hitting an invisible target the sound of which only is heard.
Shachidevi	The wife of Indra.
Shakti	A weapon in the form of spear, or lance. Some of them are sometimes presided over by the gods and have supernatural powers to kill.
Shambara	One of the asuras to fight whom Indra sought the help of Dasaratha.
Shankha (conch)	Refer gada.
Shanta	The daughter of Romapada and the wife of Rishyashringa.
Shantam Papam	The phrase, sometimes repeated in a dramatic way, of saying: "God forbid such an untoward or unlucky event."
Sharabhanga	One of the great rishis whom Rama visited in the Dandaka forest.
Sharad ritu	One of the seasons: autumn.
Shardula	One of the spies of Ravana.
Shastra	A sacred precept or rule: scriptural injunction: A religious treatise, sacred book, treatise.

Sharanga	The bow of Vishnu.
Shantabali	One of Sugriva's trusted men.
Shatrughna	The son of Dasaratha born of Sumitra. He was the twin of Lakshmana and was always with Bharata.
Shatrunjaya	Rama's elephant.
Shibi	Name of a king who is said to have saved Agni in the form of a dove from Indra who appeared in the form of a hawk by offering an equal quantity of his own flesh weighed in a balance.
Shimshupa	A tree in a Ashokavana of Ravana on a branch of which Hanuman concealed himself.
Shishira ritu	The last of the seasons: winter.
Shivadhanus	The great bow of Mahadeva which had been in the keeping of the kings of Videha, breaking which Rama won the hand of Sita.
Shoola	A weapon: trident.
Shrardha	A funeral rite or ceremony performed in honour of the departed souls of dead relatives.
Shravana	Name of a month corresponding to July-August.
Shrutakirti	The capital city of Guha, the hunter chieftain.
Shrutakirti	The daughter of Janaka's brother given in marriage to Shatrughna.
Shuklapaksha	The brighter fortnight when the moon waxes from a crescent to the full moon.
Shuklartha	There are three arthas: Shuklartha, Krishnartha, Chapalartha. Treading the right path is Shuklartha; the path which has a slight admixture of adharma but is, by and large, right, is named Chapalartha and the path which is entirely wrong is Krishnartha.
Shurpanakaha	The half-sister of Ravana. She can well nigh be said to be responsible for the destruction of the entire Rakshasa clan.
Shyama (tree)	The Nyagrodha tree which was a landmark mentioned by Bharadwaja to facilitate the Kosala brothers to locate Chitrakuta. The sage asked Sita to worship the tree before they proceeded further.
Shyeni	The wife of Aruna and the mother of the two eagles Sampati and Jatayu.

Siddha	A semi-divine being of great purity and perfection said to possess the eight supernatural faculties: Anima, Mahima, Laghima, Garima, Prapti, Prakamyam, Ishatvam, Vashitvam.
Siddhartha	One of the ministers of Dasaratha.
Siddhashrama	The sacred spot where Vishvamitra performed a yajna which was guarded by Rama and Lakshmana.
Siddhis (8)	Refer Siddha.
Simhika	A rakshasi who tried to obstruct the path of Hanuman during his flight across the sea.
Sindhu	The river whose modern name is Indus.
Sita	The foster-daughter of Janaka and the wife of Rama.
Sloka	A stanza or verse, usually in the Anushtup metre.
Sona (river)	Name of a river falling into the Ganga near the city Pataliputra.
Srivatsa	Said to be a mole on the chest of Narayana.
Sruva	A sacrificial ladle.
Sthulakaya	One of the warriors in Ravana's army.
Subahu	The rakshasa who was killed by Rama when he tried to disturb the yaga of Vishvamitra.
Sudharma	The great hall of Indra.
Sudarshana	Refer Chakra.
Sugriva	The younger brother of Vali, the king of Kishkindha. Sugriva and Rama became friends and Rama was able to lay siege to Lanka with the help of Sugriva and his army of bears and monkeys.
Suka	A spy of Ravana.
Sukra	The great Bhargava, the preceptor, the guru of the asuras: especially Bali.
Sumangali	A woman whose husband is alive.
Sumantra	The charioteer of Dasaratha.
Sumati	One of the wives of king Sagara.
Sumitra	The wife of Dasaratha and the mother of Lakshmana.
Sunanda	The gandharva who was the husband of Tataka.

Sunashepha	Refer Ajigarta.
Suparna	One of the names of Garuda.
Suparshva	The son of Sampati.
Surasa	She had been sent by the devas to obstruct the path of Hanuman across the sea, to test the strength of his will.
Surya	The name of the sun. He was the ancestor of the kings of the solar race: Surya vamsha.
Sushena	The physician in the camp of the vanaras.
Suta	A charioteer. The son of a kshatriya by a woman of the Brahmin caste. He is a charioteer or a bard.
Sutheekshna	One of the rishis in the Dandaka forest whom Rama visited and saluted.
Suvela	Name of the Trikuta mountain in which was built Lanka.
Svarnaroma	One of the ancestors of Vishvamitra.
Swasti	Repeating incantations to ward off evil befalling the person concerned.
Svayamprabha	Refer Rikshabila.
Swayamvara	An occasion when the princess of a kingdom is asked to choose her husband from among the princes assembled.
Swapana	One of the many astras used in the war.
Swastika	Name of the boat which carried Bharata and the other members of the royal family across the river Ganga.
Syandika	The name of a river.
Tapas	Penance performed with single-hearted concentration.
Tapasvin	One who performs tapas.
Tapasvini	The feminine of tapasvin.
Tapoloka	One of the seven lokas above the earth, Bhoo, Bhuva, Suva, Maha and then Tapa.
Tarpana	The anjali offered to the departed soul.
Tamasa	This was the river on whose banks was situated the ashrama of Valmiki.
Thara	One of the chieftains in the vanara army.
Tara	The wife of Vali and the mother of Angada.

GLOSSARY

Tirtha	A holy place, a place of pilgrimage, a shrine etc., dedicated to some holy object, specially on or near the bank of a sacred river.
Tripathaga	A name given to Ganga since she flows in the heavens, the earth and the lower regions.
Tataka	A dreadful rakshasi who was the mother of Maricha. She was killed by Rama.
Tatakavana	Malada and Karusha the two countries which she was occupying were together called Tatakavana.
Trishiras	The brother of Khara who was killed by Rama.
Trishiras	A son of Ravana was also Trishiras.
Tilaka	A small fragrant flower white in colour.
Trijata	One of the 'good' rakshasis who recounted a dream she had to the other rakshasis who were torturing Sita.
Trikuta	The hill on which was situated Lanka.
Tripura	The three cities of gold, silver and iron in the sky, air and earth built for the demons by Maya. They were burnt down, along with the demons inhabiting them, by Mahadeva at the request of the gods.
Trivikrama	The immense form the Lord assumed during the Vamana avatara.
Uma	Parvati, the daughter of Himavan.
Upamana	Refer Pratyaksha.
Upendra	When the devas were being harassed by the asuras, Aditi, their mother, prayed that a son should be born who would free them from the power of Bali. Lord Narayana Himself agreed to be born as her son and when he was born, he was named Upendra. His other name was Vamana since he was short and small.
Urmila	Janaka's daughter who was given to Lakshmana.
Ushanas	Another name for Sukra, the guru of the asuras.
Uttara	The name of a star.
Uttara Phalguni	The name of a star.
Vaijayantimala	The garland of flowers worn by Vishnu.
Vaishravana	Name of Kubera, the god of wealth. Also the name of Ravana. Both were the son of Vishravas.

Vajra	The weapon of Indra: the thunderbolt.
Vajradamshtra	The trusted commander of Ravana's army.
Vali	The king of Kishkindha: the son of Riksharajas and the brother of Sugriva.
Valkala	A coarse garment made of the bark of a tree. This is the garment worn by those who dwell in the forest: who are tapasvis.
Vamana	Refer Upendra.
Vamadeva	One of the preceptors in the court of Dasaratha.
Vanadevata	These are supposed to guard the forest. A sylvan deity: a dryad.
Vandhi Magadhas	The convention in a royal household is: the king has to be woken up with music and the songs should be made up of words in praise of the king and wishing him well. These singers are called Vandhi Magadhas and Sutas.
Vanjulaka	A kind of bird.
Vanara	A monkey.
Varaha	The third avatara of Narayana when he lifted up the earth with his tusk. She had been submerged under the ocean and he had to assume the form of a Varaha, the boar.
Varuna	The lord of the nether world and of the seas. He is one of the Dikpalakas.
Varunastra	The astra presided over by Varuna.
Vasanta	When Indra sends Kama into the world to disturb the penance of a rishi, Kama is usually accompanied by Vasanta, the god of Spring and Mandanila, the perfumed breeze which is said to aid him and make his task easier.
Vasanta ritu	The spring: the months Madhu and Madhava.
Vastushanti	Certain rituals to be observed before living in a new house. The fire should be fed with oblations and the Vishvedevas should be worshipped.
Vashatkara	An exclamation used on making an oblation to a deity: like Indraya Vashat: Pushne Vashat: etc.
Vasishtha	The kulaguru of the race of the Ikshvakus. He was the chief priest in the court of Dasaratha and the preceptor of the young sons of the king.

GLOSSARY 693

Vasus (8)	Name of a class of deities who are eight in number: Aapa, Dhruva, Soma, Dhara, Anila, Anala, Pratyusha and Prabhasa.
Vasu	Wealth, riches.
Vasuki	The son of Kadru and the lord of the serpent world. He was not wicked like Takshaka or Karkotaka. He was used as the churning rope during the great churning of the ocean of milk.
Vasumati	The earth so full of riches and wealth.
Vatapi	The brother of Ilvala who were both killed by Agastya.
Vayavyastra	The astra presided over by Vayu.
Vayu	The god of wind. The deity supposed to preside over the wind. There are seven courses of the wind: Aavaha, Pravaha, Samvaha, Udvaha, Vivaha, Parivaha and Paravaha. The seven Maruts are said to be ruled by Vayu.
Vedanga	Name of a certain class of works regarded as auxiliary to the Vedas and designed to aid the correct pronunciation and interpretation of the text and the right employment of the mantras in ceremonials.
Vedavati	Ravana mentions her name as one of those who had cursed him once.
Vedika	A sacrificial altar or ground. A raised seat, an elevated spot of ground usually for sacred purposes.
Veena	A stringed instrument which is said to be the constant companion of Narada. It was an instrument playing on which Ravana was an adept. His dhwaja was the Veena.
Vibhishana	The younger brother of Ravana.
Videha	Janaka's kingdom.
Vibhandaka	The father of Rishyashringa.
Viryasulka	A bride given as a reward for the display of prowess: like Sita or Draupadi.
Vidhata	Name of Brahma, the Creator.
Vidyudjihva	One of the henchmen of Ravana. He was skilled in the art of Maya. Ravana, when he heard about the coming of Rama's army, made a desperate attempt to win Sita over by telling her that Rama was killed by Prahastha. To prove it he had asked Vidyudjihva to make a head like that of Rama and also a replica of the bow of Rama. This only made Sita bemoan her loss and soon the Maya of the rakshasa was exposed.

Vijaya	One of the ministers of Dasaratha.
Vijaya	An auspicious hour. If something is lost at this time, its recovery is certain.
Vimana	A vehicle or conveyance in general: also a heavenly ratha moving in the skies.
Vinata	The mother of Garuda and Aruna.
Vinda	This is another name for Vijaya which is an auspicious hour.
Vindhya	A range of mountains which almost divides the Bharatavarsha into two. It is one of the Kulaparvatas and forms the southern limit of Madhyadesa.
Viradha	The first obstruction in the path of the Kosala brothers when they entered the Dandaka forest.
Virochana	The father of Bali equally well known for his generous nature. He was the son of Prahlada.
Vishakha	The star of the Raghu clan.
Vishvamitra	A great rishi who was first a kshatriya and then became a Brahamarshi by severe tapas.
Vishvakarma	The architect of the gods.
Vishvaroopa	The vision of the All-pervading Form of the Lord seen during the yaga of Bali when the Vamana grew to immense proportions covering the Universe.
Vishvedevas	A class of deities who are said to protect.
Vidyadhara	A class of celestials.
Vranakoopa	The name of the spring Drumakulya after it was purified by Rama. (Refer Drumakulya).
Vrata	A religious observance which has to follow certain rules and stipulations.
Vritra	An asura whom Indra killed with his Vajra.
Vyuha	An arrangement of the army in a particular form.
Yajna	A sacrifice. A sacrificial rite.
Yajnapashu	An animal for sacrifice, a sacrificial victim.
Yajnasala	A sacrificial hall.
Yajaka	A sacrificer: a sacrificing priest.

Yaksha	Name of a class of semi-god who are described as attendants of Kubera, the god of wealth. They are employed as guardians of his riches and his gardens.
Yama	The god who is the lord of the southern quarter. He is the god of death.
Yamakinkara	A messenger of the god of death.
Yamuna	A river which is a tributary of Ganga.
Yamunavana	The coppice which runs along the banks of the river.
Yayati	A king of the lunar race. He was the son of Nahusha.
Yoga	Deep and abstract meditation, concentration of the mind, contemplation of the Supreme Spirit which is defined as "Chitta Vritti Nirodha."
Yogi	An ascetic, a contemplative saint.
Yojana	A measure of distance equal to four krosas or eight to nine miles.
Yudhajit	The prince of Kekaya and brother of Kaikeyi.
Yuddhonmatta	One of the last warriors to die in the army of Ravana before the final encounter between Rama and Ravana.
Yuga	An age of the world. These are four: Krita, Treta, Dwapara and Kali.
Yupastambha	A sacrificial post to which the victim is fastened at the time of immolation.
Yuvanashva	The father of Mandhata.
Yuvaraja	An heir-apparent, a prince-royal, crown prince.